# THE
# SHAPESHIFTERS
## THE KIESHA'RA OF THE DEN OF SHADOWS

*Includes five complete novels*

**Hawksong • Snakecharm • Falcondance**
**Wolfcry • Wyvernhail**

DELACORTE PRESS

*Hawksong* copyright © 2003 by Amelia Atwater-Rhodes
*Snakecharm* copyright © 2004 by Amelia Atwater-Rhodes
*Falcondance* copyright © 2005 by Amelia Atwater-Rhodes
*Wolfcry* copyright © 2006 by Amelia Atwater-Rhodes
*Wyvernhail* copyright © 2007 by Amelia Atwater-Rhodes

All rights reserved. Published in the United States by Delacorte Press,
an imprint of Random House Children's Books, a division of
Random House, Inc., New York. The works in this collection
were originally published separately in hardcover by Delacorte Press
in 2003, 2004, 2005, 2006, and 2007.

Delacorte Press is a registered trademark and the colophon is
a trademark of Random House, Inc.

Visit us on the Web! www.randomhouse.com/teens
Educators and librarians, for a variety of teaching tools,
visit us at www.randomhouse.com/teachers

Library of Congress Cataloging-in-Publication Data is available upon request.
ISBN: 978-0-385-73950-4 (tr. pbk.)
ISBN: 978-0-375-89767-2 (e-book)

Printed in the United States of America
10 9 8 7 6 5 4 3 2
First Omnibus Edition

# CONTENTS

# THE SHAPE

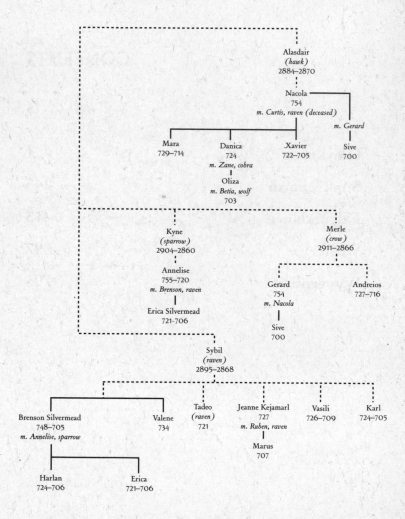

Alasdair
*(hawk)*
2884–2870

Nacola
754
*m. Curtis, raven (deceased)*

*m. Gerard*

Mara          Danica          Xavier          Sive
729–714        724             722–705         700
              *m. Zane, cobra*

              Oliza
              *m. Betia, wolf*
              703

Kyne                                    Merle
*(sparrow)*                             *(crow)*
2904–2860                               2911–2866

Annelise                      Gerard              Andreios
755–720                       754                 727–716
*m. Brenson, raven*           *m. Nacola*

Erica Silvermead              Sive
721–706                       700

Sybil
*(raven)*
2895–2868

Brenson Silvermead    Valene    Tadeo      Jeanne Kejamarl    Vasili      Karl
748–705               734       *(raven)*  727                726–709     724–705
*m. Annelise, sparrow*          721        *m. Ruben, raven*

                                           Marus
                                           707

Harlan        Erica
724–706       721–706

*Dashed lines indicate not only a lapse of several generations, but also an indirect relation.*

# SHIFTERS

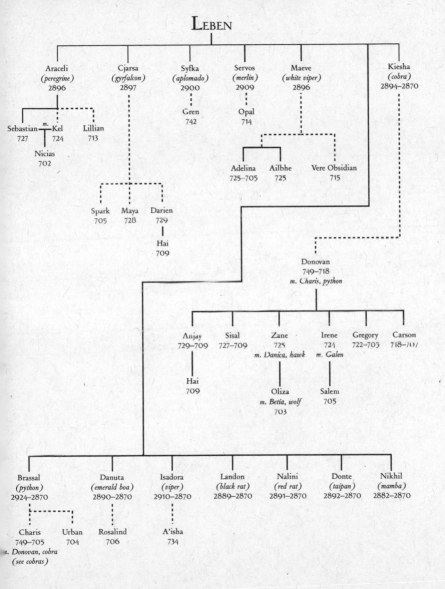

LEBEN

Araceli
(*peregrine*)
2896

Cjarsa
(*gyrfalcon*)
2897

Syfka
(*aplomado*)
2900

Servos
(*merlin*)
2909

Maeve
(*white viper*)
2896

Kiesha
(*cobra*)
2894–2870

Sebastian
727
— *m.* —
Kel
724
Lillian
713

Nicias
702

Gren
742

Opal
714

Spark
705
Maya
728
Darien
729

Adelina
725–705
Ailbhe
725
Vere Obsidian
715

Hai
709

Donovan
749–718
*m. Charis, python*

Anjay
729–709
Sisal
727–709
Zane
725
*m. Danica, hawk*
Irene
724
*m. Galen*
Gregory
722–705
Carson
718–707

Hai
709

Oliza
*m. Betia, wolf*
703

Salem
705

Brassal
(*python*)
2924–2870
Danuta
(*emerald boa*)
2890–2870
Isadora
(*viper*)
2910–2870
Landon
(*black rat*)
2889–2870
Nalini
(*red rat*)
2891–2870
Donte
(*taipan*)
2892–2870
Nikhil
(*mamba*)
2882–2870

Charis
749–705
Urban
704
Rosalind
706
A'isha
734

*. Donovan, cobra*
(*see cobras*)

# HAWKSONG

## PROLOGUE

*They say the first of my kind was a woman named Alasdair, a human raised by hawks. She learned the language of the birds and was gifted with their form.*

*It is a pretty myth, I admit, but few actually believe it. No record remains of her life.*

*No record except for the feathers in every avian's hair, even when otherwise we appear human, and the wings I can grow when I choose—and of course the beautiful golden hawk's form that is as natural to me as the legs and arms I wear normally.*

*This myth is one of the stories we hear as children, but it says nothing of reality or the hard lessons we are taught later.*

*Almost before a child of my kind learns to fly, she learns to hate. She learns of war. She learns of the race that calls itself the serpiente. She learns that they are* untrustworthy, that they are liars and loyal to no one. She learns to fear the garnet eyes of their royal family even though she will probably never see them.

What she never learns is how the fighting began. No, that has been forgotten. Instead she learns that they murdered her family and her loved ones. She learns that these enemies are evil, that their ways are not hers and that they would kill her if they could.

That is all she learns.

This is all I have learned.

Days and weeks and years, and all I know is bloodshed. I hum the songs my mother once sang to me and wish for the peace they promise. It's a peace my mother has never known, nor her mother before her.

How many generations? How many of our soldiers fallen?

And why?

Meaningless hatred: the hatred of an enemy without a face. No one knows why we fight; they only know that we will continue until we win a war it is too late to win, until we have avenged too many dead to avenge, until no one can remember peace anymore, even in songs.

Days and weeks and years.

My brother never returned last night.

Days and weeks and years.

How long until their assassins find me?

Danica Shardae

Heir to the Tuuli Thea

# CHAPTER 1

I TOOK A DEEP BREATH TO STEADY MY NERVES and narrowly avoided retching from the sharp, well-known stench that surrounded me.

The smell of hot avian blood spattered on the stones, and cool serpiente blood that seemed ready to dissolve the skin off my hands if I touched it. The smell of burned hair and feathers and skin of the dead smoldered in the fire of a dropped lantern. Only the fall of rain all the night before had kept that fire from spreading through the clearing to the woods.

From the forest to my left, I heard the desperate, strangled cry of a man in pain.

I started to move toward the sound, but when I took a step through the trees in his direction, I came upon a sight that made my knees buckle, my breath freezing as I fell to the familiar body.

Golden hair, so like my own, was swept across the boy's eyes, closed forever now but so clear in my mind. His skin was gray in the morning light, covered with a light spray of dew. My younger brother, my only brother, was dead.

Like our sister and our father years ago, like our aunts and uncles and too many friends, Xavier Shardae was forever grounded. I stared at his still form, willing him to take a breath and open eyes whose color would mirror my own. I willed myself to wake up from this nightmare.

*I could not be the last.* The last child of Nacola Shardae, who was all the family I had left now.

I wanted to scream and weep, but a hawk does not cry, especially here on the battlefield, in the midst of the dead and surrounded only by her guards. She does not scream or beat the ground and curse the sky.

Among my kind, tears were considered a disgrace to the dead and shame among the living.

*Avian reserve.* It kept the heart from breaking with each new death. It kept the warriors fighting a war no one could win. It kept me standing when I had nothing to stand for but bloodshed.

I could not cry for my brother, though I wanted to.

I pushed the sounds away, forcing my lips not

to tremble. Only one heavy breath escaped me, wanting to be a sigh. I lifted my dry eyes to the guards who stood about me protectively in the woods.

"Take him home," I ordered, my voice wavering a bit despite my resolve.

"Shardae, you should come home, too."

I turned to Andreios, the captain of the most elite flight in the avian army, and took in the worried expression in his soft brown eyes. The crow had been my friend for years before he had been my guard, and I began to nod assent to his words.

Another cry from the woods made me freeze. I started toward it, but Andreios caught my arm just above the elbow. "Not that one, milady."

Normally I would have trusted his judgment without question, but not here on the battlefield. I had been walking these bloody fields whenever I could ever since I was twelve; I could not avert my eyes when we were in the middle of this chaos and someone was pleading, with what was probably his last breath, for help. "And why not, Andreios?"

The crow knew he was in trouble the instant I addressed him by his full name instead of his childhood nickname of Rei, but he kept on my heels as I stepped around the slain bodies and closer to the voice. The rest of his flight fell back, out of sight in their second forms—crows and ravens, mostly. They would take my brother home only when it did not mean leaving me alone here.

"Dani." In return, I knew Rei was serious when he lapsed into the informal and used *my* nickname, Dani, instead of a respectful title or my surname, Shardae. Even when we were alone, Rei rarely called me Danica. It was an entreaty to our lifelong friendship when he used that nickname where someone else could hear it, and so I paused to listen. "That's Gregory Cobriana. You don't want his blood on your hands."

For a moment the name meant nothing to me. With his hair streaked with blood and his expression a mask of pain, Gregory Cobriana could have been anyone's brother, husband or son. But then I recognized the stark black hair against his fair skin, the onyx signet ring on his left hand and, as he looked up, the deep garnet eyes that were a trademark of the Cobriana line, just as molten gold eyes were characteristic of my own family.

I did not have the energy to rage. Every emotion I had was cloaked in the shield of reserve I had learned since I was a chick.

Evidently the serpiente prince recognized me as well, for his pleas caught in his throat, and his eyes closed.

I stepped toward him and heard a flutter of movement as my guards moved closer, ready to intervene if the fallen man was a threat.

With all his various scratches and minor injuries, it was hard to tell where the worst of the damage was. I saw a broken leg, possibly a broken arm; either of those he could heal from.

What would I do if that was the worst? If he was hurt, but not too hurt to survive? This was the man who had led the soldiers that had killed my brother and his guards. Would I turn my back so the Royal Flight could finish what all these fallen fighters had not?

For a moment I thought of taking my knife and putting it in his heart or slitting his throat myself and ending the life this creature still held while my brother lay dead.

Despite my guards' protest, I went again to my knees, this time beside the enemy. I looked at that pale face and tried to summon the fury I needed.

His eyes fluttered open and met mine. A muddy shade of red, Gregory Cobriana's eyes were filled with pain, sorrow and fear. The fear struck me the most. This *boy* looked a couple of years younger than I was, too young to deserve this horror, too young to die.

Bile rose in my throat. I loved my brother, but I could not murder his killer. I could not look into the eyes of a boy terrified of death and shaking from pain and feel hatred. This was a life: serpiente, yes, but still a *life;* who was I to steal it?

Only as I recoiled did I see the wound on his stomach, where a knife had dragged itself raggedly across the soft flesh, one of the most painful of mortal blows. The attacker must have been killed before he could finish the deed.

Perhaps my brother had held the knife. Had he lain dying alone like this afterward?

I felt a sob choke my throat and couldn't stop it. Gregory Cobriana was the enemy, but here on the battlefield he was just another brother to another sister, fallen on the field. I could not cry for my own brother; he would not want me to. But I found myself crying for this hated stranger and the endless slaughter that I had almost contributed to.

I spun on Rei. "This is why this stupid war goes on. Because even when he's dying, you can only feel your hate," I spat, too quietly for the serpiente prince to hear me.

"If I was in this man's place, I would pray for someone to kneel by my side," I continued. "And I wouldn't care if that person was Zane Cobriana himself."

Rei knelt awkwardly beside me. For a moment, his hand touched my hand, unexpectedly. His gaze met mine, and I heard him sigh quietly with understanding.

I turned back to the serpiente. "I'm here; don't fret," I said as I smoothed black hair from Gregory's face.

His eyes filled with tears and he muttered something that sounded like "Thank you." Then he looked straight up at me and said, "End it. Please."

These words made me wince. I had been thinking the same thing just moments before, but even though I knew he was asking me to stop the pain, I did not want mine to be the hand that ended another's life.

"Dani?" Rei asked worriedly when a tear fell from my eyes onto Gregory's hand.

I shook my head and wrapped my hand around Gregory's cool one. The muscles tightened, and then he was gripping my hand like it was his last anchor to earth.

When I drew the knife from my waist, Rei caught my wrist and shook his head.

Quietly, so Gregory could not hear, I argued, "It could take him hours to die like this."

"Let the hours pass," Rei answered, though I could see the muscles in his jaw tighten. "Serpiente believe in mercy killing, but not when it's the other side who does it. Not when it's the heir to the Tuuli Thea who ends the life of one of their two surviving princes."

We sat in the field most of the day, until Gregory's grip on my hand loosened and his ragged breathing froze.

As I had often done for dying avian soldiers, I sang to pass the time, and to distract him from the pain. The songs were about freedom. They were about children, able to play and sing and dance without worrying that they would be harmed.

The song I loved most of all, though, was the one my mother used to sing to me when I was a child, before I had been given round-the-clock nurses, maids, servants and guards. It was from long before my mother had become a distant queen with too much dignity to show affection even to her last remaining daughter. I would have given up all the pampering and all the respect I had earned those past few years if I could have climbed into her arms and gone back to a time when I was still too young to understand that my father, my sister and now my brother had been butchered in this war, which had been going on so long nobody could tell anymore what it was about or who had started it.

I had heard of avians and serpiente who had lived five hundred years or more, but no one did that now. Not in a time when both sides slaughtered each other so frequently, and so efficiently.

The only male child left to inherit the serpiente throne was Zane Cobriana, a creature whose name was rarely mentioned in polite avian society, and if he died . . . hopefully the murderous royal house of the serpiente would die with him. Yet now that Gregory Cobriana, the youngest and last brother of our greatest enemy, was dead in front of me, I could not be grateful for the loss. All I could do was sing gently the old childhood lullaby called "Hawksong" that my mother had sung to me long ago.

> *I wish to you sunshine, my dear one,*
> *my dear one. And treetops for you to soar*
> *past. I wish to you innocence, my child, my*
> *child. I pray you don't grow up too fast.*
> > *Never know pain, my dear one, my*
> *dear one. Nor hunger nor fear nor sorrow.*
> *Never know war, my child, my child.*
> *Remember your hope for tomorrow.*

BY THE TIME I found sleep that night, back in the Hawk's Keep, my throat was tight with too many tears unshed, screams unuttered and prayers whose words I could never seem to find.

# CHAPTER 2

M

Y MOTHER, LADY NACOLA SHARDAE, WAS like a bronze statue as she watched the pyre consume yet another of her children on Mourner's Rock. Firelight gave a copper cast to her fair skin, matching the gold of her hair and her dry eyes.

Earlier the Royal Flight had been present; they had flown the body here and built the pyre. But as the fire snapped in its last moments, only the family of the deceased remained. It made brutally plain how few of us were left.

My mother and I held silent vigil until the last ember had turned gray and the wind had whipped the ashes into the sky.

When the silence was broken, my mother's words were even and clear, betraying none of the pain or anger that she must have felt. "Shardae, you're not to go back to the fields," she commanded. "I know your view on the subject. I also know you will be queen in barely a month. Your people need you."

Among avians, the heir traditionally became queen when she carried her first child. That did not seem a likely occurrence for me anytime soon, but my mother had decided it was time for power to change hands despite tradition.

"Yes, Mother."

I had been preparing to take the throne ever since my older sister died when I was ten, but my mother had rarely approved of my methods. I knew going to the fields was dangerous, as was visiting anyone outside the heavily defended Hawk's Keep, but how could I rule my people if I refused to leave the safety of my home? I could not know them if I never faced the world they lived in, and that included the spattered blood of the fields.

For now, I held my tongue. This was not the time to argue.

MY MOTHER LEFT before I did. When she shifted form and spread her wings, a black cloud seemed to rise from the cliffs above us, half a dozen ravens and crows guarding her even here.

I hung back a bit, hesitating on the black rock and repeating over and over the words

*No time for tears.* I knew there would be no energy left for living if I grieved too deeply for each loss, but each funeral was harder to turn from than the last.

Eventually, I forced the creeping sorrow back, until I knew I could stay composed when I faced my people, with no trace of anxiety on my face or grief or anger in my eyes.

As I lingered, a single crow detached from the rock above me. He circled once before returning to his post, assured that I was still here, standing strong.

There was nothing left to do.

As I shifted my tired human form into one with powerful wings and golden-brown feathers, I let out a shriek. Fury, pain, fear; they dissolved into the sky as I pushed myself beyond them with every smack of my wings against the air.

It was late when I returned to the Hawk's Keep, the tower that housed what was left of my family, the highest-ranking soldiers and the most prominent artisans, merchants and speakers of the avian court.

With my mother's command, the seven floors of the Keep had changed from my safe home to my prison. Instead of being a refuge from the blood and pain, the walls were suddenly a trap keeping me from reality.

With Andreios standing near in case of trouble that never occurred inside, I lingered on the first floor, fifteen feet above the ground-level courtyards and training grounds. I watched the last of the merchants pack up their belongings, some grateful to have rooms in the higher levels of the Keep, but most wary of the world they would be returning to when they left here.

Market lasted from dawn to dusk. Merchants and storytellers would gather on this floor, along with common people, and during the day the Tuuli Thea and her heirs her only heir, now— would go among them and listen for complaints. The artisans had nearly been strangled out of avian society by the war, but my mother had started encouraging the ones who remained to show their wares. The avian market was famous for its craftsmanship, and losing those arts completely would have been tragic.

Along with crafts, custom weapons and other fine luxuries, stories and gossip could be found at the market. This was where merchants, farmers and anyone else who did not fight heard all the details.

I had seen enough serpiente soldiers fallen beside our own over the years, and now, with the image of Gregory Cobriana branded into my mind, I was reminded once again that they were just as mortal as my own kind. However, fear makes all enemies more dangerous, and the stories told in the marketplace on this night were as sickening as ever.

Parents lamented their dead children. One young man broke down in tears, a display of emotion quite unseemly in avian society, as he recalled his father's death. Gossip traveled like a river: how the serpiente fought like the demons that legends said they had taken their power from, how their eyes could kill you if you looked into them long enough, how . . .

I tried to stop listening.

My people greeted me with polite words, just as they had the day before. Another hawk child was dead, along with a dozen of the Royal Flight, a score of Ravens—another flight, just below my personal guards in rank—and eighteen common soldiers who had joined the fray when they saw their prince fall. So many dead, and nothing had changed.

"Milady?"

I turned toward the merchant who had spoken, a metalsmith of good reputation. "Can I help you?"

He was wringing his hands, but stopped as soon as I spoke, his gaze dropping. When he looked up again, his face was composed. He held out a package carefully wrapped in soft leather, placing it on the counter for me to see. "My pair bond was among the Ravens who fell yesterday.

I had been working on this for her, but if milady Shardae would wear it, I would be honored."

The gift he offered was a slender boot knife, etched with simple yet beautiful symbols of faith and luck.

I accepted the blade, hoping I would never need it, but saying aloud, "It is lovely. I'm sure your pair bond would appreciate that it is not going to waste."

The merchant replied, "Perhaps it might protect you when you go out again."

"Thank you, sir."

"Thank you, milady."

I turned from him with a sigh that I was careful not to let him hear. It was already too late for either side to win; this war needed to *stop*. Whatever the cost.

If only I knew how to end it.

"Shardae?"

I knew the young woman who approached me now from when we had both been children. Eleanor Lyssia was an eternal romantic, with grand dreams that I wished I could make come true. The last time I had heard from her had been a few years before, when she had just been apprenticed by a seamstress.

My smile was genuine as I greeted her warmly. "Eleanor, good evening. What brings you to the Keep?"

"I'm finally allowed to sell my work in the

market," she returned brightly. "I was in charge of the shop today." The smile she wore faded to a somber expression. "I wanted to tell you . . . I heard what happened yesterday. With Gregory Cobriana." She shook her head. "I know none of this is proper to say, but I like to think we were friends when we were children?" I nodded, and she continued, "When I heard what had happened, it gave me hope. If the heir to the throne can put aside the past and just comfort a dying man . . . perhaps anything is possible."

She looked away, suddenly awkward.

"Thank you, Eleanor." The prospect made me want to laugh and to cry; I settled on a tired smile. I did meet her gaze; I hoped she saw my gratitude. "Fly with grace."

"You as well, milady."

We parted ways, and now Andreios moved to my side. As always, he knew when I needed to escape. His presence would dissuade anyone else from approaching before I could do so. I wondered if he had heard Eleanor's words, but we did not speak before we both shifted form to fly above the market to the higher levels of the Keep.

Andreios stopped at the fifth floor, where his flight was quartered; I continued to the sixth. I passed the door to my brother's rooms and whispered a final goodbye before I entered my own.

# CHAPTER 3

I WAS A CHILD, UNVERSED YET IN POLITICS. The first thing that interested me in the court was a representative from the shm'Ahnmik, a group not allied with my mother, the Tuuli Thea. He was a falcon boy only a few years older than me, twelve to my eight. I was too young to know that my playmate made my mother very nervous, or that he was in the Keep for any reason different from the other children's. Too young to know that he represented an empire older and stronger than our own, without whose support we would never be able to keep our heads above water when fighting the serpiente.

I was just a child, with no responsibilities, no understanding of politics, war or pain. So I remember the falcon very fondly, as my last memory of childhood.

One of my tutors stepped out to speak with my mother in the hallway. "Milady Shardae, have you seen Andreios?" I looked up, hearing the name of my friend despite the tutor's attempt at discretion. "I'm worried that he's gone out to the field . . . to look for his father."

I was too young to understand death, but I understood that my friend was upset and so I had to find him.

I stood to sneak out before my mother returned. I had known Rei all eight years of my life, since he was three years old and I was newly born. He would listen to me more than anyone else. The falcon tried to stop me from leaving, but he had no authority over me and I refused to listen to reason.

My first breath of death hit me as I flew over the field. Yes, I knew of the war, but I had never seen the carnage up close, smelled the blood before . . . and in the middle of it all, my friend Rei, hunched protectively over his father's body, crying.

I landed at his side.

I hardly had a chance to speak before the serpent appeared. Rei pushed me behind him; they scuffled, and I saw the fangs slice into my friend's skin. Someone else attacked me from behind, but when I fought back, I was struggling with something as harmless as a wool blanket.

I realized suddenly that I was dreaming a scene I relived in my mind almost every night. I had been knocked out; Rei had saved my life. His brush with death had changed him, forcing him to grow up faster. After that day he had made a point of training. He had joined the avian army when he was thirteen and the Royal Flight when he was fifteen, and he had been the captain of that group for three years now.

Despite knowing I was asleep, I could not wake. Lucid dreams had been a curse of mine for years.

I walked the battlegrounds in my mind, through the woods and fields that I had been drawn to ever since Rei's father died. Pain, bloodshed, war. They had stained me that day.

I walked from the dream of Andreios to one of my alistair, the man who had been promised as my protector when we were both barely more than infants. Vasili had frightened me a little when I was a girl; he had seemed so cold and strong. The blood I saw in my dreams, he saw every day as a soldier. Yet I learned to understand him, and then I learned to love him—just in time to lose him, like I had lost so many others.

I pushed the phantom away and found myself face to face with the garnet eyes of Zane

Cobriana, the creature whose kind was responsible for every loss we suffered, every tear I held inside. My breath halted in my lungs; my blood turned to ice. I felt my throat constrict as I tried to scream—

"Danica, are you all right?"

I opened my eyes to find Rei searching the room for whatever had frightened me. His thick black hair had been hastily pulled back from his face as if he had been roused from sleep. He was not supposed to be on duty until this afternoon, but I was grateful he had been the one to hear me shout.

"Yes," I said, but the trembling in my voice belied my answer.

"Dream?" he asked. Rei was the only one to whom I confided my nightmares.

I nodded, sitting up. Morning was here, and if Rei was, too, then there was something important to be done.

Rei cleared his throat. "Your mother wants you to meet her downstairs, as soon as you are ready."

He left me to change, which I did quickly. My mother did not summon me for meaningless trifles.

I stepped outside my room to find the Hawk's Keep swarming with avian soldiers. In addition to Andreios, there were five other guards next to my door alone. Out on the field, I understood this kind of caution. Inside the Keep, it was unheard of.

"My mother isn't hurt?" I asked with alarm, my mind latching on to the worst possible reason for this concern.

"She's safe," Rei answered, though he didn't sound as if he was completely certain. "The rest of the flight is with her."

Of course. "Then why the sudden jump in security?" And, before he could answer, "And who in the world is guarding the outside?"

"There are about two dozen soldiers ringing the courtyard, and another few dozen in the surrounding land," one of the other guards assured me.

"They're good fighters. As for your other question," Rei answered, "we seem to have a visitor, which is why your mother requested your presence in the first place."

I had become used to having one or two guards at my sides, occasionally more if I was farther from the Keep on one of the fields. Having this many was unnerving, even though the Royal Flight were trained to work smoothly. They kept out of my way and out of each other's, but the press of their bodies in the hall was oppressive in itself. What kind of visitor required so many members of the royal guard to be in the loftiest halls of the Hawk's Keep? No one so much as got inside unnoticed. To get all the way to my chamber would be impossible.

My alarm jumped again when I realized that the guards who had preceded me had changed shape to descend to the ground floor. As a deterrent to flightless enemies, there were no stairs from the ground to the first floor. Aside from criminals and traitors, even the lowliest sparrow commoner was met in the second-floor reception hall.

"Who *is* this visitor?" I inquired softly. "Zane Cobriana himself?"

Rei did not joke back with me. He waited for me to shift into my second form, hastening what was usually a leisurely, pleasant process so that the hawk who emerged was more than a little ruffled.

My mother was standing with her back to us as we entered the enclosed courtyard. The visitor was seated cross-legged on the ground nearby, with her eyes closed as if she was taking a nap. Four of our guards surrounded her, showing just how afraid we were to have her near our queen.

Even from across the courtyard I could recognize the black hair and fair skin. As I went closer I saw her silky black dress with the white emblem sewn onto the low neckline between her breasts. On her left hand she wore an onyx signet ring.

Either she heard our quiet approach, or she sensed us some other way, for the visitor opened her eyes just then. Suddenly my cool, golden gaze was met directly by her hot flame, the color reminiscent of pure polished rubies. I looked away quickly, a shudder twisting its way up my spine.

"She's here in peace," my mother assured me immediately, but I could hear the "or so she said" in her voice even though she didn't speak it aloud. "Irene, may I introduce my heir and daughter, Danica Shardae? Shardae, this is Irene Cobriana, younger sister to Zane."

My skin chilled just hearing the name, but I answered the introduction politely. *What is this creature doing here?* I was willing to comfort Gregory Cobriana on the field, but he had been dying. Seeing Irene, alive and well and dangerous, I felt less charitable.

No doubt the guards had searched her and taken away what weapons they could—probably none, if this ruse was meant to gain our trust. But everyone knew you couldn't disarm a Cobriana unless you took its life. Their scarlet eyes alone were a weapon, not to mention their poison, which could kill in less than a minute if they struck in full serpent form, and which would kill more slowly but more painfully if they did so in a less pure form.

Irene Cobriana spoke first, for which I was grateful. If I had opened my mouth, I probably could have caused a war with what I had said, if it had not been too late already.

"We want peace," Irene said softly, not rising. In case she tried to stand, the guards were prepared to kill her instantly. "We're tired of the fighting, and the killing."

Someone grumbled; I thought it might be Rei. My mother directed a frosty glare at someone behind me.

Irene also looked up at whoever had made the sound, and her voice rose with anger as she argued, "I have lost my father to this war. Two uncles. Three brothers. A few years ago, I lost a sister and a niece at the same time when some avian soldier put a knife into her belly and killed both her and the child she was carrying. My mother is a good woman, but she is only Naga, and the people will not follow someone who is only Cobriana by name. They need their Diente. And Zane is the last true heir to that title." Her voice quieted again.

"Excuse me if we don't completely trust you, Irene," my mother said simply. "But your kind has not been known to uphold its word in the past."

Irene lowered her head, and I could tell she was trying to speak around her anger. "Gregory Cobriana died two nights ago," she answered quietly. She looked at me as she said the words. "He was only *seventeen*, and now he is simply dead. I came here, without weapons, with the hope that someone might listen. Zane wanted to come himself, but my mother argued that you would sooner put a knife in his back than listen to anything he had to say. And do you know what he replied? He said, 'Let them. If they do, someone might finally be satisfied that they've won this war, and then maybe it will end.' "

I barely managed to hold my tongue in response to that claim. Zane Cobriana was what the serpiente called an Arami, the prince first in line to the throne. Now that his father was dead, he was all but king. It was hard for me to imagine the leader of the serpiente saying anything remotely tolerable, much less blatantly self-sacrificing.

Anyone who had spent enough time in the court had heard about the exploits of Zane Cobriana. In battle, it was said, he fought with single-minded fury, and a speed and grace no avian could match. He could catch the eye of his opponent, and that warrior would drag his knife across his own throat in a killing blow. He fought beside his people in battle and had never been wounded. Whispered rumor attributed his power to black magic and demons.

"And what exactly is . . . Zane . . . proposing?" my mother asked, hesitating for a fraction of a second before she spoke the name, as if worried the word alone would soil the Hawk's Keep.

"A truce," Irene answered instantly. "Zane, my mother and I would like to meet with you, your heir, and whatever others you think necessary."

"And just where is this meeting to take place?" my mother asked skeptically.

"Before the Mistari Disa," Irene answered softly. She took a breath and then explained, "The serpiente have been fighting so long, their only reason for continuing now is to avenge the loss of so many of their kin to avian fighters. They don't trust the avians, and I think it would take quite a show of good faith from your people to convince ours that the Tuuli Thea is as honest in her desire to stop the fighting as their Naga and Arami are."

I bit my tongue to keep from demanding just what kind of "show of good faith" Irene was suggesting. When she spoke, the Tuuli Thea said much the same. "I take it Zane sent you as a show of faith from your side," my mother said. "What is he asking in return?"

Irene shook her head. "Only that you agree to meet with us on peaceful lands before the Mistari Disa. We would like to appeal to her for support of the peace talks, and whatever is involved in those."

My mother looked at me. "Shardae?"

I started to object instantly . . . but then I remembered Gregory Cobriana's blood on my hands. I remembered the battlefields, the reek and the wail of war. I remembered my own alistair, Vasili, who had once been promised as my husband. And my own brother, who had been no older than the enemy he had taken with him into death.

So my words when I answered my mother were soft, but not without emotion. "I do not trust them, Mother, but if there is any chance that they might be honest, that Zane Cobriana might want peace . . ." I took a breath, because the very thought that Zane would ever waste a breath for peace was unnerving. "Then I believe we should take it." More quietly, I added, "You know that I would do anything within my power to stop this war."

My mother nodded. "Andreios, your thoughts?"

The leader of the royal guard paused, looking at Irene. "I don't like it, but Mistari lands are neutral territory. Even a cobra would be mad to try to ambush us there; the Mistari would tear the serpents apart."

"Very well, then." The Tuuli Thea gestured for Irene to stand and held up a hand to silence the guards' protests. "Irene, please relay the message to your . . . prince that we would be willing to meet him."

"Thank you, Nacola," Irene said warmly, informally enough that I saw a guard wince. She looked directly at me as she added, "Zane asked me to convey our willingness to meet any day, any time, as soon as is possible. Please speak a date, and I will tell my brother."

Again, my mother conferred briefly with Andreios, and then she answered, "In a fortnight, on the first showing of the moon. It will take that long for us to organize our people."

If the serpiente left the instant Irene returned to the palace and were willing to ride their horses to exhaustion, their party would probably make the deadline. The serpiente would not have time to plan a sneak attack before the meeting.

Irene curtsied, her face showing no annoyance at the rush my mother was pressing her people with. "Thank you, Nacola, Danica. My best wishes go with you both until then."

# CHAPTER 4

M Y INSIDES COILED IN EXPECTATION OF disaster as I made last-minute preparations for our trip to Mistari lands. I knew the tigers would not allow anyone to bring warfare to their land, but I could not help fearing that this was a trap—just like the one that had taken my father from me. He had received a forged missive from my aunt, who lived outside the Keep, saying that she was dying and wanted her brother by her side. The ambush had taken them both from me in the same day.

Andreios had spent the two weeks all but avoiding me so he would not have to face another interrogation about the Keep's defenses, though besides small, unplanned skirmishes caused by chance meetings of our two kinds, there had been no battles since Irene Cobriana's visit.

It was only a matter of time.

"Milady? A problem." I turned, trying not to glare at the sparrow who delivered the message.

"Can it wait? We need to leave."

The sparrow shook her head. "The Tuuli Thea told me only that you need to speak to the Ravens before you leave for the Mistari lands."

Flanked by Andreios and five of his soldiers, I landed in the yard where the Ravens trained, a short flight from the Hawk's Keep.

The guilty looks a few of them tried to hide at my arrival did not bode well. The commander, a woman named Karashan, who seemed more sinew than muscle and whose arms bore many scars from her lifelong profession, approached me.

"Lady Shardae, to what do we owe this honor?"

"I was told there was some talk among your soldiers that I should be aware of," I answered honestly.

Karashan did not look away from my gaze, but she hesitated. "Well, milady—"

"Milady, thank the sky you're here," one of the younger soldiers said, giving a hasty bow before he began. "With all respect to my commander, the orders we've been given are mad—"

I could not hear the rest of his words over the murmur that started then. I held up a hand, shaking my head. "Your orders are to hold off, to defend the Keep if it is attacked but not to instigate anything. Correct?" I asked once the chaos had died down.

The commander answered, "Yes, milady. But surely there is some mistake? We'll be sitting here like lame turkeys when the serpiente attack."

I heard one of Rei's people fidget behind me.

My voice was calm, but my eyes were cold as I answered, "We are going to a meeting to discuss peace, Karashan."

The raven shook her head. "I mean no disrespect, milady, but I have been a soldier for seventy years. Serpents do not know the meaning of peace—or honor. If we do not attack soon and flush out whatever they have planned, you can be sure we will find snakes in our own beds."

I resisted the urge to glance at Rei in a plea for assistance. This had to come from me alone.

"Karashan, you have your orders. They come from the Tuuli Thea and have been repeated by her heir. Do you plan to obey them?"

She hesitated.

"Do I need to remove you from your position

to ensure you will not do anything foolish while my family is in Mistari lands?"

"No, milady," she finally answered, voice soft. "I will not give the order to attack. But, milady . . . if you do not let them move soon, my flight might not wait for my word. They are restless."

I nodded. "I trust you to keep them under control, Karashan. And if you cannot, I trust you to bring word to my mother or me before they take action. Understood?"

"Yes, milady."

I returned to the Keep feeling like a stone plummeting toward I knew not what. I ran my hands through my hair, trying not to look flustered in front of the Royal Flight.

"Shardae?"

I turned to see Karl, one of the few members of the Royal Flight who was my age, watching me with worried eyes. "Yes, Karl?"

"I will obey your orders as always, milady," he assured me, "but what if Karashan is right? You yourself agreed to go to the Mistari camps because there was a slim chance the serpiente might be sincere—so you, too, must know they probably are not. Isn't this too great a risk?"

I shook my head. "If they attack, we will defend ourselves as we have after every serpiente plot in the past. But if they don't, then maybe we can find a way to make peace. Isn't the possibility of your children never having to fight worth the risk?"

Karl nodded. "My trust is with you, milady."

I hoped I was worthy of it.

Before we could speak more on the subject, we were approached by the Mistari's avian representative, Mikkal, who had arrived earlier in the day to guide us into the foreign territory. "Are you ready to go, Lady Shardae?"

I sighed lightly, but nodded. "My mother?"

"She is waiting downstairs for you," he answered.

We joined the rest of our group: my mother, Andreios and two others from the Royal Flight. The Mistari Disa and Dio, their queen and king, had limited our number to five. We had been assured that the serpiente would bring the same. Shortly we were off to Mistari lands, with Mikkal in the lead.

The journey was not an easy one, even though my form was one of the strongest an avian could boast. The young goshawk was an extraordinary flier, and he set a hard pace. Once we had crossed the water and were over the sweltering Mistari lands, the trip was decidedly unpleasant.

The central city of the Mistari, if it could be called such, was surrounded by a natural ring of high stones. Inside those walls, the tigers of the Mistari tribes slept during the hottest hours of the day. Though the group had only been in this area for forty or fifty years, since they had been driven out of Asia by the ever-spreading human population, they had already crafted sturdy walls where the granite mounds were too widely spaced or not high enough for their liking. Built into these walls and stones were the structures where the Mistari lived and slept, some grand and brightly decorated, and some little more than tents held aloft by simple stone piles.

In the center of the ring, one of the giant boulders had been carefully hollowed out and decorated with carvings of each Mistari leader, including the Mistari Disa and Dio. This was their simple palace—the reception hall, where we would meet with the serpiente before the king and queen of these people, and chambers where the royal family slept.

Our group was instantly surrounded when we landed and shifted into human form, but the natives relaxed when they recognized us. "The Disa and Dio are waiting inside the reception hall," a tigress told us. "The others are already there."

We were hustled through the tall grasses and toward the grand stone structure that was the heart of the Mistari territories.

Most of the Mistari stopped outside, but the tigress who had greeted us initially gently pushed aside the ornate silk weavings that hung in the doorway, and invited us into the hall.

The hall was more dimly lit than outside, but carefully cut windows shrouded with white silk let in enough light to show the brilliance of the Mistari palace. The floor was black stone, polished until it shone, and the smooth granite walls were decorated with an intricate mural of the African Serengeti. Brightly colored pillows formed seats on the floor, several of which were taken by the royal family's servants. Slightly raised on a red and black granite dais sat the Mistari Disa and Dio.

All of those individuals quickly lost my interest. Within moments my attention was locked on another group, whose members were seated on the opposite side of the hall from our party.

Irene Cobriana smiled wryly when I glanced at her, but already my gaze had moved on. Another woman, wearing dark burgundy, sat nearby. Her hair tumbled to her waist, a waterfall of onyx strands, and as she turned to look my way, I avoided her startling sapphire eyes. Charis Cobriana, Naga of the serpiente. The python might not have a cobra's power, but it was never a good idea to meet a serpent's gaze.

There were three others who sat with them, one female and two male. The first man was lightly built, with ash-brown hair cut short. The woman was slender, with blond hair that was tied at the nape of her neck before falling silkily down her back. They had the casual poise and obvious attention of guards. The male guard lingered near Irene, and the female near the man, who could be none other than the Arami of the serpiente.

Zane Cobriana lounged on a cushion, his back resting against the wall, one leg bent and the other straight. The iridescent shimmer of his black slacks led me to wonder which of his kind he had skinned. His shoulders were broader than those of a common avian man, and in the position in which he sat, the black material of his shirt was pulled taut across his chest. On his left hand I could see the onyx signet ring. For a moment he was absolutely still, then he looked up and unerringly caught my gaze. Twin pools of fire, a shade of red brighter than Irene's, held me tight. Time seemed to freeze for an eternity. Then his eyes released mine and flickered down my body, a quick scan that brought heat to my face.

Andreios had caught my arm. With a glare at the serpiente prince, Rei escorted me to my seat, blocking Zane from my sight.

*We're here to try to make peace with* that? I thought frantically. My hands were cold, my face still hot. If he could affect me that strongly from across the room, without saying a word, how would I ever dare to approach him civilly?

The Mistari Disa stood and held up her hands for silence among her own people. The hush dragged my attention away from the serpiente leaders and back to the Mistari queen.

"I already know that this isn't going to be easy," the Disa began. "But so long as both of you are willing to make an effort, there is always a chance for peace."

There was some grumbling between the serpiente guards, but Zane and Irene both shot them searing looks, and they quieted.

The Disa spoke first to the serpiente. "Charis, you are Naga, are you not?"

Charis Cobriana nodded, but then answered aloud, "I am, but my Diente is dead. Zane hasn't taken the throne yet, but you should address him as our leader."

"Zane, have you not taken a mate?"

Zane raised fiery eyes to the Mistari Disa. "Taking a mate in the middle of this war would be giving a death sentence to a woman in return for her love. I've learned from experience that even a woman with child is not safe from the killing, not when she's carrying a cobra's blood."

The Disa took a breath, nodded and then turned to my mother. "And among your people, Nacola, whom should I address as your leader?"

"My daughter," my mother answered. "Danica Shardae. She will soon be queen."

"How soon?" the Disa asked gently, and my head lowered. My mother had prepared me to take the throne, but I was still uneasy about the prospect.

My mother blinked and answered hesitantly, "My daughter has no alistair. The one she was raised with was killed in this war, and since Shardae is now old enough, I want her to choose her own. When I said soon, I simply meant . . ." She paused, then gathered her thoughts and answered honestly, "I am tired of this war, tired of being queen. My daughter still has faith, and if anyone is strong enough to lead us to peace, it is her. She will be appointed Tuuli Thea on her next birthday."

The Disa nodded again. "Danica, Zane, both of you have come here, asking for peace. Both of your families are willing to follow you. Why do you need our help?"

Zane spoke first. "Even if every one of us wants peace, our people would rather fight than be taken by surprise. Among my own guards," he said, glancing at his blond companion, "there is strong doubt as to how far we can trust the avians, and among many of my people there is even speculation as to why I would want to make peace."

The Disa looked to me next, and I could only agree with Zane. "We were barely able to control our soldiers these last two weeks. They don't believe the serpiente can be trusted, and unless we either give them permission to fight again, or we

find some way to convince them that the Cobriana family and their people really want peace, my
mother and I won't have the power to keep them
from going against us."

The Disa sighed and looked at her husband.
They conferred quietly for a few minutes, and
then it was the Dio who spoke to us.

"You are both saying that your people doubt
your sincerity, and the other side's sincerity," the
Dio paraphrased. "You two are their leaders, and
if you can set the example and show them how
much you are willing to give for this peace, they
will follow." He paused and then looked at me.
"The question then is, how much are you willing
to give?"

I thought about all the battlefields, all the
dead men and women I had seen, all the dying
children and fathers and mothers I had held and
sung to. I thought about my dead alistair, Vasili,
about my brother, Xavier, and about Gregory
Cobriana begging me to stop the pain.

And I answered, "Anything."

A breath later, Zane echoed my response
with, "Everything."

The Disa took over again. "When you have
hatred, you need to start with the heart to mend
it. Similarly, when you have a rift between peoples as great as you have, the only way to bridge
the gap is to start at the center."

I glanced at Zane, wondering if he understood the Disa's advice better than I did. His eyes were narrowed slightly, as if he had an idea where this was going but didn't much like it.

"You came for our advice. All I can send you away with is this: You can only sew shut a rip by making the two sides one again. Danica Shardae, Zane Cobriana, you said you would give up anything, everything, to stop the war." She looked at me, at Zane, and then she spoke to both of us. "Never ask your people to do something you do not have the courage, or the determination, to do. If you want peace, start between the two of you."

The Disa spoke to the entire hall as she concluded, "The best advice I can offer is this: Tie the two royal families. Make the two sides into one. If you are willing to trust each other, and willing to put aside your anger and your hatred, then Zane Cobriana, take Danica Shardae as your mate. Danica Shardae, have Zane Cobriana as your alistair."

Andreios was the first to jump to his feet to protest, though the female guard shouted out not a moment after. Even my mother's voice rose, at the same time that Charis Cobriana stood. Zane's voice climbed above the others, saying, "I think that's an absurd idea," while my own objections were frozen in my throat.

Again the Disa held up her hands for silence, and one of the other Mistari touched Charis's arm and told her to sit. Another guard was doing the same to Andreios.

The Disa's voice was soft, almost sad, as she asked, "If you, the leaders of your people, are unwilling to make amends, then how can you expect your warriors to do so?" More loudly, she told the hall, "Stay here for the night, think on my words—"

Zane's voice interrupted. "Wait, please—"

"Dismissed, all of you," the Disa commanded. "You may return tomorrow at sunset if you wish to do so. For now, seek your beds, rest and think on my words."

Just like that, we were barred from the hall. The Disa and Dio left their dais as we were ushered out by Mistari guards and escorted to the rooms in which we would be staying.

A young Mistari girl brought water to wash with, as well as an assortment of cheeses, fruit and warm, freshly baked brown bread. I was grateful that the Mistari had thought not to serve meat, since like most of my kind I avoided it.

Rei stopped in to check on me once, and I had to assure him repeatedly that I would be fine before he calmed down.

He paused at the doorway and then turned back to me and apologized. "Dani, I'm sorry I lost my temper in the hall today. You know I care about you. I always have. The thought of that snake coming anywhere near you . . ." He trailed off and looked away from me as if he couldn't meet my eyes. "I should go. Good night."

"Good night, Rei," I answered with a bit of a sigh.

Then he was gone, and I was alone again, with only the flickering orange light of a solitary candle for company.

I lay back on the soft fur sleeping pallet and watched the light dance on the ceiling as I thought.

*Never ask your people to do something you do not have the courage, or the determination, to do. If you want peace, start between the two of you.* How could the Disa expect us to suddenly turn from enemies to a pair bond? She couldn't understand. The Mistari had never known the intense bloodshed and hatred our two kinds had known.

But still, there was a reason why the Disa was considered wise, a reason why warring people had come to her lands for hundreds of years when they sought peace. Never before had anyone managed to get leaders of both sides of this war together. If that was possible . . . maybe Eleanor was right—maybe anything *was* possible.

# CHAPTER 5

⚓

A CHILL DOWN MY SPINE AND A FLICKER OF darkness in the corner of my vision announced his presence, even before the figure emerged from the shadows.

Still wearing black snakeskin pants and a black shirt that I now recognized as silk, the cobra terrified me just by being in the room. Pure primal instinct forced me to my feet. The back of my neck tingled, gold eyes dilated to catch every hint of light and every inch of skin was suddenly hypersensitive. My heartbeat had jumped instantly, until I could hear it as a near buzz in my ears.

"What do you want?" I asked, choking back a cry for my guards. Zane Cobriana would not be stupid enough to kill me in Mistari lands.

Would he?

I could not read his expression as he collapsed gracefully onto one of the large pillows that lined the room. "I decided that you and I should talk," he stated simply, his voice no louder than my own. "Sit down, Danica. I'm not going to ravage or bite you or whatever it is you're thinking."

I forced myself to sit, my legs folded under me in the fine linen slacks I had yet to replace with nightclothes. My heartbeat had slowed slightly, but I could still feel the pulse in my temple and at my wrists. "Talk?"

"We were thrown out of the Mistari hall quite abruptly," he explained, "and in all likelihood the same will happen tomorrow unless we have some discussion prior."

"Continue," I said slowly, trying to keep the tremor from my voice.

"Did you know there are four guards outside your door, Danica?" Zane inquired. My expression must have appeared surprised, because he continued, "I thought not. The Mistari added their own people to yours. They're all incompetent really, or I wouldn't be here, but it would have been tricky to catch you alone tomorrow. And since you're the only one in your group who has demonstrated any sense, you seemed the one to talk to."

"It's late, Zane, and I am very tired," I sighed, my unease and fatigue joining to make me impatient. "What is it you want to talk about?"

"About life," Zane replied lightly. Before I could speak, he went on, "And about death. About the fact that my people mean more to me than anything else, and I would do almost anything to end this foolish war. I want to talk about the world, and most specifically, about you."

It took me two tries to ask, "Me?"

Zane sighed heavily. "Of course you. If the Mistari Disa's proposal is even to be considered, I would like to know what I would be getting myself into."

"I believe you already expressed your opinion on that subject," I said dryly, falling back on the cool, distant tone of a monarch. I tried not to be a frosty queen to my people and my friends, but when nothing else worked, I knew enough to use that composure as a shell.

"And I believe my first reaction is probably still correct," Zane agreed, as if he had accepted a compliment. "It *is* an absurd idea, but that is no doubt why it has never been tried. I'm not saying I'll go along with it," he said hastily, before continuing, "but it does have some potential."

There were no words to express my emotions in that moment, though I am sure they bordered between pure terror and helpless fascination.

The Disa's suggestion was impossible. It would never happen. But still . . . "And what exactly do you think you are 'getting yourself into'?" I inquired distastefully. Before this conversation went any further, I thought it best to have some idea of where Zane intended it to go, since he had surely come here with some hidden purpose.

Again his gaze flickered down my form. "If it was just your body, Danica, I would agree very quickly," he stated calmly, and despite my fine upbringing, I was not ignorant enough to keep a blush from my face. He continued, sounding slightly resigned, "But one doesn't chose a life's partner for form, and the simple fact is that your mind comes as part of the deal—and *that* is a part of you that, despite years of musing over it, I have yet to fathom."

*Years?* I did not care for the sound of his phrasing.

"I thought I understood you, once," he continued. "Beautiful and arrogant and blind to suffering. And I had almost learned to hate you. But then I heard that the pristine Danica Shardae had knelt in the blood and filth of the battlefield and held my brother's hand and sung to him so he would not die alone. It made me think that perhaps you might have a heart after all."

I jumped when he reached toward me, belatedly recognizing the movement as something casual, a mere gesture while he spoke. His hand froze, as if he had not even realized he had moved until I reacted, and then it balled into a fist.

Zane was on his feet instantly. "Damn it, Danica!" he hissed, his voice soft but full of impatience. "I'm not going to hurt you."

I stood as soon as I felt Zane's temper, stepping back from the serpiente. Fear made my voice venomous as I responded, "Forgive me if I find it difficult to completely trust the man who has had so many of my kind killed."

"If I wanted to hurt you, I would have done it already," Zane replied bluntly. "I didn't have the slightest bit of difficulty slipping past your guards. Your avian heart beats almost a hundred times a minute at rest. Poison from a cobra's bite would reach your brain within seconds, so quickly you would never have a chance to cry out." His red eyes flashed with challenge, daring me to contradict him. "Trust me, little avian, when I say that if I wanted you dead, you would have been dead long ago. I wouldn't have bothered to set up this whole meeting with the Mistari. I would have broken into your room in the dark of night and smothered you with that Chinese silk pillow that you keep on top of the trunk at the foot of your bed."

*"What?"* My voice was very faint, with shock this time instead of fear.

I knew that he was only pretending to misunderstand when he said, elaborating, "You know the one I mean—gold and red silk, with flying black and silver dragons. Beautiful, obviously handcrafted—"

"Who told you about it?" I demanded, my fear jelling with anger to form a well-practiced surface of calm.

Zane raised an eyebrow as he collapsed back onto the cushion on the floor. "About the silk pillow? Or about the oaken chest it sits on?" He paused, raising his red gaze to meet mine, and I held it without wavering. "Or maybe about the white woolen blanket you sleep with in colder weather, which is as soft as new down, and the heavy tapestry that hangs across the open balcony doors in good weather."

My voice was lodged in my throat. "How . . ."

"I've been there," he answered simply. "I've seen it. The Hawk's Keep isn't the easiest place in the world to sneak into, but I have a talent for such things. I nearly got myself caught the first time, trying to figure out how to get to the first floor, but luckily avian guards don't often look *up* for an enemy. From there, there are servant staircases. You don't even keep your door locked, Danica."

*I will now.*

Finally he lowered his gaze, and I let out the breath I had been holding. "You're making this up." It wasn't possible he could have gotten by the Royal Flight. And no matter what time of the night, someone would have seen him in the halls.

"You really think so?" Zane sounded amused. "The first time I saw you, Danica, I was sixteen. I had just lost the first of my brothers in an avian attack. Someone—I don't remember who—told me you had just turned fifteen. For your birthday, my brother died." Despite the words, his voice remained calm, tired. "I rode a horse to the old Desmodus paths, and then cut through the woods. It was an hour or so after midnight when I found myself at your bedside. I meant to kill you."

"And why didn't you?"

"Sit down, Danica," Zane requested, in almost a sigh. "Do you have even the faintest idea how beautiful you are?" When I did not respond, he closed his eyes, as if picturing a long-ago memory. "You were fifteen. Only a year younger than I was. You were wearing white lambskin pants, and a blouse made of fur-lined cotton. I assumed you had fallen asleep before preparing for bed." He shook his head, opening his eyes. "I remember thinking you were as striking as the chaste Greek goddess of the hunt. I was young. And I wasn't a killer—not then, anyway. I had never killed before, and I couldn't start by destroying something so exquisite. I reached out to touch your cheek."

I was trapped in his story, trapped in the

cool voice and hypnotic eyes. As Zane spoke, he reached out, brushing fingertips over the soft skin of my cheek. His hands were cool but not cold, the touch as light as a snowflake's kiss. Even the contact of skin on skin, so unusual among my own kind, could not pull me from the spell.

"You cried out in your sleep and pulled away from me. And then I saw the cut on your cheek, right here. Your arm had another slice, like you had been in a fight." As he spoke, he traced the phantom injuries, which had long since healed. I suddenly knew exactly the time he was speaking about, remembering as if it had been yesterday: It was the day Vasili was killed. Only quick action from the rest of the Royal Flight and the defensive tactics Rei had taught me had saved my own life.

Zane's voice pulled me from my thoughts. "For a moment I wanted more than anything just to take you into my arms, but you had pulled away from me once already, and I was afraid of frightening you. I told myself I hated you." His voice remained gentle despite the words, as he trailed fingers through my hair. "But it wasn't true. You weren't responsible for the fighting. You weren't able to stop it any more than I was."

"Why are you telling me this?" My voice seemed very far away.

Zane spilled onto his knees, which brought him abruptly closer to me; my breath hitched sharply with surprise, but the way I was sitting kept me from jumping away.

"You didn't start this war, Danica, and neither did I," Zane stated. "It's been going on for so long it's meaningless; people fight because they don't know what else to do. People fight because their leaders fight, and then their leaders are killed, so they have more reason to go on." His hands touched mine as if he could not help but reach out. "Danica, my sister Irene is carrying a child. She was white with fear when she told me. It's an event that should bring joy . . . but everyone in my family just remembers an avian soldier plunging his knife into my oldest sister's swollen belly." I started to speak, but he put a finger against my lips. "No apology is necessary from you, Danica." Again the gentle caress of hands running through my hair as he explained, "I am going back to the royal hall tomorrow evening. My mother, sister and guards will not be there to argue with the Disa and me. I hope you'll be there, and that you'll listen to what she has to say. What she suggests . . . it might work. I'm just asking you to give the idea a chance."

Giving that particular idea a chance sounded akin to giving suicide a chance, and I knew Zane saw my hesitation.

"Please, Danica," he said. "You sang to my brother of peace and hope. I can't believe that you aren't as desperate for those things as I am. Just . . . try."

Somehow, I found myself nodding. "I will try," I answered finally, struggling not to think of how Zane knew the details of those long hours on the battlefield. He ignored my uncertainty.

"Thank you." He stepped forward so suddenly, his lips a brief, gossamer touch on my cheek, that I let out an unintended cry.

That shout, louder than our hushed voices, brought two of the Royal Flight instantly into the room.

Zane tensed, backing away from me as well as from my guards, and I could see his garnet eyes flashing as they looked for a way out. Insanely, I stepped between Zane and the Royal Flight, though Rei moved forward as if to stop me.

"There's no trouble here," I assured him, my gaze cool with the warning not to challenge me on this point. "I was just about to escort Zane out, anyway."

I felt Zane's tension lessen, but even so, the feel of him behind me made the feathers on the back of my neck rise.

"Zane?" I prompted, praying silently that he would not cause trouble now.

"Thank you for speaking with me at such a late hour, Danica," Zane answered smoothly, his voice as polished as my own, betraying none of the emotion of moments ago. However, his movements were cool and languid, almost lazy—dangerous. Everyone who had seen serpiente fight knew that they could strike as quickly as the snakes that were their second forms. They appeared so graceful and slow that you felt like you should have eternity to move, but you never did.

He was prepared to fight. Despite any noble words he might have said to his sister before she came to the Hawk's Keep, if the Royal Flight attacked him, he would fight back.

The posture almost made me refuse when he offered his arm, but his eyes still held a glimmer of hope, begging me to help him keep this from becoming a battle, so I swallowed my fear and forced myself to accept.

The guard on my side stepped back to allow us to pass, but Zane had to shoulder past Rei on his way out; the crow directed at Zane a look that would have wilted most enemies in their tracks. Instead, Zane caught Rei's glare, wrapped an arm around my waist and kissed me again.

I was too shocked at first to respond. In the time it took me to blink and Rei to stride forward with murder in his eyes, Zane had already stepped back, his gaze turning from Rei to me as he nodded a polite good evening, changed shape and disappeared.

Rei scanned the area around us as he demanded of me, "Are you all right?"

"He simply wanted to talk about tomorrow's discussion with the Disa," I answered honestly. "He was perfectly polite."

Rei looked skeptical, and the coolness in his tone as he asked, "Really?" reminded me that what he had seen had most certainly not been "perfectly polite."

"He was perfectly polite until you provoked him," I amended, voice hard.

"I see," Rei said, and this time the unspoken question in his words came through to me and my cheeks colored.

I turned on my heel to return to my room; childhood friend or no, I did not need to justify myself to my guard, and on this subject I would not do so.

As I walked into my room, I heard Rei say, "Inform the Tuuli Thea. Shardae!" he called, following me in. "Danica, wait. Please. I just did one of the stupidest things I have ever done: I intentionally got into a glaring match with a serpiente. And during those moments, he could have killed you. Do you understand? You might have seen a show of serpiente bravado from a fellow monarch trying to unnerve your guards. I saw him grabbing you, cobra fangs practically brushing against your skin, as I stood there *unable to move.*"

I sighed, exhausted from the events of the day, frightened by how they were progressing and not willing to fight. "Rei . . ." I hugged him gently, a gesture too familiar for any avian setting, which made Rei tense for a moment before he hugged me back. It was nice to be in his arms and to abandon for a moment the reserve I was always expected to maintain. "Thank you for watching out for me."

"Danica—"

"I'm sorry I scared you," I continued, before Rei could finish whatever he was about to say. "But this time, you needn't worry about what happened. No threats passed between us—just talk. Two of us trying to figure out how to end this stupid war."

Rei nodded. "Danica, I—"

He broke off, stepping away from me and falling back into the formal warrior's posture as my mother entered, golden eyes cold as ice.

"Shardae, explain," she said shortly.

I resisted the desire to sigh in annoyance. "Mother, may we discuss this tomorrow? I would like some sleep before I need to speak to the Mistari Disa again."

"I would like to know what Zane Cobriana was doing in your private chambers," the Tuuli Thea responded.

"He came to talk," I answered, trying not to sound petulant when I was so exhausted that I was probably swaying on my feet. "He was worried that if we did not communicate first, the meeting with the Mistari Disa would go the same way tomorrow as it did tonight."

"And well he should be. It was an atrocious suggestion then, and it will still be tomorrow."

"Are you so certain it can't work?"

My mother's eyes widened, and she lapsed into the informal in her shock. "Danica, you can't seriously be considering . . ." She trailed off. "It's impossible, and I won't allow it."

"I will be Tuuli Thea of my own right in a few weeks," I responded. "You don't need to allow me anything."

"For the moment, I do," she argued. With a glance at my guards, she ordered, "Andreios, get your flight together, and send the Mistari Disa our apologies. We will be leaving tonight."

"Mother!"

"Shardae, there will be no discussion on this point," she said sharply. "We are bringing you home if I need to have the Royal Flight hold you by your pinfeathers the entire way."

"What about the serpiente?" I protested. "We should at least—"

"Shardae, obey me!" To that final tone there was to be no argument.

My head lowered so she would not see the fury on my face, I forced out the words, "Yes, Mother."

# CHAPTER 6

THOUGH I WAS INFURIATED BY THEIR RE-
fusal to listen to anything, I understood the
response my mother and guards had given to the
Mistari's proposal. In avian society, a young
woman was often promised to her future alistair
shortly after birth. The two grew up together, he
raised to be a guide and protector, and she raised
to trust him implicitly. He was expected to walk
the fine line of an avian gentleman, respecting
her strength and sheltering her from the harshest
of her world at the same time.

Vasili had been the son of two of the
Ravens. By virtue of his position as my alistair, I
was closer to him than any of my family or
friends.

Trying not to think of what I could not

change, for the next fortnight I threw myself into preparing for the position I would soon officially assume as Tuuli Thea. Those duties took up most of my hours, and when they lessened, I trained with the Royal Flight.

My mother had never approved of my being taught to fight, but neither had she approved of my walking the fields where the skills were necessary. Rei had long ago insisted that I learn some fighting skills, and now that I was restricted to the Keep, I used those lessons as an excuse to work off excess energy. Naturally, I could never best his people, but my skills were extensive enough to startle many members of the Royal Flight.

Half a month after our retreat from the Mistari, I was approached by a young girl no more than sixteen. She was slender and well built, and the fire in her eyes told me the question she was going to ask before she asked it.

"Shardae?" she greeted me, with the half-curtsy that was appropriate here. I nodded in acknowledgment. "My name is Erica Silvermead. I spoke to the Tuuli Thea earlier today, and she referred me to you. If there is a place available, milady, I wish permission to join the Royal Flight."

I gazed at the girl in resignation, not surprise. She was young, but no younger than so many of our warriors were when they began—no younger than so many of our warriors were when they died.

"Do you have any training?" I asked.

"Some, milady," the girl responded. As we spoke, I sized her up. Whatever training she had had was not formal, or she would have been standing at a soldier's ready, left hand gripping right wrist. "My brother taught me what he could." The unspoken words *before he died* hung at the end of that sentence.

"Follow me, and you may present yourself to the Royal Flight for consideration," I said, though I suspected this girl was of a lower class than the Royal Flight usually accepted.

Erica was a sparrow, a breed almost never admitted to the Royal Flight, since both their human and avian forms had a tendency to be light and unsuited to fighting. However, Andreios would make the final decision based on her abilities. If he thought her an ill fit for his elite group, there might still be room for her among one of the other flights.

Changing into my hawk form, I led the way down through the open circle in the floor and to the ground level, where the Royal Flight was currently sparring without weapons—a form of fighting that was an avian soldier's worst nightmare. My kind had the advantage of flight. If we were lucky, a battle could be finished with a volley of arrows shot from above. However, a clipped wing or lost bow could bring a soldier to the ground, where he would instantly be surrounded by an enemy who had every advantage.

Rei noticed my entrance and approached. I saw him take in the girl at my side. "Are you looking for me, Shardae?" he asked.

"If there is space to train her, Erica Silvermead would like consideration to join the Royal Flight."

Rei's brows tensed slightly, as if he was trying not to frown. "Silvermead . . . I believe I met your brother once, Lady Erica."

She nodded, keeping her head down a moment to compose herself. "You saved his life, nearly five years ago; he spoke of it often. I'm surprised you remember."

"He is quite a soldier, if I recall," Rei mused.

"He was," Erica amended softly.

"Ah." Rei nodded, bringing the conversation back into safe, neutral territory. "Come this way, and we'll see what kind of fighter you are, Silvermead."

He tossed her a blunted practice blade that, while not sharp enough to cut flesh, could cause plenty of bruises; I had earned enough of those myself during Rei's training sessions.

Erica's eyes lit up and she barely managed to avoid grinning.

"Try not to look so gleeful," Rei chastised

lightly. "Remember your goal, Erica: to protect your Tuuli Thea and her heirs, at the cost of your own life if necessary. You are a warrior. That means you will go onto a field someday soon, and you will kill another person."

Erica's gaze fell, but I could tell she was not overly daunted by the prospect of murder. Politely, she responded, "I apologize, sir, but one can hardly call serpiente *people*."

Rei nodded, not arguing. Erica was not unusual; this was a frame of mind most avians, children and adults, held strongly. However, Rei did ask, "If I bring you into a fight, can I trust you to retreat if ordered?" Erica tried very hard to hide her annoyance at the idea, but did not succeed. "I cannot allow you in my flight if you will not leave a fight when told to do so."

"Does this flight frequently retreat, sir?" Erica asked acidly.

Rei looked at me for a moment. "We are to protect Lady Nacola and her heirs," he explained, for what sounded like the hundredth time. "Frequently, that involves getting our charge off the field and out of enemy sights, and then following her. We are no good to the Tuuli Thea if we die for our pride."

"Yes, sir," Erica answered sullenly.

Her grin was gone, and her gaze was still down when Rei drew the knife from his side.

Erica reacted before the blade had even fully

left the sheath, and soon the two were in a flurry of attack and riposte that made my head spin in the attempt to follow. Rei was being cautious, testing his new charge, but I could tell he was using more effort to defend himself than he usually had to with novices.

To end the fight he got inside her guard and pressed the blade against her throat. Erica's blade was useless, trapped against her side.

She, however, did not admit defeat.

She passed the blade behind her back, transferring it to her left hand, and instantly it was against Rei's chest, the blade pressing just over his solar plexus.

"You're dead, Erica," Rei said.

"I'm not alone," she responded easily, slightly breathless, skin flushed with adrenaline.

Rei nodded, acknowledging the point. "You have some good moves," he admitted. "Care to try it again?"

This time he did not rebuke her grin; not waiting to recover, Erica returned her blade to her dominant hand and began the fight anew.

Rei did not check his ability in order to test hers, but while Erica did not have a chance to attack, she defended herself well.

As evening progressed, I made my way to the second-level court.

The market was peppered with gossips; the

court was filled with practiced scholars and speakers. Rhetoric replaced simple stories; ballads replaced the weepy tales. The serpiente's recent attempts at peace had already become legend, and the argument about what they really wanted was still going on. The idea that they had been honest was never considered.

After supper, the younger members of the court retired; had I not been heir to the Tuuli Thea, I would probably have been escorted out with the others. As it was, if I sat quietly I could hear the stories that the minstrels and scholars considered too indiscreet to share when the students were still in the room.

Rei usually came to court at about this time, mostly to call attention to me and hush the conversation when he deemed it inappropriate for his charge's ears, but tonight he was late. He sent another crow from his flight, but that young man had obviously not spent much time at court and was easily caught in the web of words all these speakers wove.

As I sat silently on the edge of the court, not in my place at the center table, people forgot I was present. Soon the scene in the Mistari lands was being discussed: how Zane had kissed me—scandalous!—in full view of two of the Royal Flight—shocking!—and neither one had made a move to stop him until he was already gone.

Though speculation about his motives and why the Royal Flight had reacted so slowly was a bit strong, the details were essentially correct; listening made me wonder how many of the other stories were true.

"Shardae."

I jumped at the voice behind my left shoulder, as did the guard Rei had sent to accompany me.

Rei dismissed the young guard with a displeased scowl, then simply said to me, "Considering how early you rise in the morning, I would be remiss if I did not point out to you how late it is getting." In other words, he could not order me from the court—he had no authority to do that—but he had no intention of letting me stay to listen, either.

Rei escorted me to my floor. Once, this level had housed all of my family: the Tuuli Thea, her pair bond and her sister and my own sister and brother in addition to me. Now, the empty rooms hung heavy with silence.

I bid Rei good night; then, as I had done every evening since our visit to Mistari lands, I listened to Zane's words over and over in my mind. Could he have been honest? I could not help fearing him for being the Diente, for the flames in his eyes and the fangs that were hidden but never gone from my mind. And yet I wanted so much to believe that he really wanted peace.

I slipped out of the slacks and blouse I had worn to court, and into my favorite cotton nightgown. The pale rose color always made me feel as if I was curled up in a sunrise. Small comfort, but I needed it.

# CHAPTER 7

DREAMS SLID INTO MY MIND SO SLOWLY I had no sense of falling asleep.

Nightmare chased nightmare, until finally I was ten years old, on my knees on the crimson field, with two of the Royal Flight physically restraining me so I would not run to my sister's side. They tried to be gentle, but I fought tooth and nail to get away, ignoring the chaos of battle surrounding us—

I was dreaming, I realized.

My sister had died nine years ago.

Still, the smell of blood was so strong . . .

I tried to wake up, but only succeeded in throwing myself into another lucid nightmare. I felt a serpent's blade slice into my shoulder, saw an eleven-year-old Andreios—armed only with the bloody dagger he had taken from his father's still-warm body—throw himself at the enemy to protect my eight-year-old self.

I screamed as I saw the serpent start to uncoil to retaliate; I knew Rei would carry the scars from the serpent's fangs in his skin for the rest of his life, and I could not stop myself from trying to change history.

This time, instead of being knocked out, I was struck solidly in the gut by an enemy blade, knocked down with a choked cry of pain.

Vasili caught my hand, and though his expression was usually cool and remote, distanced as the hardest warriors always got eventually, he let me see past the reserve to glimpse the affection and concern in his nearly black eyes.

I was fifteen; he was seventeen. Vasili was not the warmest companion, but as he helped me to stand—not berating me for my foolishness in trying to find Rei's younger sister even though we had both known from the start it was too late to help her—I loved him.

I knew I was dreaming, but it was so good to see him again. I had missed him so much. . . .

And then he was twisting away, his hand going for his weapon as he pushed me behind him so that he took the knife that had been thrown at me—

Gregory Cobriana, clenching his teeth and looking away as he died, slowly. Rei, comforting

as he could. I stood up as I had not done in real
life and walked away. The dream phantom called
after me, pleaded with me to stay, but I could not
stand that again.

And then it was Zane Cobriana before me,
twin garnets pinning me in place as he said,
"Please don't scream."

*Would I never wake up?*

I could never have done so in real life, but in
the dream I wrenched my gaze from his and
shoved him away. "What do you *want*?" I
demanded.

"I should think you would know that," Zane
answered simply.

This was absurd. I wondered bitterly when
this scene would turn to pain and violence like
the others had. My nightmares had visited paths
like this for years, one crystal-clear dream giving
way to another until the morning, but until now
they had always fallen apart the instant Zane
Cobriana appeared. Now that I had seen him,
spoken to him, my mind had more ammunition
for nocturnal torments.

Zane watched me, his expression wary.

"You don't seem dangerous enough to warrant my mother dragging me out of the Mistari
camps in the middle of the night," I commented
to the specter.

The real Zane Cobriana terrified me, but
this one was not overly intimidating. If anything,

he reminded me of Vasili. He projected a mask that was numbed to pain, but beneath it he was as fragile and tired of war as only a warrior could be.

"I don't?" Zane purred, a glint of amusement now showing in his red eyes.

I began to pace. If I screamed and kept screaming, would I scream aloud? Would Rei come in and wake me? Or would the dream slow like molasses, as nightmares did, until it seemed I could do nothing but choke on the silence?

"Danica, are you all right?" Zane asked, standing now, too, the skin between his eyebrows tensing with the hint of a frown.

"Is there some reason I should be?" I nearly shouted in return. Zane winced, his gaze flickering to the nearby doorway. "I just want to *sleep*. I don't want to dream, because all I see then are the people I have lost. I don't want to smell the stench of death and decay and rotten blood. I don't want to hear the wet sputter of someone trying to breathe past pain. I don't want to see dying *children* whenever I close my eyes. But I am nearly Tuuli Thea," I said more quietly, "and once I am, that will be my entire life. War. Death. And *I don't know how to stop it.*"

For a brief moment the arrogance was gone from Zane's expression, and he regarded me with what almost looked like respect.

"If I knew how to grant that wish," he finally

answered, voice soft, "I would have done so already, before this damn war had taken so many from me, too. Friends, lovers, family; I would have saved them all if I knew how. But if we both want peace, I can't believe that it is impossible to manage."

I caught him sizing me up, his gaze flickering down my form and up again. "Perhaps there *is* more to you than I see here, Danica," Zane mused aloud. "More than the stoic avian poise and emotionless reserve."

He reached up and ran his fingers through my hair, which brought him alarmingly close. His wrapping an arm around my waist brought me even closer, and then he kissed me, this time not hesitant in the face of my recoil or hurried to avoid a knife from the Royal Flight.

The sensation of his lips lingering over mine was startling; the light pressure of his body as he held me against himself was unexpected. He broke the kiss at the same time he pressed something into my hand.

"Tomorrow afternoon, Danica. I'll make sure the guards on the door are loyal and will let you in safely," Zane said, voice intense despite the fact that my mind was barely following it. I could feel myself sliding into the next dream segment, and I shrank from it, knowing the next scene would probably be a lot bloodier than this one. "We can't meet here in the open—your guards will kill me if they catch me—but I have enough control in the palace that we can make plans there . . . if you'll come."

I nodded, closing my hand on whatever he had given me.

He brushed the back of his hand gently across my cheek and then crossed the room to my balcony doors. I had a vague picture of him spreading wing and flying away.

Then I sat down to look at what Zane had pressed into my hand; before my fingers had finished uncurling, the scene changed and I was in the court, listening as Vasili debated some point I hardly understood but was willing to listen to simply for the chance to hear his smooth voice.

# CHAPTER 8

I DID NOT ATTEND MARKET THE NEXT DAY; I was so exhausted I probably would have fallen out of my seat. By midday, however, I had been summoned from my room.

I followed the messenger up to my mother's personal balcony, the open top floor of the Hawk's Keep. There was a gentle breeze today, and my mother looked like a romantic portrait, noble and sad, but beautiful. She was dressed in raw silk, nearly white, with golden threads woven into the material around her throat, wrists and the hem of her pants.

The topic she wished to discuss was far from romance.

"Shardae," she greeted me, dismissing the sparrow with a delicate nod. "I have a meeting this afternoon with the flight leaders. This is the last assembly before your coronation, and I thought it best that you joined me." I did not have a chance to do anything but nod before my mother added, "Come, they wait."

Though I was capable of putting faces to names and matching those names with the flights they commanded, I knew very few of the flight leaders personally. Most of them reported to Rei, who then spoke to my mother or me if there was a problem.

Avian flights were designed to work autonomously, each having its own specialties and tactics. Rarely did all the leaders meet unless the Tuuli Thea called them to, and since the decision for me to inherit early had only been made recently, I had never joined my mother for these councils.

We descended to the second floor, where the courtiers had been cleared to make way for soldiers. At a center table sat avian men and women from all levels of society, all of whom stood upon our entrance. Beside the flight commanders, I saw weapon smiths and a few merchants who dealt in trade not discussed in the marketplace.

Around that table, I saw eyes that reflected horrors of every scope. Haunted expressions met my gaze as I was introduced in turn to each defender and necessary killer. The only commander I felt at all comfortable with, Andreios, was the only one missing; the commander of the Royal Flight would converse with his queen alone. In the meantime, his flight was surrounding the Keep.

"Please, sit," my mother said. The simple words began a conference I had no wish to be at.

Karashan spoke first. "Milady, we have taken advantage of these last weeks' lull to train soldiers to replace those lost fighting the cobra's people. We have also recently received a new shipment of am'haj from Ahnmik."

The concoction of which Karashan spoke, more commonly called avian poison, was a falcon creation that my people had never been able to reproduce. Aside from occasional fatigue, it had almost no effect on my kind. However, a blade coated in it would cause almost instant death to a serpent even if the wound was minor—an advantage we needed against an enemy who could blend effortlessly into the shadows and who was both faster and stronger on land than our soldiers.

Many times, the Tuuli Thea had petitioned the falcons for more than poison, as they were rumored to possess magic, in addition to controlling the most deadly soldiers ever to live. The price for that aid, however, was surrendering our freedom to the falcons and accepting subjugation in exchange for victory. Like every queen before her, my mother had refused the soldiers.

However, like every queen before her, she

had accepted the poison. It was the only way we had survived this long.

Karashan continued, "I believe the serpiente are feeling panicked, milady. The only incidents that have occurred since Gregory Cobriana's death have been easily put down." She paused, looking about the table, where others were nodding agreement. "We need to take advantage of this time, milady."

"I assume you have a recommendation," my mother said when it seemed Karashan was hesitant to continue.

"There is obviously serious disorder among the serpiente. I suspect that your early return from Mistari land may have interfered with their plans. Before they reorganize, I would recommend a direct attack. . . . We won't—"

"No." My voice cut through Karashan's. Suddenly all eyes at the table were on me, including my mother's, which were full of disapproval at my interruption. I continued anyway. "Doesn't anyone have even the slightest hope that the reason the serpiente have not attacked is because they honestly want peace?"

I saw the answer to that question before I had even finished asking it. The other flight leaders agreed with Karashan. I saw fear in some of their eyes, but more than that I saw jaded surrender. Peace was a *myth* to these people. They couldn't think of any other existence but war.

There was no way to change that here, and yet I wasn't willing to let them destroy everything, either. Trying to appeal to their more rational side, I pointed out, "We have tried direct attacks before. They only bring slaughter. If we attack the serpiente in their own land, we *might* strike a blow, but it will be at an incredible cost." Knowing it was a painful subject for many, I reminded them, "It took half of the Ravens, a dozen of the Royal Flight and eighteen others to kill Gregory Cobriana. And in the meantime, Xavier Shardae, my brother, was killed." More than one of the commanders looked away as I spoke those words. I knew then from what flights those final eighteen had come from. "That was on our own land. When the bodies were counted, we had two soldiers down for every *one* of theirs, including many of our best fighters and our prince. And you are willing to take the battle to serpiente land? Willing to lose a dozen soldiers to the archers on the palace roof before you even reach the ground? And then what do you plan, to chase the royal family through their palace?" I sighed, shaking my head. "It's suicide, and we don't have a hope of doing enough damage to end this war." Before anyone could argue, I added, "It's suicide even if they are as disorganized as Karashan believes they are. If you can't believe that the serpiente want peace, then they obviously have a plan. Attacking their heart would be walking right into it. As soon as our forces were destroyed, they would take the Keep apart."

Silence followed my words, a silence that was heavy with the weight of defeat. I didn't want to *surrender;* we would fight to the last sparrow before we would give up. But neither could I allow them to begin a battle that would destroy us—and any last hope for peace.

"Shardae, do you have another plan?" my mother asked.

*Another plan?* I wished I could have stayed in the Mistari lands to negotiate—no matter how frightening their first suggestion had been—but my kind was not trusting enough to allow another meeting. The only way I could speak to the serpents again would be without the knowledge of my people. Alone, I would be shot down long before I could even reach the palace to request an audience.

Stalling for time, I threw my only thoughts out. "Something less direct. Something they wouldn't predict." What wouldn't they predict? We had been warring for thousands of years, fighting like two dancers who know each other's moves without thinking. "If we want to attack them on their land, we need to know what we are attacking. But we've never even managed to get a soldier inside the palace—not one who returned, anyway."

"We need to do something," Karashan

declared. "Soon. I would accept losing every life under my command, as well as my own, if we could deal a wound that wouldn't heal. We've always been conservative in the past, and we've always ended up exactly where we started. Isn't it time to risk a little more?" There were murmurs of agreement around the table.

In some generations in the past, the Tuuli Thea had been ruled by this group. If I didn't make a decision, the chance would be taken from me, but I was not ready to set a date for the slaughter.

"I am accepting the crown in three days," I stated. My voice was strong, and it hushed the mumbling. "Give me that time to think. In the meantime, make your plans for the attack; it will take you at least that long to organize the kind of offensive you are talking about. If by the morning after the coronation no one has come up with a better plan, I will give you the word to go."

I glanced at my mother for her reaction; for the next few days, she was still queen. I saw hesitation on her face and silently prayed that she would abide by my decision.

Finally Nacola Shardae nodded. "Three days, when your Tuuli Thea gives the word." She did not mention considering other possibilities, but neither did she override my words with a command to attack now. "Karashan, the Royal Flight is needed here, so you will lead the attack. After my daughter's coronation, you will present the plans to your new Tuuli Thea for her approval."

"Yes, milady."

"Dismissed, everyone," she said briskly when no objections were raised. "Unless another method is decided upon, we will reconvene the morning after the coronation."

I watched the flight leaders leave, feeling shaken. After the three days were over, this would be my life. The battle that Karashan was talking about would be madness, but I saw no way to prevent it unless I could think of an equally decisive way to end this war.

When we were again alone together, my mother said, "You spoke wisely today, Danica."

"Wise words won't save people's lives if I cannot think of another plan, and I have no other plan," I answered.

The Tuuli Thea looked at me sadly for a moment. "I don't mean to hurry you, Danica," she said gently, her voice holding a rare note of affection. "But I honestly feel you are ready to take the throne, while I am long past my prime. It is a queen's faith that keeps her people alive, but mine is running out."

"You are young yet," I argued, upset by the note of finality in her tone.

"Perhaps, but some days I feel so washed away. You still have dreams, Danica. I have faith in *you*, and in what you can do. So does Karashan, or she would not have let you stall her plans today. She has been planning this offensive since Irene Cobriana first entered our courtyard."

I shuddered at the thought that different words might have sent us all to battle today.

My mother changed the subject to lighter things. "It occurred to me while you were speaking that when you accept the position of Tuuli Thea, you might also announce your choice for alistair. It would help the morale of your people," my mother explained.

I nodded, though with reluctance. This was her way of assuring herself—and the rest of our people—that the idea proposed by the Mistari queen was preposterous. "I will consider it," I allowed.

"Have you given any thought to whom you will choose?"

The question was just a formality, since we both knew the answer was Andreios. His lineage was almost as pure as my own, and as leader of the Royal Flight, his loyalty was unquestioned.

"I will be able to give my decision after the ceremony," I answered, thinking how very short the next three days were likely to be.

When she did not speak for a moment, I inquired, "Is there anything else you would like to discuss?"

She shook her head. "I wish I could have given you peace," she said with a tired smile. "Fly with grace, nestling." It had been so long since my mother had spoken to me with anything but detached civility, a queen to her subject, that hearing her speak so fondly made my throat constrict even though the words were a dismissal.

"And you . . . Mother."

After the words, I did not return to my room, but instead sequestered myself inside the library on the third floor. If I could not think of a way to reach the Cobriana peacefully, then perhaps these books of tactics and descriptions of past battles would at least help me think of something less mad than Karashan's plans.

Instead, I found a dusty copy of an ancient text written in the smooth, flowing symbols of the old language. Supposedly, the original text had been written by the brother of Alasdair, who had been the first queen of my kind.

No one could read the old language anymore, but when I absently flipped the pages, I found a few paragraphs that had writing above them—a translation, done by a raven named Valene. She had been a highly regarded scholar, until her quest for knowledge had led her to the serpiente. She had been exiled from the courts long ago, but apparently she had translated some of this text first.

*My sister is a beautiful queen. She has seen only fifteen summers of life, but she has taken us from famine to abundance, and transformed us from a poor village of beggars to an empire to rival the falcons'. They call her the golden one.*

A bit later, another piece was translated.

*Against my counsel, Alasdair has allowed the serpents into the city. Their reputation is not kind, and I do not like their presence inside our walls. They say they are only here to trade. My sister insists they are as human as we are, and should be trusted as we trust our own.*

A few lines were translated on each of the next few pages, and then came the words I did not want to read.

*In the back. She showed them only kindness. She treated them only warmly. They have nothing to gain. Trust a snake to attack just because a trusting back is turned.*

I shuddered, putting the journal aside. Was I following in my ancestor's footsteps, giving trust to a cobra despite every warning? Was I making the same mistakes, to ultimately end with the same fate?

# CHAPTER 9

THE NEXT TWO DAYS PASSED TOO QUICKLY. Between preparation for the coronation and the looming war I felt powerless to stop, I had no time even for nerves . . . for which I was grateful. Neither did I have time to formulate a plan.

The morning before the coronation, I found on my bed two gifts, one from Eleanor Lyssia and one from the Aurita, a small shop run by a family of jewelry makers whose craftsmanship I favored but whose work I owned only one piece of. The family was too poor to be giving many pieces away but refused to sell anything to me at its full value.

I opened the package from Eleanor Lyssia and found inside a beautiful silken dress, the quality of which amazed me. The material was so soft it seemed to flow across my hands, alive, as I held it; the color was a beautiful burgundy that complimented my golden hawk's tones perfectly. I wondered how many hours she had dedicated to the intricate feather design carefully embroidered around the waist. Surely this was the work of the master seamstress, not the young girl I knew was the apprentice?

Yet there was Eleanor's signature, discreetly woven into the hem of the dress in matching burgundy thread.

The jewelry sent by the Aurita matched the dress beautifully. A fine gold chain suspended a garnet above the hollow of my throat; wisps of gold little wider than threads hung below the stone and made my skin seem to glisten.

The only other piece I owned from the Aurita was a delicate handflower, with similar fine gold chains trailing from a ring on my middle finger and across the back of my hand to a bracelet of twisted gold. The ring had been inset with a garnet that would match this, and as I recalled it, I decided I would wear that as well—if I could remember where I had put it.

Carefully, I removed the dress and laid it across the foot of my bed. The delicate necklace I placed on the nightstand nearby, and then I went to riffle through my jewelry box to find the handflower.

When I could not find it there, I checked my nightstand and the trunk that sat at the foot of my bed. Neither surface held the elusive hand-flower, but a brief search under the bed revealed something that glinted in the faint light.

I reached for it and then frowned as I realized it was silver, not gold.

As I pulled the ring into the light, it took me several long moments to realize what it was . . . and several more moments to convince myself I was right.

The stone was an oval of black onyx, inset in silver, and as I held the piece in my hand, I felt suddenly light-headed. The ring was heavy and larger than I wore—designed for a man's hand. It fit loosely on the first finger of my right hand, where it sat in satirical challenge.

I dropped heavily onto the bed, unsettling the beautiful burgundy dress. Without a doubt I knew that this was what Zane Cobriana had pressed into my hand, most likely intended as a symbol of his protection if I ventured into serpiente land. And of course, if this was real, if I wasn't dreaming now—and for a moment I hoped wildly that I was— I had not been dreaming then. I must have half-woken, roused by his presence.

I felt the heat rise in my cheeks as I reexamined my fuzzy memory of that night. I recalled my outrageous behavior and of course the neither brief nor chaste kiss with which Zane had ended the encounter.

He had asked me to come to serpiente land, and I had nodded; what had he thought when I had never appeared?

Dear sky above, he probably thought I had refused his offer to negotiate, his attempt at peace. After the fury with which my guards and family had dragged me out of the Mistari camps, Zane probably thought my nod had simply been a device to get him to leave, and of course he would not dare to return without knowing whether I had informed the Royal Flight of his presence. They would have posted guards on the servant's stair if I had mentioned Zane's nocturnal visits, and if he tried to return they would kill him on sight.

I knew what I would think, were the tables turned. For the sake of all my people, for the safety of the Hawk's Keep, I would be forced to assume the worst: that the serpiente were unwilling to consider an end to the war, and that indeed they were planning to retaliate.

Even if the serpiente had been sincere in their offers of peace, my lack of response would force them to attack before we could.

I could not afford to waste time.

Swiftly, I searched for suitable clothing: something that would not be ruined by a short walk in the woods but that was appropriate for meeting with another monarch. I settled on a soft blouse of woven raw silk the color of dark sage honey, and a pair of slacks of lightly tanned lambskin that would provide adequate warmth against the slight chill of the night. I reached for the boot knife the merchant had given me, but if I was going in peace I would need to go unarmed, as Irene Cobriana had arrived in avian land.

Unfortunately, I had no natural defenses to rely on, like a serpent's gaze or venom. I had wings with which to flee and hand-to-hand training that would never match a professional soldier's or guard's. A natural hawk takes its prey with talons and beak, striking too swiftly for resistance, and that is how my kind preferred to fight: from the sky. If I was attacked on the ground, any serpiente opponent would make it a point to keep me there.

Still, I put the knife aside.

There was, as always, a vase of flowers on the table beside my door. Remembering a signal I had developed with Rei when we were both mischievous children and I had constantly been sneaking out of the Keep, I moved the flowers from the doorway to the trunk at the foot of my bed. If he came looking for me, Rei would see the flowers and know I had not been abducted.

He would still worry, but this was the best I could do. There was no way I could ask him to come with me; bringing the Royal Flight would be suicide. Even if Zane had given his guards express orders to let me come with an entire regiment, no loyal guard would allow the cream of the avian army to enter serpiente land.

Taking a deep breath to gather my thoughts, I changed shape, luxuriating in the wonderful feeling of sliding from the awkwardly shaped human form into the beautifully streamlined, graceful one of a golden hawk.

Swift wing beats took me over my balcony, and within moments I was gone above the treetops.

I LANDED AND returned to human form several minutes' walking-time south of the serpiente palace. I knew there were archers stationed on the roof of the palace; if I tried to fly closer to the building, I doubted that even Zane's promises of safety would keep them from shooting me down.

Of course, Zane's promises still might not protect me on the ground, if he had even been honest in the first place. By this time, he probably did not think I was going to answer the invitation. If he had posted his loyal guards, the ones he trusted to greet me, he would have done so in the days after he had spoken to me. Now . . .

The woods were too quiet, and as I moved

through them toward the palace, gooseflesh rose on my arms.

"What do we have here, Ailbhe?" I jumped at the sound of the voice, and turned just in time to see a fair-haired woman step out of the forest shadows behind me.

Her white-blond hair was tied back in a loose braid, and her slender body was sheathed in smooth leather that laced down her back and both legs, tanned and darkened in a pattern so as to make her nearly invisible in the forest. Knives rode in sheaths on her thighs and at her mid-back, and a stiletto was bound in her hair. She also carried a stave as long as she was tall, the end of which was tapered and affixed to a silver blade. I recognized her as one of the guards from the Mistari palace and saw her eyes narrow as she recognized me.

Before I could move, I felt the sharpness of a blade at my mid-back. "What are you doing so far away from your flight, little bird?" a male voice inquired from behind me.

The woman stepped forward and nodded toward a wide tree nearby; a light prodding from the blade pressed against my skin moved me against the wood.

"Turn around," the woman commanded, and I did as ordered.

The guard behind me wore a similar outfit to

the first, altered to fit his gender, which I knew was the traditional uniform for the serpiente equivalent of the Royal Flight. He had the same striking white-blond hair as the woman, and features that suggested they were related.

"I'm trying to reach Zane Cobriana," I attempted to say as I turned. "He—"

The woman pressed the tip of her blade against my throat. "Quiet, hawk. Ailbhe, search her."

The man moved forward, and I tensed as he skimmed his hands over my body. The search was thorough; had I attempted to hide a weapon, it would have been found. As it was, the man seemed dissatisfied to find me unarmed. He ran his fingers through my hair as if I might have hidden a knife there, frowning at the feel of the feathers that grew at the nape of my neck. As he passed his palms over my chest, he found the pouch I wore underneath my clothing. I had hidden Zane's signet ring within it in order to avoid awkward questions in case I ran into another avian on my way here. The guard tucked the pouch into the bag he had slung across his back without looking into it.

I opened my mouth in another attempt to explain myself, but the woman shot me a glare that stilled my breath.

She spun her stave and struck me in the backs of the knees, smacking the joint with enough force to bruise. I tumbled to the ground, teeth set against the moment of pain, and the serpent addressed her fellow. "Ailbhe," she ordered, "tie her wrists." To me she added, "I'm tempted to kill you here, but Zane would be cross if I didn't let him interrogate you first."

With my wrists bound behind me, I was led by the two guards to the serpiente palace. Another pair eyed us dubiously at the front gate and followed my guards in.

Four guards for one unarmed hawk?

I remembered how Irene Cobriana had been treated when she had visited the Hawk's Keep, and realized that I was receiving the serpiente equivalent of that treatment. Did I really seem so dangerous to them?

I was led along winding paths I would never remember later. Finally we turned into a larger hall, but before I could take stock of my surroundings, one of the staves struck me in the back, knocking the wind from my lungs and sending me stumbling to my knees. Only Ailbhe's stave, positioned carefully in front of me, kept me from tumbling to my face on the mosaic floor.

Despite abused knees that protested the action, I attempted to stand, only to be struck again, this time across the shoulder. I bit my lip against the pain, trying to keep my chin up and my expression calm even though every cell of my being was screaming at me that I was deep in the serpents' nest and not likely to get out alive.

"Fetch Zane," the woman ordered one of the two guards who had tagged along at the doorway. He nodded and left the room without a sound.

She spun the stave menacingly, and I returned my gaze to the golden, copper and red marble that made up the snakeskin pattern of the floor. A few moments later the door opened, and the guard nodded sharply to one of the others to take her place as she went to greet Zane at the doorway.

Her "greeting" included sliding her arms around his waist and kissing him thoroughly enough that my blush overcame the ashen paleness of my terror; no one but me seemed surprised at the display.

Zane stepped easily into the hall, his hand lingering on the woman's waist with affection for a moment as he stepped away. "Adelina, what on earth is important enough to—"

He saw me, and instantly fury rose in his eyes; I flinched, waiting for another blow.

"Get your hands off her," Zane hissed, moving with the grace I had associated for so long with killing that my heart leapt into my throat and told me death was imminent. However, Zane dragged the guards to the side, tossing each inelegantly away from me.

Then his eyes lit on the guard he had ad-

dressed as Adelina, who was protesting loudly.
She was silenced when Zane fixed his hot red
gaze on her, cut off as surely as if he had held a
blade to her pale throat.

Compared with the warmth with which he
had greeted her, his voice made me shiver as he
asked flatly, "Did you search her?"

"Yes . . . my lord." Adelina hesitated before
using the formal, as if unused to it but recognizing that this was not a moment in which she
should be familiar. "She had nothing."

Zane nodded, apparently unsurprised.
"Out."

"Zane—"

"Out, Adelina!" Again Zane's anger, even not
directed at me, made me recoil . . . and wince at
the sudden spear of pain in my knee as I did so.

Adelina called to the others in the room, and
the rest of her group followed when she left. For
a moment I savored my surprise; had I told the
Royal Flight to leave when Zane or Irene Cobriana was in the room, they would never have
obeyed.

I jumped as Zane dropped gracefully to his
knees in front of me. He drew a knife from his
back, and for the second time in as many minutes, I was sure I was going to be killed; instead
he reached around me and cut the bonds secur-
ing my wrists.

The position brought him uncomfortably

close. As I remembered the last time I had seen him, when I had assumed myself still trapped inside a dream, I realized that he probably saw no need for formality.

After the ropes fell away and I had turned to rubbing my wrists, Zane asked quietly, "Did they hurt you?" His voice was soft, but still rang with the danger I had seen moments ago.

"A few bruises," I answered, moving to stand if only to regain a semblance of dignity. "Nothing I have not—"

I bit back a rather unladylike curse as my knees went out from under me; they had stiffened in the last few minutes and were now protesting the blow Adelina had delivered to them. Zane caught me, and as I recoiled from him, it took all his grace to keep us both from falling back to the snakeskin floor.

The flash of anger in his eyes caused me to defend his guards. "They did no more than would be expected," I assured him, thinking again of when Irene had come to the Keep. "I assume they are your personal guards?"

Zane nodded once, still visibly simmering. "Their leader, Adelina, and her second in command, Ailbhe, are brother and sister—two of the fiercest fighters among the palace guards. They are also the last possible people I would have chosen to patrol if I had known you were coming."

"You had no way of knowing," I assured him,

attempting to cool his fury. "And your guards had no way of knowing I came peacefully."

Zane said dryly, "You are more generous than I am."

"Ailbhe has the ring you gave to me," I added, my terror having receded enough for me to remember that. "I had no chance to explain to them."

Zane's response was sharp. "Adelina had him search you?"

Puzzled at the question, I nodded.

Zane drew in a breath, then let it out before he said, "I'll speak to the two of them later. Now you should come sit and rest. You've been hit more than is good for you."

Catching my arm as if the movement was natural, he led me to the smooth oaken table that sat at the back of the hall. I remembered that he had offered his arm when Rei and his guards had found him in my room at the Mistari camps as well.

Touching in general was rare among my kind, even in such a formal manner. I had gripped Rei's or Vasili's arms some days when grief or war had led me to exhaustion, and that display alone had been frowned upon by most of the court. I had heard that the serpiente were freer with contact, but until now I had never needed to compensate for that particular difference.

Suddenly it occurred to me that I had no idea

exactly how far that openness extended. I recalled how Zane's guard had greeted him, and the kisses he had stolen both at the Mistari encampment and in my own room. I had thought at the time that he probably considered me either foolish or wanton not to decidedly protest such an action, but perhaps doing so was so natural to him, and he had not considered how shocking it would be to his avian counterpart.

Slightly soothed by this realization, I settled into the chair Zane offered to me, relaxing my aching body and cataloging my bruises. They were no worse than those I had gained in mischief as a child, or in weapons drills with Rei; the bruises across my shoulders and knees would heal quickly.

"Irene made me wait one more night before I decided you were not going to come," Zane stated as he swung gracefully into the chair opposite where I sat. His anger was slightly better concealed now, but it was still visible in the slick tone of his movements. "Thank the gods she did."

"As it is, I cannot stay long," I was forced to admit. "My guards do not know where I am, or else they would never have let me be here." *And if they knew how the palace guards had "welcomed" me, they would do anything in their power to keep me from ever returning,* I thought.

Zane's expression took on a hint of surprise,

and his voice was resigned as he said, "I forget how much power the Royal Flight has over its queen." He shook his head. "Adelina never hesitates to protest when she thinks I'm likely to get myself killed, but the guard doesn't dare try to stop a cobra from doing as he wishes."

Recalling how Zane had cleared his guards from the room with one word, I had no doubts as to the truth of his statement. Catching the glimmer of anger still in Zane's gaze, I was equally certain as to why the guard was so obedient to its prince.

"You're being announced as Tuuli Thea tomorrow, correct?" Zane asked, in an abrupt change of topic.

"Yes," I confirmed, slightly surprised that Zane knew the details so well. I allowed my expression and tone to carry the question, knowing that Zane would answer or not as he thought appropriate.

Zane caught the inquiry in my voice and explained, "I've people loyal to me who have access to the Keep. They keep me informed."

I swallowed a feeling of unease at the thought of the serpiente having spies in the Hawk's Keep. More unnerving was the knowledge that they would need to be avian, or else they would have been caught long before now. Zane might have been able to sneak around the Keep at night by using the stairway, but it would be impossible to follow the goings-on in the court without the ability to fly.

"And who are these ears of yours?" I asked, unable to keep the suspicion from my voice.

"If we manage to succeed in ending this damn war, I will gladly introduce them to you," Zane answered smoothly. Though he did not say it outright, the second meaning to his words was clear. If we did not end the war, he would keep his spies in place.

I had been aware that Zane's attempt at peace might be a ruse, but I had been willing to risk that on the chance that he might be sincere. It had not occurred to me until that moment how carefully Zane must have laid his plans before inviting the avian royalty to join this negotiation dance.

With painful clarity, Zane's earlier words reverberated in my mind. *Irene made me wait one more night before I decided you were not going to come. Thank the gods she did.*

If I had not come this night, would his spies have killed me in my bed? Or would Zane himself have done the honor, ending my life with the cobra's poison that he had once assured me would stop my heart more swiftly than I could draw breath to scream? Suddenly I was sure that if the time allotted to me had run out, Zane might have attempted to end the war by eliminating the leaders of the other side—namely my mother and me—with methods far more sure than any of Karashan's plans.

As if reading my thoughts in the silence I allowed to pass, Zane stated coolly, concisely, "If I give you my word, Danica, you can be assured I will keep it. I want bloodshed no more than you do, but I will do what is necessary to end this war. If that means accepting the Mistari's suggestion, then I will go down on bended knee this moment and ask you to be my Naga. If that means listening to any other suggestion you have . . . so be it." He concluded, his tone never changing, "And if it means taking the Hawk's Keep down stone by stone with my bare hands, then without hesitation I will begin."

I stood, moving away from the intensity in his gaze. If I refused to listen . . . would I even be allowed to leave?

"I came here to talk about peace, not to receive threats."

"I gave my word you would be safe if you accepted my invitation," Zane assured me, not rising from his seat, as if attempting the impossible feat of appearing harmless. "If you turned around right now and left, neither my guard nor I would stop you."

"And afterward?"

Zane closed his eyes for a moment, and when he opened them again his expression was as remote as the morning star. "I hope we can end this war with peace, not a bloodbath," he answered. "I've reached the point where I honestly think I would slit my own wrists if I thought it would end the fighting. Unfortunately, the palace guard would not react well to losing its last prince, and again we would have a slaughter on our hands." He shook his head and finished bluntly, "You are an attractive woman, Danica, but I do not love you. I do not think I ever can. I look into your golden hawk's eyes, and no matter how stunning the form they accompany, I think only of your warriors murdering my loved ones. Since you recoil every time you accidentally find your own gaze fallen upon Cobriana garnet, I suspect you feel much the same way."

"Are these statements going somewhere?" I inquired, voice detached.

"I wanted to make sure there were no misunderstandings between us before I asked my next question," Zane answered immediately. He stood, and I braced myself to keep from flinching as he moved toward me. "I have considered our options, and elected to attempt the least bloody first." Graceful as the serpent that lived inside him, Zane went down on one knee. "With the understanding that there may never be anything between us but a shared desire for peace, and my word that I will never force upon you any duty beyond the political expectations of the position,

I implore you, Danica Shardae, to agree to be my Naga."

I felt my heart skip a beat, and for several seconds my voice caught in my throat.

He couldn't want an answer now . . . but of course he did, or he would not have asked. Zane waited silently, still as a statue, as I alternated between animalistic terror, the desire to flee, acceptance of my responsibilities and the knowledge that if I said no now, I would need to return to the council and prepare for battle.

How could I possibly *consider* saying yes when I knew that with as little hesitation as he had gone to one knee, Zane could stand and slip a knife between my ribs?

How could I consider saying no, when agreeing now might end this war?

"I don't know how in the world I could convince my protectors to back my decision," I admitted, and my voice was nearly shaking. The rest of the council would follow the Royal Flight, but I felt certain that Andreios would be the first to protest my endangering myself with this agreement.

"Yes or no is all that matters," was Zane's swift response. "We'll work out the details later."

I took a breath, felt my throat constrict and had to swallow hard twice before I could answer, "Yes. I agree."

Zane stood, catching my right hand as he did so. He laid a gentle kiss on my knuckles, then turned it over and pressed another ring into my palm.

The style matched the Cobriana signet ring, though this one was smaller, designed to fit my slender fingers. The metal was the same cool silver, but instead of the traditional black stone, this had been set with a rare golden onyx, with bands varying from pale honey to warm marigold. I knew it must have come from the Mistari's original homeland in the east.

"I have informed my people that I will announce my Naga on the new moon—two nights from now. I know it is the evening after your coronation as Tuuli Thea, and if necessary I can push it back, but it seems wise to make our move as soon as we can."

I nodded, and as it occurred to me, I added, "There will be protests, but if we go through with the announcement here before I inform the court of my decision, not only will I have the title of Tuuli Thea behind me, but it will be too late for even the Royal Flight to forbid me. It is a high crime for an alistair's vows to be broken." No one would dare order the Tuuli Thea to withdraw her promise, even if it was given to the Diente of the serpiente. I could stall picking an alistair easily enough, though it would be trickier to bluff Karashan into delaying. But it would only be a few days, long enough to seal the pact on the serpiente side; I would do it, whatever it took.

"How are your people likely to take the news?" I asked hesitantly. My main concern was that someone might attempt to kill Zane if I tried to take him to the Keep and acknowledge him as my alistair; I hoped I would not be dodging weaponry when Zane made the announcement here.

"They won't like it; they'll think I'm more than a little crazy. There will be those who will worry you are going to put a knife in me one night, and some who will think a strange avian magic has twisted my mind," Zane answered easily. "But you're beautiful, and there's no reason for them to think I'm not madly infatuated even if you are a hawk. That being so, they frankly cannot afford to take the announcement badly. One can be skinned for harming the Naga or her personal guards, which for you will include the Royal Flight. They'll be wary of picking fights with avian soldiers, at least for a while."

*Skinned?* I shuddered at the thought, though I certainly did agree that such a threat would be a strong deterrent to anyone intending harm.

I nodded, accepting Zane's reasoning. "I need to get back to the Keep before the Royal Flight comes looking for me," I stated, lifting my bruised body carefully from my seat.

"Can you be here at about midday after the

ceremony at the Keep?" Zane asked. "That will leave some time to prepare you for meeting the serpiente court." The concept of standing in front of a large group of hostile serpiente, relying only on the promise of Zane Cobriana to keep me safe, made my blood run cold.

"That should be fine," I responded, my voice sounding distant to my ears. I almost felt like I was dreaming again, but even my mind could not have created a scenario as terrifying as this one.

# CHAPTER 10

B Y THE TIME I RETURNED TO THE KEEP, IT
was nearly dawn, yet I had barely returned to
human form before Andreios was standing before
me and demanding to know where I had been.

I used the pretense of catching my breath as I
thought quickly and finally settled for the closest
thing to the truth I could manage. "When I spoke
to the flight leaders, I mentioned the possibility
of a less direct solution. I have been finalizing the
details of that solution." Rei's eyes widened as I
continued, "I have a plan, but it is discreet. In the
meantime, I want you to tell the flight leaders to
stand down. I don't want a move made beyond
what I have already triggered. I plan . . . to turn
the serpiente's plot back upon them."

I knew all the ways he could take the words,

and I knew he would never translate them to mean that I had agreed to go along with Zane Cobriana's plans. Karashan thought the serpiente were standing down to draw us into a trap. Let her think I was using the same plan.

"Are you sure?" was all Rei asked.

I wanted to tell him the full truth, but revealing the real plans would ruin them. Neither my mother nor the Royal Flight would let me get away with this madness.

That very fact was what tempted me the most. If I told them and they stopped me from going through with the insane agreement I had made with a cobra, I could tell myself that it wasn't my fault. At least until I walked the next bloody battlefield, or took the throne and, like my mother, lost children to the war. The first blood I saw would be on my hands, as would any spilled afterward.

I kept my fears to myself. "I am sure," I said. "Give Karashan the orders: not a move."

He nodded, and we parted ways. I returned to my bed to get some much-needed rest before the coronation that evening.

The ceremony was simple: a few words spoken to the court by my mother of my strength and courage and faith in the future, words that felt hollow in my ears as terror beat in my heart. From her own neck my mother removed a pendant of a golden hawk with wings spread, a solitary symbol on the end of a carefully woven gold and silver chain. I was wearing the necklace the Aurita had given to me; the piece hung high enough that I could wear the hawk pendant at the same time, so that each decoration seemed made to wear with the other.

I addressed my people, and saw my mother frown when I finished without speaking of my alistair. However, it was not until the Royal Flight knelt before me to swear their allegiance to the new Tuuli Thea that the horror of what I had promised Zane was made real to me.

"Gerard Halsan." Speaking his name, the older man knelt before me, taking my hand and speaking the words he had recited when he had sworn his allegiance to my mother before me. "To my Tuuli Thea goes my faith and my trust. To her blood goes my blade, my bow and my fist, ever to defend her and her kin. To her I swear my loyalty, and to her I swear my life ever before hers."

*My life ever before hers.* These two dozen men and women, their lives before mine. I prayed they would never need to give those lives. I prayed I could stop the war before they were called to sacrifice themselves for another helpless queen.

I knew every name and face among the Royal Flight. Some of them, like Karl and Andreios, I had grown up with; some of them, like Gerard, had guarded my mother before I was even born.

The list went on, coming at last to Erica

Silvermead. The newest member of the Royal Flight, the low-born sparrow who had shocked Andreios with her ability. If I had to guess, her name would be high on my list of Zane's possible spies; she had come out of nowhere. But I knew the assessment was not quite fair. Erica had barely been accepted into the Royal Flight, and she had only been in the Keep for a few days; Zane had implied that his spies had been in place for a while. There was just something about the sparrow that unnerved me. However, Rei seemed very proud of how well she fought, so I did not speak my unease. As Erica swore her vows, her voice rang sincere.

The last to stand before me was the commander of the Royal Flight himself.

Andreios stood respectfully, but in his eyes was a look akin to pain, a question he would not ask. Still, he smiled at me as he approached and went to his knee.

"To my Tuuli Thea goes my vow to train those under me, to lead them well, so our wings may be hers if she falls, so our eyes may be hers in darkness, and our talons may be hers in danger. To her blood goes my blade, my bow and my fist, ever to defend her and her kin. To her I swear my trust and my loyalty. To her I swear my life ever before hers."

He took my hand and kissed the back of it. The movement was formal, but I wished it was not. I had sworn myself to another man, a cobra, and left Rei to wonder what had happened to keep me from naming him my alistair today as we had assumed I would.

THE RECEPTION AFTER the coronation and the vows was a farce. Every member of the avian court approached me with congratulations and words of advice, and to all of them I wanted to say, "Do you know what I have done? What I am going to do?"

My mother approached me as soon as I had a moment of peace. She offered no words of congratulations, but said, "You decided not to choose your alistair tonight?" The words asked many things.

I had practiced my half-lies since speaking to the council, and when I answered, my voice was polished. "We spoke a few days ago of acting in this war. I have been working with a select few on a plan that I hope will be less bloody than sending scores of soldiers into enemy territory." I saw a moment of surprise in my mother's face and continued. "I would like, when I announce my alistair, to announce with him a new reign of peace. I would like to announce that Zane Cobriana no longer stands as our enemy. And I intend to."

Skepticism was not hidden from my mother's voice as she asked, "What is this plan?"

"Wait, Mother," I answered with a sigh. "I will announce the outcome . . . in three days' time, in front of the court. I will announce my alistair then. Until then, I will hear no questions."

I knew she wanted to ask, but she held her tongue. I was Tuuli Thea now; she had no power to challenge me.

It was nearly midnight when I managed to sneak out to the balcony for a breath of fresh air. I leaned against the railing, staring at the line where the treetops met the starlit sky.

I was not alone long. Andreios joined me, not speaking but giving me a chance if I wanted it. I only wished I knew what to say.

I started to turn away, but his voice drew me back. "Danica?"

His features were shadowed, but not enough to hide the look of determination on them.

"It's all right," he said, voice gentle. "I understand. I love you, and I always have. What matters to me is that you are happy. If there's someone else, I wish you luck with him." My heart raced at his words. I opened my mouth to say *There's no one else*, but of course there was—a serpent. "And if you're just not ready, I can wait."

I was unwilling to lie, but couldn't tell him the truth. I reached out to him, and he caught my hand and kissed the back of it. I remembered Zane doing the same so recently and couldn't speak. Words of love seemed cruel when the next night I would pledge myself to another man.

The words I uttered were halting but honest. "You have been a friend to me ever since we were children." I saw him flinch at the words, but continued, "There is no one I trust more. No one I care for more. But . . ." I shook my head. "It's impossible to explain."

I saw a sudden hint of fear and suspicion in his eyes and turned away before he could speak again. I returned to my room and collapsed into bed, where I stared at the ceiling and tried to block my own fears from my mind.

I WOKE A few hours after sunrise. Yawning, I dragged myself out of bed and called for a cold bath to try to rouse myself.

The hawk pendant was still around my neck, and I lifted it to examine the intricate detail of the wings and eyes.

*Tuuli Thea.* Though I had been preparing for the title since my sister's death, the position still seemed unreal. The idea that I was now the one the Royal Flight would look to, the one who would hear complaints of the common people in the market and the one who would be expected to administer justice in response to a crime seemed impossible.

*And by tomorrow, the title will be Naga as well.* I did not wish to dwell on that prospect, but of course I was forced to as I took my bath and the cold water woke my mind and my fears.

The dress I had worn for the ceremony the day before had been aired and hung. Though the flowing skirt, decent neckline and low back designed to allow the Demi form's wings to grow if it became necessary was an avian style, the warm burgundy and soft silk reminded me of the outfits I had seen Irene and Charis wear. It would be perfect for the ceremony at the palace. I laid it out with a silent thanks to Eleanor, its creator.

Struggling into the complicated garment alone might prove difficult; a maid had helped me with several of the clasps in the back the first time. But I would manage.

The next problem was a slightly larger one.

I could not simply disappear all day and evening without exciting a panic among the Royal Flight.

I drafted a letter, though I knew leaving a note in my room was a rather guilty way of avoiding confrontation. I also worried that someone might find it too early. I needed someone who could cover for me for a few hours and then explain to the Royal Flight where I had gone.

Eleanor. Might she be of help? She was more open-minded than most of the court, and might be willing to be my intermediary. I summoned her to my drawing room and paced on the balcony as I waited for her to appear.

"I need a favor from you," I stated once the woman was present and the page-in-training who had brought her was gone.

"What would you like?" she answered easily, unsuspicious.

"I have been conducting negotiations with the serpiente," I explained, leaving out all specifics and watching her face carefully for signs of revulsion. Eleanor appeared startled, but did not immediately reject the idea. "The Royal Flight does not know what my plans are, but I am worried I will be missed while I am away today—"

"Won't they expect you to be at market for Festival?" Eleanor asked with wide eyed faux innocence. "I know it's supposed to be a day for merchants and children, but I've never in my life known you or any of the royal family to miss it."

In the recent days' mixture of confusion and tension, I had honestly forgotten about Festival, which occurred about two months before midsummer. Every year, market was filled to bursting with magicians, storytellers and other entertainers. Though the Tuuli Thea and her heirs were traditionally not a part of the celebrations, I had always loved the bright decorations and beautiful songs that accompanied them. Even the Royal Flight let its guard down, as it was un-likely that anyone would manage to harm the heir to the Tuuli Thea among such a press of her subjects.

"Perfect," I breathed. "Andreios won't be surprised if he doesn't see me until nearly sunrise." Pacing with nervous excitement, I asked, "Eleanor, would you be able to deliver a message to the Royal Flight? I might be back before they even miss me, but if not, Andreios should be informed of my whereabouts."

Eleanor nodded. "I can do that. Festival will last until sunrise. If I have not heard from you by then, I can speak to your protector."

"Thank you." I read over my letter one more time before sealing it and entrusting it to the seamstress.

Eleanor's gaze moved to the burgundy dress that I had not yet donned to replace the simple outfit I was wearing for the morning, and I saw her smile a little. "I know the design on that is a little complicated. Do you need help?"

"Eleanor, you are a goddess," I breathed. So far, this venture was falling into place easily—too easily. It was beginning to worry me.

Dressed and ready, I gave one last look to the letter Eleanor held. It was a concise explanation of my conversations with Zane Cobriana to date, as well as where I would be that evening, and why. *If you wish to seek me,* the letter continued,

*I recommend that you do so peacefully. I want this ceremony to proceed without bloodshed, and you are enough of a soldier to know that Zane's people will not respond well if your flight appears fully armed at the palace. I do not know what serpiente tradition expects of this ceremony; I will return as soon as is seemly.*

The letter was signed and sealed, and it would be delivered. Now all that was left was to make the words true.

MY GREETING AT the serpiente palace was much gentler this time, and it came in the form of a trio of young female guards. They said little, and while their gazes alternated between distaste and curiosity, I was neither searched nor struck, for which I was grateful beyond belief.

Once again I was led through the twisting maze of the serpiente palace, and though I tried to memorize the turns we took and the doors we passed through, I found it impossible to do so. I was glad I was a willing guest and not a prisoner trying to escape; one could probably wander these halls for hours without finding anyplace familiar.

A tendril of curiosity rose. In the past, I never could have imagined exploring the inside of the serpiente palace, which was described as a labyrinth of halls and secret passages. Now, I might have a chance.

I recognized the large honey-oak double

doors before my escort pushed them open to reveal the hall where I had met Zane the first day I had come here.

Zane was pacing anxiously, while Irene and Charis Cobriana were seated at the large table that dominated the far side of the room. Now Zane dismissed the three guards with a word and greeted me warmly.

"Danica, allow me to introduce Naga Charis Cobriana," he first began formally. "And you have met my sister, Irene."

"A pleasure to meet you." I was very proud of myself; my voice did not shake as I greeted the present Naga of the serpiente, Zane's mother.

I also forced myself to meet her gaze as I spoke, as was polite; Charis did not attempt to hold my eye. "My son speaks quite highly of you." There was some laughter in her voice, as if Zane's speaking "quite highly" might have been intermixed with his speaking quite lowly, but considering I had been on pins and needles lately, I could only imagine how Zane had been around his family.

"How shortly should I expect your guards to storm the palace?" Zane asked, his voice also holding an amused lilt that did not manage to completely cover the more serious thoughts beneath.

"The Royal Flight will be informed of my whereabouts shortly before sunrise, if I have not returned by then," I answered, my voice as light as his despite my nervousness.

One of the hall's double doors opened partially and Adelina entered. She nodded deferentially to Charis and Irene, then said, "Zane, you are needed."

"Am I?" Zane's voice was clipped, not cold but short with tension. "I'd like to know what your guard needs me for at this moment."

"*I* need to speak to you," she amended, with a look to kill directed at me.

"You can speak as freely in front of Danica as you can in front of me," Zane assured her.

A moment of awkward silence followed, stretching until Irene stood and put a hand on Zane's arm. The cobra caught Zane's eye and nodded sharply in Adelina's direction, a silent command. "She deserves a chance to speak with you before the ceremony. Mother and I will prepare Danica."

Zane hesitated, but finally led the way out of the room. They paused in the hall, and Adelina closed the door.

"She knows not to hit anywhere the bruises will show, right?" Charis asked lightly.

Irene smiled wryly. "She knows—though I doubt Zane's in a mood to tolerate it even if she is justified."

"Is there something I'm missing here?" I asked worriedly. The implication that Zane's own guard might harm him was rather unpleasant.

It occurred to me again that there were reasons beyond history behind why the serpiente and the avians were at war. If a member of the Royal Flight raised a hand to my family or me, he or she would be ostracized to human society, feathers shorn, grounded forever. Yet Charis and Irene were discussing the possibility of Adelina's striking Zane as if it was commonplace. There were so many fundamental differences between our kinds, it was no wonder we had lived so separately for so long.

"Adelina and Zane have a complicated relationship. She has been very vocal with her protests of this arrangement," Charis explained.

As if on cue, Adelina's voice rose outside the door. The words were not understandable through the heavy oak, but the tone was, and it suggested that Charis's assumption that there would be violence was not far off the mark.

The voices drifted down to silence, moving away through the hall. When it was quiet once more, Irene spoke.

"The ceremony will occur in the synkal—that's where any public event takes place and every serpiente is admitted. Zane is very popular among his people, which means the synkal will be full. You will be separated from the crowd for the actual announcement, but later you will be expected to move among them. The serpiente do not expect nor want distant monarchs; if you refuse to see your people, they will not tolerate you. No weapons are allowed in the synkal, and in addition to Zane, you will have a guard with you at all times. That should keep any surprised zealots from putting a knife in you this evening."

My blood had already turned to ice. I nodded calmly, past the point where I could be shaken. I was used to walking among my own people, but I *trusted* the ravens, crows and sparrows of my home.

"After that, the majority will be wary about starting fights. The guard will keep a lookout for troublemakers, but as I said, Zane is popular: If he seems happy, his people will follow him." Irene looked to Charis, as if wondering what she should say next.

Charis sighed lightly before asking, "Danica, how much do you know about our kind?"

The question took me aback. The answer was knowledge of how to fight them, and a hodgepodge of rumors and myths that might or might not be true. "Not much," I admitted.

"One thing my daughter would not think to mention," Charis continued, "is that there are some basic differences of behavior." At this Irene was listening as intently as I was. "In avian society—correct me if I am wrong, please—one is expected to behave with a level of distance and formality that is all but unknown among my people. As Tuuli Thea, you are expected to be more a symbol than a power, speaking with cool rhetoric and moving with simple grace. As Naga, the rules are different. A serpiente leader is a friend to her people and sometimes closer, occasionally a rival, but never detached. You've spoken with my son enough to know that every emotion he feels, he shows, and that is what is expected."

"Please go on," I said, trying to take in what she was telling me.

"Zane will not push you further than you are comfortable going," Charis assured me, "but the fact is that you are going to need to convince the serpiente that this is not a match of convenience. The Diente does not choose his mate for politics or money or whatever foolishness humans marry for. If the people think Zane chose you for any reason other than love, they will not accept you."

I tried to speak and found my throat too dry to do so.

"They will expect you to be afraid, but they will think you brave—especially since Zane plans to let it be known that you do not have the approval of your own kind yet, but are willing to go through with this and convince your people to agree with you later. He has turned this match into the very image of young, reckless love, and that is the image you will be expected to preserve among the serpiente public."

I nodded, not at all sure I would be able to follow through. As Zane had pointed out, I could not even meet his gaze without wanting to recoil. "And this will involve . . . ?"

"It will involve being closer than you are probably comfortable with," Charis stated bluntly. "Touching among my kind is not just common, it is expected. Stay near Zane; that you will need to do anyway. Forget your polite avian reserve. I'm not suggesting you two make love in the middle of the synkal floor, so you can cool that charming avian blush from your face, but you will have to touch him—even if it's just an arm around his waist. Remember, you are hopelessly in love. The two of you can't keep your hands off each other. Zane is determined not to overstep his bounds with you. He would risk the whole venture to keep from doing so. It will be up to you to take initiative and keep the masquerade going. Does that make sense?"

"I understand." Could one be cold as ice and still have her face on fire from such simply stated words? Apparently so.

Charis Cobriana nodded. She opened her mouth as if to say more, then closed it again. After a moment, she said, "Thank you, Danica . . . for being willing to do this. When Zane first suggested that we try to arrange a meeting with the Tuuli Thea and her heir, I was his loudest skeptic. When I heard the Mistari suggestion, I was horrified." She shook her head. "I would not have had the courage even to contemplate such an idea, much less the altruism to give up what you and Zane are giving up for your people."

Words tried to surface and failed. "Thank you" seemed too deferential, "You're welcome" too arrogant. Finally I settled with, "I have lost too many people to this war. There was no way I could refuse to go through with something that might keep others from the same end."

# CHAPTER 11

I WAS GOING TO FAINT. I HAD NEVER FAINTED in my life; it was not a common avian dilemma. But at the moment, it was less terrifying than the thought of walking in front of a large group of serpiente when the only people present who might consider protecting me were Zane Cobriana and his personal guards—guards I trusted to defend me in a crowd as much as I would trust them to knife me at the earliest opportunity.

Finally I heard my cue and stepped from the antechamber and onto the dais at the north side of the synkal. Instantly I heard reaction from the crowd: shouts and questions, which were muted to dumb shock when I moved to Zane's side.

Zane's words were white noise in my ears as I stood beside him. I caught my hands trembling.

I remembered Charis's assurance that touching was common and even expected in serpiente society, and I wrapped an arm around his waist in an attempt to halt my own shaking. Zane seemed startled for a moment, then continued to speak, finishing with, "Allow me to introduce my Naga, Danica Shardae."

The palace guards were visible in the crowd; though they were not in uniform for the ceremony, I had been introduced to the majority of them by Irene that afternoon and assured multiple times that at least one of them would always be at my side. They had been prepared, and even though most of them had expressed doubts earlier, they did not allow that hesitation to show now as they knelt.

Like ripples in a pond, each guard who knelt was surrounded by other serpents who followed their lead. Within a few moments of the first guard's movement, all but four figures had recovered from their shock and knelt.

"Kendrick?" Zane's voice carried over the hall, an ounce of threat mixed with light inquiry.

"I don't know what . . ." Kendrick looked around himself and seemed to notice that he was one of very few who were making a spectacle of refusing Zane's chosen Naga. As he sputtered, one of the remaining four went down on his knee. "She's a hawk. . . ."

Zane appeared amused. "Really?"

"But, sir, she's Danica Shardae!" the poor man protested.

"I just said that," Zane responded, refusing to be ruffled.

"Zane." In contrast to his easily projected voice, mine was soft, intended only for Zane's ears. He turned to face me, ignoring for the moment the serpiente he had been in the process of turning into a fool. "You can't expect everyone to just accept this."

"Of course not," he responded softly, lowering his head so his lips were just a short distance above mine. He had wrapped his arms around my waist, and it suddenly occurred to me what our pair must look like to the court. "But I can expect everyone to pretend to."

Another of the four knelt while he was speaking. Kendrick and the woman who was still standing exchanged a glance across the room.

Zane brushed a kiss across my lips, so briefly that I had no time to respond, and then he straightened to speak to the court again. "Kendrick, there's no need for jealousy; you are welcome to go out and find your own beautiful hawk," Zane said lightly.

"Zane, this is crazy!" This came from the woman, upon whom Zane turned his gaze with a bit of a smile.

"Pamela, no doubt you are right. I must be stark raving mad." There was an amused murmuring in the crowd as Zane continued. "I must have lost my mind to want someone as beautiful and charming as this for my partner. To think Danica Shardae could possibly have walked into the synkal, despite protests from her guards and family, despite the fact that they might very well throw her out of the Keep for daring to answer my dearest prayer . . ." At that he went down on one knee before me, one of my hands clasped in his. ". . . for her to abandon all propriety and become my Naga."

By the end of the speech, Pamela was actually grinning. I could feel a similar expression on my own face at the dramatic humor with which Zane had spoken. The only thing that spoiled the moment was the glimpse I caught of white-blond hair as Adelina walked stiffly out the back of the synkal. My attention was drawn to Ailbhe, who looked after his sister for a moment, shook his head and returned his attention to the crowd.

"Zane—" Kendrick broke off as Zane tugged on my hand, bringing me down to kneel with him on the dais.

"May I?" Zane's voice was soft, as he reached forward and brushed a thumb across my lips.

I nodded.

In one graceful movement, Zane wrapped an arm around my waist and pulled me toward him, then gently pressed his lips to mine.

For a few heartbeats, I managed to ignore the fact that there were probably three to five hundred pairs of eyes on us.

I pulled back first, and Zane let me go with obvious reluctance; he kept an arm around my waist as we stood side by side, and with a sweep of his free hand he introduced simply, "Naga Danica Shardae, your people."

Two of the guard moved forward to flank us as we stepped down from the dais. Musicians took our place, and we were instantly surrounded by Zane's people . . . *my* people.

I hugged closer to Zane, feeling the flutter of my heart beating so fast it was a constant hum in my ears.

Serpents *moved* differently than I was used to, and put less space between themselves and others. The colors that surrounded me were equally foreign. Used to the warm brown or gold eyes of the avian court, here I was faced by hot garnet, sapphire and emerald gazes—jeweled tones as varied and exotic as the sensual outfits and the unreserved voices and expressions the serpiente wore. I was like a child raised without color who had suddenly been thrown onto a giant painter's palette.

It was impossible not to notice the warmth with which the serpiente greeted their Diente, or the chill with which many of them regarded me. Women found every excuse they could to reach out and put a hand on Zane's shoulder or arm.

Occasionally a man would attempt to be equally familiar with me. At that point, Zane would meet the serpent's gaze with a polite smile and a spark of ice in his eye and coolly remind the man that I had been raised an avian lady and was not used to casual touch from strangers.

In general, Zane handled the crowd like a magician, shifting from whimsy to melodrama to soft threat and back to whimsy as effortlessly as water flowing down a slope. It was eerie to watch the changes come over his face and body as he moved from one emotion to the next.

A few hours later the throng started to thin out, and a midnight feast was served for those who remained—about half of the people who had attended the ceremony.

"Zane, where is Adelina?" one female serpent asked as we settled into our places around the table. "It's rare to see you without her."

Zane's light expression clouded for an instant, but he recovered quickly. "The rest of the guard is quite competent. She wasn't feeling well, and since I wasn't expecting trouble tonight, I suggested she take the night off and let Ailbhe take over for a few hours." After having watched the play of emotion on his face all night, I knew he was lying.

But the serpiente nodded, not challenging Zane's words.

"Is Ailbhe going to lead Danica's guard?" another man asked.

Zane appeared surprised. "Adelina and Ailbhe will continue to lead the palace guard together," he answered. "Danica will, of course, be guarded by the Royal Flight."

The serpent choked on the wine he had been drinking, coughing and finally sputtering, "What?"

Others at the table seemed equally shocked. "You can't allow them into the palace," one woman shouted.

Zane met the woman's eye squarely, not threatening yet but bluntly honest as he asserted, "I certainly *can*, and I certainly *will*. Danica is my Naga, and you would do well to remember that she is yours, as well. I expect no one will attempt to challenge the presence of their queen's guards."

"With all respect, Zane," the man responded, "I can't see myself tolerating a flock of birds in—"

This time when Zane rounded his gaze on the speaker, his expression was strong enough that the man bit back the end of his comment. Quietly, Zane pointed out, "If you cannot tolerate it, then you are within your rights to attempt to deal with what you find to be a . . . distasteful infestation." I felt my cheeks color and was about to protest when Zane continued, his voice as cold as steel. "In that case, I would be well within *my* rights to charge you with treason, and both my guard and my Naga's will doubtless support the full punishment for that crime."

The man's face had gone white. "I didn't mean to imply that ... Of course I wouldn't ..." He looked around as if for backup, but found none. At last he gathered himself and finished, "If you believe they can be trusted in the palace, then it is not my place to contradict."

"Correct," Zane answered. "Now, shall we eat?"

The meal was good; the dishes had been carefully arranged so I was able to avoid meat without the other guests feeling deprived. Fresh bread, fruits, cheeses and elaborate vegetarian dishes were in abundance. Venison, rabbit, pork and beef made up the meat dishes; apparently Zane had decided poultry would be inappropriate.

It was nearly sunrise when Zane led me back to a room in which I would be able to stay. We had mutually decided that going home now would be both tactless—it would appear too impersonal to leave so shortly after the ceremony— and dangerous in my present condition. I was so exhausted, drained both physically and emotionally, that I had to lean against Zane to keep from weaving in the halls as we walked. I had left the Keep early, and now it was nearly sunrise again.

Laid out on the bed was a simple linen shift to sleep in, and I was relieved that someone had realized I would not be comfortable with the usual serpiente practice of sleeping in only one's skin.

"This room is part of my private suite," Zane explained, "and thus, it is one of the most protected areas in the palace. That should keep any disgruntled vipers from breaking in during the night. My room is through that door, the bathing room there and upon any future visits you may store clothing or other possessions in the trunks behind you. I took the liberty of having a few simple outfits made up, since it seemed likely an event like tonight's would occur and you would need something to wear." He paused, as if there was more he wanted to say.

When it became evident that he was not going to speak whatever else was on his mind, I allowed my curiosity to push me into asking, "How in the world did you get my measurements to have clothing made?"

Zane flashed a disturbing smile. "From Eleanor, of course."

*Eleanor* . . . "Eleanor Lyssia?" My voice was breathy with shock.

"Is that so surprising?"

Considering how easily she had agreed to

help me that night, it should not have startled me to learn that the seamstress had been working with Zane. I remembered her greeting me in the market and remarking on how I had comforted Gregory, and the unease I had felt when Zane revealed knowledge of those hours. When we were children, she had been so prone to mad schemes and so full of impossible dreams that it had shocked everyone when she had tamely decided to be a seamstress.

Another piece of information clicked suddenly into place. "You helped design this?" I asked, gesturing to the dress I was still wearing, which had been so perfect that I had never paused to question it.

"I suggested that you should be provided with something appropriate for tonight, yes," Zane acknowledged. "Though to give the credit where it is deserved, Eleanor outdid herself." The look in his eyes as they lingered on my form said more than his words and was enough for me to want to change the subject.

Zane seemed to notice my discomfort, for he cleared his throat and said more practically, "Eleanor did mention that the dress is difficult for one person to manage. Do you need help with it?"

Having Zane's assistance was quite different than having a maid or Eleanor help. However, as

I saw no other choice but to make a fool of myself trying to do it alone, I answered, "If you could undo the tie at the back of my neck, I can get the rest."

I turned around and tried not to jump at the feel of his cool fingers on the back of my neck. I lifted my hair away and felt him hesitate at the sight of my golden feathers before loosening the tie.

Awkwardly, I managed to pull the night shift over myself before dropping the burgundy dress, very conscious of Zane's presence.

As I carefully folded Eleanor's masterpiece to store it safely in the trunk, I heard Zane sigh.

"Danica—" He broke off as I turned to face him, and took a slow breath. "May I join you tonight?" My nervous expression made him continue quickly, "I'm not asking for anything beyond your company in *sleep*. Just let me rest with the sound of your heartbeat beside mine."

The request was spoken with something like wistful innocence, and I did not have the energy to be cruel enough to refuse. After Charis's statements earlier, and my observations in the synkal, it was not surprising that the new king of the serpiente would think it natural to sleep beside his Naga, even in a scenario as strange as ours.

The serpiente bed was designed with luxury in mind, piled high with blankets of the softest, thickest wool. As I lay on my stomach, the blankets and mattress sank beneath my weight until I was enveloped in a plush nest so comfortable that I felt sleep pulling at me instantly.

Zane stretched out on his side, still wearing slacks but having discarded his formal shirt. I was suddenly very aware of his arm across the back of my waist; he must have felt me tense, because while I bit back a protest, he was already moving to put more distance between us.

A sense of awkwardness hung between us for a moment, but exhaustion was a stern master, and it was not long before I was relegated to dreams.

# CHAPTER 12

IN MY DREAMS, VASILI VOICED HIS APPROVAL of my choice, echoing Charis's words about altruism and adding to them words about courage. I took heart from his assurances, even though I knew they were only in my imagination.

When Rei appeared, furious, I listened to him rage over my decision and waited anxiously for the scene to change.

I dreamed last that I was at my own funeral. The avian court was in mourning, and as much as I tried, I could not get their attention.

WHEN I OPENED my eyes, it took me a few moments to realize that I was awake.

During my restless dreams I must have moved, and now I found myself lying on my back.

This change in position was not unusual for me. What *was* unusual was Zane resting against me, his body molded to the shape of mine. One arm was under my head, providing a soft, living pillow; the other was across my waist.

The position was so startlingly unexpected that I hardly knew how to react. I started to pull away, and then stopped as Zane turned closer to me in his sleep.

Again I shifted, and again he compensated, nuzzling against my hair, breathing in a gentle sigh. His arm tightened around my waist, hugging me close.

Asleep, Zane was not thinking about who he was lying next to, but I did not have the courage to wait and see what would happen when he woke. Trying not to disturb him, I slipped out of his arms, placing bare feet on the floor and shivering at the sudden chill.

I glanced back to see his eyes open, watching me.

"Morning," he said, voice soft. He stood and stretched, and suddenly I found myself a little too aware not just of his hypnotic garnet eyes, but of the broad shoulders and very bare chest that accompanied them.

I felt heat creep up my face and turned away, making a great pretense of searching through the trunk for a new outfit when there weren't really enough choices to make it difficult.

Zane knelt beside me. He touched my cheek gently, and for the first time his skin felt as warm as mine, as warm as his voice when he said, "Should I be flattered by that charming blush?"

*Compose yourself, Danica.* I took a deep breath, recovering the fringes of my control and poise until I could look back at him placidly. Before I could speak, Zane tensed, withdrawing his hand.

"Please don't," he said.

"Don't what?"

He stood up, putting distance between us as if I had suddenly sprouted claws. "I slept all night beside you, Danica. Please don't hide from me now."

"I don't know what you're talking about."

He sighed, shaking his head. "You breathe and move and speak, but whereas I would know a serpent was behind me even if he stood as still as a statue, when I stand in front of you now it is like I am looking at a picture, something flat. Sound and sight say you are there, but there is another sense that feels *nothing,* a sense that is completely blind."

He paused, as if searching for words to explain. Tentatively, I offered, "You can sense . . . emotion." *And sense a void when I hide that emotion.*

He hesitated, as if turning the words over in his mind. "Serpiente legend, Danica . . . says that your kind have no souls." I was about to argue, but he continued swiftly. "I believed it, until I spoke to you in the Keep. You weren't guarded then; you lost your temper with me, actually." I had thought I was asleep, but I did not say that aloud as he went on. "And for the first time, I wasn't looking at a shell; I was looking at a real person. I was looking, I think, at the compassionate woman who comforted a dying man and who would soon become a beloved queen. Your 'reserve' is like armor; it may be your strongest weapon against my people. Surrounded by such ghosts, a serpiente soldier is as off balance as any sparrow looking into Cobriana eyes. But we aren't at war anymore," he finished softly.

My heart gave a heavy thump as he stepped back toward me, as hesitantly as I had ever moved toward him. He lifted his gaze, and I forced myself to look into his garnet eyes, which right now were rife with unease and a plea for trust.

Trust. I didn't know if I had the courage for that.

He stepped closer then, and kissed me, chastely and gently.

A heavy knock, followed almost immediately by someone pushing open the door, caused both of us to jump.

Adelina recoiled at the sight of us, and with blatant disgust in her tone, said, "I'm sorry for the intrusion, but there is a bird demanding to see your Naga." She nodded in my direction, and when she met my gaze, her pale green eyes made me shudder. "Since I can't put a hand on him to detain him, it seemed best to get her quickly to avoid a nasty scene."

"Andreios?" I asked, trying to recover my composure and feeling torn because I knew that I was doing exactly what Zane had asked me not to. He pulled away from me, not looking my way as Adelina spoke.

She nodded. "He says he is the head of your guard," she answered. "I suggest you hurry, before he comes looking for you."

There was no chance to speak with Zane about what had just happened. I hurried into clean clothing while Zane dressed in the next room and Adelina waited in the hall. I tied back the chaos my hair had become, and within a minute I was presentable enough to speak to Rei.

Adelina escorted me to the reception hall, where Rei was pacing anxiously. I saw tension go out of his body in a rush when he saw me walking toward him uninjured.

"Danica, thank the sky," he greeted me. "Eleanor gave me your letter. What are you doing here? This—" He broke off abruptly, as if just realizing we had an audience. To Zane he said, "I would like to speak to my Tuuli Thea alone, if I may."

His voice was dangerous, and Zane heeded the audible warning. "Adelina." He nodded toward the door, and his guard turned stiffly and exited. "Danica, I will be across the hall when you are finished."

Once the room was cleared of everyone but Rei and me, he began again to speak. "What are you *doing* here, Danica? Trying to get yourself killed?"

"Trying to end this war," I replied instantly. "And don't you see that it's working? Adelina didn't let you in because she took a fancy to you. Do you think the leader of the Royal Flight could possibly have made it this deep into the serpiente palace if Zane wasn't trying so hard to make peace?"

"Danica—"

I interrupted him, knowing that I would need to convince him quickly or have him argue with me forever. "I knew the risks, and I was and still am willing to take them," I assured him. "The serpiente are sincere. I stood in front of their entire court, Rei, and no one tried to harm me." There was wonder in my voice. "For the first time, I walked among them safely. I spoke with them, without bearing threats. They are willing to follow Zane into peace."

Rei sighed. "But what of you, Danica?" He shook his head in frustration. "I know you will do what you must for your people, but what about *you*?" He paused to take a deep breath, and then continued intently. "The danger is not only from soldiers. You were raised a lady, and you were raised avian. Zane Cobriana . . . he will not understand that. He will expect more from you than you are prepared to give, more than any avian alistair would ask so quickly." He caught my hand, nearly pleading. "Danica, there are reasons our two kinds do not get along. We are not meant to. The serpiente are quick to anger and quick to show it. Even among friends there is violence."

"Rei, I need your support," I pleaded, letting my own self-control slip to match the emotion in his voice. "I know the serpiente are not the same as our people. I am not foolish enough not to be frightened. But I am willing to risk my life if that will keep me from holding another child while he dies."

Rei nodded reluctantly, his brown eyes still warm with worry. "I know," he said finally. "I wish I could convince you, but . . . I know. You would not be the woman I love if you were not prepared to suffer for your people. But Danica—" He broke off, shaking his head, and instead asked, "You intend to announce Zane as your alistair tomorrow, I assume?" I nodded, grateful for his acquiescence. "I would recommend bringing Zane into the Keep with as few people's knowledge as possible. I will make sure the Royal Flight won't cause trouble, and the court is too well mannered to cause a scene in front of its

Tuuli Thea. Aside from my soldiers, the most zealous of your people will be guarding the Keep, not watching the ceremony." He returned to pacing. "They won't like it, obviously. They won't trust Zane, no matter how mellow his troops have been lately. But if you present yourself the same way you have to me—determined to do anything for peace—they will follow you. I hope."

I accepted his reasoning gratefully. Even when agitated, Rei had always been a clear thinker.

"My flight might be the greatest danger toward your plan," Rei continued. "Many of them would rather go against your orders than allow a cobra near their Tuuli Thea."

"I'm trusting you to keep them in line."

Rei sighed. "You know your mother is not going to agree with you."

"My mother is not Tuuli Thea anymore." My voice was solid, and for that I was grateful.

He nodded. "She has moved into one of the suites on the fourth floor of the Keep, and the Tuuli Thea's apartment has been prepared for you. The Royal Flight is going to be hard-pressed to defend both you and her from Zane if I also need to assign a guard to protect Zane from them."

"Zane can stay in one of the side rooms in the Tuuli Thea's suite," I suggested, having thought this out earlier. Seeing the arrangements for me at the serpiente palace had made me pause to consider what might be done at the Hawk's Keep. "There's only one staircase from or to the seventh floor, so it will be easy for your flight to keep track of Zane's movements and make sure anyone likely to attempt assassination is kept away."

Rei nodded thoughtfully. "Unfortunately, that puts you in the quick of danger if Zane causes trouble or if anyone tries to harm him."

"If he wanted to kill me, he would have done it," I answered peevishly, my patience wearing thin. "There are a half dozen rooms in the Tuuli Thea's apartment, and to get from any of them to my room, someone grounded would need to pass through the central hallway. The Keep was designed so one man in that hall can guard the entire floor."

Grudgingly, Rei agreed. "There are four of my guard in the surrounding woods," he explained. "They can serve as an escort for Zane so our soldiers don't kill him on sight." Rei glanced at the doorway. "I'll need to send Erica ahead. She's a good fighter, but she's one of the ones I don't trust to keep her knife sheathed if she has a chance to put it in a cobra's back. I'll speak to her once I get to the Keep and make sure she won't get too hasty. The rest . . ." He trailed off. "You know this entire idea sickens me?" He said the words coolly, but the emotion in his eyes was anything but.

"I know."

"If this is your decision, I know you'll do it no matter what I say." He sighed. "If I fight you on it, it will only endanger you more. I'm helping with this madness for that reason alone: so in the future you'll trust me enough to let me know what you're doing." When I nodded, he admitted frankly, "I would like to put a knife in him myself, and if he makes the slightest threatening move anywhere in your direction, I will. With your permission or without, Danica. See to it that your . . . alistair knows that."

Rei paused, then added more softly, "Be careful, Danica."

Again I nodded, throat closed against any response I could make to this rare display of emotion. "We should get Zane now," I said instead. The words were harsh, but necessary. Rei looked like he was on the verge of carrying me out of the serpiente palace, without care of propriety or promises of peace.

He let out a slow breath, and then we went to get Zane.

REI SENT TWO of his flight—Erica and Karl—to accompany me from the serpiente palace on wing.

Adelina and Ailbhe had only deferred to Rei's statement that he could not allow two of the palace guard into the Hawk's Keep because

Zane had forced them to. We could probably conceal Zane, but sneaking anyone else inside was asking for trouble, and if the palace guard were noticed before the ceremony, it would cause a panic. They would travel on horseback with Zane, Rei and two others in the Royal Flight until reaching the base of the Keep.

It was afternoon by the time I returned home. A party traveling on the ground would not traverse the distance as quickly, and I did not expect Rei and Zane to appear until that evening at least. But as day fell to night, I could not help worrying.

I did believe that the serpiente were sincere, but believing them and trusting them were entirely different matters. If a scuffle ensued between Rei's people and Zane's, I did not know who would win.

Feeling vaguely ill with nerves, I sank into my bed after dinner.

It was too late to back out of this, but I could not yet force my mind to accept the arrangement I had agreed to and all it entailed.

I was startled from my reverie by a knock on the door to my room.

"Yes?"

Rei opened the door, his long hair windblown and cheeks flushed. "Everyone arrived safely. One of the maids is preparing a room for Zane in the northern set," he informed me.

"Your mother has been staying in her own rooms, so we haven't had any trouble keeping Zane out of her sight." He stepped inside and closed the door behind him. "Danica, you're pale as a dove."

I put a hand to my cheek and felt the chill of my skin. "I'm frightened."

Rei caught my hand and raised it to his lips. "I will keep you safe." The words were a promise. "Even if it means defending Zane Cobriana from my own people so you can end this war as your ancestors should have, I will protect you." He sighed. "Do you believe me?"

"I believe you," I answered. I knew my smile was tired.

"Good night, Danica."

"Good night," I bid him softly.

He left, though I knew he would not be going far. He would not leave anyone else to guard my doorway with a cobra so near.

I slept well.

# CHAPTER 13

ANXIETY WOKE ME EARLY THE NEXT MORN-ing. I bathed and dressed quickly before meeting up with Zane in the hall outside my room. Andreios was exchanging a few last words with Zane, detailing the scripted ceremony associated with the naming of an alistair, which Zane appeared fairly amused to hear about.

"Tell me, do the three-year-olds usually honor these vows?" Zane asked glibly.

Rei kept his control, but the tone of his voice when he responded was sharp enough to tell me that the comment was not the first one Zane had made. "Yes, the *decision* is usually made when an alistair is that young, but he doesn't take the vows until he is ready. Hopefully you're old enough that they're clear to you," he added between clenched teeth. "If they aren't, I'm sure—"

"Good morning, Andreios," I said loudly, drawing both men's attention to me before someone was hit. "Good morning, Zane." If the two men ever did come to blows, the fight would be serious—deadly so—and I doubted they would both walk away alive.

I glanced toward the other two guards who stood in the hall with us, and added quietly, "Karl, Erica, stand down."

Both radiated tension. Erica especially trailed Zane with her eyes as if taking a sight for a notched arrow.

Karl flashed what looked like a forced smile. "Relax, Erica. We can always say 'just kidding' and run for our lives."

One of the lightest of tone among the Royal Flight, Karl had apparently been assigned to this job today to keep my mood from bleakness. His humor and voice almost served to disguise how raptly his attention covered the area, and particularly the cobra.

Erica did not appreciate the humor. "No disrespect, milady," she said to me with harsh formality, "but I will relax only when I am shown proof that he"—she nodded in Zane's direction—"is harmless."

I glanced at Rei, silently questioning his decision. I trusted their loyalty to me, but worried that they might not go out of their way to protect Zane if someone meant him harm. In fact, both struck me as a little overzealous.

He answered the unspoken question. "I trust these two to be loyal to you without fault, and they've sworn not to harm him. When there are others of our kind around who might be a threat to your alistair, I will assign other guards. When you are alone with a serpent, I won't put someone in the way that might hesitate to fight him."

Erica and Karl both looked flattered by their commander's recommendation and unflustered by the implication that they were less than fond of Zane. Since Rei himself had for a moment sounded regretful that he couldn't let them kill their charge, I found it difficult to fault them.

Instead I looked at Zane, who offered a brave smile and a shrug.

The serpent was certainly making an attempt to look harmless. He had abandoned his normal black attire in favor of calfskin pants so light they were nearly golden, and a loose shirt several shades darker. The brown tones made his garnet eyes appear less red, and his fair skin warmer.

However, clothing could not completely disguise the smooth tension of his movements, so subtly different than any avian, or completely dim the fire in his gaze. I was dreading introducing him to my people.

"Milady, it is time." Eleanor was slightly

breathless as she darted into the room, her cheeks flushed with excitement.

Zane offered his arm, at the same time delivering to me a sardonic smile. "This is going to be interesting."

There was some carefully controlled surprise among my people when I first descended the stairs with Zane instead of Rei, but no instant fury. It occurred to me that most of these people had never seen Zane before, and unless they caught sight of the signet ring he was wearing or met his Cobriana eyes—something he had assured me he could avoid—they were unlikely to recognize him.

But as I crossed the room to the slight stage in the back of the court, I could see the ripple of unease in those nearby. Instincts. Even a sleeping dormouse wakes up and knows when the cat is nearby; so it was among the court. Zane, for all his attempts to appear harmless, would never pass for avian.

They looked at Rei, and at me, and at the other members of the Royal Flight who were standing nearby, but since my guards and I were not visibly upset, they assumed their own discomfort was imagined. Only the sight of the blood rushing from my mother's face as she fainted set my heart racing. Gerard caught her, looking a little surprised and unsure of what to do with his charge. Luckily, she had been standing at the far back of the room, and only those nearest to her had noticed. I would deal with her later. Now it was time to step onto the platform.

"Tuuli Thea Danica Shardae," Rei greeted me. "You have chosen this man as your alistair, as your protector, of your own free will and without coercion."

"I have." My voice did not tremble.

Rei turned to Zane. "Are you willing to swear upon your own spirit and the sky above that you will protect Danica Shardae from all harm?"

"Upon my own spirit, I will so swear."

"And do you swear you will never raise voice or hand against her?" Rei spoke the words calmly, but the expression in his eyes as he met Zane's gaze fearlessly was anything but calm.

Zane hesitated a fraction of a second; whether surprised by Rei's bold action or debating whether he was willing to so swear, I did not care to know. "Never would I willingly harm the woman I love."

Rei caught the wording, and for a moment I saw his jaw clench against the desire to argue. He knew as well as I that Zane had made no claims of love toward me, and that his promise not to harm the woman he loved did not protect me.

Rei's gaze flickered to me, beseeching, and I gave a nod for him to continue. I understood Zane's hesitation, despite how unnerving it was;

if it came down to a choice of him or me, he would defend himself and his people. He could not swear never to harm me without knowing whether peace between our two peoples would work.

"Danica Shardae is Tuuli Thea, and so when you swear to her, you swear to all her people," Rei continued, his voice sounding strained. "Will you protect the Tuuli Thea's people as you would your own family, and risk all that is necessary to defend them?"

"I swear upon the tears of the goddess Anhamirak, I will do everything within my power to stop the bloodshed among the Tuuli Thea's people." In those words I heard sincerity at last, and though I did not know the name of the goddess to whom Zane had made the vow, I knew from his tone that he was honest in his words.

There were scholars better educated than I among the court, and as I heard their frantic whispers, I knew that some had understood the reference. I also saw with dread that my mother was stirring. As Rei continued, I watched her set her feet on the ground, her reserve shattered and her face holding abject horror.

"Danica Shardae, Tuuli Thea, you have chosen this man as your alistair," Rei continued formally, his voice rising slightly above the noise in the crowd. "Zane Cobriana, you have sworn to defend Danica Shardae, your Tuuli Thea. Upon the words you have spoken, you are bound for life."

Those words *for life* had a fateful ring.

A hush descended over the avian court, and in those moments, as I waited for a reaction, I met my mother's gaze. She looked at me with sadness and anger and shook her head. Then she began to walk out the back of the room.

Gerard tried to stop her, and I saw her spine go rigid. "The Tuuli Thea has made her choice. My words are meaningless here," she said loudly without turning. I nodded to the guard, and he hurried after the Tuuli Thea he had first served as she left.

Her rejection cut, but I had expected it.

With a deep breath to loosen the knot in my throat, I stepped forward. The court quieted, awaiting my words, stunned by what they could not believe.

I stated simply, "Yes, it is true. This is Zane Cobriana you see before you." I had to raise my voice slightly over the protests as I continued. "Yes, it is Zane Cobriana who has just sworn to defend your Tuuli Thea—and you." That quieted them slightly, and I took advantage of the silence. "When the serpiente first spoke to me of peace, I was doubtful. But I am your queen, and as such, I am willing to do what I must to protect you, my people. That means ending this war any way I can."

I stood at attention, left hand grasping my right wrist behind my back—the pose of a soldier, which I had picked up from Rei and Vasili when I had been a girl. I knew everyone who had ever fought in our armies or lost someone from our armies would recognize the posture.

"You know me," I implored them. "You know that I do not avoid going out to the field and caring for the wounded. You know that I do not flinch from the bodies that must be brought home. I do not intend to be a queen who ignores the suffering of her people. I have held your own children's hands, and talked to them as they died, so they would not be alone. And I am tired of it."

I took Zane's hand, grasping it on the stage in the avian court, in front of so many avian ladies and gentlemen who were shocked by even that small contact.

"I feared this man, as you do. I hated him, as you do. But when our soldiers cut down his brother in the field, I was the one left to sit by that boy's side as he died. And he was no different than my brother who died the same day, or the alistair and family I lost when I was a child. Then Zane came to me, asking for peace, and I had to listen." I took a breath, trying to calm myself. I had not meant to get so carried away, but now the court was watching me in amazement. Perhaps that was a good thing. "Zane has sworn to defend my people, and as Naga of the serpiente I am equally sworn to defend his."

There was some more protest at this last statement, and I waited for it to die down before I said softly, "We have all lost loved ones. And if I need to go onto the field and disarm every frightened soldier by hand, alone in the night, I will do it. As of this moment, I declare this war over. Any injury done to the serpiente will be looked upon as injury to *my* people, and to *your* people."

The court did not know how to react. They had been raised avian and were not taught to loudly express outrage or fear. However, under the circumstances, polite caution and distaste could not cover what they wanted to say.

Finally, one soft voice pervaded the area. "Milady, how can we be sure of their intentions?" The crowd parted so the woman who was speaking could approach me. "Of course I have faith in you and your judgment, but might the serpiente even now be planning to attack as soon as you recall our soldiers?"

"I had a similar thought when Irene Cobriana first came to the Keep to ask for a meeting in Mistari land," I admitted. "The Royal Flight and my own family both cautioned me against trusting the serpiente, and I was spirited back to the Keep. But Zane was not that easily dismissed," I recalled. "And when he showed up in my suite a few weeks later, unbeknownst to my guards, my mother and everyone else in the Keep, it was hard to believe that he intended me harm."

Rei was visibly perturbed by these words, but he said nothing as I continued to speak. "Had the serpiente wanted to injure me, there would have been opportunity—here in the Keep, and at the serpiente palace on the two occasions that I have visited there. Yet I stand before you unscratched." I spoke softly, but I knew my voice would carry in the near-silence of the court. "I ask for trust. I ask that I might never again hold another dying soldier—avian or serpiente—in my arms. I ask for trust. I ask that you put away your weapons so we can mourn the dead properly, and then move on. I ask for trust. I ask that your children can learn of peace instead of war. I ask for trust. It is a lot, I know; it isn't easy to give. But it is *all I ask*."

# CHAPTER 14

Escorted by Andreios and Karl, Zane and I withdrew, leaving the court alone to make their decisions. I heard several voices raised, among them Eleanor, loudly declaring their support before anyone else could speak.

After Zane and I had settled onto the balcony that marked the highest point in the Keep, I asked, "Who is Anhamirak?" Two of the Royal Flight were waiting discreetly on the stairs down to the main apartment; Rei had reluctantly gone to bed after what must have been more than a full night and day awake.

"Hmm?" Zane's gaze was distracted as he looked out over the surrounding forest and distant mountains and doubtless wondered how the argument back in the court was going. If it went badly, there were seven floors between him and safety.

"Anhamirak," I repeated, trying to keep either of us from mulling over what was happening. "You swore to her during the ceremony, when Rei asked whether you would defend my people as your own."

"When Egypt was young, and the first pyramids were being built with the sweat and blood of slavery," Zane recited, not turning his gaze from the view, "there was a sect of thirteen men and women, the high priestess of whom was a woman called Maeve. They worshiped a goddess named Anhamirak, who ruled over life, light, love, beauty—and above all, free will."

Zane sighed. "As the myth goes, a creature by the name of Leben appeared to Maeve and instructed her to stop her worship of Anhamirak and turn it onto him. He was powerful, but not a god, and Maeve knew it. She seduced him, and in an attempt to gain her favor, he gave to her ageless beauty and the second form of an elegant viper with ivory scales. She demanded that he do the same for all her people, including a woman named Kiesha. To Kiesha, Leben gave the form of a king cobra, and from her son—or so the story goes—the Cobriana line is descended."

"Do you believe it?" I asked, rather entranced by the tale.

"I believe this." Zane held up a hand, and I

could not help stepping back as the ink-dark snakeskin rippled into appearance over his bare skin, only to subside again as if it had never existed. "And I believe this." I had been watching him so intently that I had no chance to avert my gaze as he lifted garnet cobra's eyes, halting the air in my lungs. "I have seen the serpents dance, and if it isn't magic, I can find no better word." He looked away, returning those frightening jeweled eyes to the landscape as he leaned against the balcony railing. My breath let out in a rush. "What about you, Danica?" he asked. "What do you believe in?"

The story behind my kind was equally magical, but it had always been told to me as just that: a story and nothing more. Now I moved beside Zane and looked out at the land that held his attention. "I believe in the air beneath my wings when I soar."

"Is this what the world looks like when you are flying?"

I tried to see the land below as would someone who had not seen it from this height every day. The sky was just beginning to color with the pink and violet streaks of twilight, and long shadows streaked the ground. "It's not as clear as this," I responded, trying to recall what the ground *did* look like to a hawk in flight. "When you fly, the air is mostly what you are aware of . . . how it moves, and how you move in it. The ground isn't important unless you are diving, landing or falling."

"Falling?"

I had been hit once by a serpiente arrow, clipped in the wing while I was flying from a battle. Falling, unable to steady myself for several seconds, I had only escaped the deadly impact with the ground because one of Rei's soldiers had caught me. It was not a moment I wanted to dwell on—or repeat.

"It happens sometimes" was all I told Zane.

"Milady?" The voice came from a very hesitant young sparrow, whose gaze flickered to and from Zane with bright fear. "When you have a moment, your mother would like to speak to you and your . . . alistair." She hesitated, as if my mother had used different words to describe Zane.

"She is welcome to come speak to me at any time," I responded, both relieved that my mother was unlocking herself from her room and dreading the confrontation to come. "Kindly invite her to join us here."

The sparrow bobbed a clumsy curtsy and disappeared quickly.

"I think she's afraid of me," Zane observed, a dark humor showing through in his tone. He leaned back against the railing, crossing his arms, then pausing—like a cobra, coiled and waiting, a deep stillness seeping into him as he prepared to face my mother. I wondered if he even realized how dangerous he appeared in that moment.

My kind lets off subtle signs of life even when we're not moving: the heat of our bodies and the quick pace of our heartbeat. When Zane stood still, even his breathing slowed, as if he might simply dissolve into the night. The only sign of life in him was the flash of light off his iridescent gemstone eyes.

*Please don't hide.*

I wondered if, when I looked at him now, I saw and felt what he did when I pulled on my mask of avian reserve. If it was true ... I could see how the myths had begun, saying we had no souls.

The time had passed for me to respond to Zane's forcedly light remark, and now an awkward silence stretched between us, both of us hidden behind our own shields and both unnerved by them.

"I think she's not the only one," he added under his breath as my mother ascended the stairway.

"Danica Shardae, you are Tuuli Thea now, and I have no power to override your decisions." Nacola's voice was forced, as if she had rehearsed this speech many times before coming to me. "But I will not support your agreeing to this sickening arrangement."

"I'm sorry to hear that." I truly was. My

mother's approval was something I had always strived for, and the lack of it now left me groundless. "But my people must come before even you, Mother. As your people should come before your daughter."

"Child, I would not protest so if I thought this would work," my mother argued. "I understand the sacrifices a queen must make for her people. But those sacrifices must be for a reason, and *this* . . . this is a reasonless act. Our two kinds are not meant to live together, Danica," she said softly. "From the very first we have been enemies, and so it will be until either they are destroyed or we are."

"You're absolutely correct." I jumped at Zane's voice, and my gaze shifted to him. "Snakes and birds are not creatures intended to live together. As I recall, hawks will snatch young cobras from the nest and eat them. But surely you are forgetting something rather important, milady Nacola." He paused there and waited as if for an answer.

My mother did not reply, and finally Zane just sighed.

"The first of my kind was a human woman. Surely your kind comes from like roots. We have human minds and human bodies. If we can speak as humans do, and love as humans do, then what makes us so different?" Zane's words were simple, but the anger and hope behind them were anything but. "Serpents and birds are not meant to live together," he asserted again, "but I personally like to believe that we are more than our animal counterparts."

"Your *people*," my mother spat, in a rare show of fury, "murdered my *parents*. My sisters, my husband, my son and my daughter—"

"And your *people*," Zane replied with equal vehemence, "have taken from me a father, two uncles, three brothers, a sister and a niece who had not even drawn her first breath. What possible harm had that infant done to you?"

He turned away as if he did not trust himself to face her, and he paced to the railing.

"Milady Nacola," he said tightly, "I don't want to fight with you. I fear I lose my temper too easily for your world's standards. What I am trying to say is that *I* am willing to forgive history and try to act as the human blood in me implores."

"Your temper is renowned," my mother responded, her voice once again under control, and acid in its detachment. "Your kind has never been famous for holding in check its tongue or its hands, and I wouldn't expect its king to do any better." Zane drew a breath as if to speak, but my mother continued. "With that in mind, surely you can understand my reluctance to trust you with my daughter."

"I have given my word I will not harm her,"

Zane interjected, but my mother simply shook her head.

"And when that Cobriana temper breaks loose, what then?" she argued, for all intents and purposes ignoring my presence. "Violence is common among the serpent court, or so I hear, and accepted to a much greater degree than it is in the Keep. I don't expect Danica has had much experience with being struck, and I don't wish her to gather such familiarity."

"Nacola—"

"Allow me to finish." To my shock, my mother met Zane's eyes with her own fiery golden gaze, and Zane was the one who looked away. "If I am to have no say in this decision, I would at least speak my mind to you."

"Continue." The word was tense, and Zane pointedly avoided looking at me as he said it.

My mother stepped closer. "If you ever put a hand on my daughter—"

"I assure you, fair Nacola, I've no intent to bruise such soft skin as Danica's. With that point overemphasized, is there anything else you would like to accuse me of?"

"She is not one of the casual women of your court, Zane," my mother argued next.

"Quite obviously," came Zane's silken reply.

"Your word that you will never force her to your bed."

The order came difficultly to my mother's

lips, and Zane recoiled in response, his eyes narrowing in fury.

"Would my word mean anything to you, Nacola? The word of a cobra, for your daughter's *virtue?*"

My mother hesitated, her lips parting as if she would speak and then sealing closed again without a sound passing them. Her gaze was hard, clearly speaking the answer: No, his word would mean nothing to her.

"Leave now, Nacola Shardae." Zane's voice was cold as ice.

"I—"

Zane whirled to face me, turning from my mother's protest. "Danica, get her out of here before I hurt her."

I stumbled back, but did not stop to question him. I caught my mother's arm, imploring her, "Mother, please return to your room now."

"Danica—" She broke off, and with one more fleeting look at Zane, she nodded.

We walked in silence until we reached the doorway to her room, the place where my sister had once slept, long ago when I had been a child.

"I know you will go through with this," my mother said flatly, her voice soft and sad. "Even Karashan admits that you are too brave for any of us to change your mind, Danica. But please don't let that courage make you careless. Keep a guard within shouting range, and never let the door lock when the two of you are alone. Sleep with a knife under your pillow if you must, and be careful, because he *will* hurt you if you do not protect yourself." She sighed, her voice a whisper as she added, "History repeats itself too easily."

I thought of the knife in the back that had ended Alasdair's life and nodded. The events of both this evening and the past forced me to respect my mother's words.

I returned to my balcony to find Zane gone; the guards informed me that he had retreated to his room and asked not to be disturbed until next dawn by anyone but me.

# CHAPTER 15

TENTATIVELY I KNOCKED ON ZANE'S DOOR. I do not know what mad instinct possessed me to do so, but I did not think it wise to let the night pass without speaking to him.

I implored Karl, the guard assigned to this hallway, to stand outside the room instead of following me in. I did not know what kind of mood I would find Zane in, and worried that my guard might act too hastily.

"Enter." Zane's voice was husky, as if he had been shouting, though I had heard nothing.

I pushed open the door to the double rooms that Zane had made his own. The curtains to the circular balcony were normally open in good weather, but tonight they were drawn closed; only faint streaks of twilight seeped through the woolen window covering, and it took me a few seconds to adjust my eyes to the dimness.

Zane was sprawled across the low couch in the front room, his gaze resting contemplatively upon the bands of light that fell under the window.

He raised his eyes to me when I stepped into the room, but made no move to stand.

"Questions, Danica?" His voice was light, almost musical, betraying no hint of his earlier anger. Only the scant light reflected in his eyes still showed that violent emotion. "Do you want to ask, or would you prefer not to know what you have tied yourself to?" The spark of his eyes and the singsong quality of his voice made the feathers on the back of my neck rise.

"Are there questions I should ask?"

Now Zane stood, the act as liquid and threatening as his serpent counterpart coiling to strike, and I jumped at the movement. I saw the vague amusement on his face as he noticed my reaction.

"Relax. I'm not going to bite," he said, but of course the words were not intended to relax me.

Every instinct screamed at me to run, that there was a predator in the room, but I could not have moved a muscle if I had tried.

As Zane approached, he moved with a slow beauty and deadly silence. "So easy, Danica," he whispered, and now the pain was back in his voice and in the eyes that held me frozen where I stood. "Despite how I have despised your kind for so many years...you alone are so very fragile."

He lifted his hand, and I saw it coming but could barely move. At last, too late to turn away, I managed to break his gaze and close my eyes as I prepared for him to hit me.

He checked the blow so close that I felt the air ruffle my hair, but when he touched my skin, it was not in anger; all I felt was a soft caress, the backs of his fingers brushing over my cheek.

"So easy, Danica. If I had wanted to hurt you, I would have."

I pulled away, my breath coming quickly as Zane continued.

"I can feel the beating of your heart, Danica. And I know that if I pressed my lips to your skin right now, I would taste its sweet flavor, and smell the exotic scent that makes me want to bury my face in that damnably golden hawk's hair."

I hit the wall with my back and braced myself there.

"But as much as I want you, there is one emotion alone that can overcome lust, and that is fear." His voice as he said this was almost inaudible, it was so soft. "Never, Danica, will I touch a woman who fears me. Never will I strike or otherwise harm you unless you precipitate that violence by intending injury toward me or those I love. If we are in understanding on that, then you may be assured that this serpent is no threat to you."

I had no words with which I could respond.

Finally, Zane turned his back on me. "It's late, Danica, and tomorrow will doubtlessly be a long day. Now would be the time to return to your own bed . . . unless, of course, you plan to share mine."

Even if he looked as innocent as he had the last night I had shared his bed, after the ravages of anger, threat and insinuation that had passed his lips this night . . . I couldn't imagine being bold enough to join him.

But now, as he paused in the doorway, glancing back with an expression that danced between amusement and dismissal, a flicker of anger slid over my fear. Before I thought better, I stepped forward to meet his challenge.

"Okay." I knew my tone was not friendly.

Zane tensed, his eyes widening for a swift moment. "Excuse me?"

"You are my alistair," I responded. My voice was calmer than my thoughts. "It is considered impolite to make a spectacle of it, but it is not scandalous for a lady to stay a night with the man she is tied to."

I was just in front of him now. Zane was

watching me with a shocked fascination that gave me the courage to continue.

"What *would* be considered inappropriate is venting your anger at my mother's words on me." Zane jumped when I raised my gaze to his. I knew he could hold me if he tried, but he did not, and that made me bolder. "You've succeeded in frightening me, if that was your goal."

At these words, I saw him sag. Quietly, he answered, "I did not intend to frighten you."

I let my expression ask the question.

When he spoke again, his voice was careful. "Your mother all but accused me of something that is, among my kind, the highest crime a man can commit. There is no trial, only punishment, because it is considered better to let an innocent man die than let a guilty one live." He took a heavy breath and let it out. "I know my kind has an evil reputation in the eyes of yours, but having that ignorance thrown in my face in such a way was more than unpleasant."

I waited for him to continue, forcing him to fill the silence.

"I apologize for my temper, and for being too furious to argue sanely with your mother. Among my kind, the constant control avians exercise over their emotions would be considered . . . beyond rude, a lie to those around you. So I am not in the habit of needing to conceal my emotions, even where such control is a necessity. Even so, I apologize for frightening you when you did nothing to deserve my anger."

"You are forgiven, by me at least." I was still trying to push back the rioting emotions of the last few moments, but my heartbeat had almost returned to normal. "My mother will not be so quick."

Zane shrugged, and the movement betrayed his fatigue as his words had not. "Your mother is neither my mate nor my queen." His hands on my waist were so gentle I barely noticed the touch as he drew me forward. He kissed me lightly, just the barest contact. "You, milady, are both." He released me and smiled tiredly. "We both need sleep, Danica, something you would not find in my bed tonight."

I looked away at the implication in his words. "Good night, Zane," I replied.

"Good night, Danica Shardae." He sighed, and I heard the door to the adjoining room, which Zane had set up as his bedroom, close even before I had exited the front parlor.

"Everything all right, milady?" Karl asked worriedly as I stepped through the door into the hall.

"Fine," I responded.

"You look a bit shaken," he observed.

"A bit," I admitted. "But I will be fine. Thank you."

"May I speak bluntly, milady?"

I nodded, forcing myself to gather my wits and stand before the guard as his monarch, not as a scatterbrained chick. "Go ahead."

"I understand this arrangement is very important to you." Karl spoke with slight hesitation, picking his words carefully. "I understand that some risks are necessary. But some of the Royal Flight are worried that you are endangering yourself more than the situation demands." He nodded toward the door to Zane's room, and I knew he had been upset by my leaving him in the hall while I spoke to the cobra alone. "That you might not be willing to call to us until it is too late, out of worry for the peace." He took a breath and continued. "The Royal Flight is sworn to defend you, but we cannot do that if you will not let us."

I did not know how to reassure him. I had Zane's word he would never harm me, but he had also admitted his temper. If that temper got the better of him someday, would I keep my silence, or tell my guards and let them tear our fragile peace apart?

"I will think on your words." I was certain that Karl's worried questions would reverberate through my dreams all evening. "For now, good night."

"Good night, Shardae," he bid me. I saw him glance at Zane's door as if he was considering confronting my new alistair, but he just shook his head.

I hesitated. "Your concerns about my alistair wouldn't persuade you to leave him unprotected?"

"My commander and my Tuuli Thea have assigned me to guard this door and the serpent inside. I have sworn my loyalty to you and would not renege that word now. I swear no harm will come to your alistair so long as he is within the walls I protect."

I wondered as I walked down the hall whether Zane rested uneasily within the Keep, surrounded by guards who would only defend him in spite of their hatred for him.

In my room, the curtains to the balcony were still open wide. The moon was barely a fine crescent, but the stars shone brightly.

When I was a girl, Vasili had joked with me that when I was strong enough, I could fly to the moon.

Such fairy tales had disappeared when he had died.

I had lost too many dreams to blood. If the price to end that bloodshed was dealing with Zane Cobriana ...

I lay on my bed, hoping I would sleep and dream of Vasili, that I could speak to him of all the things I could not tell people in this world.

In the serpiente court, I had to pretend to be in love with someone I could not be alone with unless I could bear his shifting moods and sudden outbursts. In the avian court, I had to pretend to be sure and self-sacrificing, when in reality I was sure of very little.

Even the questions I wanted to ask about Zane and our decisions were denied to me, for who would I ask? In the past, my mother and Rei had been those I trusted to give me answers, but they were against this venture, and I did not want to show them the depth of my fear. I considered speaking to Eleanor, as she supported what I was doing, but that thought only led me to wonder how much of what I told her would get back to Zane.

I began to pace in my room, too agitated for sleep.

I walked out to the balcony, where another guard was waiting in case Zane tried to enter my room that way.

"Good evening, Shardae," Gerard greeted me formally.

"I'm going for a flight," I announced. The guard nodded, without asking if I would like company. I would have someone with me whether I wanted to or not. The Royal Flight was not in the practice of letting its Tuuli Thea go anywhere alone.

After the strain of the day, it was a blessed relief to shift into my hawk's form and spread my wings.

My path traveled nowhere in particular, though out of habit I avoided serpiente lands. I flew until the night was deep, just a few hours until dawn, allowing the steady beat of golden wings and the movement of the air around me to be my only thoughts.

# CHAPTER 16

T HE NEXT FEW DAYS WERE FILLED WITH desperate attempts to keep the peace. To their credit, the Royal Flight and Ravens reacted quickly when news came that there was an altercation occurring on the boundary of serpiente and avian land; by the time they arrived, the serpiente palace guard had almost brought the situation under control. The leaders of the two rebel factions had been killed in the fight, including Erica Silvermead's father. She asked to be dismissed from the Royal Flight for a period so she could see to the arrangements and mourn as was proper, and her request was granted.

Zane and I made plans to travel weekly between the palace and the Keep, flanked usually by three of the palace guard and three of the

Royal Flight. Andreios handpicked the guards, to ensure that they would be vigilant about my safety and wary of the serpiente, but not hasty to cause trouble. I hoped that Adelina had picked her people as carefully; the coldness with which she always addressed me did nothing to put me at ease.

As the days passed, Zane spoke little to me beyond what was necessary to preserve the charade we held in front of his people. We avoided being alone together, unwilling to face anything more than our mutual efforts toward peace.

At the Keep, things continued as usual. Petitions were made of the Tuuli Thea, but rarely now did I receive pleas for aid against Zane's people. When such requests were made, the reaction came from the serpiente army, who took care of their own people more efficiently than our soldiers ever could have.

I explored the serpiente palace whenever I had a moment free, despite Zane's warnings of "Keep a knife handy, Danica, or better yet, a guard. There are some dark passages that would easily make an end to you if someone wanted to attempt it." I followed his advice when I was in unknown areas, though I spent most of my time in the main hallways.

I located the storerooms, the kitchen, the infirmary, the guardroom and countless other rooms. One entire side of the palace was open to the public and contained a forum, much like our market, that opened into the outside air, a gaily colored nursery and magicians and artists aplenty. At first I traveled everywhere with Rei or one of his people, but as time passed, the Royal Flight trusted more and more the palace guard to keep me safe.

Especially when I was traveling with an avian soldier, I was too often greeted with fear, but occasionally the rare serpent would approach and speak to me. These people were not surprised to see their Naga among them, but many seemed impressed that I had dared to join them. The air was rich with laughter, heady scents of exotic perfumes and the heavy web that seemed to connect all these people.

One afternoon, I watched the serpents' dance, a hypnotic and sensual ritual. The music was provided by a pair of musicians, one of whom beat out the rhythm on a low drum he held in his lap, while the other swayed with a flute.

The dancer was a young woman with eyes as bright as polished emerald and midnight black hair that tumbled nearly to her knees in wild waves. When she moved, the silken garments she wore rippled, showing as much as they concealed.

When she ended the dance, she was offered food and drink by her fans, with whom she flirted for a while before approaching me.

"That was impressive." I searched for a stronger word, but could not find one.

The serpent smiled, a playful smile that reminded me of Zane's when he was in a light mood. "That was Maeve's dance, from the Namir-da," she explained. "I will perform here in the midsummer night, for those who cannot watch the dance in the synkal." She paused, taking a sip of the rich wine someone had offered to her, and then said reflectively, "Or perhaps I might dance in the synkal this year, since Zane cannot."

"Why not?" Though I had recognized the name of Maeve from Zane's description of serpiente origins, I knew not about this dance.

The dancer seemed surprised at my question. "Because a mated man does not dance Namir-da with another woman, and, little hawk, I don't think you know the steps." She sighed. "Zane is a beautiful dancer. He performed last year with Adelina, and I much regret that I did not watch." A slight puckering appeared between the woman's brows. "We were surprised when Zane chose you. He is not known to be fickle, and he and Adelina . . ." She shrugged.

The words were a blow. I had known from

the first that Adelina hated me, but I had been too much of a coward to consider why.

The dancer did not seem to notice my discomfort. With one last sip of wine, she kissed the drummer on the cheek and began to climb back onto her stage. She paused on her knees so our gazes were nearly level. "I do not know whether a hawk could learn the Namir-da, but if you are willing to learn, I will try to teach you. Maeve was light and golden like you are," she added.

"I don't have much talent for dance."

"Perhaps not, but when have you tried? Your people do not move as serpents do. Maybe that is because they can't," she admitted, "but I should like to teach you. Come back this evening, hawklet." With those words she stood, raising her hands into the air with her palms clasped together as if she was imploring some ancient god or goddess. The drum began, and my would-be tutor closed her eyes for a moment, and then began to move to the rhythm.

I had a few hours to decide whether I would take the woman up on her invitation. I had watched her performance with envy and would have loved to replicate it, but I doubted I would ever be able to. Music was important to my people, but dance was far too raw a form of expression for it ever to be popular.

I did have one decision already made: I needed to speak to Adelina. I did not know what I would say, but I felt I should recognize her sacrifice.

I found my way to the guardroom without fault. At this time of day Adelina would probably be out, but I knew she was not on patrol, and someone might know where she was.

I knocked on her door, but received no response. The guardroom dining hall was nearly empty, and the two serpiente there knew only that Adelina had left a few minutes ago.

Another time.

Zane was attending to some routine chores, so for the moment, I had nothing pressing to do.

Perhaps the archery range would offer some amusement. Serpents, like my kind, were practiced archers. I was learning from Ailbhe how to use the serpiente-style bow, though I hoped I would never need to use the weapon as more than entertainment.

An avian archer struck primarily to deliver deadly poison in an otherwise small injury. While the wound caused was minimal, the poison could kill a serpent in a heartbeat, but do little more than cause fatigue in an avian soldier.

The serpiente bow was larger and had a stiffer draw, and the arrow was plain and smooth, designed to fly far and penetrate as deeply as possible. It shot an arrow hard and fast, so a good aim could take a bird from the sky. I had been warned more than once to be careful if I ever used the weapon to defend myself, as a ser-piente arrow that did not meet with the resistance of bone could at a close distance pierce through the intended opponent and strike any-one who stood behind—friend or foe.

I halted abruptly at a turn in the hallway as I glimpsed a couple entangled in the shadows of the next corner. I started to turn away to leave the two in privacy, but my eye lit upon white-blond hair I could not help recognizing.

Adelina?

I turned back just in time to see Zane—for even in the darkness, I knew it was him—draw in a ragged breath and push her away.

I heard his voice, soft and torn. "Adelina, we can't be doing this."

"We *are*," she responded practically.

"You know what I mean." His voice was a lit-tle more solid now, but no happier. "Danica—"

"Danica can rot for all I care," Adelina said, snarling. She took a breath, and then said more calmly, "Zane, I'm sorry. But we both know you don't love her. You can pretend to the court, but not to me."

"Adelina . . ." He sighed. A moment passed, a murmured word from Adelina I could not understand, and then, "Adelina, I wish we could, but I *can't*."

"You think the hawk would care?" Adelina challenged.

"I don't know," Zane answered. "But she is my mate. I wish . . . but wishes don't stop wars."

I had eavesdropped enough; this was an interaction more personal than I had a right to hear. But Adelina's voice rose and followed me down the hall as I walked away.

"Zane, I watch you and you are miserable," Adelina cried. "You are beautiful and strong and you should never be lonely."

"Adelina—"

"No!" She was nearly shouting now. "You are a cobra, Zane. A descendent of Kiesha. You are not a creature intended to live without the comfort of touch, yet that is what you are trying to do now."

Finally she softened her voice so I could no longer hear her. My step was quick and my route wide as I stayed as far away from that solitary corner of the palace as I could. Adelina's words were gnawing at my gut.

I didn't want Zane miserable, if Adelina was right about that, but he was still a cobra, and I could not make myself forget the power he wielded. Besides, how could I take the place of the woman who loved him?

The head of the palace guard being so vocal about her feelings for me made me nervous, too. I had no doubt now that Adelina would never warm to me. I only hoped Zane's guards' loyalty to him would keep me as safe as my guards' loyalty kept him.

I ran into Zane's sister a few paces down the hall from her room. Irene was leaning back against the wall, breathing very slowly and carefully.

Though I saw no injury, I could not ignore the sight.

"Irene, are you all right?" My other worries momentarily shoved aside, I helped her into her room, where she sat carefully on the edge of the nearest chair.

"I'll be fine," she asserted. "Just a bit of a spell." At my look of confusion, she elaborated, "I get them sometimes, with the baby. Luckily, my mother makes a wonderful raspberry-ginger tea."

I faintly remembered Zane mentioning that Irene was with child, and that she had been white with fear when she had told him.

"Don't look so worried, Danica," Irene said lightly. "I just chased the father off for hovering. I don't need you doing the same."

"Who is the father?" My relief that he was still alive was palpable.

"Galen," Irene responded, her voice carrying a bit of a sigh. "He's one of the guard. He was with us at the Mistari camps."

Thinking back, I did recall the lightly built

man who had sat beside Irene among the Mistari, though I did not think I had ever heard him mentioned otherwise.

As if reading my mind, Irene told me, "We were trying to keep it quiet—so he would not be more of a target than he already was. If things are still calm by then, we are going to make the announcement at the Namir-da."

There was that word again. "One of the dancers in the market mentioned the Namir-da to me."

"That would be A'isha, most likely; she is the leader of the local dancer's nest." Irene observed, "She is very talented, isn't she?"

I needed to confide in someone, but I had not intended the words to sound as desperate as they did when I said, "She says Zane and Adelina danced last year?" Irene nodded, her gaze distant. "Is Zane really so miserable?"

Irene looked startled by the question. She paused a moment before answering carefully, "He is very happy that the Mistari suggestion seems to be working. But peace, as wonderful as it is . . . peace does not keep anyone warm at night." More sure in her words, she continued, "Serpiente children are never alone, Danica. If their parents cannot be with them, they stay in the nursery, surrounded by playmates even in sleep, comforted by the nearness of others.

"Maybe in nature a serpent is a solitary

creature, but I can tell you that my kind is not. That is why the idea of Zane's choosing a mate for politics and not for love was so disturbing. Because no one—not myself, not even Zane— believed an avian could be a mate, not in the true sense of the word. You're blushing again, Danica," she observed. "I don't mean just physical intimacy. I mean comfort, and trust. Enjoying someone's company, and being soothed by their nearness. I suppose I mean love. Or if love is impossible, then friendship."

She shook her head, then continued gamely. "I see the way Zane looks at you when he thinks no one is watching. When we first began to speak about this, he told me flatly that he could never love a woman with feathers in her hair. But I watch him now, and . . . he was wrong. He cares about you. And that makes it harder, I think, whenever you pull away from him."

He frightened me sometimes, unnerved me often, but I didn't hate him. Zane was trying so hard for this peace, and having what he was feeling put to me so bluntly was dreadful. Meekly, I stated, "Zane mostly avoids me now. He seems to go out of his way to make sure we are not alone together."

"He doesn't want to push you." Irene sighed, and added, "Look, Zane was on his way to the market a few minutes ago, to haggle prices and settle disputes and other busywork that, for reasons beyond my comprehension, he actually enjoys. Join him there, and I promise he won't turn you away. Give him a chance and see what happens."

Suddenly Irene yawned and made a shooing gesture. "Go rake somewhere, hawk," she said affectionately. "Tell me how it turns out in the morning."

# CHAPTER 17

I DID AS IRENE HAD SUGGESTED, AND RE-
turned to the market, where shopkeepers directed me to Zane without my needing to ask.
Someone near him drew his attention to me and
I saw him tense for a moment before he turned
around. I wondered whether he was thinking
about Adelina.

"My exquisite Danica," Zane greeted me,
pulling me into a soft embrace in the marketplace. I lingered in his arms for a few long moments. Zane and I had perfected the appearance
of an infatuated young couple. I was almost
growing used to the little touches—a hand
brushing a hand, his tendency to tuck loose
golden hairs back from my face—that Zane
added so easily to the play.

Remembering Irene's words, I wondered now if what I had taken to be a flawless act might really be more. It had been so long since we had been alone together, it was hard to know for sure.

Was I to blame for that distance?

"Danica, you must know Fisk?" Zane said lightly, referring to the metalworker he had been speaking with.

I did; Fisk Falchion was an avian man from the Aurita who had requested to trade in the serpiente market. There were serpents in our market now also, including a maker of the fine flutes used to accompany serpiente dance.

"Always a pleasure to see you," Fisk greeted me.

"The trade is going well?" I inquired.

Fisk nodded. "There were a few trouble-makers earlier, but they hurried off when Zane came by to speak to me," he answered. "I don't think they will be back soon." Fisk smiled, an expression of fatigue and contentment combined. "The market here is quite impressive. I had not thought it would be so."

Bidding Fisk good day, Zane and I continued to walk in the market. "The Aurita has always been one of my favorite shops," I confided. "I'm glad Fisk was brave enough to take a chance trading here."

"He's a businessman," Zane said with obvious pride. "Our market is not famous for its jewelers, but our people are known for their love of beauty. For a man like Fisk, such an opportunity must have been the dream of a lifetime."

"Do none of the guard follow you here?" I had not seen any since I had gone looking for Adelina earlier.

Zane shook his head. "It's unnecessary. The market sometimes gets a bit rowdy, but I've never had any trouble. Very few people would risk hitting their Diente even in the hottest temper, and if it occurs, I can defend myself in a casual brawl." He added, "They are fond of you, Danica. I've had people come up to me, surprised at how much they like you. That being the case, my people—*your* people—will protect you from anyone who means you harm. Bringing the guard would cause more trouble than it is worth, because it would tell the people that I do not trust them."

THE REST OF the afternoon passed with safe, neutral conversation about pointless things like the price of ivory and how Chinese-style furniture was coming into fashion among both avian and serpiente craftsmen. We drifted from stall to stall, presented with free samples at every stop. I knew that Zane rarely dined in the palace hall for lunch, though I usually joined Irene and Charis there. After sampling the wares of every baker and chef who insisted on feeding us, I wished I had skipped the formal meal, too.

I pleaded an overfull stomach to avoid offending the chef who offered a taste of roast lamb fresh from the fire. Once we were beyond the hearing of the merchant, Zane said, "I've always wondered why you don't eat meat. I understand not wanting to dine on poultry, but even a natural hawk eats small game."

"My great-grandmother Tuuli Thea Caylan could not stand the smell of cooked meat," I explained, recalling the story. "She refused to let it be served in the Keep. Naturally, the cooks learned how to make dishes that Caylan would allow, and now meat is so uncommon in the Keep that I never acquired a taste for it."

Zane appeared genuinely amused. "How utterly odd. Understand this means I must force you to try." He paused, as if considering which of the many merchants prepared the best dish.

"Zane—"

"Now, now." He led me back to the chef who had offered me the lamb a few minutes before. "If you've no moral or religious obligation against it, I cannot allow you to be closed-minded enough not to sample one of this wonderful cook's fine creations."

The "wonderful cook" in question looked very flattered, and I had no doubt that he would have handed over the entire stand free of charge had Zane implied he wanted it.

"What is your masterpiece today?" Zane asked, his expression animated with mischief.

The chef did not hesitate to reply, "I've a wonderful piece of lamb simmered with wine and rosemary that I'm sure your Naga would enjoy."

I resigned myself to tasting the cook's food, knowing that even if it was awful I would need to swallow and smile or else break the poor man's heart. Tentatively, I took the offered morsel and tried not to laugh as both Zane and the chef watched me intently for my reaction.

*Come now, Danica,* I scolded myself. *You've walked onto the dais in the synkal, and now you need to gather your nerve to put food in your mouth?*

Appropriately chastised, I tasted the lamb.

Though like nothing I had ever eaten before, it was delicious. My surprise must have shown on my face, for the chef grinned and even Zane smiled slightly.

"Does the lady like it?" the chef inquired, though he doubtless knew the answer.

"Wonderful," I answered honestly. "Very . . . strange, but wonderful."

Zane wrapped an arm around my waist and pulled me close, a playful half-hug. "My brave Naga Danica," he said, lightly teasing. To the cook he added, "We will be going back to the Hawk's Keep tomorrow morning, but perhaps next time we are here you might be willing to prepare supper for the family?"

The chef was stunned. "I would be honored, milord. Thank you."

Zane shook his head. "My thanks."

WE DID NOT leave the market until after the sun had set. I could not imagine wanting supper after all I had eaten, and so I was glad when Zane passed by the dining hall with only a brief word of greeting to the occupants and a bid good night.

Zane's mood was still cheerful, but I felt some of the humor fade to contemplation as we walked in silent company back to our rooms.

"Your room, milady," Zane said, with an attempt at lightness, as he opened my door for me. He drew me into a soft embrace as he had in the market, one of those delicate touches he seemed to bestow without thinking.

Was it true that, beneath the volatile exterior I had come to know, he was as hurt and maybe even as scared as I was? Recalling my conversation with Irene, I was determined not to chase him off tonight.

I felt the gentle pressure as Zane kissed my hair. This was the point at which I normally would have pulled away, but I forced myself to relax. Zane seemed to feel my acquiescence; he skimmed his fingers over my cheek and jaw, and tilted my face up.

He had kissed me before—as a challenge to my guards in the Mistari encampment, when I had thought myself to be sleeping, in the synkal in front of his people, before Adelina strode in the morning after the ceremony declaring me Naga.

Now when his lips touched mine, the gesture was as intense as the time in my own bedroom at the Keep, but as leisurely as the slow kiss we had shared in his. When I did not call a stop, he pressed a hand to my lower back, pulling me closer.

My hands had risen instinctively and had been resting on his shoulders as if I would push him back. I made the tight muscles loosen, and felt my hands flutter uncertainly.

Zane's lips moved to lay a brief kiss at the bend between my shoulder and neck, and then another just over my collarbone.

I had a moment's thought, as vivid as it was brief, of a cobra's fangs sinking into the skin his lips touched. For a moment I felt myself tense, pulling away fractionally, and I felt Zane hesitate, frozen for an instant.

"I'm sorry." I didn't mean to say the words, wasn't sure what I was saying them for.

Zane raised his face, and despite my intent, I flinched at the expression in his garnet gaze, which had the heat of anger and the sharpness of pain and yet was somehow neither of those.

Just as unexpected was the sensation of falling as he released me, almost throwing himself back as he spun away. He tumbled awkwardly to his knees, breathing hard, until his forehead leaned against the wall.

Frightened and confused by the sudden withdrawal, I knelt by his side.

He recoiled and rose to his feet with the gracefully controlled violence of a serpiente soldier on the field. I froze when I saw his eyes flashing not with annoyance or amusement but anger, directed at me.

One, two, three paces backward, and then he turned from me, and I could tell he was going to leave me alone in my confusion.

It hurt to see him draw back from me, and I fought every instinct not to hide behind the comfortable reserve I knew so well. "Zane—"

He turned back to me and took a deep breath, his gaze holding me in place, frozen, as if I had met the gorgon's eyes, except for the frantic beat of my heart. "I do appreciate the effort, Danica. I enjoyed spending time with you in the market, and I'm glad to see you can be so comfortable around my people. But you're here alone with me now only despite your fear . . . and I'm not looking for that kind of sacrifice." His voice softened as his anger simmered out. "I would be your lover if you would trust me, but I don't want you to come to me because you feel like it is an . . . unpleasant duty. I would rather be your enemy than a meaningless obligation."

My heart lurched into my throat at his words, and for a moment all I could do was stand dumbly. By the time I had unraveled my tongue to argue, he was continuing, the last of his rage gone.

"If you want to make the offer someday when it means something to you . . ." He shrugged, and for a moment the brilliant, charm-birds-from-their-nests smile was back, but then he was gone and I stood in shock.

*He is wrong.* Whatever else our relationship might be, it could never be meaningless.

Heart still beating loud enough to wake the dead, I followed him into the hall, trying to discern which direction he had gone. In that moment of hesitation, my ears picked up a noise that registered as subtly wrong.

The sound came again: a familiar cry that raised the feathers on the back of my neck. Carefully but quickly I moved toward it.

Just a few paces beyond the hallway's bend, I saw two figures fighting. One was obviously Zane; his movements had the frightening fluidity of a serpiente warrior, and he fought as soundlessly as all his people. The only noise came from his opponent, and even that was so soft I would never have heard it had I not stopped in the hall.

The second figure was either a slender young

man or a plain, shapeless female; I suspected the first. The loose black clothing he wore left much to the imagination—as much as the silken scarf twined around the assassin's head, which showed only shadows over his eyes.

The word *assassin* came to my mind un-bidden, but as soon as I thought it, I knew it to be true. I also knew, from the style of his move-ments, that the attacker was probably avian. He was fighting with the long-bladed dirk many of the Royal Flight favored, and he guarded his back with the precision of a soldier who is used to de-fending wings.

Quickly my thoughts shifted. If the assassin was avian, caution made it reasonable to assume the blade of his weapon was poisoned. Depend-ing on the strength, a scratch could kill; he did not even need to land a fatal blow.

I did not wait for an opportunity. Against avian poison, I was safer than Zane, and I hoped that even an assassin would hesitate to harm his Tuuli Thea. All but ignoring the weapon, I grasped the attacker from behind and dragged him back-ward to keep Zane from the range of his blade.

The assassin whirled, and I raised an arm to defend my face. I felt the knife cut through the flesh of my forearm and the heat of poison in the wound, but I also felt my attacker recoil. He had recognized me.

Obviously unwilling to continue the fight

with me in the middle, the assassin spun and took off down the hall.

Zane moved as if to follow, but then he turned to me.

"Danica, are you okay?"

I was going to say yes, I think, but at that moment the world warped and churned around me, and I stumbled back into the wall. Zane gathered me in his arms and hurried to pound on a doorway down the hall. Almost instantly four of the guard emerged.

"Adelina, we've had a run-in with an assassin, avian, I think. Danica's hurt. He went in the direction of the north exit."

Adelina nodded sharply. "You, with me," she ordered one of her men, who I recognized as Irene's mate, Galen. To the other two she said quickly, "You, stay with your Diente, and you, fetch the doctor and Danica's guard. Keep quiet," she added, with a glance at Zane that lingered only a moment too long. "We don't want this hollered all over the palace."

"Let's get her back to her room," Adelina suggested, speaking to Zane, who nodded mutely. She added, "We wouldn't have moments like this if you shouted when attacked."

Zane shook off the criticism. "The injury isn't bad, but . . ."

Time warped a bit right then. The next thing I knew, Andreios was bandaging my arm while the doctor paced in the background. "It won't kill her," I heard Rei explaining to Zane, "but—Danica, how do you feel?" he asked, noticing I was awake.

"Not well," I responded. My throat felt dry.

"You'll be fine," he assured me. "The poison must have been nearly pure to affect you this strongly, but it isn't designed to harm avians. You'll probably drift in and out for a while, and after that you might suffer dizzy spells for a couple . . ."

Again the words trailed off.

The next time I woke, I was lying on my bed, still in the palace. Zane was sitting beside me.

"Water?" he offered.

"Please." He wrapped an arm under my shoulders to help me sit up, and I gulped down the drink he held to my lips.

"You could have been killed." His voice was carefully neutral, the same tone with which he had offered water, and I wondered what emotion he was trying not to share.

I shook my head, and that made it spin. A deep breath grounded me, and when I was sure I was not about to pass out again, I added, "I assumed one of my people would hesitate to hurt me. Even a scratch from that knife would have *killed* you."

"How were you so sure it was one of yours?" Zane answered.

"The way he moved. Did they catch him?"

"*Her,*" Zane corrected. "The guard cornered the girl down the hall." He paused reflectively and then admitted, "It surprised me, too, that she was one of my people."

"Serpent?" I thought back and remembered how the would-be assassin had fought. "But she moved as if she had avian training."

"She might have been a dancer; a good one of that guild could probably imitate an avian fighter. My guess is that she was trying to return us to war. According to Andreios, one of the Royal Flight had his weapon stolen recently. Our serpent either didn't realize how strong the poison was, or she was willing to kill me. Any observer would have blamed the murder on your people, and that would have caused havoc."

"Have you spoken with the . . . her?" I could not make myself say "assassin" aloud.

Zane shook his head. "According to Adelina, she took her own life when she realized the guard had her cornered."

My head was spinning again, and I put a hand to my temple as if that might keep the world still. "What was her name?"

"It wasn't in Adelina's report," Zane answered. "Only that the girl was a viper. Probably no one in the guard recognized her."

"Did you . . . see her?" I asked.

"No." His gaze flickered as if he was uncertain

about that decision. "If none of the guard recognized her, I suppose I wouldn't have, either. They can deal with the body. I preferred to stay here to make sure you would be all right." Regarding me critically, he said, "You should probably rest more."

"How long did Rei say it would be until I am on my feet again?" I asked as Zane helped me to lie down again.

"Not much longer," he answered. "This is the most lucid you've been since you were hurt."

"How long ago was that?"

"Almost a full day. Close your eyes, Danica. Try to rest."

I did as I was bidden, and almost instantly I was asleep.

# CHAPTER 18

ZANE DID NOT MOVE MORE THAN TWO steps from my side when I was finally well enough to walk about. My stomach was still feeling picky, so the lamb dinner was further delayed, but aside from an occasional few moments of faintness, I felt fine.

"Are you sure you're okay to travel?" Zane asked. It was the hundredth time I had heard the question that day. Rei had asked as many times as Zane.

"I'm fine." I sighed again. "We're already late arriving at the Keep, and I don't want anyone imagining I've been killed over here."

Both Rei and Zane had to agree with that reasoning. With one of them on each side of me, we rode.

It was a hard trip, but Rei had insisted that riding was safer than flying if I was still having dizzy spells. By the time we arrived, I had gained a new appreciation for how much time Zane had spent traveling this path by horse while I held to the luxury of flight.

At the entrance to the Keep, we were met by a flurry of the Royal Flight, led by Gerard in Rei's absence. Near the edge of the group was a worn-looking Erica Silvermead. She did not even seem to have the heart to give Zane a proper glare as we dismounted in the courtyard.

Gerard filled us in quietly as the horses were stabled. "Erica returned to duty a few hours ago. Her father's death has taken a toll on her. A few weeks ago, he would have been listed as a soldier in battle; now he has been labeled a traitor."

The words made me take a second look at the young sparrow who stood across the courtyard like a lost soul. She was slender, hated the serpiente and had been out of sight the past several days.

Rei caught me examining the girl with a critical eye. "Adelina caught the assassin," he said, sensing my thoughts. "But if you are still worried, I can keep a closer eye on Erica." The offer made it clear that he too was concerned about Erica's state of mind.

"Thank you," I answered.

"Shardae, did you intend to loiter in the courtyard for hours while I wondered over your whereabouts?" I turned toward my mother, feeling appropriately chastised. However, beneath the censure, her face and voice both betrayed worry. "You have been missed these last few days, and the market and court are both full of nasty rumors. Karashan was on the verge of storming the palace, sure you had been abducted or worse."

"We had some problems with a . . . would-be assassin," I answered hesitantly. I went on to explain as much of the circumstances as was my mother's business, including the fact that while the assassin had imitated an avian soldier, Adelina had reported her to be a serpent.

My mother gasped. "Did it not even occur to you that you might have been the target?"

I shook my head. "I wasn't. There was plenty of opportunity to harm me."

She frowned. "If your theory is correct that someone is trying to start the war again," she pressed, ignoring Zane completely as she spoke, "then why would a serpent have hesitated to harm you? In the heart of the serpiente palace, that would have caused as much trouble as if she had killed your alistair."

"I don't know." I glanced at Zane, wondering if he had thought this point through.

"My best guess is that she wasn't trying to kill anyone," he offered. "She was trying to make it appear as if someone had attempted to kill me, but she probably balked at actually doing the deed."

"Nice to know your kind hesitates at some crimes," my mother said dryly. "The idea still seems unlikely to me. You are certain that this Adelina didn't make a mistake?"

"Do you have a better theory?" I spoke a bit louder than was necessary and gave Zane a warning glance before he could say the caustic remark that was surely waiting on the tip of his tongue.

My mother made some reply along the lines of "I will consider it," but I did not truly heed the words. I grasped at Zane's arm, trying to remain standing as one of the now familiar waves of dizziness passed over me.

"Shardae, for the love of sunlight, go lie down." My mother's voice finally came fully to my ears. "You're frighteningly pale. Why in the world did you let her travel in this condition?" This last was demanded of Rei.

"She insisted" was his answer. "Your daughter did not want you to worry."

"I'm fine, Mother." I even managed to release Zane and remain on my feet. "The spells are not nearly as bad now as they were earlier."

My mother shook her head skeptically. "Danica, you must have ridden for hours just to get here, on top of having been injured. If your guards and your alistair cannot convince you, then allow me to appeal to your sanity. Go lie down."

I nodded finally. It *was* late, and I had ridden hard. "Fine, I will go."

"Zane, perhaps you might stay?" my mother asked as we turned to leave. "I have a question for you regarding your people down in the market. There's no trouble—Danica, please, go to bed," she interrupted herself when I paused. "This is hardly anything important enough to warrant your attention."

"Sleep well, Danica," Zane said, already turning to speak to my mother.

I knew she was just trying to keep Zane away from me. Anything "hardly important enough" for me to be bothered with was surely nothing Zane needed to hear at this moment. She wanted to make sure I would go to my room alone.

I slept poorly, with a scattering of dreams I could not quite remember, yet I woke when dawn was barely brushing the sky, feeling surprisingly refreshed.

I did not want to bother any of the Keep servants yet, so I slipped into clean clothing and padded into the hall unaccompanied.

Rei had been on duty guarding the hall, and at the moment he was deep in conversation with Zane.

"I wish I could," Rei interrupted whatever Zane had been saying, his voice slightly raised. "If you—"

"Danica." I had been seen. Zane cut off Rei's words and stepped past my guard to greet me. "Good morning. How are you feeling?"

"Fine . . . good. What were you two talking about this early?" The instant I asked the question, Rei's expression let me know they had been talking about me. In what context, I did not know.

"Idle fantasies," Zane answered smoothly. Neither his voice nor his face gave away his thoughts. However, I trusted Rei implicitly and knew that he would not have tolerated insults or threats against me. "Andreios has been telling me avian lore."

That I could believe. Andreios had a passion for the old stories that belied his otherwise reserved nature. When prompted, he spun the mythical origins of our kind in a way that could make the hardest skeptic believe for a moment that they were real.

As we descended the stairs toward the court, Rei made most of the conversation. "I spoke to Lady Nacola," he commented. "In light of the attempt on Zane's life at the palace, she has dropped her argument against allowing some of his guard into the Keep. Adelina and Ailbhe should arrive before dawn tomorrow morning, and I've asked them to report to me when they do so." Rei shrugged lightly as he commented, "Your mother wavers between threatening Zane's life and trying to preserve it. She's convinced that our people were somehow involved in the attack at the palace."

"Adelina's coming?" The words were sharper than I had intended; Zane's expression took on the barest hint of a frown.

I doubted that Rei was as oblivious to the tension as he appeared, but he answered, "She is the captain of the guard, and is more than capable in that capacity. In addition to her technical qualifications, she seems very loyal."

Rei's opinion sealed the matter. He was captain of the Royal Flight, and if he thought Adelina would benefit the Keep, I would have to accept his decision.

Though the formal breakfast would not be served for hours, fruit, bread, milk and cider were available in the court for early risers. Several such people greeted us quietly before returning to what they were doing.

I helped myself to an ample meal. My appetite had finally returned, and it had done so with a vengeance. Though Rei had already eaten, Zane served himself a meal similar to mine, and we sat at one of the side tables to eat.

"What did my mother have to say about our flute-maker last night?" I asked Zane, trying to draw him from the melancholy silence he seemed to have fallen into.

He smiled wryly, and the expression appeared forced. "Nothing important, really. I think she doesn't like the thought of my having time on my hands in which I can plan mischief."

Rei glanced at me quizzically, clearly asking whether he should leave. I didn't like seeing Zane in this mood and wanted a moment alone with Rei to ask what they had been discussing that had bothered the serpiente so much.

He made up his mind without input from me. Standing, Rei apologized. "I need to check in with my flight to make sure there won't be trouble when Adelina and Ailbhe get here tomorrow. Karl will be with you today," he added, nodding toward the doorway, where the slender raven waited unobtrusively. Quietly, so only Zane and I would hear, Rei added, "Karl's weapon was the one stolen by your serpiente assassin, and he has been doing everything he can to earn back my flight's confidence. I've never had a problem with him before; he's one of my most competent soldiers, and he is infinitely loyal. You can trust him."

With this reassurance, Rei left, and Zane and I picked at our food in silence. I made a few more attempts at conversation, to which Zane responded with what sounded like a forced attempt at lightness.

Eventually I gave up on discretion and asked point-blank, "Zane, what's wrong?"

"Why would I be bothered by anything?" he replied sarcastically. "I was nearly killed within five steps of my own bedroom, and you were injured. What one person does, several people usually consider—several people who, in this case, are considering what the benefits would be if you or I met with an untimely death." He stood from the table, and I could see he was trying to gather his self-control. "Excuse me, Danica. I shouldn't be sharp with you, of all people."

"In this situation, it's perfectly forgivable."

He just shook his head.

THOUGH ZANE MADE every attempt to hide it, his dark mood persisted for the rest of the day. In front of avians who had not spent as much time with him as I had recently, he must have simply seemed more subdued than usual—a favorable turn in the eyes of the court, with which we spent most of the day.

The two serpiente merchants, however, exchanged worried glances during the short conversation they had with Zane and me while we were circuiting the market.

"It has been a trying few days," Zane apologized as he excused himself early that evening.

The sky was well past dark and court had begun to tire when I politely followed Zane's lead. I wanted to talk to him, but what would I say? I did care for him in a way; it had not only been a fear for the peace that had prompted me to drag the assassin away from him. But I knew that wary affection was not what he sought and would bring him little comfort.

After several hours of tossing and turning in my own bed, I flew to the fifth floor and knocked lightly on Andreios's door.

Rei did not appear surprised to see me; he invited me into his study, bidding me to close the door behind me.

"You're worried about Zane," he predicted before I attempted to raise the subject. I had confided in Rei most of my life; I valued his advice even more than my mother's.

"He's been . . . tense for weeks," I admitted, hedging around the real problem, "but never so moody as he was today. You two were speaking about something this morning, something that upset him. Can you tell me what?"

"Fate," Rei answered after a moment. I could tell that the conversation was eating away at him as surely as it had been Zane. He paused, took a moment to gather his words and then asked bluntly, "Do you love him?"

The question startled me. "No." I did not need to think about the answer, which sounded so brutal that I needed to add, "I do not hate him anymore, but love . . . I believe he deserves love. But I don't know if I can be the one to give it."

"Do you trust him?"

"I trust his intentions," I answered, trying to be as honest as possible.

"But do you trust *him*?" Rei pressed. "If you were falling, would you trust him to catch you? Would you trust him never to harm you, no matter what he could gain? Would you trust him to risk his own life for yours, without hesitation?"

I had to shake my head.

I respected Zane, which seemed odd, when for so many years I had only known his name as a curse. But I knew that while we danced with peace, we were both still prepared to fight. If I was falling, I trusted he would catch me—unless it was a choice between me or one of his own people. I trusted him to never harm me, because harming me would destroy this peace—unless I reneged on this deal and my death was necessary. As for risking his life for mine . . . his people needed a king.

I found myself pacing in a most unladylike fashion. Then I stopped, not because Rei ever objected to my un-avian outbursts, but because I thought of Zane asking me not to hide.

Rei sighed. "He said that you were passionate, that he was amazed by how much you could care even for someone you didn't know but to fear."

"And he said," Rei continued, as if the words came painfully to him, "that you deserved love. That you deserved someone . . . with whom you could cry or laugh without hiding your face."

I winced at the words, closing my eyes as they rocked me. I needed to speak to Zane. I might make a fool out of myself, but I needed to. . . . In the next moment I felt Rei's arms around me, a warm comfort.

"I love you." He whispered the words against my hair like an apology, but within them was surrender. For him, the battle was already lost.

I looked up, though I didn't know what I wanted to say, and Rei's lips gently caressed mine. Time hung suspended for long moments, during which my heart couldn't decide whether to sink into my stomach or lodge in my throat, but then I started to pull away. *Zane.*

The door opened behind me, and we jumped apart. I spun around, and heat flushed my cheeks as the expressions on both of the intruders' faces made it very clear what they thought the situation to be.

Karl quickly averted his eyes while he fought to control his shock. Adelina was furious.

Karl spoke before any of us could. "She . . . I—" He swallowed heavily before deciding to ignore what he had seen and spoke to Rei. "Sir, Adelina is here. You wished to have her report to you immediately?"

Adelina's eyes flashed at Andreios. "I didn't realize I'd be disturbing you." Her voice was taut with anger. "Should I come back later?"

"You didn't interrupt anything," Rei answered firmly. "Karl, please escort Shardae back to her rooms. Adelina, I can show you to your room if you would like to rest a bit, or you can have the full tour of the Keep now."

"I would prefer to know the layout of this place before I sleep," Adelina replied caustically. "There seems to be no telling what goes on here."

I heard the words behind me as I walked out, suddenly feeling pale. Nothing had happened, and nothing would have happened, but I doubted Adelina would believe that.

# CHAPTER 19

WE RETURNED TO THE SERPIENTE PALACE A few days later. I found myself watching Zane closely for signs that Adelina had told him what she had seen, but in the flurry of activity surrounding the upcoming holiday, she and the incident both seemed to fade into the background.

I sought out the dancer A'isha during any free time I had, and she taught me a few simple steps, sensual and exotic dances that I doubted I would ever have the courage to perform—until the sun rose on the day of the fall equinox and the serpiente lands were suddenly perfumed with sweets and spices, and the air rippled with the sounds of flutes and two-toned drums.

Unfortunately, the Namir-da was still far

beyond me. A'isha's words on the subject were, "Perhaps you might learn it, in more time. You have talent, but . . . not much practice."

Throughout the day, serpiente spilled into the marketplace, their bodies, skins and belongings decorated with enough color, scent and texture to boggle the mind.

I had barely stepped into the market with Zane at my side before one of the dancers that A'isha and I had practiced with offered me a gold and crimson silk scarf called a *melos*, the ends of which were strung with dozens of tiny golden bells.

According to A'isha, the *melos* was given to dancers as both praise for their skill and a request for a performance. Zane made a move as if to decline for me, not expecting me to know the meaning of the gift, but I tugged it from his grasp. Then I did a few steps from one from the dances I knew, and saw Zane's eyes widen with shock.

Laughing a little, I moved a few steps ahead; Zane answered the challenge, and within moments we had been ushered onto one of the many daises that stood in the market. Aside from A'isha, I had never performed for an audience before. Now I met Zane's gaze and took a deep breath to steady myself.

I inhaled the festive air of the Namir-da, and we danced.

In a society that worships love, freedom and beauty, dance is sacred. It is a prayer for the future, a remembrance of the past and a joyful exclamation of thanks for the present.

Zane and I danced several times in the marketplace throughout the day. When we ran out of dances I knew, we improvised. When we were hungry or thirsty, all we needed to do was step down from the stage and we were offered more than our fill.

The day started to wane, and a circular dais was constructed in the synkal, ten paces across in every direction and a few inches higher than Zane could reach while standing on his toes. The dais had no railing, and as night fell it was lit only by the torches that burned on the floor all around it.

Finally, as the last rays of the sunset faded, I took my seat with Charis at the back of the stage as Zane spoke to the assembled crowd. With words as vibrant as paintings, he told the story of Maeve and Kiesha, of the cult of Anhamirak, of Maeve's seduction and of Leben's gifts to her and her people.

When he had finished, the doors opened in the back of the synkal. The children were escorted out to the market, where they would stay up late into the evening enjoying candies, games and magic.

The adults stayed, and when the palace guard doused all the torches in the room but those around the dais, everyone turned to Irene and Galen as they prepared to dance—everyone except Charis.

I felt her tense, but when I looked to her, she was staring off the stage at someone in the darkness. Abruptly she stood, dragging me up with her. Zane heard the movement and his head whipped around toward us.

Yet every one of these actions was a second too late.

I was struck with a pain so fierce I could not even cry out; a brutal tearing constricted my lungs and sent ripples of crimson across my vision.

Charis collapsed beside me; I felt her weight on me, and I started to fall, but then Zane caught us both. In complete silence he carried us off the stage and into the relative safety of the hall.

Beyond that, my memories are scattered.

Zane's telling the guard to make sure Irene and Galen were safe, and to lock the doors. The assassin was inside.

Zane's white face as he leaned over me, telling me I would be fine. Begging me to stay awake with him.

Andreios's normally bronzed skin, turned a sickly ashen green. His turning to Zane and shaking his head.

"No." Zane's tone was flat, as if in shock. "That's impossible."

Rei's ordering, "Someone get him out of here." The guards looking at each other, wondering who to obey. A figure being dragged away.

"You can go to sleep now," Irene said. She was still dressed in the glittering black and silver dress she had danced in. Her face was pale, and her hands were shaking.

I slept, and when I woke next, the pain was less. There were bandages wrapped around my torso. Andreios was by my side.

"Thank the sky you're awake."

"I seem to keep being poisoned." The words took all my scant air, and when I tried to draw a deep breath, the pain struck.

"You'll be okay," Rei told me. "But it will take a while for you to heal. You've had a narrow escape—any higher, and the arrow would have hit your lung. Lower would have been just as bad."

"Arrow?"

"It was avian-style, but it must have been shot from a serpiente bow—the wound is deep. You've been out for almost a full day now. . . . We weren't sure you were ever going to wake." On the last words his voice betrayed his fear.

Suddenly my fuzzy mind put together those last painful moments. My mouth was dry when I asked, "Charis?"

"It just barely nicked her arm, but . . ." He looked away. "She was unconscious before Zane carried the two of you to the hall, and she still hasn't woken. I don't think she will."

"Is Zane—" I stopped, needing to carefully draw more breath.

"Sleeping, right now," Rei answered. Wryly, he confessed, "The guard drugged him."

Someone knocked quietly on the door. "Come in," Rei called. "She's awake."

Irene Cobriana entered. Her steps dragged slightly, and her eyes were swollen as if she had been crying, but she held her head high.

"Irene, you should be lying down," Rei chastised lightly.

"I can't sleep anymore," she answered. "I came to see how Danica was doing."

I tried a smile, but was not sure whether it worked. "Can't get rid of me . . . that easily."

"Andreios was supposed to call me as soon as you were awake, but I suspected he wouldn't,"

Irene said, with what was supposed to be levity but did not quite make the mark. "If you think you can eat, there's some rather unattractive green broth you're supposed to try."

I looked at Rei, who nodded solemnly. "It's very . . . healthy, I'm sure. The Keep and palace doctors worked together to concoct it. I suspect it will taste terrible."

He was correct.

Lunch was another strange-colored liquid; this time it was gray. By dinnertime cooks had intervened, so it was a warm vegetable broth that the doctors had added their medicines to. It numbed the pain and allowed me to sleep.

I woke at odd hours, ate what was forced upon me and then slept again.

I had no idea how much time passed. I did not know what day it was when I finally woke to find Zane by my bedside.

"Zane—"

"How do you feel?"

I paused to catalog my pains, which were few at that moment. There was a curious tingle around my injury, which I suspected would turn into a throbbing pain if I tried to move. "I don't know."

Zane smiled wistfully, but then the expression faded. "My mother is dead," he said without preamble. "She died last night."

I tried to form words, but nothing was

enough. "She tried to save me," I told him, knowing the words only spoke my own pain and could never heal his. "She tried to pull me out of the way."

"I know," Zane answered, his voice dead of emotion. "If you had both remained seated, the arrow probably would have hit you in the throat, and then her in the side. It would have killed you both.

"It doesn't make any sense, you know," Zane continued. "Even if they could have gotten into the synkal without being seen, and they didn't intend for you to be hit, no loyal avian would have risked your life that way. And no one loyal to the Cobriana would have used poison that wouldn't hurt you but would kill any of my family it nicked."

"Zane, are you all right?" Through the entire speech, his face had remained expressionless.

"I'm quite sure I'm not," he answered evenly. "But I'm alive, and uninjured, and—" I reached for his hand, and finally I heard his voice choke off, as his fragile shell cracked. "Danica, I've never been this frightened in my life." The words spilled out in a flood of emotion. "The guard made the announcement about my mother this morning, and right now people are still in shock. I don't know how they'll respond when they wake up from it. . . ." He took a deep breath, and then said on a rush of air, "I think it must have been one of my guard who made the shot, or at least who organized it."

"*What?*" Instinctively I tried to sit up, and the pain returned abruptly, a spear driven into my gut, just below the left side of my ribcage.

"Careful, Danica," Zane cautioned, wincing.

"Tell me . . . about the guard." After that, he could get the doctors and they could drug me to sleep again, but first I wanted answers.

"It would have been nearly impossible for an avian to be in the crowd unnoticed. Weapons aren't allowed in the synkal anyway, and a serpiente bow is not easily concealed. Only one of my guards could have managed it."

"But the poison?" The question was short. Longer sentences took up more breath than I could get comfortably.

Zane shook his head. "I don't know. Maybe they stole it."

"How?" As I asked the question, I knew the answer. Adelina and Ailbhe both had been to the Keep. Either of them could have sneaked a bow into the synkal. Either of them would have known when the lights would go out. "But Charis . . . They wouldn't hurt her."

"There was bad blood between Adelina's family and mine for generations. My mother was the first to allow one of them into the guard, the first to trust them, and for that they were more than grateful. I can't imagine *any* of the guard being willing to hurt my mother, but I believe any one of them would before Adelina and Ailbhe." Zane shook his head, running fingers restlessly through his hair. "Andreios tells me they weren't allowed near the storeroom, anyway, and that the poison was too strong for them to have taken it from his people; it had to be mixed just for this occasion. Only someone in the Royal Flight would have had the access necessary to make the poison, but any of them would have used an avian bow. Besides, an avian who was willing to plot assassination would not have aimed at my mother; he would have gone for me." He sighed and leaned against the bed, his entire frame drooping with fatigue. "As I said, it doesn't make any sense."

My nurse, a shy little sparrow who had accompanied the Keep's doctor here, interrupted us at that point. "Milady, would you like supper?" she asked politely.

I tried to decline, but Zane would not let me. He sat on the opposite side of the bed and amused us with quaint stories as I swallowed every drop of the foul concoction. I was almost asleep before the nurse had closed the door behind her.

Zane kissed my forehead lightly, as if I was a child. "Sleep, Danica."

# CHAPTER 20

THOUGH MY KIND HEALS AT A RATE THAT would seem miraculous to any human doctor, when one is bedridden, nothing ever seems fast enough.

My mother was wary about coming to the palace herself and insisted that she needed to stay at the Keep, but she sent sparrow messengers at least once a day demanding reports on my progress. She also made sure that I had the best avian doctors in the land tending to me.

Zane rarely left my side. Occasionally he would go out to the market while I slept and arrange for dancers, magicians and musicians to entertain me, but he was always beside me as I drifted into sleep and when I woke.

Clothed in deep violet, the serpiente color of

mourning, Zane was no less elegant than he had ever been. However, there was something fragile about his movements, a fatigue no amount of sleep could cure.

Before his people, he put on a good front. Though somber, he still appeared strong and confident. I saw the mask every time someone came to visit me, and I watched it fall every time they left, as if it exhausted him to enact the play his position demanded.

One evening I woke to a sound I could not quite place. When I finally recognized it, I felt a pain sharper then the arrow that had torn into me.

Zane was crying. His back was to me, and he was leaning against the wall with his head in his hands. His shoulders shook as he tried not to make a sound.

"Zane."

"I'm sorry." His voice was muffled.

"You're allowed to cry." He still didn't turn toward me. "Zane, please, come here."

His chest rose and fell with each deep breath as he fought to gather his composure and put one foot in front of the other until he reached me.

I pushed myself up, ignoring the twinge in my side. My pain was tolerable; his was not.

"I didn't mean to wake you," he apologized again.

Zane, whose face was smudged with shadows

and wet with tears, hadn't meant to wake *me*. I wondered when last he had slept a night through.

I reached to brush the tears from his face; Zane turned toward the touch, closing his eyes.

Using the shelf beside my bed for support, I pulled myself to my feet. Standing was difficult, but manageable.

Zane caught my arm and steadied me. "Danica—"

I cut off his words with two fingertips against his lips, to which he planted a gossamer kiss.

Uncertain why, but with no thought of why *not,* I drew his face down to mine. I tasted the salt from his tears as my lips touched briefly against his cheek. Again he closed his eyes, and I kissed each trembling eyelid before finally lowering my lips to his.

Just as tenderly as he had kissed my fingertips, Zane met my lips, unhurried and undemanding.

The kiss was called short by the pain that crept deeper into my side with every moment.

"We both need comfort, and rest," I said. "I can offer one, and the night will provide the other."

Ever so gently, Zane helped me to lie back down. He lay beside me. When I leaned against him, he sighed, kissing my hair, and—mindful of my injury—carefully wrapped an arm around my waist to hold me close.

I rested my cheek against his chest and fell asleep to the gentle rhythm of his breathing and the calm song of his heart. I did not wake again until someone knocked on the door.

"Danica?" a worried voice called.

Zane answered for me, "One minute." He kissed my forehead chastely and then seemed discontented with that and so lowered his lips to mine for a real kiss—one I saw no reason to withhold.

He climbed carefully out of the bed and opened the door for my doctor, an old crow named Betsy, who had been around the Keep since my great-grandmother Caylan's childhood.

"How are you feeling today?" she asked.

I had slept deeply and naturally for the first time in weeks, which made me answer, "Quite well."

"Very good, very good," Betsy answered. "Your mother will be pleased that I finally have something positive to tell her."

The doctor left instructions that I could start on more solid food in a few days, and that I should try to stand up and walk a bit whenever I felt strong enough.

"How do *you* feel?" I asked Zane once we were alone again.

"I don't know." He stopped and shook his head. "My father died when I was a child. I've lost three brothers and a sister since then, and I mourned for each of them. When Gregory died, I decided he would be the last. I was so certain that if I tried, I could keep what was left of my family safe. . . ." He did not need to say more.

I held out a hand to him and he sat beside me.

"I forgot about her, Danica," he confided, and I heard in his voice that this above all was bothering him. "When I pulled the two of you off the stage, there was so much blood on you, and the injury looked so bad . . . I didn't even glance at my mother, didn't . . ." He trailed off again.

I leaned against him, lending my warmth as I spoke. "She was unconscious almost instantly—I felt her fall, Zane," I explained. "There was nothing you could have done."

"I *forgot* about her," he argued.

"You were scared." *As I've been scared before*, I added silently. *So scared I didn't know what to think or do*. "You did all you could."

We passed a while in companionable silence, until Zane whispered finally, "You are so patient with me."

Deciding there was a time to be somber and there was a time to lighten the mood, I responded, "I have to be. . . . I can't walk out without your help."

# CHAPTER 21

O VER THE NEXT WEEK I GRADUALLY gained strength, and finally I could take short walks with Zane to the market. I hated to return to my room so early, and delayed as much as possible, until Zane frequently ended up carrying me much of the way back.

If it bothered him, he never complained. When I was tired, he would curl up with me in bed no matter the hour and we would rest together.

I remembered once comparing him to Vasili in my mind, long ago when he had spoken to me in my room in the Keep, but now I could barely see the resemblance. Zane was warm where Vasili had been cool, offering laughter where Vasili would have given a silent smile.

Vasili and I had been betrothed when I was an infant and he was a child of three. In memory, I looked at him through a child's eyes. I loved him—as a father, as a brother, as a mentor.

These thoughts chased themselves through my mind as Zane and I lingered in the serpiente market longer than usual to watch A'isha perform the sakkri. The dance was even more ancient than the sacred Namir-da. According to myth, it had originated in the cult of Anhamirak, where it had been used to summon spirits. The haunting music and elaborate, complex movements almost made it seem like A'isha must have spectral partners dancing with her.

After it was over, I spotted white-blond hair moving through the crowd. Adelina. She approached us timidly, waiting as we both turned to acknowledge her.

"My Naga Danica," she greeted me. I had never heard her address me by title before. "May I speak to you alone for a moment, please?" The guard's expression was anxious enough to put me on edge.

I glanced at Zane, who shrugged slightly. "I can wait here for you. But this is already longer than you've been walking since you were hurt; try not to linger too long."

"I'll be right back."

Adelina led me to a slightly less crowded section of the market. We were by no means "alone," but we had as much privacy as we would find out here.

"I owe you an apology, milady." Her gaze flickered toward Zane. "After the Mistari made their suggestion, I was the one who protested loudest and longest. More than anything, I wanted Zane happy, and I hated that he would give up that happiness for peace." She sighed, shaking her head, obviously having trouble finding the words she needed. "You two had a rocky start, so I suppose it's natural you would seek comfort with someone you are more familiar with."

She hesitated, and I remembered seeing her with Zane and hearing her plead with him as he refused to go against his vows.

I was about to speak, but Adelina continued. "I still hated you for it, when you went to your Rei and Zane wouldn't come to me." I tried to argue and tell her the truth about a scene that must have been eating away at her since she had seen it, but she wouldn't let me. "What's done is done. I've never seen Zane look at a woman like he looks at you now . . . not even me." Her voice held more than a trace of longing as she said the words. "Oh yes, I'm jealous. Perhaps if I were one of your avian guards, I could pretend otherwise, but I don't have their reserve. And . . . you make him happy. So I feel that I should apologize." She added softly, "For more than you know."

"You're ... forgiven," I answered, finally finding the words to speak.

"You'll be happy to know that I'm retiring from the guard tomorrow," Adelina added. "It doesn't seem appropriate for me to stay. I just—" Her voice broke off in pain.

"Good night, Danica," she whispered before turning away.

I bid her good night, feeling more than a little dazed, and went back to find Zane. I did not repeat Adelina's words to him as we returned to our room; they were personal, and I could not consider telling them to Zane until I understood them myself.

*You make him happy.* I hoped so.

We lay down together again, side by side. He trailed his fingers through my hair, hesitating for just a moment as they passed between the golden feathers hidden there.

"I don't think I'll ever get used to these," Zane commented, "but they don't bother me nearly so much as they used to."

I smiled, snuggling closer. "Maybe someday I'll take you flying." I imagined growing my Demi-form's wings and lifting Zane into the air.

"As soon as you let A'isha teach you to dance the Namir-da," he challenged. "Until then, my feet will remain firmly on the ground."

Sweetly, I agreed, "Deal." I raised my head, and Zane obligingly met my lips with his own.

"You are too tempting," he whispered.

He wrapped one arm around my waist to hold me close as his other hand skimmed down my side, a light caress that ended at my mid-thigh.

We were at the point where one of us had always backed off before, but I didn't want this to end, not yet.

Zane's hand slid down to my knee, gently moving me so I leaned toward his body. I shifted to accommodate the new position, and with the movement came a spark of pain. The sensation was over instantly, but Zane felt me tense, and thankfully recognized the reason. He sighed, drawing back.

"Don't you dare leave me now."

"You're still healing; I don't want to hurt you." His expression told me that he couldn't believe he was the one saying no this time.

"You won't."

*Do you trust him?*

When had we reached the point where the answer to Rei's question had become yes without hesitation? When Zane had sat by my bedside for hours while I was drifting in and out of consciousness? When he had arranged for me to be visited by entertainers and friends, or had carried me home when I was too tired to walk? Or when I had first seen him cry and had wanted nothing but to comfort him?

*I do not know how, yet somehow, impossibly, we are here.*

Zane hesitated, looking at me with temptation and worry in his eyes. The decision was yet unmade when someone pounded on the door, the raps too sharp to be ignored.

Eleanor Lyssia's voice drifted through the door. "Danica, Zane, Rei told me to get you."

Zane swore, pushing himself up, and helped me to my feet. He cast one last lingering look back at the bed before turning toward the door.

Anxiety was written on Eleanor's face. She led us to the main hall, where Andreios met us outside the doors. He had a cut down his left cheek and another one across his ribs. His expression was drawn but not frightened. Still, it was enough to make me queasy with worry.

He nodded toward the closed door of the hall. "We've found our assassins," he said. "Erica and Ailbhe are holding them."

It took a moment for the statement to register. My first thoughts were of Ailbhe and Adelina's treatment of me when I had first entered serpiente land, and of Erica's zealousness against the serpiente. It seemed likely we might end up with only pieces of the assassins left.

I did not have enough time to wonder how they had been caught or who they were before Rei shook his head with a grimace and turned to

Zane. "One of them is the guard who shot Charis and Danica. . . ." He hesitated. "Zane, it's Adelina."

Zane's face whitened; my gut lurched as I considered Adelina's last words to me in a new light. *It doesn't seem appropriate anymore.*

"She wouldn't have hurt my mother," Zane whispered desperately. He pushed past Rei, and then paused before opening the door, bracing himself. "Who is the other?"

"Karl." Now I understood Rei's disgust. He had personally assured me of Karl's loyalty, only to find that the guard had nearly gotten me killed. "Both have confessed. The Royal Flight and palace guard can deal with them, if you wish."

Zane shook his head. "I'll speak to them. Danica?"

I nodded. Unpleasant as it would be, it seemed right that I should face my people—even if only to sentence them.

Rei nodded, and I could tell he agreed with our decisions. He opened the door to the hall for us.

Both assassins' hands were bound behind their backs. Erica was holding Karl's wrists, and Ailbhe held Adelina. The guards' expressions were carefully blank as they detained their own people—and, in Ailbhe's case, his own sister.

"She wasn't supposed to hurt you," Karl instantly protested, before anyone bid him to speak.

"Shut up; they don't care," Adelina responded briskly. She raised her gaze to Zane's, and then looked at me.

Now Karl pleaded with Rei. "I was trying to protect my Tuuli Thea. I knew they couldn't be trusted—"

"You're guilty of treason," Adelina once again interrupted. "No one cares why."

"I care," Zane disagreed. His voice held a wintry chill, which did not quite manage to cover his pain. "I care why you killed my mother, and tried to kill my mate."

"*It wasn't supposed to be poisoned,*" Adelina snapped, glaring at Karl. "He gave me the bolt. An avian bolt, so they would be blamed. . . ." Now her gaze turned to me, and it was all I could do not to step back. "The poison was supposed to be weak, just enough to look like someone was trying to harm Charis—without actually doing it."

"And *you* weren't supposed to hit my Tuuli Thea," Karl argued, yelling to be heard over Adelina. "You nearly killed her—"

"I was trying to!" Adelina shouted back. "It was only a mistake I didn't." Her voice softened as she continued. "I saw my Diente, the man I

loved, honoring *his* vows no matter how cold and
miserable they left him—"

"Would someone just kill her and get it over
with?" Karl asked, his calm voice causing
Adelina to turn to him.

"I should have skinned you when I first
found you in the palace," she retorted. "You were
stupid enough to slice open your own Naga. I
should have known you were too stupid to—"

"I was stupid to think a snake would keep
her word!" Karl answered. "You lied to your own
king. Why did I think you wouldn't lie to me?"

"Enough!" Both quieted abruptly at Zane's
shout. "Karl, *you* were the one who cut Danica?"

The guard answered bluntly, "Trying to kill
you, sir." I had to turn my gaze away, rather than
face the young guard's poise.

Zane turned next to Adelina. "You lied to me
about Karl."

"Yes . . . sir."

"You tried to kill my mate in the synkal, and
in the process killed my mother."

"The poison wasn't supposed to be—"

He held up a hand to silence her. "Yes or no,
Adelina?"

She swallowed hard. "Yes. And I'm aware
that it's a death sentence. Accident or not, I
would impose the sentence upon myself for your
mother's death. I only wanted to make sure

he"—she nodded at Karl—"was also caught, before he could further defend his Naga by trying to kill you again."

Zane swallowed thickly. "Andreios, can you and Erica see that these two are kept under control until they can be dealt with?"

Rei nodded.

"Good." Zane closed his eyes, drawing a deep breath, and suddenly the vulnerability in his expression was obvious. "Ailbhe, you may be dismissed. You don't need to be involved in this."

I saw the moment of hesitation in every tense line of the white viper's body before he shook his head sharply. "Thank you, sir, but I'll stay. If I can't do my duty now, I have no place in your guard."

Zane nodded gravely. Rei, Erica and Ailbhe escorted the two traitors out.

As soon as they were gone, Zane collapsed against the wall. "I should have known. Gods . . . I trusted her with your life. . . ." He pulled me closer, until I was resting against him. "You could have been killed." He kissed the top of my head.

I lifted my face to meet the kiss, wanting the comfort of his touch as much as I was willing to provide the comfort of mine. The contact was sweet and soft, yet at the same time desperate.

It was Zane who pulled away first. "Danica, I

think . . ." He trailed off and kissed me again, this time briefly, just the barest touch of lips to lips. "I love you."

From a man who frequently uttered eloquent speeches, the tentative declaration was not the most flattering of compliments—especially when every movement he made and look he cast my way had shown the truth long before now.

But coming from the serpent who had once informed me that he did not love me and did not think he ever could, whose cool, polished words could cut to the bone and freeze the Earth's molten blood—whose eyes right now were just a bit dazed, and whose expression was as open and startled as I had ever seen it—the words were more than enough.

"I know," I answered. Then, soft but certain, I answered, "I love you, too."

His smile matched mine and said the same as mine: *I know.*

*My prayer is simple, my dear one, my dear one. May you never need understand. My prayer is for peacetime, my child, my child.*
*Live it well, and this life can be grand.*

# SNAKECHARM

## PROLOGUE

WHEN EGYPT WAS YOUNG, and the first pyramids were being built with the sweat and blood of slavery, there lived a
small civilization on the outskirts of society, led by a coven of thirteen men and women called the Dasi.

It is said that these thirteen were able to read the thoughts of
mortals, and that they could bewitch any who looked upon them.
When they danced their rituals together, they could summon the
spirits of the dead, make the rain fall or cause illusions to rise from
the sand.

Among their pantheon, they worshipped the dual powers Anhamirak and Ahnmik. Anhamirak granted life, light, love and all
manner of beauty; her greatest gift to her people was free will. As
all things must, she had an opposite. One prayed to Ahnmik for
power, sleep and silent peace. He was not an evil god, but with
power came force, and so while Anhamirak gave this world freedom
and equality, Ahnmik's gifts included bondage and mastery.

Each side could not exist without the other, and so the speakers
for this darker god stood as revered in the Dasi as Anhamirak's.

The twin powers were held in a precarious balance by the high priestess of the Dasi, Maeve.

As the story goes, a creature by the name of Leben appeared to Maeve. At first she thought he was a god, an incarnation of Anhamirak's son, Namid, and she bowed down to him. Then he ordered her coven to worship him alone—at which point Maeve realized that, for all his power, he was no god, for any true god would know that only chaos would follow if the balance was lost.

Knowing the danger he posed to her people if angered, but unwilling to surrender to his demands, Maeve seduced him, and in an attempt to win her favor, he gave her ageless beauty, and the second form of a viper with ivory scales. She insisted he do the same for all her people.

Leben gave the ebony scales and garnet eyes of a king cobra to Kiesha, high priestess of Anhamirak, and other graceful serpent forms to seven of her followers. The four whose worship fell to Ahnmik—Cjarsa, Araceli, Syfka and Servos—were given the majestic wings and deadly talons of falcons.

The magic Ahnmik had given the falcons, combined with Leben's gifts, was strong and dangerous, and soon they were driven from the clan for their reckless practice of it. Maeve's ivory-scaled kin were soon forced to follow, as the white vipers too fell to Ahnmik's lures and abandoned the balance they had once revered.

Reluctantly, Kiesha rose to power, and from her son—or so the story goes—the Cobriana line descended.

My own line. The line with garnet eyes and jet-black hair, which has led the serpents since the day Maeve fell to Ahnmik. We have ruled through famine, we have ruled through fortune, and for unknown generations, we have ruled through war.

Until now. I am the first of my line to rule through peace. These last few months with Danica have gone by so blissfully that I find myself doubting fate's sincerity.

*Did Kiesha's kin feel this same queasy fear in the night, after Ahnmik's followers were driven away? Did those ancient serpents know their days were numbered by an enemy they had not yet even encountered?*

*According to avian myth, Queen Alasdair was given her hawk form after she prayed to the avians' sun god to lift her city from civil strife and poverty. She gathered her people and brought them peace and prosperity and turned a faltering city into a beautiful empire.*

*Avians and serpiente had never met before the day Kiesha was granted an audience with the new hawk queen. Neither had a reason to hate the other. Yet avian history books say Kiesha stabbed Alasdair in the back; ours say Alasdair's guards slaughtered the eight serpents in their beds. No one knows the truth anymore, only that the children of the slain retaliated swiftly, and years of bloodshed followed.*

*Ancient fears, ancient questions. Our war with the avians is over now. We do not know what hatred led to the murders of Kiesha and Alasdair, but I do know it is love that binds our realms together now. I thank the gods daily for the brilliant hawk who is my mate.*

*But older hatreds and ancient threats still remain. A missive reached us late last night: Syfka arrived at the Hawk's Keep yesterday, seeking Danica and me, and was told we were at the serpiente palace. The falcon is due to arrive here any time today.*

*During the war, the falcons supplied the avians with poison specifically designed to kill Kiesha's serpent kin—my people. Before the war, the falcons nearly destroyed the Dasi's civilization in their search for power and were exiled as a result.*

*The war is over.*

*What now?*

*Zane Cobriana*
*Diente*

# CHAPTER 1

A FLICKER OF SHADOW AGAINST THE SUN made everyone in the serpiente market pause in their business and look to the sky. The fluttering of wings and the sight of a diving sparrow chilled me.

Erica Silvermead, the sparrow who now shifted into her human form in front of me, had been guarding the front door of the palace. Her presence here meant that our dangerous visitor had arrived.

Politely excusing myself from the merchant I had been speaking with, I followed Erica into the palace.

Once we were alone, she confirmed my assumption. "Syfka, speaker for Empress Cjarsa, is at the gate. She has requested an audience with you and your pair bond."

I would have liked nothing more than to order the guard and the Royal Flight to ban Syfka from our lands, but insulting the falcons would be suicide. While the serpiente retained only ancient dances and half-remembered stories from the days of Maeve's coven, the falcons' powers were still strong. Their royal house supposedly consisted of the four falcons who had once practiced among the Dasi, kept alive by a combination of Ahnmik's and Leben's magics.

If the legend was true, Syfka was one of those four and, as such, a creature whose might was too great to fathom. Even if it was false, Syfka represented an empire we could not risk slighting.

I nodded reluctantly, taking a detour to find my mate.

We caught Danica just as she was leaving the synkal, where her lessons were held. She was languid from exhaustion, but she smiled upon seeing me, and my heart warmed just from the sight of her golden hawk eyes lighting up. Then she saw my worried gaze, and her expression suddenly mirrored my own.

"Syfka is here?" she asked.

"At the gate."

Danica shuddered, but joined Erica and me on our hasty walk toward the entryway. "Syfka was never an enemy of my people during the war, but she made it clear that falcons held no respect for avians no matter how similar our second forms may seem. Whatever she is here for now, I suggest we deal with it quickly."

"We're in agreement, then."

Ailbhe, the head of the palace guard, was waiting with our visitor by the doorway. The white viper stood at strict attention, tension wavering in the air around his silent form, his gaze fixed not quite on the falcon, but never moving far from her.

Syfka radiated an aura of heat that rivaled even Danica's constant warmth. Her hair was pale gold, and in the front it faded to silver; her eyes were crystalline blue, set in milk-pale skin. Wings rose from her shoulders and cascaded down her back, with the golden undersides and brown, gray and black markings of an aplomado falcon.

She was stunning, and like all falcons, she had a magnetic air that could draw mortals to her like moths to fire—ultimately to meet with the same demise, if they dared offend her. Right now she was standing formally with her left hand clasping her right wrist behind her back. It was the respectful pose of a soldier, but Syfka's expression told me clearly that the respect was not for me.

As her eyes met mine, it was easy to believe this creature was as ancient as myth. She gave a nod that might have served as a bow, if it had been accompanied by anything other than obvious disdain. "Zane Cobriana, Danica Shardae, I appreciate that you are prompt. I am looking for one of our people, who I have reason to believe is in this area."

"A falcon?" I could not help frowning. "Not among the serpiente. Danica?"

My mate's expression remained calm, though I knew her well enough to feel her agitation and anxiety building. "You are the only falcon who has visited our lands in the last decade," she answered.

Syfka looked amused. "The falcon could have altered its form, its coloring," she explained, her voice patient, as if she was speaking to a young child. "I hesitate even to offer a gender, as that could feasibly be hidden, too. Unless you'd seen the person's falcon form, there would be no way to know."

"Then why ask us?" I replied, irritated by her patronizing tone only barely more than by her request. I struggled to keep my voice from revealing my annoyance. "If there's no way for us to tell whether someone is a falcon, how can we help you search?"

Syfka nodded toward Danica. "Though it seemed un-likely, I thought the criminal might have asked for asylum from the Tuuli Thea, since some on the island know of our past alliance with the avian people."

"May I ask what he or she has done?" Danica inquired.

"That is not your concern." Syfka's words were brisk.

I might have argued, had I thought the falcon was some-one I knew, but I doubted that was the case. Someone trying to hide was unlikely to befriend the king of the land.

Danica also held back any protests she had. If we discov-ered the so-called criminal, we might dispute Syfka's words, but for now we might as well work with her.

Danica echoed my thoughts. "So many people pass through the court every day that a newcomer could remain unnoticed for some time unless he introduced himself to the Tuuli Thea. I can, however, see if my guards have noticed any-thing unusual."

"I will speak with the serpiente," I added. "If there are any newcomers in these lands, the dancers at least will know of them." While the Cobriana were the heart of the serpi-ente, the dancers were its blood; nothing went on in the royal house, the market or the most distant serpiente lands that the dancers did not know about eventually.

Syfka nodded curtly. "See that you do. I want this done quickly, so I can leave this *equakeiel*." The last word was in the old Dasi language, spoken in falcon lands, of which I knew a little. Syfka's description of our lands was not flattering.

"If you are so displeased to be here," I suggested deli-cately, "you are welcome to leave and let us conduct this search on our own."

"You would never recognize a hidden falcon without my assistance. Your kind is as blind to Ahnmik's magic as a worm is to the sun." I heard her add under her breath, "You notice it only when it scalds you."

Abruptly she returned to falcon form and took to the sky.

*I will return shortly to see to your progress.*

The words whispered through my mind like a line of lyrics heard even after a song has ended. I had no doubt they came from Syfka, and the sense of her even so briefly inside my mind left an unpleasant chill.

Beside me, Danica went pale, her body swaying. I moved closer, and she caught my arm, drawing in a slow breath as she closed her eyes.

"Are you all right?"

"I'm fine," she answered. "I was just a little dizzy for a moment." Danica shook her head as if to clear it. "I spent most of this morning practicing with A'isha; perhaps I over-taxed myself."

I glanced from Danica to her guard; Erica looked as worried as I felt. Then again, the sparrow's whole frame had already been taut as a wire. Facing a falcon, against whom all her fighting prowess would not let her win, had left her visibly tense.

Syfka had asked for our help, even though she had dismissed our ability to give any. Harming us now would be sabotaging herself. Wouldn't it?

Still, we couldn't be too careful. "I think we should try to get a better sense of what Syfka is capable of before she returns—and, if possible, learn something about her criminal, or at least get an idea of how and where he or she might be hiding," I said.

Danica nodded, but admitted, "Falcon contempt for outsiders is legendary. Even though we had an agreement with them during the war, we were never in a position to demand much in the way of concrete information. They certainly didn't speak of criminals or illusion spells." Her color had returned somewhat, and her voice was again confident. Only fatigue, I hoped. "Don't the falcons and the serpiente share origins?"

"Technically," I said, reluctant to revisit past grief, "but we have had almost no contact since Maeve's coven split ... thousands of years ago. Most of the records we do have are either embedded in myth, or so old that they are almost impossible to read even if one knows the language."

"Almost no contact?" Danica asked gently.

"My oldest brother, Anjay, was heir before I ..." I took a breath, trying to clear too many memories from my mind. "I don't know how he encountered Syfka, but she brought him to Ahnmik and he was allowed an audience with their Empress, so he could petition for her aid in the war."

Danica knew as well as I did that the falcons had given my kind no help. "What happened?"

"I don't know.... He never had a chance to tell us."

The moment Anjay had returned to our lands, he had been told about the death of our sister Sisal—the horrible, senseless slaughter of mother and child that had sent him in a fury to the Keep.

His body had never been recovered.

I did not tell Danica the rest of that story. Anjay had gone to avenge our sister's death by killing Danica's mother, Tuuli Thea at the time. I did not want to know whether he had succeeded in harming any of the avian people before he died. I did not want to know whether one of the Royal Flight—Andreios, perhaps—had ended Anjay's life. It was for the best that Anjay had failed, but I had still lost a brother that day four years ago.

When I had arrived home and learned of this terrible series of events, I had immediately set out for the Hawk's Keep. I had started that ride in a fog of denial, refusing to acknowledge that my brother was dead, refusing to believe that the burden of the royal seat had fallen to me so suddenly at the age of sixteen. The hours had turned my thoughts from disbelief to mad fury. I had scaled the walls of the Hawk's Keep, intent on murder, and stumbled into the room of Danica Shardae.

And there, I think I fell in love. As I beheld the avian princess sleeping so innocently, her cheek marked by a new cut—probably by one of my own people's blades—my hatred died, leaving only a desperate desire for peace in its wake. When the mad suggestion was made last winter that taking the enemy queen as my mate could end the war, it had almost seemed like fate. It had not been easy to bridge the gaps between us, but together we had managed.

Fate had given me many gifts. Danica Shardae was the one for which I would forever be most grateful.

Erica drew me from my musing as she offered tentatively, "The scholar Valene studied in falcon lands once. I lost touch with her after I joined the Royal Flight, but someone might know her whereabouts."

*Excellent.* "Danica?"

"Yes? Oh . . . sorry," she answered, smiling tiredly. "I seem to be a bit useless today. I haven't heard from Valene in years, but Andreios would probably be able to find her."

"You're dancing tonight, aren't you?" I asked. Though Danica had performed some simple improvisational dances at Namir-da eight months before, I had never been allowed to watch her practice with A'isha, leader of the dancers' guild and the only one daring enough to teach the serpiente art to

an avian queen. That night was to be Danica's first performance of the more complex, traditional dances. Even if fatigue
was her only ailment, that could stop her from taking the
stage.

Danica nodded. "The thought has me so nervous I feel ill,
even if the performance is only for A'isha, you and a few of
the other dancers who have practiced with me," she confided.

"Why don't you get some rest? I can track down Andreios and ask him about Valene. If I see A'isha, I'll also
find out whether her guild knows anything about a hidden
falcon."

"Perhaps that's a good idea."

Without being told, Erica stayed beside her queen. I
hoped this spell was truly a combination of nerves and fatigue, but I could not help the sense of unease gnawing at
my mind.

I asked two people before I believed that Andreios was
with A'isha in the synkal—where the reserved leader of the
Royal Flight apparently spent most of his free time in serpiente lands. Despite the warning, the scene on the dais was a
shock.

A'isha and Rei were facing each other with their hands
touching, poised to begin one of the simpler dances. I could
barely hear the faint melody A'isha was singing, a wordless
tune meant to imitate the flute that would normally play.

The two moved into the dance seamlessly enough to suggest weeks of practice—the last thing I would expect of the
crow. I wondered if Danica knew that her teacher had found
two students instead of one.

I closed the synkal door loudly behind me, as if I had just entered. Both dancers jumped and turned to face me.

A'isha recovered first. The viper slithered down from the synkal dais, the movement sliding the material of her dress enough that one of her legs was bared to the thigh for a moment.

Rei wasn't watching the show, which was obviously put on for his benefit. He descended the stairs with a haughty expression that dared me to comment.

I knew better than to bait him now. If I even implied that I had been watching, A'isha would probably never get the conservative crow onto her stage again.

Why she had made the effort to teach him in the first place was a mystery to me. A'isha was notoriously picky in her choice of students, and although I respected Andreios, he could not possibly share Danica's passion for dance.

Still, I was thankful that circumstances had put together the two people I sought.

"Rei, A'isha, we've just had a visit from Syfka."

All traces of defiance disappeared instantly from Rei's face. "What does she want?"

"She's looking for a falcon; she didn't say his name, or what he had done, only that he was a criminal. You wouldn't happen to know of any falcons in the avian court, would you?"

Rei cleared his throat, obviously suppressing a laugh. "The falcons are fastidiously purebred. Their kind doesn't mix with ours, no matter how similar we may seem."

A'isha responded in the same way. "I can't imagine any creature with wings masquerading as one without, though I was once told that the falcons act more like serpents in their

SNAKECHARM 257

free time than like avian ladies and gentlemen." She shook her head. "I've known most of my dancers since they were infants. No one could hide among them without being noticed. I can ask if anyone has heard anything in the market, though."

"Thank you."

"You're stealing my student, anyway. I may as well find something else to do." She kissed Rei on the cheek as she turned. "Don't work too hard." She fluttered away, leaving Rei shaking his head.

"You seem to have a new friend." I said the words with all the blandness I could manage.

"A'isha has kindly agreed to teach me her art. That is all."

I debated asking more, but unfortunately, now was not the time to push Rei, no matter how tempting. "I came to find you because Erica suggested you might be able to help us find someone—a scholar named Valene, who she says once knew a great deal about the falcons."

Rei looked surprised. "Valene Silvermead is Erica's aunt. She was a well-respected avian scholar who specialized in knowledge of other cultures. I understand she has spent time in human lands, as well as with the wolves and the falcons. She was exiled by Danica's mother for her dealings with the serpiente and ended up living as a recluse on the edge of our land. I suppose the episode dimmed her faith in the avian court somewhat, since she has expressed no desire to return since."

"Could we get her here?" I asked. "I hope to gather as much information as possible before dealing with Syfka again."

"Valene's nephew was once a member of my flight, so I've stayed in touch with her despite the scandal," Rei admitted.

"I remember her as a strong flier. We could probably make it back here by the evening meal, though that's assuming she's home and not off investigating some new land."

"Danica is performing tonight, so we have been invited to dine in sha'Mehay," I said. "When you two return, could you have Valene meet us there?"

Sha'Mehay was the name for the local dancer's nest, where the members of the dancers' guild lived, slept, dined, studied and of course danced. The name most closely translated to *the ones who dance with illusions* or *the ones who dance with eternity*. Outsiders were rarely allowed inside, and even for a cobra, an invitation was a rare honor.

Rei nodded. "I will come find you the moment we touch ground."

# CHAPTER 2

D ANICA'S NORMAL GLOW HAD RETURNED by the time evening fell, though her golden eyes still held traces of the nerves she had spoken of earlier. Her warmth helped soothe my tousled emotions as we walked together to the nest, her hand in mine.

On the topic of falcons, Danica shared one memory: that of a child the falcons had sent to the Keep when she had been too young to realize he was there to check up on her kind.

"Sebastian was only twelve when he came to us, as a sort of ambassador," she explained. "I remember teaching him children's games, and wondering why he did not know them. When Syfka arrived to check on him, he announced that he wanted to stay and be my alistair. I can still remember her horrified expression before she ordered him to return home."

Danica smiled slightly, though there was a dark shadow of loss behind the memory.

"I learned to fear the falcons later," Danica added, "when my mother first explained to me how critical their help was, and how we struggled not to offend them ... but I always remember Sebastian fondly. In a way, he was the last real playmate I had. Rei's father was killed right after Sebastian left, and finally the war seemed real to me. All my friends began to train as soldiers, and I began to walk the fields. Two years later, upon my sister's death, I became heir to the throne, and suddenly childhood was over." She shook her head. "No matter how much I've ever feared the falcons, when I think of simpler days, I still remember peregrine wings."

Danica paused, and I pulled her into my arms. She looked up at me with a smile.

"Peregrine wings and Cobriana eyes," she said, drawing herself out of the past and into the peaceful shelter of the present. "The two things that come to mind whenever I think of home and safety. Come, my love—let me dance for you."

At this she led me toward the doors of the dancer's nest, a place that held no room for melancholy or suspicion.

Sha'Mehay had been built into the forest, the walls and ceiling formed by heavy nets strung between trees and then covered with leather, clay and finally ever-growing vines. The nets in the center of the ceiling could be rolled back to let sun or moonlight in and fire smoke out.

Even while standing outside, I could hear the rhythm of drums and the flutist's tunes. Once we were inside, the world was awhirl with sound and color and movement. I had come here only rarely before, but even if I had spent all my life in the nest, I did not think I would ever become immune to its wonder. The slate floor was almost entirely covered by layers of Persian carpets, pillows, blankets and other soft material the dancers had found. The only undecorated surface was in the center, around the bonfire that constantly burned to keep the nest bright and warm.

Some of the coven were working, teaching their students not only dances, but history. Among the serpiente, these dancers preserved our myths and most ancient traditions. A few, who had been born and raised in the nest, had also spent their lives studying the language that Maeve's coven had spoken thousands of years ago.

A'isha twirled up to us in a ripple of crimson and silver *melos* scarves belted around her waist to form an improvised bodice and skirt that alternately molded to and slithered away from her skin. Each flowing movement revealed bright symbols painted onto her body.

"Danica, *ak'varlheah*," A'isha greeted her student warmly, kissing Danica's cheek as she drew her farther into the nest. "A gift, for each of you," A'isha said as she produced a pair of woven silks the color of beaten gold. She tied one around Danica's waist, then turned to do the same for me. The color symbolized an eternal tie to another; it was an instantly visible declaration of loyalty to one's mate. "Now, I must steal Danica from you," A'isha apologized, "if you wish to see her dance later."

In the back of the nest was a stairwell I had never descended. Danica stole a kiss for good luck before A'isha led her down those steps to prepare.

Meanwhile, one of the other dancers called me over to the fireside, where food was being passed in a ring around the flames, along with jugs of warm spiced wine.

"You made a good choice for your Naga," she assured me. "Danica is more graceful on a dais than half the serpents I know."

"Provided she isn't blushing too brightly to see," another quipped. "The first time I saw our queen perform, I thought she was a lost cause—far too uptight, like most avians—but I'm glad to be proved wrong."

I knew I was grinning. I had never doubted that Danica could learn the serpent art. Much of her loved my world; a part of her craved dance as surely as anyone else in this nest did. Perhaps that thirst came from her time dancing with the currents of air far above where we earthbound creatures roamed, or perhaps it came from the expressive nature her own world forced her to hide.

Similar conversation flowed among us until A'isha's musical voice commanded me, "Zane, admire your queen."

The words brought our attention to the back of the room, where Danica had emerged, looking so beautiful that she took my breath away.

In response to her teacher's words, Danica smiled and shook her head, causing her golden hair to ripple about her face. It made my heart speed and my breath still, as if I was afraid the next movement would shatter the world.

She was a spark of fire in sha'Mehay. The serpiente dress rippled around the hawk's long legs, the fabric so light it moved with the slightest shift of air. The bodice was burgundy silk; it laced up the front with a black ribbon, and though it was more modest than many dancers' costumes, it still revealed enough cream-and-roses skin to tantalize the imagination. On Danica's right temple, A'isha had painted a symbol for courage; beneath her left collarbone lay the symbols for *san'Anhamirak*, abandon and freedom.

"You dance every day with the wind. This is not so different," A'isha said encouragingly to Danica. "Now, look at the man you love and dance for him."

The nest hushed, faces turning to their Naga. Her cheeks

held more color than usual, which A'isha addressed with a common dancers' proverb. "There is no place for shame, Danica. If Anhamirak had not wanted beauty admired, she would not have made our eyes desire it. You are art."

Danica stepped out of A'isha's grip. "If my mother could see me now," she murmured, but she smiled as she said it.

"Feel the beat. It is the wind," A'isha directed. "Fly with it."

The soft beat of a drum, paired with the lilting melody of a flute, filled the room as Danica stepped onto the dais at the back of the nest.

Closing her eyes, Danica stretched upward, moving onto the balls of her feet, wrists crossed high above her head, and paused there for a heartbeat. The pose was known as a prayer—a dancer's call for guidance from the powers that be.

She moved into the dance flawlessly, the sway of her body as fluid as water over stone. This was the magic of the serpent and the snake charmer combined, as pure and intense as a thunderstorm.

The first dance was soft and gentle, a common *sakkri'nira*. I could feel the drive in the music, however, and knew the moment when the first dance would move into a more complex one.

When the flute stilled, Danica rose once again onto the balls of her feet for an instant. She smiled at me before she began the most complex of the *intre'marl*: Maeve's solo from the Namir-da.

What had been praise and beauty became passion. Maeve's dance was a seduction, and the way Danica held my eyes made me feel it. Seeing my mate perform those steps made me want to join her, as any royal-born serpiente would.

The holiday for which the Namir-da had been named was still four months away; she would be able to perform then, and I with her, in a ritual that dated back to the creation of my kind.

The music was softening, in prelude to the end, when Danica stumbled, losing the beat precariously close to the edge of the dais. I crossed the room without a thought and caught her with barely enough time to brace myself and keep us both from tumbling to the floor. My heart was pounding painfully beneath my ribs.

A'isha had followed me, and she seemed instantly relieved when she saw that I had caught her charge. "Danica, are you . . ." She broke off when it became obvious that Danica could not hear her.

There was no blood, no wound. I cradled Danica against my chest. "Danica?"

Avians didn't faint. Their systems utilized oxygen at a rate fast enough to keep the body supplied during a long flight against wind. Danica had only ever passed out from poisoning—assassination attempts, to be exact, during the tumultuous time after we had first declared the war between our civilizations over.

"Ooh." The light sound escaped from her throat, and her eyes fluttered open—golden eyes, a shade darker than her hair. Her brow creased with confusion.

"Zane." Danica's voice was tentative, as if she wasn't quite sure how she had gotten there. She smiled wryly and started to sit up.

The movement was aborted; one hand flew to her forehead, and she fell back, taking one deep breath after another.

"What happened?" I tried to keep the worry from my

voice as I looked frantically around the nest, searching for threats. The other dancers were watching us from a careful distance.

"I'll . . . be okay," Danica asserted. "I was just . . . dizzy." She accepted help standing, but once she was up, her balance seemed to return quickly; she rested one hand on my arm, though I sensed that touch was more from habit than weakness.

A'isha looked from one of us to the other, and her expression slid from worried to startled to amused. "Little hawk, you've never been faint before," the dancer said.

"It's hot in here, and I've been tired and nervous," Danica argued. "Perhaps this was too much." She tucked her head down, suddenly realizing that she had fainted in front of an audience.

"Bring her to rest, Zane," A'isha ordered, apparently not daunted by the fact that she was addressing her king. Inside the nest, no one ever was. "I hear your sister's mate makes an excellent raspberry-ginger tea. I suggest you get the recipe. Now off with you."

A'isha's hinted meaning suddenly dawned on me, and I could not help pulling Danica against me to kiss her. "Is she right?" I asked, my mind tumbling with too many thoughts to put into words.

"I don't know what she's talking about," Danica responded, leaning against me. "I hate raspberry tea."

I tried not to laugh; Danica's innocence asserted itself at odd moments, and right now nothing could keep me from grinning. "Danica, Danica . . ." Concerns returned abruptly when I touched her skin. Serpiente were cold-blooded, but Danica was a hawk; her skin was always warm, almost hot. Now it was dangerously chilled. "You're cold."

"I'm just tired," she protested, but I could feel her shivering.

All delight disappeared.

"A'isha?"

The dancer came quickly to my side. "Yes?"

"Would you send some of the Royal Flight to the Keep for Danica's doctor?" Saying the words made any problem more real somehow, more frightening.

A'isha frowned. "Of course. Meanwhile, your mate may rest downstairs."

Danica pushed away. "Zane, I'm not—"

"Danica, you can fly for hours under the Mediterranean sun without being winded; dancing shouldn't leave you this drawn," I pointed out. "The nest is designed to hold in warmth; it is never cold."

I understood her refusal to acknowledge any problem. The last thing either of us wanted to imagine was that something was wrong.

*Please, let it be simple. Please, let it be ...* I cut the thought off. I knew what I wanted Danica's ailment to be, what A'isha thought it was, still I feared the worst.

# CHAPTER 3

B EFORE WE REACHED THE STAIRS at the back of the nest, we heard bright voices by the front door, a chorus of welcomes as the dancers one by one recognized the newcomer. Danica turned slowly, forcing me to do the same.

I caught a glimpse of a dark-haired avian woman wearing a vibrant blue dress in a style I had never seen before. She was talking animatedly with A'isha, and though I recognized the old language, I could not follow a word. The newcomer spoke it fluently, as almost no one did these days.

Eventually A'isha shook her head, admitting, "I've been studying the old language since I was a child, but you've surpassed me."

The stranger beamed. "I never could have managed without your teachings."

Danica blinked with surprise. "Valene?"

The raven turned, excusing herself from the dancers to greet Danica and me with a curtsy. Rei walked behind her, obviously a little uncomfortable inside sha'Mehay. For a moment I wondered why he had been allowed inside at all—

guards were let into the nest even more rarely than cobras—and then I recalled that A'isha was teaching him.

"Milady Shardae. Diente Zane," Valene greeted us. "It is good to see you both."

A'isha followed her and gave the raven a knowing glance. "Your Tuuli Thea was about to go lie down; she was feeling faint. Zane, one of my dancers went to fetch the palace doctor, and another is off in search of a bird to fly the message to the Keep—Andreios, relax," she said, stopping the crow before he demanded an explanation. "There is no problem. Zane is simply being overprotective in the most charming way."

Rei looked at me, but Danica spoke before I could. "I think I *will* go take a nap," she said softly, forestalling Rei's questions. "Zane, Rei, I forbid you from worrying. There is nothing wrong with me that rest will not heal, and you need to talk to Valene."

"Sensible woman," A'isha asserted.

I was torn between the desire to accompany Danica and the knowledge that Syfka would return too soon.

"I'll walk her down and stay by her door," Rei suggested, seeing my hesitation. "If she wakes or anything happens, I'm sure you'll be nearby."

I would rather stay and forget about the falcons entirely, but when it came to Danica's safety, I trusted the crow unconditionally. Andreios had known and loved Danica all her life. Too much the gentleman to speak of love for another man's mate, he never raised the topic, but only continued to defend his Tuuli Thea as I felt sure he would with his last breath.

Seeing our anxiety, A'isha sighed. "I don't know what all the fuss is about," she said. "Women have been having children forever. Rei can take care of her. You have work to do and your mate wouldn't approve of you shirking your duty when she's in no danger at all."

As Rei had predicted, I arranged to have my conversation with Valene in the room next to the one where Danica was resting.

"Andreios says you have had a visit from Syfka?" the raven asked, as I tried to turn my thoughts from my mate to the current situation.

I nodded, taking a deep breath.

"The falcons have lost someone, and seem to think we might have him. Our knowledge of their world is sadly lacking, and I thought it best to learn more before Syfka returns. Erica suggested that you might be able to help."

"Thank you for the compliment," Valene answered. "Among my adventures, I spent several months as a student on the falcon island. What did Syfka have to say about the lost falcon?"

"Only that he—or she—was a criminal, that he might have changed his appearance so we would never even know what gender he was, and that he might have asked for asylum among our people. So far, no one has come up with any ideas."

Valene explained, "The falcons' easiest magics include illusions so strong they can fool every sense. We would never be able to recognize one of their kind, if he wanted to hide. As for gender . . ." She laughed a little. "I've seen such a switch made with illusions, though I've never heard of it being maintained for much time. Still, Syfka is probably certain that if she names one gender, our little minds won't think to consider someone who appears the other."

"If that's the case, how could Syfka expect us to recognize this criminal?"

Valene shook her head. "I doubt she does. Falcons aren't quick to overestimate anyone else," she added. "Most likely she asked for your help primarily as a formality."

"That kind of formality seems out of place, considering her opinion of our kind."

Valene paused as if considering. "It is hard to explain. On the falcon island, appearances and conventions are crucially important. The polite face is unnerving in a city where torture and manipulation are condoned."

"If you spent time on the island recently, do you know anything about the criminal they're looking for?"

Valene let out a half caw, a barking laugh that crows and ravens had a tendency toward. "The word 'recently' is non sense, since more than a century may go by before the Empress turns her attention to an unpleasant matter, and asking 'which falcon criminal?' is like asking 'which leaf?' while standing in the forest." She shook her head. "Falcon law is strict. So much as disagreeing with the Empress can get one executed, even if she *was* wrong. The criminal they are looking for now may have done nothing more than accidentally curse in the Empress's presence and then flee her punishment: execution by torture. Of course, no one on the island would dare argue with the sentence. Implying that the royal family is anything but flawless, just and merciful is considered treason, and punishable by death."

A chill went down my spine. Since Danica and I divided our time between our two courts, I had grown used to avian politics, which were slightly more formal than my own, but even Danica did not hold herself that far above those she ruled. Our people had the right to question their monarchs' judgment; their voices had kept tragedies from occurring in the past. The falcon civilization Valene described sounded horrific.

"I could give you a course in falcon etiquette, but no matter what you do, Syfka will find some reason to disapprove of you," Valene admitted. "You'll either be rude or obsequious, stupid or arrogant. Falcons are raised with the idea that their kind is superior to any other. When it comes to magic, strength, stamina or recall, they are."

*And well aware of it,* I thought cynically, remembering Syfka's arrogance. Even without a history of practicing black magic, the falcons gave the world good reason to hate them.

"My advice is to treat Syfka courteously, and try to see to what she wants without completely disrupting the palace. Also, if A'isha's hints are correct, it would be best if the falcon does not see Danica again."

"They might not respect either of us, but the falcons have definitely shown more of a preference for avians in the last few thousand years," I pointed out. "Might Syfka behave more civilly with Danica?"

Valene hesitated for an instant, but then met my gaze and said bluntly, "In Ahnmik, it's a scandal if a gyrfalcon has a child with a peregrine, even if both are of equal rank. A match between, say, a hawk and a falcon, two very similar creatures, is seen as disgusting; any child born of them is considered mongrel, a travesty of nature. If Danica really is carrying your child, and Syfka realizes this, the falcon will be horrified. I don't think she would harm it, but..." She trailed off, then finished, "The falcons prize children above almost anything, but Syfka might not see a cobra-hawk as a child."

I appreciated the warning, but at the same time, I knew my gaze was icy when I looked at Valene.

Would my own people see the match the same way? If our child was born with onyx hair and golden eyes, would both serpiente and avians look at her with disgust for the cross, and sorrow for the loss of pure-blooded cobra or hawk features?

What if the child was born a hawk like its mother, never to spread a cobra's hood? Would I look at it and regret the loss of my own bloodline?

A knock at the door made us both turn to find Andreios already stepping into the room.

"Betsy is here," he said. Before I could even move past him, he continued, "She was scandalized enough that I was sitting by Danica's door when she arrived; I can guarantee you that she won't allow you into the room until she is certain about Danica's condition."

Despite her petite stature and habit of smoothing down the ruffled feathers at the back of her neck when agitated, Danica's doctor, Betsy, was probably one of the most formidable women I had ever met. If Rei said she would not let me into the room, I knew I would have better luck arm-wrestling Syfka than fighting my way in.

"Perhaps we should retreat to the main nest?" Rei suggested. Even though he knew no more than I did, the crow seemed perfectly calm. Avians always appeared calm; it was a talent they cultivated and respected. In situations like this, it was also damnably annoying.

Valene took up the movement. "I will keep thinking, but I believe I've shared all the useful knowledge of falcons I have. I'm sorry it wasn't more helpful."

We started upstairs, though I paused by Danica's door,

entertaining the notion of walking in and testing whether Betsy would really throw me out. I dismissed the idea quickly. One person I would always obey was the very respected doctor who was looking after the woman I loved. I trusted Betsy's judgment, even though we occasionally disagreed on propriety.

# CHAPTER 4

ONCE AGAIN A'ISHA GREETED US as we returned to the main portion of the nest.

Her presence was helpful, as I could see most of the nest was preparing to interrogate us. Loudly enough for all those loitering nearby to hear, A'isha asked, "Betsy still has not confirmed anything, I understand?"

"That is correct," I answered. Immediately, several of the dancers who had been blatantly eavesdropping sighed and turned away.

Returning to a conversational tone, A'isha said, "My dancers seem to think they have the right to know everything the moment it happens—ceaseless gossips, all of them. Even so, our blessings go to you, your mate and, if hope proves true, your child."

"Thank you; I will pass the words along to Danica as soon as her doctor lets me see her."

A'isha laughed softly. "In the meantime, you and Andreios are both welcome to stay in the nest—as I am sure you want to."

The words caught me off guard. Despite Danica's condition and Valene's presence, I had not expected such an open invitation. I understood A'isha's allowing Danica to stay, but although no serpent was ignorant of dance, I certainly did not qualify as one of A'isha's guild.

She must have seen my surprise, because she reminded me, "It has been too long since our queen has been a student of the nest. We have been honored to have Danica here."

The simple words touched upon centuries of history. Long before my time, the palace hall had been the home of the most famous dancer's nest; the royal family had been a respected part of it. Seven or eight hundred years ago, the Diente had attempted to demonstrate his power over the dancers—and as a group they had rebelled.

No one knew for certain who had put the knife in that king's heart, though most believed it had been his own son and heir's desperate attempt to prevent a civil war. The new Diente had swiftly negotiated with the dancers, and though they had supported the Cobriana ever since, they had never returned to the palace, founding sha'Mehay instead.

Now A'isha offered a small package wrapped in white silk. I opened it to find an old coin, strung on a leather cord. The faded symbol on it was barely recognizable as *Ahnleh*. Primarily, it was translated to mean *Fate*, though like many words in the old language, it had a million connotations.

A'isha explained, "A gift, for your Naga. These coins were once worn by all of the *Nesera'rsh*, the priests and priestesses of Anhamirak during the time of Maeve's coven. The *Ahnleh* came to be known as the Snakecharm, since Anhamirak's symbol was a serpent. The *Nesera'rsh* are remembered only in nests such as this one now, but once, such a charm was the only coin a dancer needed throughout her life. It is said that even enemies at war would refuse to strike someone who wore an *Ahnleh*. And once . . . the Naga wore one, too.

"The day Danica stood in the synkal and you announced her as your mate, I recognized in her the soul of a dancer. You two brought peace to two lands that had long before forgotten the word. It is past time for other bridges to be patched; sha'Mehay would be proud to see our Naga—and, I hope, the mother of our next Diente—wearing our *Ahnleh* once again."

"Thank you," I answered solemnly. "I know Danica will be honored."

"It will be the nest's gift of congratulations, as soon as that avian doctor admits the obvious," she said with a grin.


A'isha's pure faith was contagious. As I watched her most advanced students perform complex variations of *sakkri* and *melos*—dances far beyond any ability I would ever have—I found it hard to consider that fate could do anything other than turn the right way.

I sat with Andreios, who also watched the dances with a mixture of shocked awe and clinical observation. I could see him being drawn into the dancers' hypnotic spell even while he tried to stay detached enough to examine the specific steps and moves in each variation.

The nest atmosphere and the late hour combined to lower inhibitions and make me choose my kind's blunt honesty rather than the avian discretion I normally practiced with Rei. Still, our words were light as we avoided difficult topics.

"So," I teased the crow, "what prompted your mad decision to engage in our favorite heathen activity?"

Rei laughed a little with me. "I received a challenge from

a very insistent young lady, who told me she could never re-spect a man who was ashamed to dance."

"Oh?" I prompted. "This lady wouldn't by any chance be a black-haired viper, would she?"

Voice remote, he replied, "No, actually." More lightly, he added, "And I think A'isha might be offended if I implied that she qualified as a lady by avian standards."

"May I know the name of the woman who can convince the leader of the Royal Flight to take up such a scandalous pastime?"

"She's not a serpent," he responded.

Before I could attempt to learn more, Betsy emerged from downstairs with a tired smile on her face.

"Yes? What have you—"

"Calm, boy," she interrupted. She glared at the sur-rounding dancers, who backed off, giving us as much privacy as we were likely to get. "Your pair bond is fine; I believe she is in no danger. Her 'ailment' is what I know you've already suspected."

I instantly started toward Danica's room, but Betsy stepped in front of me. "You are *not* going in there."

I towered over the crow, yet she was still a fearsome crea-ture. With a glare like that, Betsy could have been a com-mander in an army. "You said she was fine," I argued, despite Rei's earlier warning.

"She is sleeping," Betsy said. "She's still faint."

"Is this normal?" I pressed, hoping that some of my questions at least could be answered. "The chill, her faint-ing . . . ?"

"I think so." Seeing my doubtful expression, the doctor sighed. "Zane, boy . . ."

I jumped as she lifted a hand and touched my cheek.

From another serpiente, it would not have been a surprise; from the usually formal crow, it was startling.

"Does my skin feel hot to you?" she asked, already knowing the answer.

"Of course."

"Yours isn't cold to me—it's the same temperature as this room, which by the way is too hot. It's making your people antsy." I had no desire to point out to Betsy that the nest was kept this way intentionally. She continued, "I don't know much about your kind, but I know that a snake's eggs will grow too quickly and die if they're too hot. Your palace doctor has confirmed that your young are the same way. That being so, imagine a serpiente child growing in an avian womb; it would never survive." Without waiting for me to acknowledge whether I understood, she concluded, "Apparently you're both human enough to breed together. Your mate's body is adapting itself to take care of your child. She will be weak for a while, but otherwise she appears healthy. You may see her in a couple of days."

"Days?"

"I've been a doctor since before you were born, and that gives me the right to be blunt," Betsy said. "She needs a few days without excitement while her system is getting used to the changes. Having you in her bedroom is *not* going to help her rest."

Again I grudgingly accepted the doctor's orders, though I hoped that Danica would argue once she woke.

"Andreios, you'll make sure he does as he's told?" Betsy appealed to the crow.

Rei answered immediately, "You know I would never let anyone do anything that would endanger my queen."

Betsy frowned. "You've spent too much time with serpents for me to trust that means you'll obey my orders," she said. "I'll wash my hands of it until she has the sense to return to the Keep. Just make sure she is allowed to rest. I will stay in serpiente lands until she is well enough to travel, in case complications arise. Zane, your associates assured me a room in the palace."

I nodded. "Of course." I wasn't overly fond of the doctor right then, but that wasn't really her fault. Avians, and their fixation on decorum and respectability, sent me to the brink of insanity almost daily.

The moment Betsy was gone from the room, one of the dancers caught my arm. "Well?" he demanded.

The words instantly brushed my annoyance aside, leaving a swell of nervous joy that would probably not go away until the child was born. "A'isha was right; Betsy just confirmed it."

"Wonderful!" the dancer exclaimed. "Before you go disappearing to see her . . . we were wondering about your plans. If the Cobriana are really returning to the nest, the child would certainly be welcome here. I know it's irregular for the Arami to be raised in a nest nursery, but in peacetime, surely the heir to—"

Something must have showed on my face, for the dancer broke off. Serpiente children, unless they were in their parents' arms, commonly slept and spent their time in a communal nursery in the palace or—in the case of a dancer's child—in the local nest. As adults they chose lovers and sometimes mates, but even as children they were never alone.

I answered the dancer, "I don't know what Danica plans for the child." Avian children were raised very differently.

I looked to Rei, wondering if his vague answer to Betsy meant he might let me slip away downstairs, but A'isha had once again engaged him, hooking one of the many *melos* scarves she wore around his waist in an attempt to draw him into the dance.

The crow looked at it with shock. A'isha plucked the scarf away with a flourish.

"No need to be shy, little crow," A'isha said. "If the gods didn't want people to admire you, they wouldn't have made you so stunning."

I got to see Rei flush for the first time, blood creeping into his tanned skin. A'isha flipped her scarf around his neck.

"One dance," A'isha implored. "I'm sure Zane would go elsewhere; you would be performing only for the nest."

"I'm sure Zane would," Rei said dryly, glancing at me.

I shrugged.

"What is your lady friend going to think, if she hears you are learning to dance but are ashamed to perform?" A'isha goaded the crow.

"*One* dance," Rei said, relenting. "And only because I know you'll never forgive me if I don't take my opportunity to make a public fool of myself." He turned to me. "You get out of here and thank A'isha for giving me an excuse to leave you alone."

I would indeed.

Danica's eyes fluttered open the instant I stepped through the door, and she smiled softly. "I was starting to wonder if you were planning on obeying Betsy after all."

"Never," I assured her. "Though I've promised I will let you get some sleep. How do you feel?"

I went to her side, and Danica hooked an arm across my shoulders to steady herself as she sat up.

Danica winced. "I *hurt*." She rolled her shoulders, as if the muscles were sore.

"I'm sure," I responded sympathetically. Offering the

*Ahnleh* A'isha had given to me, I went on, "This is a congratulatory gift from sha'Mehay." I explained the significance of the ancient coin and repeated A'isha's words regarding why she was giving it to Danica.

She took the coin reverently, closing it in her hand for a moment before tying the cord into place. "Thank you," she said softly, as she snuggled closer. I knew the words were not for me, but for the nest around us.

I began to massage her shoulders, and she closed her eyes and leaned back toward my touch. My fingertips brushed the feathers growing under her hair at the nape of her neck. There was still a moment of hesitation in my mind every time I felt those feathers, a moment when my thoughts protested, remembering so many years of war when this beautiful woman had been my enemy, so hated that when fate crossed our paths there had been no choice but for me to love her.

She met my gaze now without any hint of the fear that had once been there. Cobriana eyes had once been for Danica what her feathers were for me. Avian legend said that a royal cobra's garnet eyes possessed demonic power, and it had taken a long time for Danica to trust me enough to look into mine. Most avians still shuddered and avoided my gaze.

"I feel ... tired, but wonderful. Betsy tells me—" She broke off, words failing her, and then gave up on speech and kissed me.

"I love you," she whispered—then yawned widely. "Take a nap with me?"

The request, as always, made me smile. When we had first met, the idea of resting with another person was as foreign to the lovely but reserved hawk as the idea of flying was to me.

I was happy that Danica had *not* yet taken me into the

air, but she had grown used to a second heartbeat while she rested. That blessing pleased me almost as much as any could.

I wrapped my arms around milady; Danica sighed, tucking her head down against my chest like a chick in the nest. Having her there calmed my fears and let me drift into sleep.

# CHAPTER 5

WE BOTH WOKE THE NEXT MORNING to an urgent tapping at the door, followed by A'isha's voice. "Zane, Syfka is back. Rei and Valene have intercepted her at the nest entry, and asked me to fetch you."

As Danica began to push herself up to join me, I explained, "Valene suggests that we keep you and Syfka apart; apparently the falcons have some atrocious notions when it comes to children."

She grimaced, but nodded. "I'll savor any excuse not to speak with her. I will probably still be here when you return."

I kissed her forehead and hurried to make myself presentable before Syfka stormed sha'Mehay. I met Valene and Ailbhe inside the nest door; they informed me that Rei was outside with the falcon.

By the time I reached Syfka, her mood was obviously foul. Her first words, as our group turned to walk toward the palace, were, "You have white vipers in the palace guard?"

Ailbhe stood his ground, not letting himself be flustered.

"I am the leader of Zane's guards," he answered the falcon, gaze challenging but voice carefully neutral.

"A white viper, a crow from the Royal Flight, and now a raven exile. Strange companions for a cobra king. Valene, what are you doing here?"

"My Diente asked me to stand with him as an advisor," the raven answered.

"Your Diente?" Syfka repeated skeptically. "Last time I checked, you still had raven's feathers on your nape."

"Milady, surely your concerns are more pressing than how I word my answers?" Valene sighed, and the falcon nodded.

Syfka turned her ice blue eyes on me, and I was almost disappointed that she was no longer studying my companions. "What have you determined?"

"I've spoken to Danica, as well as members of the Royal Flight and the palace guard. If there are falcons in our midst, none of us have been able to recognize them—which Valene assures me will come as no surprise to you."

Bluntly, Syfka asserted, "There are certainly falcons among your people. Avian and serpiente armies have been favored hiding places for our exiles since the war began; the turnover and chaos is always helpful. It is harder to hide now that you've formed this hopeless alliance, but they are still here. The problem is finding the right one."

My temper flared. Only too much time at the Hawk's Keep kept me from speaking my mind and offering dangerous insult. Instead, I asked, "If there are so many, then why put forth such an effort to find this one, at this time?"

Syfka shook her head. "The royal house of Ahnmik has reason to want this criminal back. That is all you need to know."

Trying not to lose my patience, and failing, I demanded, "If you will not tell us anything about the missing falcon, when he went missing, or what his crimes are, how can you expect us to recognize him?"

She shook her head. "I forget sometimes how helpless your people are. Whatever power you once had has become as diluted as your blood."

"Perhaps we're better for its loss," I challenged.

"Careful, cobra. You're as insolent as Kiesha herself—and are making all the same mistakes." I could not tell if the words were intended to be a threat, or just another insult. Syfka did not clarify, but instead demanded, "I'd like to speak to the members of both your armies, particularly Danica's elite—the Royal Flight."

"Surely you don't think one of your people could hide so close to Danica without being noticed," I said.

"Considering your activities until recently, the most useful skills falcons would bring to your people are our fighting abilities, which any falcon child learns early and learns well. Pride would keep most from staying a simple soldier for long, and talent would get one promoted quickly. Given the choice between serpent or avian, most would wish to retain the ability to fly. That makes the Royal Flight the first logical choice."

"Members of the Royal Flight are hand-chosen by the Tuuli Thea and the flight leader," I argued. "They come from well-known families, usually highborn ones. Masquerading as a soldier is one thing, but—"

"All that would be necessary," Syfka interrupted, "is to kill a son or daughter of one of those families and take his or her form, then go to the Tuuli Thea and ask for permission to join. A petty task."

Our conversation was interrupted as suddenly one voice in the market became louder than the others.

"Don't you *dare*!" The command was given by a woman I recognized as an artist, whose eyes were wide with shock.

Raised voices in the market weren't unusual among serpiente, but it was my responsibility to make sure such arguments didn't get out of hand.

"It was just a thought." The woman's son shrugged, continuing the discussion more calmly. "I just thought she might be curious. . . ."

"That kind of curiosity is likely to get you killed," the artist said bluntly.

I started to turn away, when someone else chimed in. "Take your mother's advice; that girl is nothing but trouble."

"You don't even know her," the son replied. "She's—"

"A bird," his mother interrupted.

"Doesn't matter."

I smiled at the son's youthful optimism, but only until his mother pointed out, "She'll have a father, a brother and probably a mate. You touch her, and who do you think will have you on a spit first?"

"No mate," the boy replied, though his voice was subdued now.

"If she told you that, she's a liar."

"Why would she lie?"

His mother threw up her arms in frustration, swearing under her breath. "You think I understand a sparrow? Forget her, boy—you can be assured she'll forget you."

Part of me wanted to interrupt them, but I wasn't sure what I would say. For all we had accomplished in the past several months, the two cultures still clashed—often. Stereotypes were hard to break. Many avian mothers and fathers worried about their innocent young daughters being exposed to immoral, womanizing serpents. That my kind generally *was* more demonstrative than theirs considered appropriate made convincing the matrons and protectors that they were wrong difficult.

By our standards, their young ladies were perfectly safe. There was no harm in a youthful fling. By the standards of an alistair protecting the virtue of his betrothed . . .

Syfka was chuckling beside me. "Well, well, well. Are things unraveling a bit in paradise?" she inquired.

I glared at her before I could help myself, and she only laughed again. "Half a year ago, that young man and the avian lady he fancies might have been enemies on the battlefield," I pointed out. "The inherent dangers of youth will never change. Volatile hearts and ill-advised flirtations can hardly be compared to the hatred and slaughter of war."

"Hmm," Syfka replied, sounding unconvinced.

"You were asking about my flight," Rei reminded her, wisely shifting the subject back to Syfka's original intent. "Though I can't imagine what you intend to accomplish, looking for traitors among that group." Rei turned from Syfka to address me. "Zane, you know there is not a member of my flight who is not absolutely loyal. Not one would hesitate to give his life for his Tuuli Thea or her alistair."

"How sweet—and unlikely," Syfka replied. "But where is the Tuuli Thea? Shouldn't she give the orders regarding her people?"

"Danica's people are mine as well, as I am sure you have heard," I said. "She is unavailable at the moment, but certainly trusts Andreios and me to make decisions regarding the Royal Flight."

"Well, then," Syfka said, relenting. "Crow, I assume you are capable of introducing me to the rest of the avian guards, so I can see for myself."

Rei glanced at me for permission before replying, "I can gather those who are available, if you would care to meet with them this afternoon."

She nodded dismissively. "You do that."

At my nod, Rei took his crow form and shot into the sky.

I needed to get away from the falcon myself, before I did something unfortunate, so I used our arrival at the palace as my reason. "Now, if you'll excuse me, I'll leave you in Ailbhe's capable hands. He can introduce you to the palace guard before Andreios returns." Belatedly, something else occurred to me. "Danica and I are expected at the Hawk's Keep tomorrow, so we can speak to the rest of the Royal Flight then." Half of that group always stayed with Danica's mother at the Keep.

Danica and I traveled frequently between the two lands, acting as Diente and Naga to the serpiente and Tuuli Thea and alistair to the avians. The plans had almost slipped my mind in the chaos of Syfka's visit, but it wouldn't do to delay them—not with the falcon hovering about and news of our child to share with Nacola.

Syfka nodded in agreement.

"Ailbhe," I said, "kindly keep our guest company, and answer any questions she might have about the palace guard."

"Yes, sir." The white viper sounded no more pleased to be left with Syfka than I would have been.

I turned my back on the pair, but had taken only a few steps inside when I heard the falcon comment to Ailbhe,

"There was a time when a white viper would be killed on sight if he dared to show his face inside these walls. How long has Maeve's kin groveled before these cobras?"

Ailbhe retorted hotly, "Charis Cobriana trusted my sister and me to guard her kin—" He broke off. His sister had been loyal in her own way, but that loyalty had led to disaster. In an attempt to defend me, she had tried to kill my avian mate and had instead caused the death of my mother. "I endeavor to be worthy of my king's trust."

I paused, wondering whether I should go back to the pair and forestall the argument that sounded ready to erupt. Syfka seemed to thrive a little too much on conflict in my lands.

"Black magic. Wasn't that the accusation that drove your kind from Anhamirak's cult?" Syfka asked. "The accusation that placed Kiesha's cobra kin on the serpiente throne instead of Maeve's white vipers?"

I spun on my heel, preparing to return, but Ailbhe did not hesitate in his answer. "Zane is my Diente. The Cobriana are the royal family I follow, and to whom I will always be loyal."

"Your own sister was executed for murdering the woman you say trusted her," Syfka said bluntly. "Do you truly hold no hatred for that? Can you really not *care*?"

"I've been instructed to answer any questions you have about the palace guard—not my personal life." It sounded as if Ailbhe was grinding his teeth a little.

"Answer me one question," Syfka pressed. "Your fighting prowess is impressive, or you wouldn't have gained this rank. The mark of a white viper is obvious enough in your features that I saw it instantly; the magic may be dormant in you, but it is in your blood. If you learned to use it—as any falcon could teach you—you would be strong. If you had that chance, would you take the power you should have had by birth?"

Ailbhe spoke softly, almost under his breath, the words cool with fury. "Treason, milady falcon, is in those words, and I'll take no part in it."

The falcon whistled low. "I could have made you a king . . . and you refused. It's good to see that Zane has such loyalty behind him." There was a pause, after which Syfka offered, "Surely you must understand my desire to test you a little. A white viper in the palace—"

"Test or not," Ailbhe interrupted, "I'm sure you'll understand when I assign a pair of guards to escort you while you're in serpiente territory."

"I would expect no less."

And I would expect no less than a push for treason by a falcon. I knew Ailbhe would approach me later about the incident. For now, I trusted him to do his best to keep our falcon's destructive tendencies in check.

My mother had been the first to accept white vipers into the palace, but so far Ailbhe and his sister had been the only ones to accept the invitation. Most still lived in chosen exile on the edges of our land, refusing to return to the people who had shunned them for generations—or to acknowledge a cobra as their king. Luckily, their numbers had always been too small for them to make a bid to take the throne back.

Would it amuse Syfka to see them try? I wouldn't be surprised to know she might try to overthrow the Cobriana out of simple spite.

As I walked the halls, instinctively returning to the dancer's nest to check on Danica, another thought occurred to me: Was Syfka's lost falcon a ruse, an excuse to get close? Might the falcon Empress have planned this interlude with Ailbhe?

If she had, casual offers of power were the least of our troubles. If a fight erupted, all the ability of the serpiente and avian armies combined might not win against Ahnmik's followers.

# CHAPTER 6

THAT EVENING, we convened in the main hall to discuss our unwanted visitor. According to Andreios, Syfka had finished her interrogation of the Royal Flight and left only moments before. Though Rei stood at strict attention, the remnants of anger shone in his eyes.

Ailbhe paced near the doorway, his white-blond hair long enough to slip into his eyes and disheveled enough to belie his strictly worn uniform. Clearly his interview with the falcon about the palace guard had been no less frustrating than Rei's.

Danica's brow was furrowed as she listened to Ailbhe's description of his argument with Syfka. Valene stood beside her, now wearing the clothing of a dancer, with shimmering violet scarves around her waist and a sigil meaning "peace" painted on the skin of her left temple.

"I don't think that Syfka will go seriously out of her way to cause trouble," Valene observed when Ailbhe was finished, "but I wouldn't put it past her to try to stir things up a little if left alone. From what I saw on Ahnmik, the falcons didn't seem that interested in our politics. Much of their magic revolves around stillness; they don't usually attempt to cause change, especially something as major as the unseating of a family that has ruled as long as the Cobriana." She seemed to consider her own words and after a moment added softly, "Though I don't know how they feel our peace affects them. The serpiente and avian people have been at war so long, the falcons may consider peace more of a disturbance than a change in the monarchy would be."

Rei sighed. "Valene may be right—Syfka certainly makes no effort to disguise her disapproval—but I'd still like to think we could manage Syfka if we keep an eye on her."

"Toward that end, I'm assigning people to watch her in revolving pairs," Ailbhe said. "I wouldn't let someone in the guard who I thought could be swayed by the falcon's words, but caution is always a good idea, just in case."

Rei nodded. "I plan to do the same if Syfka follows you to the Keep."

I knew there was also a member each of the palace guard and the Royal Flight waiting outside the door, one to be my shadow and one to be Danica's.

"Presuming Syfka isn't lying about why she is here, we should be able to get rid of her by finding her falcon. I refuse to believe there is nothing we can do to help that search," I said, opening the floor to the discussion we had gathered for.

I wanted Syfka out of my land. I wanted her away from my people, and my mate.

I looked at Rei first. "She seems to think your flight would be the best hiding place for a falcon. Is there any chance she might be right?"

Rei shifted uneasily. "She has a point there, though, as you know, it isn't one I care for. Falcons are trained in fighting skills from a very young age. If someone with their talent could impersonate a crow or raven, it would make sense for him to join a group where his ability to fight wouldn't be unusual."

"Crow or raven . . . or sparrow?" Danica's voice was tentative as she asked.

"Yes," Rei admitted, though he obviously wished he could say no.

"I hate to even suggest it, but you sound as if you're describing Erica. You said yourself that her fighting skills were amazing, though she claimed to have had no formal training. And—"

"Erica's loyal," Rei interrupted, sharply enough that people around him jumped. "I know her. She's no criminal." He seemed to realize he had spoken too hastily, and he backtracked, adding, "Valene, you would know if your niece was an imposter, wouldn't you?"

"I would know." The raven's voice was uncertain enough to worry me.

But it didn't worry me as much as Rei's words. They had been too sharp, too quickly spoken. Perhaps he was only defensive of accusations toward his guards, but that alone could be a problem. If he refused to consider that there might be falcons in his flight, he could overlook something.

Though doing so brought up a score of memories I did not want to relive, I pointed out as gently as possible, "Loyalty does not necessarily ensure innocence." I forced myself to meet Rei's eyes as I added, "We've all been wrong before."

The crow tore his gaze away from mine and looked at the floor. Rei had personally vouched for a young guard who had twice plotted assassination when Danica and I had initially made our arrangement—first on his own, and next with Ailbhe's sister.

Rei spoke slowly, every word a little tight as he asked, "What if the missing falcon *was* a member of the Royal Flight, or was even Erica? What would you do? Would you really be willing to turn her over to Syfka, for torture and execution, just because she was born with a falcon's wings?" He looked at Danica, who held his pleading gaze sadly. "Every member of my flight is loyal to you; every one of them would give his or her life and soul to protect you. Does falcon blood really have the power to negate a loyal guard's willingness to take a knife for the queen?"

He knew. Maybe it wasn't Erica, but either way, Rei knew.

"I would never endanger those I have sworn my allegiance to. I would never endanger my Tuuli Thea, or her alistair, or her people. You know that." He took a breath and said heavily, "And you both know that if you order me to tell you, I will. But I must ask you to consider whether you want to make me betray someone who would give everything to keep you safe."

In the silence that followed Rei's words, Valene spoke, her voice holding the same intensity as Rei's as she looked at Danica and me. "As long as you don't know who their falcon is, you can say so to Syfka and she will believe you, but once you know, she will know. You can't lie to a falcon."

If I knew for sure that someone in the Royal Flight was a falcon, I would want him gone. Unfair perhaps, but I didn't trust falcons. I didn't want them guarding my queen or my child. I knew I was being unreasonable, but that didn't make me any more comfortable.

The only thing that kept me from demanding that Rei

tell us everything was my knowledge that Rei would sooner turn *himself* over to torture than risk having Danica endangered. He was loyal to his queen. Could I fault him for also being loyal to his flight?

This train of thought was interrupted as something else occurred to me. "Syfka spoke to you about your flight. How did you lie to her?"

"I didn't," Rei answered. "I told her there was no way a simple crow would be able to identify a falcon unless that falcon came forward willingly, and I pointed out that a traitor hiding in our midst was unlikely to be so honest. The words were true, technically. Then I introduced her to those in my flight who were available. If nothing else, the falcon's arrogance gives her faith in my stupidity."

I looked at Danica. The Royal Flight was hers to command, which meant that, ultimately, this was her decision.

She looked at me and shook her head. "For the moment, we'll let it drop. But if Syfka does start to cause trouble, we'll need to do what is necessary to get rid of her."

Rei nodded, his expression more troubled than I had ever seen it.

"We have some problems beyond Syfka," Valene asserted. "I spoke to Ailbhe about them earlier, but you should hear for yourself." She hesitated, shaking her head. "As you know, when I'm in the market here, I'm a dancer. That gives me a chance to listen to a lot of gossip."

"Go on," Danica prompted when the raven paused again.

"News travels fast," Valene said. "Most everyone has heard that their Naga is carrying a child. But not everyone is happy." She sighed and joined Ailbhe's pacing. Her dancer's garments swirled around her when she turned, expressing her agitation. "People called it madness when their Diente proclaimed his love for the Tuuli Thea, but they thought it was romantic. A child between you two is all well and good. But many people don't want that child to rule."

My hand slammed down on the table as if of its own will, but my words froze in my throat.

Danica's voice rose as she abandoned her normal calm. "Why not? It's their Diente's child."

Danica had only scratched the surface of my horror. I *would not* allow mob rule to deny my child its rightful place on the throne.

Valene turned from Danica to me, as if seeking a more reasonable listener, but she flinched as she met my gaze. She continued cautiously. "The cobra form breeds true with any serpent, except the white viper. So the child of a cobra and a python or boa will always be a cobra. But the child of a cobra and a hawk is a less certain equation. The serpiente don't mind having a hawk as Naga so long as their Diente is pure cobra—the Naga's power is always second to her mate's. But they aren't fond of the idea of a feathered Diente. They are even less fond of the idea that any half-avian child could choose an avian mate, leaving the serpiente throne ruled entirely by birds."

"It gets more complicated." Ailbhe took over. "Many people refuse even to consider that you would let a half-avian child take the throne. They're acting as if you've already declared your sister's child your heir."

Valene nodded, adding, "They might tolerate a mixed child as your heir if he or she is raised serpiente, and if they are assured that its mate will also be serpiente, but . . ." She trailed off, not needing to say what the other side of the problem was: Danica's court would feel the same way. They would want a daughter to be given an alistair—an avian alistair. Even if the child was male, avian tradition would demand that he be betrothed to a suitable avian girl within his first few years of life.

I had worried about how our child would be raised and how people would react, but this abject refusal was too horrific for me to have imagined.

The serpiente were ruled in only a nominal fashion. Loyalty bound them to the Cobriana line, thousands of years of leaders who had treated them fairly. My family had never hidden while soldiers walked the field, or we never would have held our people's respect. They trusted their leaders to keep them safe. So the Cobriana stayed in power, and the civilization survived and thrived.

Loss of that loyalty, respect and trust would destroy the Cobriana. Loss of their royal line would destroy the serpiente. If the serpiente refused to acknowledge Danica's child as their monarch, no number of guards would be able to keep that child on the throne.

I had walked this precarious balance before, when I had declared Danica my mate.

If necessary, I would do it again.

"I don't think we can deal with this immediately." I looked at Danica as I spoke, searching her expression for agreement or argument. "Valene, the dancers have already welcomed Danica and our child. If they can circulate the knowledge that I *will* name Danica's child my heir, I can only hope it won't be as much of a shock when the announcement is made." Even as I spoke, I felt the cold knot of fear in my gut. Our child would be born in peace, but would she live in war? "Besides that, we'll have to wait until the protests are raised specifically."

"Not meaning to be troublesome," Ailbhe answered,

"but how absurd is the idea that Salem could be Diente?" The white viper's words were answered by a roomful of glares, but he stood his ground. "What I mean to ask is, what is your ultimate goal? Salem will be raised without hatred for Danica's people. He'll have no hunger for war, and what's more, he'll have a civilization at peace to begin with. If peace is your goal, your sister's child will still make a fine Diente."

"And what of our child?" Danica spoke in her calm and detached court voice, which she used among serpents only when she was too angry or disgusted to maintain rationality any other way. My hand found hers, and she gripped it tightly.

"Your child may well be born as purely avian as you are. If it takes an avian mate, its children will probably show little of the Cobriana blood. Again, if your goal is just peace, the child could be raised avian—raised to be Tuuli Thea. Each court would have its heir, an heir raised without bloodlust and hatred. You would have peace."

For a moment I could not speak. So long as I had breath in my body, I would see my child on the serpiente throne. Diente, Tuuli Thea—our child would be both.

"Are you mad?" The words escaped me as I locked eyes with Ailbhe. "How could you consider—"

"Zane." Danica interrupted me, placing a hand on my chest.

"You can't be thinking—"

"Would you rather set up our child for war from the instant it's born? If the serpiente reject our child for their throne, then you still have Salem as your heir. If my people reject it, there will be no Tuuli Thea after me."

I stepped back from her, horror seeping into my blood. My gaze flickered to the others in the room. Ailbhe's pale blue eyes would not meet mine. Rei's did, but then he looked away. Valene was watching Danica, her expression unreadable. My mate was the only one who would meet my gaze, her golden eyes pained.

"Out," I said, speaking to our audience. They looked at one another, hesitating. Valene first deferred, followed by Rei. Ailbhe lingered a moment longer, and I was not sure whether he did from guilt or compassion.

Then we were alone, and I took Danica's hands.

"Danica, do you know what you are asking of me? Giving up my child to the Keep, to be raised by strangers, to sleep in lonely silence, to be taught to be ashamed of what she feels and what she *is* ... and to be betrothed before she can even *speak*, before she can possibly understand *love*." Danica closed her eyes for a moment, taking a breath. "I will never have a mate but you. I love you. And yes, I will have an heir. But you are talking about taking away my *child*."

"What else can we do?" she returned. "Zane, I was raised in the Keep; it is not as horrible as you think. And you would still see her—" She broke off, because she knew as well as I that the heir to the Tuuli Thea saw her parents only in formal situations. She shook her head. "Please ... Zane, is there another way? Anything else that will keep our firstborn child from coming into the world only to see her land ripped apart by war?"

Silence.

"It will be months before the child is born," I whispered, pleading not only with Danica, but with whatever powers might be. "We don't have to make this decision, not yet."

Danica nodded, but still she said, "One queen cannot rule two worlds, even if she is of both."

# CHAPTER 7

DANICA AND I WENT OUR SEPARATE WAYS that evening, each needing time to think. I dined with the remnants of my family: my sister Irene and her babe, Salem. My brother-in-law, Galen, had been bitten by a petulant five-year-old mamba that afternoon, and although the poison was not nearly as deadly as it would have been to a human, he had asked to be excused from dinner.

Irene had recounted the tale with a forcedly light tone, obviously trying to keep the mood up unless I decided to share what was on my mind.

Salem lay cradled against Irene's left arm in a shawl-like carrier made of bright silk and lined with fur. She negotiated the infant and her food easily, occasionally humming softly to him when he woke, and otherwise engaging in pleasant conversation.

"Would you want Salem to be Diente?" I asked abruptly as Irene turned back from one of her interludes with the laughing child.

She glanced at me for a moment, but kept most of her

attention on Salem, who had just decided to shapeshift. Serpiente children were born able to take their serpent form, though they didn't have much control over it for the first several months and their poison did not develop for four or five years. Luckily my kind had a high tolerance for all natural venom, or childlike tantrums such as the one Galen accidentally stumbled into that morning could be deadly.

Another potential problem for Danica, I realized, before brushing the pessimistic thought aside. That was the least of our problems and could be dealt with easily enough.

After Salem had calmed down, Irene answered, "I don't know. Though these last few months have been wonderful, I've seen what you have gone through as Arami and Diente. You and our brothers."

I swallowed tightly. Irene, Salem and I were the only Co briana left. Avian soldiers were fierce fighters, and they had made every effort during the years of war to end the royal serpiente line.

"Hopefully, if Salem took the throne, he would not have to rule over war."

Irene nodded, running her hand lovingly over the black scales. Salem shifted back into human form, reaching his tiny hands up to his mother.

"I would worry for him, but I would not argue with you if you named my child your heir. I do not think Galen would object either, though he too certainly knows the difficulties that Salem would face even in peacetime," she answered plainly, either not hearing or not wanting to acknowledge how painful the question was for me to ask. "It's a bit early to worry whether Danica's child will be female or male, though I've heard that hawks have a tendency toward girls."

I had not even considered that issue, though Irene must

have thought it was the reason for my worry. Traditionally, the position of Diente was male—if only because enemy soldiers would strike first at the king, leaving a queen and any child she carried marginally safer. However, it was not unusual for a woman to be named heir if she had no brothers of age to take the throne. If she took the throne as Diente, her mate was named Nag, and the succession considered exactly as it would if she were male.

"I don't care whether my heir is male or female," I answered. "We aren't at war anymore, so I don't see that it matters. My main worry at the moment is whether people will want any child of mine to rule at all."

After that I spoke quickly, sharing with Irene the fears that had been raised earlier—what I had seen and heard in the marketplace, my fury at Ailbhe's proposal and my shock as Danica seemed ready to agree with it.

I finished, "Was I such a fool to think that things would get easier after the last arrow fell?"

Irene was again looking down at Salem—her pure-blooded cobra child. "I remember the day Anjay died, and you became Arami," she said. "You wept at his pyre, but when you first spoke as heir to the throne, you did so very clearly. You took Gregory and me aside, and you told us that we would see peace if it took your life's breath and blood and soul to find it. And now here we are."

"And Gregory?" I challenged.

She answered without hesitation. "Gregory's last sight was the golden hair and eyes of your mate, who sang to him and comforted him so he would not die alone. I think he was the first of us to see the peace you promised."

I drew a deep breath and walked away from the table— too much energy, too much agitation.

Irene watched me pace. Softly she said, "You once thought you could only hate avians. Now you love your avian mate more than life. I think this will be harder for you, but if it is the only way to preserve peace, I know you will do it. And perhaps the result will be as happy."

I shook my head.

Irene refused to back down. "Your firstborn child is a precious thing, but you won't be giving her over to death, Zane. Only to a different life than you might have wished for her. I know it would kill me to give up Salem, but I would rather lose him that way than cling to him until hatred tore him away."

I sighed. As usual, my sister was far more practical than I. Unfortunately, her practicality made the words no less painful.

Danica and I would likely have more than one child. Perhaps, even if the first was raised to be Tuuli Thea and given an avian alistair, the second could be raised to be Diente.

Of course, raising the second child as a serpent would require doing to Danica what would be done to me with our first.

Knowing there would be more children would not lessen the pain of losing my first one—and lost it would be. Even if I saw her frequently, even if she ruled in peace and visited the palace as often as Danica did, she would be lost to me. Avian children were not raised to be as close to their parents as serpiente children were. They were not raised with dance and a passion to live, but with a chaste sense of duty and modesty.

Danica had been raised avian, but now she lived in the serpiente world almost as much as I did. If this child was raised avian and forced to take an avian alistair and remain as Tuuli Thea at the Keep, she would never have that chance.

Irene interrupted my thoughts, placing a hand over mine. "Zane, you of all people know that you need to try before you decide you will fail. You have months before the child is born—if there is another way, you will find it."

I tried to keep my sister's words in mind as I prepared for sleep, alone because Danica had not yet returned to our bed. Instead I found myself counting my fears, until I finally reached the painful end of the thread of indecision: Irene was right. We could try to change the world and convince our people to accept our child's rule, but if we failed, then I would have to let her go to the Keep.

Losing her to peace would be better than losing her to war.

That thought filled my dreams during the scant hours when I managed to sleep, and it twisted into nightmares.

I dreamed Danica's death. In my nightmares she was torn apart by wolves. She fell from the balcony of the Keep, unable to spread her wings because she had to carry a serpent child.

I dreamed that the child was born dead, and I woke with a silent scream deep in my throat. I reached for Danica, but found myself lying alone.

I pulled myself out of bed and went to seek my queen. My guard followed at enough of a distance to afford some semblance of privacy, in case I wished it.

The day had recently dawned clear, and the earliest merchants were setting up their stalls in the choice spots of the market. I passed by an avian jeweler, who was in the midst of setting out his wares with the help of his daughter and her alistair. She ducked her head shyly as I passed, but her father said a polite "good morning."

The scent of baked breads rose from the next stall I passed, this one owned by a serpiente merchant named Seth.

He greeted me with a tired smile. "I don't often see you wandering here this early. Restless night for you, too?" he asked.

I nodded. "Too much so. What troubles your sleep?"

The merchant hesitated, gaze going distant. "Many things . . . nightmares."

I waited a moment, giving him the opportunity to continue if he wanted to speak, or change the subject if he thought it better left to silence.

He sighed. "There is a rumor that the falcons' Syfka is here, searching for someone?"

The skin on the back of my neck began to tingle with apprehension. I answered cautiously, "That is true. Is this . . . a concern for you?"

Again he looked away, and this time I realized what he was doing: searching the skies. He explained, "I respect your efforts, and I'm glad I can sell my goods instead of wielding a blade—I was a soldier until you and your mate ended the war, you see—but that doesn't mean I'm not nervous when I see wings in the skies."

"I see." He was lying; of that I had no doubt.

He shot me an apologetic look, turning his eyes from the dawn and back to me. "Sir, I—" He broke off and turned back to his cart. "Syfka isn't—"

The slowly filling market jumped at a falcon's screech; the merchant went white, drawing back under the awning of his stall as if to hide himself from the circling falcon's view.

Syfka banked, dove and returned to human form not far in front of me. She glanced dismissively at the merchant, then said to me, "Diente, I need to speak to you."

Instinctively, I stepped between Syfka and the vender, though suspicion about his origins made me hesitate to turn my back on him. "More plots to overthrow the Cobriana line?" I challenged.

"If I truly wanted to plan treason, I would be more careful than to do so when you are standing close enough to hear," she replied tautly. "I wanted to speak to you about our missing falcon. I'm afraid the one I'm looking for might be a little more hidden than I first thought and my patience is wearing thin. I'd like to arrange some kind of test."

I sighed, irritated that she was still going through the motions of asking for permission when I doubted my answer mattered to her at all. "So long as it doesn't endanger Danica's people or my own, or interfere with the workings of the palace guard or the Royal Flight, I don't care what you do."

She nodded. "Then I hope to be free of this backward land by sundown."

The thought occurred to me suddenly, and I asked, "Where is your escort?"

"Sleeping," she replied offhand. "Deeply. Consider it similar to the heavy slumber you find yourself in after too much wine." She brushed aside the topic, glancing at the merchant, who had been slinking away. "You were foolish enough to speak my name—not just once, but *twice*—knowing I was in these skies. You don't think I'm going to ignore you now, do you?"

Again I stepped between them, as foolish as it might have been. I did not trust any falcon, but if this man really had once been a soldier in the serpiente army, I owed him something for that service. "I thought you said you hadn't found your criminal?"

"The one I was sent for—no, I haven't. This one is . . . a nobody, half gyrfalcon and half peregrine, void of any magic and hence of any value to you—"

"Or any value to you," I interrupted. If she was insistent on taking people out of my market, I wanted at least to know why. "What is his crime?"

"That is none of your business," Syfka snapped. "And you have larger problems than one *kajaes* falcon."

"As do you," I pointed out.

She tossed her head. "At least I seek a flesh-and-blood, pure-blooded peregrine who I know exists. You—and your delusional hawk you call Naga—seek a fanciful dream of harmony as impossible as a western sunrise . . . and as volatile as Anhamirak's temper."

"I've seen my dreams come true," I replied, unchallenged by her words. "I've seen an end to useless hatred and killing—"

"An end to hatred, oh?" she challenged. "Can you tell me the future, *Kiesha'ra?*"

"No man can."

"Actually, any fool who can spin a proper *sakkri* could show you your fate. But even you, with your stunted magic, must be able to predict what is about to happen on the other side of your own market."

I turned just in time to see the young, optimistic serpent from the day before catch the arm of the jeweler's avain daughter. Her alistair looked up just in time to see his pair bond pulled aside by his serpent competition.

The young lady's face went dead white in response to whatever her serpiente companion had whispered to her.

Her soft reply caused him to turn abruptly to look at the girl's protector.

"Jenna?" the unfortunate young serpent asked, voice small and hurt.

The first tears rolled from her eyes, and though she hastily brushed them away, trying to compose herself as an avian lady is taught always to do, her alistair saw.

The alistair left off his conversation with the girl's father, striding through the crowd—which rapidly parted to allow him to approach the serpiente.

Another serpent, who was closer than I, sized up the situation instantly and stepped between the two. He might have avoided trouble, but he made the mistake of grabbing the wrist of the angry alistair.

Abandoning Syfka, I pushed through the crowd just in time for the would-be peacemaker to be shoved at me as the alistair pushed past him; before I could wrestle around the shocked serpent, I heard the impact of flesh against flesh, followed by Jenna's cry as her jilted serpiente sweetheart threw the first punch at his avian opponent.

Someone tried to call me back as I waded between the two, narrowly avoiding the bird's retaliation. I caught the avian's wrist before he managed to strike the serpent, who recoiled as he recognized me. The avian swiftly dropped his gaze before it fell upon Cobriana garnet, and he yanked his wrist out of my grip.

I directed my angry question to the girl, whose opinion probably mattered most to her competing suitors. "Is there a problem here?"

She shuddered and shook her head. Then she cast a longing, apologetic glance at the serpent before taking a tentative step toward her alistair, who took her hand and kissed the back of it. I suspected that the show of perfect devotion and forgiveness was done for the serpent's sake, to keep him from getting any ideas about the future.

The less lucky suitor shrugged, smiled and said lightly what was probably the most hurtful thing he could think of. "Well, I lost that bet."

Syfka smiled and for a moment looked gently pitying. "It isn't meant to be, *Kiesha'ra*. Why don't you give up this useless quest now, before your dreams have to be ripped from your hands?"

"Your kind hides on its island, isolated from the real world, as unchanging as your god," I challenged. "You have no sense of what war is like. You have no idea what it means to see those you love fall. You cannot possibly understand what it is to fight for what you believe, and how sometimes you have to fight with words and dreams after all the weapons have been put away. You serve a cold god, surviving on his power for thousands of years without ever *living*." Too angry about the useless market argument to be fearful of the falcons or their empire's wrath, I pushed on. "You speak of giving up my dreams. Have you ever, since Maeve's coven split, *had* a dream? Have you ever had anything worth dying for?"

"You could not possibly comprehend my dreams," the falcon replied.

"No more than you can ever understand mine."

Syfka nodded and began to turn away. Then she paused, smiling a little, and asked me, "Do you think your brother was dreaming of peace, when a hawk's knife cut into his heart?"

I went cold at the mention of my brother. "You . . ."

"Anjay Cobriana visited our lands once. He asked us for

power to help him slaughter his enemies, the woman you love among them. Did you think we would not keep track of him after he left?"

Hearing this creature speak my brother's name was like listening to blasphemy, even though she spoke thoughts I had many times considered. If Anjay had become king, would he have ended the war in blood instead of peace?

"It surprised none of us when he took his little suicide trip to the Hawk's Keep. He fought his way through half the Royal Flight—ask their captain someday which of them your brother killed. Ask them why a crow as young as Andreios was promoted so soon. Ask them how long the fifteen-year-old heir to the Tuuli Thea grieved for her slain alistair. Ask them which of the avians cheered, when the young child Xavier Shardae stabbed the cobra in the back."

I recoiled from the image she painted, wanting to challenge her and knowing it would do no good. I knew the evils of war. Danica and I had needed to forgive to end the hatred, but neither of us would ever forget.

Some things I had never wanted to know.

"Get out of my market," I snarled.

Syfka looked past me, and we both realized that the falcon merchant had fled during the earlier chaos. Syfka let out a long-suffering sigh.

"Think about my words, son of Kiesha," she bid me. "Give up before your hopes turn to dust."

I flinched from the harsh beating of aplomado wings inches from my face as she reverted to pure falcon form and again took to the skies.

# CHAPTER 8

THERE WAS A STORM OF ICE IN MY HEART, and I knew by the way my people stepped back from me as I returned to the nest that I was showing it.

The faces from the marketplace and the sound of Syfka's condescending voice jelled in my mind so that I paused to try to compose myself before heading downstairs, wondering whether I should wait until I calmed down.

A'isha intercepted me before I could make the decision. The dancer frowned a little as she said, "You're too agitated for a man who has just learned he is soon to be a father." I started to respond, but A'isha didn't give me a chance. Instead she said, "Danica is a good Naga; she will be a good mother. The falcon must do what she will do before you can react to it. Troubles will pass. You will see. Now, dance with me before you wake your Naga and leave for the Keep; it is past time to greet the day that has given you this fortune."

No verbal answer was necessary, though my gratitude for her blunt words was immense. She drew me into the nest and onto the dais where Danica had performed. Had that only been a day ago?

I stretched lightly. I had not danced recently, and I had no illusions that I could compete with those who usually performed in sha'Mehay, but A'isha knew how far my talent reached and was careful what dances she chose.

She was also careful to keep in mind which dances a man did not perform without his mate. Instead she drew us into steps of thanks, praise, joy and hope.

When I finally pleaded exhaustion, she smiled triumphantly. "I will always smile on the day I can outdance Kiesha's kin. *Now* go find your mate, with a light heart instead of a frustrated one." She all but shoved me off the dais, sending me stumbling onto the soft nest floor as I tried to find my balance.

As always, the combination of A'isha's directness and the dance had chased away old grief, irrational fears and words such as "impossible."

Stealing from the baskets kept by the fireside a small loaf of bread and a jar of honey—the simple fare I knew Danica preferred for breakfast—I made my way downstairs.

I dropped everything I was carrying and sprinted the rest of the way when I heard a cry from Danica's room. Shouldering through the unlocked door, I quickly took in the room—empty but for my mate, who was obviously in the grip of nightmares.

I pulled her into my arms, waking her gently.

She recoiled, and her eyes flew open. "Are you real?"

I knew what had happened. When Danica was stressed or frightened, she was tormented by dreams that were so vivid, waking only brought more doubt as to reality.

"I'm real," I assured her, and finally she relaxed and let me hold her. "What was the dream?"

"The first one . . ." she answered softly. "I haven't had it in . . . months. Since I became Tuuli Thea. All this with Syfka brought the past to mind."

I knew only too well what she meant. "Tell me?"

"It happened when I was . . . eight, I think. Back when my sister and brother were both still alive. I overheard one of my tutors speaking to my mother, telling her that Rei was missing, that she thought he had gone to . . . to look for his father." She leaned her cheek against my shoulder, dropping her gaze. "I had never seen the aftermath of battle before. Never seen death. I found Rei . . ." She shook her head violently, saying, "It was stupid of me to go. Stupid. There were still serpiente there, though they weren't fighting. They didn't care about a crow-child. But a hawk . . ."

She shuddered. "We were both nearly killed. I remember seeing a viper sink its fangs into Rei's side, but . . . not much more. I was knocked out. Rei carried me back to the Keep. Everyone was amazed that he lived. He was only eleven, but he started training to join our army the next day." Softly she added, "We both changed after that. I couldn't get away from the blood even in my dreams, but I felt as if I had to keep going back to the field . . . to try to help, even if it meant just holding someone's hand so they wouldn't die alone."

She closed her eyes, leaning heavily against me. "At least now it's only dreams. I never want to face that reality again."

Fate willing.

Moments passed in silence before she reluctantly asked, "How are things going with Syfka?"

"Intolerable," I admitted. I did not want to detail my

most recent confrontation with the falcon, and Danica did not press. "Luckily, she seems to have hope that she will find her criminal soon. I look forward to being done with this. Do you feel well enough to travel back to the Keep today?"

"We need to," she answered, but despite her tired tone, she was smiling.

"We can postpone the trip if you're not feeling up to it. You and our child's health are more important than indulging Nacola." *Or Syfka,* I thought. She could speak to the rest of the Royal Flight when Danica was ready.

"Don't worry; I feel fine," Danica assured me. With wide-eyed innocence, she added, "I know how much it would disappoint you not to see my mother."

# CHAPTER 9

TOO SOON, it was time for the journey to the Hawk's Keep—a ride I normally enjoyed despite my lack of fondness for the destination. I had become used to avians, in general; it was just Danica's mother who made every visit to the Keep a trial.

I put the thought aside, catching Danica's hand to brush a kiss across the back of it as we walked to the stables.

We traveled this route by horseback, accompanied by four of the Royal Flight and two of the palace guard. Betsy, who had never learned to ride, had already flown ahead and planned to meet us at the Keep. Valene had politely asked to remain in serpiente lands, expressing a preference for the company of dancers to that of the woman and court who had shunned her years before.

The mood for most of the trip was light. Our guards spoke among themselves as they rode, sharing stories as we passed through a wood that had once been fraught with death.

"How goes the dancing, Rei?" I heard Erica ask.

The crow reddened, but he answered, "I don't exactly have a knack for it, but I'm enjoying myself." Was she the lady who had challenged him? Combined with Rei's sharp defense of the sparrow when we had been discussing potential falcons, this light conversation made an excellent case that *something* was going on between the two.

"When do I get to see—" Erica broke off, frowning, and said without changing tone, "A couple more just appeared."

At the same time, Ailbhe pulled up alongside us, his brows tense with concern. When he glanced at me, I saw that his eyes had turned pure blue, save for black slit pupils— snake eyes. Even before he spoke, I knew that his doing so would display fangs. Once, I had always traveled in a similar half form, but I preferred to stay in a purely human form when around Danica.

"There's a group in the woods, shadowing us," Ailbhe said softly. "It started as one, but others have just joined them."

I nodded, then sped my horse up slightly to ride alongside Danica. My voice was light, so anyone following us would think it casual conversation if they caught the tone. "We're being followed."

Her eyes widened fractionally. "Who?"

"Not sure." I cut the conversation short, moving slightly ahead of my mate. As Ailbhe had done, I shifted partially, utilizing the natural weapons and armor I always had available. More importantly, the slight change brought with it a cobra's senses.

There were six figures moving together, trying and failing to be stealthy. At least two were serpents; I knew that only by smell. I could feel the four avians by the heat emanating from their bodies. None of them was moving as if familiar with the forest, which meant they probably had not been professional soldiers.

Rei whistled to his people, and we kicked up our pace to one that followers on foot would be hard-pressed to maintain.

A sharp *caw* from the left attracted the guards' attention. I felt the wind on my face as the members of the Royal Flight grew the wings of their Demi forms, elegant feathers spreading in a defensive posture. Ailbhe and Kyler, his second-in-command, followed suit, each unclipping from the side of his saddle the long, blade-ended stave the palace guard used in close combat. I saw scales spread across their skins, Ailbhe's as white as morning frost, and Kyler's brown and golden.

The serpents came from the left, taking the attention of two of Rei's people, while Ailbhe and Kyler confronted winged attackers.

Rei shouted to Erica, "Get Danica and Zane out of here."

Any other time, I would have stayed to fight, but with Danica's and my child's lives at stake, I wanted to take no chances.

Before I could kick my mount into a canter, I heard the fateful *twang* of a serpiente bowstring, heard the whistle in the air, and the wet sound of wood striking deep into flesh.

Danica's horse went down, an arrow deep in its shoulder. I rolled from my own mount as I saw her fall and landed on the soft ground with panic in my chest. Before I could rise, one of the avians thrust a blade toward me.

Had I been in full cobra form, an observer would have seen the famous flared hood with its infamous markings. Quickly I let my natural snakeskin armor ripple into place across my arms and throat, then faced my attacker with slit garnet eyes and a cobra's fangs.

The shift made my attacker recoil. Instinctively I caught his gaze, drawing my blade in the instant my would-be murderer was off guard. Before he could recover, Ailbhe had engaged him, leaving me free to look at Danica.

Two of the Royal Flight knelt beside her, their wings spread across her body, protecting her against other arrows. Was she hurt? Unconscious?

Dead?

*She can't be dead.*

Rei started giving commands again before I could get to Danica's side. "Erica, get Zane. I've got Danica."

He shoved through the crowd, pausing only to extract his blade after it met an opponent's throat. I only saw him lift Danica in his arms before Erica spoke to me, but I heard the beating of his wings and felt the wind from them. He had her safe.

"Change shape," the sparrow ordered.

*"What?"* If she intended to fly out of there with me, she was out of her mind. Even to save my life, I never wanted to have my feet more than jumping distance from the ground.

A sound to my left caused me to spin, just in time to face another avian. I felt the sting of a blade breaking through my snakeskin before I could raise my own blade and make a killing blow.

It was not pain that hit me, but something close, something suffocating and wrenching that froze my breath and darkened my vision, as suddenly I found myself recalling that avian blades were often poisoned.

I heard Erica curse as she grabbed my arm, but then the pressure of her fingers on my skin faded . . . along with sight and sound and everything else.

# CHAPTER 10

W HEN I WOKE, I found myself wondering whether my head had exploded—or whether perhaps that would be preferable. I rolled onto my stomach and had to grip the edge of the bed until I could convince the furniture to stay still.

It couldn't have been poison. Only one poison existed that affected a cobra that strongly, and if it was mixed strongly enough to knock one out, it was mixed strongly enough to kill.

Was it something Erica had done?

I started to push myself up and suddenly felt hands on my arms. I heard a voice saying, "Don't try to sit up yet."

Warm hands, avian hands. Doctor's voice. Were we in the Keep? We must be. How had I gotten there?

I sat up anyway. The doctor, an avian I didn't know, pulled back from me a little, but offered me water, which I drank greedily.

My senses were returning slowly. Every muscle ached, but seemed to work. I managed to stand when I tried, though I had to grip the bedpost to keep from falling.

The doctor implored again, "Please, you aren't well."

My memories returned, and I demanded, "Where's Danica?" My voice was hoarse, my throat as dry as ash.

The doctor's hesitation made me start to push past her to the door despite the way the world rocked and swayed around me.

The avian finally started talking. "She is still unconscious."

There was more worry in her voice than I cared for. "What's wrong?"

"Her . . . temperature is rising," the woman said hesitantly. "Betsy is worried the child was—hurt."

*No.*

I shouldered my way past the doctor and down the hall. We were on the Tuuli Thea's floor, and there was shouting coming from outside Danica's door.

"Let me see her!"

Erica. The sparrow's voice was strained as she argued with four members of the Royal Flight.

"She's not to be disturbed," the guard answered. I didn't know these four well, and Rei wasn't with them.

"What is going on here?" I demanded.

I saw the guards' hands fall to the handles of their weapons, but none were drawn.

Erica spun around to face me. "Please, Zane, you have to let me see her—"

"Explain why and I'll consider it," I answered. "I'm still trying to figure out what you did to *me*. That doesn't make me anxious to let you near Danica."

Her gaze flickered from the guards, to me, to the door they were guarding, and back to me again.

Then I felt a rush of power, and the backlash of it as it struck the four guards, sending them falling unconscious to the floor. "I can knock you out, too," Erica said, "or you can let me go to my queen and *help* her."

*Falcon.*

I knew it, and I had a moment of indecision. Did I trust her?

Did I have a choice?

"Go. I'll be beside you."

Betsy was asleep in the chair next to Danica's bed. The way she was slumped implied that she had fallen asleep as abruptly as the guards outside—probably at the same time. It reinforced my desire never to be on the opposite side of a fight from Erica.

Danica's skin was even hotter than usual, and chalky. It was bruised and scraped from her tumble. Worse was the blood. I smelled it before I saw it, and I had to lean against the door frame, dizzy with fear.

I knew what this blood meant: Even if Danica lived, the life inside her was not going to.

I heard Erica whisper, "Milady."

"Can you do anything?"

"I think so. Give me space."

I retreated to the sitting room, leaving my mate with the only person who could help her—a falcon.

An hour passed as slowly as an eon before Erica emerged, faint and shaking with exhaustion. She barely made it to a chair before she collapsed.

"She'll be fine," she breathed.

"And the child?" I demanded. I didn't know what even falcon magic could do to heal that kind of damage.

Erica looked up. Her smile trembled at the edges, but she said again, "She'll be fine."

I panicked for a moment, thinking she was consoling me

by assuring me again that Danica would be fine, but then I understood. "My daughter?" I asked hopefully.

She nodded. "Your daughter. Thank the sky, she'll be fine. They'll both be fine."

"What did you do?"

Erica frowned a little. "I don't know how I can explain it. I . . . put the hurt pieces together again." She bit her lip, and a little fear was in her eyes as she said, "Your daughter will be fine, but falcon magic is . . . not always the best for a mother. It won't hurt Danica, but this child will be the only one. I'm so sorry."

When the words hit me, I felt too numb to know how to respond to them. Only one child meant only one heir. It meant that if this one was raised in the Keep, no child of mine would ever be Diente. It meant that there was only one chance. Yet I said to Erica, "Would she have lived without your help?"

Erica shook her head. "Danica might have, but not the child."

"Then don't apologize." Death was by far a worse separation than the distance between the Hawk's Keep and the serpiente palace. "Don't apologize for saving my daughter's life. Thank you."

"How do *you* feel?" Erica asked.

I paused to catalog my injuries. "Like I fell off the Keep. What did you do to me?"

"Do you know the concept of force-changing?" Erica asked. When I shook my head, she explained, "It's not a commonly used tactic even among my kind, because it leaves a mark on the user's magic, but when necessary, it can be used for fighting, healing or hiding." Perhaps seeing the confusion on my face, she went on, "Normally you change instinctively, taking with you any injuries you have, and any poison. There was poison on the blade that cut you. If it had spread through your blood, it would have killed you. I forced you to change before it could do much harm, but instead of letting the poison enter your second form, I brought it into myself. *Am'haj* was designed by falcons to harm serpents; it's harmless to my kind."

I would never grasp the mechanics of falcon magic, but death was something I understood very well and was grateful to avoid for now. "Thank you again." Curious, I asked, "Hiding?"

Again the sparrow—falcon, I corrected myself—looked nervous. "Like I said, when you reach that deeply into someone else's magic, it leaves a mark. The power remembers that which it touched. If it remembers enough . . ." She held up a hand, and for a few moments black snakeskin shimmered across the surface. "That is as much as I can replicate of your second form."

"Is that how you became Erica?"

She nodded. "The Silvermead family took me in when I fled the island. Valene's niece and I were very close for a while, but then Erica was hurt. I tried to save her, like I did you, but she was too injured, I was too slow." She shook her head. "It was too late. I barely needed to brush your power to take the poison back, but I immersed myself in Erica's, trying to heal her. When she died, the magic clung to me, so when I opened my eyes . . . they were Erica's.

"Valene knew what had happened. She let me stay, as Erica, so I could hide from the Empress but still live as a free woman. Later I got restless and joined the Royal Flight."

"And you told Rei who you were?"

"He is my commander," she answered. "I told him, and let him decide whether to accept me. I'm as loyal as any member of the flight, sir. You know that."

I knew it, but what would it change? Valene had said one couldn't lie to a falcon. Rei had played on Syfka's arrogance to evade the truth, but I did not know whether I could do the same.

"When Syfka speaks to me again, I can try to—"

Erica was shaking her head. "When Syfka speaks to you again, tell her who I am. She's strong; I don't know how she didn't recognize me already, except that I have not used my magic in years. She'll see it on me now even if you don't tell her, and if she thinks you're protecting me, it will put you and my Tuuli Thea in danger. And I won't allow that."

"What will happen to you?"

"For fleeing the city, and stealing a sparrow form?" Erica answered. "I don't know."

I had a feeling she *did* know. The fear in her eyes said more than her words. But if she didn't want to tell me, I wouldn't force her.

Maybe I didn't want to know.

Before we could speak again, the door opened.

Danica wasn't just "fine." Her cheeks were rosy again, and she stood as if she wasn't the least bit tired. Even the minor cuts and bruises I had seen were gone. She was wearing a simple cotton shift that looked as if it had been pulled on hastily, and the only signs of that morning's disaster were the small bits of pine needles and leaves still tangled in her hair.

She hurried to my side, asking, "Zane, are you all right?"

Her hand fell to my arm, and as I looked at it, I realized I was still wearing my snakeskin—along with the rest of my half form. No wonder the doctor and the Royal Flight had been hesitant around me.

I let the snakeskin recede, as well as the other less-human attributes of my fighting form, and saw Danica smile a little.

"I'm . . . fine." The wound on my arm was minor, especially considering there had been enough poison on the blade to end my life. "How are you?"

Danica hesitated, confusion on her face. "Strikingly well, considering I recall falling off a horse."

I nodded at Erica. "You can thank your guard."

"Erica?"

"Our resident falcon," I clarified.

Danica leaned back against the wall. "Oh dear."

"I'll turn myself over to Syfka," Erica said. "I won't cause trouble."

Danica's eyes widened. "I'm not letting her take you."

"If I may be blunt, milady, I believe this is up to me," Erica argued. "I've sworn my life for yours. I won't ask you to protect me, not when it would only get you killed."

Danica nodded reluctantly. This was Erica's decision, and not one that either of us would be able to change.

"Who *was* trying to get me killed?" she asked finally.

"We don't know yet," Erica answered. "Your guards took down five of them, and dragged the sixth one here. They are waiting with her downstairs."

"We'll speak to her now," Danica decided before I could. I wanted a moment alone with her to tell her what Erica had said about our daughter, but I understood the need to solve this problem first.

Before we could turn to go, Erica suggested, "The doctors ordered your mother from the sick room, but I am sure she will want to know that you are—recovered."

I heard Erica hesitate before the last word, as she realized that Danica did not yet know the extent of her injuries. She looked at me, and I nodded; I would tell Danica later.

"If you will speak to Nacola and assure her that Danica is safe, we can deal with our would-be assassin."

Erica nodded.

"One last question?" Danica asked the falcon.

"Anything you want to know."

"If you aren't Erica Silvermead . . . what is your name?"

"*La'Kel'jaes'oisna'wimheah'ona'saniet,*" she answered quickly, with tired pride. Then she winced and corrected herself. "Or, I used to be. None of those titles are mine any-more . . . so I guess it's just Kel now."

"Thank you, Kel."

Kel left us, and I turned to my mate, catching her hand and drawing her toward me. Again the knowledge that I had almost lost her washed over me.

I would have liked to put off telling her, but I knew this might be the last chance I would have to be alone with Danica before her mother and the rest of the avian court descended. For long moments I struggled to form the words, and I watched as the worry in her eyes turned to fear.

Her hand pressed to her stomach. "The child. Kel didn't mention—"

"The child is fine," I assured her quickly, cursing myself for letting that thought spring into her mind. "Kel says it will be a girl."

Danica sighed with relief. "Then, what . . . ?"

"You were very hurt," I explained. "As was our daughter. Kel saved both your lives . . . but the magic she used makes it unlikely that you will be able to carry another child." *Unlikely.* I used that word to try to soften the blow, but Kel had been honest with me. I needed to be honest with Danica. "Not just unlikely. Impossible."

Danica closed her eyes and drew a breath, leaning against me. "This daughter was infinitely precious yesterday," she finally said, "and she is just as precious now that she will be an only child. As for her future . . ." She swallowed hard. "I want to talk to the monster who tried to prevent her from having one."

# CHAPTER 11

WITH DANICA BESIDE ME, I descended the stairs to the Keep's ground-level courtyard, bracing myself for whatever might await me. I had dealt with traitors before. Rarely were motives clear. Rarely was justice easy.

I stopped in my tracks when I saw the woman crumpled on the ground between two members of the Royal Flight. She could not have looked further from the part of murderess. She was avian, but despite the breed's famous stoicism, the face she lifted when she heard us approach was streaked with tears.

"Milady Tuuli Thea, thank the sky you're all right," she cried, lips trembling as she spoke. "Oh, thank the fates, thank the wind, you're alive. And, my lord, I saw you fall; it's a miracle. . . ."

This litany of thanks continued for a while longer, as Danica and I looked at each other and then at the guards. The spark of fury in Danica's gaze had turned to wary confusion.

"She fought all the way back here, sir," one of the guards

explained. "Then the instant we entered the Keep, she stopped. We explained the charges to her, and she started this. We've been careful to keep her away from the court; we didn't think you would want rumors to start before you could even speak to her."

"I never meant—" The woman cut off her protest. "I complained about the child—everyone has been—but I never meant to hurt it. I'm loyal to my Tuuli Thea, to her alistair; I swear it. But . . . she suggested it, how easy it would be, and I don't know how it sounded so reasonable—"

"She?" My tone was sharp, and the woman winced. I found it difficult to feel sorry for her, though I was beginning to form a bitter suspicion about the true culprit.

"I don't know her name," the frightened avian replied. "Either way, my hands held the bow, and I know I deserve any punishment you—"

"We'll deal with that later." Suspicion was boiling into hatred, and I had no patience for pleas and rambling. "First tell me about the woman who spoke to you."

"None of us knew her really, sir," she replied. "She was tall and fair, avian, foreign. . . . She suggested how easy the plan could be, and after she left we continued to talk and somehow it made sense—"

I didn't need to know more. I nodded at the guards, instructing them, "Take her someplace . . . safe. I don't think she's entirely at fault here. Then find Kel. She . . . went to speak with Nacola Shardae." At their looks of confusion, I clarified, "Erica. Tell her I need to speak to her."

Danica touched the back of my hand as the guards moved to obey. "Zane?"

"Yes?" I turned to her, again feeling a rush of amazement and gratitude for her miraculous recovery. Thanks to Erica.

*And fury for her near-death, thanks to another falcon.*

"Why Kel?"

"Does that woman seem like someone who maliciously planned to attack her king and pregnant queen?" I asked. My voice was calm, frosty calm—shocked calm. Too much was becoming clear, and all of it was combining to form a shell of ice on my mind. "I suspect Syfka was her mysterious avian co-conspirator, and Kel is the only person I know in these lands who might be able to confirm that."

"Zane, she admitted it herself; she held the bow," Danica argued. "Syfka wasn't even there."

Was I overestimating the falcon's ability? I didn't know how far her magic could stretch. If Erica could shape flesh and blood to draw a deadly poison from me and save my queen's and child's lives, not to mention knock out trained soldiers without lifting a finger, how much more might a royal falcon be capable of?

Ahnmik had once been worshipped by those seeking power. Could a falcon of Syfka's strength control others to the point of making them think that something they would never have *considered* seemed reasonable?

Did that make any less sense than what I had just seen? Perhaps anyone facing a traitor's death might weep, but terror had not been on that woman's face. She had worn the mask of guilt, grief and gratitude when she saw her Tuuli Thea alive and well. She had made no excuses, only tried to explain something she hardly seemed to understand. If she was lying, the ruse was pointless; as Danica had said, she had admitted her guilt.

I shook my head. "At this point, I'm not willing to say whether Syfka could or couldn't have somehow controlled the six who attacked us . . . but even if she didn't give them

the idea, I'm willing to bet she messed with their minds a little. The whole group needed indifference to their own lives
and callousness toward our child's life to do what they did,
and the woman we just spoke to had none of that."

Syfka, I suspected, was more than capable of planning
this crime. She had made clear her thoughts about our efforts
toward peace, and I believed what Valene had said: Syfka
would spare no concern for an avian-serpiente child.

Shortly the guard I had sent returned with Kel. The falcon still looked pale and exhausted, but she had recovered
enough of her poise that she did not seem like death walking. Andreios accompanied her. His earlier absence was explained by a bandage on his shoulder; the skin surrounding
it had the dark blush caused by poison. He was lucky it
hadn't been stronger.

"You want to know about Syfka's relation to our attackers," Kel predicted before Danica or I had a chance to speak.
She shrugged and added, "I assume? After all, I'm the only
falcon expert you have on hand, and there was falcon magic
all over that group." She frowned a little. "I should have reported that earlier. I'm sorry."

I shook my head, dismissing the apology. "You had other
things on your mind. What can you tell us?"

"I don't know the exact Drawing—spell," she clarified.
"The royals work their magic differently than the lower
ranks. But that alone means it had to be Syfka's—unless
someone else in the royal house has decided to visit, which I
doubt. The last time any of the other three left was—" She
broke off, averting her eyes before she said softly, "Back when
Alasdair and Kiesha still lived."

Before the avian-serpiente war, then, before a time remembered by any living creature aside from the royal falcons.

"Rationally," Danica pressed, "could she have influenced six of our people so they would be willing to attack us?"

"It would be nearly impossible to influence someone who never had the thought. You needn't worry about Andreios turning against you, for example, no matter what Syfka tried. But if they had considered the act, it wouldn't be too difficult to remove whatever moral or practical inhibitions were stopping them."

"So she could make them bolder, but only if they might have done it anyway?" I asked.

Kel shook her head. "If I took away your love for your mate, your respect for life, your fear for your own life, and your desire for peace, maybe you would kill Nacola Shardae. Not because you would ever rationally do it, but because you would have no reason not to when she next baited you."

I frowned. "So you're saying these six . . . were essentially innocent?" said Danica.

Kel nodded. "By falcon law they would be guilty—guilty of succumbing to another's magic if nothing else, and beyond that, guilty of disapproving of the actions of their royal house. But by your laws, they're innocent."

"And five of them are dead now," Danica sighed.

Every one of us was thinking the same thing, but Kel was the first with the courage to say, "We need to give Syfka what she is looking for, and send her away from these lands. If I had imagined for a moment that she would go this far to find me, I would have—"

Rei interrupted. "You can't be the one she's looking for."

Kel turned toward him, eyes wide. "Is there someone else you know of . . ." She trailed off, shaking her head. "Selfish, idiot hopes."

"You can't be important enough to—"

"Yes, I am," Kel answered bitterly. She took a deep breath and said to me, "You should know. The Empress Cjarsa and her heir, Araceli, command a group known as the Mercy. Before I fled, I was part of that group—specifically, one of Empress Cjarsa's four personal guards. The only people who outranked us were the four members of the royal house. I, along with my working partner and one of Araceli's guards, discovered something the Empress wanted to be kept secret. Araceli wanted me executed just for knowing, but Cjarsa protected me."

She looked away and took a deep breath before she continued her story.

"The Mercy works in pairs. My working partner was like a very close, dear sister. We had known each other since we were seven. She decided that the rest of the Empress's people should know. . . ." She shook her head. "The Empress called it treason. When one of the Mercy falters, her partner delivers the punishment. I refused to bring her in to the Empress. I fled so I would not have to torture to death the woman I cherished most in the world."

Kel continued, "In the Empress's eyes, I am the worst kind of traitor. She had given me her trust and her protection, and I betrayed her to protect someone who had turned against her."

"You can't be the one she's looking for, believe me," Rei implored. "You said so yourself, the Mercy deals with the Mercy's faults. The Empress would not have sent Syfka for you. Turning yourself in would be useless."

As I watched the argument progress, rising in emotion on each side, I could not help feeling Rei's desperation.

Kel could have run when Syfka first appeared. She could have left Danica to die, and stayed hidden. Torture and death—that was what she once had fled. That was what she was willing to turn herself over to now—and I didn't know of any way to help her. I could not protect her at the expense of the safety of my people, my queen and my child.

Kel explained, "My partner—the one who would have been sent to bring me home—is only a step away from death, bound by her own magic in a madness that Cjarsa's wrath forced her into. Even if she was not, do you think they would send any of the Mercy for me, knowing that I left when I refused to turn in another member?"

Rei took a deep breath, trying to regain his composure, and then said very clearly, "If Syfka tries to take you, I will fight her."

Danica began to raise her voice in protest, but Kel was faster. "She'll kill you!" the falcon nearly shouted. "And then she will take me anyway."

"I am your commander," Rei pointed out. "I'm sworn to defend you."

"Not from my own people," Kel argued. "Not when you can't win. You are sworn to defend first your Tuuli Thea and her alistair—and you *cannot* do that if you are dead."

The argument was interrupted as Gerard, one of the Royal Flight who normally stayed in the Keep as part of Nacola's personal guard, landed among us. "Sir, Syfka is here. She is demanding her falcon."

Kel took a breath and looked at Rei with a cool, sad gaze. "Don't fight for me." Then she knelt, taking Danica's hand. "You are my queen, and I have been honored to serve you. If that makes me a traitor in the Empress's eyes . . . I will accept that charge and trust myself to her mercy."

# CHAPTER 12

LEAVING DANICA SAFELY BEHIND, I returned to the courtyard to greet our villainous falcon with Kel, Rei and the rest of the Royal Flight to back me. Rei had agreed not to fight, but he had insisted that if they needed to turn one of their own over to the falcons, they would all be there to witness.

The instant Kel had reached the courtyard, she had closed her eyes and her figure had rippled. Erica had faded away, replaced by a woman a few years older, with dusky blond hair, deep blue-violet eyes and the Demi wings of a peregrine falcon.

Syfka landed and returned to her half form with her usual hauteur, rustling her falcon wings as if she was shaking off some miasma from the Keep. The skin between her brows tensed as she scanned the guards and noticed Kel behind me. She seemed to deliberate for a moment and then said, "With such a welcome, you would think I came to take a royal hawk away, not a traitor."

"She is no traitor to us," Rei answered, voice softly dangerous.

Kel put a hand on his arm, urging him to hold his peace, as she stepped forward. "Lady falcon, I would be careful who you call a traitor. The Empress is a just woman. I doubt she would be pleased to know the lengths to which you went to find me."

Syfka tossed her head. "I doubt she will care," she replied. "And as you are no longer among her favored, you will have neither the chance to tell her about it nor the power to level an accusation."

"Are you sure?" Kel asked. "Lady aplomado, you of all people know how precious children are to the royal house. My crimes may seem trivial, if the white lady learns you deliberately—"

"Enough," Syfka snapped. "The child you accuse me of harming is even more of a mongrel than the one your partner bore, and it will suffer the same fate."

I saw Syfka raise her arms in an ineffective defense as Kel lashed out not with steel but with magic. Syfka stumbled, dropping to one knee as indigo bands appeared across her arms and around her throat.

Kel snarled, "Do you think I will stand here and allow you to malign that child? Did you think I would allow you to threaten my king and queen's daughter?"

Syfka had been caught off guard, but now she peeled Kel's magic from her skin. Kel winced as each band shattered, but she let no sound of pain escape from her lips.

"You dare attack—"

"I am already accused of treason," Kel whispered, her breath scarce after whatever Syfka had done to remove the magic. "The sentence is death, and not an easy one. I am prepared for that. I will answer to my Empress when I return to the island, but until then I will not grovel to you at the expense of my Tuuli Thea and her alistair."

The royal falcon's expression shifted from enraged to amused. "You are too willing to be a martyr, Kel."

"I am, as always, what my Empress made of me."

She said the words as if by rote.

When Syfka answered, her voice was cutting. "Then know this: Cjarsa never cared that you left her city. She has not spoken of you since your foolish rebellion. She has forgotten you already."

Kel recoiled, looking more stricken than she had when she had agreed to turn herself over.

Syfka continued, "Did you think a stolen form was capable of hiding you from my eyes? I recognized you the moment I saw you—I simply did not care. You are not the falcon I was sent to retrieve. The Empress has more important matters to deal with. If you are what Cjarsa made of you, then you are *nothing* anymore.

"Stay here if you like. Stay in this backward land, never again to set eyes upon the white city, never again to hear the magic sing. Stay with your rat snakes and sparrows, always remembering you are not one of them, can *never* truly be one of them. Stay with your Diente and Tuuli Thea until fate catches up to them and the bloodshed begins again. Live among strangers and die alone."

She spat the words like a curse, and Kel reacted to them as such, crumpling to the ground as Syfka finished her speech. "Should you return to the city, I will see that you are turned over to my Empress's Mercy and treated as any outsider would be. And of course you know that any child you bear with these savages would be put to death for its mixed blood."

Kel nodded.

Finally, Syfka looked at me coldly. "I leave this criminal with you, but be assured, someone will come for the one I have sought. The white lady will not give up just because I have lost my patience for this search."

The falcon's wings nearly struck me in the face as she departed. She shrieked as she took to the skies, and I heard Kel gasp. When I looked back at the exiled woman, I saw new marks across her shoulders, as if something had clawed through her shirt to draw blood from her skin.

Kel's head was down, her face buried in her hands, and her shoulders trembled as if she was weeping. The Royal Flight retreated, giving her privacy. Rei looked shocked, as if he did not know whether to leave her alone or kneel beside her.

Before either of us had made the decision, the sound changed, and I realized that Kel was not crying. She was laughing, a brittle, hysterical kind of laugh of one who has had a narrow escape.

"Kel . . ."

Rei knelt beside her, and finally she lifted her head.

"I should be dead—for what I did, for what I said to her." Her voice held shocked wonder. "I should have been dragged back to Ahnmik. Never . . . Why would she leave me here?"

Rei answered, "Because she is a falcon, and cannot imagine anyone being happy, exiled from the city."

Kel nodded slowly and reached up to brush her hair from her face. Suddenly she froze and haltingly explained, "I tried to take my natural form, to face her. But I couldn't." She shook her head, grasping a dusky blond strand of hair in her fist. "Once I had beautiful pale blue streaks like Syfka's . . . but not now. I've lost that. My skin's too dark, too. I can't remember how it was. I don't know if my face is right; I can't remember Kel, not exactly. I've been Erica too long. Are my eyes right?"

"They're violet," Andreios answered. "Dark, blue-violet."

"At least I still have that." She lifted her head, suddenly defiant. "And I have my freedom. That is all I ever wanted." Then she turned to look at me, with a bit of a smile. "That and to serve a royal house I respected and trusted."

After the tumultuous scene I had witnessed, I barely had the energy to deal with the supposed traitor whose actions had revealed Kel to us in the first place. Especially if she was innocent, as Kel had claimed.

"Andreios, if Kel can assure us that Syfka's influence is gone from her, you may release the woman your flight is holding. She should be harmless now."

The crow nodded, but he looked preoccupied. He took Kel's arm to help her stand, and she leaned against him for a few moments before she took her own feet.

The immediate trauma was over, but I still felt as if I was falling. Syfka had promised that someone would come. Would we lose even more to that search?

We had already lost too much.

"Sir, is Danica well enough to receive visitors?" Rei asked.

He had hardly finished speaking before Danica hurried down the stairs and joined us. Gerard shadowed her in avian form, shifting a discrete distance behind her.

She brushed tousled hair back from her face, then held out a hand to Kel.

"It's so good to see that you remain with us, Kel," she said. "Dare I hope this means I have seen the last of your people?"

Rei tensed, but Kel answered, "I wasn't the falcon they were looking for. . . ." She shook her head. "Someone else will come. Maybe not soon, but someday."

Rei cleared his throat. "Milady, I . . ." He dropped his gaze. "With your permission, I would like to resign from the Royal Flight."

I was as shocked by the unexpected request as Danica looked. She answered instantly, "Permission not granted. Why, Andreios?"

He shook his head. "I've failed you more than once. You have nearly fallen to assassins, and you and your child were both just almost killed. Further, I lost objectivity regarding Kel, and would have endangered you further. I should have told you about the falcon. I should have—"

Danica interrupted him. "Rei, I know you. I have known you all my life." He looked away, but she took his hands and forced his gaze back to her. "You are the best captain the Royal Flight has ever had. You couldn't have done anything differently regarding Syfka, and though you posed your objections vehemently, I don't believe you would have endangered us even if we had not spoken against them. May I also point out that I am *not* dead?"

"Milady, please," he answered. "I am good at tactics; I served you through war and could defend you there. More often now you face deception and disguised enemies, and that is not the art I know."

"And who knows better than you?" Danica argued. "You aren't making sense."

"If you are willing to accept a falcon into your ranks, Kel

would be a worthy leader. She is the best fighter we have. And, while this might not seem like a glowing endorsement, her former position on Ahnmik has given her more experience dealing with problems by means less direct than battle. If you have any questions about her loyalty—"

"I don't," Danica answered.

"Or, if you would prefer another, Gerard has always served well; he is the oldest of the Royal Flight, and—"

"Rei," Danica interrupted. "I will allow you a *temporary* leave of absence, so that you may consider this decision, but then I expect you to return to your duties. The falcons are powerful adversaries, and I have a feeling your faith in yourself has been somewhat shaken. But I remember the day you decided to join my guard; you told me your dream the instant you woke up, after fighting a serpent's poison for days. You took that poison to save my life. You proved yourself that day, and I will not allow a crisis of faith to destroy you."

He looked away again, and his eyes met mine, pleading. I shook my head; this was Danica's decision.

"Leave granted," Danica answered. "In the meantime, if she will serve, Kel may fill in for you. You," she finished affectionately, "may come back as soon as your senses have returned."

# CHAPTER 13

"E XCUSE ME."
The cold voice behind us made me cringe for reasons that had nothing to do with falcons or Rei's abdication. Danica turned with a smile, and I struggled to do the same.

Despite how well the recent months had gone, Nacola Shardae still refused to believe that a serpiente man could possibly be the right mate for her only daughter. Because of that, she hated me as only a mother could.

I couldn't quite summon such a powerful emotion for such an emotionless woman, but all things considered, I did not know whether I would prefer to face the former Tuuli Thea or the falcon Empress herself. Unfortunately, I needed to tolerate Nacola for Danica's sake, despite the way her golden eyes never quite met mine. She was discreet about it, but eventually one comes to notice these things.

"Mother," Danica greeted Nacola warmly.

"You have a bad habit of allowing your guards to inform me of important events," Nacola chastised. Her tone was carefully controlled, but it held a hint of the fear she must have felt.

"I am sorry to have worried you; you have found us in the first calm moment since Syfka's plans . . . delayed us."

I regretted that fact even more than Danica did. Immediately our disagreement surfaced in my mind, as I realized that Nacola would ask questions we had not yet resolved.

Nacola just nodded. "You are queen; you had to see to your people first. The falcon problem has been worked out, I hope?"

"For this moment," Danica said. "Kel, who you knew as Erica"—she nodded at the sparrow-falcon—"was not the falcon they sought."

Kel interjected politely, "The Empress is more than two thousand years old. She does not make decisions quickly, nor does she ever hurry. To her, a day, a month, or even a century may as well be an hour. If she is the one who pressed to have this falcon returned, then you may not see the falcons again for generations."

"If?" I queried.

"To Empress Cjarsa, time is all but meaningless. Her heir, Araceli, is more driven. People speak of the Empress's will, but often it is Araceli who gives the orders. If she is the one who seeks your falcon, you may still wait years, or her Mercy may arrive at the Keep tomorrow. And unlike Syfka, they will not be subtle with their methods, or leave until they have succeeded. The Mercy does what is necessary to fulfill their orders." She stopped abruptly, swallowing hard, perhaps as she pushed back memories of her own time in that lofty group. "I'm sorry. I'm so exhausted, I'm having trouble holding a train of thought. Do you have any further questions, or might I be excused?"

"We can speak more of this after you rest for a few hours," I answered. And we would. Kel's descriptions had soothed none of my worries; they had given me new ones instead. "I have a feeling Nacola wants to speak to her daughter now, anyway. Thank you, Kel."

"*O'hena,*" she answered. "You're welcome, always."

Our conversation with Nacola was likely to be every bit as unsettling as Kel's ominous words about the royal falcons.

"Danica, you seem to have recovered well?" Nacola asked first, as we walked back toward a more private area.

"I understand that Kel saved my life," Danica replied. "I feel healthier than I have in years."

"And you, Zane?" Nacola asked, somewhat reluctantly.

"Again, thanks to Erica—Kel," I replied as we stepped into an empty sitting room.

"For that, I am grateful." The moment we were alone, Nacola prompted, "Gerard tells me that I am going to have a grandchild soon?"

"Yes," I answered, and for all my fears, I could not help smiling. "A granddaughter, according to Kel."

Danica moved slightly toward me, and her hand touched mine.

"I didn't think it was possible," Nacola said frankly, "for a child to be born between our two kinds."

"Apparently we've enough in common for it to work," was my terse reply. Both our kinds had human roots. In the best of worlds, the knowledge that we were not so different would dim Nacola's distaste a little.

In the best of worlds, many things would be different.

"I . . ." She trailed off and hesitated for a moment. "I am pleased to hear it." The words came out a bit rushed, as if her determination would only last so long. "I would not wish to see my line end, even . . . I *am* pleased."

Neither of us commented on what we knew was the reason for Nacola's hesitation. She was pleased to know that her daughter would have a child. She was not pleased to know that her daughter would have a *half-serpiente* child.

As Nacola began her questions, I felt as if I was watching a bird of prey circle in the skies, coming ever closer to the moment when it would dive.

"You'll have the babe here, of course?", Nacola said. "Even if the father is . . . not, it still seems right that avian doctors should attend to an avian mother."

I felt myself tense as Danica answered, "Most likely, yes."

I understood Danica's desire to give birth surrounded by doctors of her own kind. The question was what would happen after that.

Nacola let out her breath softly, clearly relieved. "If you know for certain that the child will be female, have you considered an alistair?"

This time I felt Danica's body tense. She answered carefully, "Zane and I haven't decided how we will raise the child."

"Shardae, surely you understand, if you don't give the girl an alistair, she will be seen as outcast from the court. It isn't proper—"

"And if I do give her an alistair, she will be outcast from the serpiente," Danica interrupted. "I said we haven't decided yet, Mother. Once we make our decisions, I hope you will respect them."

The hawk respected very little that had to do with me, but she wasn't about to say that aloud. Gods forbid she say what she was thinking outright. "Of course I must," she replied. Her voice remained even as she went for the kill. "But have you considered what your people's reaction will be, if their next Tuuli Thea is raised as a serpent? The war is over, thank the sky, but it takes more than a few months for the hatred and fear caused by generations of bloodshed to end. Your child might be able to end it, after she is queen, but this first generation will be in a very precarious position. The serpiente have an heir to the throne, I believe. Would you, Zane, be selfish enough to keep this child for your world if doing so risks her right to the throne of the land that needs her?"

Nacola Shardae, damn her feathers, was a true queen. In that single little speech, she managed to hit every vulnerability and fear Danica and I had regarding this child.

Danica stayed silent, leaving me to answer Nacola.

"We will do what is necessary to assure our child's prosperity." The statement hurt as I recalled my conversation with Irene. "We have some time before the decision must be made. If we can find no way to raise the child so both our kinds will accept her . . . then she will be raised to be Tuuli Thea, and I will name Salem my heir until—"

*Until another child is born,* I had been about to say, but there would be no other child. Danica wrapped an arm around my waist and gave me a half hug, despite how scandalized her mother would be by the contact.

Nacola nodded, and for the first time, I saw a glimmer of respect in her eyes.

"We will decide what we must, when we must." Danica's soft voice cut through the silence. "I hope you will trust us to do what is best. For the moment," she said, changing the subject deftly as her tone lightened, "my most pressing concern is that this has been a long and difficult morning, and I've yet to have breakfast. Perhaps you might join me?"

One thing was true in both our cultures: When a woman carrying a child said she was hungry, people listened. Danica had no shame in ruthlessly using that fact to disengage us from her mother's interrogation.

# CHAPTER 14

A S SOON AS THE COURT REALIZED that Danica was well enough to be social, they dragged her into the midst of their gossip, advice and congratulations. The next several days seemed surreal contrasted with the encounters of the ones before. Danica handled the crowds well, though I noticed her harried expression whenever she caught my eye across the room.

I recognized her people's need to be reassured that she was all right. Rumors traveled as fast through the Keep as they did in sha'Mehay, and as much as I wanted to speak to her privately, I knew I could wait until the evening. For now, Danica needed to be queen to her people.

Kel approached me at dusk to discuss falcons and her temporary position as flight leader.

"Every now and then I sense a falcon in the marketplace," she admitted when asked, "but these falcons are always powerless. When they escape the island, the Empress lets them go. So long as they are careful not to have children here, they are no threat to her. I have never recognized one of my own here who would be worthy of Syfka's attention. Whoever it is must be well hidden, or not in our courts at all. If the falcons send anyone else, you may want to suggest they look among the wolves, or other local groups."

I remembered Syfka making a similar comment regarding children when she had described Kel's sentence. "Valene told me that falcons prize children. Even you said to Syfka that the Empress would be upset that our child was endangered in her schemes. Why would a child born here be such a threat?"

"Children on the island are rare," Kel explained. "Ahnmik's magic is based on stillness, death; it does not give life. For any falcon in the upper ranks to be blessed with a child is a miracle. So children are infinitely precious." She shook her head. "Pure-blooded children, that is. Mixed blood children are more easily conceived, but far more dangerous. The magic gets warped in them, and it drives them mad. They usually die by their own hands, but only after they destroy everything around them." Kel shuddered. "I was part of the Empress's Mercy for nine years. Twice I had to bind such children, to try to keep them from harming anyone. It is a horrible thing to have to do to a child whose only crime was his parents' folly."

Bile rose in my throat. I could almost understand why the falcons hated outsiders and mixed-blood children, if they were forced into actions such as Kel described.

"Might the criminal Syfka was looking for have had a child here?" I asked. "Would she have been sent to locate it?"

Kel shook her head. "The Empress has other hounds to do that cruel work."

Her voice was sharp, again laden with bitter memory. I found myself wondering aloud, "Kel, was there ever anything beautiful on Ahnmik?"

"There is *nothing*," she answered instantly, "more beautiful than the white city when the dawn hits it. No dancer I have seen in the serpiente market can compete with the *jaes'oisna* when they perform beneath the triple arches, and no musician in the Keep can ever reproduce the way the magic sings. Those memories echo in my dreams and my every waking moment."

She lifted a hand, and an image appeared, hovering in the air before her: buildings that glistened like the iridescent inside of an oyster shell, roads sparkling with colors too spectacular to name and what I guessed to be the residents of Ahnmik. Each person wore falcon wings, even the little children who ran and tumbled about the streets. As I watched the illusion, I could faintly hear music that was unlike any voice or instrument I had ever known.

"The triple arches are where the dancers and choruses perform. I used to dance there," Kel confided when she saw me watching the city. It turned and tilted to show each piece she described. "Inside the three white towers are the private rooms of Cjarsa, Araceli and, finally, the Mercy. *Yenna'saniet.* When the city is silent, you hear screams from that last tower."

*I used to dance,* she had said. Suddenly it was clear to me that this must be the lady who had challenged Andreios to learn.

"There are things about my life before I came here that I wish the void would take from my mind. Things I've seen, heard . . . done, in the Empress's name . . ." She shook her head violently. "There is no place more beautiful, but at the same time, there is no place more horrible. And even if I had the choice, no power in this world could convince me to go back."

In the silence that followed, a new question gnawed at me. It had nothing to do with falcon traitors or Kel's future, but instead dealt with my past.

"Shortly before he died," I began, "my brother found a way to visit the falcon city. Were you still there when . . ."

I trailed off, because Kel's face was suddenly stricken.

She hesitated so long that I thought she would not answer; then she said, "Anjay Cobriana. My partner and I were assigned to be his guides as he waited for an audience with the Empress. He tried to change things, in a land that has not changed in thousands of years. It was brave of him, at least. His death . . . was a tragedy."

"Kel?"

We both turned at the sound of Gerard's voice.

"Can I help you?" I asked, giving Kel an extra moment to remove the traces of sorrow from her expression before she faced this man.

"Primarily I've come to deliver a message to the flight leader. Andreios would like to meet with her regarding the position."

Kel smiled. "Hopefully the fool has remembered that his place is as one of us," she said affectionately. "With your permission, sir?"

"Certainly," I allowed.

"Sir, I also have a . . . personal request," Gerard said hesitantly once we were alone. At my nod, he continued. "Traditionally, a member of the Royal Flight must have permission to court a lady, since he cannot swear to guard and protect with his life both his pair bond and his queen."

I had no answers to notions of protection. I still did not understand what differentiated a proper lady from a lady soldier, unless it was the same as what separated a proper gentleman and a gentleman soldier. It seemed to me that avian women needed little more protecting than the men.

I held my tongue.

"It has been difficult to secure a private audience with my Tuuli Thea, and I did not wish to ask inside a room full of court gossips," Gerard explained.

"Will permission from the Tuuli Thea's alistair suffice?" In the Keep, Danica and I seemed to have equal power. The only difference was that in a disagreement, Danica's word won out. The arrangement was much the same as that between Diente and Naga in the serpiente palace.

Gerard suddenly glowed with joy. "So long as Andreios— I mean, Kel—and milady Shardae do not object, your word is certainly good enough, my lord."

"Then court your lady," I encouraged.

"Thank you, sir."

The raven turned as if to start obeying my words that instant, but as I watched him go, a shriek of *ky-eee* froze us both, halting Gerard's steps and draining the smile from my face.

Heads in the market were upraised, and an open area quickly grew as five peregrine falcons dove into the center, each taking human form as she hit the ground near where Danica had been standing with her gaggle of court ladies. The crowd parted like water as I hurried down the stairs to greet the unwelcome visitors.

Combined with such a formal escort, peregrine wings could mean only one person: Araceli of Ahnmik, heir to the falcon Empress—and one of the three who Kel had assured us had not left the island in thousands of years.

# CHAPTER 15

THE HEIR TO THE FALCONS' EMPRESS was an imposing woman, with silver-blond hair pulled back in a tight, waist-length braid, and eyes as clear and pale as the purest blue opal. Strands of hair in similar shades of blue had been pulled out of the top of the braid to frame her pale face. She wore the wings of her Demi form as gracefully as a cloak; their violet-black tops contrasted with her fair skin, while their reddish undersides gave her a nefarious halo.

She wore boots laced to her thighs over black suede slacks, and an ivory low-backed silk shirt with golden embroidery. More disquieting were gauntlets that looked like the golden snakeskin of a Burmese python, and a simple dagger at her hip, no doubt coated with the deadliest of the falcons' poisons.

Her carriage and expression warned that she needed no physical weapon, as did the four guards who accompanied her, all standing at strict attention.

"What urgent business brings the Lady Araceli and her

Mercy to the Hawk's Keep?" I asked, half shocked and half angry.

She met my gaze instantly—a fear of the Cobriana garnet was not for this woman—as she stepped forward and brushed her guards aside. "Cobra, do you claim this palace as yours now?"

I bristled at the words, but forced myself to remain as calm as circumstances allowed. Danica stepped forward, and though she wore a mask of avian calm, I could see the tension in her shoulders and the anger in her eyes.

"I am Tuuli Thea here," she answered, not quite able to conceal her fury. "Zane Cobriana is my alistair, and I am sure you are aware of that. If you are still seeking your lost falcon, Syfka must have told you—"

"Syfka told me many things," Araceli interrupted, "and none of them convinced me that she tried very hard. I want my falcon returned. The aplomado has failed in finding him, and while she faces the Empress's tender mercy, I'm forced to go after the brat myself."

Looking into her pale eyes, I was as lost as any sparrow whose gaze fell on cobra garnet. I found myself recoiling with a hiss when Araceli had done nothing more threatening than look at me. Danica's hand touched my wrist, calming me.

What would the world be like if Kiesha and the other eight serpents from the Dasi had survived as the royal falcons had? Or Queen Alasdair and her first avian kin? What magic might our people have had if we had not wasted thousands of years and countless lives in war?

"It's a pity you aren't still," Araceli murmured. "You might actually remember some of Anhamirak's magic if you stop slaughtering each other for long enough. Still, I see no reason to hurry you back into war; you'll manage it on your own in time. Now, my falcon?"

"We don't know who you're looking for," I answered, glad that I could be honest on that point. Unless I had spoken aloud without realizing it, the falcon heir had read my thoughts a moment ago. Lying to her seemed like a bad idea.

She sighed and then glanced at her guard. "You sense him here, too?"

He nodded. "Well shielded, but yes. Higher."

Araceli nodded. "Excellent." She took a breath as if to sigh, but instead let out a piercing call any avian, serpent or landlocked creature could recognize—a hunting falcon's war cry. Only shock held me still as everyone else in the room jumped, some gasping. Danica went rigid beside me, but before we could consider protesting, Araceli issued an ultimatum.

"If my falcon is not standing before me within the next two minutes," she declared, "I will take this Keep down stone by stone and timber by timber, slaughtering those inside until I find the right one. I suggest you spread the word."

"Araceli—" said Danica.

"You had better hope he's loyal to you," Araceli said calmly to her, eyes glittering with ice. "Otherwise he might just leave."

"Araceli," I said, "you can't intend—"

"I never make a threat I don't intend to keep, cobra. Though, honestly, I don't think it will be necessary. He will come."

I caught Danica's eye, imploring her silently to get out of harm's way. We could not both leave—not with Araceli standing before us—but one could go, if only under the pretense of searching for the lost falcon. Ever so slightly, Danica shook her head.

Out of the corner of my eye, I saw other, less faithful avians shifting into their second forms and either disappearing into the surrounding land or flying to higher levels to spread the word of Araceli's threat.

Kel was the first one to return, her sparrow's form coming to a hasty halt as she shapeshifted at Araceli's feet. "My graceful Lady aona'la'Araceli—"

"You are not the falcon I seek," the heir interrupted her. "You have received your sentence, and Cjarsa has supported it despite my protests. Now take your leave of me. Even this face is tainted by your stolen form."

Kel recoiled, then collected herself and stood at attention beside me. "My graceful Lady Araceli, heir to she who shines in beauty and power, loyalty forces me to inform you that I have sworn myself to Danica Shardae and her mate, and that if you attempt this fight, I will defend this Keep and those within it with my life."

Araceli barely raised an eyebrow. "And you will die, little girl."

"And will I, heir to the kingdom of moon and mountain?"

The new voice behind me made the hair on the back of my neck tingle as I recognized it, but I did not turn away from Araceli. Kel tensed, and I saw Danica's face turn white. Instinctively I stepped toward my mate as I felt her sway.

Again the man spoke. "I'm here. You knew I would be. I too swore loyalty to the Tuuli Thea; you know I did so years ago. I'm sworn to Alasdair's heir, I'm sworn to the descendent of Kiesha and I'm sworn to their people. I never swore to you. So will you take me home to our Empress's mercy? To her torture?"

Kel hitched a breath in as if with horrified shock, spinning to face the speaker. "Rei, careful—"

Araceli was hardly bothering to hide her rage. "Speak not of your Empress that way, nestling."

"I'm no nestling," Andreios sighed. "I may be young compared to some, but I am no child."

"Impertinent—" Araceli stepped forward, her hand rising as if she would strike the crow, but then she stopped, her voice halting. She swallowed tightly before she said, "You're coming back to Ahnmik. Now."

Rei stepped toward her, his face grave. "Milady, you know I will not endanger my people, and I know you will not hesitate to use that to coerce me. So I can only ask you—beg you, if that is what you wish—to allow me to stay. You sent me here when I was still a child. You made no attempt to bring me home when I refused to answer your summons. I hardly remember my falcon form, hardly remember my magics—"

"You're royal blood, Sebastian. You'll remember, when the need arises, and we cannot allow rogue falcons of your strength to wander outside our control."

"When the need arises?" he echoed. "Milady, if I had any shred of power, do you think I would have let my queen fall to Syfka's tests? Do you think I would have let her bleed while I—"

"Enough." Araceli's voice was cold.

"Please, milady, heir to the land of air and cloud, heir to the kingdom of sun and summit, let me remain," Rei said. "Do what you think necessary, but let me remain. Ahnmik was never my home."

"Sebastian—"

"Milady . . . my mother. I beg you."

*My mother.* The son of the Empress's heir—indeed he must be strong. I could only imagine what he feared, what he was running from, that made him stay here, where he had to hide that strength. There was fear in his voice now, fear not just of losing this life but of whatever would come next.

What *would* come next? Death? Torture? Or simply life in a civilization no person with reason could possibly abide?

"It is unbecoming of you to whine this way, Sebastian," Araceli said. She spoke without warmth to her son. Did her voice hold regret, loneliness, guilt? I couldn't hear any.

"Araceli—" Rei said.

"Enough!" the heir snapped. "My patience is through. Guards, bring him. If he fights you, bind him. Tuuli Thea, Diente, I hope we need not meet again."

Horror lashed me, along with a sick sense of helplessness, as I watched the guards grasp Rei's arms. No words would possibly convince the heir to the falcon throne to give up her only son.

Rei must have felt the same way as I did. He did not fight, but walked with them until they reached the center opening in the floor, where he fell gasping to his knees.

"What are you doing to him?" The pain on Rei's face ripped the words from me. Kel grabbed my arm to keep me from stepping forward.

Rei's form rippled, contorting without any of the smoothness usually associated with a shapeshifter's change. The falcon that finally emerged, wearing the same peregrine markings as Araceli's Demi wings, shuddered as if in pain.

"Force change," Kel said softly. "It hurts, as you have experienced."

"No!"

Danica's shriek—a sound of pain and loss, and absolute hatred—turned my blood to ice. Kel and I were both too late to pull her back as she ran not to Rei, but to Araceli.

"You pompous *hoverhawk*," Danica spat. "You sent him here, you *left* him here, and now after he has proved himself one of us, you *dare* to demand—"

She did not get further. Before Kel or I could reach the pair, I saw the indigo-black tar of falcon magic strike across Danica's face and arms, knocking her onto her back. A wall of Araceli's magic held me in place, so I could only stand by in horror as she drew a dirk from her back and placed the tip against Danica's throat.

"I could simplify so many things by pushing this blade through you," Araceli whispered. "No one would miss you or the mongrel creature you carry." She paused and with the blade of her weapon lifted the cord on which Danica's *Ahnleh* hung. It shone in the light like a mocking symbol of the hope we had held. "Since when does the Tuuli Thea wear a Snakecharm?"

She looked at me, and I forced myself to meet her cold gaze without flinching.

"Danica is also Naga, and a dancer," I said, because Araceli seemed to be waiting for an answer. "The leader of the local nest presented her with the *Ahnleh*."

"I see."

Araceli glanced at Rei, who was being restrained by her quartet of guards, and then at Kel, who was on her knees, shivering as if held by stronger magic than I was.

Finally Araceli looked back at me and sheathed her

blade. "I am a patient woman, cobra." I did not dare to argue with that statement; I barely dared to breathe. "I can wait, and allow you to regret not having me destroy her for you. *Saniet'la!*" she called to her guards and Andreios. "We leave here now."

# CHAPTER 16

A T ARACELI'S DEPARTURE, the air thinned; breathing again became easy, and I fell to Danica's side.

I was barely aware of the guards around us, who had come to their queen's defense and been held just as helpless as I.

Danica reached up and wiped a single bead of blood from the hollow of her throat, where the tip of Araceli's blade had rested. Her chest rose as she started to push herself up—and then she paused, dropping her head into her hands.

I waited for her to look up again, my mind following a train of thought that must have been the same as hers.

Araceli had called her son "Sebastian": the sweet young falcon who Danica remembered with a bittersweet smile because he was her last memory of childhood.

Danica had always wondered how she had survived a serpent's attack, with Rei poisoned and her unconscious. Had Sebastian tried to save Andreios from the serpent's poison by force-changing him and earned a crow's form in the process? Or had the shift been more deliberate, a young man's desperate attempt to keep from going home? Syfka had ordered him to return to Ahnmik on the day Rei was hurt, so no one would have thought to question his absence when the substitution was made.

His recent erratic behavior had now been explained, though I wished it had not. No wonder he had wanted to leave the Royal Flight. If Danica had released him from his vows as captain of her guard, he could have returned to Ahnmik—to protect her, as he always had.

"Danica?" I touched her arm and felt trembling beneath my fingertips. She did not respond, not yet.

Now Nacola hurried into the room and knelt beside her daughter. "Shardae?"

Danica balled one hand into a fist for a moment, shaking . . . and then relaxed as with a conscious effort. She took another deep breath, and suddenly I felt her force back the grief that had been rising—force it back and lock it tightly away.

As if I was suddenly struck blind, I lost her; she hid her soul from me even more carefully than she had when we had been enemies conversing for the first time.

She lifted her head finally, smoothing her hair back with her hands. For a moment, her face was vacant of expression. Then I saw the blankness drop, and it was replaced by a casual façade that was even more disturbing.

"Well," she said, without a tremble in her voice.

"Danica—"

She shook her head, cutting me off. "There was nothing we could do."

This calmness frightened me more than any blade I had ever faced. "I know." Again, I implored, "Danica, are you all right?"

"Fine," she answered. "It's ... difficult to imagine, that's all. Rei, being someone else for all these years. And now gone." But still there was no more tone in her voice than if she had been speaking of the weather. "It will be awkward losing him."

*Awkward?* I couldn't even reply to such emotionless words.

Gerard stepped forward, just behind Nacola.

For an instant his concern for his queen was obvious, but then he hid himself as flawlessly as she had and addressed her. "Andreios was a good leader, and very organized. We can make Kel's position as flight leader permanent, and I know at least a half dozen fighters who are eligible for promotion to fill the missing spot."

Danica nodded while I continued to watch the conversation with ever-growing horror. Surely this controlled calm had helped during times of war, when they had faced so much death every day, but I would never be able to endure it comfortably.

"Danica, we can deal with these things a little later," Nacola said gently.

Danica nodded mechanically, standing without assistance. I looked away from her to Nacola, hoping for some words of help.

"Watch out for her," Nacola commanded me, speaking past Danica as if she was not present. "I have not seen her this way since her alistair died when she was fifteen. The only person able to draw her out last time was Andreios ... Sebastian, and it took him weeks."

Andreios—and that was how I would always think of him, regardless of what name Araceli used—was not here this time. Though there had been jealousy between us on more than one occasion, Rei and I were friends. Losing him could not hurt me as much as it did Danica, but it hurt all the same. I prayed to any gods and goddesses who might hear for the strength to see my mate through this. I prayed for the strength to deal with it myself—for my sake, Danica's sake and our child's sake.

Two slightly ragged-looking guards approached us, one limping. They hesitated, looking first at their queen, at me, at Nacola, and then at Gerard, as if not sure who they should address—if anyone.

"Yes?" Danica asked.

"Milady, I'm sorry to have to tell you this, but . . . Kel is gone." The guard swallowed tightly before continuing. "She took her falcon form and went after Araceli and Andreios. Two of us tried to go after her, but we're no match against a falcon. She made us turn back." How she had *made* them was evident in the stiffness of their movements. "But I saw her overtake Araceli's group. She didn't stand a chance. They've taken her with them."

I was too shocked by this second blow to know how to respond. Beside me, Danica also stood silently.

Nacola stepped forward to take charge. "Gerard, you're the senior member of the Royal Flight. I expect you to make sure this doesn't cripple the Keep's guard."

"Yes, milady."

She gave her orders with a natural air of command that I had not seen her assume since Danica became Tuuli Thea. "You two, you've been injured. Patch yourselves up and get some rest," she said to the limping guards. "Everyone else who knows what's going on, get to the market and the court and spread the word that we have lost two of our people. Hear me, I want them spoken of as *our* people, not Araceli's;

they were loyal and deserve to be remembered so. Zane, get your pair bond to Betsy."

Danica tried to protest, but Nacola held up a hand to silence her.

"I will believe that you are fine when your doctor tells me it is so," Nacola stated. "Now go—if not for your sake, then for my granddaughter's."


Betsy commanded Nacola, the Royal Flight and me not to leave Danica alone, and to make sure she ate and slept, two things that she skimped on whenever she was upset. I knew about the sleeping; I had a feeling I would be faced with several more of her bouts of lucid dreaming over the next few days.

Danica's grief at losing Rei was enough to break even the coldest heart, and mine could never have been icy enough.

She spent the first few hours leaning on the balcony, with only her mother for company. I suspected they were sharing stories of the loyal falcon-turned-crow, private stories I had never heard and likely never would.

Hoping my mate was in good hands, I found Gerard in the study reserved for the leader of the Royal Flight, poring through the notes Andreios had left for Kel.

"Andreios was a good leader," he said as soon as I entered. "His files are well organized. He kept up-to-date lists of potential new members—when they first requested consideration, their history, their schooling and his observations. We can never replace those we lost, but I can start interviewing and testing potentials to fill the positions this afternoon." He paused, finally looking up from his lists. "Danica is with her mother, I assume?"

"Yes," I answered. "My presence seemed . . ."

"Intrusive," Gerard filled in when I floundered for words.

*Intrusive,* yes. I had not grown up with Andreios or ever known the falcon Sebastian before he stepped into the crow's life.

And I could not stand there and share recollections as if he and Kel were dead. I *couldn't.*

"I am glad the Royal Flight is in good hands," I said. "Do you think there is any way for us to get our people back—if not Andreios, at least Kel? Whatever crimes she committed were slight enough they left her here once. Is there any chance . . ."

I trailed off, because I saw the doubt on Gerard's face.

"I have never been to Ahnmik," he answered. "I have, however, had the honor of drilling against both Andreios and Kel, and that was enough for me to know that I would never want to fight a falcon seriously—without even taking into account falcon magic. Araceli held you, me, Kel and the rest of the Royal Flight from going to our queen's side, without even looking strained. Confronting them on their territory would be suicide. If they send our people back, it will be because they choose to."

I began to pace, because this feeling of helplessness was driving me mad. "There has to be *something.* . . ."

"There isn't always a way," Gerard pointed out.

"Not always," I admitted, "but blind determination hasn't failed me so far." As the thought occurred to me, I added, "There is another falcon in the serpiente market, who was luckier than Rei and Kel. Maybe he will know something. I can also speak to Valene Silvermead, since she is still staying in the dancer's nest. One of them must know something that can help us."

"I wish I shared your faith."

"Only Danica needs to. I will see if she is well enough to travel tomorrow morning."

The conversation lapsed into silence for a few moments, and I struggled to find a lighter topic.

Finally, I inquired, "How is your lady love faring in all this?"

His expression shifted, betraying the smile of one happily besotted despite the circumstances. "I think she is as stunned as everyone else, but she is a very strong, capable woman."

I couldn't resist the urge to tease a little. "Strong and capable? Flattering descriptions, but hardly warm enough to merit the soft look in your eyes."

"She isn't a serpent, who wears her passions like jewelry and dances barefoot in the morning," Gerard answered. "She is an avian lady, serene and composed even when she is upset. Strong, and capable." More softly, he added, "She guards her heart and soul tightly unless she is around those she most trusts . . . so every little glimpse she allows me is like the silver moon rising over the sea."

"*A'le-Ahnleh*," I responded with newfound respect. "My best wishes to you both."


I spent the rest of the day alternately checking in on Danica—who spent the hours either with her mother, or in solitude—and drilling with the Royal Flight. Gerard had sent out missives to a few of the most promising recruits Rei had named, so I was called in to help test their skills.

The loss of its leader was a harsh blow, but the Royal Flight was not easily defeated. Discerning eyes, however, could see the forced bravado and enthusiasm the more sea-soned guards showed their newest members.

As evening fell, Danica drifted to my side. Finally true darkness overtook the Keep, and we were alone for the first time since the falcons had been taken away.

I stood on the balcony outside our room, watching Danica stare out over the forest, and not so much as sigh. *Avian reserve,* her people called it, but it spoke of denial, and the circles under her eyes belied her calm.

Although she let me draw her into my arms, she otherwise barely acknowledged my presence.

"Danica, are you . . ." I trailed off, because there was no reason to ask such a question. She was not all right, and if I asked, she would simply continue to deny that she wasn't.

"My mother told me today that one of the Royal Flight has begun to court her," Danica said, and for a moment the statement seemed so inane and out of place that I hardly realized the importance.

Then I made the connection. "Gerard?"

Danica nodded. "I told her there was no reason for him to leave the Royal Flight. He is sworn to protect the royal house anyway, and has always been one of her guards. Swearing his vows as her alistair does not seem like a conflict."

I could see many reasons for it to be perceived as a conflict, but Danica continued before I could voice them.

"She says she is too old to hope for more children," Danica added, "but I doubt that is true. Maybe it would be better for her to have more. Life is safer now that we are not at war, but having only one potential heir to the throne is . . . hazardous. And we will not have another."

The words, and the offhanded way in which they were spoken, made me cold. Logically, yes, I understood the desire for multiple children in the royal house. However, any child of Nacola Shardae would be a pure-blooded hawk and, as such, as capable of usurping the throne as safeguarding it.

Danica must have thought of this, but just as she remained silent about her feelings on losing Rei and Kel, she refused to speak of it.

I broached the first painful topic, because I had no idea yet what to do about the second.

"If you feel up to traveling, I think we should go back to serpiente lands tomorrow. I haven't given up hope that we may be able to somehow bring our people home, and I'd like to ask Valene, at least, if she has any suggestions."

Danica nodded mechanically. "My mother and Gerard have things well under control here, if we travel to the palace."

Her eyes followed a natural bird as it skimmed over the treetops in the warm night air. It dove, disappearing into the forest, and Danica said, "Araceli took them so easily. You really believe that we could somehow take them back?"

"I am not ready to give them up as lost," I answered. I pulled her closer, and finally she leaned against me.

"Idiocy," she sighed, as pain leaked into her voice for the first time. "First I *miss* Andreios, and then I feel foolish for missing someone who was never who I thought he was ... and then I feel ghastly for being angry with him, when I think of all the times he protected me over the years, and what he is probably going through now."

I stroked her back and she continued. "Then I think of Gerard, and my mother, and I think I should be happy for them. I know I should be glad if my mother has a chance at more children after having lost so many ... but I hate the thought that our child might then be denied the title she should have without question."

Though relieved that Danica shared my concerns, I wished this blow had not come so soon after the last. Neither of us was ready to face it.

She turned to me and rested her cheek against my shoulder. "You're supposed to be the one going to pieces, not me," she teased.

"You have every right to be upset, and every right to show it, with me if no one else," I assured her.

"It's so hard," she whispered, "adjusting to the fact that the real Rei has been dead for more than half my life. He died protecting me, and I never even knew to mourn him. I was so young, but even so, I feel as if I should have *known*. I always thought his father's death and our brush with our own had changed him . . . but it didn't just change him. He wasn't even the same person. I grew up with Rei, and I couldn't even tell that someone else had taken his place."

Suddenly she shook her head and pulled away from me. "If you want to travel to the palace tomorrow, we should probably sleep." Once again her voice was calm, and once again I hated hearing it.

"Come to bed, then."

She hesitated at the balcony, but then turned and followed me inside, keeping a careful distance.

Even more than I wanted to bring Rei and Kel home, I wanted to see Danica smile again—or even cry. *Anything* would be better than this emotionless poise. Perhaps sha'Mehay and its dancers could revive her, unlike her mother and the solemn Hawk's Keep.

# CHAPTER 17

M<small>Y FIRST STOP</small> once we got to serpiente lands was sha'Mehay. The dancers greeted us warmly, though we were hardly two steps inside the doorway when I saw the first nervous, questioning glances. We were the first to return from the Keep since Araceli had come. I did not relish the news we brought with us.

"I need to speak to A'isha and Valene."

Instantly, the two were before me. A'isha started to usher us to one of the more private rooms, but I shook my head. The more minds on this question, the better.

"The falcons found their people," I said. Valene winced, and I saw A'isha pale.

"Who?" the dancer asked softly.

"Syfka organized a 'test' to out the falcon. Erica Silvermead revealed herself, while saving my mate's and my daughter's lives."

"Oh, gods," Valene whispered, dropping her head into her hands. "Is Kel . . . they took Kel back?"

"She wasn't the one they were looking for. Syfka would

have left her here, but she went after them, when Araceli took Andreios."

A'isha let out a cry, her face going white. One of the other dancers steadied her, and I could see in his gaze the same pain.

"What was he accused of?" Valene finally asked.

"It doesn't matter," A'isha replied, speaking loudly to the whole gathered group. "He was one of ours, a dancer in this nest. I won't see him slandered, even by the falcon Empress." Instantly she turned to me, demanding, "How do we get him back?"

"He is Araceli's son, Sebastian," I explained. "Her only heir. If there is a way—"

"There *is* a way," she interrupted before I could express my doubt. "Falcon or not, her heir or not, he's one of ours, *ra'o'sha'Mehay*. The Cobriana learned years ago that you don't hold a dancer against the ruling of the nest. The shm'Ahnmik might as well learn the same."

Her determination was infectious. I saw the heat returning finally to Danica's eyes—hope. False hope or true, it was *something*. At least we would do all we could.

"There is a falcon in the market," I said. "The baker Seth. As he's the only local falcon I know of, he seems a good person to ask for information."

"He hasn't been in the market since Syfka was here," one of the dancers told me. "I can check his house, though."

"Please."

The dancer disappeared out the door, but all those remaining kept their attention raptly on me.

"Valene, you're our resident expert," I continued. "Any suggestions?"

Looking the most doubtful, Valene replied, "When I

visited, I heard nothing of Araceli's having a son. Children on Ahnmik are so precious, there must have been a reason for her to let him go the first time. Considering how reluctantly changes are made by the royal house, and how much effort was put into bringing him home *quickly*, there must also have been a reason they wanted him now. I don't know how any of us could discover those reasons, though."

"Any thoughts on Kel?" I asked, though I knew it must be a painful subject for her. "I assume you know more about her history than I do."

Valene shook her head. "I doubt that. She told me once that knowing the reason for her exile was dangerous."

"What do we hope to accomplish here?" The voice rang out from a python in the back of the room. "We've all heard stories about Ahnmik. We all know the myths. We all know— or more rightly *don't* know—how powerful the falcons are. It's sickening that they can just say someone is a criminal and take that person away, but it's not as if they picked up a serpent. They took *falcons*. Two people who, as *loyal* and *wonderful* as everyone keeps saying they were—and I'm not forgetting that Erica, or Kel, or whoever she was, hated serpents vehemently when I first met her—lied to everyone around them about who they were. People call them brave, but does a brave man hide who he is behind a disguise? Everyone gets venerated once they are gone. But all I know about these two is that they were cowards and liars who, a year ago, would have killed me without hesitation. Why should we risk angering the falcon Empress for people who were never ours?"

"I'm sorry, I thought we had accomplished something these last months." Danica's voice was level as a blade. "I thought maybe we were past feathers and scales. We are not talking about two *falcons*, we're talking about two *people*.

"We are talking about Kel—a young woman who abandoned everything she knew to save someone she loved from torture and execution. A young woman who entered our world—hidden, yes, because she had to be—in a desperate attempt to have the kind of life we all take for granted. A young woman who used to dance in her homeland, and who teasingly challenged the man she fancied to learn. A young woman who again lost everything, this time because she saved the life of her queen—and couldn't stand to see Andreios taken away without fighting for him. And we are talking about Andreios." Danica choked up for a moment, but before the serpent she was challenging could speak, she took a deep breath and cut him off. "The falcon who became Andreios was twelve when he first saved my life. You call him a liar, and you call him a coward, but you are oceans away from the truth—"

"I'm sorry," the serpent whispered, his quiet words silencing her more quickly than any angry protest could have. "Maybe I'm wrong; I didn't know them. But I still don't think we can save them."

"If they were serpents," Danica asked, "would you be so willing to give up?"

Silence, broken by the return of the dancer who had gone to look for the falcon merchant.

"His house has been cleared out," he announced, oblivious to the tension that was in the room when he entered. "It looks like he ran as soon as Syfka found out who he was." Belatedly, he looked around. "Is there a problem?"

The serpent who had challenged us shook his head. "Just me, being . . . me." To Danica, he explained, "I shouldn't have spoken as I did. But I think I'm not the only one who still holds a little natural distrust of an avian soldier. Add to that learning they were falcons to begin with..." He shrugged. "My nest leader, my Diente and my Naga all speak for Kel and Andreios. That's enough. It's not as if I know anything helpful to you anyway; it's none of my business."

Once again A'isha took charge, though this time she did so in a decidedly cooled atmosphere. "The dancer's guilds are as old as Maeve's coven. Any obscure information we have about falcons and falcon laws would be in the texts downstairs. Even if we can't find a way to bring our dancers home, we may find something helpful for the future."

As nice as that sounded, it was less helpful than one would imagine. Of the writings done by the ancient coven, all that was left were copies of copies of words written in the old language, and much of them were obscured by mythical fancies.


The sun set over the nest, and dancers around the room stood and stretched, arching their bodies as the red light trickled into the room from the open ceiling. A pair went around the room and lit lamps, then stroked the embers of the previous night's fire into full bloom again.

Danica lay beside me as I pored over one of the many inscriptions, tired eyes befuddled by the whirling designs the letters formed.

"Well, I feel useless," Danica sighed.

"I'm not doing much better," I admitted. "I studied the old language when I was younger—every cobra does—but only enough to have the barest understanding. All this is written using more complex forms, and many of the symbols seem to have been either embellished or abbreviated. *This* squiggle, for instance, is completely meaningless to me."

Valene shifted to peer over my shoulder. *"Lar,"* she translated. "I think. *She'maen'ne'lar.* Or—wait, I see it. Someone copied the breaks wrong. *She'maen'nelar."*

Danica rolled onto her back, running her hands through her hair as she yawned. "Valene, I'm suddenly even more impressed with you than I ever was."

The raven smiled at the compliment. "On Ahnmik, it's traditional to fill the space around letters with further designs that complement the lines of the writing. I think a few of these were copied from writings like that, which means it's very likely mistakes were made. I've been reading one where half the marks don't resemble any symbol I've ever seen in my life."

"I found a description of Queen Alasdair," A'isha called. "Whoever copied it made a note that the first draft was attributed to Kiesha."

Danica brightened, moving over to where A'isha was reading. "What does it say?"

*"Mana'o'saerre'la'Alasdair* . . . the hawk queen, Alasdair . . . *rai'maen'ferat'jaes'girian* . . . golden lady . . . hmm . . . Valene?"

The raven took over, skimming the piece a few times before she read it slowly. "The hawk queen, Alasdair, is both a golden lady and a young girl, with too much power for her years. She is serene, but there is a sadness in her eyes I cannot speak to. She is the same age as my son, and I pity her for not ever sharing his freedom to be a child."

The words were bittersweet, and familiar to us all. Everyone born during war knew what it was to see childhood fade too quickly as pain and loss stole the years away.

"The serpiente were only in Alasdair's city for a single night," Danica said softly. "How could words like those have been written just hours before the avian-serpiente war began?"

I shook my head. We would probably never know what really happened that night, or why. We would only ever know the aftermath, and hope we could reach past it.

# CHAPTER 18

"ZANE! DANICA!"

I groggily lifted my head as I heard A'isha's and Valene's excited cries. Danica did the same beside me, blinking sleepily as we were both awoken. Judging by the otherwise silent nest, it was probably barely before dawn.

A'isha brushed aside the bits of writing we had been working on when sleep had taken us, and she tumbled to sit in front of us.

"I kept thinking last night that Rei was my student, one of my dancers, and so I should be able to protect him. Like I said yesterday, the guild has *always* dealt with its own. Nest justice *always* comes before outside rule. With very few exceptions, even the Cobriana have acknowledged that."

I found myself wondering whether she ever slept, as my own sleep-deprived brain fought to catch up with her thoughts. "Unfortunately, serpiente tradition won't stay a falcon's hand," I said.

"That's what I first thought, too," A'isha answered. "Valene thinks otherwise."

The raven's voice was excited despite her obvious fatigue. "The dancer's guild originated with the *Nesera'rsh*, a powerful group from the time of Maeve's coven. From what I can tell, they're the modern equivalent among Anhamirak's followers of the falcons' Mercy. I didn't think much of it until A'isha found this." Valene began to read the flowing, slippery words of the old language excitedly.

*"Maeve'hena'o'Dasi'mana-La'pt'hena'o'itilfera'alistair . . ."*

Danica and I both blinked at the incomprehensible language. Valene translated swiftly. " 'Maeve stands as leader to our thirteen, and we as guides and guardians to the village. We speak our rituals to the realm of the divine, but it is the Rsh who hold the records, and speak law and justice to the land. Each'—the closest translation I can think of is *nest*—'is a realm unto itself, and *its rule over its own is undisputed even by our voice.*' "

I stared at the page, desperately wondering if what I thought was true.

Valene confirmed my suspicions. "The original was written by one of the thirteen members of Maeve's coven. Specifically, by the hand of shm'Ahnmik'la'Cjarsa—the falcon Empress. Kel could be a trickier case, but Andreios was studying with A'isha. Cjarsa herself acknowledged the independent law of the *Nesera'rsh*, and in current day, that means this guild."

Their excitement was infectious, but I struggled to stay reasonable. "These words were written thousands of years ago. Much as I would like to believe them, it seems unlikely that the falcons will relinquish Araceli's only child because we discovered words that were written before the Dasi split."

Valene listened to my doubts, but spoke calmly once I was done. "There's a line in the old myths about how

'Ahnmik turns all vows true, all lies apparent, and the written word as blood in stone.' It would seem reasonable that some of that would carry over into their magic. I would have mentioned it earlier, but I never imagined we would find proof of any vow we could possibly hold the falcons *to*."

Still, I found it hard to believe that these powerful creatures could be so easily manipulated by ancient texts. "You sound more certain than I would be, if I had only that one line of myth to go on." I tried to make my voice gentle, because I did not want to destroy what was so far our only hope, but I also could not let them charge into a plan with no basis in fact.

"I've seen for myself how a falcon treats promises as irrevocably binding, whether she wishes to or not. . . ." Valene took a breath and continued, "Erica was thirteen and Kel sixteen when Kel first came to us. The night Erica's brother died, Kel held the girl and told her, 'The sun will rise tomorrow, and life will go on. It will still hurt. You will still miss him. But eventually things will get better.' Erica asked her, 'You promise?' "

Valene shook her head. "Kel just turned away, and I was furious. She told me later that she couldn't make that promise, because we were in the middle of a war. We could all be killed, and even if we weren't, she wasn't sure things *would* get better. I told her Erica needed hope. I asked her, 'Would it have killed you to make that promise?' She looked away from me and said, 'Maybe.' "

The raven's lip began to quiver. A'isha went to her and held her hand as she drew several deep breaths.

A'isha spoke while Valene composed herself. "If it's true that Ahnmik's magic forbids even that kind of white lie, then maybe it really would hold Cjarsa to these laws. No matter how long ago she wrote them, she signed her name and made them her vow."

Something else occurred to me as A'isha spoke. "When you gave the *Ahnleh* to Danica, you said the charms used to be worn by the *Nesera'rsh*. You thought there was a time when even enemies at war wouldn't harm someone who wore one." A'isha nodded, and I turned to Danica. "None of us could have stopped Araceli from threatening you at the Keep, but after she saw the pendant, she backed off."

Danica nodded. "It seemed like a miracle at the time, but maybe . . ."

"If our charm could stay a falcon's hand, then the word of the descendants of the *Nesera'rsh* could be enough to bring one of our own home. It's still a long shot," A'isha said, though her voice was light with excitement. "It would require the royal house first listening to our petition, and then acknowledging Rei as one of ours—which I imagine they'll be reluctant to do if it means they will lose him. But it seems the best chance we have."

Valene had recovered enough to add, "I can speak for us, as a dancer and a raven, so they can't deny Rei's place in the nest because of his feathers. As for Kel—" Again she hesitated. "You said Syfka would have pardoned her?"

"She was willing to leave her with us," Danica replied. "She believes exile in our lands would be as great a punishment as any the Empress would level."

Valene nodded. "I understand Kel was once a favorite of the Empress. If Cjarsa was willing to release her once, perhaps she will allow Syfka's sentence to stand."

The hope still hung on magics we did not understand, but it was better than none at all, and every moment made it seem more possible.

"Valene, you are willing to do this?" I asked. Though Valene had not spoken of any danger posed to the messenger, I did not count on benevolence from any creature who would carry away our loyal guards and hold a blade to my queen's throat.

"I am the only dancer you have who is capable of flying to Ahnmik," she pointed out. "Further, no one in this nest is as fluent in their language or as versed in the etiquette of falcon society. I *have* to do this—for Rei, and for Kel."

"Very well, then. When do you wish to leave?"

"As soon as possible. It will take me a few days to get there, and I do not know how long I will need to wait before I am allowed an audience."

"I have one question before you go." Danica's eyes were focused on the paper the dancers had found. "Valene, would you read this line again?"

"*La'pt'hena'o'itilfera'alistair,*" the raven answered.

"That's the line about guides and guardians?" Danica asked.

A'isha finally made the connection Danica had as her finger hovered over the letters. "Yes. This word is alistair."

"And this?" Now Danica pointed to a series of symbols at the bottom of the page.

Valene answered, "*A'le-Ahnleh.* It is a blessing, and means, more or less, *by the will of fate.* Ahnleh is hardly legible anymore on the ancient coins, but it is the Snakecharm on your pendant, from the nest. Among the serpiente, it is used at the bottom of many documents, as a mark of promise, truth. As you can see, it's also nearly identical to the Seal of Alasdair, which has always been used on binding works among the avians." Her joking tone poorly masked a certain resentment as she warned, "Though be careful not to point it out to the Tuuli Thea. The last one exiled me from the courts for daring to point out the similarity."

Danica smiled slightly, lifting her gaze from the page. "I will be sure not to let her know. Is it coincidence?" she asked.

Valene shrugged. "Your mother wanted it to be. I prefer to think that our records are wrong—that, before the wars, perhaps Kiesha's and Alasdair's people lived together peacefully. Something went horribly wrong somewhere, but before that, there must have been a time when the serpiente and avians were close enough for words and ideas like *Ahnleh* and *alistair* to become shared."

"Our history books say that the word 'alistair' is a variation of Alasdair, as she was the first true protector of her people. Perhaps it was the other way around, and she was named protector from this word," Danica theorized.

The glow was back in her face, and she was not hiding her excitement.

Abruptly, she turned and kissed me. "Zane, if this is true . . ." She trailed off, her golden eyes so wide and bright that I drew her closer to me. "Can you imagine what kind of world it might have been?"

I tried to picture a time when avians and serpiente lived side by side. Not as they did in this wary peace we held, in which intrepid scholars and merchants sometimes dared to visit the other side, but coexisting in one land where they weren't afraid of each other.

I wondered if re-creating that world was possible.

It seemed like such an incredible idea, but I couldn't help entertaining it. "We were worried that our child would need to be either avian or serpiente, because the two lands she would rule would be separated that way. What if we could let her be both, and give her a world that is blended just as surely as her blood will be?"

A'isha asked, "Just build somewhere that isn't Keep or palace, but both?"

"Why not?" Danica asked. "A'isha, your nest has serpents, falcons, ravens and hawks sharing it now. If that is possible, then how impossible could it be to re-create a world where they don't just dance together, but live together? We're stymied now because people are afraid to immerse themselves in another world, leaving the Keep for the serpiente market or the other way around, but a third court wouldn't be specifically one or the other. We could design the court so it's only a small step from home to . . . to a land where a queen can be both cobra and hawk, because her people are just as mixed."

A'isha paused, contemplating, and we all waited for her response. If she refused, then this hope was all but lost. The dancers were among the most tolerant of my kind; if their leader could not imagine that this place Danica and I had suddenly invented was possible, then no one else would.

"I would join a dragon's nest," A'isha affirmed finally. "If only for the challenge."

"Dragon?" I asked.

"A dragon is a winged serpent, isn't it?" A'isha replied.

"I've always thought of them as winged lizards, though I've never seen one myself."

"A wyvern, then," A'isha corrected. "Wyvern's Nest. Perhaps some of your avian scholars could share their myths and stories for a *she'da;* I should like to create such a dance someday, maybe one that will rival the famous Namir-da." She frowned, adding seriously, "Though it would have to be very subtle to be acceptable to an avian audience."

"Do you think the rest of your nest would be willing?" I asked.

"Honestly? Not all." She shrugged. "But you do not need all; you need only a few, who have the courage to try to show our beliefs to a feathered audience so they can understand and perhaps join us. Give us a nest, give us a fire and the audience that would come with your new land, and we will be honored to dance for a Wyvern's Court. Sha'Mehay has become too small, anyway."

I continued pondering. "Merchants would come if there was a market for them. If we dedicated some land for schooling, we could bring in the scholars of both our courts—who, hopefully, would be willing to try to learn from each other."

Danica echoed my thoughts from her own perspective. "The avian court follows the Tuuli Thea. They would be hesitant to bring their families so close to the serpiente, at least at first, but hopefully future generations won't be as frightened. And if we let it be known that we will raise our child there, I think that plenty of avian scholars would be willing to go, if only in hopes of 'protecting' the queen's heir. Then of course there may be those who simply wish to curry favor with their monarch, even if it means supporting what they will doubtless see as another mad scheme by their Tuuli Thea."

"Another?"

"Of course," she answered sweetly. "You may recall the last one, since it involved announcing you as my alistair."

# CHAPTER 19

OUR ANIMATED CHATTER awakened the rest of the nest, most of whom took it as a cue to rise and begin their rituals to greet the day. Danica and I were each drawn into the simple, slow moving dances. As soon as those morning dances were done, Valene left for Ahnmik. We watched her take to the skies, the rising sun on her heels, as powerful black wings carried her into the west.

Afterward, Danica and I sought breakfast in the market. It was a slightly more peaceful place to pause and contemplate the ideas the night had brought us.

"It seems like such an incredible plan, I find myself wondering if it is even possible, and struggling to conceive of how to begin such a project," said Danica. Testing the sounds for not the first time, she sighed, "Wyvern's Court."

"We'll need to speak to Irene, and your mother," I asserted. "If either one of them rejects this idea, there is no way we will succeed. Any potential heirs to either throne—hawk or cobra—must be raised in the same mixed-blood land, or people will feel they can still choose to be apart."

Danica nodded, so I continued.

"Then I suppose we seek the approval of our respective courts, and allow the information into the markets. Once we are sure we have support, we can consult with architects, artists, whoever we need to try to bring this place we are imagining to life."

After that, we ate breakfast in silence, sifting through our thoughts like children going through colored stones—optimistic, because although some were too dark and some were too sharp, many glittered like precious gems.

"I have an excuse to be up at this mad hour." Irene yawned as we located her in Salem's nursery. "Why are you looking so bright-eyed?"

As she spoke, she rocked Salem in her arms. The babe kept shifting from boy to cobra, trying to wriggle out of her grip, then turning back to human form to pout when she wouldn't let him.

"We're plotting reformation of life as we know it," I replied, somewhat flippantly.

"Oh, is that all?" she teased. "Why not start with breakfast?"

"Thank you, but no," I answered. "Danica and I actually wanted your feedback on an idea we had."

Quickly, we detailed the conception of Wyvern's Court, from finding the two symbols to getting A'isha's support. Irene listened quietly, nodding every now and then as she finally managed to settle Salem down.

When we paused for her response, she looked hopefully at the face of her child. "If you can create such a place," she finally answered, "I would be honored to raise my son there.

And I have never seen you two fail to achieve any dream you strive toward."

We arrived at the Hawk's Keep the next evening. Nacola greeted us the moment we stepped into the courtyard, with Gerard by her side.

"I hope this unexpected visit doesn't mean that there is a problem," Nacola said firmly.

"Nothing is wrong," Danica assured her as we walked past the first-floor market to a private parlor on the second floor. "Zane and I simply wanted to speak to you about an idea we had."

"For Rei—" Gerard cut off abruptly, as if deciding it wasn't his place to question us, no matter how much he must have wanted to know about his former flight members.

"The dancers found something we hope we can use to force Cjarsa's hand, at least regarding Andreios," I said. "Actually, Valene Silvermead was the one who made that discovery. She has gone to Ahnmik to petition the falcon Empress for his return."

"Thank you, sir."

After Danica shut the door, I broached the reason for our visit.

"While we were looking for something to use against the falcons, we found something else—something that might be even more pertinent to our current situation."

Danica and I went on to explain her discoveries in the texts, and Valene's theories regarding a possible history together. Then we described our new dream.

When we were done, Nacola drew a deep breath and said, "It seems I do owe Valene an apology. She has obviously done much for these lands in the time since she left my court—though I am not sure whether I agree with it all."

Nacola sighed. "Your dreams are vast, Danica, but they include as many obstacles as rewards."

She went on to list all the problems with a Wyvern's Court. "People from both groups will be hesitant to bring their children to a place such as Wyvern's Court. You may create one generation, but for such a place to prosper, you need families. And I can think of many reasons any avian mother would pale at the thought of her daughter being surrounded by dancers and—" She cut off, then continued, "And serpiente pastimes our people long ago deemed inappropriate for young children. Zane, I believe your people have an equally unflattering view of how we raise our children," she shot at me.

"Beyond the question of how to bring up children, you face the problem of now needing to juggle three lands, trying to shift power from the old two to the new one without forcing the destruction of the originals—which I assume is not your intent, as it would ruin the homes and livelihoods of many who live and work in those places.

"Finally, you are still faced with the problem of whether your child will, in the future, have an avian pair bond or a serpiente mate."

"We are hoping," I interrupted, trying to stop her tirade, "that by the time our child chooses her mate, whether he is scaled or feathered will not matter."

Nacola frowned, but before she could object, Danica spoke. "And she *will* choose her own partner. I chose my alistair, as you have now, too, Mother. If the next queen is raised as a member of both societies, to be Tuuli Thea and Diente both, then any man who wishes to court her will need to accept and love both sides of her—especially if he wishes to rule beside her."

Nacola countered, "You will still have trouble with families. I am certain you have realized that if all the Shardae and Cobriana children are raised well in the new land, it will encourage other parents to trust your Wyvern's Court. If any royal parent refuses, it will cause doubt among your people. I assume that is why you are speaking to me: You wish to know what I would choose, should I be lucky enough to bear another child. The answer . . ."

She paused, contemplative. "I may never have that joy," she finally said. "That means that you, Danica, are the only child I need to protect at this moment. I have seen you flourish these last several months, despite my objections and my hesitation. Should I have another child, I will raise her to be loyal to her Tuuli Thea, and her Tuuli Thea's heir. If that means raising her in a land where serpents and avians dwell side by side, then I imagine I will do what I must to support your efforts.

"However," she added swiftly, before either of us could speak, "I will make no promises as to the future until I see this dream made real."

"It is too late to gather our people this evening, and we are anxious to return to serpiente lands at first light," Danica said. "If you would speak to the court for us, showing your support, it would mean so much."

Nacola nodded. "I will present your Wyvern's Court, with all my blessings. Fly with grace."

# CHAPTER 20

WHEN WE RETURNED TO SERPIENTE LANDS the next morning, we found a debate raging in the market. A group of serpents had gathered around a stall I knew belonged to an avian artist, completely obscuring her from our view. In the midst of all our hope, the raised voices chilled me.

"This is exactly why I didn't want to do this here!" A'isha's voice rose above the others. "Back up, back up!"

With Danica on one side and me on the other, we quickly formed a path through the crowd, to reveal a blushing artist with a stripe of gold paint on her cheek.

"I didn't mean for my little sketch to create such a stir," she said quietly, before I could ask what was going on. "I heard the rumors about a Wyvern's Court . . . and my imagination got the better of me."

"Show him," A'isha encouraged, because the artist was still standing protectively in front of her creation.

"It isn't finished," the woman said as she stepped shyly out of the way.

The background had only barely been sketched—a blue sky, and what looked to be the beginning of a market. But in the middle of the white slate plaza was a green marble mosaic. The design formed was similar to *Ahnleh,* but subtly different; the artist had overlapped the serpiente *Ahnleh* with the avian Seal of Alasdair. The two symbols were so similar that they fit together as if first designed as a single glyph, reformed here after more than two thousand years.

At the center of the symbol was a young woman in the midst of shifting shape; from her back grew golden wings, but her body was sliding into a serpent's form, and her head was thrown back so that her face was bathed in sunlight.

*Wyvern.*

Even with rough details, the image took my breath away.

"The dancers say that you and your mate hope to form a combined court," the artist said. "I heard the story of where the idea came from, and I could just . . . see it. I wanted to create it."

"So do we," Danica whispered.

Her quiet reply, confirming the rumors, brought a barrage of questions. Several minutes passed before I could quiet the crowd enough for me to speak.

"Apparently you have already heard about Wyvern's Court." I had not expected our dream to stay a secret for long. Few things did once the dancers knew of them. "It's true. We intend to create a place where avians and serpents live together. Nacola Shardae has given her blessing and is speaking to the avian court on our behalf. Irene Cobriana has also agreed, as has the leader of sha'Mehay. I hope you will, too."

Again, the simple words brought a storm of replies, so much that eventually A'isha invited us, along with the avian artist, back to the nest, where we could think without being questioned. Before we had reached sha'Mehay, however, we were approached by a young raven I knew as Tadeo.

"My Tuuli Thea, Diente . . . I heard A'isha speaking to my father—he's a weaver?" he offered hopefully.

"I know your father," I answered, which made the raven blush like an adolescent corn snake. "He was one of the first avian merchants in our market."

Danica paused, and then exclaimed, "Of course! Tadeo. The last I heard, you were in the midst of another apprenticeship."

"Mm." The raven ducked his head for a moment. "Yes, milady. I've . . . had some false starts."

That was an understatement. From what I'd been told, in the past three years, Tadeo had shifted his apprenticeship from the study of music, to philosophy, to history, to architecture and now to art.

Tadeo continued without encouragement. "The artist I've been working with most recently—well, before my father called me home—lives beside a small lake, about half a day's flight from here. There's an area nearby where the land sinks, forming a valley with hills on three sides and a cliff on the fourth."

"I know where you're talking about," I answered. The valley was a beautiful area, with granite too close to the surface to allow for the deep-rooted trees of the surrounding forest, and wildflowers everywhere.

"I was thinking of it, especially when I saw that painting. It's about the same distance from the Keep and this market, just a little farther east. It's on the edge of the land claimed by a pack of wolf shapeshifters, but they don't hunt in that area, and according to my teacher, they have started to express interest in trading with us since the war ended. . . ." He looked at us hopefully.

"Why don't you come inside with us?" Danica suggested. "You can tell us more."

I looked at A'isha, expecting her to protest our inviting more avians from the Keep to her nest, but she just nodded. "This seems as good a place as any to confer—plenty of room to work, and rooms downstairs for anyone who is traveling and does not feel like sleeping in the main room like a dancer."

"In that case," I suggested, "we should see about bringing in other artists and architects who are interested in helping, and inviting some others from the Keep. I know the area Tadeo is describing. If he is correct that the wolves would not object, then I agree it might be the perfect place to create Wyvern's Court." Tadeo blushed again at those words.

"Pardon me, but I am well acquainted with both the court and the market," someone said. I turned to see Fisk Falchion, another avian merchant, behind us. "If you would like, I would be honored to fly to the Keep for you and see who would be interested in coming to work with us here."

I did not relish the thought of yet another long ride on horseback, so I accepted the offer immediately, as did Danica. Fisk took to the skies, promising to bring back the best artists and architects he knew, as well as some teachers and merchants whose ideas might prove useful in the creation of the markets and schools.

Our remaining two avian guests entered sha'Mehay as if they were stepping into a temple, their eyes wide as they took in the studying dancers. A'isha, Danica and I discussed which of the serpiente we should invite, and as the afternoon lengthened, the crowd around the fire grew.

Oddly enough, it was Tadeo who shone the most, taking the role of organizer. By the time Fisk returned with a group of avians, Tadeo had already set people into groups, each working on a different part of the new land.

The merchants were put together to discuss how the market would be designed. Avian and serpiente scholars sat down together warily, but with some encouragement, they began to debate how best to combine their skills. A'isha led a group in designing Wyvern's Nest, and in choosing who would be allowed to travel to the new nest to found it. Artists and architects claimed by far the largest area, as they created sketch after sketch, trying to blend the two distinctly different styles.

The day turned to night, as it was wont to do even among the most inspired. The nest quieted, a few dancers performing their last stretches and prayers of thanks before they curled up around the fire. Most of the avian consultants left for their own homes and beds, but a few—Tadeo included— collapsed where they had been working, sleeping in the nest as the dancers did.

I saw one serpent lie down not far from where the raven was curled up asleep. She drew a blanket over them both and snuggled against his back.

Amazing how far we had come. A few days ago, I had been surprised to see Rei and Valene accepted as dancers in the nest; now anyone who wanted a part in this project was welcome. We had achieved half the goal of Wyvern's Court simply by dreaming of it.

# CHAPTER 21

OVER THE COURSE OF THE NEXT FORTNIGHT, the dream flourished. Soon one could hardly walk across sha'Mehay without dodging notes, charts, lists, diagrams or designs.

Tadeo continued as the leader, working with his previous teacher to measure out the valley and mark the locations of pathways, houses, shops, the market center and a three-story structure built into the northern cliffs that would serve the same purpose as the Hawk's Keep and the serpiente palace.

Pointing to his sketched map of the area, Tadeo explained, "The brook and pool don't have the best drinking water, but there are three springs in the cliffs that are cold and fresh. One is higher up—a couple of sparrows found it. It's about the right height for us to build a fountain around it, and have it central in the top story of the Keep—or palace, or whatever you want to call it. The building is going to be worked into the side of the cliff. In the end it will stand tall and grand, but still be rooted deeply in the earth—a perfect combination of avian and serpiente ideals."

He continued his updates, which he had given us every evening since the project had begun.

Danica and I both turned at a shocked cry from Lincon, one of the avian merchants from the Keep. "Not in the middle of the market!" He looked horrified by whatever his serpiente companion had said.

"Where else would you put them?" the serpent replied, sounding genuinely puzzled.

"I thought A'isha was dealing with your dancers," the avian said, gesturing vaguely toward A'isha and her group.

"They *are* designing the nest, but there needs to be somewhere for them to perform."

Fisk joined the discussion. "The dancers are a crucial part of serpiente culture, not to mention a beautiful addition to any public area."

"They may be important to the serpiente, but making their performances so accessible to our children just isn't appropriate," Lincon said. "Wouldn't it make more sense for the dancers to remain in their nest, so the more impressionable of our . . ." He trailed off, because the room had suddenly gone very quiet around him.

A'isha flitted over to the avian man, wrapped in quiet anger. "Have we harmed you in some way while you have been here? Has one of my dancers offended you?"

Lincon pointed out, "It is not your hospitality I question, but your regard for propriety. I was propositioned within moments of entering your nest."

A'isha chuckled, shaking her head. "You are a pretty man, and you walked in alone."

Lincon cleared his throat. "I don't think this is a laughing matter. Our young men and women should not be exposed to such—"

I stepped between the two before the argument could go further. "Wyvern's Court is not going to be a place where avians and serpents can turn their backs on each other, like neighbors who never speak. Our artists can't be the only ones here who are willing to compromise. Every teacher, parent, child and merchant will need to do the same. A'isha, that may mean teaching your dancers to exercise care around avians new to Wyvern's Court." To Lincon, I added, "Compromise may also mean letting unattached ladies and gentlemen make their own decisions and mistakes."

I looked at Danica, remembering the first uneasy months after she had agreed to become my mate. She smiled encouragingly.

"We come from different worlds," I said, "but each has so much to teach the other. There will be moments of dissonance, when people struggle to understand each other's ways, but once we get past our misconceptions, imagine the reward.

"The dancers *will* perform in the market of Wyvern's Court; they will be beside avian poets, singers, philosophers and storytellers or we cannot hope to succeed. Merchants will haggle prices and barter goods as they have in both our markets throughout history. Scholars will work to impart their valuable knowledge to their students. Artists will create beauty. And our children will grow up together, playing the same games, taught by the same teachers, *living* side by side until as adults, I pray, they laugh at the petty arguments we had in this nest while we designed their world."

"And ravens will dance, and serpents will fight for the lives of falcons." The soft voice drew our attention to the doorway of the nest.

Valene swayed by the door, her face pale and shining with sweat.

"Valene, are you all right?" Danica darted past me to take Valene's arm and lead her inside.

The raven nodded. "It is . . . a long flight. I just need to rest." Despite her obvious exhaustion, she said, "I spoke to Empress Cjarsa. She said she would consider my words; then she sent me home. . . . I don't know what she will do."

"Thank you."

"I heard you speaking when I came in," she said, lifting her head enough to look at me. She gestured to those surrounding us. "Is this a dream?"

"This is real," I assured her.

She smiled, but her eyes were heavy-lidded. "I thought I might have fallen asleep already."

"That might be a good idea," A'isha said. "You're shaking with exhaustion. Let me help you downstairs, so you can rest. You have done much for us."

Danica, A'isha and I helped the exhausted raven downstairs and saw her tucked securely into bed.

As we turned to leave, a serpent approached. Her expression held a bit of nervousness, as did her voice. "Zane, Danica, do you have a moment? I'd like to show you something."

A'isha returned to the main nest as we followed the new serpent to one of the other rooms downstairs. I spent the brief walk trying to place her face, which seemed familiar in one way, but completely alien in another.

She stopped in the empty hall before one of the bedroom doors. The illusion rippled away at the same time that she said, "Before you act, remember that it was not I who took your people. Nor was it I who sentenced Kel to death."

Danica and I both recoiled from Syfka as she shed the

magic that had hidden her. The falcon held out her hands, palms up in a timeless gesture of harmlessness—one that was an utter lie—and said before either of us could speak, "Your raven speaks the old language almost like a falcon, and she is as quick to twist ancient laws to her advantage as Empress Cjarsa herself."

"And what of her request?" Syfka's dark words about Kel made Danica's voice soft. Danica's hand again found mine, seeking support.

"Though Sebastian was well hidden, Kel does not have the power to veil herself from royal blood," Syfka explained. "I did everything I could to avoid bringing either of them home, and believe me, the Empress was not pleased with my failure."

"You did not seem so anxious to help us while you were here," Danica pointed out.

"I have no desire to *help* you or them," Syfka answered. "But a crow has no right to the royal house, and despite his birth, Sebastian is far too tainted by his life here to be called anything else. And despite Cjarsa's blind affection for the girl who was once hers, Kel will cause nothing but problems among our people. I would have gladly abandoned them both here, but Araceli was not anxious to give up her kin."

"So what now?" I demanded. "You would not be here if you—"

"Araceli ordered Kel executed," Syfka interrupted. "I convinced her that there were better ways to deal with the girl that would not martyr her. Eventually she concurred with my sentence."

"And Rei—Sebastian?"

"Sebastian is dead," she said. Danica's hand gripped

mine more tightly, until Syfka added, "In his mother's eyes, anyway. I give your Andreios to you, provided you assure me you will keep him."

"Give . . ." Danica's eyes widened.

"It was lucky that Valene spoke to me first, and I decided to take her to the Empress. Cjarsa honors such ancient laws, but Araceli might have been inclined to make your raven disappear. Fortunately for you, the heir still must answer to the Empress, no matter how disinclined she was to give up her only son." Syfka nodded at the room behind her. "Your people are there, somewhat worse for wear—and officially barred from our lands. Should they return, the raven dancer included, they will be executed on sight."

"Thank you," Danica managed to reply.

The falcon tossed her head. "Don't thank me. They both paid the price for their crimes. Though considering what I see here, they may soon regret your efforts to regain them. Snakes and birds," she spat. "It was never meant to be."

"Somehow, I don't find your opinion important," Danica replied. "Now step aside so I can see my people."

As I watched, Syfka's form again shifted to that of a familiar-seeming dancer. I had no doubt that she would walk out of the nest as easily unnoticed as she had come in. Danica rushed past me to the room where Rei and Kel were supposed to be.

Kel was kneeling as we entered, bending over Rei's still form.

She looked up as we came closer, and I winced at what I saw. Her violet eyes were dull with fatigue; only a hint of triumph in her gaze kept me from hating myself for not fighting more to keep her. The left side of her jaw was the sickly green-yellow color that a bad bruise turns before it heals.

Strands of hair had fallen out of her ponytail and hung around her face.

She was wearing a falcon shirt, which left her arms and most of her back bare, and the skin it revealed had livid welts, bruises and deep cuts that had yet to fully close. Her shoulders glistened with what looked like faint silver lines drawn across her skin to form symbols that were both familiar and strange.

Rei was resting in Kel's arms, unconscious but breathing. His face was shadowed by his nearly black hair, but like Kel's, the skin I could see was bruised, cut or shimmering with what I suspected was some strange falcon magic.

"You're truly with us?" Danica whispered. "Syfka said . . . I barely believed her." Danica fell to her knees beside the pair, reaching forward and then pulling her hands back as if afraid she would hurt them. "You need a doctor."

Kel shook her head sharply. "I'll heal. Some of these will scar, but . . . they're meant to. No doctor will keep my skin from being marked when Araceli went out of her way to make it so. Rei will be fine, too. He passed out barely after we touched the ground here; please let him sleep."

Kel lifted Rei, gently laying him on the bed before she begged of us, "Please, water?"

"Of course," Danica answered, standing quickly. "I'll bring it. Rei can rest here, and you are welcome to use one of the other rooms. Do you want anything to eat, or should we let you sleep?"

The falcon hesitated. "Food. I don't think I've eaten . . . in a very long time. Thank you, milady. . . . Danica, my true queen."

# CHAPTER 22

K EL INSISTED ON GOING UPSTAIRS into the nest instead of staying downstairs, where it was calmer.

"I need to prove to myself I really am back here," she explained softly as A'isha chastised the people who had immediately descended with questions. "The nest is so infinitely different from the white city."

She broke off the instant food was presented to her, staring at it for long moments as if not believing her eyes. After that, she ate with a hunger that reminded me more of wolves than of graceful falcons.

She also drained glass after glass of water and finally slowed enough to sip a hot tea. The color began to return to her skin, though in places the change served only to accentuate her injuries.

"Feathered Hades, girl, when did you last *eat*?" Tadeo gawked. He was almost hustled out of the nest, but Kel smiled wearily.

"Before I left the Keep," she answered. Her voice was as

dry as dust, and she took another sip of her tea, which was flavored generously with honey and sage.

"It's been weeks," I protested. She was obviously thinner, but not so much—

Kel managed an expression too tired to be patronizing, then answered simply, "When I was four years old, I stood in the Ahnmik courtyard for a fortnight, not moving, drinking or eating, just focusing on my magic. The test is one all falcon children take, to see whether they have the power to be—oh, but you don't care; it doesn't matter now. That world is gone to me and good riddance."

With these last words, she emptied her tea and sat back in her chair, closing her eyes.

"How good it is to be here," she sighed.

A small sound brought our attention to where a much-bedraggled Andreios stood in the doorway. He was gripping the edge of the frame, but his eyes took in everything around him, as if he was as starved for the warmth and companionship of the nest as Kel was for food.

I offered him my hand, too grateful to have him back to speak.

Rei looked at it for a moment as if not understanding, then gripped it as if he would lose the earth if he let it go. Leaning on me, he made it with near-grace to the fireside.

As Kel had, Rei put away more food than I had ever seen him eat in one sitting, and he drained water glasses as fast as they were set before him. Every now and then he would stop, his eyes lifting and lingering on something with disbelief—sometimes Danica, sometimes me and quite often Kel.

Only after the food was gone did he ask Kel, "You came after me?"

She nodded.

"I'm sorry," he whispered.

"Don't be." Her voice was also soft, but it held no uncertainty. "You are needed here."

"My mother was not happy to part with me."

"No," Kel answered, "she wasn't."

For a while, there was no conversation, as no one wanted to be the first to question the falcons about what had happened, and everyone wrestled with curiosity.

Finally, Danica raised her voice in one word to Andreios: "How?"

I knew she wasn't only asking how he had gotten out. Rei started at the beginning, the part Danica was most curious about.

"We were together in the Keep's library when you heard that Andreios was gone. Remember I tried to stop you from going after him," he answered, voice pained. "I followed you, to keep you safe, but I was too slow. One of the serpiente struck you across the head. Another bit your Andreios. I fought them off, but you were unconscious and Andreios was poisoned. I tried to force-change him, but . . ." We already knew the result. "It was too late, or I wasn't strong enough. I had just enough energy to bring you home, and then I collapsed. I had taken too much of the poison from Rei trying to save him; it nearly killed me. It was days before I was fully awake, and then I was locked in Andreios's form for days before I regained my strength."

He took a deep sip of his water, looking at Kel to continue for him.

"He had already disobeyed a direct order to return, insisting instead that he wanted to swear his loyalty to a different queen. For most falcons, that would have been enough to merit death. No one would dare execute Araceli's only child, even for treason, but then he stole a crow's form," she explained. "It is one thing for a guard to acquire another form in the service of her Empress, as sometimes happens, but quite another to sully the royal house. It took them years to come searching for him because it took Araceli that long to convince the Empress that he should still be considered a falcon, and not put to death as a mongrel."

"I knew I could not go home," Rei continued, "and I was terrified that you would force me away if I told you what had happened." Finally he raised his eyes to Danica, his expression pleading. "I swore my life and my loyalty to you, to protect you no matter the cost, no matter the situation. I stayed as Andreios first because I was frightened not to be him, but later because he gave me an identity. I could not save him, but he could save me."

Danica brushed her fingertips across his cheek. "You are Rei. To me, you will always be Rei." She shook her head. "I understand. I forgive you."

"Thank you, Dani."

Danica smiled at the nickname, but then the expression faded as I asked, "What now?"

Defiantly, Kel asserted, "They hold no claim to either of us now. Our magic is bound. Our falcon forms are bound. I have my sparrow and Rei has his crow, and we have the forms you see now, but that is all."

"Just mortals now," Rei whispered. He watched Kel as he explained, "The Empress had her Mercy take from Kel what she had learned that threatened the island."

Kel briefly touched a mark on her left wrist, which I had not noticed since she had returned to her true form. I did not recognize the symbol. "The Mercy works in pairs; if one strays, her partner reprimands her. The Empress broke the bond, and she took the memories . . ." She paused, then finished, "to protect Ahnmik, and to protect . . . I don't know." She dropped her head, leaning it on her hands for a moment. "I don't know. 'Just mortals now.' "

Rei stood and wrapped his arms around her. "Thank the sky, just mortals now."

Kel laughed a little, but it was bitter laughter. I suspected the memories behind it would only give me reason to shudder in the dark as I imagined what these two loyal souls had endured, together.

"A finer mortal I've never known," she replied. She turned to Danica and asked with a rhetorical, detached air, "I suppose my stint as leader of the Royal Flight was very shortlived?"

Rei shook his head. "Take the position."

"Either way, I won't have it long," Kel replied. "I'd like to ask milady's permission to court an alistair."

Danica raised one brow, and I could not help smiling at Rei's shocked expression.

"That's not exactly the way it's usually done," Danica answered, though her tone was light enough to say she would not deny the request.

"Commonly, I believe an alistair courts a lady, but I'm tired of waiting for him to pick up on my hints," Kel said.

Rei still looked a little scandalized.

"Of course, Kel," Danica answered, squeezing my hand. "Though the Royal Flight will miss you and your alistair."

Kel immediately turned to Rei, teasing, "I believe I can only have a falcon for my alistair, and since you're the only falcon present—"

"No," Rei interrupted, shaking his head. "This isn't right

at all. An alistair is sworn to defend his pair bond, to protect her with his life."

*Are you willing to swear upon your own spirit and the sky above that you will protect Danica Shardae from all harm?* I recalled vividly the day Andreios had asked me that, in front of the avian court, as the first of the vows sworn by an alistair.

Without hesitation I answered that question again in my mind:

*I swear it.*

I wondered now only why Rei would not, when it was obvious that these two souls were perfect for each other.

"Is that a problem?" Kel asked, her voice suddenly sounding a little more fragile than before.

"It is when *you* came after *me*. So long as we're altering tradition, I do believe I should be asking you, Kel, to be my alistair."

Kel paused for a moment. "Faultless logic. With milady and my lord's permission," she said, glancing at Danica and me to receive our nods of encouragement, "I accept."

Kel leaned over to kiss her pair bond. I spun Danica to her feet, leading her in a few steps of the Namir-da before simply holding her close. Someone behind us in the nest cheered, and others picked up the cry—avian, serpiente, falcon, scaled or feathered, for tonight the differences didn't matter.

*In the temple of Anhamirak, the steps were different each day and each eve, but each dance was still one. They danced the only dance, the one Anhamirak weaves.*

*Hope, trust, love, life.*
*Sha'Ahnleh: They danced with Fate.*

# FALCONDANCE

## PROLOGUE

**H**ERE WE ARE, among the lucky ones who live in times of peace, in times of hope and dreams and laughter. Here we are, in the glimmering Wyvern's Court.

Yet my dreams are not of the slate walks and marble plaza of my home. They are not of the velvet floor of the nest, of the exotic serpents' dance or the haunting melodies that can be heard at all times from the southern hills. Nor are they of the glint of sunlight on soaring wings, or the smooth hum of avian voices.

Ahnmik. That is the city of which I dream. Ahnmik, the falcon land of which I have learned so much and so little all at once. My parents refuse to speak of the land in which they were born. They have accepted this avian-serpiente world as the only one they will ever have.

But Lillian has painted my dreams with images of a city that glitters with magic. She speaks hesitantly of her homeland, because she knows that my parents' crimes will forever keep me from the island, but each word twines around some part of my heart.

I will always be loyal to Wyvern's Court, but how can I fail to think about the tall white arches that are said to be created not by *any creature's hand, but by pure strength of will? How can my nights not hold roads that sing a melody no voice or instrument can produce?*

*Ahnmik.*

*Of course I have learned of the city's namesake, the god so powerful that even those who laugh at myths fear to call his name in vain. Ahnmik is shown in art as a white falcon, diving through sky and sea alike, and his domain is power. It is control. It is magic.*

*The serpents of Wyvern's Court worship Anhamirak, the goddess who grants free will, and they fear Ahnmik. The falcons, however, believe that Ahnmik has a gentle side, just as the serpents' Anhamirak has a violent one. Ahnmik is the one who can grant sleep, and silence. When whatever nightmares plague my mother's sleep have become too much, I have heard her call to Ahnmik—and I have seen my father's look of horror.*

*Long ago, the serpiente and the falcons made up one civilization. They worked and worshipped together, until something caused the two sides to clash, and the falcons were driven out of the land. Serpiente history books say that Ahnmik's followers practiced black magic, endangering the falcons and the serpiente, and were exiled for that reason.*

*Lillian always shies away from the subject of the conflict, saying only that history is easily distorted by years, and by the teller.*

*As a falcon raised in Wyvern's Court, I do not know what I believe. I try to base my decisions on facts, but what facts are left from a fight that occurred thousands of years ago?*

*I ramble. I find that I do that more of late, as I think of things I will never have and never know. I am posted in Wyvern's Court as one of the princess's personal guards, a lofty rank of which I am proud. But contentment . . . that is beyond my grasp, drifting away as though in a gust of Anhamirak's storm winds.*

*Anhamirak's domain is also of spilled blood.*

*Of fire that sears.*

*Of tempests that drown.*

*Beauty and light and passion are hers, but simplicity she can never grant.*

*Nicias Silvermead*
*Wyvern of Honor*

# CHAPTER 1

M Y BREATH STILLED for an instant as I watched the blade
slice a hairsbreadth from the fair skin of Oliza Shardae
Cobriana, nineteen-year-old princess of Wyvern's Court.

"Relax." The reassurance came from the cobra beside me,
Oliza's only cousin, Salem Cobriana. "I've seen her perform
this blade dance a hundred times in the nest." He shot me an
amused look as he added, "With dulled blades."

The dagger went up once more as Oliza sank to the
ground, closing her eyes and bowing her head before clap
ping her hands behind her back to catch the weapon one
final time.

Members of the audience approached the dais, where
Oliza remained perfectly poised as her fans placed flowers
and small gifts in front of her. This had by no means been
her debut, but it had been her first time performing the
*jaes'falnas*—the blade dances that her parents had almost forbidden her to learn.

After seeing her perform, and seeing just how sharp the
performance blades were, part of me wished they had.

A serpiente dancer could, and often did, risk her life in pursuit of her trade. Oliza Shardae Cobriana, however, was not just a dancer, but heir to two thrones. Her mother, Danica Shardae, was the avian Tuuli Thea, and her father, Zane Cobriana, was Diente to the serpiente. Oliza's reign would mean the merging of two monarchies that had, until our parents' generation, been at war for thousands of years. But first Oliza had to choose her king, a decision for which all of Wyvern's Court waited anxiously, and one that had led many a young man to try to court her.

Oliza smiled at me, meeting my gaze just long enough to express her exhilaration before a petite golden-haired girl managed to slip through the crowd to stand next to me. Surprise washed over Oliza's face when she saw the unexpected guest, and she quickly came toward us.

"I can see why your parents objected to your studying these dances," Sive Shardae remarked, admiration clear in her voice despite her chastising words. "My mother would never have allowed it." Sive was three years younger than Oliza, but was the younger sister of Oliza's mother. Though still very avian in her mannerisms, she had made a point of stepping away from her avian tutors and spending more and more time with the serpiente in the past few years, learning their ways. She had not bridged the gap between the two cultures as completely as Oliza had, but that she was here at all spoke volumes. Twenty years earlier, a young avian woman would not have been permitted to walk alone through the market—much less watch the "scandalous" dances of the serpiente.

*She's not quite alone,* I thought as I scanned the crowd. Sive's alistair, Prentice, was standing just beyond the edge of

Oliza's audience, his gaze never leaving his charge. I watched him carefully, for out of this group, he was always the most likely to cause a disturbance.

The raven had made his distrust of serpents very clear, and he became especially irritable when Sive insisted on spending time with the dancers. Serpiente hugged and flirted casually with almost everyone, but Sive's alistair bristled at having to tolerate that kind of attention being paid to his pair bond.

Salem, leaving on his way back to the dancers' nest, greeted the raven politely. Prentice nodded curtly at the serpiente. He had argued with Salem in the past, but that day they managed to walk by each other without raised voices.

Progress, at least.

"Ridiculous," Oliza said to Sive, oblivious to the frosty moment between the two men. "No one has died performing a blade dance in sixty years."

Sive looked at me as if seeking reason, before realizing that Oliza was teasing her. Sive's scandalized expression made her appear even younger than her seventeen years.

It made me think back to when I had been a child and my parents had first brought me to see Wyvern's Court. I remembered the day fifteen years before as vividly as if it was playing before me that moment.

I stood beside my parents, trying to mimic their careful attention as they watched Oliza and her family. My mother, Kel Silvermead, was captain of the Royal Flight, one of the elite guards who protected Oliza's mother, the Tuuli Thea; my father was her second-in-command. Their attention never strayed from their charges, but mine shifted momentarily to the rolling hills and gentle valley where architects had been laboring for years.

Oliza's grandmother, Nacola Shardae, was there, with a nurse next to her holding the sleepy infant Sive. Salem, exactly twenty months older than Oliza, suddenly pulled away from his mother and father to whisper something in the princess's ear.

Without warning, both royal children took off down the hill. Adults tried to follow, but Oliza and Salem thought it was a great game to hide in the empty market stalls from their parents and guards, deaf to all the worried shouts.

***

Oliza touched my arm, startling me from my memories.

"You look skies away," she said softly. I realized suddenly that the crowd had dispersed.

"I was thinking about our first day here," I said, though I knew that wasn't enough of an explanation. It was not my habit to let my mind wander—not when I was with Oliza. I looked around uneasily and tried to account for the missing minutes.

"I hardly remember it," Oliza admitted, not noticing my disquiet as she led us from the market. This was our ritual; we walked and talked until we reached the woods, and then, beyond the edges of the court, we changed shape and spread wing. "We were so young. I just remember you finding me, after I got lost in the woods. No matter what kind of trouble I got into, it seemed you were always there."

I didn't say aloud that I could still find the exact tree beneath which she had been cowering, though it was true. My parents were the only people I knew who had never been surprised by my memory.

*Of course*, my mother had replied once, when questioned by my teacher about my fast progress. *He is a falcon.*

She had never said those exact words to me, but they always hung in the air, every time I shot past my peers in class. I had begun training with the royal guards when I was nine, while others my age were still studying . . . or playing. Many of the children had been wary of me, a falcon in their midst. They knew the falcons' history of black magic, and they knew that the falcons had sided with the avians—against the serpiente— during the war.

And none of them liked being around someone who made them feel stupid.

By fifteen, I had become a Wyvern of Honor, one of the dozen members of Oliza's personal guard, and that position meant more to me than any teacher's praise. Again, my parents had been proud, but not surprised; standing side by side on the street, we looked nothing alike, but I would always be their son.

Before I had even been born, my mother's falcon magic had given her the visage of a sparrow, and my father's had made him a crow. But their power was bound now. That was why my pale golden hair did not match my parents'; my mother frowned at the way it lightened to silver in the front. Beneath my hair, my feathers were blue-violet. When I grew the wings of my Demi form, the markings were peregrine. My parents' magic had altered their forms irrevocably, but genetics had made me the child of what they had been: falcons.

"Nicias?" This time Oliza sounded worried. "Is something wrong? You've seemed so distracted lately."

For the past several nights, my dreams had been filled

with the white towers of Ahnmik, and my nightmares had been stained by cobras trapped in ice and whispering voices I strained to hear, which made me stumble in the cold darkness.

"I haven't been sleeping well," I said, not elaborating. Oliza had her own burdens. She didn't need my troubles. "I must just be a little tired."

"Too tired to fly?" she asked, her tone light but her expression more serious. "I'd like to get out of here for a while."

Unspoken between us were the many reasons she usually asked me to stay beside her instead of one of her many other guards.

I was only one year younger than she was, and we had grown up together. I was also the only person in the court who didn't call her Wyvern, a nickname she hated but would probably never shake.

The serpents in her guard could never follow her in the skies, and I knew that Oliza disliked flying with the pure-blood sparrows, crows and ravens that filled the avian side of town. She preferred to fly with a falcon, someone who not only could match her pace, but also was just as out of place among the avians and serpiente as she was. But the most important reason, the one she would never speak aloud, was that she preferred to fly with someone who wasn't courting her—and never could.

Soon the serpiente were going to stop treading lightly around her half-avian parentage and start pursuing her, and the avians were going to start panicking. I saw that Oliza was always cautious not to show more favor to one male friend than any other now.

With me, she never had to worry. She would be queen of

the avians and serpiente, and so she must have one of them as her king. And I . . .

I was a falcon, and my parents had cautioned me many times about the dangers of choosing an avian or serpiente pair bond, regardless of how I might feel. The other falcons would never allow such a union.

Oliza and I would always be friends.

Once we reached the woods, Oliza stretched her arms above her head and sighed. In the afternoon sunlight, she was beautiful in the most uncanny way. Her black hair glistened with red highlights; the feathers that grew on her nape ranged in color from deep copper to rust. Her eyes were as golden as the rising sun and were surrounded by long, dark lashes.

And here, out of sight of the rest of the world, she shifted form.

Her serpent body was as flexible as a whipcord, its scales the same color as her hair—black with glints of red and gold. A ruff of avian feathers grew across the hood, spreading onto the powerful wings that unfurled from her back.

*Wyvern.* She cut through the air like lightning.

I followed her as a peregrine falcon, shrieking a cry of triumph to the sky that Oliza answered with a call too musical to be called a hawk's screech.

*Absolutely, without compromise, unavailable.*

I knew it; she knew it. It made our relationship safe.

We landed on the shore of a distant sea, hours away from Wyvern's Court. Oliza's talons dug furrows in the loose sand before she returned to her human form, shaking her ruffled hair out of her face. We had passed high above many human villages, too distant for their inhabitants' weak eyes to perceive Oliza's form as unusual.

"Sometimes I consider just flying and flying until I find someplace I've never even heard of," Oliza confided, her face still flushed from the flight. "Then I would land, take my human form, and live there the rest of my life."

I laughed a little. "Humble goals for the princess of two worlds."

She joined in my laughter. "I must seem terribly spoiled. Arami of the serpiente, and heir to the Tuuli Thea, and I want something else completely. No one's ever happy with what they have, I suppose."

"True," I answered, thinking of my own dreams of flying and flying . . . until I reached the white shores of Ahnmik, an island that lay in a sea I did not know.

Time passed in companionable silence as we sat on the beach, waiting for the tide to come in and the waves to lap across our toes.

I found that when I looked into the sea just the right way, the ripples where the sun hit the water looked like writing. I mentioned it to Oliza, but she just shook her head.

"Not from this angle," she answered. She leaned toward me, black hair brushing my shoulder. I caught the faint fragrance of almond, a scent she often wore, and had a momentary desire to wrap an arm about her waist.

I fought down the impulse.

It was impossible to count how many times over the past few years I had been tempted to say or do something just as stupid as putting an arm around her now would be.

Finding nothing in the waves, Oliza shook her head again. "I think perhaps you've had too much sun, Nicias Silvermead."

"Perhaps."

She looked at me strangely for a moment, maybe hearing something in my voice—a hint of longing for all things impossible.

"We should get back," she said as she stood. "We'll be late for dinner as it is. Again."

I pushed myself to my feet, brushing sand from my clothing. "Race you?" I challenged her, to break the tension.

Her eyes lit as she teased, "Do you need a head start?"

"Hardly," I answered haughtily, which earned me a handful of sand in the chest.

"Fine, then."

She took off like an arrow in flight, gaining air on me almost immediately. The lead she had now would diminish later; Oliza was always the faster flier at first, but she paced herself poorly, and during a longer flight I was almost always able to overtake her.

I let her pull ahead, not pressing my speed yet, and heard her challenging cry as the wind carried it back to me. The air was clear, and I kept an eye on her, but did not fret about the distance between us; I did not fear for the wyvern's safety, not in these skies.

One thing I would never regret about being a falcon was flight: the warmth of the sun even as it was quickly sinking in the west; the ground rushing by, far below; and the steady beat of wings. I complained about my falcon blood some times, but never would I complain about having a falcon's power in my wings. I let out a whoop of joy as my sleek feathered body cut through the air.

# CHAPTER 2

R IVERS, MOUNTAINS, fields and trees stretched out below me, their contours forming complex patterns I could never quite follow. And around it all danced the wind, moving east and west, dragging the clouds above and the leaves below.

That day it seemed almost as if I could see the lines as they formed, rippled, moved and reset. If I could only pause to look at them—

And suddenly I lost the rhythm not only of the Earth but of the sky and felt myself falling as fast as a stone toward the ground that seemed to rush up to catch me.

With too much effort I twisted in the air, changing the fall to a dive. A natural peregrine falcon can stoop at two hundred miles an hour as it dives for its prey, and I used every ounce of that ability now.

When I reached the ground, I slammed into human form, my heart pounding, breath labored, palms on cool dirt below me as I fought to keep from retching.

What had happened?

One doesn't *forget* to fly any more than one forgets to

breathe. I could think of a million things and never miss a wing stroke. So what had happened?

I tried to stand and found that I was trembling not with shock, but with pure exhaustion.

I caught my breath as my gaze fell upon a pair of eyes the color of blue opals. There seemed to be nothing beyond them—no forest, no sky—just those icy gems looking at me from some world beyond this one as if startled by my presence. The air seemed frozen, and I recoiled—

Then the eyes I saw were not blue, but liquid silver. They regarded me with curiosity, and a woman's voice said gently, "Nicias—"

Mercury bled into garnet as her silver gaze gave way to twin pools of blood, still as death, and furious at my intrusion

*Get out.*

The words shot through my mind, the woman's voice familiar but at the same time unlike any I had ever heard.

*** *** ***

Again I was on the ground, as if that third woman had shoved me away. Illusion, hallucination—I didn't know what to call the visions. That final gaze had looked like a cobra's. I pressed my cheek to the rough bark of the tree, trying in vain to figure out what was going on.

Oliza must have arrived home by now and hurried to dinner, either expecting me to follow or thinking I was already there. Again, I had left her unguarded when it was my duty to protect her. There was no room for a weakness that left me unable to do that.

Another, more chilling thought occurred to me. What if Oliza had been under this spell, too?

I pushed myself up, forcing my limbs to stop shaking. I needed to find Oliza. I changed shape and pressed into the skies, cursing the lethargy that seemed to make my wings heavy and awkward.

*What had happened to me?*

I knew one person who might be able—and willing—to explain. Lillian. But I wouldn't be able to speak to her until later that night.

Now I had to find Oliza. I went straight to the Rookery and was relieved to find her safe in the dining area. Her cheeks were still flushed from the flight, so I could not have been out as long as I had thought. She shot me an amused, triumphant glance that said she would needle me later for having finally lost a race to her. Then she politely turned her attention back to the crow with whom she had been speaking.

My mother had been at the Hawk's Keep with Danica Shardae the past few days, but she did not leave the Tuuli Thea to greet me, or even to ask why I was late. My father was engaged in a conversation with the Diente, Zane Cobriana, and looked up only long enough to frown at my tardiness.

I would hear about it later, but duty had always come first to both of my parents.

Oliza *did* walk over to me, which prompted Gretchen—the python who led the Wyverns—to do the same.

"Silvermead—"

Oliza's friendly voice cut off what would probably have been a chastisement of me. "Next time we race, I'll give you a head start," she offered. To Gretchen, she added, "You can hardly blame him for being late when I'm the one who kept him, can you?"

If only that were the truth.

Dinner, despite the presence of the Tuuli Thea, the Diente, most of the royal family and a few members of the court, was a relatively informal event. I would have liked to talk to Oliza more, but most of her attention was dedicated to her parents and her more insistent suitors.

A crow named Marus pulled Oliza aside when we were through. Though he had been born in the Hawk's Keep, Marus had moved here with his family when he was ten, and he had been courting Oliza with all the careful charm of an avian gentleman for the past few years. He was among the most tolerable of her suitors, and tried to be open-minded despite his very conservative upbringing, but I doubted he would ever care to watch Oliza perform one of the serpents' dances.

In some rumors he was named the next king, but those were rumors started by gossips who knew nothing. Oliza spoke of Marus the same way she spoke of many of her suitors—with some fondness, but nothing more.

"If you have the time," Marus said, any nervousness flawlessly hidden behind a shield of avian self-control, "I was wondering if you might like to walk with me this evening."

"Unfortunately, I've promised my night to the dancers," she answered. "But if you would like to escort me to the nest, I wouldn't mind the company."

Marus hesitated, as I had known he would. The nest was located on the southern hills of Wyvern's Court, in an area that was primarily serpiente. Although avians were not banned from the area, they were somewhat out of place.

Wyvern's Court was not yet a perfect blend of the two worlds. Many serpents were just as hesitant to walk the northern hills as Marus was to walk the southern ones. I believed, however, that every generation would step farther across the valley. Many others of my generation would make the effort specifically for Oliza.

Then Marus nodded, as if he had weighed the benefits of walking with Oliza against the unease he still felt around serpents and found the former worth the latter.

I followed them to the doorway, then saw Oliza take Marus's arm and felt a pang of envy.

"It kills you to watch her walk away with him, doesn't it?" The soft voice startled me so much that I jumped, though by then I should have been used to Lillian's quiet coming and going.

I turned to Lily with a sharp look, then regretted it as her gaze dropped.

"I'm sorry," she said. "I just hate to see that expression on your face, knowing that she either doesn't see it, or doesn't want to."

"It's better that way," I said.

"Better . . . yes," she echoed, the words hollow. "I hope this evening is your own, at least. I need to talk to you."

"I'm not on duty tonight." Oliza never took a guard to the dancer's nest. Looking more closely at Lily, I realized that there was sorrow in her gray-blue eyes. "Is something wrong?"

Lily lived in constant fear of what might happen if someone discovered that she was not the simple raven most people saw when they looked at her.

I had tried many times to convince her to tell Oliza the truth, but she had refused.

*Perhaps you are right*, she had said once when pressed, *and your Oliza would never betray me to the rest of her people, but I cannot afford to take that chance. A falcon will always be an outsider here, someone to fear and hate and avoid.*

She had apologized almost instantly, but her words had still cut deeply. Too true. At least I was familiar in these lands, the son of two respected members of the Royal Flight, and one of the princess's elite guards. Otherwise, I doubted my living here would be tolerated.

I was not prepared for Lily's answer.

"I've just received a summons from Araceli," she said. *Araceli.* It was always jarring to hear Lily say, without hesitation, a name my own parents never dared utter. The heir to the falcon Empress was my father's mother—and she had disowned and exiled him before I had even been born. It took a moment for me to register the rest of Lily's statement: "I'll be returning home within the next few days."

Lily had never pretended that she would be in Wyvern's Court forever, but the suddenness of this hit me like a shock of cold water.

"Will I see you again?" My voice sounded faraway to me. I knew what the answer would be.

"Probably not," she replied. "I was granted this leave to see Wyvern's Court because I lost someone very dear to me in Araceli's service, and she believed I should be given some time of my own. You must agree that two years was a very generous reprieve. Now I have responsibilities to which I must return."

I did agree, and I did understand. I just didn't know what to say now. When Lily and I had first met, she had been like a window to a land that had always fascinated me. In the past two years, she had become one of my few friends in Wyvern's Court. Besides Oliza, Lily was the one person who looked at me not as a falcon, but simply as Nicias.

"Nicias!" Her sharp tone made me jump. "Have you been this distant all day?"

"I'm sorry."

"What happened?" I did not want to burden her with the events of my day, but before I could change the subject, she caught my hand in hers. "Nicias, you aren't normally distractible, yet I can see that it's taking an effort for you to keep your attention on me. You look exhausted. Please, talk to me."

I took a deep breath and tried to focus. "It's probably just fatigue. I've had nightmares the last several nights, and haven't been sleeping well." I shrugged. "I keep thinking about things that happened years ago and completely losing track of time."

I tried haltingly to describe what had happened during my flight with Oliza, and watched her face turn pale.

"Nicias ... have you spoken to your parents about this yet?"

I shook my head.

"*Que'le'kaheah'hekna-a'tair'ferat'jarka-takmu!*" Though I was not quite fluent, I had studied the old language for years; what little I could understand of the string of profanity Lily spat out made it clear why my tutors had not taught me the rest. "You have to tell them," she asserted, in a more familiar language. "They might have left Ahnmik, but they're falcon-born, and they deserve to know. I need—I need to speak to my lady."

Despite the fear I could hear in her voice, she sounded excited. "Wait," I called as she turned to leave.

She darted back and kissed my cheek. "Go, speak to Kel now. I must speak with your father's mother."

I winced as Lillian evoked my lineage again.

My hand lost its grip on Lily as she shifted shape and a raven shot into the air. Even though I knew that the bird I saw was a product of magic, an illusion, I could never make out the peregrine falcon she said was her true second form.

I watched the raven disappear on the horizon, fearing that I would never see her again or have a chance to say goodbye.

Suddenly I heard her voice, as clear as if she was standing beside me. *Do not worry, Nicias. I have easier ways of speaking to my lady than flying all the way back to the island. I will stay near, and you will see me again, soon.*

Magic? Lily had always been discreet with her power. But now she had given me a taste of what I had never had . . . and had assumed I never would.

I took my own falcon form, obeying her command to seek my parents. An idea, a strange hope, was beginning to take shape in my mind, but I didn't know whether it was a combination of dreams and fatigue or a reasonable conclusion.

# CHAPTER 3

MY MOTHER WAS still deep in conversation with the Di-ente and the Tuuli Thea when I returned to the Rook-ery, and even if I had been bleeding to death, I would have hesitated to interrupt. Fortunately my father noticed me idling there and excused himself from the others.

"What's wrong?"

I hardly knew how to begin. I could not use Lily's com-mand as an explanation, since my father would not even know who she was. I had known that my parents would never trust a falcon as my friend, and so had never mentioned her to them.

"Something strange happened to me today, on my way back with Oliza."

"Strange how?" he prompted when I hesitated, hating to trouble my father.

"I was flying behind Oliza, and suddenly I . . . fell." I struggled for words that made sense. "I was watching the ground, and then it was like I forgot where I was. I barely managed to land safely, and then I saw something; at least, I think I did. Something that wasn't there."

Sometime during the speech, my mother had joined us at the door, perhaps to see what was keeping my father. He did not seem too disturbed by my words, but my mother's expression was grave.

"Has anything else happened?" she asked. "Strange dreams or nightmares?"

I nodded.

*"Vemka'mehka'Ahnleh,"* she swore under her breath. "Rei, say what you must to Zane and Danica. I'm taking our son home."

"Kel—"

"They'll understand; they're parents, too," she argued, never raising her voice from a fierce whisper. "Nicias, let's go. We need to talk."

I followed her from the Rookery to our home on the northern hills. My father caught up with us by wing as we mounted the two steps to the doorway.

Both my parents normally conducted themselves like older-generation avians, controlling their expressions and their voices, but right then they both looked tense and worried. I could not remember another time when my parents had excused themselves from our monarchs to attend to *me;* their doing so now, when I was almost twenty years old, could not be a good sign.

My mother began to pace in our living room. The restless action was so unlike her that it ripped the question from me: "What is happening to me?"

"When your father and I were exiled from the island," my mother began slowly, "the Lady Araceli, heir to the falcon Empress Cjarsa, bound us into the forms we had used to hide among the avians when we first left Ahnmik. She stripped us of our falcon forms, and took away our magic." She looked to my father for support as she summarized the tale I knew, then moved on. "As you know, falcon magic—*jaes'Ahnmik*—is so powerful that the serpiente and avians have feared it for thousands of years. That magic runs very strongly in the royal house of Ahnmik, where your father's mother is heir. It also ran very strongly in me. After our magic was bound . . ."

She swore again in the falcons' language, trailing off with a whispered prayer of *"Varl'falmay."* Help me with this.

"That magic should never have showed in you," she continued, "not with both of your parents locked from it. But everything you have been experiencing lately I have seen in others, when they first discovered their power."

Chills ran down my spine. I had suspected something like this from the moment Lily had told me to go to my parents.

"Even if I do have this magic, why does it frighten you so much?" I asked. "I would never use it to harm anyone; you *know* I would never use it against Wyvern's Court."

"I know," she said, shaking her head. "But I worry it will use you."

"Kel," my father finally spoke, putting a hand on my mother's arm to still her pacing, "what if all this worrying is premature? We both left the island when we were younger than Nicias is now, and neither of us ever had a problem."

She looked at him as if he had gone mad, then sighed, her gaze turning distant. "Sebastian of Ahnmik . . ." He winced when she called him by the name he had once used, as Araceli's son. *"Sebastian* would have passed the four summers Trial without effort. He was royal blood, after all—"

"As is Nicias—"

"It doesn't matter." My mother spoke over my father's protests. "I never knew Sebastian. But I can say with certainty that he had years of training before coming to avian lands. I passed the Trials when I was seven; it was another nine years before I fled. And both of us stole avian forms within a month of arriving, which kept the magic in check until Araceli bound it. Neither of us has the ability to teach our son, or to bind him."

"What do you propose we do, Kel?" my father asked, his voice strained. "I know the danger as well as you do. What I don't know is the solution."

"I might not have been raised on Ahnmik studying this magic," I said in the ensuing silence, struggling to keep my voice respectful despite my irritation, "but I'm not an idiot and I'm not a child. Would one of you please speak *to* me, instead of arguing as if I am not here?"

My mother looked at me for long moments, then said to my father, "We have to send him to Araceli, ask her to—"

"No." My father's response was swift. "Sending him to my mother would be madness. The only reason I got out when I was young was that Syfka convinced Araceli to let me spend some time off the island, and taught me to force-change so I would be able to hide from her—"

"Isn't it madness to keep him here?" my mother demanded. "I've known that this might happen from the time he was three and I saw the first silver in his hair. I assure you, I have considered every option."

All that time, and she had never told me, warned me? My father spoke before I could.

"Have you considered that we are both outlaws, Kel? There is no assurance that Araceli will even agree to see Nicias, or that she won't execute him on the spot as the son of traitors. If she *does* see him, *and* agrees to teach him . . . it will be because she sees herself in his face, a pure-blood falcon with his beauty still intact, unmarred by a crow's features. I am my mother's only child, but I am dead to her. In our son, she may see a villain or she may see her *heir*. If she agrees to teach him, it will mean she has no intention of letting him go."

"She won't force him to stay," my mother said. "Nicias will be powerful. If she does not bind his magic, she will need to teach him, and once she teaches him, he will have the strength to resist her."

"I'm not worried she'll force him," he said, though his voice had the tone of one who had given up.

Finally, *finally,* he turned to me, as if realizing that I deserved to have some part in this conversation about my life.

"Nicias, Ahnmik's magic is powerful enough to destroy its user, if he cannot control it. Most falcons begin to study almost as soon as they can walk, just to keep it from killing them." His voice was level, as controlled as any avian's, but I could see the effort that control took. "Most royal-blood falcons use their magic innately, and so it may be with you. . . . But your mother is right. As a child, even I was given exercises to help me focus my mind and keep me from losing myself in the magic."

"Rei—"

He cut my mother off with a look. She sighed, but allowed him to continue.

"It may be that this fall today was a fluke, caused by your magic waking when you weren't expecting it. It may be that this will be all, that your magic has been crippled by the bonds put on your mother and me, and it will never grow stronger; that would probably be for the best. Or, your power may simply have been hidden all these years, and now it will show as true as any falcon's. If it does grow, you may be able to control it effortlessly—or you may not." He drew a deep breath and then continued. "If you can't, it will destroy you. It will numb your body and mind, until it drives you into what is called *shm'Ecl*. There are rooms on Ahnmik filled with those who have succumbed to it, those who could not learn to control their power. They are neither alive nor dead, neither awake nor asleep. . . ."

His voice wavered, his gaze turning distant. He shook himself, as if to clear away something foul that clung to his skin.

"There are two people I know who are powerful enough to bind a falcon's magic," my mother finished for him. "The Empress herself, and her heir, the Lady Araceli of Ahnmik."

"My grandmother."

She nodded.

My father spoke again. "My mother is a devious woman, Nicias, not a kind one. If you go to her, I don't know what will happen. I worry . . . I worry you won't return." I could not tell whether he feared that his mother would kill me, or something worse. Did he really think anyone could convince me to abandon my home?

He added, "But you may be in just as much danger staying here. I don't know. But as you've said, Nicias, you're not a child; your mother and I can't make this choice for you."

At once I regretted those words, because now I *wanted* to be a child again, so that I would not need to face this decision. Stay here, where I might be fine or I might decline into madness, or go to Ahnmik, where I might be executed or I might finally see and study in the city that had haunted my dreams?

"I need some time to think," I said. "If it's true that today might have been a fluke, can we wait, and make this decision after we see whether it happens again?"

"Maybe," my mother answered. "But if that is your

choice, I would recommend you ask for leave from Oliza's guard for a while, until we know whether your magic will interfere with your duty. And, Nicias, please try to avoid activities that could be dangerous if you were . . . distracted."

Distracted. I remembered falling in the woods, and the time I had lost after watching Oliza dance, when anything could have happened to her without my noticing. Yes, my mother's suggestions made sense.

"Tonight we should all get some sleep," my father said. "Fatigue doesn't help anyone keep alert—or make decisions."

✳✳✳

I tried to obey, but as I tossed and turned in bed, images from the day and visions spawned by my parents' words kept shifting through my mind.

When I finally did drift into sleep, those visions invaded my nightmares, twisting around everything. I found myself locked inside black ice, frozen and still, unable to escape—

Garnet cobra's eyes, staring at me with fury. A cobra's fangs, bared and glistening with poison—

Ice, rippling with white lines like a million silver scars; it cracked and shrieked and bled—

*My prince,* whispered a voice—the same one that had shouted at me in the woods, angrily telling me to go away. *You are too brilliant for this dark land. . . .*

Then Oliza stood before me. She touched my hand and then there was fire—

I scrambled away, choking on the smell of burned flesh, and slid on the ice. A black cobra coiled around me, the scales cold against my skin.

*Why am I drawn to your dreams?* she asked. *What vows bind you to me?*

"You're a cobra," I managed to whisper. "I am sworn to the royal house."

*My prince, do you think me a fool?* she snarled.

Abruptly the cobra became a python. It wrapped around my body, binding my arms and constricting my chest until I struggled to breathe.

*You* are *the royal house. Your royal blood infects this land like a virus—*

✳✳✳

I woke, gasping and coughing as I tried to draw air into my body. For long moments I could only feel the cold coils of the serpent, pulling me back.

Finally I became aware of a gentler voice.

"Nicias, Nicias, come back to me," Lily was whispering. Her hands were warm on mine, which made me realize that I was shivering.

I forced myself to open my eyes, disoriented by her presence as much as by the dream.

"You cried out, with your magic," she said. "I felt you fall, felt you go cold—did you speak to your parents?"

"I—" The effort of trying to speak made me cough again. My ribs felt bruised.

As if reading my mind, Lily placed one hand gently on my chest. "There isn't too much damage," she said after a moment. Warmth seemed to spread from her touch, dispelling the lingering chill from the nightmare. "I was so frightened—"

The door opened.

"I thought I heard—" My mother broke off, looking from me to Lily and then back to me. Her obvious conclusion, though false, made me blush and pull away from Lily slightly.

Lily didn't look embarrassed or bother to explain who she was or why she was there. Her fear for me became anger as she demanded, "You left him alone? The evening after his magic awakened, you let him sleep with no one near to pull him back?"

"I didn't realize there was anyone in the area who—"

"You and your pair bond hid for years among the avians," Lily snapped. "You of all people must know that there are at least half a dozen of us in the area—"

"And who exactly are you?" my mother finally asked.

Lily drew a deep breath, visibly struggling to control her temper. "A woman who cares about your son," she said softly. "I would think that is something we share."

My father joined my mother in the doorway. He glanced at her questioningly, and she shook her head slightly.

"Nicias, I can fly with you to Ahnmik if you would like, to show you the way and keep you safe from your magic over the open seas," Lily said.

My father cleared his throat, attracting our attention. "Have you already made your decision, then, Nicias?"

"What other choice is there?" Lily asked. "I felt his magic clear across Wyvern's Court. Even among your avians and serpents, you will hear people speak tomorrow of their nightmares from this evening. Maybe you don't have the power to sense his magic pressing him, but I can tell you without doubt, if he does not begin studying the *jaes'Ahnmik,* he will fall within the week."

Still my parents hesitated, as if they were hearing different words than I was, less frightening ones.

"You would allow him to stay here, knowing . . ." Lily let

out an angry cry. "How selfish can you be? You know that he will not survive here. He needs—enough!" She ran her hands through her hair, drawing my attention to the tangles in the blond strands. I realized then that she must have come here from her own bed; her hair was tousled and she was wearing a very simple linen gown. "Nicias, do you wish to come with me? I will leave immediately. Every hour you are here puts you further at risk."

"I am not going to let my son leave with a perfect stranger," my mother interrupted.

Lily turned to say, "This is not your decision to make." She took a deep breath. When she spoke again, her voice reminded me of the black ice from my dream. "I lost my mother to *Ecl* before I was old enough to know her, and my twin brother several years ago. I have seen too many loved ones fall. I will not lose someone whom I have the power to save." More gently, she added, "Nicias will be safe on the island. He is of our blood, and has our magic; that means he will be allowed to study. I do not know what crimes led to your exile, but they don't matter. The Empress's laws do not allow any falcon to be held to the crimes of his parents." She sighed. "Have faith in your son. Recall that you are the ones who taught him about duty."

Turning from my mother, she touched my hand and said, "If you want to come with me, get dressed. I will go to my home and do the same, and then meet you here."

I did not need to tell her or my parents that I would be leaving for Ahnmik that morning. The decision was already made, and we all knew it.

"Wait," I said as one complication occurred to me. "I need to speak to Oliza."

"Of course," Lily said. "You are sworn to her. I will meet you outside the nest, then."

She kissed me on the cheek before pushing past my parents on her way out.

My mother sighed, her head bowed in defeat. She touched my cheek, almost whispering, "She's right, Nicias. It's fools' hopes that make us want to keep you here."

"May I speak to Nicias alone for a moment?" my father asked. My mother nodded and drifted back into the hallway without another word.

"Are you really worried that I won't return to Wyvern's Court?" I asked. "This is my home. I consider myself a subject of the Tuuli Thea and the Diente and their heir, not of some empress I have never met. And though Araceli may be family by blood, the falcons have never claimed me as kin. All the family I care about is here."

My father drew a deep breath.

"Ahnmik is, despite all its other traits, a beautiful land," he finally said. "It is a realm where you would be revered instead of shunned, where your falcon features would be seen as a thing of beauty instead of proof that you are different. That alone can be a powerful lure."

I shook my head. "Vanity isn't enough to make me betray Oliza."

"More than that, on Ahnmik you would be royalty. You would be able to use magic that few people here can even begin to comprehend." I had no desire to rule over anyone. And although I was curious about magic, I wasn't curious enough to give up everything—and everyone—for it. "And then, of course, there is—what is her name?" he asked me softly.

"Lily," I answered. "She has been my friend for two years. I know I should have told you, but . . ."

My father shook his head. "I speak to you now because I know Araceli will offer you everything and more to keep you by her side, and I hope you will have weighed all the possible temptations against your love for and duty toward this land." I nodded, knowing what he was implying. "Before you go, there is something I need to show you, for you to remember when Araceli tells you of the wonders of the white city."

He unlaced the throat of his shirt and pulled the cloth over his head.

I knew many men in the local guard who practiced bare-chested in the summer heat, and even more who wore the low-backed shirts that allowed them to grow the wings of a Demi form at any time, but I had never seen my father dressed either way.

Now I realized why.

Complex designs had been etched into his skin; scars covered his back and crept onto his shoulders and upper arms. Some were fine and neat, as if from a sharp blade, and some were broader and appeared burned in—as if he had been branded.

I stepped forward, horrified not only by the cruelty of whoever had left these marks, but by the artistry of the marks as well. Shimmering lines of what had to be magic twined with the scars, continuing and layering the designs in iridescent silver, blue and violet.

Someone had created a work of art on my father's skin, with blades and power.

"It is a crime to imply that the royal family can be cruel, so on the island punishment is referred to as the Empress's or Heir's mercy. It equates to torture. Many things on Ahnmik are equally honey coated—especially when it comes to the royal family. Keep that in mind. Keep in mind that if you choose to stay, you will be tying yourself to leaders who condone such things."

"What did you do?" I asked in shock. I had never dared to question either of my parents about why they had been exiled from the land of their birth. But I had never seen the punishment they had received, either.

"My crime was wanting to live off the island, among those the falcons consider savages—the avians and serpiente you have been raised with. Your mother wears similar marks, though hers are worse. In addition to leaving, she argued with my mother to let me go. After Araceli decided we were no longer suited to life on Ahnmik, after she had decided to let us go, and bound our powers, it was pure spite that led her to mark us both."

Suddenly the idea of visiting the white city filled me with dread.

My father grasped my shoulders in a brief and uncharacteristic embrace. "You've falcon blood, but your heart is avian, Nicias. You'll come back to us."

✳✳✳

The dancers in the front of the nest tried to keep me from entering at first. They relented only when I pressed upon them that it was an emergency, and even then they did so reluctantly.

No, a falcon was not welcome in this place.

I found Oliza still sleeping, resting innocently in a tangle with several other dancers. I couldn't reach her past the others, so I called her name.

"Oliza?"

"Nicias?" She sat up so quickly that one of the serpents who had been lying against her whispered a sleepy complaint before another shifted to fill in the gap Oliza had left behind. "What's wrong?"

I winced, knowing that anything I said in the dancer's nest would become common knowledge within a day. The dancers were revered in serpiente society as historians and storytellers—which made them tend to be insatiable gossips.

When I hesitated to explain around company, Oliza stood and followed me to the edge of the nest. Out of earshot of the rest, I said simply, "Apparently I inherited my parents' magic. It seems to come with some disadvantages."

Oliza's eyes widened. "I hope it doesn't pose a danger."

My gut tightened. "My parents think it does. I don't understand it all, really. But I'm traveling to Ahnmik, as soon as possible." Belatedly, I added, "With your leave?"

"Permission granted, of course, especially if your safety is at stake," she answered swiftly. "We will see you again, I hope?"

"I'm one of your Wyverns," I answered without hesitation. "And I would far rather live in a realm you rule than that of the falcon Empress."

"Take care of yourself, Nicias," Oliza said, with more warmth in her voice than she ever allowed herself to show around her many suitors. She hugged me tightly and kissed my cheek. I heard one of the serpents who had been watching us say something that sounded like "Lucky falcon."

Lucky. At the moment, *lucky* was not a word I would apply to myself.

# CHAPTER 4

"T HE FLIGHT is long," Lily warned me, barely a single step
outside the nest, "and there aren't many places to rest.
We'll be able to stop and relax our wings, and perhaps eat
something, only once during the journey—provided we make
good enough time to get to the island at low tide, while it's
above water." Her eyes widened. "Nicias . . ."

She reached forward and tugged my hair loose of the tie I
used to keep it back.

"What are—"

She laughed. "I was too preoccupied in your room to notice earlier." She pulled forward some of the front strands, allowing me to see for the first time that what had previously
been silver-white was now pale blue, just a shade lighter than
my eyes.

Normally the change would have irritated me, since it
set me even further apart from the serpents and avians who
already looked at me as an oddity. However, Lily's delight
was infectious.

"A falcon's magic marks his body," she explained. "Your

mother's violet eyes are one example. The blue in your hair is another. It will probably darken a little more when you begin to study, though the royals don't seem to show their power as overtly as some of the others. But I'm delaying us; we should be gone. Are you ready?"

"I hope so," I answered.

She didn't wait for more, shifting immediately into a sleek peregrine falcon a little smaller than me.

The first leg of the flight was less terrible than I had imagined, despite Lily's being able to hold an even faster pace than Oliza had ever managed. At the beginning, I delighted in spreading my wings, delighted in the ocean breeze and the smell of brine. I settled into a peaceful reflection, caught between sun and sea.

Then Lily bumped against me, her talons catching my wings to steady and lift me. With a start, I realized that I had dipped dangerously close to the waves. I shook my wings vigorously, both to gain altitude and to dry my feathers.

Though we had left shortly after dawn, we did not reach the island Lily had spoken of until nearly dusk. The little bit of volcanic rock, worn smooth and covered with shelled creatures and seaweed, was an inhospitable place to rest, but I was still grateful for the chance to return to human form for a while.

I arched my back, stretching my spine and then rolling my shoulders, unable to focus on fears or hopes while my heartbeat was still pounding from the exertion of the day.

As she landed, Lily shed the last of her illusions, then for the first time stood before me in her natural form. She ducked her head self-consciously as I stared, shocked by the transformation.

Her face and form were very similar to before, but her

skin had paled to cream. Her hair was a shade darker than mine, but still the color of honey in milk; in the front, it became cobalt and indigo, like gemstones spun into silk. Her eyes, previously a very ordinary blue-gray, now picked up the colors of the ocean and of her hair, so that they too shone like fair jewels.

And she was wearing her wings, enormous peregrine wings that tumbled down from her shoulders and nearly brushed the ground at her feet.

"I know it is rare in Wyvern's Court for one to wear her wings openly," she said shyly, "but on Ahnmik, very few do not. This is what I consider my true form."

She knelt and brushed a hand over the kelp that covered the island, clearing a bare, smooth space large enough for both of us to sit in.

"I hope I didn't overstep my bounds with your parents earlier," she said. "This must be very hard for them. They both left Ahnmik when they were young, and having their magic bound would have been terribly painful. It is not surprising that they would not think well of the royal house."

"How could they?" I almost asked, thinking of my father's scars. But I kept my questions to myself when I saw the fear in her eyes. "I saw them hesitate, and all I could think was that they couldn't possibly know . . . They hadn't felt your heartbeat slow and your skin cool as your magic tried to drag you down. I shouldn't have taken my fear out on them." I reached out, and she took my hand. "You're safe now. And you probably have questions."

Questions. Where could I begin? "Until last night, my parents had always refused to speak of Ahnmik—or magic."

My parents had tried to forget their pasts, and who they used to be. My father had changed his name entirely, from

Sebastian to Andreios, which he had been known by for all the years he had hidden among the avians as a crow. Both of my parents had chosen to use the surname Silvermead after their exile, in honor of the avian family that had taken my mother in when she had first fled the island, and of the dancer Valene, who had petitioned the Empress for their pardon.

"What would you like to know?" Lily asked, startling me from my thoughts. I had to stop drifting off. Of course, that was exactly what this trip was about, wasn't it?

"That moment in the woods—the one that made you so sure I had this magic—can you explain it to me?"

How could I possess something I barely understood?

"When a falcon's magic first appears, it often does unpredictable things," she said. I could see her struggling to find the right words for something that was common knowledge among her people. "The three visions might have been images from your future, necessary sights, catalysts with the power to irrevocably alter your path." Then she added with a wry smile, "Or they might have been nothing more than ghosts, people you might see, or even ones who sensed the sudden shift in magic and happened to look back at you. Blue and even silver eyes are so common on Ahnmik that I couldn't begin to guess to whom they might belong. And cobra eyes are certainly not unlikely in your future." She dismissed it all with a shake of her head. "I won't go so far as to say that all visions are without meaning, but those that come unsummoned to an undisciplined mind are most often nonsense."

"Is there anything you think that I should know, before we get to Ahnmik?"

Lily paused, fiddling with a razor-shell she had taken from the rocks. "The island may seem very overpowering when you first land. People will be able to tell that you are royal blood, and they may not know how to treat you. The royal court of Ahnmik is not as informal as the one you are used to, and people are likely to err on the side of caution.

"Araceli will probably give you leave to address her familiarly, but usually any member of the royal house is addressed as lady or, in Servos's case, as sir." Slanting an amused gaze in my direction, she added, "I suppose that means I have been horribly disrespectful with you these two years, calling you Nicias."

The suggestion made me laugh and shake my head. I was the son of two guards, and only a guard myself, which placed me one respectful step *below* the lords and ladies of Wyvern's Court. I couldn't imagine being treated as some kind of royalty on Ahnmik.

"Aside from you, the royal house has four members. Cjarsa is Empress, but she rarely grants audiences, and it is Araceli who rules the island day to day. Syfka is right hand to both Cjarsa and Araceli, and often speaks for them when they are otherwise occupied. She is also the one who normally sees to any business off the island." Syfka was rarely spoken of in Wyvern's Court, though I recognized her name from my parents' conversations. I understood that she had enabled my father to leave Ahnmik the first time and helped my mother and father both return from the island after Araceli had taken them. If Araceli proved herself as malicious as my father had painted her, then perhaps I would find an ally in Syfka. "Servos, the last of the four, is guardian to the *shm'Ecl*."

As my parents had, she spoke the word softly, her gaze haunted.

"You should recall that we falcons share history with the serpiente, not the avians," she continued. "If I had considered more carefully, I would have disguised myself as a serpent instead of an avian in Wyvern's Court, so I would not need to deal with men who felt like they had to protect the honor of a woman living alone and were shocked if I displayed an unseemly emotion." She shrugged, but I understood her point. Only the serpiente influence in Wyvern's Court had given her the freedom to maintain her independence while utilizing such a disguise. "You'll find that most falcons are as free with their emotions as the serpiente.

"Hmm, what else?" she asked, pondering. I saw her gaze at the edge of the island, which had already lost several inches to the rising tide. It would not be long before our dry resting place became ocean once again. "Of course, the old language is spoken on Ahnmik. You've been studying it in your history lessons at Wyvern's Court, but it might take you a little while to perfect its use."

Not too long, I hoped.

"Ahnmik is in your blood," Lily added, as if she could read my mind. "His words will feel natural to you."

She leaned on me, her body warm against mine. "It is a beautiful land, Nicias. Though I have enjoyed seeing other places these last two years, I have missed the white city. I have missed hearing her sing, and seeing the magic dance, and being among others who see my blue and know what it means instead of simply fearing it. You will see. Wyvern's Court is a lovely place . . . but it is not Ahnmik."

# CHAPTER 5

W E SHIFTED INTO our human forms just above the
ground and landed on a marble terrace. My knees almost went out from under me, I was so exhausted. We had
flown throughout the night, and it was now well past sunup
once again.

I was barely aware of the audience we had attracted, until
someone spoke to me.

Even once I had lifted my head to listen to his words, I
had no idea what he was saying. If I had been less exhausted,
I probably could have translated the old language, but right
then my mind refused to obey.

I blinked at him for a moment, trying to figure out what
was going on.

Thankfully Lily noticed my confusion. "He wishes to
know if you need anything," she told me.

I knew what I needed: sleep. I was having trouble standing upright; I felt as if I was being buffeted by winds from all
directions, and my vision was blurry from exhaustion.

*I should greet the Empress first,* I thought. *Or—*

Lily stepped forward to answer for me. Her voice rang with authority, the rolling language of Ahnmik coming easily to her despite the two years she had spent in Wyvern's Court. After a moment, she turned back to me and added, "They will find you somewhere to rest, and something to eat if you wish it. I apologize, but I must leave you in the capable hands of our welcoming committee, so I can present myself to my lady and let her know I am ready to return to my duties. Get some sleep."

"I can help you to your rooms, sir," a young man offered, making an effort to speak a language I knew.

As tired as I was, I did not fail to notice that the rooms I was given were more elegant than the ones Oliza occupied back in Wyvern's Court. If the pale stone and crystal sculpture lacked some of the warmth of that place, they made up for it with sparkling beauty.

My guide left me in the hands of two women, each wearing loose slacks and backless shirts, and each graced with wings that matched my own peregrine. Everyone I had seen so far had worn Demi wings, as Lily had said.

And everyone, in either the language I knew or the language I could barely understand, seemed to want to know what I needed. While I fought to stay awake, being waited on was fine with me. I wouldn't be able to exert any kind of effort if I tried.

The meal I was served was simple but delicious: freshly baked bread still hot from the oven, a savory fish soup that warmed me to the core and hot cider to drink.

As I ate, I was entertained by a choir somewhere outside the building. The words faded in and out of my awareness, but the melody was haunting.

Food and a moment to regain my bearings had helped

enough that when I was asked, "Would you like a bath readied, sir?" I had the sense to answer, "My name is Nicias."

The woman nodded. "Yes, sir."

Being called sir again sent a chill down my spine. "You can call me Nicias."

Her eyes widened a little, but she repeated, "Nicias. Would you like—"

"I think I'd rather sleep first, if you don't mind."

"Of course," she answered. "You have been shown your room?"

"Yes, I'm fine. . . . Please, I'd just like to sleep now."

Within two breaths I was left alone to seek my bed, accompanied only by the distant singing.

The bed was larger than I was used to, as everything here seemed to be, but firm enough to be comfortable and piled with the softest blankets I had ever touched.

Only as I was looking for a lamp or candle to snuff out did I realize that the abundant light seemed to be coming from the walls themselves. More specifically, from intricate designs etched into the stone.

*If I knew how to use falcon magic, I would probably be able to turn them off,* I thought, with as much humor as I could muster.

For now, I would have to be content with light. But the instant I lay down and got settled, the lights dimmed and finally shut off. The effect startled me so much that I stood up, prompting them to gradually brighten until I lay down again.

The colors in my dreams seemed brighter than usual, and the sounds softer. A melody wove itself through everything, sometimes sounding like a chorus of hundreds singing in harmony all around me, and sometimes sounding like a lone child far away. No matter how I tried, I couldn't quite make out the words.

Visions came and disappeared throughout the night.

A woman was kneeling on a floor of pure white stone with her head bent forward. Her hair was so white it seemed almost translucent, except at the front, where it darkened to violet and, finally, almost black; it fell forward, hiding her face and pooling on the floor around her. Silks that shimmered from deep indigo to silver wrapped her form in a complex gown.

Suddenly I realized that those silks not only clothed her, but bound her. Her wrists were crossed behind her back and tied there. Her eyes were covered and her ankles were pressed together.

Despite the blindfold, she looked up as I approached.

*"Hehj-ale'heah-gen'lo'Mehay?"* the wind seemed to whisper.

I found that I understood her words easily: Do you desire to know your future?

"No," I answered.

She gave a tight-lipped smile. "No man, no woman, can see the future in truth. It is all the same illusion. *Hehj-ale'heah-gen'lo'Ecl?"* Do you desire to know your past?

"No," I answered again.

"We will be here before," she said.

"I don't understand."

"You didn't," she answered. "Now you do." She began to sing, a melody slightly different than the ones I had heard earlier. It made the air ripple around us.

Then the world changed, and we were standing on the cold black ice I knew from my nightmares, with the bone white moon above. The woman's gyrfalcon wings were spread, her hair whipping around her in a wind so strong, I stumbled and tore the skin of my hands on the sharp ice. The silks that had bound her were gone, and now she was wearing a gown that looked to be made of woven gold.

Her song had changed into a scream, one that made the ice shudder around us. "This isn't your place, Nicias," she shrieked, voice like the wind. "Leave now. Dance with the light, falcon child."

I was thrown from my dream with the force of a thunderbolt and woke breathless. I flung myself out of bed and was grateful when the light snapped on. The door to the next room had been left partially open, revealing a bath that had been prepared recently enough that the water was still perfectly warm. Or perhaps magic had kept it that way for hours. I didn't know or care.

I scrubbed my skin and hair, dried with a soft towel and dressed in clothing that had been hung while I had slept.

The pants were made of a material that was softer and warmer than any I was familiar with; in lieu of a belt, they had a silver clasp on each side. The legs were comfortable and unrestricting, but laced tightly at the calves. The shirt was similar, designed to be loose around the shoulders and in the upper sleeves, but tight at the forearms and wrists. The upper back was open to allow for wings. There was no footwear, but thinking back, I didn't recall seeing any of the falcons wearing shoes the day before.

I had just finished tying back my hair when the first knock came on my door.

"Yes?"

The young woman who entered was the one I had instructed to call me Nicias the evening before. She curtsied deeply, bowing her head.

I stared at her for too long, waiting for her to rise, before it occurred to me to say, "Stand up. Can I help you?"

She stood with a smile, as if she could have knelt on my

floor all day. "I hope the room merited your approval, and you found everything you needed this morning?"

Even if something had bothered me, I wouldn't have dared to say no—not to someone who was trying so hard to please me. "Everything was fine."

"The Heir would like to see you this morning," she said, "as soon as you are ready."

Before I could say that I was ready, she reached forward to change how the cuff of my shirt was laced.

I pulled back so quickly that she dropped her gaze apologetically. "Please, my lady will be very cross with me if I let you go about Ahnmik and the palace looking like a mongrel. You don't know our ways yet. Let me help?"

Despite the sincerity in her voice, I did not care for the term "mongrel." I lived in a mixed blood land. Moreover, I knew that the word's equivalent in the old language, *quemak*, was considered by the serpiente to be uncivil. A fight would have broken out in Wyvern's Nest if one of the serpiente dancers had used it as casually as this woman just had.

She must have seen my displeasure; I saw her pale ever so slightly. I recalled my father's warning about the Empress's "mercy" and realized exactly why she was so desperate to please me—and Araceli.

I bit my tongue. I didn't want to be responsible for getting this girl—or myself—into trouble.

"I would appreciate your help," I said finally. "But please teach me so I can do it right on my own in the future."

She clapped her hands lightly, a gesture of relief and joy. "Of course!"

Over the next few minutes, I learned one crucial thing: Falcons valued appearance far too much. I had always cared somewhat about how I looked, but that was mostly out of respect for Oliza. As one of her guards, I reflected upon her.

I would try to extend that respect toward the Empress and her heir, but I couldn't help complaining when my tutor took down my hair so that she could clasp most of the blond bulk back while leaving the newly blue strands loose around my face.

"A falcon's blue is a thing to be very proud of," she explained when I reached forward to tuck those irritating strands back, "not something to be hidden."

I didn't have the heart to contradict her. I was beginning to look forward to meeting Araceli for only one reason: I wanted to have my powers bound, so that I could get off this island and go back to being Nicias Silvermead, Wyvern of Honor, instead of some preened and pampered prince of an empire ruled by fear.

Finally she asked me to grow the wings of my Demi form. "People will be very confused if they see you without them. They will wonder what you and the Lady could possibly have fought about this soon."

"Fought?" I inquired.

"Those who are a danger to the city or endangered by the city are not allowed to spread wing above her, or wear their Demi forms. That includes criminals, Pure Diamond, outsiders, and mongrels. But you are pure royal blood; the only reason you would be denied access to our sky is if the Empress or her heir barred you from it."

I frowned at the way she separated the classes of the city so easily.

"They're restricted for different reasons, of course," she added, apologetically. "Pure Diamond is a rank for falcons who learn their magic too young. They are often . . . disturbed, and need to be bound as children to keep them from harming themselves or others. Empress Cjarsa prefers that they stay on land, so that it is easier to reach them if they need her.

"As for outsiders, they are kept grounded mostly for their own protection. The city is not kind to those it does not consider its own, and it can be very disorienting from above.

"As for those with mixed blood . . ." She hesitated, and I wondered if she had intentionally changed her phrasing due to my response to the word *mongrel*. "They often have trouble controlling their magic. It makes them dangerous to others, and to themselves. They must stay on the ground, where the city's power protects them somewhat."

And what would Araceli think of me? I wondered. Despite this girl's assurance that I was royal blood, I was most certainly an outsider. I was sworn to a mixed-blood queen and I was the son of two of Ahnmik's exiled criminals. How long would it be before I was thrown into one of those sharply defined categories?

# CHAPTER 6

**B**EFORE I COULD LEAVE my room, I had to have my hair put up, my clothing corrected and my feathers carefully preened. If this was a taste of royalty, I would have no difficulty refusing any offer Araceli might make. This much attention was more than I'd ever wanted, and stepping into the open streets was a blessed relief.

In the first breathtaking moment, I realized how little of Ahnmik I had seen the day before.

The road, the walls, every building about me glistened with the same kinds of designs as were in my room; only here, instead of simply remaining silver, the patterns shifted from sea foam and emerald to coral pink and bruised cranberry. The designs seemed to dance to the music that I suddenly realized was coming not from a chorus, but from the walls.

*Magic.*

The road beneath my bare feet was warm, and though it looked as hard as crystal, when I stepped down, it felt as soft as a carpet.

"What are the towers ahead of us?" I asked, pointing to three pure white spires in the north.

*"Yenna'marl,"* my guide answered. "They are called simply the white towers, and they mark the boundaries of the testing yard. The rest of the city holds spells to keep her inhabitants' magic in check so that they can learn faster than their power can grow. But in that yard, the magic is even stronger than it is in the outside world. Careful not to stray there; the way the magic flares can be dangerous, until you have more control."

I nodded, appreciating the advice.

We had reached the arched doorway of a grand building that seemed to be made entirely of crystal, perfectly clear save what must have been hundreds of layers of magic.

We paused at the doorway, and I tried to follow the patterns as they wove under and over each other.

Suddenly it seemed so obvious. "It's writing, isn't it?" I asked in surprise. "What does this say?"

My guide looked startled. "It's not writing in the sense that you know."

"But . . . here," I argued, tracing one line. I couldn't make my eyes follow it exactly, but I still understood. "It's a prayer."

"We should go inside," she said.

"One moment, please." I struggled to grasp what I was "reading." The longer I watched the pattern, the more loudly it seemed to speak to me.

A prayer to Ahnmik.

Then the voice from my dream the night before whispered, *Nicias, child of she who is heir to the domain of ice and night, you sing here so clearly. So, careful, Nicias, remember.*

*We will be here before.*

"Nicias!"

I was wrenched back by the shoulders, spun around so quickly that I felt dizzy and reached out a hand to support myself.

Someone grabbed my wrist, steadying me as I blinked away my confusion.

*"Vesake-mana,"* my guide was mumbling from where she knelt beside us.

*"Ka'gen'lakin,"* the woman who had caught me replied.

It took me a moment to translate the brief exchange—*I'm sorry, Lady. Not your fault*—and meanwhile the woman caught my arm. *"Sine'le,"* she said, dismissing my guide, before addressing me. "Nicias, come inside."

I did as instructed, my throat parched and my eyes unfocused. "Careful, Nicias, or we'll lose you to the *shm'Ecl* before the day is out. Do you know *nothing* of your magic? Did your father . . . Of course not." She sighed. She pressed a cup into my hands and said, "Drink."

The liquid burned my tongue as I gulped it down too quickly, but it also managed to clear my head.

Suddenly I realized that my guide had addressed this woman as Lady; she was either the Empress or her heir, then. My gaze snapped up, and instantly I knew which one.

Those eyes. I knew them from that moment in the woods; when my magic had first appeared, it was her gaze that had first looked upon me.

Furthermore, these were the ice blue eyes that looked back at me from the mirror every day. Softened in some places and sharpened in others, her face was nearly the female version of my own. She smiled as I looked at her, scanning my features as I did hers.

"Son of my son," she greeted me. "Nicias of Ahnmik."

"Silvermead," I corrected automatically before it occurred to me that I might offend her.

She shook her head, laughing a little. "Your mother might have taken the name Silvermead, but your father was my son. You have the powerful wings of a peregrine, as he did, and as I do. If you did not have our magic, the songs would not call to you the way they do. Ever since I felt your magic wake a few days ago, I have known that you are worthy of your royal blood. On this island, that makes you Nicias of Ahnmik, nothing less."

I wanted to ask what she'd meant when she'd said she had felt my magic wake, why I had seen her so briefly, and who the other eyes had belonged to, for if hers had been real, then perhaps the others had been, too.

Instead, I hardened my heart against the joy I could see in her face and forced myself to say what I needed to. "I'm sorry, Lady, but I don't want to be Nicias of Ahnmik; I want only to be Nicias Silvermead. My parents sent me here to have my powers bound, so I can safely return to Wyvern's Court."

Araceli winced. "Nicias, why? What can you have there that is more than we can give you here? You weren't raised to rule, so I can understand your being daunted by that. You weren't raised in luxury, so I can understand your not desiring the finer things Ahnmik can provide you. But what does *that* world offer you? Not even love, Nicias, unless you are willing to kill any child your mate would have."

Her voice softened as she implored, "Give this world a chance." I started to argue, but she shook her head. "Nicias, I've lived nearly two millennia, and have had only one child. Letting him leave was the most painful thing I have ever done."

"Painful for whom?" I asked, knowing that my voice was harsh, but the image of my father's scars was still bitter in my memory.

"You have no concept of what our magic can do if uncontrolled," she snapped. "Your mother might have survived, though few born with power can survive long without this land's magic to protect them. Your father certainly would not have. He didn't have the training, and royal blood cannot protect one forever. The only way I could bind their magics as tightly as I needed to was to etch the spells into their skin. Even what I did might not be enough; the marks clearly weren't as strong as they should have been, or you never would have been born with power."

She spoke with such pain in her voice, I couldn't help wondering if it was true. What if the wounds she'd dealt *had* been part of the spell to keep my parents' magic from killing them? Who was I to call her a liar, I who knew nothing about this dangerous power except that even my parents were frightened by it?

"I'm sorry, Lady," I replied, shamed by my arrogance.

She sighed. "Forgiven. And please, Nicias, to you I am Araceli."

I nodded. "Araceli. I'm sorry for my impertinence a moment ago. But I still don't think this place is right for me. As you said, I wasn't raised with luxury, or servants hovering over me and calling me sir; I don't think I would become used to it, or even want to."

Again she laughed a little, the sound like bells. "Nicias, consider for a moment. For one, you are fascinating to most of the people of Ahnmik; very rarely is one of us born off the island, much less one of royal blood. Furthermore, they didn't know how much attention you would demand. If you were spoiled and arrogant and wanted to be pampered, but they ignored you, you would be far more cross than if you were modest and kind and wanted only to be left alone while they hovered. If you let them know that you prefer to be treated like an equal, that is how they will treat you."

It was difficult to reconcile the horrible person my father and mother had warned me about with the woman I was speaking to now.

"Come walk with me, Nicias," Araceli requested. "Let me present you to Empress Cjarsa, and then I shall show you around our island. You can tell me this evening whether you want your powers bound so soon. I'll warn you now, it will hurt, and it will leave you marked, and it will be irreversible. To bind your magic, I must bind your falcon form. You'll never be able to spread wing again, Nicias. I pray you will give this world a chance before you decide to throw it all away."

We walked through the palace, but its wonder was lost on me.

Pain I could deal with, if I had to. My training in Oliza's guard had taught me how to brace myself against necessary pain. Marks I could deal with. My falcon blood had already marked me, setting me apart from the others at Wyvern's Court both physically and mentally. I could stand losing magic I had never expected, and a royal position I had never wanted, too.

*But never to fly again?*

Never to set off into the sky I loved, alone or with Oliza? Never to return to the distant lands that could be reached only by wing?

I wouldn't lose just the air. I would lose Wyvern's Court. With none of the strengths of a falcon, a serpent or an avian, I would have nothing to offer as Oliza's guard. They might let me stay out of pity, but living the rest of my life in the face of that pity would destroy me.

Yet both of my parents had avian forms, even though their magic had been bound.... "How did my parents get their winged forms?"

Araceli winced as she answered, "Force-change. It is one of the higher-level abilities, and forbidden on the island in all but the most desperate situations. It is a way to temporarily take control of another's magic and body. Afterward, a skilled user of our magic retains a memory of the forms of the person he changed."

"Why is it forbidden?"

Araceli looked at me as if I was mad. "To violate another's body, magic and mind so intimately is . . ." She shook her head. "Among my people, force-change is seen in the same light as the serpents you were raised among see rape."

"If it is so abhorrent," I said tightly, "then why was it taught to both of my parents?"

"Kel was taught to force-change because she was one of the Empress's personal guards, and although the Mercy almost never need to utilize such a skill, a guardian of the royal house must be armed with as much knowledge as she can have. Sebastian . . ." Her voice wavered as she said my father's falcon name. "He was royal blood, as you are. I had no need to teach him any specific pattern; he could discover it on his own, as in time you probably will be able to, too. If you decide not to go through with this self-destructive binding, I will teach you the discipline you need to keep your magic from harming you. The rest, for royal blood, comes naturally."

"I still have trouble imagining my parents doing something they were raised to feel was so evil."

Araceli backtracked gracefully, but the distaste was not completely gone from her voice as she added, "I am sure your parents did it out of desperation. I understand both of them were attempting to save another's life. Even in this city, they would not have been reprimanded for that effort."

I wanted to ask more about that story, but Araceli's tone made it clear that the discussion was over. We walked silently for a minute and soon approached a pair of doors, each pale blue with a pattern like silver frost on the glass. A falcon guard stood on each side of them, watching us warily.

"Please tell Cjarsa that I would like to introduce her to Sebastian's son," Araceli told the guards.

"I regret to inform you that the Lady is not receiving today," one answered. Both dropped their gazes as Araceli frowned.

"I'm not some mongrel seeking to petition for a favor," she said coolly.

The door opened, and out stepped a falcon I recognized from history-book sketches: Syfka. She bowed respectfully to Araceli, but her voice held poorly concealed annoyance as she explained, "You won't be able to speak to her. I've already pushed my way past these guards; the Lady is occupied, with no time for conversation." Under her breath, she grumbled, "As she has been for weeks."

Araceli sighed and glanced at me apologetically. "Nicias, allow me to present Syfka, aplomado of the royal house and our ambassador on the mainland. Syfka, this is Nicias, son of Kel and Sebastian."

Syfka's gaze fell on me, and I saw a hint of regret in her eyes as she greeted me politely. "An honor to be introduced, sir." Before I could reply, she turned back to Araceli. "My lady, might I have a few moments of your time?"

"Can it wait? I would rather not leave Nicias alone on his first day in our city."

"As you wish, but it is a matter of some importance to both of us. I had wished to take it up with Cjarsa directly . . ." She shrugged. "It seems the Lady has more pressing concerns than her own kingdom." Araceli looked at Syfka sharply, and the aplomado quickly assured her, "No disrespect intended. As for Nicias, he is blood of our house; the land and his people will protect him, if he needs it. Ahnmik would never betray its prince, so he is in no danger wandering alone. And perhaps he would appreciate a few minutes unchaperoned, to think."

Seeing my dismissal very near, I interjected, "If I might ask one favor?"

"Yes?" Araceli replied.

"Before I make my decision on whether to stay or go, I would like to speak to my parents." They had warned me not to trust this woman. I didn't know whether she was speaking the truth about my magic and my falcon form.

"Nicias, Nicias." Araceli sighed. "When you leave this island, it must be with your magic either bound or mastered. Right now, the island is protecting you from yourself, and yet you were still hypnotized by your power at the doorway to the palace. If you try to leave now, you'll fall and drown while you're busy listening to Ecl's whispers and watching the paintings in the waves."

I recalled the way Lily had needed to grab my wings so I wouldn't fall on my way to the island. I didn't think I could risk a return trip. "Then might one of them come here?"

"Your parents are both in exile," Araceli told me bluntly.

"But you are the heir to the Empress. You must have the authority to lift that sentence long enough for them to speak to me. If you have been honest so far, then there is no risk to you in my speaking to them."

Syfka took a step back as I made that statement, even before Araceli tensed, looking as offended as if I had struck her.

"I do *not* have that authority. That is my lady Cjarsa's decision to make, as she is the one who put down the sentence upon each of them. Even if it *was* my decision," she continued, "I would not allow them back. When they fled this island, they endangered themselves, and they endangered those they'd sworn their loyalty to on the mainland.

"Your mother fled her responsibility to the Empress Cjarsa the first time she was called upon to protect her liege. Tell me, Nicias, what is the sentence among Oliza's Wyverns for a guard who abandons his post and allows his monarch to face an assassin alone?"

She did not wait for me to unravel my tongue and attempt to answer. Among the serpiente and the avians, what she was describing would be high treason, and punishable by death.

"In the years since they left," she said more softly, "it seems that both of your parents have matured. Their positions among the avians are respected, and their loyalty is unquestioned. Perhaps they have learned their lesson. But that does not excuse their first crimes. They abandoned this land when it needed them. If you stay as prince, you might have the power to pardon them someday, but until then I will not allow either one to set foot in my city."

"And what unforgivable crime did your son commit?" I asked tentatively.

Araceli's tone when she spoke of my father was like ice.

"Sebastian of Ahnmik is dead. There is a crow who holds his memories, a crow who holds his blood but not his features—the features I see so clearly in you. But my son, my only son, is dead to this world, dead to my people, and dead to me."

"What—"

"Silence," she snapped, and now the pain in her eyes was apparent. "On this topic, I demand it. We do not speak of that which is too late to change."

"My lady, I hate to interrupt," Syfka said softly, stepping forward awkwardly, "but I must speak with you, *now*."

Araceli nodded. "Walk our city if you like, Nicias," she said, distantly. "I have business I must attend to. I will summon you this evening to hear your decision. Dismissed."

I took a step away from the pair, somewhat dazed by the argument. When I had just turned the first corner, I heard Araceli say to Syfka, "I suppose it is too much to ask for his trust, when his parents have surely been speaking ill of me throughout his life. Even though I speak honestly to him and say things he would accept as reasonable if they came from a serpent or an avian, he assumes they are lies."

"Doubtless his parents think many of their words are deserved," Syfka answered.

I hesitated, curious what else they would say when they thought I was not listening.

"Perhaps some of them are," Araceli admitted. "But our war with the serpiente was over thousands of years ago, and yet they still teach their children a hatred of us." After a long silence, during which I almost continued on my way, she added, "I cannot stand to lose another child to ancient conflicts, Syfka. But how can I compete with a hatred that has endured thousands of years?"

The raw pain in Araceli's voice cut me more deeply than anything she had said so far.

As a child of Wyvern's Court, I was far too familiar with her sentiment. I had seen serpents wary of avians, and avians wary of serpents, despite the efforts our leaders had made to bring the two groups together. I had thought myself beyond that hatred because I had been born a falcon. Instead, I had learned to hate my own blood.

I continued on my way out, tracing the halls I had come through with Araceli, and resolved to try to look upon what I found here with a more open mind. I would not dismiss everything my parents had told me, but I would try not to be as biased as an avian matron watching the serpents' dance.

# CHAPTER 7

O NCE BACK OUTSIDE, I hesitated at the foot of the palace. I might have dreamed of the chance to explore this city, but to stand at its edge with no destination and no guide was overwhelming.

In the distance, I caught a glimpse of an elegant spire shimmering like a violet mirage on the horizon.

Thinking that landmark as good a destination as any, I started forward, only to find that the roads of Ahnmik twisted in unpredictable ways. What had seemed to be a straight path only moments before turned out to curve so that after several minutes I found myself on the cliffs where the ocean met the island.

Turning back, I could see the city: the three *yenna'marl*, bone white and sharp against the sky, and a trio of arches that seemed to be in the center of the city. Again, I could see only the edge of the strange violet spire.

I tried following the beach and found myself by a bridge that seemed to connect Ahnmik to another, smaller island, one peppered with lush greenery.

Exploring that area would have to wait. I had a feeling I was lost enough as it was. I glanced behind me, wanting to confirm that I could still see the *yenna'marl* and get my bearings from them.

The odd tower that had caught my attention was practically brushing against the road on which I now stood. How could that be?

It seemed almost as if the walls were made of liquid, and the violet that had seemed so bold at a distance was muted up close. The arched doors were smoke black glass, slick and ominous in the white city. They had no handles, though I could see the seam between the two. Two symbols marked that doorway: *shm'Ecl.*

*If you can't, it will destroy you,* my father had warned me. *It will numb your body and mind, until it drives you into what is called* shm'Ecl. *There are rooms on Ahnmik filled with those who have succumbed to it, those who could not learn to control their power. They are neither alive nor dead, neither awake nor asleep.*

I pushed against the doors almost in a daze, bracing myself for whatever lay beyond and yet needing to see the fate my parents feared so much.

Inside, the building was completely silent. All day I had been listening to the songs Ahnmik sang, music that seemed to seep from the walls and roads, but now I felt as if I had been struck deaf. The air was heavy, so thick with power that walking was like trying to move underwater.

The hall in which I stood was round, with a silver domed ceiling, and walls that were pale at the top but darkened to nearly black where they touched the floor. A spiral ramp circled along the edges of the room, ascending to where it hid the rest of the ceiling from my view and descending beneath the level of the floor. All along the walls were doorways, some open and some closed.

"*Maenka'Mehay-hena'hehj? Meanka'las?*" a deep voice asked. What lies beyond *Mehay*? Beyond eternity? The old language came more easily to me now, and I understood what he said as he continued. "Nothingness, *Ecl*. That which never was and never can be. Commonly, it is translated as destruction, but more accurately it is lack of existence."

I turned to find a man whose body and face made him appear a few years younger than I, but whose eyes, liquid blue like the ocean, gave him away as being ancient.

"The minds of the *shm'Ecl* are lost somewhere that we in this world can never hope to reach. Their magic is unpredictable. In some moments, they lash out at hallucinations, nightmares, pain that drives them ever further from us. But most times, they are simply still, their minds as numb and empty as the womb of the void."

"Servos?" I asked when he paused and stared into the distance.

He nodded, not seeming to focus entirely on me. "And you are Nicias."

*Nicias?*

A voice whispered through my mind, making me jump. It was one that I had heard several days before, when I had first fallen in the woods, and then again in my dreams.

Servos sighed.

I heard the song from my dream, heard it and for the first time understood the words.

*Of eternity, of silence, of coldness, of stillness. Of* Ecl. *He who dwells with* Ecl *knows of void. He who dwells with* Ecl *knows of death. But he who dances with* Ecl, *he is lost, for he who dances with* Ecl *brings to life the world of death. So dance.*

The song sent a shudder down my spine.

"You hear it?" Servos asked.

I nodded, searching the room for the singer.

"You can't see her from here; her room is near the top of this hall," Servos explained. "Her name was Darien. She was a dancer, and part of the highest choir. Most people cannot hear her voice, even when they stand beside her."

*Of eternity, of madness, of heat, of movement. Of* Mehay. *He who dwells with* Mehay *knows too much. He who dwells with* Mehay *knows of creation. But he who dances with* Mehay, *he is lost, for he who dances with* Mehay *cannot leave the dance and will face the fire. So dance.*

"If you'll excuse me," Servos said abruptly, "I need to see to one of my charges."

He did not wait for a response from me, but turned to descend the ramp underground.

Darien's song stopped and was replaced by a whispered chant:

*Nicias Silvermead, Wyvern of Honor, Nicias of Ahnmik, heir to the heir of she who shines in darkness, Nicias fool child, Nicias wise one.*

The words fluttered in my ears, almost teasing, sighing along a few notes from on high. Irresistibly drawn, I started up the ramp. I thought that the *shm'Ecl* were not aware of their surroundings, yet this woman who was supposedly one of them called me by my name and by many titles, some of which I used for myself and some of which I wanted no claim to.

My gaze was drawn to one of the open doorways I passed. Inside, a figure was lying on the floor, her ink-dark falcon wings crumpled behind her, broken and scored by tarlike bands of black and crimson. Unlike the graceful, delicate designs that painted the white city, these marks were vicious and ugly, but they shone with the iridescent sheen I had come to associate with falcon magic.

I did not know her by name, but I recognized the familiar line of her jaw, texture of her ebony hair and warmth of her fair skin. I was sworn to the royals of Wyvern's Court, which included the Cobriana, and I could not fail to note that this young woman had cobra blood.

I knelt and put a hand on her arm, needing to try even though I had little hope of stirring her.

Without warning, I found myself back in my nightmares. The black ice rippled and warped, jutting skyward to form razor blade walls, uneven and mazelike. Beneath it, I saw shadows moving, talons and fangs scraping the ice as they reached for me, and I shuddered.

I leapt aside as a serpent reared its head, blocking my path, the tips of its milky fangs glistening with drops of venom. As I stumbled, my arm brushed against one of the jagged walls of ice, and I gasped in pain as my skin was sliced open.

*It is only illusion,* I told myself, hoping that was true.

I stepped toward the serpent. There were glints of red in its eyes, like the vermilion magic on the girls' black feathers.

It spread its hood, but there was no crest on its back as I was used to from my dealings with other cobras. Only this slick black on black.

*I see you've met my daughter, Hai.* Darien's voice whispered through the land. *Her father was . . .* The cobra slid soundlessly into the ice, and the jagged landscape smoothed as Darien trailed off, leaving a lingering sense of sorrow.

*Your mother could walk the minds of those no one else could touch,* Darien told me. *It seems you have inherited her skill. I don't recommend it, not here in the Halls of* shm'Ecl. *The minds of* Ecl's *lovers are unfriendly places.*

*Come to me. We need to speak.*

She pushed me from the illusion.

The first thing I realized when I returned to reality was that my arm truly was cut. The cloth of my shirt was not torn, but the skin beneath was; my own blood had darkened the fabric. A black coil of magic, like that which wrapped Hai's wings, had twined around my hand, and I could feel where it snaked up my arm and across my shoulder. Cold seeped from the tarlike bands.

I stood unsteadily, holding my hand against my chest and wondering whether Servos would be able to explain all this to me. Or maybe Darien herself.

A few wobbly steps up the ramp took me to another doorway, and beyond this one, I heard a voice I knew.

"My lady suggested that I visit you this morning, to make sure I am ready to return to her side. I had a dream last night, you see," Lily was saying to a still form before her, "in which you woke. You came back to me. . . ." She sighed. "This morning when I first opened my eyes, I thought for a moment that it was true. We—"

She tensed and without turning said, "Nicias, meet my brother, Mer." Lily pushed herself to her feet, so I could see her brother clearly.

Mer's features would have given away their relationship even if Lily had not spoken of it. He knelt on the floor, his wings tucked behind him, his head bowed and his hands on his knees.

The posture was so relaxed and peaceful, he looked as if he was about to draw a breath and stand.

"Oh dear," Lily whispered as she took in my condition and swiftly crossed the room to take my hand. "Someone should have warned you. The *shm'Ecl* who respond to nothing else can sometimes still sense royal blood. Not all of them are happy to be drawn from their dreams. Hold on a moment, and I can fix this."

As she spoke, she unlaced the cuff of my sleeve and pushed the material off my arm to assess the damage. The bleeding had already stopped, and now the black lines on my skin began to fade away. Even the bloodstains on my shirt disappeared.

"Who was it?" she asked.

"A girl, further down. She looked like she had cobra blood."

"Hai," Lily said softly. "Her father was a serpent who came to this land several years ago; her mother—" She shook her head. "The Empress's laws forbid our kind from having children with outsiders, because they always turn out this way. Their magic grows too quickly, too wildly. As a young child, Hai would become lost in illusions no one else could see. One day she stopped speaking. Finally, a few years ago, she fell while dancing. She lost control of her magic, and you can see what it did to her. Even if she regains her mind, her wings are broken; she will never fly again."

"With all the magic on this island, there is no one who can heal her?" I asked.

"Hai is . . ." Lily hesitated, seeming to look for words that wouldn't offend me. "It may sound harsh, but she *is* mixed-blood. The cobra blood in her is like a poison. It will always burn her, and it will burn anyone who tries to save her. Those few who are strong enough to mindwalk the *shm'Ecl* are needed elsewhere. They cannot afford to risk themselves trying to save one *pt'vem* dancer."

She might be "one *pt'vem* dancer" on Ahnmik, but all I

could see were her torn wings and tortured body, and the pain she must be in.

Walking out of those halls with Lily, while leaving that broken cobra behind, went against every vow I had ever taken as a Wyvern of Honor, but I had to do it. There was no way to help her.

# CHAPTER 8

AFTER WE LEFT the hall, we did not speak of Hai, and for some reason I felt oddly reluctant to speak of Darien.

"Are the roads really singing?" I asked instead. I had heard my parents and Lily say that they did, but I had always assumed that the phrase was a metaphor for beauty.

Only when Lily looked at me with surprise did I realize that I had fallen into the old language without thinking. It simply felt natural to me, like something remembered instead of learned.

My own surprise made her laugh. "Ahnmik's voice is the one spoken by your magic, by your blood and your dreams," she explained in the same language. "I told you that you would learn it swiftly, once you were here." Returning to my original question, she said, "Outsiders don't hear anything, but to one who is falcon-born, they sing. They also shift position. And some say that if you close your eyes and walk blindly down them, they will lead you where you should go." Wryly, she added, "But I don't recommend it. They have a dry sense of humor, and a tendency to dump unsuspecting zealots in the water, or lead them into very awkward positions. Though there is a story of a young man who found his true love when the roads led him through the back door of her house and into her bedroom."

I laughed, my curiosity piqued. Perhaps that was why I had been unable to find the halls that had caught my eye from across the island until I had turned my attention elsewhere.

"So the roads are alive in a way?"

"They're imbued with thousands of years of magic from those who live here, soaked with their dreams and thoughts, and thus given a personality of their own. Sometimes if you sing, they will sing back to you. Or sometimes they will knock you off your feet, depending on whether you can carry a tune."

"Dangerous paths to walk."

Lily stopped, tilting her head as if she had heard something. "If you would like to begin your study, Araceli is available now."

"How . . ." I trailed off because the question seemed stupid in this realm.

Lily answered anyway, though not how I had expected. Her voice brushed across my mind, as it had at Wyvern's Court.

*It is a skill you will learn swiftly*, she told me. "This way," she added aloud.

How long had it been since Araceli and Syfka had left me alone in the city? I had not managed once to think about the consequences of having my magic bound. How was that possible?

I had thought us far from the *yenna'marl*, but we turned a single corner and were only a few steps from the courtyard.

There was no visible fence or wall around the testing

yard, just the abrupt change from the crystalline roads to the white sand. In the center of the triangular yard was a pool of water, its surface like glass; offset around it were three white birch trees, each reaching toward the sky like a pale hand.

Araceli was kneeling there, her fingertips trailing through the still water. When she saw us, she stood and approached.

As she crossed the shimmering sand, it held no footprints, no sign that anyone had been there only moments before.

She nodded at Lily, but spoke to me. "Nicias, I apologize for leaving you alone earlier, but my meeting with Syfka could not wait. I am glad to see that you found a capable guide in my absence. Are you ready for your first lesson?"

She said this as if we had not argued the last time we had spoken, as if we had agreed and the decision had been made.

"I have some questions first, if you don't mind," I said, though I didn't know what she could say that would make me feel more certain.

My choice was either to master my magic, or to have it bound. If I had it bound at this point, I would be giving up everything. Perhaps I could learn just enough to be able to do a force-change. I recalled the harsh way Araceli had spoken of that magic. I knew that even if I found someone willing to donate his wings, I would never be able to take them.

"Yes?" At Araceli's prompting, I struggled to put my thoughts into coherent order.

"I do still intend to go back to Wyvern's Court," I asserted.

She nodded.

"By studying here, am I tying myself to this land? Or will I be able to leave when I choose?"

"I learned from your father that one does not attempt to imprison a prince in his own kingdom," Araceli said, her words obviously chosen with care. "Once I believe you have enough control over your magic to survive off this island, I will let you leave. You are lucky in that your royal blood will *enable* you to gain that kind of control. Most falcons are never able to safely leave the island."

I heard the prerequisite in her promise. "And if I chose to leave today?"

"I wouldn't need to stop you," she said. "I would need only to send Lillian to pick you up out of the ocean, hopefully before you sank too deep for us to bring you back."

I shuddered at the unpleasant image. "Can you give me some idea of how long it will be, then, before you will deem it safe for me to leave?"

"Falcon children are tested for their magic for the first time when they are four years old. They grow up using magic; they begin to memorize its patterns as naturally as they learn to speak and walk." She paused to consider. "The bonds on your parents and the way in which you were raised denied you that early training. I don't doubt that once you gain *any* control over your power, you will learn its finer points quickly. However, I don't know how difficult that first step might be." The first hints of impatience slipping into her voice, she added, "The sooner you allow me to begin your instruction, the sooner we can find out."

She was right. I didn't really have a choice, except for whether to keep fighting the inevitable.

I had one more question, though, about a term I had heard recently. "What is mindwalking?"

Araceli looked startled. She looked at Lily, who said, "I

mentioned it to him. He had done it accidentally and run into a little bit of trouble."

"I see. Well," Araceli replied, "a mindwalker is someone who can step into another person's thoughts, to speak, or to see what they see. It is a required ability for anyone in the Mercy, so naturally your mother was quite talented in that area. It can be a dangerous pastime when used idly, so I recommend avoiding the *shm'Ecl* until you have more control. In the meantime, if we have trouble reaching your magic through traditional lessons, perhaps we can see whether you can recreate the fluke that led you to mindwalk the first time. Assuming you intend to study, of course."

She said this in such a way that I knew she had seen my decision on my face. I nodded. I would study my magic, and then I would return to Wyvern's Court. Perhaps somewhere along the way, I could learn something that would help Hai.

"Excellent," Araceli said. "Come with me, Nicias. Lillian, would you care to assist us?"

"As you wish, my lady."

Araceli started to lead us both toward the courtyard.

When I hesitated, recalling the warnings I had been given about this yard, she turned. "Most of the city is wrapped in spells to keep you from drowning in your power before you can control it. Unfortunately, those same spells will hamper your ability to learn, until you have the conscious control to reach past them. In this courtyard, your magic will be at its strongest, stronger even than it would be off the island."

That was exactly what I was afraid of.

"You won't be able to come here without me for a while yet," Araceli assured me, "but so long as I am with you, I will be able to protect you."

I winced as the light seemed to brighten and the air warmed around me the instant I stepped onto the soft white sand.

Araceli took a deep breath, closing her eyes for a moment, and all at once I sensed the magic that she exuded. I fell instinctively into a soldier's ready, right hand grasping left wrist beneath my wings. I waited for her instruction.

"Put your hands up, mirrored to mine," she told me.

I did as she ordered, moving into what I knew only as a common starting position in serpiente dance. Arms crossed at the wrists, the backs of my hands and forearms lightly touched the same on her.

"Ahnmik's symbol is a pure white falcon, diving through a black sky. Close your eyes and see that," Araceli ordered.

I did as she said, and found that the image came easily to my mind's eye. I hoped that I would do as well here as I had elsewhere throughout my life. My parents had feared for my safety in sending me here, and if I did not return in a few days' time, they would begin to worry that I was not going to.

"I'm going to blindfold you now," Araceli said. "You are used to using your eyes. I hope to make you learn to see another way."

Her arms once again pressed lightly against mine as she tied the blindfold and returned to our original position.

"You were raised a warrior, so this exercise should be easiest for you," she said.

That was the only warning she gave. I felt the flare of her magic as if it lashed out in an attack—and I knew I had to respond.

If she had thrown something at me, my arms would have lifted to catch it. Now my magic did the same, and I had no conscious thought as to how.

I knew we never moved physically, but we might as well

have fought, danced, run, flown. The magic rippled between our still bodies.

The activity stretched until I had no sense of the world Araceli had blinded me to. There was only the power, shifting and swirling in patterns complex and simple at the same time, bright and dark, silent yet singing.

Sweat was beading on my brow, and my breath and heartbeat were racing when she finally broke contact. My body swayed with exhaustion and I stumbled down to one knee. Lily was there immediately, her touch soft and familiar as she offered me a cup full of cold, clear water. I reached up to remove the blindfold, thinking the lesson was over.

*Not yet, Nicias,* Araceli said. *Stand up.*

I hesitated, feeling every ache in my body all at once.

*Stand up,* she ordered me again.

Standing right then was perhaps the most difficult thing I had ever done, but I forced myself to obey her command. The sun, which had previously warmed the front of my body, was now an unwelcome weight on my back.

Araceli's magic struck me harder, and it was Lily's hand on my arm that held me up, even as I felt my magic sluggishly respond.

*Release him, Lillian,* Araceli said, sternly. *Nicias, try to push back at me.*

Tentatively, I reached out, trying to do consciously what I had done instinctively before. I managed . . . something, I thought.

*Again.*

I tried again, and when I fumbled, I felt Araceli's power slap across mine.

"Enough," she finally declared, pulling back. I felt a tug as she untied the blindfold; then I was blinking against the light of Ahnmik. The day had disappeared while we had been working, but the white towers glowed softly, as if reflecting moonlight that the clouds above concealed.

It felt as if the ground shifted beneath me; I braced myself against the dizzy spell, closing my eyes and breathing deeply. Araceli nodded to Lily, who came back to my side, steadying me. I flinched when she first touched my arm. My skin was badly sunburned, but it healed instantly at her touch.

Again she offered water, and I drank greedily.

"Ahnmik's magic is not gentle and its study is not easy. We will need to work on your endurance before you can master it," Araceli said. For the moment, all I desired was sleep. "I will see you tomorrow for your next lesson. For now, rest. Lillian, help him get home safely."

# CHAPTER 9

LILY AND I walked toward my rooms mostly in silence. Part of me felt exhilarated by the lesson, and the memories of the shifting power. Another part felt acute frustration. Never in my life, in classes or training or any other form of study, had I worked so hard and accomplished so little. I didn't know what I had learned, if anything.

Lily put a hand on my arm, drawing me back from my bleak thoughts as we reached the doorway to my rooms.

"Careful," she said. "You've burned a great deal of power today—more than you're used to losing so fast. Sometimes it can lead to melancholy. Are you hungry?"

I shook my head. "Strangely, no."

"Not strangely," she corrected. "It's normal, especially the first few days. You will learn quickly that your magic can sustain you. But watch out; as soon as your body remembers that it requires food, you'll wake up starving."

She pushed open the door, and I followed her in, watching the lights emerge from the patterns in the walls as we entered.

"Why don't you take down your wings and relax?" she suggested. Her own wings slid against her body and faded away as she spoke, hidden until she was ready to walk about the city again. She stretched, arching her back and twining her fingers together behind her.

I did the same, but flinched as I discovered a sea of pulled muscles. They would stiffen that night and ache the next day.

"I've never worn my Demi form for this long in my life," I said, carefully rolling my shoulders to try to work out some of the kinks.

Lily winced in sympathy and moved behind me.

"If you'll lie down, I'll rub your back for you."

"That would be wonderful," I said before I'd had a chance to think the answer through.

I had been raised close enough to the serpiente that casual touch did not shock me, but I was still very avian at heart, and I had a moment of unease as I lay on the bed, head resting on my hands, with an attractive woman beside me. Even more so the first time her palms smoothed down my back.

I had never thought of Lily that way before, because neither of us had ever been available. I had always known that she would have to return to Ahnmik. And I had always been one of Oliza's Wyverns.

"You are either angry, frightened, or nervous," Lily said. "I don't think I frighten you, and I certainly hope I don't anger you."

She left unspoken the last possibility. As she sat on the bed beside me, I started to push myself up.

We *still* were not available.

Lily's gentle hands on my shoulders directed me back

down. "Relax, Nicias." Her voice betrayed the laughter she was trying to subdue. "Relax."

I took a deep breath and concentrated on doing as she said. Eyes closed, I let myself think of nothing more than the feeling of sore, tense muscles being worked out.

Beyond where her hands touched my skin, I felt a faint tickling sensation, a warm buzz that made me so calm I thought I might sink through the mattress. Magic. I recognized it, but the desire to question her drifted away.

"Much better." She sighed. Her hair swept across my skin as she leaned over my back, and I would have tensed again if I could have summoned the energy to do so.

She brushed my hair to the side, and her fingers slid through the indigo feathers that grew at my nape. "Relaxed now?"

Suddenly . . . not exactly.

And even less so when her lips touched my shoulder, silently offering and asking at the same time.

I sat up, and this time Lily did not stop me. She just flopped onto the bed, letting out a heavy breath.

"Nicias—"

"You know I have to go back to Oliza," I said. I pushed myself to my feet, wanting very much to hold Lily, but fighting not to. "I can't stay on Ahnmik. And I know you need to stay. So we can't—"

"Nicias, I'm no avian sweetheart," she said softly. "I'm not offering marriage. I'm offering companionship, a heartbeat beside yours." She sighed, her blouse stretching taut across her chest, which did not help me keep control. "You've lived so close to the serpiente, how can it still be alien to you to sleep with another life beside you?"

I took a step back, needing to put more distance between us.

The problem was that it *wasn't* completely alien to me. As a child, I had shared a serpiente-type nest with Oliza; her cousin, Salem; and a few others. I had stopped doing so before I had joined the Wyverns, but I often missed the warmth and company as I slept.

"I know I will never be first to you," she said, as if reading my mind. "You have sworn your loyalty to Oliza much as I have sworn my loyalty to the white Lady, and nothing—*nothing*—will ever precede her in your heart. Duty will forever come first to you; I admire that because it is the same for me. But loyalty does not have to displace every other kind of love. For right now, neither of us is called upon. For tonight, we can just . . . be."

There was no arguing with that.

Lily was right. Oliza had my vow. I would give my life for my queen. Until that day, however, that life should be mine to do with as I chose.

Before I could speak or make a move, Lily let out a frustrated prayer of *"Ecl* spare the girl who waits for you to make up your mind."

Then she kissed me, standing on her toes and leaning against my body. Tentatively, I let myself put an arm around her back, holding her close, and I felt her lips smile against mine before she drew back just enough to speak.

"If you want me to go, I'll go," she said, softly, blue eyes vulnerable. "But I would rather stay. And I think you would rather I stayed."

She stayed. I stayed. The night was marvelous, and I had one vivid thought before I fell asleep: *I could get used to this.*

And then I was somewhere else entirely, back upon the nightmare landscape that was now familiar to me: Hai's world. Black sand dunes appeared, frozen forever in place. Far away I could see the high turrets of a castle, but when I took a step toward them, I heard an ominous hiss.

The black cobra reared its head.

I took a step back, willing myself elsewhere, and soon found that I stood before another figure.

Darien was pacing furiously, dressed in suede slacks, vest and boots. Her white-gold hair flowed behind her, loose and wild, not quite in time with her movements.

"Before you ask," she said sharply, "yes, you are asleep. And yes, I am really speaking to you. It is difficult to do so here. You should come back to the hall where they keep me."

She paused and looked directly at me with eyes that seemed to shift color: from green, to blue, to violet, and finally to pale gray.

"I can't right now," I said, my own voice alien to me. "I'm not quite sure why I *should*, either."

"Fool child," she spat. "Trusting fool child. A woman bats her eyes at you, and you think she's harmless." She shoved my shoulders, sending me stumbling on the ice, which was suddenly slicker than before. "Another woman shares stories of how it hurt—oh, how sad she was—when she tortured her son for days and exiled him from his homeland. And you trust them both with your body, your mind, and your magic."

"Do I have any more reason to trust you? You're supposed to be mad."

Her face fell. As she sighed, a cold wind whipped across the ice, making all the hairs on my arms rise as I shivered.

"Yes, mad," she whispered. "Mad for challenging the white Lady, for daring to defy her. For daring to despise the woman your father once called mother, and your lover calls Queen. You didn't realize that, did you? When Lillian speaks of her Empress, she means *Araceli*. She is guilty of treason in her heart if not in action. If I was still sworn to my lady Empress, I would have brought dear Lily before her long ago."

"You're not endearing yourself to me," I said coldly.

She looked at me as if I had not even spoken. "But you, Nicias, you are not the Empress or her heir. You may even have some sort of a heart, despite the poison from your royal blood."

*That* was a rousing endorsement. "Why do you hate Araceli so?"

"Why does the cat hate a mouse?" she returned. "Why, more like, does the mouse hate a cat?" She whipped her head to the side, as if hearing something else. "Not now."

"Darien?"

"I thought no one remembered my name anymore, save Servos," she said, softly. "All those who mattered have forgotten. It is nice to hear you speak it."

Darien's eyes burned violet as she looked at me.

"A word of advice, *prince,* for your travels in our fair city. Everyone on this island is a pawn. You, me. Syfka. Cjarsa. Everyone. It's accepted; it's *expected.*" She sighed and whispered, "I borrowed a feather of your soul, son of the son of she who shines in the darkness, she who glints on ice. I borrowed it and kept it safe."

"What are you talking about?" I demanded.

"I borrowed it and made it dance for me, and it said . . ."
She let out a falcon's shriek that made the ice shatter in all directions. I struggled to stay out of the water underneath, but felt myself falling.

"It said, son of the son of the Lady, that you would destroy an empire."

I fell into the water and felt it close over my head before I struggled back to the surface to find Darien kneeling on a patch of unbroken ice, offering her hand.

"I could never forgive myself if I let Kel's child drown here," she whispered.

I took her hand, and she pulled me up, whispering, *Come to me, Nicias. We need to speak.*

Then I was awake, shuddering from the dream that wasn't a dream. I needed to go to her. I needed to know what she meant.

Lily snuggled against me, her eyes heavy-lidded with sleep, looking much bluer at this hour. "Something wrong?"

"No, no," I answered, perhaps too hastily. "Go back to sleep. I need to talk to someone."

She threw an arm around my waist, snuggling against my side as I tried to stand up. "It's the middle of the night. You don't need to talk to anyone right now."

"I should—"

"Nicias, go back to sleep," she said, laughing and reaching toward me to run a hand up my chest. "Or, if you don't want to sleep, I'm sure we can find a way to pass the time. But if you wander around Ahnmik alone at this hour, you're asking the roads—if not *Ecl* herself—for trouble. Whatever it is, it can wait."

I sighed, relaxing back into her arms. I didn't even know

anymore why I had wanted to see Darien. She hated Araceli and Lily, and her own daughter had shown me how dangerous *shm'Ecl* were, despite their apparent stillness. I had no sane reason to go to Darien now, and plenty of reasons to stay with Lily.

# CHAPTER 10

THE NEXT MORNING dawned cool and misty—or so I was told. By the time Lily and I woke and greeted the day, most of the fog had burned off and the air was as pleasant as in springtime. I awoke to find slender silver lines along my chest and stomach. When I asked about them, Lily blushed.

She brushed a hand across the marks, making my breath catch as the magic oscillated. "Harmless," she said. "Think of them as . . . love marks. Though I can remove them if they worry you."

With her eyes that beautiful indigo, her hair still rumpled from sleep and her hands on my chest, there wasn't much that could worry me.

We bathed and dressed, then emerged into Ahnmik with the languor that always follows deep sleep. Lily unfurled her wings as soon as we stepped into the outside world, reminding me to do the same.

It also reminded me of a question. "I was told that outsiders and mongrels"—I still hesitated to say that word *quemak,* though I had accepted that the falcons used it differently—"are not allowed to wear their wings in the city, but when I saw Hai among the *shm'Ecl,* she was wearing hers."

Lily's expression was grim as she said, "The Empress favored the girl, and made an exception to the law. She regretted it when Hai became a poignant example of why mongrels are forbidden in the sky. The city is not kind to those it does not consider its own."

*More say that they are imbued with thousands of years of magic from those who live here, soaked with their dreams and thoughts, and thus given a personality of their own.* Lily had said that to me earlier, when I had asked whether the roads were alive. Now the memory prompted a dark thought.

"You said the city's mind comes from those who have lived here," I said. "Wouldn't that mean its actions toward outsiders are inspired by its inhabitants' feelings toward them?"

Lily laughed, shaking her head. "Oh, Nicias." Her amused tone seemed to say "You are being terribly naïve, and it's terribly cute." I found that when she looked at me with eyes that were nearly violet in the morning light, I lost my breath as well as my desire to argue.

For now, I was content to listen to Ahnmik's music and watch the people who passed, all of them wearing the wings of gyrfalcons, peregrines, aplomados and merlins.

One of the buildings we passed was a kitchen, and Lily picked out two small freshly baked bread loaves with honey for us to nibble on as we walked. I wasn't particularly hungry, but made myself eat anyway. Maybe food would fortify me, in case that day's lesson with Araceli was as rigorous as the one the day before.

It didn't—at least, not enough for me to notice a difference.

Around noon Araceli called for a break, and we sipped mint tea as we discussed things of great and little relevance.

The conversation turned to my life in Wyvern's Court. "The two civilizations aren't exactly combined," I explained. "But they've come a long way since the wars. Right now, the northern slopes are primarily avian, and the southern slopes are primarily serpiente. The two groups do gather in the market, though, and many of the younger ones share classes. The older generation has bent as far as they are able just by moving there, but their children will go further," I said confidently. "It's a slow process, but I have faith in them, and faith in Oliza to lead them."

Araceli sighed. "It's amazing to the point of frightening, those two working together."

I nodded. "My parents have told me enough stories of war to make me glad that I was born in peace."

I instantly regretted mentioning my parents. To Lily and Araceli, they were very different individuals from the ones I knew and loved.

"I remember your mother a little, from when I was a child," Lily said, tentatively. Araceli sighed and nodded for Lily to continue. "But then, watching the Indigo Choir dance is not something anyone could forget, no matter how young."

"The choirs dance?" I asked, confused.

"Each choir is a rank, and each rank is defined by how many levels of our magic its members can weave," she explained. "It takes most people centuries to master as many layers as your mother managed in the sixteen years before she fled. Kel was among the Empress's favored from the time she was seven. I remember how much I envied her for that as a child. No one ever spoke Kel's name without pride, without respect." Softly, she added, "And then she left it all behind."

I wondered if Lily shared Araceli's opinion about my mother's actions. "Do you know why?"

"No one's ever content with what they have, I suppose," Lily answered carefully. It was the same thing Oliza had said to me on my last day in Wyvern's Court.

Araceli scoffed. "Kel had earned the highest rank a non-royal peregrine can achieve in a fraction of the time such prowess usually takes. That power, along with the Empress's favor, and her fame as a dancer, gave her a great deal of arrogance."

"But how can you say—"

She put up a hand to silence me. "Your mother was always restless, but she had sworn herself as one of the Empress's personal guards. When she began to feel the weight of the duty she had chosen, she fled rather than face it."

The picture Araceli painted was so different than any I would ever have associated with my mother. It chafed so much that I couldn't help challenging Araceli. "And my father?"

I expected her to silence me again, but instead, Araceli looked away, drew a deep breath and attempted to answer me.

"First Sebastian wanted to learn about other places. I was wary of letting him go, but Syfka argued reasonably on his behalf, so I allowed him to act as a kind of ambassador to the avians. Suddenly he announced that he was in love with a hawk. It was a childhood infatuation, and if I had treated it as such, it would have blown over, but I overreacted, demanded he return home, pressured him too much. And lost him."

Both my parents sounded like impulsive children running away from home.

*"I do not care for the girl I used to be,"* my mother had said to me once, when I had asked why she never spoke of her past. My father had said almost exactly the same thing: *"Sebastian of Ahnmik, if he had survived, was not a man I would have wanted to know."* I had always assumed that they hated their past selves due to the land that had shaped them. Was it possible that they had disowned their pasts because they *had* been as flighty and immature as Araceli described? They had grown since and learned the ideals of duty and loyalty and honor that they had taught to me. Surely they would hate remembering that they had once fled their responsibilities rather than facing them.

I was grateful when Araceli asked, "Are you ready to return to training now?"

I stood up and stretched, then answered bravely, "Anytime." I would rather be buffeted by her magic than by these dark thoughts.

Once again, we stood in the sun, my eyes blinded by what Araceli called falcon's silk—a silvery, shimmering piece of cloth that Lily had summoned effortlessly when Araceli had asked her to, weaving the fabric with nothing but air and magic.

Araceli began the same exercise we had performed the day before, this time without her arms against mine to guide me.

*Good*, she said, encouragingly. *Again.*

We continued, the dance performed without either of us moving.

*Again.*

*One more time.*

*Nicias, Nicias Silvermead . . .*

I felt myself pull back as Darien's call echoed in my mind.

"Nicias of Ahnmik, focus!" That command came from Araceli.

I felt Darien slip in between Araceli and me. I was distantly aware that *she* was dealing with Araceli now, mimicking my faltering attempts at the magic to keep Araceli from sensing that anything was amiss.

*Nicias, leave them and come to me tonight,* Darien crooned. *If you want power, I can give you power—*

Her voice faded away, then came back sharper than before.

*Nicias, you wear lines of magic on your skin. Are you fool enough to think they are harmless?*

For a moment, I felt uneasy. What did I really know about falcon magic?

*Tonight, Nicias, come to me.*

Then she was gone, and I staggered under Araceli's magic. The blindfold was pulled away, and I blinked against the unexpected light.

"That's enough," Araceli said. "You did well. Within the next few days, perhaps, we can start working on simple Drawings."

I wasn't paying much attention to her, just nodding mechanically to acknowledge the compliment.

What if Darien was right? My mother and father had warned me about Araceli, as Darien was doing now.

But Darien was mad.

Yet she had given me very real and sane doubts. "I think I'm going to—"

Lily leaned against my side, sighing tiredly, before I could finish my sentence. I needed some time to walk around the city on my own again, but I didn't have the heart to send her away.

"If you aren't too tired, you would probably enjoy watching the dancers," Lily suggested. "Indigo Choir performs tonight."

Araceli nodded. "I know that the serpents you were raised with still dance, performing what they recall of the ancient steps, but you have never seen a true *sakkri* performed. It is a sight you should not miss."

# CHAPTER 11

AS DUSK FELL, Lily hurriedly led me through the glitter-ing streets and toward the triple arches I had seen from a distance, but had never tried to locate.

"There are three arches, at different heights," she explained as we approached. "Talented air-dancers test their wings by trying to fly through the tiny space between where the arches almost intersect. I've known more than one arrogant dancer who has lost pinfeathers and pride to that trick—myself included, I admit. The air-dancers we will see tonight are all of the highest rank." She squeezed my hand. "Trust me, you will be amazed. Especially since you have only seen the dull imitations done by the serpiente. These are real."

I was about to defend the dancers I had grown up with when we passed through the veil of magic that separated the arches from the rest of the city. The air changed, cooling slightly. The music around us also changed, from the indistinct singing of the roads to the murmur of voices hushed in anticipation.

The five dancers were gathered at the center of the arches,

facing each other with their arms crossed at the wrists and their fingertips touching those of the person next to them. They stood like statues, moving only to breathe, which they did in perfect unison.

"What do you mean, these are 'real'?" I asked.

"Serpiente dance with their bodies, and that is it," Lily said. "A falcon dancer uses her body to weave magic. When the serpents perform the *daraci'Kain*, you watch and perhaps enjoy the dance. When Indigo Choir performs the *daraci'Kain*, you feel the rain on your skin. You are the thunder. The magic speaks of love, and you feel love so powerfully, you would give everything to keep it; it speaks of fear, and you shake in terror. Wait and see."

Lily's description didn't make me eager to experience this, but in that moment the last of the day faded, and the five dancers hit the first note of the music together. They were answered by the arches themselves, which began to sing as the five moved into the first steps of the dance.

The first turn left a trail of silver magic. The dancers were like shadows, silhouettes against the colorful patterns the dance left behind.

I closed my eyes for a moment and could still see the dance and the magic, ripples of silver, plum, violet, burgundy, deep sapphire and rich emerald building and hanging in the air.

Suddenly I could feel more than myself, more than the dancers; I could feel the breath of the city, how the magic was wrapped into everything—even the *shm'Ecl*. I felt pure love as the city kissed its sleeping kin.

I dropped to my knees, and I felt Lily do the same beside me. We were breathing in sync, hearts beating together. I opened my eyes and nothing changed.

There were tears on my face, and I did not brush them away.

The performers sang another note and moved into another dance, and now it was not perfect love I felt, but awe. Within a few moments, I recognized the steps of the *daraci'Kain* from serpents' performances, but as Lily had said, serpents simply couldn't do *this*.

As Lily had described, I felt the fury of the storm, and when I closed my eyes, I could feel the warm rain. I was a wave in the ocean, thrown to the shore and then drawn back out again and again.

I saw lightning, and my breath caught until a roll of thunder reverberated through me.

Still trembling from that shock of power, I felt the dance shift once more, to a *sakkri'teska,* a dance of thanks. Calming, soothing. The magic fluttered across my skin like the wings of a thousand butterflies, cooling that which the storm had scorched.

I was filled with gratitude, and again I felt tears in my eyes.

When the dance broke, I found myself on my knees with my hands splayed before me and my head bowed. I was not alone; some had bowed even lower, so that their foreheads pressed against the ground.

Each of the five dancers turned to face us and sank into a similar bow, returning the honor.

A few of the audience stood, including Lily, who stepped forward. *"Varl'nesera-fm'itil,"* she said, praising the dancers and kneeling before one of the women. You bless us, dancer.

*"Fm'varl'nesera-hena,"* the falcon replied. Be blessed.

By the time Lily returned to my side, I felt almost capable of standing. Offering me a hand, she said, "You do the dancers a great honor by attending the performance. It is not often that any of the royal house are present."

"I'm not—"

She put a finger to my lips. "It may seem unimportant to you, but you are still the Lady's blood. It means something to those who performed for you tonight. It means much to them that you were so moved. Most of the strongest do not allow a dancer's magic to touch them. I believe they miss a great deal." Shyly, she offered, "Perhaps someday I can perform for you. I would do a *harja*, though you might accuse me of trying to use magic to seduce you."

I laughed a little, hugging her close. "Do you need magic, Lily?"

With her eyes so fair they were almost gray, she asked softly, "Do I?"

The moment hung heavily, words unsaid. She looked away first, turning the conversation back to a neutral topic. "The dancers will stay here for the next several days as they recover. It takes a great deal of energy to spin magic as they have tonight."

"I can imagine," I answered. "Was my mother really once able to do that?"

"That and more," Lily answered. "She was one of the best. I once saw her dance a *sakkri'a'she*, when I was a child. . . ." She shuddered. "A dangerous dance."

"*Sakkri'a'she?*" I asked. *A'she* meant future, but I did not know what it meant in this context.

Lily's gaze lifted, and she scanned the skies as if for inspiration. "Some of the most powerful magics are the *sakkri'sheni*, those that deal with time. Most easily, the past can be viewed—though never changed, of course. I can spin that form, though it is difficult. Then there are those dances that show the future: that which might come to pass. They're unpredictable, and show unlikely events the dancer fears as often as they show nearly certain futures." Softly, she added, "No one foresaw that Kel would run."

The mention of my mother's name was jarring. My skin was still tingling from the Indigo Choir's performance. I didn't want to think about home right then.

I was enjoying Lily's company; I had even enjoyed Araceli's. I tried to keep my father's words about Araceli in mind, but that day she had seemed so different to me from the cold woman my father had portrayed. And then there was the city, its songs and its living roads. I understood now why my parents could not speak of this place without sighing.

Once Araceli had taught me my magic and I was able to safely leave, I would have to go back to Wyvern's Court. I was loyal to Oliza. I had sworn my life to her. But I was beginning to feel reluctant about abandoning all I had learned, abandoning the city and the company of both Araceli and Lily.

Oliza would want me to be happy. She of all people knew what it was to be an outsider; she would understand the appeal of a world for my own kind.

I winced. When had *my own kind* stopped meaning the avians and serpiente I had been raised with and started meaning this civilization I was related to by seemingly little more than blood?

Again, Lily drew me from my dark thoughts, hugging me as she kissed my cheek.

"I'm sorry; I did not mean to upset you, especially after a day as long as the one we've just shared."

We returned to my rooms together. This time there was

no debate. Already it felt right to have Lily beside me as I slipped gracefully into sleep—and onto the familiar black ice, lit only by the silver moon.

"The night on ice," came Darien's voice. I turned, but could not find her. "That is how *Ecl* is described. Just as Ahnmik is the white falcon, diving through the midnight sky."

I heard a screech and looked up to see the image she had described, the falcon diving . . . diving until it slammed into and through the ice, sending fractures out in a million directions, a million fingers of gray in the blackness.

"*Shm'Ecl.*"

I felt her breath on my neck, and I turned to find her standing close, dressed in a traditional falcons' outfit like one Lily had worn earlier. Her image blurred before my eyes, and then it *was* Lily standing there.

But when she spoke, the voice was still Darien's. "Do you like this form better? Do you trust it more?"

I stepped back, unsure of how to deal with her icy rage.

"Do you notice the way her eyes change color?" Darien asked. "The magic stains a falcon's body. The magic is what puts the blue into your hair. What do you think makes her eyes violet? And why do you think you turn from your questions the instant she wishes you to?"

"I've known Lily for years," I replied. Why was I arguing with Darien? Why did I feel the need to justify myself to a specter I had never even met in the flesh?

"Two years," Darien said. "Two years are nothing in this world, especially when the prize is the trust of a royal falcon. Look at me, Nicias!" she commanded when I tried to will myself out of this dreamland. "Look at me and listen to my words with all the intelligence and reason I would expect from Kel's child."

"What do you know about my parents?" I demanded.

"Enough to know that neither of them would have fled this island if there was nothing here to flee," she retorted.

Darien turned, as if startled by something. "You don't speak of a mindwalker without her knowing, especially when you lie so close to her, but what choice did I have? Nicias, Nicias, if you want to learn your magic, I could teach you . . . everything," she whispered. I could feel the effort it was taking her just to maintain contact with me. "I could teach you in one night what it may take you a hundred years to learn from Araceli."

*Come to me.*

The ice shook at her command, and I was lost again, surrounded by black mountains. The serpent who had haunted me was before me again, but as Darien's voice echoed, it recoiled.

*Come to me.*

I pushed past the cobra, following the only path I could see as the ice began to shatter around me.

*Come to me.*

When I woke, it was because Lily was shaking me.

"Who calls to you?" she asked.

I blinked in disoriented surprise.

"I grasped the barest tendrils of the magic," she explained. "It is a powerful call. Who is it from?"

I answered, "One of the *shm'Ecl*. Darien, she is called."

Lily's eyes widened, and she snuggled closer to me. "I am glad I have never heard that one sing . . . not since *Ecl* took her. Be careful, Nicias, and take her words with a grain of salt. Darien hates the royal house. She was one of the Empress's Mercy, until she turned on her liege. I was there the day Darien attempted to assassinate Araceli." Lily twisted, and I noticed for the first time the faint scar under her right shoulder. "Her blade ripped through my back, into my heart. My brother saved my life. Mer fell to *Ecl* that day, but at least he took that bloodless creature with him."

I shivered, thinking of how close I had come to trusting Darien.

"That's why Darien is bound now," she explained. "Even if she recovers from *Ecl*, she won't be able to leave those halls."

"Why wasn't she executed?" There had to be more to this tale, but I didn't know what.

"The Empress is merciful ... and she has always been very fond of Darien, despite all the traitor has done," Lily said bitterly. "Be careful. Until you learn to protect yourself, I fear that even bound Darien could wrap you in persuasion magics so strong you wouldn't hesitate to hold a knife to your own throat."

She tucked her head into my chest, and I felt a wash of guilt. Her brother's fall was what had driven her to Wyvern's Court. Now that she had returned to Ahnmik, what right did I have to make her face her demon again?

"If you will let me," she said, "I can share with you dreams more pleasant than those of the black ice."

I nodded.

As we drifted back to sleep, I thought I heard one last faint whisper from Darien.

*I am not the only one on this island capable of such magics, Nicias,* she warned. *Even my enemy has told you that I am bound and helpless. Now come to me.*

# CHAPTER 12

THE REST of the night passed blissfully, but we had barely stepped through the door of my rooms the next morning when Lily was pulled away.

One of the Pure Diamond falcons who I had seen guarding the palace delivered the summons. "Your lady would like to speak to you."

Lily looked surprised. "Is it time for Nicias's lesson already?"

Now it was the messenger's turn to look surprised. "Your lady the *Empress Cjarsa* has requested your presence," he clarified.

Lily's eyes widened. "I apologize. The Empress so rarely grants audiences, I didn't imagine she would have reason to summon me. Nicias, I'm sorry, I must leave you for a while. Please, be careful."

She kissed my cheek and then changed shape without another word.

"Is something wrong?" I asked the Pure Diamond falcon before he could leave, too.

"I do not know the circumstances of the command, sir," he answered, watching me with an eerie focus. It took too many moments for me to realize that he was standing at attention, a guard before his monarch, awaiting either further commands or permission to leave.

"Dismissed," I said, not at all comfortable with the turnabout. I had heard that word many times from Oliza, my commander and the Tuuli Thea and Diente; I had never expected to speak it.

"Thank you, sir." He changed shape, spreading black-and-white gyrfalcon's wings to take himself back to the palace.

Only after he was gone did I realize we had had an audience. Instead of greeting me, Syfka said, "Pure Diamond falcons are bound magically to obey anyone of royal blood. That you have not decided to stay as Araceli's heir doesn't change that."

"Can I help you?" I asked, still distracted. Syfka had shown no interest in me since I had arrived on Ahnmik, but now she obviously had something she wished to say.

"Your mother left some things here when she fled," she said briskly. "Rightly, they're yours now. If you'll come with me?"

She turned without waiting for me to respond, and I hastened to follow. I thought she would lead me into the courtyard, but she passed by the white sands, and instead we went to one of the three *yenna'marl*.

"This is the Mercy's tower," Syfka explained as she led the way up a spiral staircase formed of smoky glass. We passed by several doorways, each marked with a different pattern. "And this was your mother's room. It has been locked since she disappeared."

She touched the doorway, and the patterns shifted until

the door clicked open and Syfka stepped back to allow me access.

"Thank you."

She shook her head. "If it was my choice, I would have had these things destroyed years ago. It was Cjarsa who favored Kel and Darien, Cjarsa who ignored their treason as if they were children and not guards of the royal house, and Cjarsa who commanded that your mother's possessions be passed to you." She snapped, "Help yourself," before turning and abandoning me with the remnants of my mother's old life.

I pushed the door open the rest of the way. As they did in my room, the walls began to emit a soft light. In here, the marks were not just silver, but also violet. I wondered whether my mother had been the one to create them.

Though most of the bedding had been stripped away long before, a silky shawl had been left behind. I picked it up and realized that it must be a *melos*, one of the scarves given to dancers as the highest praise for their work. It felt as light as air in my hands and shimmered with all the colors of the sky at sunset.

In one of the corners, the artist who had woven it had left a note:

*a'sorma'la'lo'Mehay*
*ka'hena'itil'gasi'ni*
*la'gen-Darien*

I translated the words swiftly. To the sister of my soul: a more beautiful dancer there never was. Yours, Darien.

I put the *melos* down, wondering how my mother had known this woman well enough to merit such words.

On the far wall stood a vanity made of pale birch wood. Its surface held a silver hand mirror, an assortment of hair clips and a portrait—a ghostly image etched into a glass surface.

At first I didn't think I knew either of the two women in the picture. They were both sitting on the edge of the cliffs, looking out at the ocean and laughing at something. Then I recognized my mother's violet eyes, in a falcon's face I had never known.

The other woman, I realized with a start, was Darien. She seemed so happy and carefree in the portrait, I almost couldn't believe she was the same woman who haunted my dreams.

Next to the portrait was a small box, with a hastily scrawled note beside it: *I go to confront Cjarsa today. Please keep these for me. They should go to my daughter when she is old enough to understand.—Darien*

Underneath the box was a letter, unfinished and unsigned, but in Darien's handwriting. It was a letter to Hai's father, informing him that Darien carried his child, but most of what she had written was crossed out.

A self-mocking scrawl at the bottom of the page read, *Why should I bother to tell him of a child who the Lady will never let him know? A child the Lady will never let study magic, but would rather sentence to* Ecl *for the misfortune of having her father's blood?*

Darien had trusted my mother with these things, and with her daughter's future. My mother had kept them, as well as the *melos* and the portrait, and displayed them as cherished belongings.

Darien had called to me many times, but I had never thought I had a reason to believe her words. Now I realized how close she had been to my mother, and it made me reevaluate everything Lily had told me.

I used my mother's *melos* to carefully wrap up the box of

Darien's belongings, along with their picture. I planned to take the scarf and portrait back to my mother when I went home, but the other things belonged to someone else. Someone I had just decided I should see.

✳✳✳

This time, I found the Halls of *shm'Ecl* without difficulty. Servos greeted me, but did not ask questions as I walked past him.

Shortly I began to hear Darien's voice again, a haunting singsong.

*Foolish child, foolish child, you tread in power and greed. Foolish child, foolish child, you tread in blood and darkness. Nicius of Ahnmik, Nicias Silvermead, destroyer of an empire. Come to me.*

Though magic held them all, Darien was the only one of the *shm'Ecl* who was physically bound. I could hear her chanting as I approached.

"Finally the great prince deigns to speak to me," she said once I stood before her. "He lets them mark his skin and use persuasion magics on him first, but finally he comes to me."

"How did you know my mother?" I asked as I knelt before her.

"Will you remove this blindfold?" she replied. "You know that sight only hampers our magic. If I wished to harm you, a blindfold would only make it easier. I would just like to look at you as we speak."

That made sense to me. I put my mother's belongings down between us and reached to pull the blindfold away. The cloth seemed to dissolve beneath my touch.

"It's falcon's silk, woven by Pure Diamond," she explained as I stared at the remnants of the fine material. "It can't be untied, removed or cut, except by one of royal blood."

She kept her eyes closed for a moment, as if bracing herself for light, and then slowly lifted her gaze, uncertainly.

I felt a rush of familiarity. When I had fallen in the woods, the silver eyes that had looked upon me, the curious voice that had spoken my name, had surely been Darien's.

"Nicias, you wear your mother's blood so visibly on your face. Even if she no longer does."

"How did you know my mother?" I asked again as Darien looked at the objects I had set between us.

She smiled a little. "Kel and I were ever rivals for the favor of our Empress. And yet we were friends, closer than any among the Mercy had ever been. Her friendship was the brightness of the life I led. Mine was the brightness of hers, I believe. But then we found ... what we did, and I fought the Empress.

"Cjarsa does not acknowledge friendship or loyalty to any but herself. Kel would have been the one to give me the Empress's mercy. She fled Ahnmik rather than put me to death the way Cjarsa would have it done. And I let *Ecl* take me, rather than give my *Empress* the satisfaction of hearing my screams," Darien said.

"What did Cjarsa do?"

"You want to know?" Darien asked, voice lilting. "Will you believe me? You will not want to believe it; I did not want to believe it. And you have lived among the serpiente and the avians, as I never did. . . ."

I knew of the falcons' ancient feud with the serpiente, but Darien's anger spoke of something more tangible in our current lives. What horror could this woman know that would force her to turn on her empress and would drive my mother from these lands?

"Tell me, please," I implored her.

Darien nodded and then closed her eyes.

"When the followers of Anhamirak left those of Ahnmik in the days of the Dasi, they kept their serpiente magic. Cjarsa and Araceli, falcon priestesses of Ahnmik, worried that the serpiente, being more prolific than the falcons, and more active, would be a danger.

"So they took in a young human child and raised her, to be like themselves but different. They brought her to power, and helped make her empire as strong as that of the serpiente, their natural enemies. Then they used their persuasion magics to convince one of the serpiente to stab this leader in the back. Her name," Darien said slowly, "was Alasdair. The first avian. Her people retaliated swiftly. The avians slew the eight original serpents of Anhamirak's clan. And the war that began between the avians and serpiente has continued ever since, generation to generation of blood and hatred.

"The royals of Ahnmik will do the same again, if your Wyvern's Court grows too strong," Darien warned. "Because they know that if the slaughter stops and the two lands finally find true peace, the serpiente will regain their magic and be a threat. If your wyvern Oliza comes to the throne, they *will* destroy her—but so subtly, blame will never fall on their shoulders. So many generations more of cobra, python, boa, taipan, rat snake, mamba and viper will be lost, and so many more generations of crow, raven, sparrow and hawk will fall. Perhaps Araceli will find a new pawn, maybe the wolves.

"But the royal falcons will do it. And they leave me here, locked and bound and blinded, because they know I know, and they *pray* I will be truly lost to the void and never bare the truth to the light of day."

I wanted to shout at her, to demand that she take it all back. I had not been alive during the war, but I had heard enough about its horrors. I had seen the hatred and fear that generations of fighting had left behind. Too many people my age and older were missing mothers, fathers and siblings.

I didn't want Darien to be telling the truth, but her story made too much sense to be ignored.

No one knew how the ancient war had begun—no one except the falcons.

"My mother was aware of this?" I whispered. My ears were ringing, and my voice seemed unnaturally loud.

"Once, she was," Darien said. "But no one in the avian court would have believed the truth even if she had tried to tell them. They would not have wanted to believe. Now . . ." She shook her head. "Years ago Kel came back to Ahnmik to plead with Araceli to let Sebastian, your father, go free. She bartered her magic, her mind, her knowledge. Araceli burned from her memory the worst *and* the best. Kel doesn't remember anything having to do with those days. She doesn't remember what we learned . . . or who she learned it with. She doesn't remember the torture she dealt . . . and she doesn't remember me."

I winced, needing to look away, as if that could change anything.

"How did you learn all this about the falcons?"

Darien's gaze turned distant. "My daughter's father was serpiente. After he returned to his home, I used my magic to keep an eye on him. I saw him killed during an avian attack, and I reached out to save him. I think Cjarsa might have let me, but Araceli pulled me back. She told me not to interfere, though I could feel the avian poison—unmistakably one of Araceli's creations—burning through his bloodstream as if it was my own. In fury, I turned on her, demanding to know *why* we had to let him die, when it was easily within our power to end the avian-serpiente war entirely. She told me it was their choice, and not our place to interfere."

She paused and looked away. "I have never been as talented with *sakkri* as your mother was, but when Araceli lied to me that day, for a moment I could see the past as clearly as if it was marching before me. And I knew what she and Cjarsa had done. The vision was so powerful that we all knew, everyone who was in that room. Some of us chose to forget, or ignore. I couldn't, not with my child's father dead because of Araceli's ego."

What Araceli had done to Darien was unforgivable, but I was more horrified by what she had done to the avians and the serpiente. Wyvern's Court would forever be stained by their war, a war intentionally begun to cripple my world. For the first time in my life, I believed absolutely in evil, for there was no other word that could describe such an act.

"Confront Araceli if you need to," Darien said. "I see in your eyes that you are thinking of it. I can protect you from her persuasion magics."

Desperately, I asked, "How do I know you aren't using the same magics on me? Making this sound more . . ."

Darien shook her head. "Because then you would never have been able to question me. If you can consider both sides of an argument, no falcon magic has been used on your mind." She admitted, "I tried to use magic to bring you here, but others did their best to keep you from me. Araceli suggested that Lily come to the *shm'Ecl* that first day because she realized that you were on your way, and she hoped that your 'friend's' presence would distract you until her meeting with Syfka was through. And Araceli has done what she could to distract you every time you have seemed inclined to return here. But now, Nicias . . . I do not think I need magic to make you see the horror of what Ahnmik's royal house began with the murder of the young queen Alasdair."

I nodded, still not sure I fully trusted her, but shocked by her story just the same. My body was shaking, a fine tremble. I needed to compose myself. Needed . . .

Needed to confront Araceli.

✳✳✳

I stumbled down the hall, away from Darien, almost running.

"Nicias, are you all right?" Servos caught my arm as I started to brush past him, and I looked at him without a tought of what to say.

"Darien is awake," I said, finally.

Servos winced as he searched my gaze. "She spoke to you directly?"

I nodded, wondering how much he knew.

"She is mad," Servos said. I was about to argue with him when he added, "But she is also very sane. Have care with her, Nicias of Ahnmik. She is an injured bear, just as likely to turn on the ones who try to help her as on the ones who hurt her."

*And who is he to speak?* Darien sighed in my mind. *Servos, guardian to these still halls. He has been kind to me, true. But he worshipped Ecl in his youth. The only reason she does not take him is that he already loves her darkness.*

*Go to Araceli, Nicias. Soon is best.*

My steps through Ahnmik were long and quick, yet at the same time they got me nowhere. It seemed that the three white towers that marked the courtyard of the Empress's palace were never in front of me no matter how I turned.

*The roads fight you,* Darien said. *They fight you because they know you are going to challenge Araceli and Cjarsa, and though they do not have lives per se, they protect the royal house—as the Mercy do. Luckily, you are of royal blood too. Araceli's chosen will not hasten to break you.*

As I tried to shake those dire words from my mind, I finally saw the path to the palace. I simply turned a bend in the road and it was before me, as if the roads and the city had given up protecting me or Araceli.

I pushed open the grand doors and found Lily standing at the base of the stairs, interrogating the falcon who had given her the Empress's summons.

"You *lied* to me."

"I gave you the message that the Lady Syfka gave to me. I do not know why the Empress would not see you," he said, defending himself.

"My lord, can I help you?" the other guard said, a little too loudly, as if to alert the others that I was present.

*Lillian, now the youngest yet most powerful of Araceli's Mercy,* Darien shuddered as Lily turned around, seeming startled by my presence. *She, Kel and I did always compete.*

I wondered just how old Lily was. She looked my age, but in a realm where most never aged after their twentieth year, that meant nothing.

*Lily was nine when Kel fled the island and I fell to Ecl. Only twenty-nine now,* Darien informed me. *Too young to know what she does.*

I did not mean to speak aloud, but could not stop myself from asking, "Did you know?"

Lily's eyes flashed from gray to violet. "Did I know what?" Her voice was fragile, her expression almost wounded. "Why are you looking at me as if I've drawn a knife on you, Nicias?" She stepped toward me.

*She might as well have,* Darien snarled. *Tell the two-faced little fowl that she deserved the knife I once managed to give her.*

Darien's fury toward this woman I cared for made me wince.

Lily put a hand on my arm. "Nicias, what's wrong?"

My stomach clenched with guilt. Darien's words were persuasive, but I had known Lily for—

*Nicias, get control of yourself,* Darien commanded. *She's put persuasion Drawings on your skin. Of course you hesitate to—*

*She's used more than magic on me,* I responded.

"Nicias . . . did something happen while I was gone?" Lily asked, fearfully. "Dear sky above, Nicias, *what is it?*"

Darien's shouting in my mind strengthened. *So what if she does like you? You're an excellent catch. You are the only male child of the royal house; you are powerful and influential and beautiful. None of that matters, because Araceli ordered her to seduce you, to make you want to stay on Ahnmik, and to keep you away from me.*

I tried to push Lily away, not sure whether to believe Darien, but shocked by the implications.

Lily held my arm. "Nicias—"

"I've been speaking with Darien," I said, allowing her to take the words as she wished.

Her eyes widened in fear. "Oh, gods, no." She stepped closer. "*Tasa'Ahnleh,*" she whispered. *Ahnleh* could mean many things, but in the form that Lily spoke, it meant all things evil. "Nicias, she could *kill* you."

"Were you ordered to keep me away from her?"

"Of *course*," she answered vehemently. "Nicias, Darien is *dangerous*. She hates the royal house, of which you are a part. Araceli wanted to protect you—"

I recalled the words Lily had spoken two days before: *I know I will never be first to you. You have sworn your loyalty to Oliza much as I have sworn my loyalty to the white Lady . . .*

"Did she also give you other orders?" I demanded.

Lily crumbled, stepping back from me. "Do you think it was all an *act?*" she whispered.

*Of course,* Darien responded, though I tried to close my mind to her barbs.

"Why were you sent to Wyvern's Court?"

Had the tale she told about her brother been true at all? Or had she lied about that, too?

Lily drew a deep breath. "I told you the truth about why I visited your lands. If Araceli had other intentions, I never knew them."

*That lying little fowl,* Darien snapped. *I may not be privy to Araceli's commands, but I know how her mind works. You were coming of age, Nicias. Of course Araceli would have sent someone who could be a suitable mate, if you proved worthy—or could put you down, if you tried to tie yourself to a serpent or avian.*

I recoiled mentally from Darien, and physically from Lily. I didn't know who to trust anymore. Darien hated Araceli, and I did not think she would hesitate to warp the truth to get me on her side. Lily was working for Araceli, and I had no idea how far that loyalty went.

Araceli wanted me to stay on Ahnmik.

But why had she called Lily back before I had mentioned my fall in the woods to her?

*Araceli knew that your power had awakened. She felt it that day in the woods, just as I did. What better way to make it easy for Lily to guide you here, without anyone asking questions, than to command she return? Araceli would not even have needed to tell Lily her intent.*

Even now, the suggestion seemed contrived. I wanted to believe Lily; I wanted to erase the hurt from her violet gaze. She put a hand on my arm, and I opened my mouth to apologize.

*Trust yourself,* Darien snarled, fiercely enough to make me flinch. *Trust what you know to be true. And never trust a falcon whose eyes flash violet, for it means she is using the strongest of her magic. Is it so hard to imagine what for?*

How many times had I lost my train of thought when Lily looked at me with such jewel-colored eyes?

*Ask one of the Pure Diamond if he can see Drawings on your skin,* Darien suggested. *They cannot lie to you.*

I glanced at the two guards, who had been standing in silent ready positions throughout our brief conversation.

If they could see magic on me, did I really want to know?

*Your hesitation itself is due to magic.*

I turned to one of the Pure Diamond. "Could you see, if someone had used magic on me?"

The pain on Lily's face cut me inside. "You don't trust me at all, do you?"

"Of course I—"

"You think I've been using magic on you," she said. "You think . . . what? That Araceli ordered me to befriend you? *Sleep* with you? Fall in *love* with you?"

"No!" I protested, at the same time that Darien answered

viciously, *Yes, of course, save the love part. The Mercy isn't encour-aged to love. It would be awkward, if she was later ordered to skin you or some such. If Lily is foolish enough to actually care for you, she will regret it when Araceli calls her.*

"What am I supposed to think," Lily said, "when you start asking Pure Diamond to read for magic on your skin?"

*Try this one*—Darien pushed at me, and I found myself saying words she was inventing. "I told you I spoke to Darien. I think she might have used magic on me. You might not be able to see it since she was a higher rank than you."

"How much did Darien tell you?" Lily asked, quietly. Her face held an odd lack of emotion; those gray eyes were shuttered.

"About?"

"Everything."

I had to tread carefully. "I think you know what she told me."

Lily nodded. "Darien, Kel, Mei and I found out together."

"And yet you still work for Araceli."

Lily's eyes had returned to pale blue, and the expression in them was cold as hail clouds. "Did Darien tell you what her fighting won? How many innocents were destroyed by her treason before the Empress had the heart to sentence her favorite to death? Did she tell you that Kel had to leave be-hind a sister and a lover when she fled the city and put herself into exile?

"Did Darien tell you that a few years ago Lady Cjarsa took pity on her and drew her from the *shm'Ecl* and offered pardon—and that Darien repaid the favor by trying to kill her? Did she tell you how many of the Mercy died or fell to *Ecl* that day, my brother included?" She insisted, *"That* is what Darien's struggle got her, Nicias. So don't look at me with disgust for refusing to wage that war."

*Look what it got you, Lillian,* Darien sighed.

*Is it true?* I asked her silently.

*In part,* the gyrfalcon acknowledged. *What she does not mention is that the Empress's pardon came with conditions. But that is history and this is now; that is my life and this is yours.*

"What other orders did Araceli give you, regarding me?" I asked, as gently as I could. I needed to know. Had any of it been real?

"It doesn't matter now, does it? It's over, *sir.*" She spat out the title, then turned on her heel and walked away from me. "Guards, Araceli and Cjarsa are both occupied. If you let him pass, it will be your hides."

Lily's wings were trembling slightly, betraying the tension in her body.

That morning, in ignorance, I had been happy. Part of me wanted to reach for her and push away the knowledge I had gained.

It *did* matter now, more than it ever had.

I called out as she ascended the stairs, "Araceli ordered you to keep me from Darien." Lily hesitated for a moment. "What will she do to you, knowing you failed?"

Her magic lashed back at me, making me stumble and strike the wall, every hair on my body standing on end. "I am no longer your concern, my lord. You have made that much clear." She pushed open the silver double doors at the top of the stairs and shut them behind her so hard that I heard them ring.

The Pure Diamond guards were watching me warily. Death to them if I forced myself past. Painful death, probably.

I had hurt enough people that day. I did not need to give myself more nightmares by fighting these two.

*Then come back to me,* Darien whispered in my mind. *Let me teach you our magic, teach you what Araceli should be . . . could be, if she didn't fear Ecl.*

# CHAPTER 13

I WANTED to go *home*.

I could not undo the evils of the past, or forget the horrors I had learned. I could not undo the hours spent in Lily's arms, or forget the ice-cold expression on her face. I could not forget, though I wished to.

I did not want to be a royal falcon, a prince of this bitter island. I did not want their power. I wanted only to return to Wyvern's Court.

*Araceli won't help you.* Darien's voice in my mind was now gentler, almost apologetic. *She was pained by the loss of one heir. If she was less obsessed with purity, she never would have given up Sebastian. But she refuses to see a man with a crow's face as her son. She will not part with another child. She never intended to.*

Everything felt like it was crashing down around me. How could I learn to control my magic under these circumstances? I had been raised to be loyal and honest, and I did not have the wiles necessary to manage the game Araceli had begun.

*I can teach you your magic,* Darien promised. *If you have the courage to ride the Ecl, I can teach you.*

Darien was using me even as she offered to help me. Lillian had been manipulating me even as she'd shared my bed. Araceli had been engineering my thoughts and actions from the moment I had stepped onto this island. And Syfka . . . anyone who had seen my mother's belongings would have known that they would lead me to seek out Darien. Either Syfka or the Empress who commanded her had planned for me to visit the halls.

*Syfka has her own agenda, though I do not know what it is,* Darien agreed. *But if her plans force her to help you, and help me, then we can use her as she uses us.*

Did anyone here ever work under pure motives, or was it all a façade, layers upon layers of deception?

*We are Ahnmik's chosen, and Ahnmik is god of control and power and the mind. These games are the way of our realm. Now come.*

*You,* I replied tiredly, *want no less to use me than Araceli does.*

*Certainly,* Darien answered lightly. *But that being so, can we not use each other, too? You take what I teach you. I have faith that, with knowledge, you will do what I hope. If you do not . . . then perhaps it was not meant to be. I, however, will only manipulate you with the truth. Araceli has no such qualms. I will manipulate you with what is and what could be. Whether you choose to follow where I lead, or lead where I suggest, or fly another sky altogether will ultimately be your own decision.*

*Come to me. Now.*

✳✳✳

Servos was not present as I entered the halls and immediately walked up the winding ramp to Darien.

Without either of us speaking, I untied the bonds on her wrists and ankles. The knots that had held her for so long separated almost instantly at my touch, and Darien sighed.

Once free, she stood, stretched and unfurled strong white and black gyrfalcon wings. She let out a cry, half pain and half triumph. She stretched and flexed her magic as she had her body, and the sheer power made my breath catch before she finally turned her attention back to me.

*Nicias.*

*Darien.*

*I thought for a while that I would never be free of my bonds. Many times, over many years, I almost gave myself to* Ecl *in order to escape this imprisoned flesh. Then I felt you, when your magic woke, and . . . remembered why I'd chosen this path.* She stretched once more, arching her spine and reaching her hands above her head. *You are Kel's child,* she said, approvingly. *But I think you may be stronger than she is. You can handle what I have to teach you.*

"And what is that?" I asked aloud, for seeing her standing perfectly still while I heard her voice so clearly was unnerving.

"Magic," she answered. "Science. Religion. Whatever you call it. The void. The *Ecl.* I can teach you to ride it."

"And then?"

"Ride the *Ecl,* and it can never rule you," Darien explained. "If you go willingly, if you dance with its darkness, then you will keep your own mind. Your anchor. That will be enough to keep your magic from devouring you.

"If you are brave enough to begin."

She put her hands up as Araceli had the first day, then paused, allowing me to either mirror her or not. No more words were spoken.

I hesitated, but not for long.

I pressed the backs of my hands to hers.

*Now dive,* she commanded.

✳✳✳

Once again I was on the black ice with Darien, with the harsh wind ripping at our clothes and hair. The full moon was circled by rings of plum and cranberry, the only colors on the landscape.

"*Ecl'gah,*" Darien said, naming the land.

*Illusion.*

"Those the Empress calls *shm'Ecl* are the ones who have fled from a world that holds too much, into a world where they can rest. Sometimes they do so intentionally—it only takes an instant, a single thought that perhaps nothingness would be easier—and sometimes they do so unintentionally, overwhelmed by their own magic until they forget where the real world is. They get caught by illusions, which are created by their minds to protect them from oblivion.

"Finally, even the illusions fade, and there is only *Ecl*. It is *nothing,* but it is beyond that. It is the absence even of emptiness. It is what is before existence, what is after annihilation. There is no desire to return, and even if one does find a mote of self-awareness, struggling is futile. The more you fight, the more painful the illusion becomes, until you sink back into oblivion because you cannot face what you have created."

Darien smiled softly.

Then, at a flick of her hand, the ice shattered. I tumbled into the cold water beneath, choking on it as I had in my nightmares, and struggled to remain afloat. The ice cut into my hands as I tried to grasp it.

"Fight and you will fall here," Darien snapped. *Now dive.*

I *can't.* My heart pounded as if it was trying to escape my chest, but as much as I shared its desire to flee, there was nowhere I could go.

"Nicias of Ahnmik, son of Kel of the Indigo Choir and Sebastian of the heir to the white Lady, mindwalker—Nicias Silvermead, sworn Wyvern of Honor. You can drown here, or you can dive. Make your choice. *Now.*"

If I did not follow Darien, I would be trapped here, one of the unmoving *shm'Ecl*, forever.

I let go of the ice, and then there *was* no ice, just the water, sucking me down. Neither cold nor hot, it engulfed me instantly. I forced myself not to struggle to the top and found myself sinking ever deeper.

My need for air disappeared, until I realized it had gone and I panicked, afraid to draw the blackness into myself as breath, but afraid not to just the same.

Again I was thrashing against nothing.

*Calm yourself, child of Mehay. Fearing her darkness only drives you closer to her.* I wasn't certain I could even call it a voice, let alone Darien's. *Let yourself fall. See where the darkness takes you.*

I imagined for a moment that I was back at Wyvern's Court, at the end of a long day of drills, and then I brought my mind further back, to my days in the dancer's nest. I remembered the exercises the serpiente taught, designed to relax one's body and mind.

A sigh seemed to brush against me, like silk in the darkness.

*Why do you walk here, stranger?* a familiar, resigned voice inquired.

Suddenly, in the distance, again I saw the black castle. I

was back on the ice, surrounded by dunes that began to ripple, smoothing and shifting so that no matter where I stepped I could not move closer to the distant castle. *You aren't wanted . . . not by me, anyway. Stay here long enough and Ecl will keep you. So why do you walk my kingdom?*

Abruptly I stood before a scene held in ice like a frozen tableau. In it were the triple arches where the dancers performed. Above the arches, a black-winged dancer lifted her face to the moonlight and stretched her body as if weightless. Her hair was black, but held scarlet highlights. Her eyes were closed.

I recognized Hai, Darien's half-serpiente daughter. My thoughts of the serpiente must have brought me to her—or her to me. There was no distance, no "here" anyway.

"Is this your kingdom?" I called. "Or is it your prison? Can you leave?"

*Why would I want to leave?* Hai replied.

I jumped back as the image before me shattered, shards of ice slicing my face and arms before they fell to the ground, where they turned into black and crimson feathers. I knelt to pick one up and found that it was broken and twisted, its edges seared.

*What are you waiting for? Me to invite you in for tea? Go away. You shine too brightly here.*

Ignoring the dismissal, I asked, "What do you mean, I shine too brightly?"

*You—are, you've . . .*

As if my question had distracted Hai from maintaining her defenses, the path to the castle appeared before me. I could see her, again, standing at the top of one of the turrets, her body a gray silhouette against the white moon.

*My mother comes here, sometimes, but I can hardly see her. She is never . . . really here. She is surrounded by nothing and she is nothing. But you make all this seem fake. Illusion.*

"It is."

"Don't patronize me!" Her voice reached me this time, not in my mind, but carried on the air. "I know this is illusion . . . sometimes, anyway. When nothing reminds me, when you and my mother don't barge in here and try to pull me out, I forget. But when you walk in, you shine, and then—" The ice around me glittered with a million colors, before it once again faded to black. "All my world fades."

"Why do you stay here when you know it's fake?"

She turned from me. *Why not?*

"It isn't real!"

There was a pause, and for a minute, I thought she had left, withdrawn into the palace. But finally she responded, *When you are not here, I can forget that. Color, sound, touch—I forget it all.*

Horrified, I asked, "And you're happy that way?"

*Of course not,* she answered, very matter-of-factly. *But at least I am not in pain.*

I reached the castle, only to find the drawbridge closed and the moat filled with serpents, all with their fangs bared as they moved through a vile liquid that stank of brimstone.

*Is the real world so awful?* No pleasure might mean no pain, but I had never imagined pain bad enough to make me pay that price. *There are beautiful things there. If you can't stand Ahnmik, you would be welcome in Wyvern's Court—*

The air laughed, an eerie giggling that came from nowhere and everywhere. *Wyvern's Court, yes. Beautiful, doomed Wyvern's Court. Leave now, Nicias. Before I need to kill you to get rid of you.*

*I think your death would stain this world, but so will your life if you linger long . . . so leave now.*

*Hai—*

*You speak of illusions, my* prince. *but you cannot recognize the truth. Go now, Nicias. Leave me to my sleep, and I shall leave you to your waking dreams.*

She pushed me away, and again the world around me faded. I fell into *Ecl* without any defenses, forgetting everything I was and had ever known.

There was only the void I drifted through—

Yet there wasn't, because there was no *I*, and the void can never be.

Occasionally I became aware of something more, something

*Mehay*

beautiful and horrible. *Ecl* rippled for a moment.

And then I remembered *pain*. I screamed and remembered *sound*.

I drew a breath and remembered *taste* and *smell* as I inhaled the dry air.

I remembered *sight* as the light blinded me, and I pressed my hands to my eyes.

Then a hand touched my shoulder, and I remembered comfort. "Mehay." A voice spoke, and I remembered music.

Still, I longed for the *Ecl*, wanted to reach out to it, because I knew it was near and inside it I would never know hurt.

"Nicias, stay with me."

And hearing my name, I remembered *I*.

I remembered my vows, every one I had ever made in my life.

Darien's voice seemed very loud, even though I knew she spoke softly. The smooth floor on which I knelt felt coarse against my knees, and the air in the halls was suffocating. *The halls*—we were back in the Halls of *shm'Ecl*. Again I saw droplets of my own blood on the floor beneath me, too real after the void. My arms were striped with the black and scarlet magic I had come to associate with Hai.

I didn't want to be here. . . .

I ran myself through the dancers' exercises. As I forced myself to relax, I found myself smoothing out the marks Hai had left on my skin. I realized I was doing it only when I saw the marks begin to fade, and I was so startled that I snapped my gaze up to Darien.

She smiled tiredly. "You have touched *Ecl*, and yet you have returned. If ever again you embrace her, you will be able to find your way back. Fear is what drives you into the darkness, beyond where any voice can reach. Relax your mind, and you will be drawn back toward this world like rain to the earth.

"Without your fear in the way, and with your royal blood to guide you, you will quickly learn how to use your magic with finesse. Simply put your body in balance, close your eyes and focus on the intent. If the spell is within your grasp, you will be able to see the pattern. Depending on the complexity, it may take you minutes to memorize, or centuries. Even if you never learn more than I have given you, it will be enough to keep you from drowning in the void."

"If what you have taught me is such an effective way to keep someone safe," I asked, "then why doesn't everyone use it?"

Darien shook her head. "And deprive the Lady and her heir of so many years during which they can brainwash their subjects?" she said bitterly. "Truthfully, most falcons discover their power when they are still children, some before they are four, and hardly any after their ninth year. But, Nicias, you are nearly a grown man. You have a lifetime of bonds holding you to this world, vows you've made and connections you've forged. Even more important, you are old enough to have a strong image of who you are. A child lacks all that. They would never have the strength to return from the void if they dove in as deeply as you and I have," she said sadly.

"Why do you sound pained?"

She sighed. "Mehay is pain, inasmuch as pain is part of existence."

"There's more to it," I pressed.

"I, too, have bonds here," she said, her gaze distant. "Vows I made in blood and magic, which lock me to this world and will for all eternity. Particularly, they tie me to the Mercy. That is a group you leave only in madness or in death."

"My mother left."

"She left physically," Darien said, "but it was not until Cjarsa stole her memories that she was truly free. It is a bit death, a bit madness."

"What pains you now?"

"When one of the Mercy feels pain," Darien said, "all do."

I knew who she meant before she said the name.

"Lillian, of the Elite Silver Choir, Mercy to Araceli," Darien whispered, "I am sorry. But Araceli put you in my way to Nicias, and I could not spare you."

"Why is she being punished for my actions?" I demanded. "I may not like the job she was given, but she did it. She obeyed Araceli. She did everything she could. I am the one responsible—"

"You only as much as I," Darien said. "Neither of us holds as much blame as Araceli. She gave the orders."

"What is happening to her?" No matter where the blame fell, I felt the guilt.

"If you want to see, reach into the Now and look," Darien snapped. *"Sakkri'equa.* That is within your power, *Nicias'ra'o'aona.* Follow your own blood. Your father's mother is with her."

It was easy.

Too easy.

I thought of doing it, and it was done. I stood— immaterial, helpless to act—by Lily's side.

There was no sound. Lily uttered no scream and gave no pleas for lenience. Instead, what seemed to grip her was sweeping despair at her failure.

She knew she would survive this.

To her, that more than anything else was agony. She had disappointed her lady Araceli. How could she ever stand to face her again, knowing that she did not deserve Araceli's forgiveness?

Her infinite mercy.

Beside me, I could feel Darien struggling with her own memories, her own feelings of guilt when she had first failed her Empress Cjarsa. There had been no torture then, but I sensed that she might have preferred it.

I tore myself away from the scene, almost back into the *Ecl,* where there was no suffering or guilt or fury. Lily had be- trayed me for a monarch who had repaid her loyalty with . . . this horror.

Darien's voice reached me just before I crossed into the void, commanding, "Never flee to it. *Ecl* asks a price when you use it. You do not want to enter it to hide from pain—not if you want to return complete."

This she knew from experience.

"Always enter *Ecl* willingly, and without demands," Darien advised. "Then it will never hold you. If you seek to abandon your senses, you will lose your soul and self as well."

I nodded mechanically and then turned when I heard a swiftly indrawn breath behind me.

"Hello, Servos," Darien said.

Servos nodded respectfully, as if it was perfectly natural for him to be greeted by a woman who had previously been bound and lost to the void. "Darien." He looked at me and said, "It has been three weeks since you first came here. We had given up hope that you would wake."

"Three weeks?" I gasped. I had thought hours, maybe a day, but not *weeks*.

"You spent much time in the *Ecl*," Darien explained.

"Araceli thinks you are lost," Servos said.

How many people thought the same? After all I had experienced in this land, I finally understood why my parents had doubted I would return. Were they now convinced that they would never see me again?

What about Oliza? She would not believe that I had abandoned her—would she?

"Darien, would I survive off Ahnmik if I left now?"

She frowned. "Your magic would not kill you."

I nodded, grateful.

Darien, however, did not leave it at that. "Then you are going home now?"

"If Araceli does not try to stop me."

"Araceli does not visit these halls," Servos said. "If you

can work illusions to hide yourself, you could leave and no one would be the wiser."

"Why wouldn't you tell them?" I asked.

"I've been the guardian of these halls for too long," he answered. "I wish this madness on no one, and I wish Araceli's mercy on no one. If you stay here, likely you will suffer both." After a moment of contemplation, he added, "And I would hate to see the destruction of two who are so deft in managing *Ecl*'s swift currents. *Mana'Ecl*. Masters of the void. The title is rarely given these days, with Cjarsa and Araceli valuing mindwalkers and weavers of *sakkri* more highly, but both of you have earned it. Now . . . I will leave you two to your own futures."

Darien nodded as he retreated.

Then she demanded, "Nicias, knowing what you do, you are just going to run?"

"I have no reason to stay."

She looked appalled. "Return to Wyvern's Court and you will be just another bird, your talent and power wasted. You will not be able to use your magic lest Araceli sense it and drag you back here. You will never be able to take a mate, because Araceli *will* know if you have a child, and if it is half outsider, she will kill it. You could do so much here, *be* so much. You could be—"

"Prince," I interrupted her. "I did not want that power when Araceli offered it to me, and I do not want it now."

"But you could fight in ways that I never could," Darien argued. "And still you will not even confront Araceli?"

I met her gaze and asked bluntly, "Could we win if we fought her?"

"You are Araceli's grandson. You are perhaps the only one who *could* challenge her, could show the world what she has done—"

"And if we did *win*, what would the reward be? Would we destroy Ahnmik? What would our rebellion win us?"

"Justice to the falcons," Darien answered. "For creating a race designed to slaughter. For murdering any who could compete with them."

"You're talking about vengeance," I argued, "not justice."

She let out a frustrated screech that drew Servos back. Turning to him, she said, "You know what Araceli and Cjarsa have done. How can you live with them?"

"I am aware of their experiments," Servos admitted. "However, I am also aware of their motivations. You may want to ask Araceli about those someday."

Darien laughed, a sharp and biting sound. "I was Cjarsa's Mercy, not the Empress herself. Those two answer only to themselves."

"They would explain themselves to Nicias."

It was my turn to argue. "I don't want their explanations. I won't fight them unless they try to harm Oliza, but I won't listen to any defense for what they did. Araceli has manipulated me too many times already."

Servos sighed. "As you wish. Fly with grace and luck, Nicias Silvermead." He changed shape and departed.

"You were raised among the warring two," Darien said, "and yet you aren't even going to challenge the woman who orchestrated their ancestors' deaths?"

"I am not willing to lose my life for my pride," I answered calmly. "Why should we sacrifice more lives to avenge the lives we lost before?"

"If the avians and serpiente knew what she did—"

"Wyvern's Court is prepared to defend itself if falcons try to interfere. If Araceli was not lying, then most of her people cannot even leave this island. If we take a stand here, we will lose. But if we take a stand only on our own land, and only if forced, then we have a chance."

She frowned, but did not argue.

"I was raised a warrior," I said softly. "Any in my position would do the same. The avians and serpiente just ended their war; they want to forget, not rehash old wounds, and the last thing they want is to start another battle."

Darien paced anxiously. For the first time, I noticed the clothing she wore, which had once been very elegant, but now held fine particles of dust. "I will stay here. Maybe I can't win the fight, but for me, this is home even if it is a hated one."

"Araceli will demand that you be turned over to the Mercy the instant you leave these halls."

"Araceli will demand it, yes," Darien replied without seeming to care. "But I am sworn to Cjarsa, and so it is Cjarsa who will decide upon my sentence. If I can remain calm this time, I believe I can convince her to pardon me." Softly, she added, "If I can't, I will make sure that they kill me instead."

"That is your choice," I said, chilled by the simple determination in Darien's voice. "Though, if you would not endanger my people, you would be welcome in Wyvern's Court."

Darien just scowled and started down the ramp.

I hurried after her, wanting to say goodbye in a friendlier way before we parted.

"I told you I would only offer you the truth," Darien said when I caught up to her. "You don't agree with me. At least you don't agree with Araceli. That was my first fear, that Kel's child would turn into a creature like—"

She stopped abruptly, and all the color drained from her face. She took a trembling step forward and then fell to her knees in front of the battered young woman who had commanded all of her attention: Hai.

"My beautiful daughter," she whispered as she drew the girl into her arms, careful not to crush the magic-burned wings. "I never saw her dance. She was only an infant the last time I . . ." She shook her head. "Except for dreams in the void, I have never even seen my own daughter. I knew she was here, so vulnerable, but I could never . . ."

"I spoke to her," I said. "In those moments in *Ecl*, somehow I spoke with Hai."

Darien smiled, though it was obvious that her thoughts were far away. "Royal blood calls strongly to *Ecl*'s chosen. And you are not only a royal-blood falcon, but sworn to the Cobriana. If anyone could reach my daughter, it does not surprise me that it would be you."

"Isn't there some way to save her?"

"She has no reason to come back," Darien admitted after long, painful moments. "Her magic will always burn her, because of her mixed blood—and this city and its inhabitants will always hate her because of it. She loved to dance and she loved to fly, but these injuries have stolen both those passions from her." She touched a gentle hand to her daughter's crushed black feathers. "I don't know what either of us could say that would give her any reason to return."

There were tears in Darien's eyes when she finally looked at me, but behind them was a fragile hope.

"I can help you return home, Nicias, without Araceli even knowing that you are gone. Once I come back here, I will do all I can—and if I do win a place by the Empress's side again, I will be able to do much—to veil you from Araceli's senses in the future. Otherwise, she will notice your absence swiftly no matter how quietly you leave. All I ask is that you take my daughter to Wyvern's Court with you. I don't think she will wake; there is too much pain for her in this world. But maybe being among her father's people can help her more than I ever could."

I nodded, though it chilled me to realize that Darien never would have offered her help if she had not desired this from me. What she didn't understand was that I would have agreed to take care of Hai without receiving anything in return. Darien was very much a product of this land.

"I will do what I can for her."

# CHAPTER 14

DARIEN WRAPPED the three of us in illusion, saying, "Watch and remember what I do," but warning that I would probably not be able to follow her Drawings beyond the first layers.

She was right. I could understand the pattern that hid us from view, and I thought I might be able to recreate it with practice.

After that, as Darien wove spells to fool each sense, I was lost.

I ended up sitting on the floor of the hall, Hai next to me, for I did not know how long. Sometimes it seemed that time dragged, and others it seemed that it was moving quickly. There was no way to tell. Nothing moved but my own breath. Even the signs of life that every creature emits seemed frozen in Hai and Darien.

Finally Darien gasped, her eyes opening.

They were not the liquid silver I had become used to, but indigo so dark it was almost black. She hesitated, struggling to focus.

*Now*, Darien said, *I need your help. Servos will not betray us, and Cjarsa never looks at the skies anymore. Araceli and Syfka are in conference.* She paused, then commented absently, *They have conversed often of late, though when I stood by Cjarsa's side, they hated each other.* She shook her head, turning her attention back to the present. *I can hide us from the Mercy, but I cannot conceal us from the Pure Diamond without your help. They are sworn to the royal house. If I use your power, I can command them not to see us, and they never will.*

That was all the warning she gave before she sent me gasping to the floor, weaving my power into her illusions to veil us from that last threat.

Eons later, she stepped forward and helped me to my feet. She handed me a small soft bundle—the belongings I had rescued from my mother's old room. Then she knelt again and lifted Hai into her arms.

"We will need to fly in Demi form if we are to carry her," she said, mentioning nothing of the time that had passed or the effort either of us had put forth. "It will not be quick, but we won't be seen—at least, not as what we are. We may appear to be clouds or swift-flying birds or shadows—what people expect to see when they look at the sky. Once we reach Wyvern's Court, we will be avians, familiar and unthreatening. The illusion will hold long enough for us to do what we must."

I nodded, hoping she was right.

✳✳✳

How we made that flight home I do not know. Demi form is not well designed for swift or sustained travel, so it took us far longer to cross the ocean than it would have if we had been in pure falcon form. Without sleeping, eating, speaking or touching land, we flew for nearly six days.

Sometimes it seemed I was far away from myself, only dimly aware of the beating of my own wings. Sometimes I felt every aching muscle, every breath in my lungs.

By the time we reached Wyvern's Court, I was so tired that it took all my energy to guide Darien and myself to the Rookery. I knew only that I needed to check in with Oliza and let her know I was home safe.

My legs collapsed under me the instant my feet touched the familiar ground. Beside me, Darien wavered for a moment before one knee went out and she fell into a trembling kneel, Hai held protectively against her.

Though Darien's magic should have kept anyone from noticing us while we were in the air, we had definitely been spotted. Almost immediately, I saw a familiar wyvern diving toward me from the skies. An equally familiar sparrow followed her closely.

*My magic cannot conceal a loyal guard from the one to whom he is sworn,* Darien said apologetically. *Nor could I possibly hide myself from the woman who used to be my partner in the Mercy. Though perhaps it is best that the first to see us home are your queen and your mother.*

Once my mother returned to human form, she protested to Oliza, "I think it would be best if you would allow me to call for your Wyverns."

"The best of my Wyverns is already here," Oliza replied sharply.

Darien observed with dark humor, *It seems my magic has not failed to hide you from Kel. If we were still the friends we had once been, she would have laughed when she realized what a fine prank I had managed. . . .*

I pushed myself up, wincing as I discovered that my whole body ached, especially my back and shoulders. I withdrew my wings carefully and struggled to present myself to both my monarch and my mother.

For a moment I saw Darien's look of confusion, and I clarified, *Most don't wear their wings openly here.*

*Of course, your land with serpents and hawks.* Her wings rippled and disappeared with far more ease than mine had.

My mother drew her blade then and stepped between us and Oliza.

"Kel!" Oliza shouted. "Stand down."

My mother stepped back a pace, but not quite behind Oliza.

Darien had fallen back into at-ready, the respectful position of submission. With the off hand gripping the wrist of the weapon hand, it left her physically defenseless.

When Darien spoke, her voice was soft with resignation. "Kel of Ahnmik, Indigo Choir, mindwalker, beautiful dancer and once Mercy to the Empress, you don't recognize me, do you?" She spoke my mother's title in her native tongue, then switched to the language of my home, perhaps in deference to Oliza.

"I don't use that title here," my mother said curtly. "And I do recognize you, vaguely. Enough to recall that you, too, were among Cjarsa's Mercy. It's unusual to see one of that group off the island, but when it happens, it is never good."

"You are here."

She stiffened. "I am an exception. You still wear your falcon form."

"Only to you," Darien sighed. She held out her arm, palm up, displaying a very faint scar on the underside of her right wrist. A symbol of some sort. "Do you recognize this?"

My mother rubbed absently at her own wrist, but she didn't speak.

Oliza stepped forward, greeting me formally as she took command of the situation. "Nicias Silvermead, please report."

My mother frowned, and I saw her eyes widen. She had looked at me before, but Darien's magic had kept her from truly *seeing* me until Oliza had called me by name. I wondered how my connection to my mother could be less strong than the connection she shared with a falcon she barely even remembered.

"Nicias?" she whispered. Her blade lowered a fraction, but then she strengthened her pose.

I swallowed tightly, watching my own mother face me with a bared weapon. "Mother, I'm—"

She brought her weapon up as I tried to move closer, and I saw in her the lessons she had taught me many times. Defend those you are sworn to defend. Do not let yourself be deceived by what you wish to see. Err always on the side of caution. She still did not know whether I was an enemy or her own son.

I looked at Oliza. If vows of loyalty were what made the magic shiver, then perhaps this would help.

"*You* know me, Oliza," I said. "And I know you. I know that although the young men who court you give you exotic, spicy perfumes, you wear only the mild scent of almond that your mother gave to you. I know that you love to stay up all night listening to the wolves sing. I know that you dream of flying from this place and living in some faraway land." I went to one knee, looking up at my monarch the way I had when I had first gained my title as Wyvern of Honor. "I am sworn loyal to you and would swear the same again."

My mother's blade wavered.

"I know you, Nicias," Oliza said. "I never doubted who you were."

"And the woman with you?" my mother asked.

"Would like to see the Empress rot," Darien replied, causing my mother's eyes to widen. "And you know none loyal to Ahnmik would speak such, even in an attempt to fool you. I was your own partner in the Mercy, Kel—Darien, of the Indigo Choir. I know why you left, though you do not. I would never harm you."

My mother hesitated, but she sheathed her weapon. "That being so . . ." She glanced at me. "What are you doing back here? I hate to say it to my own son, but if Araceli and Cjarsa are hunting you, you bring grave danger."

Though I would rather have heard assurances of safety and a mother's love at that moment, I understood her concerns. Darien answered for me. "They aren't hunting us. They think Nicias has been lost to *Ecl*, an illusion I am happy that they maintain, and I am here only long enough to see your son and my daughter safe; I will return to Ahnmik long before anyone notices I am gone."

She spoke simply, and I knew that the impassive words were all my mother heard. She could not feel the regret and sudden, sweeping loneliness that I sensed from Darien as she looked at a woman who had once given everything to save her.

"Your daughter?" Oliza asked.

Darien stepped back, to kneel by Hai's side. "Oliza Shardae Cobriana, may I present *quemak'la'Hai'nesera* . . . Hai, daughter of Anjay Cobriana, late Arami to the serpiente."

*Oliza's uncle.* I had known that Hai was a cobra, but I had never had a moment to wonder who her father was. For an instant, I was washed by fear. Darien had shown herself to have many motives, none of them selfless. Had I brought home with me a pretender to the throne I had sworn to protect?

Darien dispelled some of my fears as she added, "Her condition, unfortunately, is likely irreversible, but I hope Wyvern's Court may at least make her dreams warmer than they would be on the island."

Oliza nodded, looking as dazed as I felt.

"Kel, please go with Darien and see that suitable arrangements are made for Hai's care," Oliza commanded.

"Are you certain—"

"Anjay Cobriana was my father's older brother," Oliza said, sharply. "By law, that would make this young woman Arami before either Salem or me. Circumstance denies her that birthright, but regardless, she is a cobra, she is family, and she is one of my people. If we deny Hai the sanctuary of her rightful home then we are no better than the empress who turned her out.

"Dismissed, Kel. Take care of my . . . cousin. I wish to speak to Nicias alone."

"As you wish, my lady," my mother replied, subdued. "Nicias, I hope I will have a chance to hear your story soon."

Darien gathered Hai into her arms, along with the bundle of belongings we had brought back with us. My mother's gaze fell on the *melos,* and she frowned, as if it seemed familiar. Then she nodded at the doorway, indicating that the falcon should leave Oliza's presence first.

*She knows she should remember me,* Darien sighed. *She wonders why I am one of the memories the Empress so carefully removed from her mind. She starts to reach for them . . . and then pulls back.*

As soon as they had left, Oliza sighed and leaned back against the wall. "Nicias . . ." She shook her head and began again. "I would like to question that girl's parentage, but it is as clearly written on her face as mine is. Anjay is the only cobra who ever traveled to Ahnmik. He returned only hours before he fell to the war. Looking at this girl now is like looking at a ghost ... a ghost from whom I seem to have stolen a throne. What is wrong with her?"

Now the questions began. This one would be the easiest.

"The magic the falcons use makes them susceptible to something they call the *shm'Ecl*; Hai's serpiente blood makes her even more vulnerable. I don't know how to explain it, except to say that Darien was telling the truth—it is very unlikely that Hai will ever recover." Addressing the worries that had crossed my mind, I added, "Know that she has been raised as a falcon. In the unlikely event that she wakes, I doubt that she will want to acknowledge her serpiente blood, and even if she does, your people love you. They know you. They would never support a stranger as their queen before you."

Oliza nodded slowly. "Honestly, this silent cobra is the least of my concerns. There have been three fights in the market since you left, all between serpiente and the avians. I fear that perhaps my hesitation to declare my mate and take the throne is hurting my people, and keeping them apart."

This was the moment when I could say, "I learned on Ahnmik what caused the war." I could tell her what Darien had told me, that the old war and the hatred we still battled had been specifically engineered. I could tell her, and then I would no longer have to hold the dark knowledge alone. But what would that solve?

Oliza was my queen-to-be, to whom I was sworn, and she had for many years been my friend. I had vowed to protect her, and to protect Wyvern's Court, and I would. Sharing this with a people who had only come together now that they had forgotten it would be an evil I did not want to commit.

If anyone could heal the schism that falcon magic had created, it was Oliza.

"Fights in the market are still only fights; they aren't battles," I assured her. "We have come a long way. When you take the throne, you will move this land even further along."

"Soon," Oliza whispered. "I need to speak to my parents. They should know who Hai is . . . and if ever I have needed advice from them, it is now." She hesitated. "Nicias," she said nervously, "do you plan to remain among my guard, here at Wyvern's Court?"

"Of course," I answered. "If you'll still have me."

"Of course," she answered, as quickly as I had. "It's just that I wonder—now that you've seen what you have of the world, and with your magic—whether you'll be content. I want you to know that if you do ever choose to leave, I would not fault you for it. Wyvern's Court is a very small piece of the world you have access to."

Chilling was the thought that if she had said this to me before I had left, I might have taken her up on it. Without my vows to Oliza making me hesitate, how much more open would I have been to what Araceli offered?

"Either way, you should get some rest before you report to your commander. You still look exhausted."

I wondered if she was giving me time to change my mind if I wanted to.

The freedom did not comfort me.

✳✳✳

I returned to my home, intending to follow Oliza's advice, only to find Darien there settling Hai into the spare bedroom.

"Hello, Nicias. I assured Kel that you would not mind having Hai near you," Darien said. "Of anyone in this land, you best understand what is wrong with her, and the little that can be done."

I nodded. Even though the idea of Hai living in my home, forever still and silent, unnerved me, I could think of no one else I would trust with her care.

"I must leave now," Darien announced. "I am too tightly bound to the white land to leave it for long." She sighed. "And I have no place here. I envy your mother's freedom, but I cannot stand to look at her as what she now is, and have her look at me as a stranger. She has assured me that Hai will be taken care of, as much as one so deep in *Ecl*'s realm ever can be." She paused, then said, "The magic on you will fade in time no matter what I do. If you wish to remove the illusion spells earlier, I am sure you will be able to."

"What is it you plan to do on Ahnmik?"

She raised a brow. "Commit treason, naturally, with no less than the Empress's blessing." She smiled wickedly. "This is a suggestion I do not make lightly," she added more seriously, "but if ever you return to Ahnmik, you could yet claim your place as Araceli's heir. Return to the center, and see what you can do from there."

I shook my head. "It isn't my world. I won't join it to change it."

"Pity. I will probably not see you again for a long while. Don't forget me."

*Forget* this falcon? For better or worse, I could not imagine ever forgetting my encounters with Darien. "I won't," I vowed.

"If something does go wrong, and Araceli finds you gone, I will do my best to warn you, so that you will have time to flee Wyvern's Court before the falcons come for you." Unexpectedly, she hugged me. "I borrowed a feather of your soul once, borrowed and kept it safe," she whispered in my ear, as she had during our first meeting. "It told me that you would destroy an empire. Perhaps that empire was not the white towers of Ahnmik or the walls of Wyvern's Court. Perhaps it was the black castle of *Ecl'gah*. If you ever do manage to wake my daughter, call to me, please."

*Goodbye, Nicias.*

The last words floated back to me like an afterthought as Darien disappeared out the door. I watched her form shimmer into that of a beautiful black-and-white gyrfalcon and slice through the sky like an arrow.

*Goodbye.*

# CHAPTER 15

KNOWING THAT I had done my duty—reporting to Oliza and ensuring Hai's safety—I was finally able to relax. I could barely stay on my feet long enough to reach my own bed, where I collapsed, still fully dressed.

I fell instantly into soft, sleek oblivion.

I dreamed of a beautiful dancer, with wings as black as night. She performed on a dais in the center of Wyvern's Court, so beautiful and yet achingly lonely.

Around us, the day began to dawn, warm and golden. Her eyes were closed, but she shuddered when the first light touched her.

Abruptly, her eyes shot open, as if she had just realized where she was—not in her dreams, but in mine. She turned to me with an angry hiss.

The world shattered, and I threw up my arms to protect my face—

***

Again I woke with blood on my skin, though the marks were not as bad as they had been in the past. At least this time Hai had been pulled into my dreams, instead of the other way around.

Over time I hoped I would be able to protect myself from her better as I slept. For now I did what I could to heal the marks she had left behind—both the cuts and the visible black bands.

Though I had not been hungry before, I was suddenly famished. Lily had warned me that this would happen.

The thought of her was like a knife in my stomach. I forced it away as I dressed and stepped out of my home.

After I ate, I would try to remove Darien's illusions from myself, and then I would seek out my parents. After that, I would ask my commander's permission to return to my post.

***

For now Darien's magic was still hiding me, and walking through the market as a nondescript avian man was an unnerving experience. I smiled and chatted about the weather with the merchant who sold me my breakfast, and then I continued through the crowds.

For the first time, I wasn't an outsider, a falcon in a realm of serpents and avians. I wasn't known as a Wyvern of Honor, one of Oliza's personal guards.

A group of avians were gathered near the majestic statue that marked the center of Wyvern's Court, talking quietly among themselves. They nodded polite greetings to me as I passed, then continued to speak.

"—but imagine, my son on a dancer's stage," one woman was saying. I slowed slightly, to listen. "Naturally, his father would have forbidden it outright, but I thought it best to let the boy try." She shook her head, making a *tsk-tsk* sound. "I worry for him, but you have to let them out of the nest someday. A more dignified pastime would have been my preference, but he just tells me I'm old-fashioned when I say things like that."

"Boys will be boys. He'll come home soon enough. Though let me say, I am relieved to see that our princess's interest seems to be focused on a young man with nicely traditional values," one of the women replied. "I saw her with Johanna's son Marus the other day. They make a simply splendid couple. He's just the type to help her settle down."

The conversation was drowned out by a pair of serpiente. The two were laughing so hard at something that they had thrown their arms across each other's shoulders just to remain standing. The three avian matrons glanced at them disapprovingly.

"Jaye, I've been looking all over for you," someone said, grabbing my arm.

I turned to him, sure he had mistaken me, and for a moment my head spun. Out the corner of my eye, I saw a wreath of falcon magic, and inside it a fair, slender young man with pale violet eyes. As soon as I was looking directly at him, however, the illusion of an avian youth returned.

He pulled me away from the crowd, and I went willingly, curious. As soon as we were away from the group, he asked softly, "Who is the black-winged dancer?"

*What?* I thought, mute with shock.

*You're not the only one hiding here,* the stranger said. *Now tell me who the black-haired dancer is. She was dreamwalking last night, and it wasn't pleasant for any of us. You're the only newcomer here, so it seems likely that you might be responsible.*

I did not know or trust this young man. I wasn't about to confide in him about Hai. I tried to change the subject instead. *Others are here?* He had to be talking about falcons.

We had left the crowded areas, and he returned to normal speech. "You're here. Why should it surprise you that others are, too? Though I will admit that I had been worried. I had heard that the Heir had bound her, to stop her from helping others flee the island. No one else has come here in years."

"Her?"

He gave a long-suffering sigh. "Darien. I can see her magic on you. I would not have spoken to you if I hadn't."

So Darien had smuggled a couple of falcons out of Ahnmik over the years. It did not surprise me. But the knowledge did make me a bit more at ease with this stranger, enough so to answer his question.

"The dancer is named Hai," I answered. "She is Darien's daughter."

He winced. "She is lost, then?"

I nodded. "Darien says royal blood might call to her strongly enough—"

The falcon snarled a curse. "True, but the royal house does not risk itself by wading into the void. The blood of royals may be strong with magic, but it's very thin when it comes to compassion."

Clearly Darien's magic had not completely failed to hide me. This stranger knew that I was a falcon, but he did not know that I was Nicias, Araceli's own grandson.

He continued to vent. "Even Servos, the guardian of the

halls, will *watch* them for a million years more before he ever considers trying to save one of them. Darien is the only one I've known who is brave enough to swim the still waters, but even she is barely strong enough to keep from drowning. It cuts her every time she tries."

He shook his head as if to shake loose a dark memory. "I wish I—any of us—could walk the *Ecl'gah* like Darien can. Maybe we could bring Hai back to her. Nothing less could possibly repay her for all she has done." He sighed. "If wishes were feathers, vipers would fly. None of us share Darien's talent in the *Ecl*, or her ability to mindwalk. We'd need both to even seek Hai out."

There was a moment of silence as we walked farther, toward the primarily avian section of the area. I spent it considering this new information. I had thought that Darien's fight on Ahnmik was active. It had not occurred to me that her "treason" consisted of smuggling others into Wyvern's Court or rescuing them from *Ecl*.

"I must get back to my shop," the falcon said. "If you have a few moments, many of us gather there at midday for lunch; I could introduce you to the rest."

"Thank you." The temptation to meet others who knew the place I had fled, and who understood what it was to be a falcon in this land was overpowering. "If I'm not imposing, I would be honored."

"Never imposing," he assured me. "Hiding who you are gets lonely, and loneliness is the fastest way to join the *shm'Ecl*."

My guide knocked on his own door. A petite girl, with blond hair tumbling loose across her shoulders, barely silvered in the front and showing no hint of blue or violet, answered the door.

She stepped back warily after recognizing my host, watching me with open distrust and revealing two others: a woman tending the fire across the room, and another young man who had yet to acknowledge my entrance.

"Who's he?" the woman by the door asked.

"Darien's newest, apparently," my host replied. "And he brought Hai with him."

I offered my hand. "I haven't introduced myself—"

"Not to be rude, stranger," the woman replied, "but I would prefer not to know. The less I know, the less valuable I am, the less of a danger I am to the Lady, and the less reason she has to find me. Understand? So don't tell secrets here, and that includes who you are. Just be content that we know the white city as you do."

I hesitated, debating whether I should leave. I craved this company, but these people would not be so welcoming if they knew who I was.

"Pardon my friend's melodrama," my host said, chuckling. "She's been the most affected by the black dancer's dreams. It's true we don't share the names we were known by on Ahnmik here; no need to give that away in case one of us was found. But I'm called Gren in Wyvern's Court. That is Spark. Maya was the charming young lady who greeted you first, and that sullen fellow in the corner is Opal. That done with, would you care for anything to eat, or drink?"

"Gren, why are we being so polite to this stranger?" The question came from Maya, who was eyeing me warily. "We know nothing about him."

"He wears Darien's magic," my host answered. "That's enough for me."

"He also wears some other magic," Opal broke in. "Or am I the only one not blind to that?"

Gren frowned. "Don't try to make trouble again here. I won't have it."

Opal stood up and walked through a back door without a word, leaving his companions shaking their heads.

"Opal is not the friendliest of us," Gren said, apologetically. "But considering our situation, his suspicion is natural."

"Your situation . . . Hasn't anyone ever considered speaking to Oliza and asking her *permission* to be here? I'm certain she would grant it, and then you wouldn't need to hide so much—"

"Ask protection from the near-queen of a civilization on the verge of suicide?" Spark laughed. "Obviously you haven't been here long. No one knows who will rule next, or if this court will even still exist. It has already segregated, avians on one side of town, serpiente on the other. I've heard the dancers threaten to leave Wyvern's Court if it's true that Oliza plans to make that crow Marus her king. Of course, those threats are no worse than the ones started by avians a while back, when it seemed Oliza might choose a serpent. The turmoil makes it *possible* for us to hide, and we're grateful for that, but when the wyvern chooses her mate, she may well push this world back to war—and you should never trust yourself to someone who might be powerless."

Her matter-of-fact words were a kick in the gut. I knew the politics that would confront Oliza when she wanted to take a mate, but the casual assumption that Wyvern's Court was doomed was chilling.

"Perhaps the two cultures can keep from killing each other for a while," Spark stated, "but from birth to death they are as opposite as they can be. They can't exist together, and if they try to force it, the result can only be bloodshed."

Designed to be enemies.

There had to be a way to derail Araceli's plots, but I didn't know what it was. Not yet.

I tried to argue. "If they've come this far—"

"They've come this far only to find that they can't go any further," Spark interrupted. "The two cultures are able to co-exist temporarily—they've shown that—but asking them to combine like this land does is asking a snake and a bird to live together. Either the bird needs to give up the sky, or the snake needs to give up its earthen den. Both options demand too much."

Opal had returned to the doorway and was studying me. "I've realized where I've seen those marks before."

"Where?" I asked without thinking, but as I met his gaze, I instantly regretted it.

"On the Mercy," he said angrily, "when someone fights them. When they mindwalk and something goes wrong. On the Lady's chosen executioners."

Swiftly I realized what he had seen: some lingering vestige of magic from my moments with Hai in the *Ecl*. And I knew what he was afraid of. "No," I said quickly. "I know what you're thinking, but—"

"I don't care if you have Darien's magic on you," Opal challenged. "The only ones who come here with your power are from the Mercy, or are Pure Diamond. The Lady's hand, either way."

"I'm *not* working for Cjarsa or Araceli or any falcon," I protested. "I was born in Wyvern's Court—"

"Mongrel?" Maya interrupted.

"What? No," I answered, hastily enough to make even me flinch. When had I picked up *that* prejudice? "I tried to introduce myself earlier. My name is Nicias Silvermead—"

Gren rose to his feet so quickly that the stool he had been perched on toppled over, his mouth opening and closing in silent protest.

"Tar and feathers," Opal cursed. "Gren, you invited a *Wyvern* here? Why not invite the princess herself?"

Maya snarled, "Kel's son. Your mother is the Lady's Mercy and you have the gall to tell us—" She stopped when Gren caught her wrists, keeping her from moving toward me.

"Quiet!" Spark shrieked, sending the room into stunned silence. "Nicias, get out of here. *Now*. You're not welcome here." She started to reach forward as if to push me, but then recoiled.

I didn't feel the need to stay. I stepped outside, into rain that had started to fall heavily, and heard raised voices behind me.

Spark followed me out, making shooing motions. "Keep moving."

She kept pace as we crossed the market, and only when I was back on the doorstep of my own house did she speak again. "Maya has felt the Mercy's wrath before, as has Opal," she said. "Maya's punishment came at the hand of the woman you now call mother. One of them would have attacked you if you had stayed. You're just lucky they didn't make the connection to who your father is, and who his mother is."

"I wouldn't hurt any of you," I assured her. "Neither would my parents."

"Blood will tell, *sir*," she said, with none of the respect usually associated with that title, but with a substantial amount of venom. "Mercy's blood and royal blood. You'll be as useless as the rest. I trust," she concluded coldly, "that we won't be seeing you again." Under her breath she added, "And you can be certain that you won't see us, either."

Shocked speechless, I could do nothing but retreat with whatever grace I had left. I entered my home, shaking Darien's illusion from myself as I crossed the threshold. How could I have thought, even for a moment, that I might find acceptance among falcons? I was too much a part of Wyvern's Court to be one of them.

No, that excuse was a lie. I was too much a part of Wyvern's Court to be happy on the island, but here among the exiles, I was too much a part of Ahnmik. *Mercy's blood and royal blood,* Spark had said.

*You'll be as useless as the rest.*

What had I done, really, besides run from Ahnmik? I had run home to Wyvern's Court, away from the place where I might have been able to make a difference.

It wasn't my fight.

*The blood of royals may be strong with magic, but it's very thin when it comes to compassion.*

I still needed to speak to my parents, yet I found myself drawn to Hai. If anything was my fight, she was, a cobra locked in a falcon's madness.

Arrogance, for me to think I could help her—but what choice did I have? Who was I, if not Nicias Silvermead, Wyvern of Honor, sworn to protect the royal houses of Wyvern's Court with every strength I possessed?

I put my hand on Hai's arm, closed my eyes and for the first time reached intentionally toward her nightmares.

The *Ecl'gah* in which Hai hid from the world had changed since I had left, but I was not sure whether the changes were for the better. Instead of the stark hues of last time, I found technicolor that dazzled the mind.

All around me were rolling fields of what seemed to be crystals as sharp as razors, which glowed in the light and bent in the intermittent wind like blades of grass. The sky was too vivid, a sunset gone mad with scarlet, amethyst and ginger, flames and waves swirling in no natural pattern. High above, a falcon circled, waiting, waiting to descend.

The cloying smell of sodden roses stuck to the back of my throat. The wind came from random directions at unexpected times, sometimes warm and sometimes frigid.

"Hai?" I called.

My own voice startled me. For all the disturbed beauty of this illusion, Hai had not woven sound into it. The wind was silent even as it danced past the same black castle I had seen too many times before in the distance.

I walked carefully through the crystal flora, to the moat that still circled the castle. The brimstone and serpents were gone, but the sparkling blue water steamed, and every now and then I glimpsed the back of some great scaled beast as it touched the surface of the water.

I could once again see Hai's silhouette looking down at me from the tallest tower.

"Hai?"

*Why do you do this to me?* Her voice was strained. *Why do you give me these dreams? Why must you wrap me with impossible illusions of wyverns and dancers and wings in the air?*

I staggered as the ground beneath me shifted. A raven screamed above me, and I looked up just in time to see the poor creature snapped from the air by a gyrfalcon. The falcon broke its prey's neck, scattering black feathers and blood to the ground.

Where they landed, the flowers and grass blackened as if brushed by a flame.

"It isn't impossible," I said to her, trying to turn away from the ugly sight. Again the illusion shifted, and baby cobras emerged where the raven's blood had fallen. "Hai, Wyvern's Court is real. I've seen—"

One of the cobras, now fully grown, reared up and hissed, flaring its hood.

*If you believe in such bliss,* Hai responded, *then I will pity you, poor hopeful boy. I pity you the fall you must soon face. Perhaps you should let the gentle void take you now, before you have to watch your world burn.*

"I'm not about to let it burn," I asserted. "And I'm not about to hide here from a difficult path."

She laughed, but the sound was like hot sand across my skin. "Nicias, you are already hiding. You walk in my world and tell me not to hide from my problems, but look what you have done. You are Araceli's only heir. She is not likely to give up on you so easily. Soon she will dare to enter the silent halls, and she will realize that you are not there. She will come to Wyvern's Court, and she will drag you back with her. Perhaps while she is here, she will execute the traitors who hide in the candle shop. Perhaps she will rid the world of your precious Oliza, whose reign she fears so much.

"You swore to defend Wyvern's Court, with your life if necessary," she said, accusingly. "Do not wait until it is too late."

The temperature dropped as if to match the sudden chill that had taken me as I heard the truth in her words.

*No one has danced your future for you, have they?* she asked. *Most fear the* sakkri'a'she. *It can burn one's mind, they say, but I spun that magic with almost every breath as I walked the streets of the white city. Let me see if I remember the steps . . .*

"Hai, wait—"

I was caught by her magic like a swallow taken by a hawk,

slammed from this *Ecl'gah* and onto the familiar green marble of Wyvern's Court's market plaza, where I held Oliza in my arms. My hands were marked with the blood from her wounds; she was cold and still. As I lifted my gaze, I saw that the land around us had been charred.

Oliza's body fell, listlessly, away from me as I stepped back in horror, wanting to flee the image.

"Hai!" I screamed. "This isn't real! Take it—"

*Take it away?* she asked me. *This may not be real, but trust me, sweet prince, it is a likely enough future.*

"Not one I will allow."

*But you have no idea what causes it.*

With that reply, she turned the vision, so that instead of being by Oliza, I knelt before Salem Cobriana. Near us, I could hear the shouting of a mob calling for blood, but my magic had pushed them back.

Too late.

Hai knelt next to me, but she did not lift her eyes to mine.

"Hai—"

*Would you prefer a path less bloody? You could always walk this one . . .*

I was gone from Wyvern's Court in an instant and then stood in one of the *yenna'marl* with Lily. When someone knocked at the door, I called out, "Come in," wondering what horror Hai had spun into this threat.

The man who opened the door knelt, not lifting his eyes as he spoke to us. "Sir, the Empress has requested your presence."

"We will be there shortly," Lily said when I hesitated. "We shouldn't keep Araceli waiting."

Then the vision ended, and I was back in Hai's illusion. I

could feel her agitation in the way the ice around me began to shiver.

*What have you done, Nicias, that topples my Empress from her reign and puts your father's mother on the throne? Or, what have you not done?*

Around me, I saw a million versions of myself, a million moments and possible futures. In some, I was Nicias of Ahnmik, heir to the Empress. In others, I stood beside Oliza in Wyvern's Court. In too many, I was left alone with the bodies of those slain.

*Fail, Nicias . . . and the white towers fall. And the golden air of the wyvern's rule becomes a hell of silver ice. Swear to me, Nicias, that you will never betray your wyvern queen.*

"You know I will not."

*Swear it!*

The creature in the moat lashed out, wrapping me in a serpentine body covered in blue and silver scales. I tried to retreat from Hai's mind, but found myself held fast; she had taken control of this moment, and I could only struggle feebly against the iron coils.

"I swear I will never betray Oliza."

The world shimmered as I spoke the words.

The creature set me down, and Hai spoke once more.

*Then you must never become Ahnmik's prince. Know this, Nicias: There are already very few futures in which Oliza lives to rule—and there is not a single one in which you sit on the white throne and the wyvern survives to take her own.*

*What does that have to do with the Empress?* I asked.

*Araceli desires an heir before she betrays my Empress,* Hai whispered, as if in a trance. *Right now, she believes that Darien lured you into Ecl. She believes that she can rescue you, and you will be grateful, and she will be able to win you back to her side.*

*When my mother returns to Cjarsa's side, Araceli will be angry. When she next enters the Halls of shm'Ecl and finds you gone and her plans in ruin, with Cjarsa's favored Mercy to blame, her fury will have no equal in this world. She will turn that anger upon Wyvern's Court as she seeks you, and when Cjarsa tries to calm her, Araceli will turn on my Empress and the white city will turn black. . . .*

*If you hide, both our worlds will crumble.*

*You swore to defend Wyvern's Court, with your life if necessary,* she repeated. *Now it becomes necessary.*

"Please, Nicias, do not do this to me," someone whispered, the words making Hai's illusion shiver. "Sweet Ahnmik, I have given you everything. Please, do not take my son from me."

My mother's prayers gently pulled me back from Hai's world. I was back in my home, at Hai's bedside, as if I had woken from a strange dream instead of the violent nightmare I was used to finding in Hai's realm.

I could still feel Oliza in my arms, her body limp and cold.

I looked up to find my mother and father both near me, my mother crying with relief. "We came to speak to you, and found you . . ." She gulped.

I lifted a hand to my mother's cheek, hating what I was about to do to her.

Despite her madness—or because of it—Hai was right. I couldn't stay here.

"Nicias, please, be careful," my father said. "When your mother told me that you were home, I thought it meant—"

"I am safe," I interrupted. I could not stand to hear his hopes when I was about to destroy them. "From my magic, at least. But I can't stay here. I was a fool to think I could.

Araceli will come looking for me sooner or later, and I cannot hide here when it puts all of Wyvern's Court in danger."

I looked at Hai. If she was right, I would not only be endangering my own world, but others' as well.

My father drew a deep breath. "What is it you intend to do?" he asked me.

"Go back." I could hardly say the words aloud. "Confront Araceli, and either convince her to let me go, or—" *Or what?* If I could not convince her to let me go, I would need to stay on Ahnmik to keep her from threatening Wyvern's Court. How long would it take for her manipulations and persuasion magics to soften my resolve and convince me that I had a place on the white throne of Ahnmik?

I asked my mother, "How true is a vision seen in a *sakkri'a'she?*"

She winced. "No vision seen in a *sakkri* is impossible at the time it is woven," she answered.

If that was the case, then there was still a possible future in which I sat on Ahnmik's throne—and, according to Hai, somehow led to Oliza's demise.

If Araceli would not let me go, then I had only one option: I would give myself to *Ecl*, before I could do more damage.

"Nicias," my mother said, perhaps seeing the dark resolve on my face, "a *sakkri* can be wrong."

"And it can also be right—and that is not a chance I can take. I will not endanger Oliza that way. I will return, if I can, but for now I must leave."

My father caught my arm as I turned to go, and I thought that he would argue with me. Instead, he hugged me. "You could not be our son and do less," he whispered. "Even if, right now, I wish you were a little less noble."

My mother added her blessing. "Ahnleh protect you . . . and bring you home again."

I stepped out my door, instinctively reaching to Oliza even though I knew she had no magic and would never hear me. *I will always be loyal to you. But right now, I must leave you.*

Somehow she did hear. I even felt her reply, faint as it was. *Nicias, what . . . no, I trust you. Fly well.*

I didn't have time to question what power allowed her to answer me, or whether perhaps the words were a gift of my own imagination, trying to comfort me. I changed shape, spread my wings and shot into the sky.

The island where I had rested with Lily was drowned in water when I flew over it; no stopping there. I didn't think I could pause even if I wished to. My heart was pounding with fear.

The flight was a battle through rain and wind that made every stroke of my wings heavier and tried to drive me into the sea.

The destination, I knew, might be worse.

# CHAPTER 16

ONCE AGAIN I landed in Ahnmik's plaza, crumpling to the ground as I returned to human form and desperately tried to catch my breath. The city was dark at that hour, except for the *yenna'marl*, which reflected the blush of dawn that had not yet crept past the horizon.

I started toward the palace, but hesitated when around a corner in the road I heard the soft conversation of a trio of falcons who had not noticed my arrival.

"I swear it's true. She was wearing the Mercy's uniform," a young man said, his voice hushed. "And arguing with Syfka, loudly enough that everyone on the street could hear her."

"Cjarsa must be mad," another responded. Hastily she added, "Far be it from me to question my Empress's judgment, but to place a traitor back into her favor is . . ."

"Suicidal?" the third, another man, suggested. "I've heard some say that Cjarsa is all but lost to *Ecl* already. Maybe she hopes Darien will kill her before the void finishes the job."

*Darien?* Wanting to know more, I turned the corner, not anticipating the kind of reaction my presence would produce. All three falcons paled at seeing me and went to their knees.

The one who had called the Empress suicidal spoke swiftly, pleading, "Sir, forgive me for my rashly spoken words. I am only a simple man. The decisions of my royal house are surely beyond my understanding."

Their fear only made my own worse. If they were so terrified by being caught speaking as they had, what would I face when I spoke to Araceli?

"Stand up," I said. "Please, tell me—Darien is back with the Empress?"

"Yes, among her Mercy," the man answered. "She is working beside Lillian."

But they hated each other.

"Lily was part of Araceli's guard," I challenged, trying to work out this puzzle.

"The Heir dismissed Lillian," the woman explained.

Probably because she had failed to keep me from Darien.

And now they were working together, beside the Empress. What next?

"Where can I find Araceli at this hour?"

The man who had begged my forgiveness seemed very happy to be able to answer me. "She is meeting with Syfka, once again. You could wait for her in the forum of the palace; I understand she is supposed to see the Empress next, and the Mercy would not refuse admittance to Araceli's own grandson and heir."

Did I really want to do this?

No.

Did I have a choice?

No.

"Thank you," I said. They seemed startled that I would bother, and even more startled when I walked past them on my way to the palace without saying more.

I had not even reached the base of the palace when a pair of guards moved to flank me, shimmering with Pure Diamond power. Before I could speak to them, they broke formation, to allow a quartet of women and men to approach.

Each wore a slender blade on his or her left hip. Gauntlets graced their wrists—some leather, and some appearing to be snakeskin—and they wore vests of the same material over their looser clothing. Their wings gave them away as peregrine, and the way they dismissed the Pure Diamond who had brought me there gave them away as something else: Araceli's Mercy.

A line of sweat formed between my shoulder blades as I fought the instinct to flee. I faced them with no way to defend myself against what was to come.

"Welcome back to Ahnmik, sir," one of them greeted me. Her eyes were liquid cobalt and flashed with distaste. "The Empress and her heir are separately occupied at the moment. They asked us to detain you and ensure you do not wander off again."

It occurred to me that if these four had felt Lily's "punishment" as Darien had, they might have good reason to hate me. "I didn't mean for her to be hurt," I said, raising the topic that I feared was on their minds. "I didn't know—"

One of the men glared. "Don't worry, sir, Lillian is fine. We're always careful not to irreversibly damage one of our own."

"Follow us, please," another said impatiently.

I followed; I saw no choice, even though my stomach was twisting as if it would turn itself inside out. This was a group of trained fighters, well practiced in magics that I was only beginning to grasp. Even if I fought, I would have no place to go unless I settled things here first.

My parents had found leniency. Painful as it had been, they had received their desired banishment. I hoped I could do the same.

My heart was pounding as I was led to the Mercy's tower. I doubted that if Araceli still hoped to have me as her heir, she would want permanent physical damage done. How much freedom did the Mercy have with me?

The anger I saw in their eyes said they would use all they could.

I felt the air pressure build as we walked up the weathered stone staircase to the top of the tower. There were no windows here, and the only light was provided by silver marks that snaked along the walls.

A force hit me, and with it I stopped seeing, hearing, knowing.

I couldn't scream, even though the world around me seemed to twist, compressing my lungs and lashing my skin.

In the midst of this, I was blindsided by a sickening guilt for what I had caused to happen, not just to Lily, but to every person I had ever judged. I thought of Araceli and could not summon my fury. I could not summon my resolve or remember why I had made the decisions I had.

She was my father's mother, after all. She had offered me everything, and I had spat on it like an ignorant, ungrateful child.

*Vemka'tair'ka'o'ha'nas* . . . Someone was cursing in my mind, sputtering, *Weakling fool, are you going to let them mind-walk through your brain until you may as well be one of them?*

I felt this angry presence fight back, startling the Mercy enough to let me slip momentarily from their grasp.

Ice sliced open my hands as I fell gratefully into the *Ecl'gah*, suddenly the sweetest place I had ever been. I wanted to sink into the ice and stay there, numb.

Someone kicked me viciously, flipping me onto my back as I let out a yelp.

"You stain my world, *ruin* it, and then have the gall to try to give up?" These words were followed by a string of harsher ones, coming from a female figure who was slowly edging into focus. "You invade my dreams and tell me I am a fool for staying here, but the first time you are tested, you hide yourself away and dare to stand before me as a *hypocrite*."

She dragged me to my feet and pinned me against the cold, black walls of her palace.

"Hai." I blinked in surprise, staring into a pair of furious garnet eyes—the ones I had seen long ago in the forest.

She smacked me, and I couldn't help wondering if staying with the Mercy would have been better. "Someone is calling you. Get back there."

I shuddered. Maybe I *would* rather she kept hitting me.

"I *will* keep hitting you," she snarled. "Ecl wants you, Nicias. She wants her price for saving you, and that price might be hundreds of years, enough to destroy your mind completely. Unless you get out *now!*" More gently, she said, "The worst is over. Go back."

I swallowed hard, then forced myself to agree, with a condition to make it worthwhile. "Only if you will."

She cursed and shook her head. "It's been too long. I can't."

"Darien seems to think you can."

"My mother is a fool."

We hung in silence for a moment. Again I felt the tug of the void, so inviting, painless and . . .

"You must go back," she whispered. "Don't fall here."

"What do you care?" I challenged.

"Damn you," Hai whispered. "I have danced a thousand futures and lived a thousand lifetimes and all I have seen is ashes and ice. You are too—You don't belong here. You have things you need to do, out there. Go, Nicias, *please.*"

"Only if you will."

"Swear you'll go back, and I'll try." Her voice was soft and frightened, but the words were enough.

"I swear."

"Then I swear as well."

✳✳✳

There was blood on the floor when I returned to the *Now*—my blood, from a dozen lacerations across my back and my hands.

There were two women standing above me: Darien and Lily, I realized with relief.

"He's ours now," Lily said, "until the Lady and her heir return."

Darien took my hand and pulled me to my feet, smiling a bit. "The Empress believes in keeping a serpent close so she can watch it." She added silently, *No better place for me.*

Lily regarded me with cool detachment. "You might say thank you."

"Thank you?" My voice broke in my dry, tight throat.

"They would have done worse," she said.

"Why . . . did you stop them?"

"Nostalgia, maybe. Believe me or don't, but I did care for you." She shook her head. "Forgive me for saying, *sir,* but I've recovered from the affliction."

Darien prevented me from replying. "Cjarsa wants to meet with you before Araceli returns. Can you walk?"

"I can walk." I was still dazed, but I recalled enough to say to Darien, *Hai saved me.*

She gave me a sharp look. *She spoke to you?*

*She made me swear to return. If she would.*

Darien paused, swaying with shock. *She said the words?*

I went over the conversation with her as we walked.

*A vow spoken to royal blood will bind her to this world,* Darien whispered in my mind when I was through. *She will try. And she . . . may succeed.*

We reached the door to the reception hall of the palace, and I felt both Lily and Darien hesitate.

"I do not know how the Lady will receive you," Lily told me. "She and Araceli have been . . . displeased with each other, lately. I do not know what Cjarsa wants from you."

We stepped inside with the care of ones crossing a battlefield.

"Nicias of Ahnmik, you stand before the Empress Cjarsa, she who rules the white towers, lady of moon and mountain, sun and sea." Lily and Darien knelt at the Lady's feet, and Lily continued, "Great lady, allow me to present Nicias of Ahnmik, Nicias Silvermead, mindwalker, *mana'Ecl,* son of the son of your heir and of Kel, once of the Indigo Choir and of your Mercy."

"Stand aside," Cjarsa said.

They obeyed, moving to the edge of the doorway, though Darien sent me a wry *She usually will not lie outright. I hate her and she knows it, but even I must respect her.*

I faced the Empress of this cold, white land, unable even to imagine what the next few minutes might hold.

# CHAPTER 17

CJARSA WAS AN eerily beautiful woman, with skin like milk and hair the color of white gold. Her eyes were the same mercury as Darien's, and her lashes just dark enough to set them off, hints of gold in a porcelain face. She wore a gown of deep violet, and the color was striking against her pure fairness.

"Nicias Silvermead, she forgot to add your title Wyvern of Honor." Her voice was musical, as haunting as wind whistling through barren cliffs. "I believe your post as the wyvern princess's guard is the one you respect."

"That is true, lady."

"I am sorry about your rough reception," she said, though there was no regret in her voice. There was no emotion at all. "Araceli's chosen are rather cross with you. I have had to take Lillian into my own employ, as Araceli refuses to forgive her. Though, of course, if you choose to stay, you may have her join yours."

"I have no desire to stay."

She sighed, but again the emotion she tried to portray

seemed forced, as if she was not attached to this world enough to feel the way we mortals did.

"Oh, yes, I am far detached from this realm," she said, as if I had spoken my thought aloud. "In my youth I spent time in the void, too much time exploring the illusions of *Ecl*. Darien will never forgive me for not reaching in and saving her daughter. She knows that I could. But Ecl is a temptation too strong for me. I am already too weary of this realm."

I shivered involuntarily, glancing at Darien without meaning to. The gyrfalcon averted her gaze, jaw set. *Ignore me, Nicias. Speak to Cjarsa*, Darien commanded. *I do not know what she wants, but I do know that she is the only one with the power to keep you from Araceli.*

"Nicias, please sit," Cjarsa said, gesturing to a chair to her left. "There are things I need to discuss with you. A proposition I must make."

"Pardon me for being blunt, Lady," I said, "but after my other experiences in your land, I do not entirely trust your intentions."

She shrugged. "Sit, listen. I am not holding you, and I do not plan to. You know too much already about incidents that should have been forgotten in the past. Since our history seems to have proven that the truth has a way of finding the light, it seems best to end this problem here not by stripping that knowledge from your mind but by tempering it with understanding. Listening is not going to hurt you." She glanced at Darien. "We both know that my less-than-loving Darien will warn you if I lie or try to persuade you magically. Her candor is unusual in this land, and one of the reasons I asked her back to my side."

Darien nodded.

"I am listening," I said.

Cjarsa smiled a little, her expression still somehow cold. "I know that Darien has told you of our actions regarding Kiesha's and Alasdair's peoples. While I may not always approve of Araceli's *methods*, her motivations—in this case, at least—were correct. If you had lived through the early days after the Dasi split, you would understand the necessity of what was done. You only hate it because you were raised among those you see as most harmed."

"Are you going to argue that they weren't most harmed?" I asked, trying to keep my words even and my head clear of the anger that was surfacing.

"The magic of Ahnmik balances itself," Cjarsa explained. "Ahnmik is the energy of stillness and silence. It will bring one to *Ecl* when it is too strong, and he succumbs to sleep.

"Anhamirak's magic is different. It is a magic of wildfires, tornadoes, thunderstorms, bloodshed. Yes, she represents freedom and beauty, but she also represents chaos. When her magic is out of control, it burns. First it will burn out the mind of the user, and then it will destroy what is around him.

"Back in Maeve's coven, Ahnmik and Anhamirak's powers balanced each other. Kiesha and I worked side by side. When the serpiente forced us out, they destroyed that balance. Their magic became as unsteady as ours, but theirs had the power to destroy more than ours ever could.

"When we created the avians, it was more than a way to keep the serpiente from remembering Anhamirak's magic. Avians are *part* of the serpiente magic, a part we removed but could never destroy. That is why, though they have hated each other for ages, they are drawn together. Each is the missing half of the other's magic. When the pair breeds together, the magic joins in the child. Likely, that first child's magic will never awaken. Even if it does, it will be stunted and sluggish. But over generations . . .

"If Oliza takes the throne, her heirs *will* have Anhamirak's magic. It will destroy first them, then their people, and quite possibly the rest of their world as well, until stopped by the only thing that *can* balance Anhamirak: lack of existence. Lack of anything left to burn."

She shifted her gaze from one of the swirling patterns of magic on the walls to me. "Can you understand, Nicias?"

*Could* I? Did I?

Perhaps the ends *did* justify Cjarsa's means, but even if they did, what was there to do? I would still not be part of an effort to launch the avians and the serpiente back into war. Nor could I refuse to let Oliza come to the throne where she belonged.

I was no prince, no king; these decisions should never have belonged to me.

Cjarsa continued, "We designed the avians to be opposite from all the serpiente believed in, so that even if they were not at war, they could not become one race again. Neither civilization will bend; the only way your Wyvern's Court could truly combine them is to entirely destroy the culture of one. That was intentional. Perhaps they do not need war, but they must not be allowed to keep forcing this merge, either."

"I am not loyal to you, or to Araceli, or to Ahnmik," I answered. "I have already refused to be part of an uprising in your land, so you need not fear that from me, but never will I betray my queen-to-be by helping sabotage the people of Wyvern's Court. So, please, tell me plainly what you want with me."

"How far does your loyalty stretch?" Cjarsa challenged.

"Even in Wyvern's Court, there are many who are wary of the time when Oliza will come to the throne. No matter who she chooses, there will be those who hate her mate enough to consider killing him, and maybe your queen as well. And after that, will your loyalty stretch so far that you would let a wyvern's blood destroy the world she rules?"

"I find it difficult to believe that you could perform a magic strong enough to rend the serpiente of half their power and give it to another race," I said defiantly, "and yet you cannot do anything to protect this potential child from herself."

"I am no longer the young fool who once dove recklessly into *Ecl* and warped Fate herself to her will," Cjarsa sighed, her voice distant once again. "I have neither the strength nor the power to do such a thing a second time."

"Araceli bound my parents' magic so that it would not destroy them," I said, thinking aloud. "If the child showed magic, couldn't it too be bound?"

"Nicias, it has been many long years since I have been able to feel a summer wind on my skin, or hear the music of a choir, or savor fresh fruit. I can see Ahnmik's power, and so I can control it, but I am blind to Anhamirak's warmth. Asking me to bind her power is asking me to paint in red and blue a sunrise that I can see only in gray. I could rip the magic from the child entirely, but I could never control it otherwise."

"If that is the only way you will let Oliza's child live, the people of Wyvern's Court could live without magic. They always have."

Cjarsa shook her head sadly. "The serpiente, the avians, they are creatures of Anhamirak's fire. They may not use it consciously, but it is what gives them their scales and their feathers. It is what makes them immune to the plagues and weaknesses that infect humans. If you take it from them, they will die. That is what *am'haj*, the poison Araceli designed and gave to the avians to help them fight the serpiente, does: rekindle the dormant magic that long ago split Anhamirak's power between Kiesha and Alasdair, and allow that ancient spell to destroy what is left."

I lay my palms flat against the wall, thinking of all the lives that had been lost. There had to be a way to solve this that did not involve the destruction of Wyvern's Court and a return to the horrors of the past.

I jumped as the doors to the hall slammed open. As I turned toward the violent intrusion, I saw Darien and Lily draw their weapons, moving between Cjarsa and the interlopers. Though I would have sworn that the four of us had been alone, two more guards appeared as if they had melted from the walls.

Araceli stood with her wings held tightly to her back in the way of an avian warrior. Syfka stood to her left; two of Araceli's Mercy were to her right.

"This is low, Cjarsa," Araceli spat. "You stay in your palace hall all day and night, drifting almost as badly as the *shm'Ecl*. When you emerge, first you take traitors under your wing—traitors who should be shorn of their wings for treason and worse crimes. And now you try to turn my own blood—"

"You are looking for an excuse for your uprising," Cjarsa interrupted. "Nicias was never loyal to you; do not accuse me of turning him against you."

"I can accuse your precious Darien of that crime," Araceli answered hotly. "And we all know to whose hand she has always belonged."

Darien laughed, never allowing her blade to waver or her attention to falter from Araceli and her guards.

If this became a battle, who would I fight for? Would I fight, or could I flee?

*Araceli wants Cjarsa dethroned. She accuses Cjarsa of being an idle Empress over a stagnant land,* Darien whispered to me. *She wants to take power, and build Ahnmik in the great image she sees. She wanted you for her heir, a loyal addition to her power after she disposes of her obstacles.*

Obstacles like Cjarsa.

I jumped as Cjarsa spoke to me, her voice like ice. *Araceli craves power; she has no understanding of balance. And it looks as if she has turned my Syfka against me now, as well.*

She spoke on this point. "Syfka, beautiful aplomado, has she wooed you to her madness as well? Has your time off Ahnmik stained you so badly that you cannot see the danger in Araceli's plans?"

Araceli did not allow Syfka to answer. "Your aplomado was the one who first considered destroying you."

I saw Darien frown. Her command was like a shove. *Look at Araceli, Nicias, and tell me what you see. Araceli is power hungry, but she has never been insane. If she fights here, even if she kills Cjarsa, she will fall.*

When Darien said *look,* she meant with magic. Cjarsa and Araceli continued to argue, the Empress's voice getting softer as Araceli's grew louder, but I ignored all that as I tentatively reached out to my father's mother.

*Movement.*

I stumbled as a wave of Darien and Lily's magic crossed the room, knocking back the two Mercy that Araceli had brought with her. I reached out at the same time that Araceli retaliated. Her magic slammed into me like a tsunami, forcing the breath from my lungs.

As the power flooded over me, I recognized the pattern

hidden in it. The design was infinitely complex, woven through thoughts that Araceli had long harbored, but on the most basic level, it was the same as the persuasion magics Lily had once used on me.

They were well disguised, so subtle and yet so tightly wound that their creation had surely taken years, decades perhaps. Araceli was blind to them the way I had been blind to Lily's. Cjarsa could not delve deeply into this power without drowning, and so she must not have seen it. And the Mercy could not read the lines because they seemed to have been put in place by one of royal blood. Darien only suspected their existence.

I threw the knowledge at Cjarsa and her four guards and felt them react. The two in back had gone to Cjarsa's side to defend her, but Darien and Lily moved forward. When Darien knelt and touched my brow, I shuddered, drawing breath for the first time since I had fallen.

"Would you kill your own kin to win this fight?" Darien asked softly, eyes lifted to Araceli. As she forced me to breathe and my heart to beat, I felt her using my power to read the magic Araceli wore.

Araceli shuddered. For the moment of indecision, the persuasion magics wavered.

Suddenly I made the connection.

Darien had said that Araceli would not survive if she forced this fight. If she and the Empress both fell, Syfka would be next in line—unless I stayed as Araceli's heir. No wonder Syfka had wanted me gone and had "helped" my father to flee years before. She had been planning to destroy both royals for years, but new ones kept appearing.

Lily walked past Darien. I caught a glimpse of a peculiar magic, which could be only the bond among the Mercy, being funneled into Lily. It left three of Cjarsa's Mercy all but defenseless, but Lily as strong as all four combined.

Lily spoke to Syfka, as quietly as Darien had, "Beautiful aplomado, there's no need for you to fall with the heir."

Syfka's wings snapped open, aggressive. "Drop your weapon, Lillian," she commanded.

"I guard the Empress first," Lily answered, "and her house second. You are part of that house, and I hesitate to fight you unless I must. So I ask you, stand down."

Araceli must have felt the strands of Syfka's magic and was unraveling them slowly, because she was shuddering like one coming out of a deep, cold sleep. She was watching Syfka warily, too, and I knew that she had also realized why the aplomado had worked so hard to send Araceli's heirs away.

"My lady," Syfka began. She never finished.

Lily and Araceli both turned on the traitor at the same time. No physical weapon was ever used, but Syfka crumpled, her wings dissolving back into her body. Magic wrapped around her, a net to hold her in place.

"Nicias Silvermead," Cjarsa addressed me as her guards hauled the still form up. "You've already seen more of our quarrel than you should have."

Araceli opened her mouth to protest, then shook her head, averting her gaze. "Lady . . ." She did not say more.

"Say goodbye to Sebastian's son, Araceli. Nicias must return to his own people." Cjarsa looked back at me. "He is an intelligent child. When the time comes for him to choose whether to follow his queen or not, he will choose well."

I would have to tell Oliza what I knew and give her Cjarsa's warnings, but she was my queen, and it was not my place to make decisions for her.

Hopefully I could get her to delay the day she would

choose her mate and take the throne. In the meantime, I would practice what I had learned from Darien. Cjarsa might be too lost to *Ecl* to touch Mehay, but I was not. I hoped that by the time Oliza reigned, I might have the control to protect any child of hers from itself.

Araceli sighed and knelt beside me.

"May I leave now?" I asked. "With your blessing?"

She hesitated. Then she kissed my forehead and withdrew the magic she had harmed me with.

"One last word before you go, Nicias," she answered. "Oliza is very fond of you, true? I know she sees in you a kindred spirit."

I swallowed tightly. "I like to think that is true. We have been friends most of our lives."

"Be careful that someday soon that interest doesn't turn into more than friendship," Araceli warned. "I'm sure you understand how deadly it would be for you to take her as your mate. Adding falcon blood to a wyvern's would be a poor idea. But not so much a problem, as both the serpiente and the avians would kill you before they would allow you to stand as king."

Of *that* I had no doubt. "I love Oliza in many ways, Lady, but I have no desire to be her king. If I wanted to rule, I could stay here." That would not change, though Araceli's warning had made me think of something else. "But if in another world it was possible for falcons and serpiente to be together, wouldn't our magics balance each other, as they once did before Maeve's coven split?"

"Perhaps," Araceli admitted. "Perhaps the child would be able to wield both magics, without losing control of either. Imagine the kind of power she could have, and combine it with the right to reign she would inherit. Neither you nor your mate would have the strength to control her, and absolute power is as dangerous as Ahnmik's ice and Anhamirak's fire combined."

"Absolute power like you and Cjarsa have in this land?" I asked.

Araceli looked amused as she answered, "I know what you think of our realm, *ra'o'ra*. Go now, Nicias. If you return to Ahnmik in the future, you will always be greeted as my heir, whether you choose to stay for an hour, for a year, or forever. Cjarsa will not allow me to hold you here, so I will leave the decision up to you. Perhaps if the offer remains open, you will one day accept. Until then, fly with grace, fly with purpose, fly with strength."

When I returned to Wyvern's Court, I paused only to change my clothes quickly and wash the blood from my skin before I sought Oliza.

She was sitting on a grassy knoll with her cousin Salem, and a couple of their friends. Marus was also sitting with them, close enough to Oliza for his hand to touch hers.

She was so young, I realized as I approached her. What I had seen and learned on Ahnmik made me feel ancient.

I had removed all magic from myself, so the crowd recognized me as I approached. Oliza smiled when she saw me.

I tried to smile in return.

"Are you finally back for good?" she asked. "I have been worried about you."

"I think so," I answered. "And I have permission from

both Cjarsa and Araceli to be here, so I am not a danger to anyone."

*I hope.*

"Welcome home, then."

She stood to hug me and invited me to sit with them as she returned to Marus's side. There was so much more I wanted to say, but there would be too many people listening.

Hopefully later would still be soon enough.

✳✳✳

I returned again to my home, where I checked in on Hai.

She lay on her side on the guest room bed, one hand tucked beneath her head, looking as peaceful as I had ever seen her, but as pale and still as ever.

I felt a crush of disappointment, though I tried to push it away. Darien had given me hope, but what had I expected? I started to turn away, and then I noticed a *melos* and a small open box that had been set on the bedside table. Both were from the collection of belongings I had taken from my mother's room.

Someone sighed behind me. *You're here. I suppose that means I must cease dreaming that I am not.*

I turned back to see Hai pushing herself into a seated position. Her face was falcon fair, her hair dark as *Ecl,* and her eyes the deathly still pools of blood that I had looked into weeks before, when I had fallen in the woods. Only as she leaned back against the headboard did I realize that she had taken down her wings. She pulled her knees up to her chest as if she was cold.

She looked very fragile in this world.

"Welcome back," I said to her.

*Your wyvern pretended to be glad that I have "recovered," but she is a poor liar compared to a royal falcon.* She peered at the possessions that had drawn my attention a moment before. *A father killed within days of my conception, and a mother who would rather have vengeance than raise her own daughter. Such a legacy I am honored to have.*

She opened one of her hands, to reveal one of the Cobriana signet rings.

*I suppose it was my father's,* Hai whispered, slipping it on just long enough to see that it was far too large for her. She took it off and closed it in her palm for a moment. When she tried it on again, it fit as if crafted for her hand.

The casual use of power unnerved me no less than her idly adorning herself with the symbol of the royal serpiente house. What had I done?

*You are the one who woke me, my prince,* she reminded me. *A'she'hena; the rest is in the future's hands.*

o'Mehay
shmah'Mehay-hena'keyika
ka-shmah'Mehay-jacon'itil
a'quean'enae

But he who dances with Mehay, he is lost—
For he who dances with Mehay cannot leave the dance
And will face the fire.

*Nesera*
So dance.

# WOLFCRY

## PROLOGUE

*A*nother day, and Wyvern's Court still survives. Sometimes I fear that we are held together by nothing but hope and desperation, but those bonds have held us for a score of years.

Tomorrow is the holiday that my mother's people call Festival. It is a day of storytelling, laughter and song for the avians. Already the northern hills of Wyvern's Court are bright with decorations.

Meanwhile, my father's people, in the southern hills, prepare to celebrate a serpiente event. My cousin, Salem Cobriana, will take vows tomorrow to become a full member of the dancers' guild. He will be the first cobra in more than eight hundred years to be embraced by that venerated group.

I speak of my mother's people and my father's. To which group do I belong? Both—or neither?

I have four forms in addition to my human one. One is that of a hawk as pure and golden as any avian queen who soared above the land. Another is that of a black cobra, like every heir to the serpiente royal house. I also have a form that is a blend of all my traits—a human body with wings the color of sunset, scales black like night, garnet eyes, a hawk's vision and a cobra's poison.

*My last form is that of a wyvern, a perfect blend of serpent and avian—a form that is of all my people and like none of them. The wyvern's cobra body is ruffled with feathers at its hood, spreading into wings that can drive me through the air faster than any hawk.*

*I am the princess of Wyvern's Court, the wyvern for which it was named, and my reign will mean the union of two worlds that warred for two millennia before my birth. Tomorrow, Festival, marks twenty-one years since my mother and father made what many considered a mad plan to bring peace to their people.*

*My parents ended the slaughter, the battles, the clash of armies and the generations of widows and orphans. They swore to end the killing, and for that I sing my thanks to the avians' gods of the sun and sky, and dance it to the serpents' goddess of freedom and passion. But hatred takes longer to die, and I fear sometimes that my parents' bloody memories blind them to the fear and anger that still stain this world. I see it all too clearly.*

*Their reign ended the killing. I pray for the strength I need for my reign to be the one to end the war.*

*Oliza Shardae Cobriana*
*Heir to the Tuuli Thea*
*Arami of the serpiente*

# CHAPTER 1

The northern hills of Wyvern's Court were filled with the trills of tiny bells, the lilting words of storytellers and the songs of choruses. Enraptured children sat in front of me, waiting for me to begin the story of the first avian queen. Blatantly out of place among them was a friend of mine, a serpiente dancer named Urban, who was lounging near the back, managing to look bored and nervous at the same time.

"Many, many years ago, our ancestors were a collection of small tribes, each led by a different captain and each squabbling with its neighbors over food, water and shelter. When drought caused famine, they became afraid and so were more protective of their scarce belongings.

"In the middle of the worst winter, when early snows had destroyed too many of the crops, a woman named Aleya gave birth to a daughter. She loved her child, but she knew she could never take care of her. So Aleya brought the beautiful golden girl to the mountains and left her there, praying that the wild spirits would care for her.

"The infant began to cry, and soon a pair bond of hawks

landed beside her. They cared for the child as one of their own, teaching her the language of the forest and giving her their most precious gift: the skies. They gave the girl some of their magic and taught her how to change from her human form into that of a golden hawk."

I paused there, looking into the wide eyes of my young audience. One of the children had moved closer to Urban and was trying to examine the silk scarf he had tied around his waist—a *melos*, one of the accessories worn by professional serpiente dancers. Urban glanced at her and she jumped.

"But there comes a time when every chick must leave its nest, and as she grew older, the hawk-girl began to wonder about her true mother. Finally, when she was thirteen, she returned to her homeland. She found her mother and her younger brother, whom she had never known, but was horrified by the conditions in which they lived, by the fear and anger that seemed ever present among humans.

"The girl led first her family and then the rest of her mother's tribe into the woods and taught them how to reach the skies. She showed them better ways to hunt, with a hawk's vision and talons, and so they became healthy and well fed once again.

"Later, other tribes joined them, and each took a form from the wilderness—ravens, crows and then sparrows. For the first time, these tribes lived peacefully together, led by the young queen they named Alasdair, which means *protector*."

The children clapped happily, making the bells hanging from their wrists jingle.

I smiled, enjoying the story almost as much as I had during my first Festival—until one of the adults who had been nearby noticed her child reaching for Urban's *melos* again and darted forward to scoop her up and away from Urban. Urban pretended not to notice, but I saw his back tense.

I had told the story of Alasdair the way my mother had used to tell it to me, but I knew that some of these children had learned a darker ending from their parents. Just twenty years before, the myth always would have included the death of Alasdair at the hands of the serpiente. Tales such as these fueled avians' hatred from the cradle.

I tried not to let the avian mother's reaction to Urban ruin my mood. I knew that many people did not approve of his presence there; Urban was not just a serpent—an apprentice dancer, at that—he was widely known to be my foremost suitor among the serpiente. As such, he faced the wrath of mothers with eligible sons, and of course the jealousy of avian men our age, in addition to the general prejudice of avians against serpiente.

Still, I was glad he had come. Suitor or not, Urban was one of my closest friends. We had grown up together. It meant a lot to me that he was willing to be there even though he knew how the avians might react.

"Bit of a dull story," Urban remarked as he came to my side, trying to keep a careful distance between himself and the avians around us. "Lacks intrigue, danger, scandal."

"Well, I'm sorry that the way my ancestor saved her people from starvation and war isn't racy enough for you," I said, teasing.

Serpiente history—which, unlike the avian stories, was regarded as fact, not myth—involved the brave leader of a clan known as the Dasi seducing a powerful creature called Leben, who had impersonated one of their gods to demand their worship. The story, which was told each year in the dance named after the winter solstice holiday Namir-da, described how Leben had given all of Maeve's people second forms to try to win her favor. Maeve had been given the form of a white viper. Kiesha, the high priestess of Anhamirak, had been given the form of a king cobra. Seven others had been given serpent forms, and four, the followers of the god Ahnmik, had been given falcon forms.

The *Namir-da* did not tell the falcons' story. It also did not include the part about the Dasi being torn apart by a vicious civil war shortly after the gifts had been given. Maeve and the four falcons had been exiled on charges of black magic. The white vipers still lived on the fringes of our society even in modern day, while Cjarsa, Araceli, Syfka and Servos made up the royal house of the falcon empire. Kiesha's people became the serpiente; my family were her descendents.

"Unfortunately," Urban continued, his tone making clear that he found nothing unfortunate in it, "I need to run to the nest now. I'm hoping to catch Salem before he is surrounded by people." Only the full members of the dancer's nest had been invited to Salem's initiation ceremony, and though Urban had grown up in the nest, he had not yet taken his vows. However, the reception that night would be open to anyone who wanted to attend, including apprentices and wyverns. "You will be there later, right?"

"Of course. I think my parents have already headed over."

He looped an arm around my waist and kissed my cheek. By serpiente standards, the gesture was friendly and casual, but by avian standards, it was shockingly forward—so much so that someone immediately grabbed Urban's arm to drag him away from me.

"I'm sorry," Urban instantly said, smiling at the young

man who had come to my unnecessary but well-intentioned rescue. "Did you want a kiss, too?" Marus, the avian, blushed the color of a robin's breast, which prompted Urban to add, "Hmm. I'm sure you did—just not from me."

As Marus stammered, Urban raised his hands innocently. "Sorry, Oliza, Marus, but what can I say? I agreed to be bored to tears all day. You can't blame me for slipping up. Now I really do need to run. I'll see you later, Wyvern." He blew me a kiss on his way down the hill to the dancer's nest on the opposite side of Wyvern's Court.

"I apologize if I overreacted," Marus said to me before I could even begin to speak. "I saw him put his hands on you as I walked by, and responded without thinking."

I had known Marus for years, and while I was glad he understood that *I* would think he had overstepped his bounds, I knew he didn't really think it was inappropriate to pull an assertive suitor away from a lady.

"I appreciate your concern, but according to serpiente custom," I explained patiently, "he might as well have just smiled at me. It would have meant the same."

"According to *serpiente* custom, perhaps," Marus said, "but Urban knew where he was."

"The laws are the same on both sides of Wyvern's Court, and he hasn't broken any."

"They might be the same on both sides, but they change according to blood. Urban took advantage of the fact that you allow a serpent to behave in a manner that you would consider utterly inappropriate from an avian like me—and he did it specifically because he knew that it would offend the dozens of people who were watching."

What he said horrified me, because to a large extent it

was true. I wanted my people to be treated equally, but even I dealt with avians and serpiente quite differently, assigning to each a different set of rules.

What choice did I have? I couldn't judge my people only by avian or serpiente standards, and asking them to behave according to the customs of the area they were in meant that we might as well still have two courts. Between a culture in which it was inappropriate to display strong emotion and another in which it was rude not to, one world where touching was vulgar and another where lack of contact was an insult, there was no easy middle ground. There certainly wasn't one that wouldn't be considered offensive by *everyone*.

"The moral of this story," came a calm, diplomatic voice, "is that Urban can steal as many kisses as he likes, and regardless of his intent, she will always see his actions as one of a friend." I turned and was immediately face to face with seventeen-year-old Sive, the youngest daughter of my grandmother, Nacola, which technically made Sive my aunt, despite her being three years younger than I was.

Sive's hair was long and golden, and her eyes were the same color. She wore a softly flowing cream gown and her feet were bare aside from the fine golden anklet that chimed as she walked. She said, "Serpents may be freer with physical contact, and I'm sure that is a perfectly valid choice, but I imagine it is difficult to court a lady if there is nothing romantic and daring left to do."

Hearing sweet, docile Sive say the words *romantic and daring* almost made me laugh. Although Sive had grown up in Wyvern's Court, she had been raised with the strictest avian traditions. Right now Sive stood beside her avian alistair, Prentice—the nineteen-year-old man to whom she had been betrothed at her birth, a raven who had never done anything that was not careful and reserved.

Sive's comment pacified Marus, but it did not settle my own thoughts—partially because I continued to worry about my own prejudice, and partially because I wasn't certain I wanted Marus to take Sive's thinly veiled advice to be "romantic and daring." In avian society, a lady who accepted a kiss on the cheek from a suitor might as well have accepted a proposal. I wasn't ready to choose my king.

I could think of only one way to avoid the potential problem: give Marus something to do before he thought up something on his own.

"Unfortunately, we must continue this conversation later," I said, "since I plan to attend Salem's reception."

"I thought you said you couldn't go," Marus said.

"To the ceremony itself," I clarified. "Salem's initiation is a major event—not just for the dancers but for all serpiente, since it means the return of the royal family to the nest. The reception is open to anyone who wants to attend."

Marus's eyes did not quite glaze over, but despite his best attempt to show an appropriate level of interest, it was obvious that he cared as much about the formal ending of an eight-hundred-year-old feud between the nest and the Cobriana as Urban cared about famine among Alasdair's warring tribes.

"You're welcome to join me," I offered.

"Us," Sive corrected. "I promised Salem I would make an appearance."

"Sive . . ." Prentice's cultured tones didn't quite conceal his distress. "Didn't you decide not to attend?"

I wasn't surprised by the raven's reaction. Prentice was horrified anytime Sive chose to be around serpents.

He didn't care for me, and I didn't care for him, but he and Sive seemed to get along well enough. If the hawk resented having no choice in the matter, she did not express the sentiment aloud. Avian ladies had always had their pair bonds chosen for them by their parents. I was thankful that my parents had decided to follow serpiente tradition, allowing me to pick my own mate—though occasionally I wondered if it would have been easier if the choice had been made for me.

Sive arched one golden brow. "No," she said, "I believe I told you that *you* did not need to attend, if you are so uncomfortable around serpiente. Since Salem, Oliza and her parents, Zane and Danica, will be there, I am sure to be quite adequately chaperoned."

"Marus?" I prompted.

He started to shake his head, then paused, taking a moment to evaluate my very serious expression. "This isn't just a friendly invitation, is it?"

I shook my head and answered honestly. "Marus, you were upset that Urban kissed my cheek because you know that he is also courting me, and you fear it means that I allow him more liberties than I do you. Sive and I both told you that it meant nothing. I'll go one step further in telling you why:

"I'm not an avian lady, to be courted with poetry and flowers. I'm not a serpiente dancer, who can be impressed by a *harja* and a gift of a handmade *melos*. I am the wyvern of Wyvern's Court, and I cannot afford to choose as my king a man who is not able to accept both sides of me, and both sides of this land. If you are going to feel threatened by Urban, it shouldn't be because he kissed me. It should be because he came with me to the northern hills during Festival.

Avian merchants watched him as if certain he was going to steal from them. Alistairs and parents stepped between him and any lady or child he stood too near or—sky forbid—tried to talk to. In short, they treated him worse than they would have treated a beggar wolf from the forest. But he stayed.

"You say you are trying to court me. So, if you're going to feel challenged by anything, feel challenged by *that*."

What could he possibly say?

He drew a deep breath and then nodded. "Then . . . I accept your invitation."

# CHAPTER 2

E ven for someone raised partially in the serpiente nest, as
I was, there were sights capable of stopping thought and
even breath. A professional dancer who takes the stage to
perform a *harja* for a man she desires is one such sight.

As we moved through the crowd, Marus followed me
closely and tried to stay calm. We had almost reached Salem
when I saw Rosalind Lakeyi step onto the dais. If her relationship with Salem had not already been common knowledge, it
would have been made clear by the lingering look she sent
his way as she rose onto the balls of her feet, stretching her
spine and arching her back in a pose I recognized. It was the
starting position for the solo in the Namir-da dance: Maeve's
seduction of Leben, one of the most famous and most complex of the *harja*.

The dance was accompanied only by a single drum,
which pounded like a heartbeat, driving the pulses of the audience faster as our minds and bodies were hypnotized by
each dip and turn Rosalind took. At some point I heard Sive
whisper, "Oh, my," and turn away, as if her instinct was to

give the dancer privacy for such a display, but my gaze was as firmly locked as that of any cobra who swayed to the rhythm of the snake charmer's dance.

When it ended, we collectively let out a breath. In such a moment, it was easy to believe that our ancestors had possessed magic powerful enough to command the gods themselves.

"If I dance for you, will you look at *me* that way?"

I jumped at Urban's voice, then blushed at both his suggestion and my reaction. "You know I wouldn't let you."

An adult dancer could perform a *harja* or a *melos* at any time, technically, but it was almost always intended for someone special, and it usually ended with the new couple seeking a private alcove, and the nest elders sighing about young love. If I danced those steps, it would be taken as a sign that I had chosen my mate, or at least that I was ready to do so.

I longed to dance as freely as Rosalind did, but while friendly kisses were nearly meaningless among the serpiente, dance never was. I could let Marus steal a dozen kisses before I could let Urban get on that dais and perform a *harja* for me—much less stand up and perform one myself.

The decision I would someday make was too crucial. I wished I could base it on the pull of my heart, but there had never really been anyone who had drawn my passion in that way—not even my two foremost suitors.

I turned my attention back to Marus, who had gone pale. My guest started to speak, thought better of it, and then abruptly turned from white to crimson.

Urban whispered to me, "I bet you his last thought was 'What would Oliza look like doing that?' "

I frowned and hushed him.

Prentice approached with Sive and, looking at Salem, asked dryly, "Is that appropriate?"

My cousin had responded to Rosalind's performance in the only way serpiente *would* consider appropriate. Their kiss had gone on long enough for one of the other dancers to spin a *melos* around both their necks. Normally I would have assumed the gesture to be idle teasing, but the black silk *melos* had been decorated with intricate stitching in gold— a color that among the serpiente represented an eternal mated tie. I wondered if I would be hearing an announcement sometime soon.

Salem must have heard Prentice's question, because he focused his garnet cobra's gaze on the avian.

I stepped between the two men, clearing the way with inane chatter. The two of them had never gotten along.

"Salem, congratulations," I said. His smile warmed and he stepped forward to hug me.

Behind me, Sive was whispering to Prentice: *"Behave."*

*"I will if he does."*

"Thanks," Salem replied, looking around searchingly. "I saw your parents a couple of minutes ago."

"Then Rosalind distracted you?" I asked.

"I have my priorities straight. And it looks like you've brought your own distractions. Marus, this is a surprise."

"I hope I am not intruding," Marus said.

"Do you really?" Salem asked, teasing. Without giving Marus a chance to come up with a polite reply, he shook his head. "You are of course welcome, especially since I imagine that you are my cousin's guest. I have nothing against feathers. Speaking of, my blushing aunt, I seem to recall that you promised me a dance. Prentice, mind if I borrow your lovely lady a minute?"

Prentice looked like he minded quite a bit, but when Sive shot him a pointed look, he gritted his teeth and shook his head. In the spirit of the moment, I turned to Marus and offered my hand. "Care to dance?"

"No." His response was so instinctive, so abrupt, that we both laughed. Color crept up his face. "I'm no expert on serpents, but I know that almost everyone here learned to dance while learning how to *walk*."

"Not everyone." I nodded at Salem and Sive. This was maybe the third time Salem had convinced Sive to try dancing. She was abysmally bad, but Salem led well enough that she didn't embarrass herself. Despite Salem's keeping to dances that were tame by serpiente standards, appropriate for siblings or friends who weren't intimate, Prentice watched them with a scowl.

"I don't know how to dance," Marus said.

"I'll teach you." There were plenty of fairly innocent dances that were also simple enough for Marus to learn.

He was so nervous that I almost felt sorry for him as he followed me to the edge of the plaza where serpents were dancing informally. Had I not had so much invested in that night, I might have told him he could leave.

"I can't handle watching this disaster in the making," Urban announced as he jogged to catch up with us. "Marus, relax. If I can tell you're tense by watching you *walk*, you're going to have a lot of trouble dancing."

Marus looked mildly affronted, but before he could react, a shadow brushed across the ground. I looked quickly at the sky, where a single peregrine falcon was circling.

His voice a little too hopeful, Marus asked, "Do you need to go?"

The falcon was not simply any bird, but Nicias Silvermead,

the second-in-command of the Wyverns—my honor guard on the few occasions when I needed one, as well as the rarely necessary police of Wyvern's Court. Gretchen, the commander of the Wyverns, was a serpent and had requested the evening off for Salem's reception. That left Nicias in charge, which meant that his seeking me out was for official reasons. Not a good sign.

My parents also must have seen the signal. They slipped through the crowd.

"Urban, Marus, good to see you both," my mother greeted the young men politely. "Oliza?"

"Go," Urban said. "I'll take care of Marus while you're gone."

"Excuse me?" Marus chirped in surprise.

"I spent all day at your avian Festival," Urban informed him. "You aren't getting off so easy here just because there's an emergency. Give me your hand. By the time Oliza gets back, we'll have you ready for a dance."

They looked at each other for a moment, Marus shrinking somewhat with acute discomfort, and Urban's blue eyes shining as he challenged his primary competition. I could almost hear them both thinking, *Is this really worth it?* I worried about leaving them alone together, but if Nicias was looking for me, then I had bigger problems than male egos.

"I'll be back as soon as I can," I told them.

"Do you have any idea what's going on?" I asked my parents as the three of us pushed through the crowd to clearer ground.

They both shook their heads, but the answer was not long in coming. As soon as we were outside the mass of serpents, Nicias dove to the ground, transforming from a falcon into a young man with blond hair that turned silvery blue at the front, and worried icy blue eyes.

Nicias and I had been friends since infancy. The only falcon in Wyvern's Court, he was as much an anomaly as I was as the only wyvern, and that bond had made us very close. That he was the only male my age who I knew would never try to court me also helped.

He had gracefully offered to take over for Gretchen for the evening, without speaking a word of regret about not being welcome at the reception. Salem might not have anything against feathers, but many serpents were still uncomfortable around a falcon—even one born and raised in Wyvern's Court.

"Something wrong?" my mother asked. As always, Danica Shardae seemed to embody the blending of the two courts that I often tried to mimic. Her gold hair was pinned up with combs decorated with images of the serpiente goddess Anhamirak, exposing the hawk feathers at the nape of her neck and a necklace of twisted gold, with a pendant in the form of an *Ahnleh,* an ancient serpiente symbol meaning Fate. The necklace I wore every day had a coin stamped with the same symbol; it had been a gift from the dancer's nest to my mother when they had ceremonially welcomed her into their ranks, shortly before my birth. Even though my mother was dressed like a serpiente dancer right then, she held herself with the calm poise of an avian lady while listening to Nicias's report.

"I'm not sure," Nicias said. "A pride of lions entered our land a few minutes ago. The leader says he has a message for the royal house of Wyvern's Court."

All the lions I knew of worked as mercenaries. Wyvern's Court had never needed them, though they had offered to serve both the avians and the serpiente at various times during the long years of war and had occasionally been hired.

"Are they waiting in the Rookery?" I asked.

"In the courtyard, yes."

As we started toward the eastern cliffs, my mother hesitated, glancing back at Marus and Urban. "Is it a good idea to leave them together?"

"Probably not," I admitted.

"An avian and a serpiente dancing together to impress the recipient of their mutual affection," my father mused. "It is bold, but not the most surprising thing I've ever heard of young men doing in their efforts to show off. They will probably be fine."

"Probably?" I asked. The words were not as comforting as I would have liked.

# CHAPTER 3

We entered the Rookery courtyard to find six well-armed men and women watching us with a neutral attention. Every time I had spoken to the lions, they had been the epitome of courteousness, but even so, the sight of their soldiers unnerved me.

Their leader stepped forward and bowed. "Diente and alistair Zane Cobriana; Tuuli Thea and Naga Danica Shardae; Princess Oliza Shardae Cobriana. And Arami'ka Irene Cobriana," Tavisan greeted us formally as my father's younger sister—Salem's mother—stepped into the room.

"I saw the three of you leave and came in case I was needed," Irene explained when we all looked back at her.

"That's yet to be seen," my father said. "Tavisan, I understand you have a message for us?"

"I'm here on behalf of Kalisa, the alpha of the Vahamil pack," Tavisan said. The wolves' territory brushed against the northern borders of Wyvern's Court. We had always had excellent relations with them. "My pride recently stopped in Vahamil land to trade. As you know, it is our way to ask the permission of the leader of any territory we stop in, so I requested an audience with the alpha. It was . . . not entirely what I had expected.

"Kalisa has been injured, severely. I was told that it was a hunting accident. It is possible that a successor will be chosen. Kalisa says she would like her allies to be present, so that if necessary she can introduce them to the new alpha and help ensure a continuing alliance between the Vahamil and Wyvern's Court."

*I was told. Kalisa says.* He was being very careful with his words.

"Why does it take six soldiers to deliver a message?" I asked.

"I have given you the message, as I was requested," he replied. "Anything else I might tell you would be speculation."

I glanced at my parents, but they both nodded for me to continue. "Is there other information you feel we should know?"

"It seems odd that the Vahamil would hire an outsider to deliver such important news. Normally my pride is asked to carry messages only across terrain that those sending them could not easily cross—which is not the case with the wolves—or in times when one does not want to place an important missive in the hands of someone of questionable loyalty. I do not know exactly how precarious Kalisa's position is, or how many wolves are currently vying for leadership, but my impression is that there are not many she can trust."

The Vahamil had flourished under Kalisa's leadership, but if she was perceived as weak, under their laws any wolf would have the right to challenge her. She might have said she was sending for the rulers of Wyvern's Court to introduce us to a potential heir, but it seemed more likely now that she had called for her allies to try to protect her own throne.

My mother must have come to the same conclusion at the same moment, because she nodded and said, "We will go tonight. Our alliance with Kalisa has always been valuable to all of our people. It is important to make sure that any potential heirs appreciate that. Oliza, would you please give our regrets to Salem and the nest for needing to leave so suddenly?"

"Of course."

"Do you need me to stay in Wyvern's Court?" Irene offered reluctantly. She and my uncle, Galen, had intended to leave for the serpiente palace immediately after Salem's reception that night. From there, they were headed east and wherever Fate took them. Their plans had been nearly half a year in the making, since Irene had announced her intent to take advantage of this era of peace by traveling the world with her mate.

My father shook his head. "Oliza will be here."

I often acted in my parents' stead when they were away. As they often reminded me, I would inherit the throne as soon as I chose my mate and was ready to claim it. In the meantime, I needed to live up to my position.

"I'll send for the members of your guard to travel with you," Nicias said to my parents. "I imagine you will want to leave immediately."

"That would be best."

"If you do not require our escort," Tavisan said, "I would like to respectfully ask your permission to remain in Wyvern's Court and visit your market tomorrow to replenish our supplies. We did not have time to trade with the Vahamil."

The lions had occasionally passed through our lands for various jobs and had never caused trouble, so I said, "As long as your stay is peaceful, you are welcome in our market."

"Thank you, milady."

Irene stayed to confirm plans with my parents, assuring me that she would return to the reception before going on her way, and I started back toward the southern hills. If the events in Wyvern's Court had been anything other than the initiation of a cobra into the dancer's nest, I would have asked to go with my parents, but I understood why my remaining there was important. The dancers were the heart of the serpiente; it was essential to make clear that Salem could join them and still be part of the royal house.

Serpiente celebrations frequently lasted until dawn, but anxiety about Kalisa had stripped me of my energy. I wondered how early I would be able to leave without causing concern.

The first person I saw was not Marus or Urban but a young woman with the black hair and garnet eyes of the serpiente royal house—a cousin I had learned of only a few months before, when Nicias had brought her back from the falcon island of Ahnmik. She seemed to be watching the dancers from the edge of the crowd.

"Good evening, Hai," I said. "It is good to see you out and about."

When she did not reply immediately, I thought she had not heard me, and I wondered whether I should speak again. Hai was the only daughter of my father's oldest brother, but she had been born and raised on Ahnmik. She could pass as Cobriana, but I knew she considered herself a falcon, like her mother.

The combination of these two heritages had nearly driven her mad. When Hai had first arrived at Wyvern's Court, she had been comatose, and most people had assumed she would never recover. Even now that she was awake, it was evident that her mind was still not completely right.

"Oliza," she said to me after a moment. "Don't patronize me."

"I didn't mean to. I simply do not see you in the market much. I'm sure Salem is pleased that you are here."

She shrugged. "I'm sure the cobra has other things on his mind . . . like flirting with a pretty hawk and waiting for her alistair to hit him."

I sighed, deciding to end the conversation while it was still sane and mostly civil. I had known Hai to break into periods of complete incoherence.

"If you'll excuse me, I need to find Marus."

She nodded and replied loftily, "You're excused."

It didn't take long to find someone who could point me toward Urban and Marus. My two well-known rival suitors' attempting to dance together was a spectacle even by serpiente standards.

Aside from his jumping whenever Urban moved closer and they accidentally touched, Marus seemed to be dealing well with Urban's instruction. Every now and then one of the young men would murmur something, usually too soft for me to hear but clearly less than flattering.

Watching them gave me some hope. Neither looked exactly *happy*, but I would have been shocked if they had. After all, they were not just from opposite sides of the court, they were rivals. However, the competition seemed to have driven both of them to do something they otherwise would not have considered; Urban had issued this challenge, and Marus had accepted it.

Urban noticed my presence. He smiled at me and then moved a little closer to Marus to say something that made the raven blush. A moment later, the sound of a familiar, bell-like laugh drew my attention to where Sive and Salem were still dancing together. Prentice looked as if he was on the verge of reclaiming his pair bond, but Rosalind was doing her best to keep him occupied.

I looked away from Urban and Marus only for an instant, and in the next moment, I heard a sound that could only have been a punch connecting with skin.

I spun around just in time to see Urban stumble back, one hand going to his bleeding lip. Serpiente tempers being what they were, I had time to take exactly one step forward before Urban retaliated with a blow that sent Marus to the ground.

"I forgot. You're a bird," Urban spat. "You wouldn't rec-ognize a come-on if it bit you."

"And you wouldn't recognize a *lady* if she slapped you," Marus retorted as he pushed himself up.

"Sure I would—one just did."

Marus made another move toward Urban, but Salem grabbed the raven's arm. That prompted Prentice to come to Marus's defense, and practically the entire population of the southern hills to come to Salem's.

Recognizing the possibility for real violence, I took a deep breath and let out a wyvern's shriek. It was sharper than the hunting cry of a golden hawk and more dangerous than the hiss of a king cobra, and it made everyone freeze in their tracks.

"Salem, do you really want to let your reception turn into a brawl?" I asked. My cousin shook his head and took a step away from Marus and Prentice. "Do you want that to be the memory your parents take with them when they leave tonight?" I was aware that my voice was less than warm, and

I didn't care. "Prentice, perhaps you should talk to Sive before you put her in the middle of a riot." Prentice's eyes widened, and he turned his head to locate his pair bond. Sive had pressed herself against the edge of the dais, trying to get out of the way of the crowd. "Marus. Urban. What happened?"

"Oliza, he . . ." Marus hesitated, as if realizing that his excuse was not enough to justify the fight. "I lost my temper."

"So I saw." I sighed. I doubted that Urban was entirely innocent. No doubt each of them had been trying to bait the other. Marus had just been unlucky enough to throw the first punch.

Marus stepped forward. "Oliza, you didn't hear—"

"Don't bother," Prentice said. "You're an avian and you hit a serpent. That's all anyone here cares to see."

"Prentice!" Sive exclaimed.

Prentice looked at his pair bond briefly, but his next words were for me. "Are you going to say otherwise?" he challenged. "Tell me it matters to you that the snake was making intentionally inflammatory remarks."

Urban protested. "I wasn't—"

"Or are you just going to say, 'That's their way,' and ignore it," Prentice continued, "the way you always ignore the culpability of serpents when their behavior becomes more than one of *us* can stand?"

"Thank you," Marus said respectfully to Prentice, "but you don't need to defend me. I could have walked away. I shouldn't have hit him." The words obviously pained him. I suspected that this, like the apology he had offered back on the avian hills, was a bow to my sensibilities and not an admission of his own beliefs.

"Urban hit back fast enough," Prentice muttered.

"Prentice, I think it's time we left," Sive suggested, taking his arm. "This is a private matter, and it seems to be under control."

As they left, I noticed that sometime during the argument the rest of the serpents had backed off as well.

Marus shrugged. "Even I know enough about serpiente culture to know that you don't hit one without expecting to be hit back."

"Either of you have anything else to say?" I asked.

They both shook their heads. "But I'm not going to volunteer to help any of your other suitors in the future," Urban said. "I don't know where I came up with that idea in the first place."

The night had been a fabulous disaster. Most serpiente would continue to celebrate for hours yet, but Urban spoke for all of us when he announced with obvious frustration, "It's been a long day. I'm going to bed."

He and Marus exchanged one last look, too tired to be quite hostile, before he turned back toward the nest.

"I'll see you in the morning, Oliza," Marus said hopefully.

I nodded, and he changed form and took wing back to his home in the northern hills.

I used the disruption both as an opportunity to pull Salem aside and summarize what Tavisan had told us and as an excuse to leave early without offending anyone. I had spent many nights curled in the arms of the dancers, enjoying their warmth and company, but that night quiet solitude was all I wanted.

# CHAPTER 4

At the last moment, I changed my direction so that instead of immediately going to the Rookery, I stepped into the forest beyond the northern hills. I needed to calm down before I would be able to sleep.

I was not surprised when Nicias landed by my side a moment later. He was my guard, and he would not leave me alone, especially while there was any rumor of unrest among the nearby wolves. He gave me distance as I picked my way through the darkened woods, lost in thought, but he came to me when I sighed.

"What happened?" he asked. "I saw your parents off and then flew over the southern hills just in time to see you come out here."

I briefly described the fight, trying to keep the bitterness from my voice. After I was done, Nicias let a few moments pass in awkward silence before asking softly, "Do you want to talk, or should I give you space?"

Though I knew he could not go far enough for me to be truly on my own, I appreciated the offer of privacy.

We had been friends for so long, I chose instead to tell him the fears that I rarely shared with anyone. "I love the serpiente, the dancers, the silken *melos* scarves and the Namir-da," I said. "I love the avians, their singers, the sky, the poetry and the philosophical debates in the northern side of the marketplace. I love both sides of Wyvern's Court . . . enough to admit that despite their sitting on opposite sides of a single valley, intended to be one society, they might as well sit on opposite sides of the world. They are two completely different civilizations, and neither wants to change to accommodate the other—and I don't feel I have the right to tell them to."

Nicias looked away, and I regretted how frustrated I had sounded. I tried not to burden others with these fears. I might have apologized, but before I could, he said, "You're right. But we've come so far by not killing each other. There *has* to be a way." Thoughtfully, he suggested, "Your parents went to the Mistari. Perhaps an outside perspective would help again?"

"Perhaps, but what if the tigers agree with all the others? The wolves don't understand why we bother to try; Kalisa and I had a long discussion about this when her pack was visiting the market a few months ago." Kalisa and I had always gotten along; I respected her. I hoped she was not as badly injured as the lions' message had indicated. "Kalisa said they respected our efforts but it isn't natural for two people who are so different to mesh. And the falcons?" Nicias winced.

"Think it can't be done," he said, as he had many times before. That was one of the very few things he had told me of his days on Ahnmik.

He would tell me the rest, if he ever thought I needed to know.

Nicias had seemed older since he had come home from the falcons' island four months before. When he had returned to Wyvern's Court, he'd had wounds that spoke of torture. Those injuries had since healed, but whatever he had learned had marked him permanently.

He had continued studying magic, but I had never met his teacher, and he seemed reluctant to speak of her. I had put enough together from his vague references to know that she worked with him from the city of Ahnmik, without needing to come physically to Wyvern's Court.

"What if I go to the Mistari, and they say the same thing?" I challenged. "It can't, or shouldn't, be done? People see the Mistari as almost infinitely wise. If I brought that message back with me, it would fracture the court further. I can't risk that kind of damage." But doing nothing meant risking the kind of damage that could have occurred that night. "Maybe I should just give it up," I said, joking. "Shock everyone and elope with a falcon."

There had never been anything between Nicias and me beyond friendship, and yet he tensed, moving away from me.

"Don't, Oliza," he said.

"Wyvern's Court isn't something I should joke about," I said, concurring. "I just get so frustrated."

"I know," he answered, "but it's not a safe joke to make, even in frustration. There are too many people who would take you seriously."

Too many people, in these woods? What had happened to the days when we could share our dreams and he didn't chastise me about the shadows overhearing us?

I frowned, hurt. I knew what would happen if I *did* take a falcon for my mate. Both serpiente and avians would probably rebel. I would have a civil war on my hands. Even if that wasn't the case, everyone knew that a falcon couldn't take a pair bond from another breed without the risk of having a child whose magic was too strong to control. Hai was a vivid example of that madness.

The impossibility was what made my friendship with Nicias safe. There had never been a chance for a relationship between us, so we could both tease and not worry about it going further.

I supposed he had stopped teasing after his trip to Ahnmik. I hadn't noticed until just then.

"It's late," Nicias said softly, "and it has been a long day. Maybe it would be best to face these questions in the morning."

I nodded. "You're right. It's too late tonight to make any decisions anyway, too late to do anything but turn over the same fears."

We said our farewells, and I changed shape and stretched my wyvern's wings, circling once over my home, as if to bid it good night. The dancers would keep the southern hills bathed in light and music until nearly dawn, but the rest of my world was quiet and peaceful.

Almost. Shifting shadows drew my attention to something out of place in the avians' northern hills, a figure lying on the ground, curled on its side on the cobblestone path between the houses. My pulse sped as I dove toward the unusual sight. It was common for people to sleep outside on the southern hills in good weather, but it was unheard of *there*, on the hard cobbles of the north.

I fell into human form near enough to make out dark

hair. Fair skin. Clothes that could pass for acceptable in either court. A *melos* tied around his waist, with a fringe of silver thread. A dancer.

*Urban.*

I tumbled to his side, skinning one knee when I saw the blood on him.

"*Urban!*" I shouted, but was afraid to touch him. He was curled in a protective ball, one arm over his head, his hair in his face so I couldn't see it. *Please don't let him be . . .* "Urban, please . . ."

Tentatively I touched his shoulder and turned him toward me, and though it made me cringe, the pained sound he let out was the sweetest thing I had ever heard. Thank the gods at least he was alive.

"Urban, it's me, Oliza. How badly are you hurt?" I was torn between wanting to stay with him and wanting to take to the skies to drag back a doctor *right then*.

A doctor, and guards. If someone had done this to him, it had happened just moments before. Whoever was responsible had to be nearby still. I couldn't leave Urban alone, unprotected.

"Oliz—" He hissed in pain and then slowly, agonizingly, tried to lift his head.

"Don't move yet," I told him. "I'll be right back."

I rose to my feet and shifted back into my wyvern form, propelling myself into the air, with one eye still on Urban. As I shot above the mist, I let out a shriek capable of shattering glass.

Within seconds, two of my avian guards took to the sky. Other avians rose from their beds and came to doorways. All the serpents who were celebrating in the southern hills, including Gretchen, looked up.

Half a minute had passed since I'd left Urban, but by the time I landed beside him again, I had six of my guards with me.

Nicias took charge. "Get to the Rookery and bring back a doctor *now*; I don't care who you have to wake up," he ordered two of the avians, who instantly returned to the sky. "The rest of you, spread out, try to find sign of who did this. Try not to panic people." Meanwhile, he knelt by Urban to assess the damage.

By this time, Gretchen had reached us, her face flushed from the run. "Oliza, what's—" She went pale when she saw Urban, but her first question was for me. "Oliza, are you all right?"

I nodded sharply, even though I understood why I had to be her priority. "I found him. I wasn't here when it happened."

"It's all right," Nicias was saying to Urban. "You're going to be all right." He lifted his gaze to me, and I could tell he was worried.

"Is there anything you can do?" I asked.

"I'll try."

He brushed the hair out of Urban's face, revealing bruises and a long cut down his cheek. One of Urban's eyes was swollen shut, but the other eventually focused on Nicias, and Urban cringed, perhaps anticipating the touch of what the serpiente considered falcons' black magic.

"It'll be all right," Nicias said again before he closed his eyes, drew a breath, and then went impossibly still.

By the time the doctor arrived a few minutes later, Urban's eyes had closed again, but he was breathing regularly. Nicias looked up, finally releasing the long breath he had held, and reported, "I can't do any more. I don't know how. I managed to stop the bleeding inside, but he has broken bones, things—" He pressed a hand to the ground as if to steady himself. "I'm not a trained healer."

The doctor, an avian named Rian, nodded. "I'll take care of him."

The next two hours were torture. I waited in the Rookery library, my head in my hands and my body shaking with adrenaline, while the doctor tended to Urban.

"Oliza?"

I looked up when I heard Gretchen. "Urban is awake. He wants to speak to you."

"How is he?"

"The doctor is . . . optimistic." The careful words made me pale, and she quickly clarified, "He'll live. But the doctor is avian. I do not think she understands that Urban is more concerned about the broken leg and the dislocated knee than he would have been about a potentially fatal injury."

"Gods," I whispered. Gretchen was not exaggerating. A dancer's craft was his life. Who had done this?

I stood to go, and Gretchen added hesitantly, "Urban also wants us to speak to the nest and bring a serpent here to stay with him."

I began to nod, surprised that Gretchen had even bothered to pass that request by me instead of simply fulfilling it, and then it hit me. When the dancers heard about the attack on Urban, they would be furious and assume that avians were to blame. We needed to find out who had done this before word got out, or the dancers might take matters into their own hands.

"I'll speak to Urban," I said, "and then we'll figure out the rest."

# CHAPTER 5

"How is he?" I asked the doctor as she stopped me in the doorway of Urban's room.

"He'll make it," Rian said, "but not thanks to any craft of mine. Nicias minimizes his skill. Judging by the injuries I saw, if the falcon hadn't been on the scene, I'm not certain I would have been able to do anything. I know you'll need to talk to Urban, but make it quick. He needs rest now."

I didn't bother to try to explain that Urban would not be able to rest well until he was back in the nest and safe in the arms of his fellow dancers. That would be my problem. "Can he be moved?"

"If he must be, but he won't be able to walk. He'll need to stay off that leg for a week at least if he wants it to heal right."

She left the room, and I went to Urban's side. I had to bite my lip to keep from cursing when I saw him. I wanted to weep; I wanted to scream. *What kind of monsters could have done this?*

I forced myself to remain calm when I said, "I hate to have

to question you so soon, but I need to know what happened, before the rumors start."

"You mean," Urban said, "before the dancers learn that one of their people was jumped by a group of avians?"

I winced. "You're sure they were avian?"

"Yes."

"What happened?" I didn't want to know, but I needed to.

Urban shut his eyes and took a shaky half breath. "I'm not sure. A little while after you left, I walked over to the northern hills. Figured I should go by Marus's house to see if he was still awake, and apologize."

"Apologize?" I asked, impressed but surprised that he would have decided to do such a thing, especially since Marus had hit him first.

"I might have baited him—just a bit," Urban admitted.

"So you walked to the northern hills."

"There isn't much more to tell," he said. "I thought I remembered where Marus's house was, and I was on my way there. It was dark. I felt a couple of people nearby—avians." He didn't need to clarify how he knew they were avians. Serpiente were cold-blooded; if he had felt their body heat, they couldn't have been serpiente. "Someone hit me with something. . . . I don't know. I don't remember much more. I remember someone saying . . ."

"Go on."

"Just, 'Stay away from her,' " he mumbled. "I'm sorry."

"You're sorry?" I whispered. "Urban, this is my fault if—"

"It's not your fault. It's their fault." He coughed before muttering, "And they call us violent."

"Do you remember anything else about the people who attacked you?"

He shook his head and then cringed as if the movement

hurt. "I don't remember. There were two. Maybe three, but I think two."

"Marus?" I asked hesitantly. An even worse possibility . . . "Prentice?" Both had been directly involved in the violence earlier.

He started to smirk. "I'd love to say yes, but I don't know."

"I need to talk to my parents."

Had anyone sent for them? It had been only a few hours since they had left, but it would be difficult for even an avian to locate them until the sun was up.

Had any night ever been longer than this one?

"If the doctor says it's all right, I'd like to go back to the nest . . . but I'm going to need help."

I hesitated a little too long and saw his eyes widen.

"Oliza—"

"Will you wait until I talk to my parents?"

"Oliza, I've done nothing wrong."

"Of course you haven't—"

"If the nest learns that you refused to let one of their dancers go home—if you *lie* to them . . ."

I pressed a hand to my forehead. "You've done nothing wrong, and I have no intention of holding you against your will or lying to anyone. I am *asking* you to please wait until I have spoken to my parents and the Wyverns, so that I will have something to tell people."

"That wasn't meant to sound like a threat," Urban assured me. "I'm on your side. I'd like to wring the necks of the mangy fowl who hit me, but I can't stand the idea of letting them create a rift in the nest. Salem Cobriana was the first member of the royal house to join us in twenty generations.

Don't betray that—not to protect a bunch of birds too cowardly to even show their faces."

He was right. As much as I would have liked to keep this
quiet until I had more answers, serpiente did not tolerate deception from their royal house. Too many people had seen me
shout for help. Too many people would notice that Urban
was missing, and would start asking about him, if they
hadn't already.

"I won't." I stood up, touching his cheek gently on one of
the few unbruised spots. "I'll be back as soon as I can, and
I'll help you to the nest. In the meantime . . ." The promise
that there would be guards on the door would be of little
comfort. They weren't his nestmates, the people a serpent
went to when hurt or scared.

"Hurry back."


"Gretchen, I want to see all the guards who examined the
scene earlier," I told the python after I left Urban's room.
"We need to get Urban back to the nest as soon as possible,
and I want to know *something* before we do. I need to talk to
Salem right away," I added. I would need him to help keep
the dancers calm in the next few hours. "And then I'm going
to need to speak to Marus and Prentice." That was going to
be unpleasant. "And please get someone with wings who
can find my parents." *Now,* I wanted to add, or better yet,
*Yesterday.*

As Gretchen jumped to respond to my commands, I
walked with rapid strides to one of the empty classrooms. I
needed to get myself under control, needed . . .

I screamed, muffling the sound with a cushion so that my

guards wouldn't come running once again. There was no way to beat down this horror, this fury—this *terror*.

My fault, my fault. I wasn't the one who had hit Urban, but I was the one who had insisted he come to Festival. I was the one who had laughed and assured him he would be fine.

I screamed again. I felt blind, and helpless.

"Don't do it."

The voice from the doorway made me jump. Hai. I turned toward her with a glare hot enough to melt steel. She looked back at me with an absolute lack of concern.

"Don't do what?" I asked when she did not speak again.

"I don't know. What are you about to do?"

I struggled to compose myself. "Hai, can you act sane for just a moment—please? I don't have it in me right now to play riddles."

"How nice for you."

"Hai—"

She made an abrupt motion, cutting me off. "A *sakkri* isn't neat like a letter. I was never trained; I can't control it. At least I remember mine. Most without training cannot."

"*Sakkri?*" I knew of them from my studies in the dancer's nest. The various forms of *sakkri* performed by serpiente were the remnants of ritual dances that had once been used to conjure powerful magic long ago. Some *sakkri* had called the rain; some had been used to create illusions; some had been prayers for divine assistance and some had summoned spirits of the past and future. There were dozens of varieties, some of which I had performed and many that I would not even begin to study for years yet.

Unlike the serpiente, the falcons had never lost their magic. My cousin, despite her cobra features, claimed to wield a falcon's ancient power. "Magic. Vision. *Sakkri'a'she.*"

She tried to explain. "You are about to do something that changes everything."

The *sakkri'a'she* was one of the more intricate *sakkri*, which I vaguely knew but had never performed. If one believed the stories, this particular form had been used to ask the future for guidance.

"How can you be warning me not to do what I'm about to do when I don't even *know* what I'm about to do?" I snapped.

"Your not knowing what the weather will be tomorrow does not change it."

"Presumably my knowing what I'm about to do would affect *that*."

Why was I arguing about this? I didn't believe in prophecy, and even if I had, I wasn't certain I would have trusted a prophecy told to me by my crazy cousin.

"Of course. This is why I came to speak to you." She waved a hand dismissively. "The mind barely comprehends its own yesterday, but *sakkri* force on it other times, other places, other people, visions it tries to shake away because to hold them all would only court madness. A single soul is not meant to know every *is* and *was* and *may be* and *could have been*. What I see is never as clear as *why* and *when* and *where* and *how*. Just pieces of a memory that aren't meant to be mine. All I know is that within the next few minutes, what you do what you *did*, or will do, in the future I saw . . ." She closed her eyes and let out a heavy sigh. "I do not know."

Regardless of whether I believed her, I thought I understood the warning: consider carefully before acting. I needed to calm down so that I could think rationally.

"Thank you for trying," I said. "I will be careful."

She shook her head. "I hope so."

I closed my eyes and drew in a deep breath, meditating the way dancers did before a performance. Those mental exercises included envisioning the steps the body would soon take; now I forced myself to think of a plan for Wyvern's Court.

Urban was right that we could not put the dancers off for long, but it would be equally dangerous to speak to them without some kind of reassurance. *Damn* Kalisa for calling my parents away. How would I deal on my own with the only suspects we had so far?

Speaking to Marus would be hard enough. After all, he was a longtime friend. Worse, though, would be confronting Prentice. I doubted he would react well to the accusation. Avians considered themselves above the vulgar passions that led to violence; they would not want to believe that an alistair to the royal house could be responsible for such a vicious attack. If Prentice *wasn't* found guilty but word got to the serpiente that he had been questioned, they might jump to the conclusion that he had been protected because of his position.

There was no good way for this to end.

"*Vemka!*" I snarled a curse I had learned in the nest. *Calm down, Oliza. Calm down, and think of a plan.*

I opened my eyes. Hai was still there, watching me with an utterly inscrutable expression.

"Hai, thank you for your concern, but would you please leave and let me think?"

"If I thought you were capable of such, I would," she said, "but I live in this place, too, and I would rather it still be here tomorrow."

I needed something to calm my rioting, exhausting

thoughts. Prompted by Hai's warning, I chose the *sakkri'a'she*. *You're thinking too much about what you are doing,* my teachers always told me. *You aren't comfortable with it yet.* Right then, I needed something that would take all my concentration, something that would force my fears from my mind long enough for me to relax and step back.

I took another deep breath, calling to mind what the music would sound like, hearing the rhythm in my head before I began to focus all my attention on the subtle, tricky ripples of the dance. I was vaguely aware of Hai nearby; she sighed, and I remembered that she had once been a dancer herself. She took a step toward me.

If I had Hai's power, could I use this dance as my ancestors had, to beg the spirits of the future for guidance?

I felt at peace, as if all the world was held at bay for a moment.

But then it was as if I had been struck by lightning, and I found myself with my palms pressed against the ground, tears in my eyes, my whole body shaking, unsure of exactly where or when or who I was.

Hai recoiled from me. "Whatever you have just done, I'll thank you not to do it again," she choked out before stumbling from the room.

Whatever I had done . . . Thoughts lingered in my mind like a dream. I needed to—

*This is madness—*

I woke in the Rookery courtyard, to the sound of Nicias calling my name. An instant later he was beside me, whispering something in the old language that had to be a prayer.

"Where am I?"

"Are you hurt?"

"I—no. How long have I been—"


"*Oliza!*"

"I—what?" Gretchen was with us now, and Nicias sounded slightly frantic. He had put a hand on my shoulder, and I pushed it away. "I'm fine," I said. "I think."

My head was spinning. How had I gotten there? I remembered talking to Hai, and then . . . a vague sense of knowing I had to do something, go somewhere . . .

"You're pale," Nicias said. "Does anything hurt?"

I shook my head and pushed myself up—


I was standing; we were at the stairs to the Rookery. I was holding Nicias's arm for support.

"Oliza?" Gretchen asked when we paused abruptly.

I felt as if I had been dreaming and was waking up in stages. At least I remembered now when it had begun. "Remind me never to let Hai 'help' me again."

"What about Hai?" Nicias asked.

*What* about Hai? She had come to the library. "*Sakkri'a'she,*" I said. "She was talking about something I was going to do. She wasn't making any sense."

"*Sakkri'a'she* are rarely worked even on Ahnmik," Nicias explained. "Of all the versions of *sakkri*, the *a'she* is among the most difficult. It allows the user to see possible futures, ranging from those that are likely to occur, to those that could occur only if a very unlikely series of events took place. Falcons have been known to go mad struggling to fight Fate to bring about events that they would never have known could occur if they hadn't seen them. And Hai . . ." He sighed. "She has no way to control it. She has told me that she gets lost in time constantly. The past and the present and the future overlap in her mind, so sometimes she sees the consequences of her actions before she has even decided what to do, and sometimes she sees her own 'free will' as nothing more than a result of the choices of those who came before. You didn't try to perform one in her presence, did you?"

The concept made me shudder. I recalled thinking how valuable it would be to know what the future held, but I would never want to pay that price.

The deeper explanation of Hai's madness, though chilling, did not explain the loss of time I had experienced, and my lingering disorientation. As I recalled the strange, painful incident, Nicias went a shade paler.

"The magic that still lingers in the Cobriana line disturbs falcon magic; it acts like a spark," Nicias said, sounding shaken. "If Hai were already half-caught in a *sakkri'a'she* when you began to dance one, your being there might have triggered something. Or her being there might . . ." He trailed off. "I have to tell you something I've put off. It can wait until after we deal with Urban, but tomorrow, I need some time."

"Yes, of course."

He shook his head as if to clear it. "Salem, Sive, Prentice and Marus are all here, waiting for us—for you. Do you need to rest, or are you ready to speak to them?"

"I'm as ready as I'll ever be."

I wasn't losing time anymore, but the night continued to progress in a kind of haze. I felt as if there was something I was missing. My sense of frustrated ignorance was not helped by the meetings that followed.

None of the guards had seen anything. Marus and Prentice, both of whom had been pulled from their beds, seemed legitimately horrified as they swore their innocence. Salem first reacted as I feared all the dancers would—with pure fury, which he immediately directed toward Prentice—but he responded to my appeals that, in this, he needed to be a cobra first and a dancer second. We needed him on our side.

We had no proof of guilt, very few suspects and even fewer leads. The only concrete decision that we were able to make involved Urban and the nest.

"Salem and I will help Urban back to the nest and explain that we're doing all we can. We need to make sure that the dancers know we're on their side so no one will think about taking justice into their own hands. We can't afford vigilante retaliation. My parents should be here soon. They . . ." What could they possibly do to make things right?

*Nothing can make this right.*

# CHAPTER 6

Urban, Salem and I were welcomed into Wyvern's Nest with anxious eyes and horrified questions. Rumors about what had happened had already reached the southern hills, and the only way we could calm people at all was to beg them to be quiet for Urban's sake, so that he could rest.

Salem helped Urban to a comfortable spot near the central fire as I faced the questions I had anticipated. *Who did it? Were they avians? Was it Prentice? Of course it was Prentice; everyone knows he hates dancers. Was it Marus? Everyone saw him hit Urban earlier. Will the attacker be turned over to the serpiente for nest justice?* Everyone had a theory and a proposed solution. Urban freed me from the interrogation; Salem took over for me, as if he had not nearly come to blows with Prentice in the Rookery just minutes before.

I joined Urban on the pallet of blankets and cushions that the other dancers had put together in front of the fire. Mindful of his injuries, I nevertheless lay as close to him as I could without pressing against him, knowing that he would want that comfort even more after having been denied it among the avians.

Almost immediately, he shifted to close the distance, my warmth and companionship more important than bruises.

I only meant to lie down for a few minutes, but the night had been too long. I didn't even realize I had fallen asleep until a wolf's howl startled me awake.

Urban woke when I stirred, and he asked, "Something wrong?"

"No," I answered. "Just the wolves. Go back to sleep; you need the rest."

"I've been 'resting.'" He shifted and winced. "I don't think that doctor remembered that she was talking to a dancer when she told me to stay off my feet for a week. I feel like I'm going to crawl out of my skin if I don't move, and it's only been a few hours."

Carefully, I put an arm around him. Worse than the doctor's orders to stay off the injured leg, no doubt, was her warning that it might not heal right if he didn't.

He sighed and closed his eyes again to sleep. As I did the same, he ran an idle hand through my hair, tickling the feathers at the nape of my neck. It reminded me of when we had been children, curled together in the nest at the end of a day of mischief. He had always been fascinated by my feathers.

"Oliza?"

"Hmm?"

"I . . . never mind." He sighed.

I opened my eyes and saw in his gaze something unchildlike.

Abruptly the mood changed. Though I knew that Urban considered himself one of my foremost suitors, I had always seen him as a friend, nestmate, safe companion when the rest of the world was cruel. That safer world fractured into sharp, fragile pieces as he turned my head so that he could steal a very *adult* kiss.

I pulled away instinctively. "Stop."

I had no doubt that he would, no fear. He smiled sadly, knowing the answer before he asked, "Don't suppose you're just saying that because I'm injured and you're worried about hurting me?"

I shook my head.

"Can't blame me for asking." In the space left between us, the night air suddenly felt colder.

A few minutes crept by in near silence, broken only by the chattering of predawn birds, as we both pretended to re turn to sleep. I don't think it surprised him when I stood up, saying, "I'm going to see if my parents are back yet."

Not far away, Salem was watching us. Rousing Rosalind, who had been curled against his chest, he hurried to meet me before I reached the doorway.

"I need to see if there is any news," I said. "I shouldn't have stayed as long as I did."

Salem sighed. "Good luck. Urban's not just any dancer. He grew up in Wyvern's Nest; he's like everyone's little brother."

"Which means he's going to have a lot of big brothers looking for payback," I said. "I know."

"Oliza . . ."

"Yes?"

"He *is* a good man. Don't let a bunch of thugs scare you off."

If only it was that easy. "I have to go. Take care of him."

"We will."

As I paused at the doorway to glance back, Salem and

Rosalind repositioned themselves so that they bracketed Urban. He wouldn't be alone.

Once outside the nest, I walked silently toward town. My parents would have come to the nest if they were back, but I could still go to the Rookery to see if anyone had learned anything. Maybe there had been a witness. Maybe . . . maybe so many things that seemed unlikely.

I had just needed to get out of there.

I touched a hand to my lips.

My parents had married for politics and then fallen in love. If I had to do the same, would I be as lucky as they were? I wondered how many generations of ruler had made the same decision.

As if to match my bleak thoughts, the clouds opened up and the first spatter of rain landed just as I crossed the market center.

I walked quickly across the green marble plaza in which the symbol of *Ahnleh* was combined with an equally ancient avian sigil, the Seal of Alasdair, and paused before the white marble statue that stood at the center: a true wyvern, slightly taller than I was, its tail curled around the base, its wings spread proudly, and its head raised as it shouted to the sky. It had been built the year that I had been born, when the idea that avians and serpiente could live together was new and so many had been filled with hope.

I couldn't remember what it felt like to be that proud and sure. Maybe one could manage it only when caught in the coldness of stone. I stared at the wyvern, envying her, as I let my body shift into *my* half form.

The wings that tumbled down my back were the same color as the feathers at my nape, varying from gold to rusty red to nearly black; the snakeskin that covered my body from my ankles to my neck was black with a red sheen. My eyes shifted to a deep amber, the whites disappearing and the pupils becoming slit; my fangs were filled with a cobra's poison.

My full wyvern form was similar to the statue, but this was my half form, my monster, a form no one I knew could see without flinching.

I leaned against the cold marble wyvern, putting my arms around her lithe body.

In half form, my senses were almost as keen as those of a pure cobra and those of a hawk combined. That was why I heard the sound of bare feet slipping slightly across the rain-slicked marble plaza floor, and why I felt the body heat of several creatures suddenly surround me. I turned to flee or fight, but I had no chance to even recognize my attackers before their hands slammed me back into the statue. One of my wings smacked into the ridge of its back, and I gasped as I felt bones break, my vision wavering so that the figures around me were nothing but vague outlines in the rainy morning.

Before I could recover, one of my attackers grasped my wrists, and others extended my wings without care for the broken bones. The pain made my stomach roll and I choked back bile.

"I'm sorry," said a voice that seemed familiar as I felt a blade begin to cut my long flight feathers.

My gasps were halted as someone put a cloth over my mouth and nose, muffling me and cutting off my breathing until I spiraled into unconsciousness.

# CHAPTER 7

Time passed in an odd, warped way, so that I could not tell how long I was in my strange, rocking prison, less than half-awake. Sometimes I would open my eyes and there would be light; sometimes it would be dark as pitch. Most of the time, my vision was too blurry to tell any more than that.

The first time I woke with any true awareness, I found myself lying on my stomach in human form, though I did not remember returning to it. I tried to shift, and the combination of pain and dizziness forced me to stop and cry out as I clutched at the wooden planks beneath me.

Sometime later I came to again. My world wasn't swaying as badly, but my head was pounding and my mouth felt cottony. People were talking nearby in loud voices, which seemed to warp and waver, swirling in the air. Someone asked, "Can't we let the princess out now?"

646    AMELIA ATWATER-RHODES

"This whole area is infested with wolves," someone else responded. The voice . . . I knew that voice. "No need to let them see her."

There was a pause; then someone else said, "She's moving around again."

"Bring her something to eat and drink." The speaker was Tavisan, the leader of the lion mercenaries. But why had they done this? Had the wolves hired them? Kalisa wouldn't have; who were her rivals? I did not know what might benefit them.

The wall of my tiny little room was peeled back, letting in a bit of light from their fire. The lion who blocked the doorway was broad shouldered, and his gaze never left me as he put a canteen of water and a plate of simple food in front of me.

"Wait!" I called after him as he started to move away. My voice cracked; my throat was so dry. He ignored me and carefully fastened the leather wall back into place. "Tavisan!"

I could barely speak above a whisper. I grabbed the canteen of water and chugged half of it before I even noticed the smell of roasted meat. Starving, I shoved food into my mouth. I needed strength to . . .

Needed to . . .

The thought drifted away. Woozy, I lay down again, and belatedly the word came to mind: *drugged.*

When I slept, my dreams were hazy visions not just of home but of whatever fate I was going toward. At one point, I woke, screaming, from a nightmare about butterflies.

*"Milady, I cannot possibly—"*

*"Tavisan, please."*

When I fell asleep again, the image changed to Urban,

bleeding—and then it was Marus instead. Sometimes others; sometimes all of Wyvern's Court. The dancer's nest was on fire. Sometimes there were falcons, and occasionally lions.

I knew I had to get away. To *run*. Far away, because someone had me, and they weren't afraid to use violence—I remembered my wing breaking—or to drug my food. The haziness left from the drugs made it impossible for me to concentrate for very long, and I struggled to keep from drowning in fear.

Finally I woke fully enough to realize that I was inside some kind of covered litter. The walls and the top were leather, and they were attached so firmly to the heavy wood floor that in my weakened state I could not pry them away. I still worked at it, trying to ignore the way my stomach rolled with every movement, and I nearly collapsed as the vertigo hit me.

The drugs were in the water, I decided. I had to stop drinking it, to clear my mind so that I could make a plan instead of continuing this useless scratching.

Eventually it occurred to me that mercenaries worked for payment. Surely Wyvern's Court could offer the lions more than their current employers—and if prizes would not work, a pride of lions was not stronger than the serpiente and avian armies.

"Tavisan!" I shouted again. "You know who I am. Talk to me. We can work something out." I waited but heard no response. "Tavisan, you were in Wyvern's Court the day before I was taken. When my people find that I am gone, they will quickly discover your role in my abduction. Is the payment you have been offered enough to risk the wrath of Wyvern's Court?"

I heard whispering among the lions carrying my litter then.

"Tavisan, she has a point. Wyvern's Court—"

"I know what I'm doing." The leader's voice was certain.

"But what if—"

"Do not question me," he snapped.

"Tavisan, you are destroying your own people," I argued. I had a vague memory of arguing with him before. How many times had I woken, in my drugged state, and perhaps said these exact words?

"Oliza, I apologize for your rough treatment. I wish it had not been necessary. Even so, you are wasting your breath."

I continued to call to him, alternating between threats and promises, sometimes trying to bargain with Tavisan and sometimes appealing to his people, but I received no more answers. Eventually my throat was again too raw to continue shouting, and I dared not drink to soothe it.

I avoided the drugs long enough to clear my mind, but after two days without water, the cramping in my body became so severe, I knew that dehydration might kill me. I curled up in a ball in the corner of the litter, trying to concentrate on something productive.

They had clipped my wings. They had clipped my wings and then fed me a poison to force me back into my human form. I knew the process because it was one of the most severe punishments meted out in avian society.

It permanently locked someone out of both her half- and full-avian forms. Locked me from my wings. My serpiente form would be unaffected, but my hawk was gone.

Grounded, forever. There was no cure; there never had been. That was why the avians used it as a final punishment, and only for the most extreme crimes.

*Stop it, STOP IT!* I tried to force the thoughts away.

Suddenly the ground was tilting, and I heard yelling, mostly in a language I did not know. Howls, shouts, sounds of fighting. My litter swayed again as whoever was holding it stumbled.

Instinctively, I threw myself to the side that was tilting. The impact of my body against the wood made me see stars, but I did it again, and again—

Until my litter tipped and hit the ground *hard*, one side splitting as the wood broke with a crack as loud as a thunderclap. I blacked out for a moment but was too frantic to do anything but drag myself up afterward. I crawled through the split, gasping at the cold outside. Instantly soaked, I forced myself to move. Water, on my hands; I licked it off gratefully.

I didn't know who was fighting, and I didn't waste time looking. With the drugs slowing me down, I rose to my feet, sprinted, stumbled, rolled as I fell and fought to my feet again. *Woods.*

The forest looked like a haven and I scrambled into it, cutting open my hands, knees and arms on brambles in my mad flight.


Later I collapsed, choking on my own heavy breathing; body cramping, demanding water, food and sleep. I could give it two of those. There was water everywhere; I scooped it up in my aching, frozen hands. Cold.

Sleep.

I hoped I wouldn't be found. I curled up to conserve as much heat as I could, but I wasn't even shivering anymore. That was good, I decided. Not so cold now.

Sleep.


It felt as if days had passed, but all I knew for sure was that the sun was out when I opened my eyes and sneezed on fur that was across my face. There was some animal next to me, giving me its warmth. I had enough clarity of mind now to realize that the creature—a wolf, I realized as I turned—was the only reason I *had* woken. I must have been on the verge of freezing to death when I had fallen asleep.

*Snow.* That was why there was water everywhere. I had seen snow once, when I had gone with the Vahamil pack far to the north, but that had been nothing like this. This was deep and thick and still falling from the gray sky above.

I looked at the wolf, not for an instant believing that it was a wild beast, though unable to tell if it was from the pack with which I was familiar.

"Thank you," I said, shivering.

The wolf tilted its head, questioning.

I could feel the human in it—in *her*—and I knew that my savior was a shapeshifter. But she was looking at me without any human comprehension. "My name is Oliza. You saved my life, I think."

The wolf stood up and started plodding away from me. I stayed where I was, and she paused, looking back. She didn't need to speak; her warm brown eyes seemed to laugh at me, saying, *Follow.*

Where was I? I could remember only the last couple of days with the lions, after I had stopped taking the drugs, but the change in weather was drastic enough to make me think that we had traveled weeks away to the north. Weeks that I had been away from home, weeks during which my people should have come after me and found me.

I was too lost, and too weak, to travel on my own. So I followed my silent guide, though my steps dragged and my stomach rumbled. The drugs still felt thick in my system; I was perspiring even as I shivered, the winter air slicing through my clothes and freezing my sweat. The world kept turning to fog around me, but whenever I drifted, the wolf was there, bumping into my legs and guiding me in the right direction.

When I stopped, unable to move any farther, the wolf nudged me into a hollow where the snow was not so thick and the wind could not reach. She brought down a rabbit and we shared it, the raw meat disgusting to the "civilized" part of my mind but a welcome meal to the sensible, *starving* one.

My guide did not let me sleep. I suspected that she was worried I would not wake. After our meal I dragged myself back to my feet and we kept walking.

I spoke to the wolf as I walked. My stories were disjointed and often trailed off as I forgot what I had been saying, but my mute guide didn't complain. She made no indication that she understood, but the words helped keep me focused.

"I walked away, that was the last thing I did," I said, thinking of Urban. "He was hurt because of me but . . . I couldn't stay . . ."

Why had no one come for me? They had to know that the lions had taken me.

"My Wyverns. Gretchen, and Nicias—did I tell you about Nicias?" I thought I had. I had talked about magic . . . or something, earlier . . . "My best friend," I whispered. "The only man in Wyvern's Court not related to me who I can be alone with without causing a scandal. Shouldn't be a scandal." I had never been tempted to do anything scandal worthy. Oliza Shardae Cobriana, her mind always on her throne. It might have been nice to be a carefree child for a while, chasing butterflies in the summertime.

I envied Salem and Rosalind. What I wouldn't have given to look at someone with—"they love each other so much." Had I said the beginning of that thought aloud?

I was getting confused. I was repeating myself at times, but other times, I knew I was saying only fragments of sentences.

"I need sleep," I said. "I'm so tired."

I stumbled, going to my knees in the snow. My legs were numb. At least they didn't hurt.

The wolf nuzzled my shoulder with a whine. I put a hand on her shoulder and pushed myself back to my feet.

"It would be nice to be in the nest now," I mused. "A fire to keep warm. People around. Sometimes it drives me crazy. Serpiente don't believe in privacy, and it gets so that even your thoughts don't feel like your own, but it would be nice to be warm. Nice if Marus and Prentice didn't look horrified when . . ."

I realized I had stopped walking again only when the wolf bumped against the backs of my knees. She whined, trotted ahead a few paces and tossed her head in a way that made me look at the horizon.

The fires burning in the distance were the sweetest signs I had ever seen. Desperation gave way to hope, and I started moving faster, stumbling forward because I couldn't run with legs that had gone numb hours before.

Someone saw me and called out, and in that moment, my energy fled me. I had held on to it only because the wolf had demanded I keep walking. Poison, malnutrition, dehydration, exhaustion, cold and injuries caught up to me just in time for me to collapse into the arms of a young man I had never seen before.

# CHAPTER 8

I woke warm and dry, if still a little woolly-headed. A fire was crackling, and as I opened my eyes, I found myself inside a small cedar hut decorated with furs, leathers and odd silver and bead ornaments. I sat up slowly, glad that the world did not spin too much, and looked around for the owner.

He sat in the corner, wrestling with some bit of leather that refused to do what he wanted. Intent on that project, he had not yet noticed that I was awake.

What if I wasn't safe? For all I knew, this was the mercenaries' destination. If Kalisa's rivals were responsible for my abduction, it would have made sense for them to place me in the power of their own allies—who were probably wolves.

I didn't know what I would do if these people were unfriendly. I thought about the weather outside.

And the wolf who had saved my life.

"Hello?" I said tentatively.

The man in the corner looked up and smiled. His striking amber eyes—which I had only ever seen on wolves—gave away his breed. Remembering how the wolf outside had not talked to me during our journey, I wondered if these people spoke a language I knew.

He paused a moment before answering. "Hello. Are you feeling better?" He had a heavy accent, but I could understand him easily enough.

I tottered to my feet a little unsteadily, but once I was up, the ground stayed solid. "Much better. Do I have you to thank?"

He gave a little shrug. "You have Fate to thank, for taking you to the edge of our camp. You were half-frozen, and poisoned. It is not all gone. Our doctor is not sure what it was. Eat well, stay warm, rest for a few days." He shrugged again. "You will be better."

"What about the wolf?" I asked. He looked amused, so I clarified. "Another wolf. I was farther away. One of your people saved my life; she brought me here."

"Ah," he answered. There was a long pause, and I did not think he would say more, but then he sighed. "That was Betia, perhaps. She is . . . feral?" he said hesitantly, as if unsure that he had translated right.

I nodded, unnerved. When a shapeshifter went feral, it meant that she had spent too much time in animal form. Eventually the human characteristics eroded, along with the memory of her original form. Usually a feral shapeshifter was volatile, without an animal's sense of balance or a human's sense of morals, prone to attack those who had been closest to her.

"Has no one tried to bring her back?" I asked. "She did not seem too far gone to me."

He shook his head. "Betia was my sister. I have tried all I could think of, but she lets no wolf speak to her, or touch her. She had a falling out with the alpha's son, Velyo," he confided, "and she ran away. I do not know what the fight was about, only that her animal mind associates our kind with pain now. So she will not let us near." Again he shook his head, admitting, "It should be my job to hunt her down like an animal for the safety of the pack. But I can't, and so far our alpha has not forced me to."

The door opened, letting in a gust of cold air and an older woman who was speaking swiftly in a language I did not recognize.

The woman was plump in a comfortable sort of way and carried a bundle that smelled wonderfully like food. The man I had been talking to winced and nodded as she seemed to berate him.

Finally he turned to me. "My mother says that she is glad to see you awake, that I should not have let you get up, that she has brought breakfast, that I should have offered you something to eat and that she is sure my manners are terrible and I have not introduced myself or told you where you are." He smiled and then continued obediently. "I am Pratl; I am head huntsman. This is my mother, Ginna; she is doctor, advisor and anything else she believes is her role. Right now, you are in the huntsman's hut of the Frektane tribe. I believe it means *blue eyes* in your language."

I knew the name. Wyvern's Court had never traded directly with the Frektane, but the Vahamil occasionally brought their wares to our market. I wondered where the pack's name came from; I had never seen a wolf with blue eyes.

Another round of commentary from Ginna, and Pratl sighed. "Now I am talking too much. May I ask your name?"

I had to conclude that these people were friendly; they had given me help, and I had certainly needed it. So I answered honestly. "Oliza Shardae Cobriana. Arami, and heir to the Tuuli Thea."

Apparently Pratl's mother had understood at least some

of that, because her eyes widened and she stared at me. Then she shrugged—and continued talking.

Pratl laughed. "My mother says we are flattered to have you in our camp, even if you did . . ." He paused, working on the wording. "Did get dragged in from the blizzard looking like a winter rat. What brings you to our camp in such a condition?"

"Honestly, I am very lost," I answered.

Pratl frowned. "You weren't with that group of lions we intercepted?"

"Were you the ones who attacked them?"

He bristled. "Of course. They did not ask permission to hunt on our land, they were loud enough to scare away all the game for miles and their reputation is as foul as their mange-spotted coats. If you are with them—"

I held up a hand, shaking my head. "No, not like that. I was brought here by them. Against my will. I escaped when something attacked them—your pack, I assume." His vehement response comforted me. If this pack had been involved in hiring the mercenaries, Pratl at least had not known the plan.

He nodded, content now. "I believe that. I did not know who you were when we first found you, but I did not think any bird would be with them," he said, gesturing toward the feathers on the nape of my neck that must have made him assume I was avian even before I woke.

"How far am I from Wyvern's Court?" I asked, dreading the answer. How many days had I been traveling, semiconscious, while people from home had been searching for me?

Pratl conferred briefly with his mother before turning back to me and shaking his head. "The Frektane visit Wyvern's Court rarely, though some of our people winter with the Vahamil. It is probably not a long flight." He considered. "Maybe three weeks, traveling by land."

"*Three weeks?*" I gasped. I had feared that I had been drugged for that long, but I had hoped otherwise.

The lions had asked to trade in our market after they had delivered Kalisa's message. Had they been hired by someone while they had been in Wyvern's Court? I still did not know who had attacked Urban. What if the same culprit was responsible? And how could I take three weeks to get home?

"Lions travel quickly—faster than you would if you walked. But by air the time will be much less." He was right. I could probably travel that distance in a day, two at most . . . if I had my wings. I didn't have my wings.

Ginna interrupted with some sharp words to her son and started opening the bag she had brought.

"Breakfast," Pratl said simply. "She is concerned that if you get weak, the poison will make you sick again."

"Tell her thank you, please."

Pratl conveyed this, and then Ginna left us as Pratl and I sat down to eat.

"And thank you, for acting as translator," I added. "How is it that you know our language so well?"

As I ate with an appetite I had not expected, Pratl explained, "Among my pack, there is someone who studies each culture we might deal with, so that we can speak with them. Mostly we deal with Wyvern's Court through the Vahamil, but it is best to be able to speak for ourselves if we need to. My sister had that post, until recently. She taught me most of what I know. Our alpha's son saw your feathers, so he had you put here. He and his father are the only others in this area who speak your language besides me. Frektane will expect me to be able to tell him who you are, why you are here and how long you wish to remain with us."

From dealing with the wolf tribe near Wyvern's Court, I

knew that the leader of a pack was formally addressed by the pack name. The formality was often dropped among Kalisa's people, but apparently Frektane's alpha did not allow such familiarity.

"Frektane does not like strangers, but his son argued that it would be unwise to leave an unknown guest out in the snow. Now that we know who you are, I think Frektane will listen to his son."

Pratl's mother returned then with a bundle of clothing and a pair of fur-lined boots. She said something brief to him, and he nodded.

"Your clothes are not designed for this area, or for travel," Pratl told me. "These were Betia's. They should fit you, and you may keep them when you leave."

"How long has she been lost?" I asked.

Pratl winced. "Four months."

"So there's still hope for her."

"No," he sighed, and stood without elaborating. "Frektane is expecting you. Dress, and I will be back to take you to him."

I was happy to have the warm, dry clothing. The base of the outfit was a pair of wool pants and a loose, comfortable shirt of the same material. A heavy jacket, lined with some kind of fur, laced over the blouse. I pulled the boots up over the pants to just beneath my knees; they too were fur lined, amazingly warm and comfortable. Once I was ready, Pratl escorted me to the largest hut at the center of the camp, to meet with the leader of the Frektane. I could only hope that Pratl was right and I would be allowed to stay; I did not know what I would do otherwise.

# CHAPTER 9

Frektane was still physically young, his body lean, but his face was marked by a series of scars across his left cheek and brow. I had never seen a wolf with such striking blue eyes; they had to be the reason for the tribe's name. If I had not been raised among serpents and falcons, whose eyes were often jeweled tones seen nowhere else in nature, I would have called such eyes impossible.

"Oliza Shardae Cobriana," Frektane greeted me stiffly.

"Forgive my father for not standing," another man said, making me jump as I noticed him for the first time. Also whipcord lean and obviously strong, and with the same vivid blue eyes as Frektane, this had to be his son, Velyo. "He injured his leg earlier this winter, and it still pains him."

The words were polite, but something about his tone made me feel as if an insult had been spoken.

Frektane responded by instantly rising to his feet. "My son makes much of a minor ailment," he responded, glaring at the younger wolf before he turned to me.

Sensing an argument I did not know the heart of, I did

my best not to get into the middle of it. "If I have come at an awkward moment, I apologize."

"My father and I were simply discussing . . . matters of little importance," Velyo answered. His father said something to him in their native tongue, and he smiled. "Kind, Father, of you to offer. But since I was the one who insisted we let Oliza stay, I will assume full responsibility for her."

"How long *are* you here?" Frektane asked me, ignoring Velyo.

"I was brought into this area against my will," I explained. "I fear traveling too soon may make me sick again. If it is not a hardship, I ask your permission to remain for a few days, until I am stronger."

Frektane made a disgusted sound, but before he could speak, Velyo assured me, "A few days will prove no hardship for us."

Again Frektane grumbled to his son in their language. This time, Velyo replied, "You are alpha, leader of this land and its people. Say the word, and I will see to it that *everyone* too weak to provide for the pack is removed."

He had hit a nerve, for suddenly Frektane crossed the room, favoring his right leg just slightly. "Watch yourself, Velyo."

"You're weak, Father," Velyo snarled. "This winter has been good to the pack, because *I* have led the hunts down the river. Hunts your injury kept you from. Before you talk of denying Oliza a few days to rest, consider how many of our resources you devour. You've been slower every run this season. The cold is in your bones. You're *old*, wolf."

I jumped back as Frektane threw Velyo into the wall. "Not old enough that a pup like you can challenge me."

Velyo snarled at his father as he pushed himself back to

his feet; then he glanced at me. "I'll escort Oliza while she is here."

"See that you do."


"I apologize for that little scene," he said, as if I had witnessed some minor spat, instead of part of an ongoing power struggle between father and son. "You may think our ways harsh, but in this kind of world, it is necessary to rule firmly. Laxity is what causes a pack to starve in the winter. My father's strength has been failing since he was injured last fall. I won't let him bring our entire pack down by refusing to admit it."

"I suppose I'm lucky to live in a more moderate climate," I answered, trying to remain polite despite my desire to argue. The wolves had different values than I did. As Velyo had said, this pack lived in a difficult land, where strength was necessary for survival. "Wyvern's Court has never had problems with starvation, for which I am grateful."

Velyo nodded. I couldn't tell if it was in agreement or approval or neither.

I wondered how Kalisa was doing. If she had needed my parents' support, what had happened when they had suddenly been pulled back to Wyvern's Court to deal with events there after I had disappeared?

Velyo seemed to be waiting for me to speak again, so I searched for a safe, neutral question. "How many people are in Frektane? It seems so quiet."

"Few more than a dozen winter here," he answered. "The weaker ones separate and travel south, nearer to your court. They trade among the human cities or stay with other, more southern packs. You have probably seen them with the

Vahamil, though I imagine your position leaves you little time to idle with common wolves. In spring or summer they will return here to the main encampment."

"What about the children?"

"They travel if they are old enough," he answered. "Otherwise, they stay here and people such as Ginna take care of them. Mostly they stay out of the way. Father does not like for them to get underfoot." Wyvern's Court had such a different opinion about children that I could not immediately think of an appropriate answer. Luckily Velyo chose that moment to offer, "If you would like to get word to your people, our relations with the Vahamil are good enough that they would not object to our sending a messenger through their lands to Wyvern's Court. You can wait here until your guards arrive to see you safely home."

"I would appreciate that," I said, and felt some of the tension in my neck begin to dissolve. A messenger from the Frektane could travel more quickly than I would be able to even in perfect health, which meant that my people would hear from me sooner. It had already been too long. "Do you know anything about Kalisa's condition? She was injured shortly before I was taken from Wyvern's Court."

"Injured?" Velyo asked. "I hadn't heard. Do you know how serious it is?"

I shook my head. "Serious enough that she wanted to meet with my parents, but I don't know more than that."

"Perhaps I will accompany you when you travel south, to check in on Vahamil." His thoughtful tone gave me a chill before his expression cleared. "In the meantime, join me for some dinner. You look half-starved."

The main encampment of the Frektane tribe was a very somber place, especially compared to the Vahamil's near my home. In addition to despising little children running about, making noise and getting underfoot, the alpha also disapproved of "frivolous" activities such as dancing and singing, which had always kept Kalisa's tribe active and alight with laughter.

"Someone will bring my father his supper. He prefers to eat in solitude," Velyo explained to me as we entered a central hut where the air was filled with the scents of roasting meats.

A young woman tended the hearth, but she stood the instant she saw Velyo, brushing ash from her hands. Two others sat at a long table in the back of the room, and they also stood hastily.

"This is Lameta's first winter in Frektane," Velyo told me, nodding to the hearth mistress. He greeted her in their native language, and she gave a half curtsy, never looking away from him. There was respect in her eyes, but I could tell she was also wary. I tried to keep an open mind, though from what I had seen and heard so far, I would not have wanted to be one of Frektane's and Velyo's subjects. They ruled with a fist that was a little too iron for my comfort.

We were served roast venison, with a warm, sweet sauce, and hot spiced wine.

"I'll warn you, meals in the winter can be somewhat repetitive," Velyo said apologetically. "I suspect Lameta dipped into the fruit stores tonight after she heard we had company."

As we turned to sit at the table, the two who had been sitting there went to serve themselves. Others came in from outside, as if they had been waiting for a dinner bell, and finally Lameta herself took a plate.

They had been waiting for Velyo, I realized. The pack didn't eat until its alpha had taken his share. I knew that law from my studies, though it was one of many that Kalisa enforced only in formal situations. Usually she preferred to give the first share to whichever hunter or tradesman had contributed the most to the meal.

"I have never been to your Wyvern's Court," Velyo said. "Tell me of it?"

I did my best to describe my homeland, from dancers to singers, merchants to scholars. Velyo listened quietly, nodding occasionally or quirking a brow when I said something he found curious.

"Do you have a mate waiting for you at home?" he asked finally.

His tone was innocent enough, but there was something about the way he looked at me that made my skin crawl, as if a hundred spiders had suddenly scampered across it.

"I have not yet chosen my king," I answered.

"I had forgotten that your people are born to royalty, or marry into it. It is a precious luxury."

"I assume that the alpha position in the Frektane must be hereditary, since the pack's name obviously refers to your line."

He sounded as if he was reciting as he explained, "It is not a matter of birthright, but breeding and education. If one of my wolves proves himself better qualified to lead the Frektane after my father no longer can, I will have to step down, but like my father, and his before him, throughout my childhood I was given the lessons I would need to take over as alpha once it is time. For nine generations we have led this pack, each Frektane alpha choosing a strong mate who will add worthy qualities to the bloodline. My mother could bring down a wild boar in her human form while armed with no more than a dagger. She could track antelope through pouring rain, and shoot an owl from the sky in the dead of a moonless night. My father has done a great many unwise things in his life, but choosing his mate was not one of them. I only hope I can choose a mate who will prove as fine a queen as my mother was.

"She truly earned the right to run by my father's side. It is good that she did not live to see him in his current state." He hesitated, then added, "Though at least she would have had the courage to put him down."

I had no desire to address the possible euthanasia of a man who by my standards was perfectly healthy. No wonder Kalisa had called her allies to her side when she had been injured, if this was how neighboring packs—not to mention her own—would view her weakness.

I steered the conversation back to a topic I understood all too well; I was the heir of not just one but two monarchies, and I understood the care that had to be taken in choosing a mate. "Have you made your decision?" I asked

"No." He stood up abruptly, without bothering with the dishes. Someone would clean up after him, I was sure. "There are women in the Frektane who are good hunters, women who are good leaders, women who are intelligent and women who are brave. It is rare that one finds all those traits in a single place. I thought I had once, but . . . I was incorrect."

*Betia?* I wondered. Pratl had said that she had had a falling out with Velyo. But the look in Velyo's eyes warned me not to inquire further.

# CHAPTER 10

I was exhausted from my travels, even more tired by how carefully I had tried to watch my words with Velyo, and worried I had accentuated Kalisa's troubles by revealing her possible vulnerability. I was relieved when Velyo offered to escort me back to my room, because I would be able to rest.

The doorway was covered by heavy furs, and Velyo brushed them aside, allowing me to slip through the narrow opening. Someone had built the fire up before we arrived, so the room was warm despite the winter chill outside.

Velyo followed me inside and then, as if just deciding, said, "I think I'll join you."

"*Excuse me?*"

Had he been serpiente, accustomed to sleeping innocently among friends, I might have assumed that his offer was platonic, but as far as I was aware, the wolves did not share that particular custom.

He walked toward me, his stride graceful and soundless. "I said, I think I'll join you. It's a cold night."

I took a step back, but the room was small, and I only succeeded in hitting the backs of my knees on a trunk that sat at the foot of the bed. "I'm sorry if I somehow gave the wrong impression, but—"

He caught my hand and kissed the back of it. "You are half serpiente, are you not?"

Insulted, I fought the urge to deliver an equally offensive and thus hardly politic reply. Instead I used his own logic against him. "I am also half avian."

He shrugged. "You are also a guest in my camp. I thought you would be grateful."

"I am grateful," I answered, trying unsuccessfully to take my hand back. "However, I also—"

He stepped forward despite my protests, trapping me against the trunk. "You also?"

"Let go of me."

"Relax," he whispered.

"I am not interested," I said bluntly, feeling my heart trapped in my throat. "Now kindly release me."

I caught his wrist when he reached for me with his other hand, which made him chuckle a little. "Princess—" He yanked his hand back as he tugged on my wrist, so I ended up stumbling and falling against his chest. "I'm not sure you appreciate your position. There are many women who would be jealous of—"

"I'm not one of them," I growled. The last of my respect for him had disappeared, and with it my trust that he wouldn't force this. "I said, *let go.*"

When he didn't, I twisted, driving an elbow into his stomach as I attempted to hop over the trunk and back into the center of the room. His grip loosened for a moment, but he didn't quite release me; instead, he twisted my arm behind my back so that I fell, barely avoiding hitting my head against the corner of the trunk when my knees struck the ground.

Before I recovered, he pulled me to my feet and then shoved me toward the mound of blankets piled on the bed.

Furious and frightened at the same time, I managed to lash out once more, striking him in the chest with the heel of my boot. He doubled over, spitting out a string of curses in his own language that I never wanted to have translated.

I hurried back into the cold night before he could follow. I would just have to hope I was well enough to get by. I couldn't risk staying at the mercy of Velyo Frektane. One or the other of us wasn't likely to survive it.

"Oliza?"

I hesitated when I heard Pratl's voice. "I have to leave," I said quickly. "Thank you for your hospitality, and please thank Ginna."

He glanced toward the cabin I had just fled, and winced. Then he drew a knife, and for a moment I thought he meant to stop me. Instead, he offered it to me, handle first. "Just to help you hunt on your way. Don't use it on him." He looked again toward the doorway as I took the weapon. "Go. I'll try to delay him if he comes after you."

"Thank you," I whispered.

"You should not travel long alone," Pratl warned. "You are not well."

"I don't think I have a choice."

He nodded reluctantly. "Go. Be well."

I ran, for the moment concerned more with removing myself from Frektane land than with choosing a destination.

Only after I was back in the woods did shapeshifting occur to me, and then I remembered that I did not have my wings.

Three weeks to Wyvern's Court, Pratl had said; it would

be more than three weeks if I had to travel alone without supplies through unfamiliar land. I knew that Wyvern's Court had to be south from here, but I had never made such a trek by myself.

I tried desperately to take my wyvern form but again felt only a queasy rolling in my stomach. Desperate to reassure myself, I reached for my cobra form—and found nothing. *Nothing.*

*The poison lingers. Dear sky, I hope it won't linger forever.* I knew that a similar poison was used by the dancers' guild when a punishment required someone to be held in one form for some time, but that wore off in a few days at most. I hoped this would be the same. I had lost my avian form; I could not lose my cobra, too.

Had the lions stolen the poison while in Wyvern's Court? I wondered. Or had their employer given it to them? They might even have had it already.

*South, Oliza,* my scattered wits reminded me. *You don't have the information you need to find answers, and you won't have any more information until you get home. Your people need you. You've no choice but to walk, so walk.* My fury at Velyo and at my situation in general kept me warm, and I made good time as I jogged and walked south through the night.

It was nearly sunrise when I grudgingly accepted that I needed to sleep. I wished I could make a fire, but my hands were shaking and I could barely keep my eyes open; the idea of searching for dry wood and struggling to make a spark was overwhelming. Fortunately, this night was not as bitter as the one before, and I was able to find shelter in a warm nook where a pine had been knocked down across a boulder.

I curled up inside, my stomach rumbling. I would need

to figure out how to find food and make a fire later. But for now, sleep.

I woke near noon to find a furry gray-brown ball at the entrance to my little den. It lifted its muzzle and licked me when I blinked at it in confusion.

"Morning, Betia," I greeted with a smile of relief. "Thank you for finding me and guarding my rest."

The wolf yawned, stretched, shook herself and let out a little bark. Then she plodded to a large deer that she had obviously taken down earlier and saved for me.

"Thank you," I said. *And thank you, too, Pratl, for the knife,* I thought as I clumsily butchered the deer. The tree I had slept under provided dry wood, so I managed to cook as much of the meat as we could consume right then.

Betia watched me with an intelligence and patience that said she knew what I was doing. I spoke to her as I worked, and while she didn't respond, I had a feeling she understood much of what I said, too.

"I can understand why you ran away," I confided when we began to walk again. The afternoon was bitter, but at least it wasn't snowing. "I couldn't stand Velyo, either."

Betia growled beside me, and I laughed a little.

"I think that's a good way to put it."

She growled again, and as I turned, I realized she was looking into the trees. I did not have a wolf's sense of smell or hearing, but I could hear . . . something.

Something unfriendly, by the sound of Betia's growling. Someone shouted deeper in the woods, and I recognized the voice of one of the lions.

I looked at Betia, my heart racing, and then we ran, slipping through the trees, stumbling over downed logs and brush. In their lion forms, my hunters were much faster than I was; I wished again that I could shift.

We were going to be overtaken, and I didn't stand a chance with just my knife against the claws of a pride of lions. Even if Betia helped me, she was only one, and I knew there were at least a half dozen of them.

"Oliza!" Tavisan's voice floated through the trees. "Stop running!"

He had broken a bone in my wing, clipped my feathers, drugged and poisoned me; I wasn't anxious to talk about it.

Suddenly Betia and I were tumbling down a bank I had not noticed. Betia let out a yelp, and then I was back on flat ground, the air knocked out of my lungs. The wolf nosed my rib cage, encouraging me to get back up; bracing myself on her shoulders, I dragged myself up again.

Luckily, our pursuers were delayed by the drop-off. Maybe they weren't being paid enough to risk broken necks—but who could have hired them to go this far? They knew who I was. What payment could possibly make it worthwhile for them to risk both the serpiente and avian armies' coming after them?

I didn't know how long Betia and I had run, using stream banks to obscure our footsteps and distort our scent, sleeping for only a few minutes at a time before my pounding heart woke me again.

Two sunrises, three sunrises. The world began to waver under me and finally I forced myself to slow our pace. I did not know how near the lions were, but I knew I couldn't go on that way.

With someone after us, I knew better than to go due

south as I had planned. Betia and I varied our direction; I mostly followed as she led us to streams with fish, rabbit burrows, brooks with fresh water and sheltered spots where sleep was easy to find.

Evenings, I lay awake in whatever hollow we had chosen for a bed that night, shivering from chills caused by more than the winter air. I kept food in my stomach through sheer force of will, fighting the twists in my gut because I knew I needed the energy the food provided. I needed my strength. I needed to make it home.

# CHAPTER 11

I didn't know how long we had been traveling—a fortnight, maybe—when the day turned black without warning. I fell to my knees and heard Betia's frantic bark. Despite my best efforts, when I tried to push myself up, I couldn't find the strength. I was dizzy and sick from poisons and too many days of running.

Betia whimpered and nuzzled my shoulder, but my abused body had had enough. My stomach cramped as a bout of heavy coughing made me curl into a little ball on the cold ground. I coughed until I gagged, and even afterward I couldn't keep my body from shaking.

The wolf was running in desperate circles around me, barking every now and then to encourage me.

She disappeared, and I was overwhelmed by another coughing fit. I had to stand up; we had to keep moving.

I had pushed myself to my knees by the time Betia returned, her coat dripping wet and her brown eyes apologetic. She must have run back to the river, to try to bring me something to eat.

I lifted a hand and put it on her shoulder. She licked fever sweat from my cheek, and I closed my eyes.


I was on the ground again, and I was sick, and I was cold, and I was lost, and I was frightened. Betia was frightened, too, and I wanted to say something to comfort her, but I could think of nothing.

What was happening in my home while I was lying there? What had happened with the dancers? With the Vahamil? For all I knew, I might return to a war.

Suddenly hands were on my shoulders and someone was lifting me into a sitting position. For an instant I thought the mercenaries had found me, but I couldn't summon terror. I felt only protected. Gentle fingers brushed my cheek, and then someone was holding a cup of cool, sweet water to my lips. I realized then how tight and raw my throat was from coughing. I tried to stand again, but strong arms held me still. When I shivered, they held me more tightly.


Night fell, and those arms kept me warm in the darkness. When I woke, I was offered more water. As if by magic, a fire had appeared. When I woke again, sometime after sunrise, it was to the scent of cooking meat. I ate a little, though my appetite was still poor, and drank more water; then I slept once again.


It was another day before the fever broke, and I opened my eyes and finally looked with clear vision upon the woman who had cared for me.

Her thick hair was light brown, with darker, ruddy shades. Her skin was tanned, and her arms and face had streaks of dirt. Her eyes were a familiar, warm brown, with dark, heavy lashes.

"Good morning, Betia," I said.

She looked at me and yawned and stretched, just as she had the first morning. She did not speak aloud, and I didn't know if she even remembered how. Speech was one thing that most shapeshifters who went feral never recovered. Still, that she had been able to recall her human body was a good sign. Her concern for me and her need for a form more suited to caring for me must have driven her back from her wolf.

She put a hand to my brow to check my fever.

"You keep taking care of me," I remarked as she turned to tend the last flickers of the fire with easy skill.

Betia glanced back at me and tilted her head the way a natural wolf would have when puzzled. I wondered what thoughts were passing behind those earthen eyes. She smiled and then returned to the rabbit she had set to cook over the low-burning embers. Had she caught it before she'd returned to human form, or was she still an excellent huntress even without a wolf's speed, strength or ferocity?

Of course she was, I decided. The Frektane tribe belonged only to those who could take care of themselves and their pack—and Velyo would never have been interested in a weak woman with nothing to offer him.

The thought gave me a chill that had nothing to do with my illness. I realized for the first time that Betia was dressed in simple pants made from soft wool and a loose blouse of the same material, with fluffy sleeves and an airy fit. Her feet were bare, and her hair was down around her face in tangled waves.

Dressed like that, she had probably been alone in her

own room, relaxing or perhaps preparing to sleep, before she had taken her wolf form and run from her people. Alone—or with someone she had trusted.

By the next day we had started moving again, more slowly this time. Each day took us farther south, though we kept an ear out for signs of pursuit.

If I had worried about Betia's ability to travel in human form, I had been wrong to. Not even bare feet seemed to bother her, though I was glad we were no longer in the snow. She ran ahead occasionally, slipping through the trees like a sprite but always returning before peaceful solitude turned to loneliness.

I saw my reflection in a pool where we stopped for water, and I grimaced. I was beyond lean—thin, dangerously so. The drugs should have worn off weeks before, but I hadn't had enough food or rest, and my body simply didn't have the resources to fight the poison. I could still feel it in my blood, and with every step, I knew that I risked bringing the fever back. I simply didn't have any choice.

I was lucky to have Betia with me. She had a knack for finding drinking water, as well as caches of nuts hidden by squirrels. She also could tickle fish from the streams, seeming not to care about water or mud—and I had not forgotten that she had somehow caught that rabbit, alone and unarmed.

I still did not know what had possessed her to follow me, or to save me in the first place. I wondered if I was doing her a disservice by taking her with me. She obviously did not want to return to the Frektane, but was Wyvern's Court, in its state of distrust and turmoil, really a place where she could be happy?

More and more I wished I could join her in the forest, as serene and natural as she seemed to be.

"Your brother, Pratl, was the one who told me your name," I said to her in the midst of one of our many one-sided conversations. "He cares for you a great deal, it seems."

She tensed beside me, her step faltering, and did not even look my way.

"Your mother also seems to be a kind woman." I described the odd morning when I had met both Pratl and Ginna, not moving on to discuss the rest of the day. I knew that Betia didn't want to hear anything about the leaders of her pack.

"They must love you," I mused aloud, thinking of my own loved ones. My parents—not to mention the rest of my family, and most of the court—would be frantic with worry over my disappearance.

Everyone would be, except whoever had paid to have me removed. . . .

"I know you were hurt, and you're frightened, but couldn't you still go back—"

Betia shot me a look that clearly said, *Do not speak of that.*

"Betia . . ."

She dropped her gaze for an instant, then looked at me with a plea in her eyes, reaching out to touch my arm.

"I didn't mean to upset you," I said. "I was just thinking about the people from my home, who I love, and who I miss, and who must be so frightened for me. If you never want to return to the Frektane, that is your choice. If you want to come to Wyvern's Court, you can have a new life there, or if you want to be with other wolves, Kalisa's pack would probably take you in." Unless, of course, Kalisa was no longer in charge of the Vahamil when I returned.

Kalisa, injured. The dancers, demanding answers. Wyvern's Court, torn by violence.

And me, wandering around in the endless woods.

I let out a frustrated cry, and Betia leaned against my side and put her arms around me.

The mercenaries never should have been able to take me from Wyvern's Court. They never should have been able to take me through forests patrolled by my guards and occupied by the Vahamil.

They never should have *wanted* to. Who could convince the lions to risk the wrath of a realm such as Wyvern's Court? We were a peaceful nation, but we had warred for many years; the death toll on both sides showed just how skillful my people had been at killing each other. It would take a lot to force Wyvern's Court to turn back to war, but kidnapping the heir to both thrones was a good start.

Or was that the point?

Someone wanted me not just removed but transported a great distance. Someone had gone to great trouble and great expense to meet that goal. Someone . . . was behind me.

I froze, then moved only my arm to reach toward my knife. Why hadn't I heard them approach?

Betia snarled, and bush branches snapped as she pounced. I spun toward the interlopers, raising the knife, evading one attack.

Serpiente—at least three of them in my immediate view. The real criminals?

*No time to wonder,* my mind snapped. *Defend yourself first.*

Betia and I moved back to back as if we had rehearsed it. "Three on my side," I said aloud, though I didn't expect a response from her. A quick glance revealed another two on hers. The serpiente in front of me had the palest blond hair I had ever seen, and light blue-green eyes.

Two against five. Not good odds, especially since the serpents wore two knives crossed on their backs, and three of them were also armed with strong wooden staves tipped with blades that gleamed wickedly in the sunlight. One wore a bow in addition to this.

"Drop the knife," the man in front of me said.

I didn't have a choice, really. Fighting now would probably get me killed. If these were the people who had had me abducted in the first place, they wanted me alive, and dropping the knife would be the better option.

Before I could act, Betia snarled and someone behind me cried out. Seizing the moment of surprise, I leapt for a man holding a stave; I knew how to use it. I hit him in the gut, knocking us both to the ground, and reached for the weapon with my free hand.

We rolled, and I came up with the stave, which I tried to snap down across my enemy's head. He blocked, rolling enough to deflect most of the blow, then came up with a snarl. White scales coated his skin, and his eyes became pure blue except for slit pupils. Snake eyes, in his fighting form. I wished I could summon my own, with its increased speed, flexibility and reflexes, as well as enough poison to make any enemy hesitate.

I rolled away, swinging the stave; I felt it strike one of the other attackers across the ribs.

Someone pounced on me from behind; an arm wrapped around my throat, and I turned the knife in my hand to drive it backward. I felt it hit something, but then my wrist was grabbed and the knife was wrenched from my hand. An elbow to my attacker got me dislodged and tossed into an inelegant heap on the ground, nearly at the feet of a woman.

She gripped the front of my shirt, then froze and let out a piercing whistle.

Startled, she half hissed, half shouted, "Peace! Weapons *down*." There was an *oomph* as someone behind me was hit, and the woman said to me, "Call off your friend." She stood, dropping her stave. "I didn't realize who you were."

"Betia, stop!" They had us outnumbered and out-armed. There was no reason for them to let us go unless the woman was being honest. Looking around, I saw that we had done a surprising amount of damage, but I had no doubt that we would have lost eventually.

Betia was still in her human form, thank the sky; if she had returned to her wolf to fight, I would have worried that she might not come back again.

The woman who had pinned me offered me a hand, saying, *"Fm'itil-varl'nesera."*

Shocked, I took a moment to translate the words. You bless us, dancer. My hand went to the coin at my neck, the *Ahnleh* my mother had passed on to me, and I gave the traditional reply. *"Fm'varl'nesera-hena."* Blessed be.

# CHAPTER 12

My heart was still pounding, even though the fight was over. I had been formally greeted as a traveling dancer, based on an archaic law that almost no one remembered these days.

"I apologize," my former opponent said. "Normally we do not tolerate strangers in our lands, but anyone with a Snakecharm is welcome here, and safe—as in days before. I am sorry I did not see it sooner."

"And my friend?" I asked. "She is not a dancer."

"If she is your friend, she is ours."

I brushed myself off and went to Betia's side unchallenged. I had not known there was any place left that still honored such old traditions, but as it seemed to be working in my favor, I would not argue.

"Betia, are you all right?" I asked.

A man knelt beside us. "She's bleeding," he said. "Come, let us care for her wounds—yours as well, dancer. And our own," he added wryly. I realized he was the one whose skull I had tried to knock in with a stave. "You fight well, especially considering that you look half-starved and exhausted. We will see to your injuries; then you will eat and rest here."

Their generosity forced me to be honest. "I am being hunted. And I am not really a dancer. I have learned some, from Wyvern's Nest, but I am not even officially apprenticed."

He smiled anyway. "Someone thought you worthy of wearing the *Ahnleh*. So you are welcome. As for your hunters . . ." The smiled changed to a hungry one. "You are among the Obsidian tribe. We have more than steel to keep you safe, if need be."

"Are you the leader here?" I asked tentatively. Perhaps I was not so safe. The Obsidian guild was a group of outlaws. The nearly colorless hair and eyes of some, if not their ivory scales, should have told me. White vipers, Maeve's descendants, they had lived as outsiders since their ancestors had been driven away for practicing dark magic that endangered the serpiente. They had defied Cobriana rule for millennia, occasionally joined by other serpents who had either chosen to leave serpiente society or been exiled for crimes.

"Perhaps," he answered, with a teasing smile. "Perhaps not. You are looking at me as if I have sprouted wings— though for you, that might not be strange." He tickled the back of my neck, ruffling the feathers there and making me jump. His expression turned serious. "I know who you are, Oliza Shardae Cobriana, princess of Wyvern's Court. I recognized you as soon as I saw you. But you still wear the charm. That grants you safety, a meal and a bed, no matter whose blood you carry or who travels with you."

My whole body sagged with fatigue and relief. "Thank you. Your generosity will not be ignored."

He laughed. "Oh, ignore it, please. We've no desire to join your court. Certainly no desire to come to the attention of your parents. You may stay as long as you like and leave whenever you like, but once you are gone, I hope you will forget us entirely. Now, please, join us for supper, *fm'itil* and *tair'feng,* dancer and wolf."

Our wounds were tended, as were those we had delivered; no one seemed to hold a grudge about the injuries, though Betia delivered more than one amused look my way. She sat beside me while we ate. Although they were friendly, no one introduced herself or himself by name; I noticed that the names they used for each other shifted from one moment to the next.

"So tell us, dancer; you said you're not even apprenticed, but you would not be wearing a Snakecharm if you did not know something?" one said as the night wore on.

"I cannot officially be apprenticed to the nest because of my position in Wyvern's Court," I answered. People nodded; it seemed everyone here knew who I was. "However, I have learned as much as my nest's leader will teach me."

"What steps do you know?"

I sighed, considering. "Blade dances are my favorites," I answered, "but I love everything. I know about fifteen of the *sakkri,* and most of the *she'da.* Of course I have learned the *Namir-da,* though I have never performed it, and I know the four *harja* types and six of the thirteen formal *melos* variations, though I have never danced them outside of my teacher's class, either."

"How old are you?" someone asked bluntly.

"Twenty." I knew what the next question would be. "It's my own choice not to perform the *rrasatoth* dances." The *rrasatoth* dances included the *melos* and the *harja,* as well as certain pieces such as the *Namir-da.* That reminded me of

Urban's teasing offer to dance with me at Salem's reception. I wished my last memories of him could have been that light.

The man I had first spoken to, a white viper I suspected was the leader despite his refusal to admit it, said firmly, "Then we'll respect that choice. Though if tomorrow you are feeling well enough, perhaps we might see something you enjoy."

Dinner ended when I was just reaching the sleepy haze that follows an excellent meal. Betia and I were offered a bed in one of the few shelters. It was a beautiful night for sleeping outside, but our host pointed out that it would be best if Betia and I were not seen by anyone who passed by—namely the mercenaries who had been following us.

I spoke to Betia as we drifted into sleep—about dances, about the beautiful *melos* and about how I wished I could dance those steps without all the hassle that came with them. I told her of the *Ahnleh* and how it had come to me, and then of the history of the Obsidian guild, from the genesis of the serpiente to the modern-day position of Maeve's kin.

Betia leaned against me, snuggling closer, and I took it as encouragement to continue.

"The white vipers have never acknowledged a Cobriana as their king," I finished. "Some of my ancestors have tried to force them, and some have tried to make peace with them, but the guild stays as it has always been—a group of drifters. The white vipers are the heart of the guild, though sometimes other serpents join them." I did not explain that these were usually former soldiers who had been branded traitors for refusing to fight during war times. Criminals who were no longer accepted by their own families and friends also went into the woods sometimes. Supposedly, justice among the guild was harsh enough that these criminals were forced to reform or else were kicked out of their last possible haven.

Betia yawned beside me, and soon we both fell asleep. I felt safe and warm for the first time since I had found Urban unconscious on the cold cobbles of the northern hills.

# CHAPTER 13

The Obsidian guild implored me to stay for a few days to recover my strength before traveling, and as eager as I was to get back to Wyvern's Court, I knew they were right.

Betia bounced back to perfect health like a puppy, and soon she was laughing and occasionally humming a melody I did not know. Though she remained in human form, she still had a tendency to pounce like a young wolf at play, sending us tumbling across the soft ground until we were covered in dirt and leaves but laughing too hard to stand up. Despite the horror that had led to this situation, and despite my fears of what I would find when I reached home, I was thankful to have this time. I had never had a friend who was completely unaffected by my status in Wyvern's Court. It was nice to be a person instead of a title.

As a result of the good food, the chance to sleep well and the healthy exercise, gradually I started to feel like myself again. The nightmares that had plagued me did not completely disappear, but I was able to shake them off during the day. My serpent form returned to me, which left me both relieved and heartsick.

I could not imagine returning to Wyvern's Court without my wings. I could not imagine facing pity from the avians, or horror from those who would now consider me even more a serpent. I could not imagine facing the ignorance of my serpiente friends, who would never comprehend what I had lost.

But it was time. I had no place in this world if it wasn't in Wyvern's Court.

On the last day we planned to spend with the guild, Betia left early in the morning to hunt with some of Obsidian's people, and I remained behind, speaking with their leader. When the white viper pointed out that the winter solstice was only a couple of weeks away, I was reminded of how fast time was flying.

We would be leaving the next day. I would be home in time for the Namir-da holiday, which celebrated the birth of the serpiente people. Thinking of it made me wonder about the group I was currently with. "Tell me of your people," I said finally. "I know the stories as they have been told by my ancestors, but I would like to hear how you tell them."

He hesitated, his eyes searching the skies, and then agreed. "Long ago, there were thirteen high priests and priestesses, known as the Dasi, who were led by Maeve; there were also two groups, the Nesera'rsh and the Ealla'rsh, who were lesser priests and priestesses. Maeve and the Dasi spoke to the gods. They brought the rain, and peace and prosperity for their people. The Rsh spoke to the villagers. They made sure everyone was heard and no one was forgotten. They were the healers and judges, and they taught the common people the worship of *Ahnleh*. They answered to no one and nothing but Fate herself.

"They believed," he explained, "that every soul was connected to every other, and therefore that none was better than any other. They believed that each person was a part of the whole and led and followed as Fate decreed—and that the position of each person shifted through his life. They kept their true names between themselves and the gods, because in the wider world, we are all anonymous. When we call another person by name, it is just another name for ourselves.

"Of course you know the story told in the *Namir-da*, of how Maeve seduced Leben in order to protect her people, and he gave to her the second form of a white viper, and to the rest of her people serpent and falcon forms." He paused and finally said, "That is the entire story that the Cobriana tell. What they do not mention is that Maeve had a lover before Leben. They do not tell that part of the tale because that lover was one of the Dasi—Kiesha, the high priestess of Anhamirak."

My eyes widened. Kiesha had been the first cobra.

"Kiesha was devastated by what she thought was Maeve's betrayal. Even after Leben was gone, she refused to forgive Maeve. Instead, she took a mate and bore to him a son she named Diente. You know the rest of that story, because Diente was the first king of your line. As for our line . . ."

"Our myths say that Maeve started practicing black magic," I said when the silence grew long.

"Ahnmik, the dark god who is Anhamirak's opposite, grants the numb peace sought by a man or woman whose love has turned elsewhere. He whispers promises of rest and of release from pain, and Maeve succumbed to those lures. So Kiesha's people drove her away."

"And then?"

"The Nesera'rsh took her in. Gradually, she withdrew from Ahnmik's numbness, accepting life once again. She took a mate. Her descendants are the white vipers of today. We follow the ways of the Nesera'rsh, as well as we can."

"Two generations ago, Maeve's kin were pardoned by the Cobriana," I said, broaching the subject tentatively. "The Obsidian guild was invited to join the rest of the serpiente. Only two white vipers came. I know your people have been treated poorly in the past, but surely the time has come when you no longer need to live like outlaws."

"Wyvern's Court is already struggling to bridge one ancient rift. Now is not the time to fight to close another," he pointed out. "Besides, my people would only follow someone who they knew understood and respected their ways. The Cobriana have not earned that trust; the Shardae line of hawks certainly has not."

"I wasn't asking you to kneel to me," I said, hoping I had not given that impression. "I was just offering you a place to call home. As long as you didn't break any of our laws, no one would demand obeisance."

"You have had ancestors who promised pardons and delivered mass executions," he pointed out. "Others have invited us to their land only to decide after a few years that we were not respectful enough. It did not help that one of the two vipers who went to serpiente lands was executed shortly after. I'm inclined to believe your father's word that Adelina was guilty of treason, but my kin have learned not to be too trusting."

"Yet you took me in."

"You wear the *Ahnleh*," he said, as if that was all that mattered. Maybe it was. "And I might have wanted to meet the wyvern who would be queen of this impossible realm. I do not trust easily, but that does not mean I have no hope for the future. When I was a young child, your uncle used to walk these woods. Anjay Cobriana would spend nights here sometimes, when he could get away from his guards. He would dance with us, and for a while we could forget that by blood we were enemies. If he had lived, we might have followed him. But that *if* speaks of the past. Now I speak to the child of Anjay's younger brother, Oliza Shardae Cobriana, who has more pressing issues at the moment than my people."

Before more could be said, Betia and the others returned. Obviously impressed, her companions informed me that Betia could gather fish from the river as if her hands were made of netting. The mute wolf smiled proudly, holding up her catch.

During dinner we made light conversation that turned deeper when one of the pythons of the guild sighed. "It's a pity you don't perform the *rrasatoth* dances," she said.

I shrugged a little, though I knew it did not hide my regret. "It's a decision I've made. I don't want to be pressured—"

"That's what's so unfair," the python interrupted. "If you were forty years old and had been performing *rrasatoth* since you were sixteen, all you would need to tell a suitor is that you aren't interested. You shouldn't be denied the dances just because you aren't ready to choose a partner."

"I would think a child of Obsidian wouldn't have such a passionate belief in fairness, considering how you have been treated in the past."

She gave a shrug that conveyed the same things that mine had earlier: acknowledgement and regret. "A dancer who cannot dance because her nestmates won't respect her desire *not* to choose a lover is just as confined as an avian lady who is ostracized because she chooses to have one. That isn't freedom. Perhaps it is no wonder your people have forgotten Anhamirak's magic, if they have so obviously forgotten her lessons."

Some sense of tension I got from her made me turn to Betia then. Betia's beautiful brown eyes dropped when I focused on her, but then she smiled. So I didn't understand why she stood up and walked inside.

I wanted to follow her, but my companion caught my wrist. "She'll be back. I think I know what she's after. She was working on it earlier."

Betia returned then and placed a soft bundle that felt like silk in my hands. The material slid across my fingers, and I caught my breath as I opened it.

The *melos* was simple, a single piece of cream-colored silk with an uncomplicated boarder stitched in golden thread. There were no tassels, no chimes, no fringes or complicated patterns—and I knew that it would always be my most cherished possession.

"Dance," the python said. "No one here is going to tell Wyvern's Court that we saw Oliza Shardae Cobriana dancing a *melos*. No one would believe us anyway."

I pulled Betia into a hug. She knew exactly what this meant to me. She didn't have to speak it aloud: *Dance.*

When was the last time I had let myself feel joy without reserve? I couldn't recall. This would be one of those times.

I stepped onto the dais. I knew the variation I would perform: *hanlah'melos.* And I knew who I would be performing for. I looked into the wolf's eyes and heard the music begin.

I felt as if I moved in a sphere of fire and electricity, and anything I touched would meet that charge.

Why had I refused this feeling before? In that moment, I

believed with all my soul that any trouble it might bring was more than worth it. I could survive with nothing else if I could just dance and have someone to dance for.

At the end, I stepped off the dais and knew that every eye in the camp—far more than those of the four people who had been watching at the start—was on me.

I saw only one person.

I hooked the scarf across Betia's shoulders and grasped her hands as if I could channel into her this incredible feeling of possibility. Maybe I did.

We both jumped when a viper, one of the two professional-level dancers who traveled with the Obsidian guild, stepped toward us.

"For someone who has never performed publicly, you were amazing. Actually, that was amazing even if you had been dancing for years. Something to be said for cross breeding," she said, joking. "I would love to share the dais with you someday."

"Thank you," I said, snapping out of my trance. Betia's hand was still twined with my left one, and I gave her an apologetic smile. She shrugged off the interruption, giving me a friendly shove toward the other dancer.

The serpent laughed. "I think that was an order to do so now. Do you know the *san'asi*?"

Literally, the name meant *raising the gods*; it was one of the most exotic of the *sakkri*, and Urban, Salem and I had performed it together on more than one occasion.

"I know it," I answered.

The viper offered her hand, inviting me to join her and her companion, a man who had amused Betia and me the past several nights with stories and songs.

The *san'asi* was one of the more complicated versions of

the dance. I knew it well, but my ability to perform would be entirely dependent on how well I could sense and predict my partners' movements and work seamlessly with them. I didn't want to make a fool out of myself.

I took the white viper's hand, then glanced at Betia, who was seated in front of the dais, watching me and waiting. She flashed a challenging smile, the glint in her eyes daring.

The three of us must have been quite a sight, all balanced effortlessly on the balls of our feet, forearms crossed before us, facing each other in a triangle so that our fingertips just touched: white viper, Burmese python, and me.

*If only Wyvern's Court could achieve this.* One little symbol, the *Ahnleh* my mother had given to me, had allowed me to join this mixed group. If only I could forge such a powerful talisman for my home.

# CHAPTER 14

One of the Obsidian guild played the flute, the simple instrument that had always been the main accompaniment to the serpents' dances.

Breath attuned, heartbeats in sync, we moved into the ancient dance. There was nothing else beyond the dais.

As the three of us moved, the air seemed to ripple. It was as if we were alone, two spirits in three bodies. The pressure grew, and abruptly I realized that something was *wrong*—

*Two?* It should have been three, or one. I knew where the white viper was when I danced, but the python was a foreign entity.

I wasn't the only one who stumbled. Nothing touched us, but I found myself fighting off tremors. I pushed myself up and saw the white viper kneeling by the third dancer's side.

The guild's leader spoke behind me. "Kiesha's line hasn't demonstrated any talent with the old coven's magic since Maeve was driven away," he said, his voice holding something that sounded like awe. "I didn't imagine you would be the first, Wyvern."

"I don't have magic," I answered. My throat was dry. What had happened? I felt much the way I had when Hai's power had overwhelmed me before I spoke to Marus and Prentice.

Betia put a hand on my arm, questioning.

"I'm all right," I said softly. "It was . . ." Already the sensations were fading. I felt as if, for a moment, I had touched something incredible, but then it was gone.

The white viper came to my side, her face glowing with admiration. "That—" She laughed. "I've read descriptions, of course, that say a true *sakkri* is too powerful even to be recalled by the mind without practice. But I never imagined—"

She stopped when she saw the confused expression on my face. "*Sakkri.* These days they're just a type of dance, but once they were powerful spells. No serpent has been able to spin one since Maeve's time. And even if we could, I understand that the mind can't see them or make sense of them without training. They fade away like dreams."

That was certainly one way to describe this lingering feeling; it was as if I had woken abruptly, just as my mind had reached for sleep and the land of dreams. Was this what Hai had tried to explain to me? *The mind barely comprehends its own yesterday, but* sakkri *force on it other times, other places, other people, visions it tries to shake away because to hold them all would only court madness.*

"You seem much less confused by this than I am," I said, trying to make sense of what had happened.

"A white viper is no stranger to magic. We never lost ours the way Kiesha's kin did. But Maeve's position in the Dasi was as one who preserved *balance*, not as one who worked the higher magics," the white viper explained patiently. "Even in the early days, we never possessed the sheer power that could be woven by Kiesha or Cjarsa."

Never in all my days in Wyvern's Court would a serpent have casually said the name of the first cobra and the name of the falcon Empress in the same breath. Hearing them together now, in this context, made me feel a little lost. On the other hand, the connection did make me remember something Nicias had said.

"A falcon once explained to me that their magic is disturbed by what is left of the magic the Cobriana once had. The remnants act like a spark. Maybe it does the same with yours."

One of the other vipers nodded thoughtfully. "That's probably all it was, then. After all, it isn't often that a cobra dances with a white viper. It seems to have taken a toll on you, though. Maybe you should lie down for a few minutes."

"Yes. Yes, I think I will."

Betia and I returned to the tent that had been set aside for our use. "I'm . . . all right," I assured Betia, who was watching me with a worried expression. "I don't think wyverns are cut out for magic." I briefly described the unpleasant incident with Hai that had occurred while we were trying to deal with Urban.

He would be walking again by now, I realized. I leaned against Betia with a sigh. "I wish there *was* some magic that would let me know what was going on at home. Being here, dancing, almost makes me forget how scared I am of what might be happening while I'm gone, but then it all comes flooding back."

The tent flap opened just enough to allow one of the Obsidian guild vipers to slither inside. The serpent returned to human form to explain swiftly, "Intruders, lions. They look like they might be the mercenaries who have been after you. We can deal with them, as long as they don't know you're here, so stay quiet for a little while, all right?"

We nodded, and she left the same way she had come, discreetly in case anyone was watching the camp.

It wasn't long before we heard loud voices outside. It sounded as if the Obsidian guild was inviting the mercenaries to join them for supper.

"We're looking for a pair of thieves," the lions' leader said. "Two girls—a wolf and a bird. One has dark hair, gold eyes, real distinctive."

There were some questioning murmurs as the Obsidian guild consulted its own people.

"No thieves here," someone answered. I had to bite my hand to keep from laughing. The Obsidian guild, while friendly to a traveling dancer, was generally considered a group of outlaws.

"You sure? Mind if we look around?"

I held my breath until I heard an indignant, "Yes, we mind. We offer you hospitality, and you offer mistrust in return. Sit!" It wasn't an invitation. "Maybe if you join us for a spell, we might be more inclined to believe you're friendly. Especially if you have something to trade for the information."

The mercenaries mumbled an apology. I gathered that they agreed to join the guild for a meal.

"I know you aren't looking for thieves," I heard someone say a bit later. "You're mercenaries; you've passed through here before. Who are you working for now?"

"Can't tell that," one of the lions answered gruffly.

"Honestly, you must know," the serpent said, pushing.

"*I* know; my men do not," the leader said before anyone else could speak. "And it is not information I am at liberty to give out, no matter how . . . grateful . . . I am for your . . . hospitality." There was an odd hesitation in his response, as if he was having trouble speaking.

"Someone must want these two pretty badly," a serpent observed.

"Yes" was the only reply.

A while later everything was quiet. Betia and I waited until our host stepped into the hut with a smirk and a chuckle. "I hate rude people."

"Where—"

"Drugged," he answered simply. "Sleeping off some of their own poisons, from their own bags, which my people have lightened just a little. There's no reference in the leader's bags about who hired him, but we did find this. I believe it's yours." He held out a sheathed dagger that I instantly recognized as one my mother had passed on to me. It had been given to her on the day the last avian-serpiente battle had been fought, and it had never once been drawn. She had handed it to me with the prayer *I hope you need it as often as I have.*

"It is." I tied the dagger to my belt to keep it safe. "Why would the lions have had it?"

He quirked one brow and admitted, "Probably for the same reason that one of my people took it. It's very well made, a work of art in addition to being a weapon, and therefore valuable. If the lions found it while they were looking for you, I imagine they didn't hesitate in taking it. And they're going to be cross when they wake up and find it gone. We can defend ourselves without any problem, but I would rather you and Betia weren't caught in the middle of it. I think it's time the two of you moved on."

It had been one of the most amazing days of my life. I had the *melos* that Betia had given me tied at my waist, and all I needed to do was touch it to break out in a grin. But all good things must end.

I had another life to return to, one with responsibilities and expectations. I reached for Betia's hand as I stepped out of the hut, and tried to remember the optimism and faith that she had brought out in me.

"Thank you, for everything," I said to the members of the Obsidian guild.

Our host shook his head. "Our hospitality was nothing more than the *Ahnleh* should ensure you anywhere. Though if gratitude will keep you from speaking to your parents of us . . . ?"

I nodded. "If you wish to be unknown, it would be a poor reward for me to go against that wish."

"I'll send a couple of my people with you, to guide you until you meet up with the Vahamil. They should be able to take you the rest of the way to Wyvern's Court."

"*Teska.*" Thank you.

The leader of the Obsidian guild smiled. "*A'le-Ahnleh-itil.* If ever I would acknowledge a queen, perhaps it would be you. But that time isn't here yet. *Wimashe.*"

"*Wimashe-lalintoth.*" Goodbye, friend.

# CHAPTER 15

We reached Vahamil land sooner than I'd expected. Betia scented wolves before I had a chance to warn her, and she went rigid, recoiling. I had just turned to encourage her when a familiar male voice shouted my name. At the sound, Betia whimpered, turned on her heel and ran. *Velyo.* I turned to go after Betia but stopped when I felt pressure on my arm, a hand restraining me from running. I shook off Velyo's grip, but Betia had too much of a head start, and a wolf running in fear would always be faster than the human who followed her.

Surrounded by unfamiliar woods, I shouted, "Betia, please! You're safe with me; you know you're always safe with me—"

"Oliza?" Velyo said again, drawing my attention back to him.

Furious, I spun about. The other wolves that had been around us backed off, including some that I recognized from the Vahamil pack.

Right now I wasn't interested in them—only the man I had hoped never to see again. "What kind of leader *are* you?"

I demanded, shaking with rage. "She runs from you in *terror*. What did you do to her—or do I have to ask?"

I shoved past him, remembering the last scene between us. He refused to move, and my shoulder caught him in the chest, knocking him back.

Betia would never come to me, not while he was there. "What are you doing here, anyway?" I snapped as he walked after me. "Following me?"

"Believe it or not, I do take my responsibilities rather seriously," he replied. "You might not have wanted our help, but I felt that it was important to tell your people what I knew of your situation. While I was here, I wanted to see to my people who winter with the Vahamil, especially since Kalisa isn't certain she will be continuing in her position. Now, if you're done with your tantrum, there are some things you should know."

"My *tantrum*?" I shouted, feeling every inch a coiled serpent preparing to strike. "Your own people are terrified of you, Velyo. Has that occurred to you?"

"They should be," he replied frankly. "I am their leader, and I have control of their lives or deaths. It is a weak leader whose people do not respect him."

"My people *respect* me," I spat. "Respect and fear are not the—"

"Aren't they?" he asked. "And do they?"

I was filled with cold rage, and I spoke the words I knew I should not. "What you tried to do to me—what I suspect you did to Betia—would carry a death sentence in Wyvern's Court. How long do you think you would survive if I told my guard? That is not because they fear me; it is because they care for me."

"How long do you think you would survive if you declared war on my people?" he said. He held out a hand to me, challenging. "We both know that you won't do it. So why don't you play nice and come back to the camp with me? Your people have been looking for you, frantic as a child missing his blanket. They were not happy to learn that you were traveling alone."

"Thank you," I said, hating to acknowledge his help but knowing that he had not been obligated even to tell my people that I was alive. I did not take his hand, though I tried to force myself to appear calm as I walked back to the camp.

I was not so furious about what he had tried to do to me. I despised him, but I had no authority over him. I could not change his world when I was trying to fix my own.

But I hated him for Betia. I had no doubt that he had frightened her into her wolf form, and even as I walked to Kalisa's camp, I was gnawed by the terror that this might have been too much for her. If she fled into her wolf form now, she might never return.

I stroked the *melos* she had given me, which was still tied at my waist. Though the colors were not the vibrant reds, greens and blues traditionally used, any of my people would recognize it for what it was. I thought about hiding it before I ran into any serpiente, so that I wouldn't have to face their questions, but I couldn't. I might have lost Betia already. I would not put away my only remembrance.

The Vahamil camp was quieter than I had ever heard it, and I quickly realized that Velyo was the reason. His own people watched him with fear; Kalisa's watched him with wary disdain. Kalisa herself greeted him with a polite nod as she stood and walked toward me. Her movements were tight, and they betrayed that she was still in some pain, but her expression was one of welcome and relief as she grasped my hands in her own.

"Kalisa, it is so good to see you," I said to the alpha. "I had heard that you were injured."

"It remains to be seen if I will continue as alpha of the Vahamil," Kalisa replied. "Frektane's presence has intimidated many of my challengers—but only because he has hinted that he is interested in the position. Velyo is not someone I would wish as my successor." She glanced at Velyo, who had gone to speak to one of his wolves. "Fortunately, unlike Frektane's, my position rests on a little more than brute strength. My people are far better off, due to our relationship with Wyvern's Court. Your parents' support has been a great help to me during my recovery." She admitted, "Seeing your parents as terrified as they've been since you disappeared has been heartbreaking. I am very glad to see that you are all right and will be back home soon. We are still a couple of days away by land, but it would not be a long flight."

I shook my head. "I can't fly."

"Velyo was right, then, about the drugs? But they will wear off eventually."

I nodded, though I knew that the drugs were no longer holding me in this shape. I had recovered my cobra form when the drugs had worn off; my wings would not be coming back.

"In the meantime," Kalisa said, "I will send one of my fastest wolves to tell your guard where they can find you. Whoever was responsible for taking you away will probably feel threatened by your return. I think it would be best if you wait until your guards are with you before continuing on your way, I wouldn't travel alone through these woods until the villain is found."

It seemed to be sound advice, though if Velyo had offered it, I probably would have refused. "Thank you," I said. "Can you give me any word on what else is going on in Wyvern's Court?"

I worried that other violence might have followed the attack on Urban, such as serpiente retaliating against those who had harmed one of their own—especially while my parents and I were gone.

"We haven't been in the area recently," she answered. "Your guards came here to ask if we had seen you, but we knew nothing until Velyo arrived. I was horrified to learn that you had been taken through our land without our knowledge."

Looking up from his discussion with another wolf, Velyo said to Kalisa, "I may disagree with your belief that it is not necessary to patrol the border you share with Wyvern's Court, but it is hardly the Vahamil's fault that their neighbors can't keep track of their own princess. Especially when all the pack's resources were dedicated to the welfare of its alpha."

Kalisa refrained from responding, and Velyo, apparently bored of the discussion, turned and left us again.

"Two alphas is too many for one camp," Kalisa said softly after he had gone. "Blue-eyes is a little too eager for me to pass on my authority. The Frektane pack has always been ambitious enough to keep the rest of us on guard."

"He treats his own people like dirt," I said, tact leaving me.

Kalisa shook her head. "The northern packs need to be a

little harsher to survive the winter," she said, though the expression in her eyes did not match the tolerance in her voice. "It isn't my place to question how Velyo runs his pack, only how I run mine."

"But you let them winter with you."

"Should I punish the Frektane people because I don't like their leader?" she asked.

"Leader? What about his father?"

"Dead," Kalisa informed me. "Shortly after you left."

"Frektane did not seem that unwell when I saw him," I said, wondering if Velyo had added patricide to his list of crimes since we'd last met.

"This isn't really a conversation for you, Wyvern," Kalisa replied, confirming my suspicions. "Pack business is pack business, not meant for the ears of Wyvern's Court."

I nodded, accepting the dismissal. Unlike among the Obsidian guild, here I would always be Oliza Shardae Cobriana. When Kalisa spoke to me, it was queen to princess, and that was not a relationship that allowed for idle talk.

"Just . . . be careful," I couldn't resist adding.

"I always am."


Time passed differently among the wolves than inside Wyvern's Court. The days were marked only by sunrise and sunset, and the meals by when a hunter returned. The mellow rhythm was a poor match for my anxiety and frustration. As long as I was with the wolves, I knew that Betia would not come back to me. I was the only one she seemed to trust. And as long as I was away from Wyvern's Court, I would not be able to eat or sleep without the queasy feeling that my world might be crumbling.

# CHAPTER 16

A flurry of wings woke me early on my third morning with the wolves. I opened my eyes to see the descent of ten avians, including a peregrine falcon and a golden hawk. I was desperate to see my own people again, and I hurried to meet them.

With a falcon's ability to dive swiftly and gracefully, Nicias landed and returned to human form first. He practically lifted me off the ground as he hugged me with truly serpiente abandon. I noticed a couple of avians averting their gazes as they landed around us, but I tried to ignore them. Birds would forever look away at displays of affection, just as serpents would forever indulge in them. Some things would never change.

Someone behind Nicias cleared her throat, and he sprang away from me to give her room. The other avians—a half dozen from my mother's Royal Flight, and the rest from among my Wyverns—also stepped back, fanning out protectively around us but giving us space.

My mother hugged me so tightly, I feared for my ribs; I hugged her back just as tightly. "We feared the worst," she whispered, refusing to let me go. "Are you all right? Can you fly yet?"

"Yes and no," I answered, trying to keep up with her quick, anxious questions. Though she had been raised avian and was perfectly capable of assuming their poise, my mother was making no attempt to be calm just then. "I'm fine, mostly, but I can't fly. Did any of you see a wolf on your way here?"

"We saw a lot of wolves," my mother answered, stepping back with a puzzled expression. "Kalisa's people?"

"No, a . . ." I sighed. She wouldn't have known Betia from anyone else. "We'll look for her later. What's going on back home?"

"You *are* coming home, right?" my mother asked suddenly.

"Of course. How could you think otherwise?"

She relaxed. "Someone went to great lengths to convince us you left willingly. I can't stay long; there are too many destructive rumors going around in Wyvern's Court. Not to mention your father wanted to go tearing off after you. Nicias can explain everything you need to know. I just had to see you alive and well, and hear from you that you are coming home."

She glanced back at her guards, who were standing at attention. Kel, the sparrow who led the Royal Flight, was quietly conferring with Nicias; he was nodding, listening to her without ever taking all his attention from me. I wondered where Gretchen was.

Nicias excused himself from Kel and crossed toward us. "I apologize for hurrying you two, but Kalisa's runner said that it was lions who kidnapped you." He looked at me for confirmation.

"Yes, the mercenaries who came to Wyvern's Court."

"That being so, I would like to send a few people to track

them as soon as possible." He did not add aloud that he could not do that when all the avian Wyverns were needed to guard me, and the Royal Flight was needed to guard my mother.

My mother nodded, grasping the problem quickly. "Of course. Oliza, we can speak further when you get home; I need to let your father know that you are okay before he goes and does something foolish. *For the gods' sake be careful*," she said imploringly before hugging me again.

"I will be."

"Fly with grace," she bid me before nodding to Kel and shifting back into her hawk form. About half of the remaining guards from the Royal Flight followed her, and the rest stayed with the small number of my Wyverns who were left.

I turned to Nicias then. "Now, tell me what is going on."

"People are frantic," Nicias said, as soon as we had some privacy. "When we found the note—"

"A *note*?"

"In your handwriting," he continued, "explaining that you had left of your own free will. People saw it before the guard did, and half the court was sure— You *didn't run*, right?"

I shook my head, a little dazed. It was the perfect scheme, convincing people that I had left willingly, so that there would be no conflict when Salem and Sive took their respective thrones. But who?

"Who?" I asked aloud.

Nicias shook his head. "We don't know yet. The runner Kalisa sent told me only what they knew—that you had been taken by mercenaries, and that you had been drugged and couldn't fly. Now that we have found you, we *will* find them. Their leader will know who hired them."

"And if Tavisan won't tell you?"

Nicias hesitated, reminding me that some falcons were more than capable of finding the information they desired in someone else's mind.

"I'll bring him back to you," Nicias answered finally. "It will be up to you to decide how we deal with him."

"What else am I going to find when I get home? What happened with Urban?"

"There haven't been any serious injuries since the attack on Urban," Nicias said, "but the marketplace has been volatile enough that I've had to assign a couple of my Wyverns to monitor it during the day." I closed my eyes and concentrated on my breathing. I was a child of peacetime; imagining soldiers policing my home made me sweat. "The three avians who attacked Urban came forward and were arrested. They were all from the Hawk's Keep and had come to Wyvern's Court to visit family during Festival."

"They just confessed?"

"I understand that Prentice put some pressure on the avian community. Your mother dealt with them."

"Severely, I hope."

"Serpiente law would have indentured the three of them to Urban for twice the time that he was unable to work—in this case, until he could dance again—but Urban wanted nothing to do with them. Your mother claimed the time instead and has required them to spend two hours each morning in Wyvern's Court with the scholar Valene, learning about serpiente culture, history, myth and language."

"A fine and cultural tutoring?" I said, incredulous. What could my mother have been thinking? "If they had assaulted an avian, they would have been exiled from the court, possibly grounded. But they can beat a dancer and get away with it?"

"If they had assaulted an avian," Nicias said, "other avians would have been calling for their blood. As it is, your mother feared that exiling them would turn them into martyrs."

Martyrs. What kind of world did I live in, where there were people who would defend three men viciously beating someone? "I want to speak to them when I get back to Wyvern's Court."

"You will have a lot to handle once you are home. Your mother—"

"I *need* to speak to them," I said. "I am sure my mother has addressed the issue to her satisfaction, but I need to look into the eyes of the monsters who would attack a young man just for walking on the 'wrong' side of the court."

Nicias nodded slowly. "Of course." After that, he changed the subject to one that obviously had been gnawing at him the way the attack on Urban had been at me. "Oliza, when you were taken . . . all your guards thought you were sleeping in the nest, and everyone from the nest thought you had gone back to the Rookery. You were abducted from the middle of Wyvern's Court." His voice was raw with guilt. "There were signs of a struggle by the statue in the market, but there were dozens of scuffles that morning and the rest of the day, once word got out about what had happened to Urban. We were so focused on minimizing those fights that it wasn't until midday that anyone even noticed you were missing. And once we found the note, half of your guard—including Gretchen— refused to search for you, saying that if you had left willingly, it wasn't their place to drag you back like a disobedient child. Others hesitated because they wanted to obey our captain.

"Actually, I have charges of mutiny and treason hanging over my head right now for blatantly ignoring Gretchen's orders and convincing others to follow me," he said, "though your parents won't support a trial for either. Unfortunately, by the time I convinced people to look for you, the rain had washed most of the lions' tracks away. We sent out search parties by air and land and found almost nothing. We failed you."

"It sounds," I answered, "more like you were one of the ones who didn't."

Nicias shook his head. "I swore to protect you, Oliza—not the Arami, nor the heir to the Tuuli Thea, but *you*. Even if you *had* left Wyvern's Court willingly, I would still have been bound to protect you. And not to judge you." Reluctantly, he added, "I didn't know whether you had wanted to leave, but I didn't want to lose you either way."

The trip home was long and dismal. Within a couple of days some of the serpents from my guard met up with us, but even then we were short several Wyverns.

These were the only ones who had looked for me, I knew, the ones who would not let me disappear into the night. None hesitated to consider Nicias their leader; apparently he had earned the position. They watched me vigilantly, never leaving me by myself for a moment. I appreciated the security, even though I desperately wanted to walk away from the group a little and call for Betia.

None of the serpents had seen a girl by her description on their way here, and while they had seen wolves, they admitted that they couldn't have recognized Kalisa from Velyo in wolf form.

A few of the serpiente glanced quizzically at the *melos* I wore, but they never asked their questions aloud, so I never had to answer them.

Being surrounded by armed guards made me uneasy. In Wyvern's Court, I had rarely been guarded unless I was somewhere secluded. Never had this many been around me at one time, and never had they been so heavily armed. There had never even been an incident in Wyvern's Court in which my guard had needed to draw a weapon. Ours was not a warriors' society.

Right now, we looked like one. Any stranger who approached us would be seen as a threat, not as a visitor.

Sitting by our campfire and thinking my dark thoughts, I shuddered and felt Nicias put a hand on my shoulder. He sat beside me and stirred the fire in silence.

I needed to tell him the one thing I hated to admit even to myself. He was the only person I knew who might have the power to do something about it. Softly enough, I hoped, that my other guards would not hear, I said, "Nicias, when the lions took me, they . . ." It hurt to face this, as if saying it would make it real. "It wasn't just the drugs that stopped me from coming home sooner. Those wore off days ago. They clipped my wings."

He tried to hide it, but there was a moment when I could see his horror, the very response I was afraid I would get from all my people.

"Is there anything you can do?" I asked. "I don't know much about falcon magic, except for how powerful it can be. There *has* to be a way—"

"I wouldn't even know how to begin," he admitted.

"I know you've been studying further since you came home. I know you have some kind of a teacher. Isn't there someone you can ask?"

"I have been studying," Nicias answered carefully, "but along very different lines. And as much as I hate to admit it, no one on Ahnmik would help me with this."

"Why not?" I demanded.

Nicias averted his gaze, the way an avian guard would when he suspected that his monarch was near to hysterics and he wanted to allow her some dignity. The instinctive, infuriating gesture made something inside me snap.

"Nicias, you are one of my oldest friends, and one of my personal guards. You told me that you preferred not to discuss your time on Ahnmik, and I accepted that, because I trusted that you would tell me anything I needed to know. You brought home Hai, a half-falcon heir to the throne, and I accepted that because I knew that your vows left you no choice but to help a cobra in need. You continue to study falcon magic and continue to tell me little about it or about your falcon tutor, and I have accepted *that* because I trust your loyalty. But now, I ask you a direct question about a relevant, necessary topic, and again you refuse me?"

"Oliza, maybe this isn't the best time for—"

"Nicias Silvermead, I am not asking you as your friend. I am giving you an order, as your princess. What is it that you learned on Ahnmik that pertains to me, that makes you step away from me, that makes you study so hard—and makes you so certain that the falcons who seem perfectly willing to teach you whatever it is you are learning will deny you this?"

"They fear you," he finally answered, looking at me defiantly. He drew a deep breath, trying to get control of himself before he continued, in a softer tone. "You're right. You need to know. Oliza—" He bit his lip, hesitating. "According to the falcon Empress," he told me finally, his gaze distant, as if he hated to say it, "the Cobriana still possess some of the magic of their ancestors—a dormant power that they can no longer use. The Shardae line also carries latent magic, though again, they cannot use it. The falcons believe that, should those avian and serpiente powers combine, they would become active."

He looked at me as I struggled to unwind his nervous words.

"*You* carry that magic, Oliza, but thousands of years have passed since anyone has wielded it, and so it is still sluggish in you. The experience you had with Hai after Urban was hurt—the disorientation and lost time—resembles the episodes many falcons have when their magic first wakes. Often they perform incredible, or devastating, feats of magic they would never be able to replicate. Fortunately, yours was fairly mild, which supports the falcon Empress's belief that even if your magic wakes, it will never be strong or reliable. Probably nothing would have happened at all without Hai's magic acting as a catalyst. But when you have a child, he or she will also be born with avian and serpiente power, and the falcons believe that that child *will* be able to wield it."

I stood and stepped away from him, trying to clear my head. What had happened with Hai and the Obsidian guild had seemed like a fluke, perhaps with a simple and reasonable explanation. I had been raised in Wyvern's Court, not in a falcon's land of magic.

It didn't make sense to me.

"Avians and serpiente are so different," I argued. "They may live together now, but they come from completely different worlds. How could my parents' joining possibly have bred something neither side had in the first place?"

Nicias winced. "Wasn't it the dream of a history where avians and serpiente lived together that led your parents to found Wyvern's Court?"

Only then did it occur to me that Nicias's time on Ahnmik was spent with the only living creatures who could remember the days when the wars between the avians and the serpiente began, who might know *how* they began. "Is it true, then?"

"Not in the way your parents envisioned," he replied. His words seemed carefully chosen. "But both powers, from Kiesha and Alasdair, originated in the same place, two halves of a whole."

There was something he wasn't telling me, and I truly wanted to *shake* him and demand that he stop evading it, but I refused to get sidetracked.

"So my child may have magic," I said, keeping my mind on the future.

"The falcons believe that the power she might have would be dangerous," Nicias explained. "I don't know whether I believe that, but I know that they do. I know that if you have a child and she shows an ability to wield the serpiente magic that you carry, the falcons intend to kill her."

*Dear gods.* I had ordered him to tell me this, but it made the air seem dense and suffocating. They would kill a child? *My child?*

Nicias caught my hand, drawing my attention back to him. "I may be able to bind the child's magic, or at least control it. I have been working with a falcon named Darien, to try to find a way."

"And when were you planning to tell me all this?" My voice sounded hollow.

"When you chose your mate, so you could discuss it with him. I had hoped that I would be able to give you some assurance of safety by that time."

I couldn't help shivering. "I assume it's occurred to you that if the falcons are so opposed to my rule, they could easily have orchestrated recent events."

"That's true; they could have," he admitted softly. "I can't say that they didn't, even though they assured me they will not interfere yet. On the other hand, if falcons had chosen to remove you . . ." He took a deep breath, his disgust obvious. "Urban wouldn't have been the one who was beaten and nearly killed. You would have been, and it would have been fatal. Further, they would not have gone to great lengths to soften the blow by convincing us that you had left willingly; they would have left us with a serpent or an avian with blood on his hands, to drive us into a civil war."

"You know this of them, and you still trust them?"

"I trust Darien's motivations," he said. "If I didn't, I wouldn't be working with her."

"And despite that, you know that she wouldn't help you with my wings?" The horror of being grounded was something I could wrap my mind around, whereas the atrocity Nicias had just described was beyond my comprehension.

"Darien probably would, but the Empress and her heir would never let her. I had to bargain to keep you safe from *them*. They won't help protect you from anyone else. And if Empress Cjarsa forces Darien to stop working with me, it won't matter if your wings are clipped or not. When your first child is born, if the royal house of Ahnmik does not believe that I can make the child safe, they will kill her, and you, and anyone else who stands in their way."

I tried to calm myself, practicing avian control, wrapping reserve around me like a cold blanket. I couldn't let this information break me.

"We can discuss this in more depth when we need to," I said. "When I declare my king, I will ask you to explain this magic to me: why I have it, why my ancestors had it and why my child will have it. After . . . after I have a child," I said, willing my voice to be level, "we will take precautions, to either control her power or control the falcons if they will hurt her."

The thought made me shudder. We had just ended one war. I was not enough of a fool to try to preserve a child's potential magic at the cost of a war with the falcons. I said, "We will do what we must to persuade them that she is not a threat. Without bloodshed. And as for my wings . . ."

What was losing the sky if I could lose Wyvern's Court entirely?

"I will make do. I need to."

He nodded. "I'm so sorry."

I shook my head.

"Try to get some sleep," he suggested. "We will probably be back at Wyvern's Court by tomorrow evening. Someone there might know something about your wings. But, Oliza?"

"Yes?"

He met my gaze with his very blue eyes, and asked not with a guard's examination but with a friend's regard, "If you don't mind my asking, who gave you the *melos*?"

My hand brushed the soft cloth as I remembered dancing for Betia, and I once again hoped that she was okay.

Softly, Nicias asked, "Have you made your decision already, then?"

I shook my head. "Just a friend," I told him. I was going to have to explain the *melos* to the serpiente when I returned to Wyvern's Court, or risk everyone there jumping to the same conclusion. A female wolf—wouldn't that shock the court?

It was no wonder that, when I slept, the old nightmares invaded my mind.

I was back in Wyvern's Court—and I was armed. I was wearing the blade my mother had given to me; the steel shimmered as if new when I drew it. The instant the blade cleared the sheath, I saw the first wound appear on my own skin. The blade was already bloodied, even though I could find no enemy to slay.

"Oliza, this is madness," someone said, pleading. "There has to be another way—"

I woke with a gasp, shivering even in the warm air, but before I could sit up, someone was beside me; arms were going around me and guiding me back to sleep. For a moment I thought Betia had returned, but I quickly realized that it was just Nicias lying against my back, protective and friendly—the way we had once slept as children in the nest.

I needed that comfort now.

This time I dreamed of the sky as it could only be experienced in flight, something I longed for. I dreamed of the Obsidian guild, and the *melos* I had danced for Betia. I dreamed of running with a wolf, and then of running *as* a wolf.

I half woke once again, wanting to weep at the dreams lost. What wouldn't I give to have those days back?

I turned in Nicias's arms, tucking my head down against his chest, and closed my eyes one more time. I matched my breathing to his, allowing his peaceful sleep to guide me back into the realm.

My dreams were those of an unborn infant, the sound of a heartbeat, and the gentle rhythm of breath indrawn and exhaled.

# CHAPTER 17

We returned to Wyvern's Court at midday. For a moment I paused on the hills, watching my people go about their lives, almost as they had every day before. The scene was marred only by the soldiers I could see patrolling the public areas, serpiente on the ground and avians either perched or circling the skies above. A fierce protectiveness swept over me, as well as anger, and fear. This was my world. These were my people. And someone had threatened them.

*What do you want from me, Wyvern's Court?* I demanded silently. *What can I possibly give to you that will let you be free to live, and love, and dance and sing? Anything you want—except to hurt each other. How can I spare you this pain?*

I jumped when I heard a wolf's howl; I took a step in its direction before I heard a response from another direction, and then another. Just the Vahamil. They used this music to communicate over great distances.

"Oliza?" Nicias asked. I wondered what he had seen in my face.

"Let's go," I answered.

With Nicias beside me, I walked hesitantly into the reception hall in the Rookery, where my mother and father were waiting for me. I knew I was about to face an interrogation.

I had one foot in the door when my father dragged me farther in, lifting me in his arms as if he couldn't believe I was real. My mother followed suit, whispering praise for answered prayers.

I learned from their hasty words that when they had discovered "my" note in my room, Urban had told them of the awkward scene between us in the nest.

"You *didn't* run away?" my father asked finally, his hands on my shoulders as he looked at me intently.

"No," I answered.

"What happened with Urban wasn't—"

"Let's let Oliza talk," my mother suggested, slipping her arm around my father's waist to pull him back and give me room. "What happened, Oliza?"

The answer to that question was trickier than I had imagined it would be. The four of us sat around a small conference table at the back of the hall, and I described as well as I could the attack and what I remembered of my captors, which wasn't much.

"Is anyone tracking them?" my father asked Nicias.

"I've got three of my people on it," he replied. "The lions are a practical group; they won't fight when they know they can't win. That they accepted an assignment to abduct Oliza in the first place shocks me. I didn't expect them to tangle with Wyvern's Court."

Again, Nicias sounded disappointed in himself.

"Continue," my mother said to me.

I described stumbling through the snow, not knowing what it was, sick from the drugs. I told them about Betia saving my life by bringing me to the Frektane. I explained about the poison and for the moment left them to assume that it was why I still could not shapeshift; I wasn't ready to deal with that loss yet. There were more important things to discuss.

I hesitated when I got to the incident with Velyo. Among both avians and serpiente, what Velyo had tried to do to me was a crime punishable by death. Even if my family and the new head of my guard were willing to ignore it—and even that much I doubted—they would not forgive it. It would fracture our peace with the wolves, and in this time of unrest, we could not afford to alienate our allies.

I tried to gloss over the moment, but my mother noticed. "You were in such a hurry to leave that you brought *no one*? I might not agree with Frektane's arrogance, but at least he would have provided you with an escort."

I shook my head, forming my words carefully. "A disagreement arose between Velyo—the new alpha, now—and me regarding a matter I was not willing to compromise on. As an outsider far from home, I was not in a position to question their customs, but neither was I willing to accept them. I thought it best to leave."

My mother sighed, shaking her head. I knew that my explanation sounded like atrocious diplomacy, but I could not defend myself with greater detail.

"Betia walked most of the way with me," I continued. Just saying her name made me feel a little ache in my chest, so I gave as little detail about her as I did about our trek home. "Whenever we heard the lions, we ran," I explained. "So I can't tell you anything more about them from my trip home. Eventually

I ran into Kalisa's tribe, and they sent for the Wyverns. That was when Betia stopped traveling with me."

My story was full of holes. Omitting the Obsidian guild had caused that. I was uncomfortable lying to my parents, so I tried to account for some of the brevity by explaining, "I did receive some other help on my way home, but from a very private group who requested I not discuss them."

Nicias asked, "Are you certain they were not involved with the abduction?"

"I am."

My father said, "I won't insist on knowing why you ran from the wolves; the Frektane are willing to overlook the slight, and I have faith in my daughter's judgment. As for your mystery group, we will trust your instincts there, as well."

"Thank you," I said, before my father added, "As long as you plan to explain where you received the *melos* you are wearing, that is."

"The *melos*," I answered, "was given to me for its earliest traditional reason: as praise for my abilities, and as a request for me to dance. There is no law saying that it must mean more, even though it commonly does. As for the color," I continued, "the giver was a wolf, who doesn't know all the connotations." Among the serpiente, gold represented the bond between mates.

My father nodded slowly, acknowledging the facts but hesitating to outright agree. Even though a request of a dance was the true meaning, for centuries the scarves had been given as courting gifts.

I sighed. "Betia became a very dear friend to me during our time together. She saved my life repeatedly and traveled with me for weeks. I would never have survived without her.

She knew how much I resented the pressure I received from serpiente at home, and how much I wanted to perform."

Both of my parents looked relieved the instant they realized that Betia was a woman, though Nicias was still looking at me with an expression I could not quite place.

What if I *had* fallen in love during my travels? What if I had brought home a white viper from the Obsidian guild? All things considered, bringing that group back into the court would have been an amazing political accomplishment.

Further, what if I had just danced, and some young man I trusted had offered the *melos* with no ulterior motive, as Betia had—simply because he knew what it meant to me? My parents never would have believed me. If they had, they never would have trusted *him*.

There was a short period of silence, which Nicias broke for me. "Would you like to see the note?" he offered.

I nodded. "Please." He handed over the letter, which had been written on the stationery I kept in my room in this very building. "Do we have any idea who wrote it?"

"The best scholars in the Hawk's Keep insist that, as far as they can tell, it *is* your handwriting," Nicias answered. "I don't know of anyone who openly admits to such skill for forgery. Perhaps one of the mercenaries?"

"I don't know. It would probably be helpful in their line of work, but . . ." The letter distracted me, and I began to read.

*To rule is easy. To truly protect my people is harder. I write this with tears in my eyes, hoping that perhaps one day my time will come, but believing that for now we are not ready for a wyvern on the throne. We have struggled for twenty years to make Wyvern's Court one land, but one cannot perform such a marriage while both*

*parties bleed into the dirt and fight against the Fates. Let us heal;*
*let our children learn peace. And then maybe it will be time.*

*I leave now of my own free will. This is what I must do. Please*
*do not seek me.*

*Oliza Shardae Cobriana*

"I don't know who wrote it. I don't know who *would*
write it." I shuddered, standing up.

My parents exchanged an intense glance, the silent communication of a long-married pair. My father looked away
and sighed.

"What?" I asked.

"This is going to be a very delicate time in Wyvern's
Court," my father said. "Your mother and I have been discussing what could be done to calm our people."

"We know how reluctant you are," my mother said, "and
hate to press you for a decision, but we believe that it would
comfort them if you announced your choice for your mate."
She added quickly, "You don't need to go through the ceremony yet or do anything you aren't ready for. Just let our
people know that the decision has been made. People believed too easily that you had abdicated."

My father winced, but he supported my mother. "I know
I was one of those who encouraged you to wait, but perhaps
that was wrong. Technically, your mother and I still rule, but
Wyvern's Court looks to you for guidance. As long as you are
undecided, *it* will be."

I recoiled, refusing to see the sense in their words. "I have
friends and suitors on both sides of the court, but no one I
love, no one I could even *imagine* as . . ."

Protector, companion, friend and lover. An alistair, whom

I could trust with my life and my heart. A mate, whom I could turn to in any moment of joy or grief. A leader, someone to rule beside me. Someone whose *children* I would carry. Someone I would spend my life with, however many more years I had.

"I can't just pick a life partner like plucking a pebble out of a riverbed," I argued. "I know you two made the agreement without love, politically, and found it later—but you were *lucky*, incredibly lucky, and there was no other choice. I don't know a single avian man who wouldn't be horrified to see me stand on the dais and perform a *harja* during the Namir-da— and I certainly don't know one who would dance with me. And I don't know of a serpiente who—"

My mother sighed. "Oliza, I'm sorry. I don't know the answers this time. I only know that indecision can cripple this entire world. And if we can't make Wyvern's Court survive, what does that say?"

I lowered my head. "I'll consider your words," I said softly. Even if I could choose, I remembered what had happened to Urban for daring to steal a kiss. How much would I be endangering any man I claimed to love? "But for now, I need some air. Can we continue this later?"

My mother nodded. "Go. Nicias?"

"I'll be with her," he answered.

"You'll want to speak to your people soon," my father said gently. "They have heard by now that you're back, but they're going to want assurance from you that the rumors of your abdication are false."

"I will speak to them," I promised. *As soon as I know what to say.*

As soon as I knew how to tell my people that I was grounded, flightless. As soon as I could figure out what to do.

Nicias followed me out. I knew he had to, but in that moment, I did not want him near me. I wanted to be alone.

"Oliza, I know why you're panicking," he said, his long legs easily keeping up with mine. "And . . . I noticed that you didn't tell them."

"What could I say?"

"You could say what happened," he replied. "Your mother might know something that would help. More important, she would *want* to know, and you might feel better having told her."

I spun to face him. *Panic*—that was the word he had used, and maybe it was the right one. "Nicias, they want me to choose a mate. I know why they feel I need to, but for the life of me I cannot figure out who to pick. No, not for my life, but for the life of Wyvern's Court. Especially now, with my wings gone. How could I ask an avian man to be my alistair, knowing that he will always see me as some crippled creature whom he must protect and be polite to because he pities her? I *can't* ask a serpiente, not if I'm never going to take to the skies again; the avians would have objected to a serpent before, but how much more will they object if they know I'm not even one of them anymore?"

*How can I lead them if I am not one of them?*

I jumped when someone spoke behind me. "I'm glad to know you think so little of those who walk the Earth like mortals." The dry, emotionless tone made my skin crawl as I turned to face my cousin. "Don't worry, little queen," she added. "The sky doesn't really matter so much, now, does it?" How many times had Hai been told the same thing since coming to Wyvern's Court with her falcon wings broken and lost? "And at least your serpents can ignore your hawk's blood, if you never show it to them again."

I had felt pity for her before, but this was too much. Nicias must have recognized how nasty the conversation could get, because he quickly said, "Hai, maybe I should speak to Oliza alone."

She shook her head as she obediently moved toward the front door of the Rookery. She paused just before leaving, though, to say offhandedly, "If you had the skill and courage to force-change her, you could heal her wings, my prince. Though in the process Anhamirak's power might ravage your magic as bitterly as it does mine." Nicias's eyes widened in surprise, but before he could respond, she added, "Of course, never having practiced it, you might also kill both of you. And I would find that unfortunate."

Hai turned to me. "Oliza, if you're ever interested in speaking with someone who has a great deal of experience with these magics, a working knowledge of Anhamirak's fire and absolutely nothing to lose from the falcons' wrath or her own self-destruction, you know where to find me. Right now, I'm going to go for a ride. Serpents keep telling me it's just as grand as flying."

She slipped out the doorway while we were both still frozen in shock. In the months since I had met her, Hai had barely even spoken to me, much less said anything intended to be helpful. This was now the second time she had offered to help me in as many meetings.

"Could she really do that?" I asked Nicias.

"I . . . I don't know," he answered. "She *is* powerful, but I didn't think she could control her magic to the extent she is proposing. Maybe I misjudged her there, too." He shook his head. "Her magic is unpredictable, and we've already seen that combining it with yours can have unexpected results.

Just because the falcons don't think your magic is enough of a threat for *them* to worry about doesn't mean that using it can't hurt *you*."

"I know you can't work the type of magic Hai was talking about, but if you were there, would you be able to help control it?"

He paused, thoughtful. "Most of my study the past several months has been devoted to working with Darien to try to control Anhamirak's power, for the binding spell. I can try to help keep Hai's and your powers balanced, but if that doesn't work, I should be able to stop it completely."

We were interrupted by Sive's entrance. Her expression warmed as she saw me. Even Prentice cracked a smile. I tried to do the same, but my thoughts were mired in the argument with my parents, and the strange conversation with Hai; it must have shown on my face, because Sive's expression mellowed before she had even reached me.

"Oliza, I had heard that you had met up with your wyverns and were on your way back, but it is good to see you with my own eyes. Are you all right?"

Not yet, but I hoped I would be. "I don't plan to vacation via mercenary in the future, but I'll be fine. Thank you. And Prentice, I understand that I owe you thanks, as well, regarding the identification of Urban's attackers."

He nodded very slightly. "I was not blind to the fact that my name was on the top of your list. Finding the responsible parties was the only way I could clear my own name, in my queen's eyes, my lady's eyes, and anyone else's."

The response was not exactly what I might have hoped for, but what had I really expected, from Prentice?

"I have spent enough time with the dancers that I could

anticipate how they would react," Sive said. "We hoped that action from the Shardae line would help convince the serpiente that, even with you missing, we had not just forgotten the crime against them."

"Thank you, again. I am glad that both of you were here while I was gone."

# CHAPTER 18

After the conversation with Sive, I walked with Nicias along the outskirts of Wyvern's Court toward the dancer's nest. I needed to show my people that I was home, and I wanted to check on Urban.

Nicias had been right to accuse me of panicking after the conversation with my parents. The interlude with Hai and the more rational discussion with Sive and Prentice had calmed me, and now I needed to decide my path.

"The Vahamil are our allies, and though there is obviously a power struggle going on between them and the Frektane, neither pack seems a likely suspect. That leaves someone from Wyvern's Court—I hate thinking of my own people in that light, but I know I must—or the falcons. I know you feel that the falcons aren't behind this, but from what you've said, they seem to have a powerful motive to remove me. Do you really trust them?"

Nicias let out a short laugh. "*Trust?* Absolutely not. The falcons' god Ahnmik might not be *evil*, but he supposedly gave this world manipulation and deceit. If Darien had said she wanted to help me because she felt it was the right thing to do, it would have been a lie. She was in love with your uncle Anjay Cobriana; their child, Hai, is in Wyvern's Court; and Darien hates the Empress and Araceli for supporting the war. She wants to fight them, and that means she will do everything in her power to see you on the throne of Wyvern's Court. Like I said before, the royal house has agreed to give me a chance to protect your child, and I do not think they will go back on that agreement; if they did, I believe they would find a more effective means of doing it. I've been wrong about them before, but if I was in this case, Darien would let me know . . . simply because she is that vindictive."

"What about Hai? She has been here for months now and has rarely spoken to me. When she has, it has usually been incoherent or outright condescending. Now she has offered to help me the last two times I have seen her." The first time had been right before I was abducted. "Hai makes no attempt to hide her loyalty to Empress Cjarsa. Why does she claim to want to help me?"

"I don't know," Nicias admitted, "but she wouldn't do anything she thought would hurt you."

"Why not? I don't believe for a moment that she is loyal to me."

"The only monarchy Hai is loyal to is the one on Ahnmik . . . the one of which I am third in line to the throne." He cringed. "I like to believe that Hai's affection toward me is more than loyalty and magic, but even if it is, I doubt she would hesitate to turn on someone she loved if her Empress wished it. What I *know* is that the only thing that allowed Hai to wake, and allows her to survive in our world, is her tie to me. Betraying you would be betraying me, and it would destroy her."

I needed her help desperately. There was little I could do until I knew whether I had my wings. I had been straddling the line between heir and queen for years. Maybe my parents were right in saying that we had reached a point where my hesitation could hurt my people.

I needed only to decide.

"I know I need to be here," I said to Nicias with a sigh as I thought about the days I had spent in the Obsidian guild. Simpler days, without these hard decisions. "I *am* Arami, and I *am* heir to the Tuuli Thea, and I won't just *forsake* that. But is it so awful that I was tempted? I danced, Nicias, and it was so *pure*. I wasn't queen-to-be. I wasn't competing and being backed into a corner by decisions I am not ready to make. And there was this incredible, perfect moment. . . ."

I thought about the instant after the *hanlah'melos*. It had seemed as if anything was possible. It had felt like . . .

I shook my head.

"I am the leader of Wyvern's Court, and if I have to declare a mate, I *will*." I made this pledge without any idea as to how I would fulfill it. Nicias started to protest, but I cut him off with a motion. "I am terrified that what happened to Urban is just the beginning, that anyone I pick will be in even more danger. But what I've done so far hasn't worked. People believed that I had abdicated—even members of my own guard. The longer I procrastinate, the longer I wait to tie myself to Wyvern's Court, the more speculation and doubt will grow."

"Do you have anyone in mind?" he asked, neither challenging nor agreeing with me. I was grateful for his calm support.

"No," I answered. "Someone known by both groups. A

serpiente who won't be lost without constant company, who won't panic if I ask for a moment of *privacy*. Or an avian willing to learn to dance, and who won't be challenged by . . ." I let out a frustrated cry. "In short, a man who doesn't mind abandoning the culture that raised him, and is submissive enough to let me drag him about. That doesn't exactly sound like a good basis for a loving, equal relationship, does it? And what kind of king could such a man make?"

Nicias shook his head, but before he could say more, he tensed; his hand moved to rest on the knife at his waist as he took a step past me, toward something he had heard that I had not.

A moment later, we glimpsed a flash of white. Nicias unsheathed his blade and moved in front of me.

"If I meant harm, I would not be foolish enough to show myself to a loyal falcon." The voice was familiar to me. I put a hand on Nicias's arm to draw him back as the leader of the Obsidian guild stepped forward.

"*Ciacin-itil.*"

"*Cincarre*, Obsidian," I said. "Nicias, it's all right."

Nicias's expression was doubtful, but he stepped back a little.

"Don't worry, falcon. I do not plan to stay long. I am simply escorting a friend." He looked behind himself and called, "It's all right, dear."

Tentatively, another figure emerged from the woods. My breath left me in a rush when I recognized her.

"Betia."

I pulled her into my arms as gratitude overwhelmed me, washing away the dread in the pit of my stomach. Betia was still in human form; she hadn't gone back to her wolf.

She balked when I tried to draw her into the clearing,

and I spoke quickly. "Betia, this is Nicias; I know I told you about him. He won't hurt you. Nicias—" But Nicias had already relaxed and put his weapon away.

He bowed slightly. "Betia, it's an honor to meet you."

Betia gave a little nod, still watching him warily. However, she let me bring her forward.

"Are you all right?" I asked. "I was so worried about you! I will *never* let anyone hurt you, I swear it. Do you believe me?"

Her gaze flickered from me to the woods, but she nodded again, leaning against me in a way that betrayed her fatigue.

"Oliza," she whispered.

It was the first word I had ever heard her speak, and I spun her about joyfully and then hugged her tightly to myself, not even releasing her when the white viper spoke again.

"She came back to us shortly after you left," he said. "It was obvious that she regretted leaving you, but she did not want to travel alone through wolf territory to find you."

"Thank you," I said. "Thank you so much. Please, if you need anything before you go on your way—"

He shook his head. "I will be fine. You two . . ." He looked past me, at Nicias, as if debating whether to finish, and then concluded, "You should be together."

"Do you want to see Wyvern's Court?" I asked Betia. "Or first, how about a hot meal and a place to sleep?" She smiled, still holding on to me. Her body felt frail; she obviously had not been eating or sleeping well since she had fled from Velyo once again. "I'll take care of you," I promised.

I looked up, intending to thank the white viper once more, but he was already gone. Unsurprised, I turned to Nicias instead.

"For tonight, I'm going to take Betia to Wyvern's Nest. It's public enough that you don't have to worry about my safety, and I don't doubt they'll take her in. Tomorrow I want to speak to the men who attacked Urban, perhaps when they have their meeting with Valene."

"I can come find you shortly before their lesson ends."

"Would you please let Hai know that I would like to speak to her as well, at her earliest convenience?"

"I will let her know."

"Betia, how does an evening in the dancer's nest sound?"

She nodded groggily, already half-asleep in my arms. I scooped her up to carry her, and she leaned her head against my shoulder. She was so terribly light.

Nicias blinked in surprise. "Would you like a hand?"

"You need your arms free in case we run into trouble," I said. "I can carry her."

He shrugged, smiling a little. "I'll speak to Hai. You take care of your friend."

The three of us reached Wyvern's Nest without trauma. Betia found her feet again as we neared the entrance, though she put her hand in mine as Nicias left us and we stepped inside.

We had barely reached the door when we were greeted by a rush of dancers with Salem at the forefront.

"Oliza, thank the gods! I was starting to worry I was going to have to give up this life of hedonism and pick up some real responsibilities." He grinned and hugged me tightly.

"Well, you can relax now. Your future is secure."

He stepped back and regarded me with great seriousness before saying, "First I heard that you had abdicated, then that you had been kidnapped. There were rumors that Prentice— well, they were rumors. There were just as many people up north saying I was responsible, according to Sive. That's the burden of the second heir. But really . . ." His solemn expression cracked into a smile as he gestured at the *melos* at my waist. "If you were going to go off and elope, you really should have warned someone."

"I did not abdicate," I said loudly, so that everyone could hear me. "I did not leave of my own free will, but I have returned safely." I did not mention my inability to shapeshift; I would wait to see whether Hai could work this miracle she had implied was in her power. Because I knew that, like Salem, many of them were more curious about the *melos* than about the state of my health, I added, "And I have not yet taken a mate. The *melos* was given to me by a dear friend of mine, who saved my life more than once these past few weeks." I saw skeptical looks, but most seemed to accept that I was telling the truth, especially when I glanced at Betia to make it clear of whom I was speaking. "Salem, this is Betia. Betia, this is my cousin, Salem."

"Welcome to Wyvern's Nest, Betia," Salem said. "Thank you for bringing our Wyvern home."

She nodded in greeting, a little wide-eyed as she took in her surroundings. Wyvern's Nest was always filled with warmth, movement and music, but right then the air was also thick with preparation for the Namir-da. The holiday was only days away, and there was no force on earth that would stop serpents from celebrating.

Betia jumped as someone else swept in front of us— Urban. Seeing him walking again brought tears to my eyes.

"Oliza, thank the gods," he whispered, hugging me tightly. "When you disappeared, I thought . . . But you're back now. That's what really matters."

"It's good to see you up. How have you been?"

He grimaced. "A little stiff, but the doctor assures me I'll get over it. I still take an escort from the Wyverns whenever I go into the northern hills, even though the crows who attacked me were caught. Avians are being just as careful over here." He looked thoughtful for a moment. "It's odd. There were never a lot of birds around the nest, or out in the market with us in the evening, and we complained about the few who did show up. Now almost all the avians vanish at sunset, and I kind of miss them." He glanced back at someone I couldn't see over the crowd, and added with a half smile, "But then, I seem to have compensated."

*"Oliza?"* At the excited cry, Salem, Urban and the other serpents stepped aside to reveal one of the last people I had expected to see there: Marus. His jaw was darkened by a bruise that couldn't have been more than a day old, and he looked tired, but that wasn't half as shocking as the fact that the big clothes he was wearing had obviously not come from his home. They were serpiente clothes—a *dancer's* clothes— borrowed to cover an avian's more slender frame.

He stared at me with as much shock as I felt looking at him. When he realized he was doing so, he started to try to control the reaction, and then he shook his head as if recalling that members of the nest were made nervous by avian reserve.

"Marus, what are you—"

"Doing here?" he finished for me. "I seem to have moved in."

Urban stepped forward. "I know you two will need to catch up—when you have some privacy—but first, Oliza, Betia, come in, sit down; Betia hasn't even been introduced to anyone. You both look exhausted and hungry. Betia, welcome to Wyvern's Nest. My name is Urban; I'm a friend of Oliza's. This is Marus, another friend. You've met Salem. No one else really matters." A few people objected to the quip, but Urban continued, "Sit down, sit down."

Within moments, half of Wyvern's Nest was sitting or lying somewhere near me, many leaning against me, Betia or Urban. The wolf didn't seem to mind the familiarity. Marus had claimed a spot at the edge of the crowd. The serpents seemed reluctant to sit too close to him. I was still just amazed that he was there.

The time for questions would come later. For now, bread, wine, fruit and meat were passed around and shared by every member of the nest; Betia ate well, and I found that my appetite had also returned.

After the meal, the request was made: "Come, Betia, convince your lover to dance for *us*," someone teased. "It isn't fair at all that we taught her, but she'll only let you see."

My face felt hot. "She's not . . ."

Betia laughed a little, shaking her head. She leaned forward and kissed my cheek as she grabbed my hands and pulled me to my feet. Her brown eyes glittered with a devil-may-care recklessness that warmed me to my toes. If it would make her smile that way, I would dance all night.

The dancers and my mischievous wolf companion all but dragged me onto a low dais at the back of the nest.

I must have danced a half dozen times, performing a few *sakkri* and then moving on to simple one-scarf *melos* dances before, finally, someone called for a *harja*—specifically, Maeve's solo from the *Namir-da*.

"Absolutely not!" I said, laughing. A *melos* could be innocent; a *harja* never was. The *intre'marl* from the *Namir-da* was representative of Maeve's seduction of Leben; the metaphor was not hard to recognize.

There was a sound of disappointment from the audience.

"Someone else perform," I insisted, sliding off the stage near Betia. She swung me about in a fairly good mimic of one of the moves I had performed earlier. "I thought you were *tired*," I pointed out.

She laughed, but the sound was cut off by a yawn that she tried to stifle, turning it into a little squeak.

"That's enough, people; you'll dance your princess to death at this rate," one of the elder dancers said. "Oliza, Betia, everyone else, get some sleep."

There were some grumbles, but people began relaxing, lying down in twos or more. Someone dragged a blanket over Betia and me, and several dancers curled against our backs. I remembered how often a serpiente nest had been compared to a pile of kittens or puppies, and wondered if the wolves ever slept this way. Betia seemed just as comfortable with the crowd as she had alone with me.

# CHAPTER 19

D espite having danced myself into exhaustion the previous night, I woke early. Loath to disturb Betia, who was still sleeping deeply, I extracted myself carefully from the pile. Bodies shifted instinctively to compensate for the sudden chill, closing the hole without anyone waking.

I found Urban sitting by the fire, munching on bread and cheese. He offered some to me.

"Morning, Oliza. Beautiful performance last night."

"Thanks."

"I'm sorry about what happened, before," he said hesitantly. "You disappeared, and all I could think was that the last memory I had of you was—" He broke off, then blurted out, "I'm sorry for pressuring you. I didn't realize . . ." He glanced over his shoulder at Betia, and I suddenly understood why he believed I had pulled away.

"Just a friend, Urban. Really," I said.

He raised one eyebrow. "After that little display last night? I've never seen you act that way around a man, Oliza."

I blushed. "I'm royal blood, Urban. I'm in line to the throne. And a royal pair bond has to produce heirs."

Urban cursed, and my mind returned to the argument I'd had with my parents. The dancers would hate any decision that they thought had been made for political reasons instead of love, which meant I couldn't discuss my indecision with any of them—especially Urban. I had walked away from him once, and there would be no undoing that.

My gaze drifted to Betia, who was still sleeping, curled in the arms of a dozen dancers, and from there to a more solitary form.

Urban saw who I was looking at. "Marus approached me the first time I left the nest, a couple of weeks ago. Between his objections to my behavior at Festival and the fight at Salem's coronation, he felt he shared responsibility for what had happened to me, and then for your leaving. He was in bad shape about it and wanted to make amends, so I invited him back to the nest."

"And he moved in?" It seemed a little extreme.

Urban looked down. "He came by a few times. But when I went by his house to meet him one day, his parents forbade him to go with me. They argued, loudly enough that I could hear it from the next room. His mother kept shouting about how it would look, how he would never be considered a suitable alistair by any lady who knew he associated with serpents—dancers, especially—how their friends would be horrified . . . I'd never heard avians raise their voices that way. Marus and I left anyway, and when he went back later that day, they wouldn't let him in. That was about a week ago."

"He's been staying here ever since?" I wondered if talking to Marus's parents would help any or only hurt the situation more. They had both been soldiers during the war and were very conservative, as were many of the avians of their generation.

"Not all of the dancers welcomed him with open arms," Urban said. "I think a lot of them still believe he was one of the avians who attacked me. More of them think he's here just to impress you. But Salem and Rosalind have championed him, and no one has the guts to accuse him of assaulting me when I keep saying I trust him."

I realized that Marus had done exactly what I had told Nicias my mate must; he had crossed Wyvern's Court. He hadn't been accepted by everyone, but here he was anyway, in the dancer's nest.

"Looks like someone was less forgiving," I commented, recalling the bruise on Marus's cheek.

*Can I love Marus?* I wondered. I looked at my raven suitor and tried to imagine spending every day with him. Tried to imagine someday looking at him the way my parents looked at each other. I knew he was kind, and well-spoken. Perhaps he even had the traits he would need to be a king. But even as I tried to let my imagination run wild, I felt no attraction to him. I had never felt the urge to do any of the crazy things that I had seen my peers do in their attempts to impress the ones they loved.

Such as getting onto a dais with professional dancers of the Obsidian guild, or performing a *melos* in the nest in defiance of all the potential difficulties, and dancing for hours.

Urban grinned, not privy to my thoughts. "One of the others made the mistake of harassing Marus while Salem was around. Salem is such a dancer that sometimes it's easy to forget that he's a cobra, but he has a protective streak a mile wide, and when you trigger it . . . well, he never needed to raise a hand to the other guy. Just stared him down with the kind of Cobriana glare that they say used to make opponents in the battlefield drop dead from terror." He shook his head, still looking amused.

Once Betia was awake, we left the nest so that I could show myself to the rest of my court before my meetings in the Rookery. That early in the morning, the crowd was primarily avian, so our greeting there was much more subdued. The relief in the avian population was apparent in their smiles and in the warmth they allowed into their voices when they welcomed me home, most of them sparing no more than a passing glance for Betia. Wolves in this market were common enough.

Serpiente tended to have late evenings and late mornings, but there had always been a handful who were early risers: a flautist, who had discovered that, though they did not dance, avians did enjoy music; a baker, who sold spice rolls and meat pies; a weaver, famous for his *melos,* who had found a morning niche creating more subdued designs that had since become fashionable as cloaks and shawls in the avian court. That day, there were so few serpiente in the market that I might as well have been in the Hawk's Keep.

Two of my Wyverns, a crow and a sparrow, were taking turns circling above to keep an eye on things. I knew they would keep their attention on me as long as I was in the space they were guarding. Their movements were what drew my attention to Arqueete, the baker, who had drawn her stall off to the very edge of the market.

She smiled tiredly at me. "Oliza, good morning; you are a sight for sore eyes, even though you look as if you've lost a stone of weight since I last saw you. No matter; we'll fatten you up soon enough," she promised. "And is this the wolf I've heard so much about?"

News always traveled fast—none faster than gossip carried by dancers.

"Yes, this is. Betia, this is Arqueete; she has been feeding me every morning I've been home for as long as I can remember."

"Someone needs to; you eat like a bird. Betia, you're staring longingly at one of my pheasant pies. Go ahead and have one; no one else is eating them. Consider it my thanks for finally convincing our Wyvern to dance the *rrasatoth*."

"Where is everyone?" I asked as Betia nibbled at the meat pie Arqueete had shoved into her hands.

She shrugged. "Most of them stopped coming out here right after Urban was attacked—and a good thing it was, since there were dozens of fights over the next couple of days. Then about a week ago Salokin stepped away from his stall for just a minute and came back to find that someone had ruined weeks' worth of work," she said, referring to the weaver. "The rest of the serpiente refused to come out here before noon after that. They all get enough work helping prepare for Namir-da, fortunately."

"And how have you been?"

"Managing," she said. "I refuse to be chased off by a bunch of ruffians causing a ruckus. Sive comes by most mornings and buys breakfast for herself, and speaks highly of me to her associates, so that helps some."

Our conversation was cut short by an avian woman, who cried out with an uncharacteristic display of relief, "Milady Shardae! Finally, you're back. We all feared we might never see you again."

"Princess, how wonderful that you're home," an older

avian gentleman said. "At last, you can put a stop to this madness." .

"I am going to—"

"He isn't talking about fights in the marketplace," Arqueete interrupted. "I've been listening to him preach since the day you disappeared. He is convinced that those three birds they arrested are innocent."

"Innocent?" I echoed, staring incredulously at the avian man. "They *confessed*."

"Of course they did!" he said. "With an alistair to the Shardae line accused, what good man *wouldn't* step forward to protect—"

Arqueete offered, "I would believe they confessed to pro-. tect Prentice. I would believe he is *guilty*. Everyone knows—"

"It was an absurd accusation," the avian woman who had greeted me a moment before said. Voices were beginning to rise as everyone tried to talk over everyone else. "It is obscene to think that Lady Sive's alistair—"

"Lady Sive's alistair," Arqueete shouted, "would rather lock his mate up in a golden tower than let her have a life."

"Prentice only wants to protect her."

"Protect her from *what*? Salem would never let any harm come to her. He watches her like she's his own—"

"The cobra watches her a little too closely for anyone's comfort."

I imagined that this group had been having this same argument for more than a month; certainly nothing would be settled by my adding to it. I hoped I could lay some of this debate to rest after I spoke to the criminals myself.

I was just about to announce my intentions when Betia stepped deliberately into the middle of the argument. With feigned obliviousness, she nodded thanks to the serpent for her breakfast. I smiled as I realized that she had positioned herself just right: close enough to the serpent to seem friendly, but far enough from the avians to seem polite by their standards.

I took advantage of the moment of peace she had brought to say, "I have plans this morning to speak to the three men who were convicted of the assault. If a mistake was made, I will fix it. If indeed they are guilty, I hope you will trust the judgment of your Tuuli Thea and her heir. Now, if you'll excuse me . . ."

I understood now how my mother could have feared that a serious punishment would turn criminals into martyrs. I heard similar concerns about Urban's attackers as I continued through the market, as well as questions about my own absence. Repeatedly I assured people that the rumors surrounding my disappearance had been exaggerated, that the culprits would be found and that the mercenaries would be taken in for questioning as soon as my guards returned with them. Among the avians, there was no doubt that a group of guards with wings would succeed in finding a group of lions on the ground.

As in the nest, I saw nobody who was afraid, or intimidated or angered by my return—at least not visibly. Avians were better at lying with tone and expression than the serpiente were, but even so, nothing here felt faked.

Betia stayed by my side the whole time, appearing interested in all the goings-on of the market and never wandering off out of boredom as I had the same conversation again and again with my subjects. Just as she had accepted the closeness of the nest, she seemed comfortable among avians.

I thought of her as a forest spirit, a woman from a world completely different from mine, who could flutter among dancers or merchants as if her feet never needed to touch the ground. No matter where we were, she radiated calmness and acceptance.

The wolves had a harder life, yes, but I realized suddenly that they also had a simpler one. They were a people of the seasons, who followed the migratory herds, traded with every culture they encountered and lived at the whims of Fate. The difference between the southern and northern hills of Wyvern's Court, a dissonance that had been the focal strain of my life, was to her as easy to accept as the changing seasons.

I wished that the people of Wyvern's Court could accept each other so easily.

The wolf I liked least stepped through the crowd. I saw him just in time to reach back for Betia's hand.

Velyo's blue eyes widened a little when he saw Betia, and then more when he saw our hands clasped together. Her knuckles were white from gripping my hand so hard, and I could feel her pulse racing where we touched, but she stayed by my side.

"Oliza. *And* Betia," Velyo greeted us, his tone amused. "Well, this explains a lot."

"What do you want?" I asked, trying to keep my voice calm so that we would not attract more attention than we already were. The two avian guards drifted a little closer, keeping an eye on the stranger close to their princess, but they responded to my apparent calm and did not make their presence obvious to Velyo.

"I heard an interesting rumor," Velyo replied, "about you and one of my wolves."

"I would love to discuss rumors with you," I said as I

moved past him, keeping my body between him and Betia, "but I have other obligations."

"You might want to be careful of the company you keep," Velyo warned. I paused, glancing back, even though I knew better. "You're the princess of this land, soon to be queen. You have a reputation to maintain."

"My reputation is neither in trouble nor your concern. Now, if you'll excuse us—" I felt Betia's grip on my hand loosen as she tried to pull away. "Betia, it's all right. He can't hurt you."

Velyo chuckled. "Maybe it would be best, Betia, for you to come back with me, before you cause trouble for your . . . friend."

"She's no trouble," I said, nearly growling. Nearby avians were starting to look concerned, and I struggled to keep my composure.

Before Velyo could make any more snide comments, Nicias dropped to my side and returned to human form. "Oliza, Valene's lesson should be over in a few minutes. You wanted me to come find you."

"Thank you, Nicias."

Perfect timing. Finally I would be able to do something productive. I wanted to put an end to the destructive rumors I had heard that morning. My mother was a wise woman, and I trusted her judgment; I doubted she would have been fooled by a false confession. Also, as much as I disliked Prentice, I knew that he had enough honor never to have let other avians sacrifice themselves to protect him.

"I'll watch out for Betia while you're busy," Velyo said.

I couldn't bring Betia to the meeting; I needed to be the heir to the Tuuli Thea, not just a woman with a friend.

However, I wasn't about to leave Betia with the alpha who had abused her.

"Thank you, but that *won't* be necessary."

"Wyvern," Velyo said, his voice dropping somewhat, "you are aware that you have no authority over my wolves?"

I stepped closer to Velyo, so that my words would be heard only by him. "She. Isn't. Yours. Anymore. Do you hear me?"

"And she's *yours*?" he hissed. "I am trying to look out for you, Wyvern. Even Betia knows she's going to bring you nothing but trouble."

"She *saved my life*," I said. "And she—" She had never done anything to hurt me, and I believed with all my heart that she never would.

I couldn't begin to put into words all that Betia had done for me. How could I explain how it felt to have a friend who didn't care that I was Princess Oliza Shardae Cobriana? How could I describe the way she had given me courage and helped me find the faith and hope I had lost after Urban had been attacked? There was no way to explain how much it meant to me that she had walked into my world and never cringed from it, that she had drawn me up to dance, challenged me, *accepted* me.

"Your face is as easy to read as hers." Velyo sighed. His voice was almost pitying when he said, "You aren't one of my subjects. I don't care what your *preferences* are. But I know what it is to be a leader. You are the monarch of this land; you are your parents' only child. You need a king, Wyvern."

"What does that—"

He put a finger against my lips. "You are not just a woman, and your heart is *not* free to be given away. You need a king, or your parents' bloodline will die. Stop fooling your-self, and *send her away*."

"Oliza?" Nicias touched my arm. "We need to go."

I nodded woodenly.

*Stop fooling yourself.*

To Betia, Nicias suggested, "If you don't want to be alone in the market, you can wait with Hai and me in the library."

She nodded, her eyes on me. Her resigned expression stayed in my mind as I hurried to my meeting.

# CHAPTER 20

I had to put the look in Betia's eyes, and my reaction to Velyo's words, from my mind. I couldn't afford to think about it right then.

My body tight and my face stony, I stepped into the conference room where Urban's attackers were supposed to be. I was going to need every bit of reserve I had to deal with these three calmly.

I had thought that I was prepared, but what I found in the conference room was almost as horrific as the attack itself. One of the "men" waiting for me couldn't have been more than sixteen years old. The oldest—who, I assumed from the similarity of their features, was the boy's brother—was probably near my age, and the third boy a year younger.

I had expected older men, perhaps soldiers—people with memories of war and loved ones lost. These three couldn't ever have seen a battle. Two of them were too young even to have lost a parent or sibling in the war.

*These* were our vicious assailants?

A few days before, when Nicias had told me what my

mother had sentenced these boys to, I had felt it was too mild. Now, having seen them . . .

I thought about the child who had reached toward Urban at Festival, and how her mother had pulled her away. Who was really to blame here?

I looked at the youngest boy. He was pale, and though his expression was controlled, his fingers were trembling. "What is your name?"

"Shane, milady," he said, in a voice so small I could barely hear it. "Shane Tenahe."

"Brin Tenahe," the eldest said when I looked at him. Unlike his brother, he stood and spoke confidently, as if utterly certain he had done no wrong.

"Luke Redine." The third boy was soft-spoken but shared his friend's poise.

"I heard a rumor, on my way here, that you each confessed out of the nobleness of your innocent hearts. Looking at you, I almost wish it was true—but I don't think it is."

"I did come forward because I heard that Lady Sive's alistair had been questioned," Brin said. *I.* Had he confessed for himself, or for all three of them? "I would never allow my actions to harm the royal house."

"We would never," Luke said.

"Would never . . ." I trailed off, thinking of everything that had occurred since Urban had been attacked—all the violence, and guards in the marketplace. "I imagine none of you were alive during the war."

"We've all heard about it," Luke said.

"Have you?" I challenged. "The stories of forest floors so soaked with blood that the trees began to die? The stories of black smoke from the pyres, and the stench of burning bodies so constant that the living stopped even noticing it? The stories of *children* killed, of . . ." So many horrors. "We *have* all heard the stories, but *I* have never been tempted to relive them. You were the first ones in twenty years to pick up a weapon and nearly kill someone who wasn't even your enemy anymore."

I had almost dismissed the younger brother as a child, almost as much a victim as Urban, but he was the one who stepped forward to defend their actions.

"The war never ended," Shane said. His voice wavered a little, but not just from nerves. "Some people say it did, but it didn't. The only thing different now is that people turn a blind eye. We used to live in Wyvern's Court, but we had to move back to the Hawk's Keep because our sister grew old enough to draw serpiente attention and it did not feel safe for us to stay."

"Shane—"

He shook his head when both of the older boys tried to interrupt him. "My pair bond still lives here," he continued. I forced myself to reevaluate my first impression. He was young, but avian boys were raised with an intense emphasis on responsibility and the protection of their families and pair bonds. "I understand that the serpiente have different customs, but why does that give them the right to abuse her? Why does the fact that it is 'their way' mean I cannot take my lady for a moonlight walk without our being propositioned by strangers? Do you know what that is like? I am her alistair, and I am told that I must tolerate her constant *fear*.

"She is fourteen, and she cannot walk through the market-place alone after dusk unmolested. I fear what would happen to her if she dared step onto the southern hills. There is one small area of this court that is unpolluted by serpiente—the northern hills—and I will be *grounded* before I allow a dancer to skulk about in the shadows there.

"Now, if I have spoken too frankly, if I have offended my lady Shardae—my lady *Cobriana Shardae, Arami*—then I will accept the consequences. I am tired of being silent, and *accepting*."

Was this the world we had worked so hard to make? This fury had not been bred by war; it had been created in the cradle of Wyvern's Court.

I looked at the older boys.

"I have no pair bond," Luke said, "but I too have family, and friends, and have heard similar complaints."

"Are you telling me that there have been physical assaults by serpiente in Wyvern's Court, and the royal family has not responded?"

"There does not need to be physical violence for people to be harmed," Brin said. "In accordance with our Tuuli Thea's wise sentence, we have been coming here for almost a month now, and we have not ignored everything we have been told. I am aware that most serpiente probably consider their actions casual flirting, that they may have no idea that their 'friendly' jests can ruin reputations, relationships and lives. They don't understand that the pretty girl they just stole a kiss from, such as my brother's pair bond, has possibly never *been* kissed, has never had someone grab her that way and isn't blushing because she is coy but because she is terrified. They're like . . . real birds of prey, snatching mice. Maybe they aren't malicious, maybe they don't mean any harm, but that doesn't help the mice any."

I resisted the impulse to rub my temples. At least I knew they had not confessed falsely.

I considered and threw out a dozen possible responses.

Finally I sighed. "I understand your grievances. I know that Wyvern's Court is still a work in progress. But violence is not the answer."

"We committed a crime," Brin said. "I know that. Violence might not be an answer, but at least it made people recognize that there was a problem."

I took deep a breath and let it out slowly.

"I have another meeting to attend," I said softly. "Gentlemen . . ." Could they be used to help find . . . Their meetings with Valene had to help, somehow . . . or . . . or nothing. I had no ideas. "I'll speak to you again another day."

# CHAPTER 21

I drifted from the conference room to the library with my head aching and a heavy feeling in the pit of my stomach. I paused in the doorway to watch Hai, Nicias and Betia for a moment. Nicias looked amused, and Betia was smiling brightly. Hai was wearing her customary detached expression.

Hai noticed me first; she looked up and said, "We were discussing looking into the future."

"You were?"

"And the ethics of looking into someone else's past, or future." She shrugged. "Nicias moralizes like a serpent. Betia listens well, though she doesn't talk much. Or at all."

I wondered what Betia might have said on the subject, or whether there was more wisdom in remaining silent while the two falcons debated.

Betia stood and hugged me in greeting; I leaned against her, desperate for some kind of support. Suddenly a pang went through me. *Stop fooling yourself.*

*I've never seen you act that way around a man, Oliza,* Urban had said.

The truth was that I had never ever been tempted, just as I had never felt torn about performing the *rrasatoth* dances because there had never been anyone I wanted to perform *for*. Until that day in Obsidian.

I held on to Betia a moment too long, knowing I wouldn't always be able to.

I forced myself to focus on the reason we were there. I had to.

"Hai, I'm sorry for what I said yesterday," I began. "I have never thought less of you just because you can't fly, and I—"

"It would be hard for you to think less of me, cousin, since you think very little of me in the first place," she said off-handedly, as if she found the whole subject silly. "I'm not a falcon to you. I don't deserve that respect in your mind. And I'm not a cobra, either, not kin to you, not in your heart."

She was right. I *didn't* know how to think of her. I found it hard to think of her as family. I acknowledged our shared blood mostly out of a sense of responsibility to her, not out of any genuine affection. The way she drifted into and out of a room, often responding to friendly greetings or questions with an expression that conveyed something close to contempt, had alienated me from the first time we had met.

"I didn't realize you felt that way." Having recognized my mistakes, I wanted to fix them. "I don't know you well, Hai, but—"

"I spoke a *fact* to you, Wyvern," she interrupted, once again snuffing out what might have been some kind of connection before it could be formed. "It was not a plea for compassion. Were I given the choice, I would be in the white city, not here, and I would call Cjarsa my queen, not you. But I do not have a choice. You have come to ask me if I really can fix your wings, or if my offer was just the rambling of a slightly delusional mind. There is no need for this false courtesy before you ask me favors."

"Given how you seem to feel about me, why are you offering to help?"

She lifted her cobra eyes skyward. "My loyalty toward the Empress who raised me implies no hatred for you. I do not care what images of me you hold in your head. I will give you back your wings, if I can, because *I* of all people know what it is like to have the sky, your future, your place in life all torn from you by the shifting tides of Anhamirak's whims. Now, Wyvern, let us see if I can find your golden feathers."

I looked at Nicias, who shrugged, as if to say, *Your decision.* I stepped closer to Hai, and she moved into the starting position of many serpiente dances.

I raised my hands and crossed my forearms, mirroring Hai, the backs of our hands just touching. Nicias stood behind Hai, as if prepared either to catch her or to push her out of the way.

"You really think you can do this?" I asked Hai.

"That, or we could burn down the library."

"Excuse me?"

She gave me an innocent look. "Don't worry. You don't harm Wyvern's Court; your magic isn't that strong."

"Hai, you aren't making any sense."

She leaned back against Nicias, closing her eyes. "You have asked me for my help, and yet still you doubt? Every moment of every day, I touch a thousand different *a'she,* a thousand possible futures. I know that your magic is not strong enough to really burn."

"If you know these things, can you tell me who hired the mercenaries?"

She looked up at me, her eyes like pools of blood. "Now

she asks. But no, I cannot see that. The only way I think I can find your wings is by using your control, that overriding control that will forever keep your magic a whisper instead of the whirlwind it could be. Precious control, which I do not have on my own. Relax, Wyvern. This will hurt."

I was vaguely aware of Betia's warmth behind me when Hai's power first reached me, but then that faint contact, as well as any awareness of the library we were in, burned away.

*If this is what her power feels like, no wonder she is mad.*

I would have screamed if I could have found my voice, but it was gone, seared away from me. And then I felt Hai, and the power that was at the heart of this agony.

*You burn,* she whispered in my mind, and in those words I felt longing and envy and fear, all rolled together.

*Frozen.* When I reached for Hai, her power was like ice. It wrapped around me, seeping deep into my body, contorting muscle and bone.

The magic I had inherited from my parents accepted the falcon's magic like an old companion, and they fit together until I could feel my hawk form again. It had been broken and buried in pain, but now I knew I would be able to grow my wings.

If this could work for one of us . . . could it work for the other? I was not the only one there whose wings had been lost, the only one longing for the sky.

*Hai—*

*No.*

I had already reached for her. She recoiled, but it was too late.

My magic had welcomed hers, but hers—

Fractured—

Another power reached forward, something gentler, frightened but soothing: Nicias—

Someone screamed, maybe me. The sound echoed in my head until it became white noise and then hollow silence, stillness.

Like a feather skimming the surface of a sudden draft, I floated into another world.

# CHAPTER 22

The world seemed to pause. The air felt heavy and expectant; when I turned, I was hardly surprised to find myself no longer in the library but in the woods. There was a stranger before me. Her eyes widened, and her hand flew to a dagger at her waist—

Suddenly I knew that this had happened before, in some memory I could not quite reach. The instant I became aware of that, I realized that I was not part of this scene. What was happening now was an echo of the past—specifically, the moments I had lost after Hai's magic had interacted with mine for the first time.

Hai's words echoed in my mind: *A sakkri isn't neat like a letter. I was never trained; I can't control it. At least I remember mine. Most without training cannot.*

Sakkri?

*Magic. Vision.* Sakkri'a'she. *You are about to do something that changes everything.*

My past self held up her hands in a gesture of harmlessness, and the stranger paused, her blade lowering slightly. "You . . ." She looked puzzled, and lost. "This . . . who . . ."

I watched as Oliza-of-the-past spoke softly, facing the confused woman. "You're in the woods near Wyvern's Court," she said. "I am Oliza Shardae Cobriana. Are you a dancer?"

The woman she was facing raised a hand to touch something at her throat: an *Ahnleh*, like the one I wore. *Exactly* like the one I wore. Now I recognized the knife as well; it matched the one my mother had given to me.

"Not a dancer," the not-such-a-stranger sighed.

I understood now, as I had understood then. "The *sakkri*," I gasped, just as my past self had. Once again I was trapped inside the memory. My *sakkri'a'she*, meant to distract my mind and calm me, instead had summoned a vision of my future self.

"*Sakkri'a'she*," whispered the vision.

She wore the *Ahnleh* on a soft leather string. She also wore deerskin boots that went to her thighs, gauntlets of hard leather, and a vest that I now realized was armored.

Her face . . . was mine, but not the one I saw in the mirror every day. The golden eyes were hard, and her expression was painfully controlled. A ragged scar twisted from her left cheekbone, down her jaw, to the edge of her throat—a few more inches, and the wound probably would have killed her.

This was a version of me who had seen war, I had no doubt. The sorrow with which she looked upon Wyvern's Court told me more about her life than I wanted to know.

"They aren't ready," the vision said softly. "There is no answer." She swallowed hard and then explained, "I stayed. I stayed, and when pressured I took a mate. Urban." She smiled a little, but her expression was weak. "He was sweet, gentle, you know. And he was dead within a fortnight, killed at my feet in the marketplace with poison so swift no one saw the source. The riots lasted three days."

She held out her hand, and tentatively my past and future selves touched fingertips.

Vertigo, as time and Fate swirled around us, future and past and present scattering and mixing together.

Suddenly I was on the green marble of the plaza at Wyvern's Court. Sunrise was painting the hills, but I walked through a silent court. Where were the merchants, preparing to sell their wares? Where were the dancers, giving thanks in the mist? Where were the children, laughing, running?

Someone grabbed me, and I went peacefully. This was a dream. Nothing could be hurt here but my heart and faith.

"What do you want, feathered stranger?"

My captor turned me, and I blinked as I saw the leader of the Obsidian guild.

"Dancer, you aren't welcome here," he said bluntly.

Instinctively, I lifted my hand to the *Ahnleh* at my throat, and he smacked it away. "That's the only thing that keeps me from killing you on sight, Oliza Shardae Cobriana." He spat the last two names. "I don't know how you reached our land, but I suggest that you take your wyvern form and fly swiftly and high out of here. Go home to your palace, your forts and—"

Choking back a cry, I violently twisted the world about me, landing on my knees in the same spot but in another reality.

Here, Wyvern's Court was crowded, despite it probably being the middle of the night. There was a festival air that reminded me of Namir-da, and I sighed in relief, trying to shake off the vision of Obsidian.

I should have stayed to ask him what had happened, but I had panicked. I would not do it again.

Leaving the market, I walked up to the dancers' guild, ever the home of gossips. Searching revealed nothing; Wyvern's Nest was gone in this future. Scanning the market from this distance, I realized that there was not a single dais.

I lifted my eyes and saw crows and ravens circling above me, their pattern precise. Guards.

I returned to the market, letting my dream self twist so that I ceased to be Oliza Shardae Cobriana and was instead perceived as a friendly stranger.

"What happened here?" I asked the first passerby I could find. The woman looked at me as if I had lost my mind, and I clarified my question. "I've been away a long time, but when I was here last, there were dancers."

"Oh, well," the woman said, "the dancers all left years ago."

*Left* implied that they had gone peacefully. "Why?"

"There was a lot of trouble for them," the woman explained. "This wasn't really their place, anyway."

"Wyvern's Court was—"

"Hush, girl, no one uses that name anymore." The avian shook her head. "No, the dancers knew they weren't wanted even before Oliza decided—" She cleared her throat. "Before Oliza decided to do the right thing."

"Which was?" I asked.

"Where have you been, child? Why, she finally picked an alistair. The dancers just got up and left."

Someone behind me spoke up. "Don't let her fool you," the young man said. "The dancers didn't leave. I was part of the crew that took the bodies out of the nest." He swallowed hard. "Someone got it into their heads that Oliza preferred avians, and that they could get away with it. And they did. They say Oliza killed herself, though I don't believe it. I'm more likely to say Prentice killed her."

"Prentice. Sive's alistair?"

"Don't go spreading filthy rumors like that," the woman said.

"Someone killed her," a third person said. "I myself wouldn't accuse the Tuuli Thea's alistair, but someone did it. The wyvern wasn't the sort to take her own life."

I was relieved to hear it. My position in this reality shifted, and I was not surprised to see Sive, sitting in the Rookery's conference hall, a queen upon her throne. Where was the young girl I had known? This woman was beautiful in a cold sort of way, her skin as pale and flawless as alabaster, and her golden eyes fierce.

"Well?" she demanded of the three avians who stood before her, Prentice included.

"Milady, the reports were true," her alistair informed her.

Sive looked away for a moment. "I knew I shouldn't have let her go into those lands, but she had so much faith. And she loved him so much. . . ." She shook her head. "Why didn't I stop her? What kind of promise is *love*, to keep a hawk safe?" she cried out, in a shocking loss of control for a hawk.

"Milady—"

"I'm sorry," Sive said softly. "It has been a very long day. I had prayed that the rumors weren't true. Danica was almost a second mother to me."

*My mother.*

They were talking about my mother.

What had happened?

"How is my own mother today?" Sive asked. I could see

that she was bracing herself for the answer.

"Nacola is not well, milady," Prentice replied. "The poison—"

Again I pulled myself away, thinking, *Find me a time when there is peace. Please, any god or goddess that exists. Find me a time when I find love, when I take a mate and it does not lead to war.*


Wyvern's Court was gone. No wreckage remained. Instead, the buildings that stood there glittered with what could only be falcon magic.

I shivered.

A small child ran past me, her long chestnut hair trailing behind her. She laughed and turned; her eyes were as golden as my own.

I saw one of the men from the Obsidian guild—the Burmese python I had danced with once—following close at her heels. He picked her up, spun her around and then paused when he saw me.

"Is she yours?" I asked.

"Yes," he answered, warily. "Can I help you?"

"Where is her mother?"

"Ooo." The girl struggled to get down. "I want to chase the butterflies."

He sighed. "Keyi, there are no butterflies."

"But . . ." She started to cry; great big tears trickled down her face. "I want to chase the butterflies."

My eyes widened, and he looked at me with a guarded expression. "Not many people come here," he said. "Did Hai send you?"

"Hai?" I asked, blankly.

He frowned. "You probably shouldn't be here."

"Daddy, let me down!" The girl managed to get free, and she continued running. He hurried to catch up with her and scooped her up in his arms.

"She's a handful, I take it?"

He shook his head. "You really aren't from here, are you?"

"No," I answered.

This time he seemed to look closely at me; he frowned and said, "You seem familiar, but I can't place you." He tensed, holding the girl closer. "You aren't from Ahnmik?"

"The falcons come here often?"

"Look around you," he answered.

"I'm sorry; I have not been here in a very long time. The last time I stood in this spot, Oliza was the heir to the throne."

"No, *I'm* sorry," he answered. "If you are looking for Oliza—" He turned away, his breath hitching.

"Daddy, do you see the rainbow?"

"There is no rainbow, honey."

"Daddy—"

"*There is no rainbow,*" he said, too sharply. Then he fell to his knees, cradling the girl.

Tears stung my eyes. What kind of future was *this*? This was my child; I could feel it. And surely this was the mate I had chosen. But where was everyone else? Where was Wyvern's Court?

What was wrong with the girl?

"Mommy!" the girl shouted, pulling away from her father. She ran to me.

"Not Mommy," her father answered. Looking at me, he said, "I'm sorry, you never told us your name."

"Mommy!" the girl called again. "Mommy, Mommy!"

She was crying now, and I could not help going to my knees and putting my arms around her.

"Please don't encourage her," the man said. "Keyi has a poor grasp on reality. These walls keep her physically safe from her magic, but her mind has never been as safe. Please, Keyi, come here."

"Where is everyone else?" I asked over the girl's head. "The rest of Wyvern's Court?"

He shook his head. "There is no rest of Wyvern's Court. I'm sorry to have to be the one to tell you. We were warned that Keyi would be born with magic. We were warned that it wouldn't be stable. We tried . . . we tried, and Nicias and Darien tried, *everything*, but her magic was too powerful. We had no way to control her and no way to teach her. I know that Oliza wouldn't begrudge her daughter for what she did as an infant, but I think it's probably best that Keyi's mind will never grow beyond what it is."

My breath was coming in ragged gasps. *This* was the world with peace? Was anyone alive?

"What of Sive? Salem?"

He shook his head. "The falcons came."

"Why . . ." My throat closed around sobs when I tried to speak.

"Why am I alive?" he asked. "Because someone needed to care for her, because the falcons wouldn't kill a child. Just lock her in this magical prison, where she chases butterflies and sees phantoms of all the people who once lived on this ground. Hai and Nicias help. So do the rest of Obsidian, as many as Araceli allowed to live. The other serpiente and avian children were taken back to the palace and the Hawk's Keep. I suppose the falcons are raising them."

"Dear sky," I prayed, "is this my future?"

His eyes widened. "Who are you?"

"I'm . . . the past," I answered. For myself more than him, I said, "And I have no daughter. This prison doesn't exist. And Wyvern's Court *does*."

"*Sakkri*," he whispered. "Oliza?"

I nodded. He stepped toward me, hand outstretched, and then jerked away. "If none of this exists, then I pray you won't let it. *Ever*. Do we even know each other, in your world?"

"We met," I answered. "I was running from mercenaries. We danced together. That's all."

"I remember that day," he sighed. "Better if that is all."

I looked at the daughter I would never have, and held back tears. "When I leave, all this will vanish. She will vanish. And she will never exist."

"And only you will know she could have," he answered.

*Gods, why? Why do this to me?* If *this* was what the falcons feared, the reason Nicias believed that they would kill my child if she was born with magic, then this was a possibility with any man I might choose as my mate.

"Did she kill me?"

He nodded.

I pulled away from the vision, letting it dissolve, and ended up on my hands and knees, choking on tears.

# CHAPTER 23

When the visions faded, Betia's arms were around me and I wept. The wings of my Demi form cascaded down my back; I had wanted them so much, but now they were less important.

I wanted both to remember and to forget everything I had just seen; I wanted never to have known. I understood, then, more than I had ever wanted to. I remembered pulling from the trance after Urban was hurt and struggling to act even as the visions continued to barrage me, slipping me from the present to the past so that I spoke and acted in a haze that I later recalled only in my nightmares.

I struggled now to keep my resolve as the memories frayed like dreams.

"Are you all right, Oliza?" Nicias asked, kneeling next to us.

"Keyi . . ." I tried to hold her face in my mind.

"Hope?" Hai asked, from where she was leaning against the wall. Her skin was flushed, and I could see the sheen of sweat on her brow.

*Hope.* That was what the name meant in the old language.

But Keyi didn't exist.

"Please, leave me alone for a moment?" I asked of Hai and Nicias. "Thank you for helping. Thank you. But I need time to think."

Nicias nodded and said, "I will be right outside if you need me." With one last concerned look back at me, he escorted Hai out. I was certain that he had not seen the devastating visions I had seen; I did not know if Hai had.

Betia met my gaze questioningly, and I held her more tightly. I did not want to be alone, not truly. And I couldn't send her away, not when she had been gone in every world I had come across.

"Where were you?" I whispered. "Did I chase you away when I became queen, Betia? I must have . . . So much death. Where were you?" I sobbed, looking away. "I had a daughter. And she was mad. And she—"

I could not say it.

Betia lifted my face and brushed the tears from my cheek. Her voice was hoarse from the long months of disuse as she asked, "Were you in love?"

The question, the first sentence she had spoken, made a lump lodge in my throat.

Betia kissed my forehead. "I won't leave you unless you ask me to. I—" Her lips touched mine, chastely. "The future will come. I will be there, if you want me."

She kissed me again, so sweetly that I could not help crying harder. Her lips were warm, her body soft against mine.

"You don't have to speak. Words fade," she whispered. "I know that better than anyone. Words are forgotten; they are regretted. Unnecessary. I know."

So in silence, we held each other until my trembling subsided. And when she kissed me once more, I gave in to the temptation, and I kissed her back. With her presence and her touch, she gave me the hope and the warmth that I needed so much.

*I don't care what your* preferences *are. But I know what it is to be a leader. You are the monarch of this land; you are your parents' only child. You need a king, Wyvern.*

I pulled away from Betia as reality began crashing down around me—as I suddenly remembered why she had not been in the future.

*Find me a time when I find love, when I take a mate and it does not lead to war.*

I found love. And I took a mate.

They just weren't the same person.

I looked at Betia and saw the hurt in her eyes. "Betia, I can't. . . . We can't be together. Not while I'm queen. Not while—"

A vision of Keyi came to mind, and again the words echoed in my mind:

*And a royal pair bond has to produce heirs.*

"Oliza?" Nicias had entered the room and was standing beside me.

"Nicias, *please*—"

"Oliza, I'm sorry, but a group of our guards just brought the mercenaries in."

The lions. I needed to talk to them. Needed . . .

*I want to chase the butterflies.*

Again, I struggled to keep the dream in focus. But I also wanted more than anything to forget it, to curl in Betia's arms and pretend that the future was easy.

"I need to talk to the mercenaries," I said.

Betia nodded, her expression resigned. I couldn't help it; I kissed her again, tasting her lips and drawing strength from her embrace for what I needed to do. I didn't care what Nicias thought.

"The lions hunted sometimes with us," Betia said. "They only do their jobs. Don't hurt them?"

I smiled, moved by her protectiveness. The lions had no formal kingdom and had always been at the mercy of the laws of the lands that they visited. The punishment for treason was severe in both courts, but in this case I could promise. "I won't hurt them." Needing her support, I asked, "Would you come with me to speak to them?"

Betia hesitated, but then she gripped my hand and helped me stand.

# CHAPTER 24

Tavisan and nine of his people were waiting in the Rookery courtyard, surrounded by my Wyverns and additional members of the serpiente and avian guards. It was the place where I had first met him; it was also the place where I had woken up after the unintended sakkri.

"Let me through," I told my guards as they tried to keep me from getting too close to the lions' leader. Too many people were there. "Nicias, I want to speak to Tavisan alone."

"Oliza—"

*"Now."*

His eyes widened at the command, but nevertheless, he escorted Tavisan from the mass of soldiers to the far edge of the Rookery, where, if we kept our voices down, we would not be overheard. Betia hesitated and then, at my gesture, followed us.

"Betia Frektane, an honor as always. Oliza Shardae Cobriana, I hope you take no offense if I say I had not hoped to see you again." His voice was soft, and his body seemed tired.

Nicias had given us some room, but he didn't move so far back that he could not intercede if Tavisan tried anything.

I didn't have time to argue with him. Voices were echoing in my head, and I grasped at them, needing to remember. . . .

*The dancers didn't leave. I was part of the crew that took the bodies out of the nest. . . .*

Tavisan took a deep breath. "I know what you are about to ask, milady, but I cannot tell you the name of my employer. I was instructed not to tell anyone, my own people included, unless my refusal to speak put me in danger."

"You don't think you're in danger here?" Nicias demanded. "You abducted our queen. For a reason I do not comprehend, she is willing to show you lenience. I think it would be in your best interest to answer her."

*Tavisan, I need your help.*

*Milady, what is wrong?*

I finally understood the argument that had echoed in my mind frequently since Hai's magic had first triggered mine and I had spun the *sakkri'a'she.*

*Oliza, this is madness. There has to be another way.*

Almost two months before, I had woken from these visions the same way I had this time, desperate to protect the future from the horrors I had seen. I had gone to the only person I knew who might be able to help me do what Hai had warned me I would: *change everything.*

There was no time to be subtle. "I hired you."

*"What?"* Nicias asked in shock, but I ignored him. No time.

"I know it's the truth. I remember now." More important, I remembered *why.* I couldn't let the horrors I had seen become reality, and there was one thing they had all had in common.

The one thing I had begged Tavisan to help me remove.

Tavisan hesitated but then nodded. "You told me that you needed to leave Wyvern's Court, but that you feared you would soon lose the knowledge of why. You were the one who ordered me to strip your winged forms, so that you would not be able to return easily." His gaze dropped. "We did not anticipate that the Frektane, whom we have worked with before, would be a problem."

*I want to chase the butterflies. . . .*

"Nicias . . . release them, all of them. I need to go."

*I want to chase the butterflies.*

I grasped at the memory but couldn't quite find it. Why did those words bring an ache to my chest?

*I want to chase the butterflies.*

I kissed Betia's cheek and whispered, "I will meet you . . . in the nest. There is something I must do now. I love you."


I needed speed; I needed my wings. I shifted into my wyvern form, nearly shrieking with the relief of finally unfurling my wings again. I would have loved to take to the skies and soar, but in that moment, I had other things to do. I whipped out the doorway, past Nicias, who I knew would follow me as soon as he had changed into his own form for flight.


Sive let out a little gasp as I landed inches in front of her, finding my human form again; I had stopped and shifted so swiftly that she had to grab my arm to steady me. She was alone, luckily. I did not want Prentice as an audience just yet.

I swallowed thickly. Could I really do this?

I asked, "Could you do it, Sive? I've heard how highly your people speak of you, and I know that you would treat them well; you think swiftly and are as polished as any hawk ever was. Could you rule if you had to?"

She froze. "Oliza, are you all right?"

"Never mind me," I answered. I couldn't think about myself right then.

I couldn't think about how I had always expected to one day be their queen. All my life I had considered Wyvern's Court mine.

Mine to protect, before anything else.

"Both of our mothers are still alive; you would not need to take a throne immediately or even soon. I assume you would inherit it when an avian queen traditionally does, when you have your own child, years from now.

"Would you do it?"

She nodded slowly. "If I had to, Oliza. But you are the wyvern of Wyvern's Court. I could never replace you."

"I'm not asking you to replace me."


I found Salem in the market. This time I landed a little ways back. The cobra was engaged in lively banter with a pair of merchants, both of whom were looking rueful but honored by his presence.

He stepped back from them with a self-satisfied nod and quickly noticed me.

. "Good morning, cousin." The lighthearted sparkle in his eyes almost made me forget my purpose, almost made me remember simpler times.

The burden I was about to put on him . . .

"What would you have done if I had never returned to Wyvern's Court?"

He frowned. "You don't think I believed that nonsense about your abdicating, do you?"

"No, I don't," I said. "I'm just asking what if. If I was gone, what would you do?"

Slowly, now visibly worried, he answered, "I'm no wyvern."

"I'm not asking you to be," I said. "Could you be Arami for the serpiente? Lead this generation, in peace, so that maybe in the future . . ." My voice was wavering.

Salem began to pace, his garnet eyes flashing. "Oliza, you will be a good queen. *No one* cares more about Wyvern's Court than you do, and—"

"If I rule them, it will *destroy* them," I said. "I would be their queen if they would allow me, if Fate would allow me, but my first duty as their leader is to keep them safe. Could you do it?"

He sighed heavily, running his hands through his hair. "They like me, Oliza, if that's what you're asking. If anything ever happened to you, they would accept me as Arami, as Diente. But, Oliza—"


I didn't wait for him to protest any more. I returned once again to Wyvern's Nest. I kissed the doorway, knowing that I would probably rarely see it in the future. I could not be in Wyvern's Court without usurping power from Sive and Salem. I wouldn't be able to stand it.

There could be no indecision.

I was trembling as I walked into the nest, because I knew that I could not change my decision, no matter what answer

I received there. I could not keep Wyvern's Court or my place as its princess; I could not keep any of the things I had assumed would always be mine. I could only pray that there was something—*someone*—I loved that Fate would not rip from me.

Betia greeted me hesitantly. I caught her hands and pulled her to me. I sensed her concern and support for me, and they calmed my nerves as I kissed her. I remembered those simple words she had spoken, when she had promised never to leave unless I asked her to.

And then I went down on one knee.

"I don't know what kind of life we might have together," I said, never looking away from her warm brown eyes. "But I know I would protect you with the last scrap of my soul. I know I want to *be* there for you, to hold you, to dance for you, to hunt with you, to be with you no matter where Fate takes us, because it's the sound of your heartbeat that comforts me when I drift off to sleep, and I know I—I cannot offer you royalty. I'm not sure what I *can* offer you—but myself. Hopefully that is enough, because I love you, Betia, and I do implore you to be my mate."

Tears gathered in her eyes, and my stomach twisted and my heart pounded in panic. I had to give up Wyvern's Court. The decision was made and set in stone, no matter what happened.

She knelt in front of me and squeezed my hand gently.

"Wolves mate for life," she said softly.

I smiled and said, "So do wyverns."

"I love you," she whispered. "I . . ." She shook her head and said again, "Words fade so easily."

Her lips touched mine, and she held me as if she would never let go—not even when her fingers found the feathers at my nape, or the sparks of red and gold in my hair. She had not pulled away from me in the closeness of the nest or objected to the calmness of the avian market; she knew every side of me, had listened to all my dreams and had never rejected any part of me.

She didn't have to say the words aloud.

Someone behind us whistled, which made us both recall at the same time that the nest was rarely empty. Even though I had paid it no mind when I had entered, there was a crowd watching us.

Betia laughed.

"I'm going to need to talk to them," I said apologetically.

She nodded, not quite giving me up yet; she slid her hands down my arms to twine her fingers with mine again.

"Betia, you're the one who has been with me this entire time. You know what I'm about to do?"

She nodded. "Speak to your people. I will wait for you."

Suddenly panicking again, I gripped her hands. "Am I doing the right thing? It kills me to give them up, but I really think this is the only way. I know what people will say. They'll accuse me of being afraid. Am I just a selfish coward giving up because it's getting hard?"

"Selfish coward?" she repeated with some confusion. "From the time I met you, you have spoken of Wyvern's Court with love, and pride, and a sense of home that I envy. You have spoken of yourself as belonging to them. Wyvern's Court is your world. It is *you*. It . . ." She shook her head. "Words, words. I just know that it can't be selfish or cowardly to give up everything you ever thought you were, in order to protect them."

We kissed again, quickly, and then looked up at the dancers, who had backed off enough to give us some privacy.

Urban took my glance as an invitation to step forward. His limp was a dagger to my heart, but it reinforced my determination.

"I'm sorry" was the first thing he said. Only then did I realize that much of the nest must have seen the pained look on my face in addition to the interlude with Betia. "I know we teased you two a little, but I don't think anyone really thought—" He looked stricken as his gaze fell to Betia, and I realized he was apologizing to *her*. Turning back to me, he said, "I take it this means you've made your decision?" I struggled to come up with an answer as he shook his head and said gently, "I can recognize a goodbye when I see one, Wyvern."

He thought I was saying goodbye to Betia and preparing to declare a mate. That was what the apology was for—Wyvern's Court's taking me from her. If only he knew how much I was really saying goodbye to.

"Would you help gather the serpiente in the market?" I asked him. "I need to make an announcement."

He nodded. "I'll tell the others. And I'll bring Marus."

"Thank you." I separated grudgingly from Betia. "I'll meet you there?"

She nodded, and again I found my wyvern form. I stopped briefly to inform Nicias that I needed to address my people, and I asked him to gather the avians.

Then I sought my parents. A courier, whose eyes were wide as he beheld my rumpled hair and harried expression, hurried to fetch them once I reached the Rookery.

"Oliza?" My mother sounded worried as she and my father came into the room.

My father took one glance at me and then poorly suppressed a smile as he came to the obvious conclusion. He cleared his throat.

"I've made my decision," I told them. "I need to address our people. I'd like to do so from the market, unless you have another idea."

My parents looked at each other.

"Do we get to know the outcome, or shall we also wait?" my father asked, his smile suddenly a little more strained.

I hesitated. I wanted to tell them but was worried that they would try to talk me out of my decision. The images from the *sakkri* had already faded to a point where the strongest thing I remembered was the sense of absolute desperation. I remembered what I had thought of them, remembered that I had seen the devastation caused by every choice I made, but the specifics . . . the faces . . . they were disappearing.

I was happy to lose the details; they had hurt too much. I was also happy that, unlike last time, I was not losing time—perhaps because Nicias had been there to balance the vision and cut it off cleanly at the end.

"I will speak to you along with our people as soon as they have gathered—which, hopefully, they are already doing. If you're willing to wait."

They both looked worried now. I remembered the stories I had heard of the last such "announcement," when my parents had told their respective people of their choices: to get married and unite the avians and the serpiente. Many people had been horrified.

But in the end, the war had stopped.

"We can wait," my mother said, and I knew that it had taken all her avian poise to say that. She grasped my father's hand. "As long as you are certain."

"I am."

# CHAPTER 25

Within the hour, I stood on a dais at the center of the market, near the glittering wyvern statue. I took a deep breath, seeking strength.

My eyes fell to the small group immediately in front of me: my parents; my mother's mother; Salem; Rosalind; Sive; Prentice; Nicias; his parents, Andreios and Kel; and of course, Betia.

Hai was conspicuously absent.

*You are about to do something that changes everything.* Her words had begun all this, and now I wondered if she had known that it would lead to this moment. What had she wanted?

Had she spoken as a cobra, protecting Wyvern's Court, or as a falcon?

What I needed to do remained the same either way.

Behind my family and all around the dais was a seething mass of curious avians and serpiente, who had all hushed the instant I had landed and taken human form.

In the sudden silence, I could feel my heart pounding and hear my blood rushing.

"Twenty-one years." I sighed and then cleared my throat before beginning again. "Twenty-one years ago, in the *sha'Mehay* dancer's nest, the dream that would become Wyvern's Court began." My voice carried this time, ringing through the market. "The dream was inspired by a symbol, and by the word *alistair:* protector. It spoke of a beautiful world, a peaceful world—one in which serpiente and avians lived side by side long ago. More important, it spoke of another world in which they would do so again.

"I look into this crowd today and see vipers and sparrows, taipans and crows, and all these faces prove how far we have come." At that moment I saw Marus at the periphery of the crowd. He was staring longingly at his parents, who were standing farther off. "Simultaneously, they prove how much further we still have to go."

My people were watching me, their faces curious and excited. I knew that what I was about to say would change those expressions.

"I've been a fool."

Those who had been silent and attentive began to shift and grumble as they sensed that this announcement was not about to go the way they had expected.

"We dreamed of a world in which these two kingdoms would become one. But that's all it was—a *dream*, ruled by the logic of dreams.

"I love the southern hills of Wyvern's Court. I love their dance. I love their laughter, their comfort, their expression. I love their passion." I continued with just as much sincerity, "And I love the northern hills. I love the rhythm of the skies. I love the debates, the music. I love the *simplicity*, and the beauty of shy romance.

"I love this entire world.

"I love these *two worlds*.

"And that is what they are.

"Nearly two months ago, a young man, a dear friend of mine, was severely beaten for daring to cross the market from his world to the northern hills. More recently, another friend lost his home, his family, for trying to do the same.

"Every day in the market reveals the segregation and the prejudice that we have almost come to take for granted. We say, 'That's their way, not ours,' and we walk away ignorant. Or worse, we say, 'Well, at least we aren't at war,' when we are *killing* each other with fear and hatred. We ignore the slander because at least it isn't blades. We ignore the pain because, thank the sky, it isn't blood."

I fought the urge to pace on my dais. People in the crowd were averting their gazes as they recalled their own actions. Only Nicias kept his eyes on me.

Marus's parents noticed him in that moment. But when Marus took a step forward, his mother turned her back on him.

"I am of you, of all of you, avian and serpiente. I have for all my life wondered how, beyond my very *existence*, I can prove to you that we can live together. In my parents' time, the mission was to stop the bloodshed, but in mine, my goal has always been to stop the *hatred*.

"And I have never known how."

I paused to gather my thoughts, drawing air into my lungs, which felt constricted. Betia smiled up at me, her eyes holding absolute trust.

"These two worlds are different, so different that I do not know if they can ever be made one. I cannot say that one set of values is superior. I cannot say that a child should be raised one way or another. I cannot destroy one culture to assure that there is no strife.

"I should not. And I *will* not.

"So all I can do is give you to yourselves and let you live side by side, each generation trusting a little more."

I saw confusion in my people. My mother was gripping my father's hand so tightly that her knuckles were white.

"I would be your queen if you would allow me. I would be honored to lead you. But now, I do what I must."

*What do you want from me?* I had demanded of them once. I had prayed to the Fates for guidance, time and again, screaming to them, *How can I give peace when they do not want it?*

"My generation has tasted peace, and I have faith that they will safeguard it. And I have faith that someday, when the past is further behind us and fear and hatred have been supplemented by understanding, the time will come when a wyvern can grace your palace.

"But that hour is not now." It was time to change everything. "We have tried to marry two worlds, but one cannot perform a marriage while both parties hold knives to each other's throats. One cannot sew two pieces of cloth together while both unravel. Let us heal. Let the land know peace."

I stared at the faces around me, and I announced, "As of this moment, I formally renounce my claim to both thrones, avian and serpiente."

I tried to avoid looking at my mother, but I could still see her sway, then lean against my father's tense form.

"I name Irene Cobriana's son, Salem, Arami, next to be Diente of the serpiente."

I held out my hand to the cobra, and he stepped onto the dais, face composed so that his people would not be troubled.

I knew that he would have liked to argue with me, to shout and rail against my decision. He hid his emotions from the rest of his people, comforting them, his first sacrifice of *self* for the throne he had never expected to hold.

It would not be the last. This title I gave him was no gift.

He said softly, for my ears alone, "They need you, Oliza."

I shook my head, but like him, I could not let our people see me breaking inside. "I've given them what I can. It's up to you now." Turning to the crowd, I continued, "And Sive Shardae, my mother's sister, shall rise as Tuuli Thea of the avians."

She nodded as Salem helped her onto the dais. She was as externally composed as we were—as if we had planned this months before, and neither dissented. We needed to be in agreement in front of our people. They both knew that.

"I share blood with both of them," I concluded. "I am living proof that we can live without hatred. So I give you to yourselves and ask that you remember, and you teach your children, and they teach their children. Learn, trust, just . . ."

I would have given them everything: all of me, all I had and all I was. Instead, all I could give them was my faith and desperate hope that they would—

"Just *try*. The future, my people . . . the future is all we have."

I stepped down from the dais, leaving Salem and Sive to address our—*their* people. My mother and father instantly came to my side.

Both looked as if they wanted to speak, but neither did at first.

"It was the only choice," I said.

My mother swallowed hard. "Oliza, I know how hard leadership can be, and how impossible the future seems sometimes, but—"

"*Staying* would have been easier; it's leaving them that will break my heart. But it would have been selfish to keep them. I can't give them what they need. Please, trust me." I drew a breath and added, "And even if you can't . . . Our people are going to be scared. I know that. They need to see that you believe in them. Sive and Salem are going to need your support. So, please, don't fight me. It's done."

"But what are you going to do?" my mother asked. There were tears in her eyes.

"I'm going to leave for a while, so Sive and Salem can show Wyvern's Court that it can survive and prosper without me. I'll be with friends." I thought of the Obsidian guild as I said it. They would take me in. "And I'll be with my mate."

Betia had pushed through the crowd to reach me as my parents and I spoke, and now she took my hand. My mother closed her eyes a moment, speechless.

Finally my father sighed. "Oliza, this isn't necessary. If you aren't ready, then—"

I winced and said, "If you are referring to my leaving, it *is* necessary. I know that you may never understand it, but please, *trust* me. I am the daughter you raised, and I am doing what I must for the sake of our people." He started to argue, but I continued, "And if you are referring to Betia, you should be careful. I know you are upset, and shocked, but I love her. I won't have you treat her like she's some kind of excuse."

My mother broke out of her paralysis. "That isn't what we . . . who we . . . Oliza, are you *certain*?"

"More certain than I have ever been about anything."

She started to speak again but then hugged me instead. She looked at Betia and said to me, "We love you, Oliza. And we trust you. We just— Good luck."

My father nodded and seemed resigned when he said, "Treat her well, wolf."

Betia and I walked through the market toward the edge of town in silence. I was barely aware of Salem, who spoke behind me to a crowd that was growing more and more restless, or of my people as they moved aside to let me pass. Some of them called my name, but I had to shake my head and keep walking. I saw several of my Wyverns—mine no longer, but performing one last duty—lining up to try to hold back the avians and serpents who were trying to follow me.

Suddenly Marus and Urban stood before me, side by side, as if they had planned this final vision of the world of which we had all once dreamed.

Marus started to speak, stopped and then drew a deep breath as if to compose himself. Urban said, "Oliza, I know we aren't perfect, but . . . don't give up on us. We can still—"

I touched his face, silencing him before he made me cry. "I have all the faith in the world in you, both of you, *all* of you. If I was needed, I would never leave. If ever I *am* needed, I won't be far. I'm not abandoning you. Just . . . letting you spread your wings."

Urban smiled wryly. "But I don't have wings."

"I do," Marus offered, voice slightly choked. He gave up on the idea of reserve and hugged me. "We'll make you proud," he whispered. "Take care of yourself."

Then it was Urban's turn. He kissed me on the cheek and smiled at Betia. "Take care of her, Betia. She's precious to us."

There was one last person I needed to speak to. Nicias caught up with us just before the woods' edge.

For a moment, we regarded each other in silence.

"I understand," he said at last, quietly. "I hate it, but I understand."

"You may be the only person in Wyvern's Court who really does."

"People are going to be angry. Hurt."

"I know. I wish it wasn't so, but . . ."

"There's no other way," he finished for me. "I don't know all of what you've seen, but I've seen enough myself to understand. We'll manage; don't worry about us." He added, "And I'll feel better knowing that you and your mate are taking care of each other."

Tucked against Betia's side, I said, "Thank you for that, too. My parents were a little shocked."

"Your parents," Nicias said, "haven't heard the way you've talked about her. They haven't seen the way you look at her. I think I knew before you did."

"She *was* a little slow," Betia said, teasing. I started to defend myself—and then just kissed her instead. She was right.

Betia led once we were in the woods. I knew she would find our destination without difficulty. This was, after all, her realm of expertise.

I was not surprised when Velyo intercepted us. With an arrogant smirk, he said, "I listened to your little speech— quite heartwarming. It's nice to see that you can justify walking away from them to be with your fling."

I went rigid.

This time, Betia came to *my* defense. "He will never understand," she said. "He doesn't know what it means to sacrifice to protect your people."

Velyo's eyes were blue flames as he turned on her, clearly

as furious as if she had struck him. "Do not speak to me about leadership. You turned down my offer when I would have made you queen of the Frektane. Is this what it takes to win your hand? A queen abandoning her throne? I should have had the pack hunt you down, before—"

My fist met his jaw, hard enough to send him stumbling backward.

"Don't you *ever* threaten her," I snarled. "In fact, I think it would be best if you just left us alone."

He regained his balance, his hand going to his face.

"Abdication means I'm free to make my own choices, for myself," I pointed out. "It means my word isn't that of my courts. It's simply mine. Tempt me, and I'll dance this dance with you."

"So you're proposing what—to kill me?" Velyo asked. "You won your place as princess by birth, Wyvern, and you weren't strong enough to hold it. I won my right to rule through blood and my own strength. You have no chance of winning, but you want to try to challenge me for one of my own people?"

Fury rippled through me, and I leaned toward him. With my lips only an inch from his throat, I whispered, "You should know, Velyo, that a cobra's bite while you sleep will kill you before you can wake."

He jumped back from me, and I smiled, betraying a cobra's fangs. My eyes, normally a hawk's gold, had become a sea of blood marked only with slit pupils.

He was caught in my gaze like a baby bird. Like prey.

I added, "And Velyo? Everyone sleeps sometimes."

Betia growled, on the verge of shifting into a more deadly form. Velyo looked back and forth between us, not quite managing to hide his fear.

Finally he stepped back.

"She's yours, Wyvern. Seems you two deserve each other." He shifted shape and loped away in his wolf form, with his fur bristling and his tail down.

I turned to Betia and pulled her into my arms. "Thank you," I whispered.

But Velyo's words still bothered me. How many people thought that I had abandoned all of Wyvern's Court just to follow my heart? It was a beautiful, romantic idea, but leadership left no such luxury. How could Betia respect me, respect *us*, if she thought—

She shook her head. "I would have said no."

"What?"

"If you had wanted me despite what you needed to do," she said, "I would have said no. I am too Frektane" she grimaced a little as she said it—"to love someone who would betray her duty. You are too Shardae Cobriana to love someone who would ask you to. And I love you. So ignore Velyo."

Wise words, very wise words.

We returned to the Obsidian guild, who took us in as friends and dancers without asking questions that I suspected they would quickly learn the answers to anyway. In the abandon of the evening, I performed blade dances and *melos;* after a long, lingering look at my mate, I performed the sensual *harja* for the first time. I danced *sakkri* of thanks and love and passion and freedom.

Betia shared myths and stories from her people and taught us songs she said were often sung on the cold nights. Her voice was a husky alto and blended with mine very well. When pressed, I shared some of the songs and stories of my mother's people, which the Obsidian guild had never heard.

As the dawn neared, I curled against my mate's side, listening to her heartbeat and enjoying her warmth. Sleepily we murmured of the future to each other.

I did not know what the next days would hold, for me or for my world. The next night would be Namir-da, and the serpents would dance as they always had and they always would. Avian parents would whisper to each other about scandal in the knowing way that elders had; meanwhile, their children would sneak out to watch the rituals with wide eyes and fascinated minds.

I had to trust Salem, Sive and my parents to take care of Wyvern's Court. I had to trust Wyvern's Court to let them. I had not left them an easy path, but at least now they had one.

*Toth'savirnak*
*Savirnak'toth*
Sacrifice of love, sacrifice for love.
Fate is gentle and harsh; she gives and she takes.
*A'le-Ahnleh*

# WYVERNHAIL

## PROLOGUE

W ho am I? Lately I have wondered this, as I've struggled to discover my place in the world in which I find myself.

Mongrel, exile, stranger. I have always been tolerated, wherever I've been, but I have never been welcomed except by Ecl, the void darkness. And what does that mean, to be wanted by Nothing?

My father was Anjay Cobriana, a serpiente prince, the heir to the cobra throne. He was loved by his people and his family. Though it has been twenty-five years since Anjay's death at the hands of the hawk prince Xavier Shardae, my father's followers still say his name with reverence. They look to me, as his only child, with respect, even though I never knew him; my father was killed within days of my conception.

My mother was the falcon la'Darien'jaes'oisna'ona'saniet. Darien was young, and she was powerful. She swore her service to the Empress Cjarsa when she was still a child. Years later, she conceived me during Anjay's visit to our falcon land. The trauma of his death triggered in her a vision of events the Empress had long before struggled to hide: the creation of the ancient avian-serpiente war.

Darien stayed quiet for the months before my birth, but once I was no longer dependent on her mothering body, she began her treason, which culminated in an attempt to kill the Empress's heir, the Lady Araceli.

That was the last time my "mother" bothered to care for her child.

I was raised a mongrel in the beautiful white land of Ahnmik; I was a flaw in the center of an otherwise priceless diamond. The Empress herself took a hand in my upbringing. She alone showed me tenderness during my childhood.

My earliest memory is of my Empress holding me after my magic overwhelmed me and filled my mind with images no child should ever see. My memory is of pain and blood—and of my Empress's gentle arms and the sadness in her eyes when I burned my voice away with my screams.

After that day, Cjarsa allowed me to grow the wings of my Demi form, so that I could take to the sky. She taught me to dance, and for a few brief years I was a child. I ran with the dreams of others, laughing with the spirits of the past and the future that always walk the roads of the white city, invisible to most—but never to me. I made friends with those who did not exist, with those who might never exist, and with those who had died millennia before. I remember one woman, who most frequently filled my constant waking dreams. Though born of mixed blood, she had learned to control her power. I wanted so badly to know her—to be her—but like all my ghosts, she never looked at me.

Sometimes, when I danced, I could feel my Empress watching. She was one of the very few people who were fully real to me. When she smiled, I felt Ahnmik's magic shimmer with pleasure as if I had been granted a gift by the divine.

Then came the day when—

Ahnmik' falmay'la. *Ahnmik, help me; grant me your black peace. Do not make me think of that day.*

I can speak for ages about the lives, the hopes and fears, of others; please, keep me from my own nightmares.

I can speak of the Dasi, the ancient coven from which the falcons and the serpiente both come. I can almost feel the hot sand of the Egyptian desert beneath my feet and smell the Nile. I can see their altars. I can see them dance and pray.

I was lost in the darkness of Ecl for so long, and I was content there, until a guard sworn to my father's line—a guard with royal falcon blood I could not ignore—called to me. Duty compelled Nicias to try to pull me from my void, but it is hard to say exactly what compelled me to return.

And now here I am, a mongrel in a land of mongrels and yet still an outsider. All I have from my mother is a broken falcon form I cannot call upon, and all I have from my father is cursed blood and a black onyx signet ring to symbolize the family that I've no desire for.

She'ka'hena.

*We are not.*

O'she'ka'hena-a'she'ka'hena.

*We never were; we never shall be. We return to the void we never left, for* Mehay *is the center of all, and all is the center of nothing.*

em'Ecl'la'Hai

# CHAPTER 1

Fire.

Serpiente who held to the old myths believed that the world began in fire. Out of the numb void came passion and heat, and Will too strong to be denied. Order and chaos— Ahnmik and Anhamirak—began their eternal dance, and from the embers of their battle, the world was born.

So perhaps it was not surprising that the world would end of that same heat.

I was pulled from my musings as the door opened, drawing my attention to the small two-room building in which I had been sitting cross-legged before the hearth, perhaps for several hours. I looked up as a trio of falcons entered the candle shop, their steps uncharacteristically light and their expressions unguarded.

*"Hanlah'ni-aona'pata'rrasatoth-rakuvra'pata'Diente."* Cobras change kings, Spark observed with some amusement, as easily as the white Lady's heir changes lovers.

The four falcons who frequented this shop at the edge of the avian hills of Wyvern's Court were in hiding, criminals who would probably be executed if they ever showed themselves in the white city again. Though Spark, Maya, Opal and Gren disguised themselves as simple avian merchants in the public areas of Wyvern's Court, here they switched back to the falcon language *ha'Dasi*.

I enjoyed hearing the language of my home, even spoken by these exiles. Some of the serpents of Wyvern's Court tried to use it, but *ha'Dasi* always sounded stunted and twisted to me when it came from the tongue of a snake.

Opal emerged from the back room, his eyes heavy lidded from sleep. Without sparing a glance at me, he asked, *"Hehj' hena?"* What happened?

Gren, the owner of the candle shop, answered in the same language. "Oliza Shardae Cobriana," he announced, "has just abdicated the throne of Wyvern's Court. She and some wolf have run off in the woods together, leaving Salem and Sive holding the bag."

The words stole my breath, not because they shocked me but because they left me with a powerful sense of déjà vu. Months before, I had seen a vision of the wyvern princess dethroned. The image had been unclear, and all I had been able to do was go to Oliza and warn her: "You are about to do something that changes everything." I had hoped to make her think through her actions.

Instead, I had triggered the very events I had sought to avoid.

Around me, the falcons continued their conversation. "Changing leaders like autumn leaves is better than letting one rule for a thousand years," Gren observed.

"It makes you wonder, though, how easy it might be to put someone on the serpiente throne who would turn this land in a more favorable direction." Maya looked pointedly at me.

This was not a new argument, and Opal dismissed it before I even needed to reply. "Makes *you* wonder, perhaps," he scoffed. "One would think that several days of punishment by the Empress's Mercy would have taught you not to speak treason with every word."

"The Heir gave me to her Mercy for conceiving a *child*," Maya spat. This was the crime that had led her to flee from the falcon island. "If that is treason—"

"Which it is," Opal said, interrupting, "seeing as the Empress forbids *kajaes* from breeding."

*Kajaes* were falcons born without magic, freaks in a city whose inhabitants breathed power and worked spells as if they were weaving baskets. But Ahnmik's magic was poison to new life; the royal house had had only one child in the past thousand years: Araceli's son, Sebastian. *Kajaes* children were conceived more easily.

Almost as easily as *quemak*, mongrels like Opal—whose father was human, leaving Opal with the stigma of mixed blood in addition to no magic—and of course me.

"If that is treason," Maya said softly, "and is deserving of what I suffered for it, then do you think I fear a cobra's punishment? Besides, I speak only of replacing one cobra with another. It's nothing new for serpents."

Sometimes I envied Maya for the fire of her hatred. Though *kajaes*, and therefore powerless to make any change, she maintained an incredible passion that I was no longer able to feel, no matter how I tried.

"Sebastian's child guards the new serpiente king," Opal pointed out. "Nicias sees us all for what we are, and don't think he doesn't watch us carefully. You don't think he would stop you if you tried to—"

Maya uttered a curse. "Then we get rid of him—"

"At which point you consign to the Ecl the false queen you wish to place on the throne," I said softly, interjecting. This argument was old, and I was bored of it. "But not until I teach you agony the Mercy never dreamed of."

Silence crashed down. Unlike these four, I was not harmless *kajaes*. I had the full ability to carry out my threat, if I chose.

"Salem Cobriana is beloved by his people," I said. "The dancers adore him, because he is the first in more than eight hundred years to be raised in the nest nursery. He follows their most ancient traditions and knows them all as well as any dancer. He is supported by the previous Diente, by the beloved princess Oliza, and by the avian Tuuli Thea. Most serpents tolerate me, but only because I do nothing that offends them . . . that they know of," I added. If they knew I spent my free hours with falcons and the white vipers of the outlaw Obsidian guild, they would tolerate me far less. "Sive Shardae, on the other hand, can barely stand to be in the room with me—"

"Who cares what the hawk thinks?" Maya asked, challenging me.

"Everyone who does not wish to return to war," Gren answered for me.

I nodded. "And as you mentioned, Salem will now be guarded by Nicias Silvermead. I will kill any who touch the falcon prince. That is, if they aren't first killed by either the Wyverns or the serpiente palace guard."

Maya tossed her head. "You are forgetting that you are the rightful heir to the serpiente throne. You are Anjay Cobriana's only daughter—"

"And Salem is his nephew," I said. "*You* are forgetting two very important things. First of all, the serpiente would rebel and dethrone any who dared challenge their beloved king. No matter what my *birthright*, they would never allow me to take the throne from the one they want there."

Again Maya argued. "There are traditionalists among the serpiente who think you should be queen. I have heard them speaking. Whether or not they approve of you specifically, they think that Anjay's daughter—not the son of his younger sister—should take the throne. You are the oldest and the first in line. Blood may not matter to a serpent as much as it does to a falcon, but a cobra's blood still matters."

"The second and most important thing you are forgetting," I said, ignoring the valid but irrelevant argument, "is that I have no desire to be queen. *Breathing* is a bother to me. Why would I wish to rule?"

"*Think what you could accomplish,*" Maya said, impassioned. "Imagine a world where the serpiente followed you. Imagine if you could rally your Nicias to our cause, or—"

"I could, what, topple the white towers?" I asked. "Survive, Maya. That is all you and I can do. And for some of us, survival takes enough effort. Let it be."

"If nothing else," Maya said, "you would be able to protect those of us who are here. We would be able to live our lives without constantly fearing that the serpiente will discover us and send us away, or that the Empress will remember us and have us dragged back to the island to be put down like feral dogs. If you would not or could not fight Ahnmik on the island, you could fight the Mercy if they came for us here. The serpiente army would be able to win if you showed them how to fight a falcon. We're all *kajaes*. Our children would have no magic. They would be no threat to this realm. As Diente, you could give us a chance to have normal lives."

Tears glistened in Maya's eyes, no doubt as she remembered the infant the Mercy had ripped from her the moment it was weaned of its mother's milk.

Had my own mother ever cried this way? I thought not. Darien of Ahnmik had shown more compassion to these *kajaes*, whom she had smuggled off the island beneath the veil of her own magic, than she ever had to me, her own misbegotten child.

"Go to Salem, while he is holding his first child in his arms and feeling how precious it is," I said to Maya. "Or go to the Tuuli Thea Sive, when she is first a mother. Tell that monarch your story, and speak your plea."

"Trust a hawk?" Maya replied incredulously. "Or a cobra? What would stop them from turning me in?"

"Honor?" I suggested.

"Cobras have no honor."

I couldn't help smiling a little, though most wouldn't at that thought. "I am a cobra," I answered Maya. "*Quemak*, remember? And the other half of my blood comes from one of the Empress's Mercy. Not a good lineage for a woman you would like to place in power."

"You're a gyrfalcon," Gren argued. "And your mother isn't just one of the Mercy; she is Darien, to whom we all owe our lives—"

"Darien," I said, "who tortured your mother, Opal, for her dalliance with a human. Darien, who—"

"People change. They learn," Opal asserted. "Darien most of all. She wants to—"

"My mother *wants* a lot of things," I said. "She speaks about a great many dreams as she stands in the white city, by the right hand of the Empress, while we rot in this mongrel land."

I tried to turn away, but Maya gripped my hand.

"Hai, please, try to imagine—"

" 'Try to imagine' a world where she cares," Opal spat. "Imagine a world where our mongrel cobra has the courage and conviction of her mother. But the Empress long ago wrote that a *quemak* child will have cowardice and treason in her blood—"

"The Empress says a lot of things about *quemak,* things that may serve her agenda more than the absolute truth," Maya snapped. I tried to pull away, and she held more tightly. "Hai, listen to me! Imagine a world where a mixed-blood falcon like you isn't automatically branded a dangerous traitor. Imagine being able to study your magic, take your wings, and dance—"

I tore away from her, aware that my garnet eyes were flashing with rare temper. "I had that," I said. "And it wasn't something my mother gave to me. My *Empress* raised me, when the woman you praise was otherwise occupied. When my first *sakkri* made me scream until I lost my voice for days, Cjarsa bent her own laws and let me grow my wings and dance so I could focus my magic on the present and perhaps not see such horrors again. What did that leniency get us? I lost control, lost my wings and endangered the woman who had raised me, all because my *quemak* arrogance convinced me that I could be more than my cobra father's mistake."

"You *are*—"

"And now here I sit," I continued, "in a room full of criminals, listening to treason. So tell me, Maya, how was Cjarsa incorrect?"

Bitterly, Maya said, "You speak very highly of *your* Empress, yet you are the only one of us who is willingly here in Wyvern's Court. If you love the city so much, why don't you go back to it?"

"Give it a rest," Opal said, placing a hand on Maya's shoulder as I turned to leave. "Sometimes the Empress *is* right. *People* change. *Snakes* don't."

I did not slam the door as I left. There was no need. We had had many arguments about this here—and we would have more.

It was true that I would be allowed to return to Ahnmik if I chose. Empress Cjarsa might send someone to carry me, since I did not have wings of my own anymore. Then I would once again be able to walk in a land where the walls glistened with magic and the roads sang a melody no voice could reproduce. I could live out the rest of my days in a land where even the prison of the mad—the Halls of *shm'Ecl*, where I had spent many years—was so beautiful to behold, it could bring tears to a mortal's eyes.

So, too, could a cuckoo be raised by robins. I loved the white city, but in it, I would be that cuckoo, put into the nest by a mother more interested in using me as a political excuse than in nurturing me. If I returned, I would be Darien's pawn to use against my Empress, and that I could not stand.

# CHAPTER 2

I was not the only citizen of Ahnmik who had chosen this exile. Nicias Silvermead was the acknowledged heir of Lady Araceli, who was heir to none other than the Empress herself. Yet the beautiful royal peregrine had chosen to stay in Wyvern's Court to serve the now abdicated wyvern princess, Oliza.

My loyalty to the Empress Cjarsa kept me from the white island, but my connection to Nicias kept me in Wyvern's Court—and indeed, in this reality.

I had languished in my silent madness for years before Nicias found me hiding from the pain of a shattered body and ruined dreams. His vows to the Cobriana line and royal falcon blood helped him pull me from that void, and for that salvation, I both loved Nicias and hated him. Ahnmik's reluctant prince had given me the world . . . or as much of it as I could hold. Visions of Ahnmik, shards of Wyvern's Court, fragments of pasts and futures other than my own.

I still felt trapped within Ecl's numbing ice, able to watch others live but not quite able to feel that life—except sometimes when I beheld Nicias's love for this land and its people. His passion for Wyvern's Court drove me now from Gren's candle shop to the marketplace, to see what would happen next.

Before I had even descended the northern hills, I could hear shouting.

I took another step forward, and suddenly the noise was replaced by absolute silence. I looked over the market that had just been filled with anxious, frightened and angry avians and serpents, and saw nothing but mist and the pale shimmer of falcon magic.

I squeezed my eyes closed, trying to clear the vision from my mind before it could overwhelm me. This time I succeeded in chasing away the *sakkri*, and I was grateful for that. Too often I became lost in other times and places, especially when I walked through the center of Wyvern's Court. Anhamirak's magic swirled so thickly there among the avians and the serpiente, it frequently robbed me of any scraps of control I might have had.

The shouting returned, and I entered the market.

Salem Cobriana and Sive Shardae were at the heart of the chaos. Salem, Oliza's only full-blood serpiente cousin, had stepped down off a nearby dais and was talking intently with the serpents, who had all but mobbed him. Sive, Oliza's young avian aunt, was struggling to keep some space to herself, but it was a losing battle, one that was obviously making her alistair, Prentice, very nervous. Oliza's parents, Zane and Danica, the current Diente and Tuuli Thea, both looked pale and tired, but they were trying to deal with the shocked crowd.

Oliza herself did not seem to be present.

Nicias, however, was nearby. He was moving from group to group, sometimes speaking to other guards or breaking up fights, but most often trying to hold the crowd back so they wouldn't completely overwhelm the royal family. Though I would have liked to go to him, I knew better than to attempt to distract him while he was working. I could more easily have swallowed the sea.

Instead, I waylaid a serpiente I knew, a flautist named Salokin. "What is going on?"

The red mamba quickly confirmed what the falcons had told me: "Oliza has announced her abdication." His voice was breathy and dazed, and his gaze was unfocused. "She stood on that dais and . . ." For the first time, he looked at me, as he said, "You weren't there. The Diente and the Tuuli Thea and Nacola Shardae and Salem and Sive and Prentice were all there."

"Apparently I don't merit an invitation to royal functions," I said without much shock. As Maya had said, my having cobra blood mattered to the serpiente. It did not, however, matter enough to make me family.

"But she *abdicated*. She must have spoken to you about it."

"Why would she have?" I asked. I had meddled too much in this drama already, helping Oliza spin a *sakkri* of her own after mine had foretold her abandonment of the throne. I had not been able to see that second vision, but I imagined that it was what had led to Oliza's abdication.

*Which one was it?* I wondered. I had seen many futures for Wyvern's Court, most of them ending with fire, as Anhami- rak's magic burned out of control, or with ice, as the falcons wielded Ahnmik's power and tried to salvage what they could from the wreckage.

Salokin's eyes widened. "Why would she . . . She *ab- dicated.*"

"So you've said, a few times now."

"The serpiente Arami just stepped down from the throne," he said, as if rewording might make the facts different.

*So did the avian heir to the Tuuli Thea,* I was about to say, before I realized what was troubling the mamba. "Salem will rule the serpiente well," I assured him.

"Salem is . . . very much a dancer." The words, though formed like a compliment, did not sound like one. "He was not raised to be king. He wasn't even in line to inherit. How could the Arami abdicate and not even *inform* the woman who, if not for falcon treachery, would have been heir in the first place?"

*Falcon treachery. Is that how they're explaining my history these days?* My father had never even known I had been conceived. Even if Anjay Cobriana had not been killed within hours of his return to serpiente land, he would not have been in- formed of my existence. Had Nicias not spied me in the Halls of *shm'Ecl,* Wyvern's Court would have been ignorant still.

Some, I supposed, would consider that treachery. After all, according to serpent laws, I should have been my father's heir.

"I would have to be more than half cobra to be heir to the serpiente throne," I pointed out. "Certainly I would have to be less than half falcon, since most serpents still hate and fear my mother's kind."

"Oliza was only half cobra herself," Salokin said, "and

she was beloved as Arami, despite the fact that we warred with the avians, *her* mother's people, much more recently than we did with the falcons."

I smiled slightly, somewhat amused. "Fine, perhaps it was . . . rude," I allowed, "but though Oliza and I are cousins, we aren't close. I imagine she had larger things on her mind than the guest list when she planned her abdication."

"Maybe."

My gaze drifted back toward the crowd, to where Salem had regained the dais. The cobra reached down to pull a lovely auburn-haired dancer up with him.

At first, the dancer's face seemed to be streaked with tears. She was dressed in a gown of dark plum, the serpiente color of mourning, and her skin was pale and blotched from weeping.

Then the brief vision faded, and she was vibrant and beautiful once more.

"Rosalind," Salokin said when he saw what my attention had turned to. "I imagine she is the one Salem will name serpiente queen." He shook his head.

"He will be a fine king," I said. The words were mostly empty comfort; what did I know of kings? "It isn't as if he will be without guidance. The Diente and the Naga are both still alive."

"I suppose."

"Hai!" The anxious voice that cut through our conversation belonged to Sive. The hawk had somehow struggled away from the near mob around the dais and now came to my side, perhaps out of courtesy or perhaps to take advantage of the space that most serpents gave me, wary of the "black magic" falcons could wield.

Sive would become the next avian queen, and though

she was young still, she was too old to be called a child. Her alistair, Prentice, hovered beside her, as protective as a mother hen.

"Hai, how are you?" she asked me. She reached out and took my hand in greeting, betraying her frequent contact with the serpents.

For a moment I could not answer, because at Sive's touch I saw her, several years older, glowing with joy as she held her infant in her arms. The beloved queen presented her child to her people and said her name: Aleya. She handed the babe to her alistair, and as their hands touched, I could feel the love that stretched between them.

In contrast to the earlier visions I had had, of Wyvern's Court after its destruction and of Rosalind's tears, this one was comforting.

"I . . . You will be a beautiful queen," I said, still half within the vision. "Aleya . . . the name means 'given to us.' "

Sive recoiled from me, breaking the trance.

"Th-thank you," she said, but I could see the fear in her eyes.

I was glad she stopped me, because I knew what I would have said next: *You are very much in love, but there is sorrow in your heart, too. You remember the man who was your alistair when you were a child. He often frustrated you, but you loved him despite his awkwardness.*

Prentice . . . gone, to where?

Right then he came forward, guarding his pair bond from whatever threat he felt I projected.

I started to reach out for the rest of the vision and barely managed to resist. Sive could rule peacefully with or without this man. I did not need to know when or how they would separate.

I shook my head, backing away.

"Excuse me," I said.

"Are you all right?" Salokin put a hand on my arm, and that was enough to trigger another vision of Wyvern's Court, this time in flames.

I shuddered, pulling back mentally and physically, trying to fight the *sakkri*. There was too much going on in the market. In the language of Ahnmik, Oliza's abdication would be referred to as a *sheni'le*, a decision that drastically altered the path of Fate. I had foolishly come here to see the present for myself but was on the verge of being swamped by futures.

I turned abruptly, not bothering to beg leave of the heir to the Tuuli Thea or explain myself to the flautist. I needed to be somewhere quiet.

If only I had not lost my falcon form long before, I could have grown my wings. Within minutes, I could have been beyond the bounds of Wyvern's Court, beyond the influence of Anhamirak's magic, and beyond the pulse of these visions.

Instead, I walked—agonizingly slowly, step by weary step—back to the small house I kept at the edge of Wyvern's Court, and there I collapsed into sleep.

# CHAPTER 3

"*Ahnmik, I have always been yours, your voice, your tool. Help me now, I beg you. Give me the strength to do what must be done today.*"

The falcon Cjarsa whispered the prayer as she pushed open the doors of the temple. Araceli was deep in meditation and did not notice the intrusion, even as a shaft of sunlight fell across the altar—a simple black silk melos scarf draped across cold gray stone, with a single alabaster statue, symbol of the god Ahnmik, on it.

The rest of the room was equally stark, except for one corner, where a three-year-old child with fair hair slept upon a soft violet cushion. Araceli had found the girl abandoned in the jungle, far from the desert lands of their home, and had named her Alasdair.

Protector.

"*Araceli, it is time.*"

Kiesha, the cobra high priestess of Anhamirak, stood in the doorway to her temple, holding her head high despite her obvious exhaustion. Cjarsa remembered this woman as having mahogany hair, sun-touched skin and brown eyes, but Anhamirak's fire had dyed Kiesha's body as surely as Ahnmik's ice had dyed Cjarsa's. Kiesha's warm earthen eyes had become lakes of blood, and they were no longer kind but eerily piercing as she beheld Cjarsa, whose power had once been the opposite–the balance–of hers.

Many things had changed since Maeve had abandoned their coven. Once, they had been the protectors and leaders of their people, priests and priestesses of the eight great powers, led by Maeve and kept in balance by her guidance. Now the powers were unbalanced.

The stain left on Kiesha's hair and eyes was nothing compared to the terror of the uncontrollable magics that had ripped through each of the Dasi in Maeve's absence. The serpents had blamed the falcons for the first assaults, saying that their worship of death and darkness had led to this destruction; Cjarsa's followers had retaliated, spilling their own accusations against the chaos-worshippers.

"You say you wish to end this," the cobra said to Cjarsa and Araceli in greeting.

"Before more lives are lost," Araceli said.

They had been fighting for years. What else could they do? Anhamirak's domain was wildfire and war. As long as her magic was left unbalanced, there could never be peace.

"Yes," Cjarsa whispered. She had seen the future, seen the final fire that would consume them all. She knew that this had to be stopped. "Come forward, child," she said.

When Alasdair stepped out from behind Araceli and held up a curious hand, Kiesha knelt down and let the tiny fingers wrap around her thumb. "Yours?" she asked Araceli, her expression softening.

"No," Araceli said, blinking back tears. "Brassal killed my

daughter last night. Odd that it would be a priest of Namid, giver of life, who would destroy a child."

The python had crept into Ahnmik's temple, probably hoping to kill Cjarsa. Instead, he had found Araceli and her young daughter.

Araceli was convinced that he had killed the child intentionally; Cjarsa believed it had been an accident. Like all their powers, Brassal's magic had grown beyond his ability to control it.

"Now," Cjarsa whispered, throwing out her own magic like a net. Araceli, Syfka, Servos and Cjarsa had spent the past three years concocting this spell, and now it drove Kiesha to her knees. The cobra screamed.

And the child screamed as well.

Oh, gods . . . hearing that scream, Cjarsa wanted to leave this world. The spell the falcons had created shredded Kiesha's magic, tearing it into two. One half of Anhamirak's power remained in the cobra; the other half burned its way into the child's soul. As it had painted Kiesha garnet, so it stained the child, darkening her white-blond hair and pale blue eyes to the color of beaten gold.

It was too late to bring back the balance, and no one could control Anhamirak's chaos, but they hoped that this would cripple the serpents' magic before it could destroy even more.

Araceli was the one who took the little girl's tiny hands in her own and whispered gently, "Now you'll be able to fly, like we can."

"Don't be kind," Cjarsa said. "If you are kind, we will never be able to do what must be done."

"Come, Alasdair," Araceli said, taking the young hawk's hand before Kiesha could recover and realize what they had done. "You have much to learn before we take you back to your people."


No, this wasn't me. This wasn't my time. All this had happened long before to Cjarsa, before she had raised the island from the sea and become Empress of the white city. I'd seen it before; the first time, I had screamed with Kiesha, screamed for days until Cjarsa had helped me escape the vision.

Where was I . . . oh, there . . .


Even generations later, the Cobrianas' garnet eyes had not faded. As Anjay rode in a fury to the Hawk's Keep, they burned with the same intensity that had made Cjarsa cringe when she had faced Kiesha in the temple of Anhamirak.

Some of Anjay's soldiers had followed him, and they fell by the dozens as he thrust forward into avian lands, but no bow or blade seemed able to pierce his pain and hatred.

The cobra had returned from falcon lands only hours before. He knew nothing of the child he had sired, and if he had been lingering on recollections of the falcon lover he had left behind, those had been shoved aside by the news of his sister's assassination.

Anjay did not dismount as he reached the courtyard of the Hawk's Keep, but boosted himself up to stand on his horse's back; a raven tried to stop him from grasping the balcony floor above, and Anjay quickly drove a blade into the man's ribs.

As Anjay hoisted himself over the balcony rail, a young hawk girl shrieked the raven's name with enough pain in her voice that Anjay knew that the man he had just killed had been her mate. Fine; he would end this hawk's pain, too, as her people had ended the lives of so many he loved.

All the while, the falcon Darien shadowed him, and she let out a cry that echoed the girl's as the youngest avian prince defended his sister, Danica, by driving a soldier's blade into Anjay's back. The avians had lost scores of their own people to this mad rush, and now they cheered as a serpent's blood flowed over the child's hand.

No, no. Why was I forced to watch this, again and again, every time I closed my eyes? I shared Anjay's blood. Did I need to share his death?

And now, finally, I remembered who I was: the unwanted child of a doomed cobra prince, and a falcon sworn to the Empress Cjarsa, who had ripped Anhamirak's magic in half. Had the avians and the serpiente known, all those years as they had warred, that they had slain the other halves of themselves? Was that why peace came with such difficulty: not because they hated each other, but because they could not forgive themselves?

*I was a young child, dancing the skies above the white city, lost in the endless tides of magic that whirled through this land like storm winds. The wings I spread showed the taint of my father's blood— the color of tar and lava. Anhamirak's stain.*

*My father's magic was not powerful; a cobra did not have enough power on his own to be a danger. But when what remained of Anhamirak's magic needled the falcon magic I had inherited from my mother, Ahnmik slashed back. I spent most of my days struggling to control these combinative powers, but in the middle of this sky-dance, I lost that battle.*

*The two magics fought, tearing and slicing, ripping at my body and my wings. Dark flight feathers cascaded to the ground even before I fell screaming.*

*Cjarsa caught me before the crystal-hard ground shattered my plummeting body, but though she mended my flesh, she could do nothing with my ravaged wings. As for the rest of me . . . the agony from my magic was as deep as my blood, and even my Empress could not heal that.*

*She cradled me in her arms as I shivered and cried, my magic striking her blindly no matter how I tried to keep it in check.*

*"Sleep now," she whispered to me. It was all she could do.*


Yes, I would have liked to sleep, to rest, to finally be away from the sharp edges left behind by that ancient rending. But . . . I had made a promise. I needed to find my way back to *here* and *now*, in Wyvern's Court, such a strange and un- likely place. The two halves of Anhamirak were trying to shove themselves together, but it was like trying to return blood to a wound.

Back to Wyvern's Court . . .


*Salem Cobriana, the heir to the serpiente throne, lay in my arms, dying. His blood felt cold on my skin; his red eyes had turned a tawny brown. His heartbeat was so faint that even with my cheek pressed to his chest I could barely hear it.*

*I knew I could save him; I had that power, always had. I could use my magic, patch his bones, slow the bleeding, force his heart to beat and his lungs to stir the air . . . but terror gripped me. I could ask my magic for that much, and Ahnmik would grant the favor, but the white falcon's power ultimately came from the void, from Ecl, and that dark goddess would ask even more in return. If I swam her dark, still waters, I would drown. I shrieked for help, but none came.*

*The mob was seething. How had the crowd turned so vile so quickly?*

*An arrow pierced my back, slicing under my left shoulder blade. I covered Salem with my body but did not reach out to him with the greedy magic that could save his life. I couldn't. Please . . .*

Another arrow sliced through my arm before burying itself in his side.

"Hai!" Someone shouted my name. At that moment, I felt Salem die, felt the last spark go out as Brysh, goddess of death, claimed her own.

No, not her own. This wasn't natural; this was a travesty. I screamed and then let the magic free, lashing into the crowd.

Hai!

Shm'Ahnmik'la'Hai. Kiesha'ra'la'Hai.

Pain. Fear. Not from me or from Salem but from someone else, someone who knew all my names.

Stay here, Hai. Stay here, with me.

Only one person ever called me by both sides of my blood: Nicias. He named me shm'Ahnmik, a falcon, and Kiesha'ra, a cobra.

I wanted the serpent throne no more than Nicias wanted his throne on Ahnmik. We would never claim our royal birthrights, but our magics would forever tie us to them. The words—his bond to me, and mine to him—drew me back to the real world.

# CHAPTER 4

I lifted my head, in the place and time most call reality, in the bedroom of my little home at the edge of Wyvern's Court, and found Nicias standing across the room from me, one arm held protectively in front of his face. His forearm was bleeding in four places, as if scratched by the claws of some great cat; I could see a dark stain on his shirt where his chest had been similarly torn. A cloud of angry magic—my magic, which I had lashed out with during my unwanted visions—stormed around him.

I curled into a ball, trying to draw the magic back from Nicias and into myself and knowing that I might have killed anyone else who had woken me. I shut my eyes for a moment and again heard the whisper of Ecl, who for so long had been my keeper . . . my guardian, my kingdom, my ever-jealous lover. Her voice was soothing, and I felt myself falling back into sleep.

Nicias touched my arm, terribly trusting even with blood trickling down his skin. "Hai, stay with me."

"*Quemak*," I said. He had called me a falcon and a cobra, but I was neither really. Opal was right. *Quemak*, mongrel. That was the only title I could claim.

Nicias winced when I said it. The word was not a polite one, and I knew he hated to hear me apply it to myself, but how could he argue? We both knew it was true.

"You're hurting yourself," he said. The magic I had been trying to pull away from him had cut into my own arms instead. I didn't mind the pain much; I was nearly numb to it. But I hated to see blood on his skin.

He gently ran his hands down my arms. I shivered, both at his touch and at the brush of his magic, which felt like cold water in the scalding desert. He smoothed the cuts I had created, transforming them into something harmless that quickly faded.

I doubted that Nicias could explain how he had done it. He had begun to study his falcon magic only within the past few months, but he was royal blood, so his power responded freely to his desires. Simple things like this he could do instinctively.

"Nightmare?" Nicias asked as he healed us both.

How I envied people who dreamed, who could have nightmares and know that in no world were they real.

"*Sakkri.*"

Nicias resented anything resembling prophecy. He had not been raised with the assumption that if one was strong enough, one could look forward in time and see what Fate had planned. Not every *sakkri'a'she*, vision of the future, came true, but every one had the potential to do so.

Few people had the power to weave such *sakkri*, and among those who could, even fewer had the strength to recall them. I was one of the few, but even I had trouble sometimes; I would remember single images or driving desires instead of whole scenes. Most of the time, I let the future-memories fade.

But this time something had caused me to wake screaming and struggling.

I had seen my father killed—no, I saw that frequently, almost every time I slept. It no longer had the power to—

*Salem.* His was the death that had disturbed me. The memory of it made me shudder. I could almost taste the helpless terror and fury I had felt in the vision . . . *almost.* The emotions were already fading, returning me to my more familiar state of numbness. But surely in the future I had envisioned, I had felt like I was losing something far more dear than one cobra's life. *Why?*

I had once given myself to Ecl to rid myself of these kinds of visions, which were rich with emotions—most often painful ones—that had no parallel in my everyday existence. Now I had taken myself back to reality and was trying to live again. Would this be my punishment, to have this cobra die in my arms while I wept? Would I die with him?

*Will I be the cause of his death?* I wondered.

"What did you see?" Nicias asked, drawing me from my dark thoughts.

I shook my head; I couldn't speak of it. Describing such prophecies made them more real, and as I had recently experienced with Oliza, sometimes that was enough to set one into motion.

"It doesn't matter. It will fade," I said. At least, I prayed it would.

Nicias sighed and ran his hands through his pale blond

hair, which was hanging loose around his face. The blue strands were tangled with all the rest, and I wished I could reach forward and separate them, binding the golden locks back, the way they would be worn on Ahnmik.

Old habit, left over from years in the white city when I had prayed and wished I could have the pale, pale blond hair of my Empress, marked with a falcon's blue, instead of the black hair of a cobra.

Or perhaps it was a desired habit. Every time Nicias was near, I found myself inventing excuses to touch him.

I kept my hands by my sides.

"I can't stay long," Nicias said apologetically. "The court is—dear skies, you weren't even there. Hai—"

"I heard," I said. "Oliza has given up the throne."

Nicias nodded. "Salem and Sive will inherit the serpiente and avian thrones. Neither of them hates the other. Hopefully . . ."

Hopefully they would be able to maintain the peace between the avians and the serpiente and bring the two worlds together so that someday a wyvern queen might be able to rule. Hopefully the slaughter that had lasted more than a thousand years would never begin again.

"What will Oliza do now?"

"She has taken a wolf for her mate," he said. "A woman named Betia. They left Wyvern's Court as soon as Oliza made the announcement."

It had been obvious to me from the beginning that Oliza loved the wolf. Even so, I nodded, accepting the information as if it was new.

Fate did care for its children sometimes. Long before, Araceli and Cjarsa had split Anhamirak's magic to protect this world. In Oliza, daughter of a hawk and a cobra, that magic had again combined. Love that would never let Oliza breed was a gift, as any natural-born child of the wyvern's would unleash terror on this Earth.

"Salem plans to formally name his mate tomorrow night," Nicias said. "He believes it will comfort his people if he takes the serpiente throne quickly, so they do not need to wonder if he will also step aside. I'm not sure I agree with his reasoning, but . . ." He shook his head. "Salem will be king, and once that is done, it will be harder for Oliza to return if she wants to. I think Salem would step aside if she tried, but a king cannot give up his crown as easily as an heir can give up her birthright." He let out a frustrated sound. "I don't like this. Oliza has gone off and asked none of her guard to follow her. Salem's mother is still exploring *somewhere,* and though we've sent dozens of messengers for Irene, there is no guarantee they will find her. We've spent most of the last two months trying to control riots in the marketplace, and now, with Oliza gone, it is going to be even harder. It isn't a good time for the royal house to be so scattered." Nicias shook his head again. "I'm sorry. I don't mean to burden you with this."

Nicias usually tried to shelter me from what he perceived as the more difficult aspects of this reality, as if any bad news might send me back into Ecl. Perhaps someday it would, but not right now. I attempted to find something to say that would encourage him to continue the conversation.

*She and some wolf have run off in the woods together, leaving Salem and Sive holding the bag,* Gren had said. Since Oliza's mate did not care for other wolves, they could be with only one group: the Obsidian guild. The guild, which included

Maeve's descendents, was shunned equally by serpiente and falcons. Though they had been pardoned by the Cobriana two generations before, very few of them had elected to rejoin serpiente society.

"Oliza is safe," I assured Nicias. The leader of the Obsidian guild had introduced himself to me within days of my waking in Wyvern's Court. He was another of my late father's devotees, and he had made it clear that I was always welcome in the Obsidian camp. Though only a child when Anjay had died, the white viper spoke highly of the long-dead cobra and had even implied once that the outlaw guild might have returned to ally with the rest of the serpiente if my father had survived to rule. I would not call him a friend, but I was familiar with his ways. He would not allow a traveling dancer to be threatened in his land. "I know where she was heading, and you don't need to worry about her there."

Nicias and I never spoke the word *Obsidian* between us, but I sensed he knew both of my connection with that guild and of Oliza's. My neglecting to give specifics now was enough to tell him who Oliza was with.

"She will always be my queen . . . and I will always protect her, as long as she will allow me to," Nicias said. "I know she doesn't want a guard loitering around her, but it would make me—and the rest of her guards, not to mention her family—feel worlds better if I could see for myself that she is safely settled."

I shook my head. "You wouldn't be welcome." A glimpse of a royal guard would make the entire guild disappear.

"No, of course not. You're right."

"You need to stay in the court, anyway," I said. Then,

noticing his troubled expression, I added, "If you would like, I can check on the wyvern."

"Thank you. You don't know how much it would mean to me."

*Yes, I do,* I thought.

"I need to go," Nicias said. "I shouldn't have stayed even this long."

I sent him a silent query, by magic instead of voice. At his sharp look, I repeated myself out loud. "Why *did* you come here?"

"I felt you scream." His voice was soft.

*But why come to my side?* I asked silently. *Why do you do all this for me when you know I am only a danger to you, a mongrel falcon in your world of serpents and avians?*

He ignored my silent words, as he always did. I knew he heard me, but he would only acknowledge my questions if I pronounced them.

"Thank you," I said instead.

"Will you be all right?"

"I will be fine," I answered. "I shan't dissolve away—and I will bring back news of your queen."

He kissed my cheek. "Take care of yourself, Hai."

*"Teska-Kaya'ga'la."*

He gave me a curious look when I used the endearment, which meant *my light.* He knew he was. My vow to him was what kept me in this world, kept me from the numbing darkness of Ecl.

*"O'hena-sorma'la'lo'Mehay,"* he replied. Literally, the title meant *sister of my soul,* though, like most of the old language, it had many different connotations. Some were fraternal; others were more loving, closer to *soulmate.*

He did not explain what he meant any more than I had explained what I'd said. Instead, he went back to Wyvern's Court, to continue his exhausting struggle against the future—a future he still believed he could control, though I feared we might all soon drown.

# CHAPTER 5

I followed Nicias to the front door. As we hesitated on the threshold, my eyes lingered on him in a way I could not have avoided had I tried, and for a moment I was transported to another time, another place, where this man was not Nicias Silvermead but Nicias of Ahnmik—son of the *aona*, the Empress's heir, Araceli.

The aona'ra *walked upon paths that rippled with power, two of his Mercy beside him. Nicias's footsteps were soft and echoed by music; the white city embraced its only prince, its spirits cajoling him, gossiping with him and praying to him as he passed.*

*He had nearly learned not to weep at the road's bittersweet songs, which conveyed the tears of all those who had lost their loved ones to powers like Ecl.*

*Hai had once spoken a prophecy to him. She had made him swear never to betray Oliza, and informed him that there could be no future in which he took the white throne of Ahnmik and Oliza survived to rule Wyvern's Court. What Hai had not said was that Oliza would choose to give up her throne, regardless of the choices he made.*

"Hai?" Nicias called me back to reality once more, with worry in his ice blue eyes.

"Nicias . . . what will you do now, without Oliza?"

"The Diente and the Tuuli Thea have asked the Wyvern guard to stay in the court for now," he answered. "Many of us have been offered positions with the Royal Flight or the serpiente palace guard, should we wish them in the case we are eventually dissolved."

*He still protected Oliza; he always would.*

*He wished only that he could be numb to the crying. . . .*

*He had gone into the Halls of shm'Ecl once, intending to do what Cjarsa and Araceli refused to do. Royal blood called to the shm'Ecl; he could save them, like he had saved Hai.*

*He had tried.*

*But this time he had failed, and though he had survived, three members of his Mercy—three falcons who had willingly chosen to serve him, to protect him—had lost their lives. Their deaths had taken something Ecl had not been able to, a shard of . . . something he couldn't find words for.*

*Oh . . . gods.*

*Your soul, my love,* I cried to the ghost of a Nicias I prayed would never exist. *Your soul, your compassion. That is what you lost with their deaths.*

He wasn't thinking of returning to Ahnmik—was he?

"You've mentioned the plans for the Wyverns. I was asking about *you*. Will you stay in Wyvern's Court?" I asked, somewhat desperately. *I* longed for the white city, but the falcon land wasn't for Nicias. Ahnmik would destroy him. It nearly had before; it would for certain if he went back there.

"I imagine so."

If he, like my mother, believed that he could do the most good from the white city, no power on this earth would stop him. Prophecy certainly would not.

He looked at me with concern. "What's wrong?"

I shook my head. "Nothing. Just—nothing." Nothing that words would help. "You need to get back."

He nodded slowly, those blue eyes gazing into mine, before finally turning away. I watched him shapeshift into the beautiful peregrine falcon that was his second form. As he spread wing and shot into the sky, my breath stilled. How I wanted to do the same.

Instead, I saddled Najat, the Arabian mare that the serpiente royal house had given me, and headed into the woods.

Though the Obsidian camp moved constantly, I never had trouble finding it. White vipers had little active power, but Maeve's magic was like a beacon to me.

The first "sentry" I saw around Obsidian land was not a guard but a child who could not have been more than four years old. Concerned that she might be lost, I dismounted Najat and walked slowly toward her.

"Hello?"

The child, who was intently peering through the trees, did not seem to hear me.

"Hello?" I said again, moving closer.

The girl turned toward me, her eyes wide. Though her milk-fair hair spoke of white-viper parentage, her eyes were a deep, rusty red: a cobra's eyes. My first thought was *Another of my father's?*

Absurd—my father had been dead two and a half decades—but she was obviously the result of some cobra's indiscretion. I doubted that Oliza's father would have strayed from his beloved Naga, which left only Salem. I had not thought that a boy so tightly bound to the dancer's nest would wander into these woods, but how well did I really know my cousin?

"Are you lost?" I asked when the girl didn't speak. "Do you know how to get back to your family?"

She chewed on her lower lip.

"Here, take my hand," I said softly. "I'll help you get back to the camp."

She raised her tiny hand to put it into mine, and only then did I see the blood on her pale skin.

"Are you hurt—"

I had only half finished the question when she wrapped her fingers around my hand and the world shattered.

*Fire.*

I shrieked as a wyvern's untamed power tore through me, searing everything that Ahnmik had left frozen and numb and ripping from me all the *sakkri* I had ever spun.

I saw Wyvern's Court awash in scalding magic. Serpents and avians slaughtered by Oliza's child—*this* child, Keyi, who didn't exist yet, except in visions like this one. She looked different every time I saw her, but each time, the vision was so powerful I had no way to guard myself from it.

*Oh, gods.* I could see . . .

*The survivors fighting as the falcons came to try to tame Anhamirak's power before it could engulf the whole world as it nearly had once before.*

*So much screaming, so much pain.*

*Nicias, weeping as if his heart had been ripped from him.*

And then I recalled the moment, months before, when Nicias had dove into Ecl to save me and had nearly lost himself. I told him: *I have danced a thousand futures and lived a thousand lifetimes, and all I have seen are ashes and ice. You are too— You don't belong here. You have things to do, out there. Go, Nicias,* please.

*Only if you will.*

*Swear you'll go back, and I'll try.*

I couldn't stand to see Nicias fall in that dark place, but surely he would have found his way back. I could have said no. Instead . . .

*I swear.*

*Then I swear as well.*

*Why* had I made that vow? This world *hurt.* Everything was a struggle, without the possibility of any end but fire. Did these fools really think their mixed-blood world had any hope?

I tried to shove away the visions.

*Hai?* Nicias's silent concerned query reached me from Wyvern's Court. *Are you all right?*

I couldn't have him come here, this close to Obsidian land. *I'm fine,* I replied. *I'm fine, I'm fine, I'm fine.*

*Are you sure—*

*I'm fine!*

I severed the communication, one word pounding in time with my pulse: *why why why why why why?*

Why had I tied myself back to this world? I could have remained in the Halls of *shm'Ecl* for a thousand years and more, and I would never have needed to know this pain.

I had almost broken free of the *sakkri* when someone real touched my shoulder, upsetting my power yet again.

"*Nasa-Vere-nas'ka'la!*" Don't touch me! I commanded, lashing out at the white viper with my magic.

He fell back, his moss green eyes hot with fear and anger. The members of the Obsidian guild shared their names only with those they trusted most, but my power had found the viper's name—Vere—and now it was twisted into the magic that was digging like thorns into his skin.

"Remove it," he whispered to me.

I reached out to do so, and my whole body shuddered. "I can't."

He moved closer and reached toward me again but stopped with his fingertips an inch from my skin as my magical command made his muscles freeze.

"Are you all right?" he asked.

Was *I* all right? I had wrapped the leader of the Obsidian guild in falcon magic, and now he asked me if I was all right. He should have been cursing me.

"I'm—"

Again I caught sight of the girl, further back in the woods, but this time I recognized her for what she was: a *sakkri*. A vision of horror wrapped in a child's innocent form.

"Skies above," I whispered, dropping my head into my hands. "Not again."

In most futures in which Oliza took the throne, peace ended with an assassin's blade. In the handful of futures in which Oliza lived long enough to bear Keyi, the child slew her mother and destroyed most of Wyvern's Court before the falcons descended to pick up remnants of the once grand society.

I had often seen the look in my mother's eye as she realized that my Empress had been right all along in creating the avian-serpiente war to protect them from this rampant magic. Many times, I had wondered how that horror would manifest itself in her opinion of her daughter. Would she be proud that I, a mongrel, had been loyal when even her faith had wavered?

Or would I simply be a reminder of yet another disastrous mistake?

Would I still find the answer to that question? Oliza had abdicated. She did not plan to have natural-born children. Why was the vision of Keyi still coming to me so strongly?

I felt Obsidian struggle against the magic I had left on him, and shift it until he could lay a cautious hand on my shoulder.

"Talk to me," he said.

"Fire," I whispered. I squeezed my eyes shut against the image. "It's too much. I can't control it."

"Can't control what?"

"*Everything.* The future."

"No one can," he said.

The anguish I felt wasn't my own. It belonged to the serpents and the avians who would be destroyed in a future in which this child existed. Even so, it felt as if my heart had been ripped from me. . . .

Suddenly, for the first time since the day I had spun my first *sakkri*, I was weeping. I cried without tears and without sound, but still my breath hitched and my body shook. I reached for Ecl, my peaceful oblivion, but this close to Maeve's kin and the balancing magic they still held, I couldn't make myself fall into the void even if I could have forgotten that damning vow to Nicias.

Without words, Obsidian wrapped me in his arms, holding me as I struggled to free myself from the aching sorrow. Was this how other people felt, all the time? How could anyone live if at any moment they could be struck by this pain? Even when I shoved back all the screaming, wailing and weeping, I could taste tears on the back of my tongue and feel them making my lungs tight and my chest heavy.

Finally, as the dry sobs subsided, I asked, "Why?"

"Why what?"

"Why comfort a mongrel falcon who would strike you with magic just for coming near?"

He tilted his head, a quizzical, almost amused expression on his face. "You really don't know?"

"You've said you were loyal to my father," I said, guessing.

"True, I was loyal to Anjay Cobriana. If he had lived to be king, I would have followed him. When you first came to Wyvern's Court, I introduced myself to you because I knew you were his daughter. But that is not why I am still here right now."

"Then why?"

He shook his head as he rose to his feet, and offered me a hand to help me stand. "I would never be able to walk away from someone in the condition I found you in. I don't have a falcon's power, but I could feel your agony half a mile away."

When he saw my confusion, he asked, "Doesn't anyone on Ahnmik ever just do the right thing?"

I snickered. "*Right* is a relative term when you're dealing with the white falcon."

Hesitantly, I took Vere Obsidian's hand, but this time there was no flash of power. No visions overwhelmed me as I rose shakily to my feet; I was too burned out for even my volatile magic to catch a spark.

# CHAPTER 6

"I've never thought of you as a falcon until now," Vere said, "when I heard you speak of yourself as if Anhamirak has never touched you. I suppose it was arrogant of me, to ignore one half of your parentage because I was fonder of the other."

"If you have to ignore half my blood, I would rather you ignore my father's," I said, cut by his words, which I had heard in many forms as a child.

He shook his head. "Then you would have been dead long before I let you walk these woods."

"I could kill you before you could injure me," I pointed out. "I could kill you in such a way that you would feel like it took you centuries to die. I was raised on Ahnmik, after all. I might have been a dancer, but I learned many of the Mercy's tricks."

He nodded. "I suppose you could, except for one thing."

"What is that?"

"You would have to care enough about your own life, and my death, to do it. And you don't, not nearly."

I shrugged. "Perhaps."

Perhaps. I felt very tired, very worn down by the despair in my visions, for someone who couldn't care less if she lived or died.

As if summoned by my thoughts, the child darted across our path again. White-blond hair streamed behind the running figure.

"I told Nicias I would check on Oliza for him," I said, shifting the topic to something that concerned me more, "since I knew that you would not want him to come here himself." Partly I spoke to fulfill my duty to the peregrine, but I was equally interested in learning Vere's opinion of the abdicated princess. Keyi's possible fathers were many, but her white-blond hair in this particular vision could come only from one of the white vipers of the Obsidian guild.

"She's here. Heartbroken by what she has had to do, but confident that it was the right thing. Betia will help her through it." He paused, considering, before he added, "I have no objection to her being our guest, but I would like someday to know why she made the decision she did. I haven't wanted to pressure her."

"And you think I might know?"

"I *know* you know," he replied. "It's only a matter of whether you'll tell me."

"When your kin first left the Dasi, do you know what happened?"

"I suspect you're going to tell me I don't," he said wryly.

"In the ancient days, the Dasi were able to summon spirits for guidance and call the rains to feed their crops.

Namid's priest could see if a mother was kindled with life just by looking at her, and when it was time, he could usher that life into the world with ease. Brysh's priestess could take a dying man's last breath just as painlessly and wrap the survivors in peaceful mourning. When your ancestor Maeve left the Dasi, all control, all balance, left with her. Rains turned to floods that swept away homes and drowned dozens of men, women and children." *A bassinet, swept down the river, with a wailing infant inside.* "Namid's touch could burn a woman so the life inside her bled. Just a glance from the aplomado Syfka—who had been sworn to Brysh—could make a person fall, and a glance from Kiesha, Anhamirak's priestess . . ." I shuddered. "Can you imagine a cobra's being able to kindle fire with those garnet eyes?"

"They nearly can still," Vere whispered.

"Serpents don't remember what it was like in those first days, but I've seen it. If somehow Oliza and her mate survived her coronation—an unlikely enough possibility, since serpents will not accept an avian Nag, and avians will not accept a serpent alistair—Oliza's child would bring back those days of despair, which the entire avian-serpiente war was fought to keep at bay."

The war. Nicias felt that the falcons' actions had been unjust, that kindling the war had been evil, but what else could have been done, when there were no good decisions that could have been made?

"How can you know this?" Vere asked me.

"*Sakkri,*" I replied.

Why was I trying to warn this white viper of what the consequences might be if he or one of his people joined with Oliza? What did I have to lose if Wyvern's Court burned? It would possibly mean my reconciliation with my mother, and therefore my Empress, presuming I survived the fire.

It would mean Nicias's broken heart as well.

And of course, the loss of Wyvern's Court.

Our conversation was interrupted as we reached the Obsidian campsite, and I was grateful for the timing. It kept me from pondering why I found myself trying to protect Wyvern's Court when letting it burn might gain me everything.

The Obsidian camp was simple. Hammocks, designed so they could be taken down swiftly if necessary, had been strung between the trees around a central fire. The Obsidian guild was tolerated by the current monarchy, but in the past they had been actively hunted, and they had never dropped their habits from those days. All their camps were transient, and all their members armed.

As we entered, a pair of serpents was performing a flame-dance. They wove their bodies against each other, sliding around, over and through the campfire.

A mistake, and those watching would choke on the smell of burned flesh.

I closed my eyes, and for a moment I saw the triple arches of Ahnmik. The three arches were among the highest structures in the city, less only to the *yenna'marl,* the white towers. To fall from that height . . .

Some days, I felt as if I might still be falling.

I opened my eyes, forcing my attention past the dancers, to where Oliza was curled in the arms of her wolf, Betia. The wyvern's eyes were swollen, as if she had been crying, and she was watching the flame-dance intently, as if to avoid drowning in her own thoughts. Her expression, which reflected how I felt every moment of my waking life, drew me to her almost against my will.

Betia saw me first, and her gaze met mine. *Don't hurt her,* the wolf said, quite clearly, without needing to speak. *She has been through enough today.* I nodded, knowing she would sooner snap my neck than let me harm her mate.

Betia's attention prompted Oliza's, and the wyvern visibly braced herself as she watched me approach.

I almost said, *I understand.* I knew why Oliza had left, knew the horrors she had seen, which no one should ever have to face. I was probably the only person in this world who fully understood.

But as I looked into Oliza's eyes, the words fled. The once princess had her mate for understanding. She had Obsidian land for sanctuary. And, I realized, she had the blessed amnesia that came to those who worked *sakkri* without training. She remembered only enough to know that she had chosen this exile for a reason, and to fear the woman who had twice triggered the terrifying visions of the future.

I took a step back, surprised by how much it hurt to see such wariness in her.

"I'm sorry," I said, without being able to help it.

"Why?" Oliza's voice was guarded, with good reason. She had no way of knowing that I had not intentionally shown her the visions that had eventually led to her abdication.

Araceli, heir to the Empress, had hinted more than once that it would please the royal falcon house if Oliza never took the throne of Wyvern's Court. If the veiled request had come from Cjarsa, or if my loyalty to Nicias had not stayed my hand, I would not have hesitated to sabotage Oliza's reign.

Oliza was right to be nervous. She had no reason to trust me.

"For intruding," I said. "Nicias was worried. Since he can't come here, I told him I would look in on you."

Oliza relaxed a little when I said the peregrine's name. "Please, thank Nicias for checking on me, and tell him that I'm sorry I couldn't let him know where I was going. I'm with friends." She added, "I couldn't stay at court."

"He understands." *As do I.* "I'll let him know you are safe."

"Thank you."

I turned to go, but she called my name.

"Hai?"

"Yes?"

"I know my leaving hurt Nicias. Take care of him?"

The image of Nicias as Ahnmik's cold prince briefly flickered through my memory. I wondered if Oliza had seen that vision, and if it had made any difference. "I will, as long as I can."


I walked away from Oliza and Betia and back toward the dancers.

Watching their movement, I could almost read the pattern left by the dancers' bodies. The white vipers currently performing had just enough magic to lace the air with innate power but not enough to hold the spell in place. Otherwise, a *daraci'Kain* like this would have had the power to call the rain . . . or, if unbalanced, to drown the earth.

"What do you think of our dancers?" Vere Obsidian asked me.

I shook my head, trying to banish the image of dancing from my mind . . . trying to forget the white arches, where I had experienced the greatest bliss and the greatest devastation.

"They're lovely," I said, with no real emotion in my voice.

The dancers had sunk into a deep bow, feet, knees, head and hands pressed to the ground. There were two reasons for the bow: the first was to give thanks to the audience, and the second was to recover their strength.

On Ahnmik, such a bow would sometimes last days, as the dancers rested. Those dances were rare, but incredible to behold, especially when performed by someone of the upper ranks.

"Hai?"

"What?" I snapped, more forcefully than I had intended.

Vere Obsidian held out his hand. "Dance with me."

*Fool.* Didn't he know my wings were broken? They had been scarred, tortured and lost the *last* time I had tried to dance, in the skies of the white city. "Are you still courting my father, Vere, or are you courting me now?"

He arched an eyebrow. "I might do both," he admitted, "if I thought I could ever mean half as much to you as your peregrine does. But what man on this earth could hope to compete with the prince who brought you back to life?"

The honest reply, so blunt that it could have come only from a serpent, diminished my useless anger. I just shook my head. "I don't dance anymore." I rubbed my hands over my arms, smoothing away goose bumps. "Please, just . . . understand."

"It's hard to understand when you refuse to explain."

*Serpents!* Only they would insist on dragging such pain back into reality, on rehashing and sharing such vile histories.

He waited, until I found words that could answer him. "The ancient dances were meant to weave magic. I can't control my power even when I do not call upon it; if I try to dance, I don't know what will happen."

"There's more," he said softly, no doubt reading the deeper fear in my eyes.

"Another day, viper."

He sighed. "As you wish . . . cobra."

I winced as I turned away.

Better to forget.

# CHAPTER 7

In desperate need of comfort but not wanting to bother Nicias, I traveled to a still pool deeper in the forest. To detach myself from the chaos of this reality, I immersed myself in the cold water. I swam deeper, until my lungs burned and my heart raced, and then finally those physical pains faded as my magic replaced breath and blood.

I reached for the city of Ahnmik.

My two mothers—Darien, who had borne me, and Cjarsa, who had raised me—were almost always together and were almost always fighting. Few people had the power or the courage to argue with the Empress Cjarsa, but Darien was one of those rare souls who did.

I did not mean to intrude on their conversation that day, but I had carelessly reached too far. Cjarsa and Darien ceased talking and shifted their attention to me.

"Hai?" my mother said.

The instant Darien spoke my name, Cjarsa turned away,

assuming that I was not seeking her. Losing that brief moment of attention from my Empress was like having all sunlight disappear. I knew that Darien sensed my reaction; I felt her disappointment through the magic that connected us in that moment.

What did she expect from me, the daughter she had abandoned?

If my devotion had been focused on anyone but Cjarsa, would Darien have cared at all? Or was this just another excuse for her war with my Empress? Darien said she wanted to change the island; like Maya, she had lofty ideas, many of which I might have agreed with if I had believed her stated motives. However, as far as I could tell, what motivated my mother was not the desire for equality and freedom of which she spoke but stubborn spite.

I often wondered: If it had truly been love for my father that had driven her to commit treason, wouldn't she have been more concerned about that man's child?

"If you hate the white city and everything it stands for as much as you say you do," I asked my mother bitterly, "if you hate the Lady and her heir and Ahnmik, why do you stay there?"

*Why do you stay in that land, that land I have always wanted . . . that land I will never have because I was born with a cobra's blood? Why do you struggle in a place you hate, struggle and fight, when nothing will ever change? Why?*

*Why could you never just be a mother to your daughter?*

"Because . . ." Darien tried to explain. Did she herself understand it? Or was this fight just something she had started one day and now couldn't find her way out of? "I love it as much as I hate it."

"I have always only loved it."

"I would give it to you if I knew how. I *am* trying, Hai. I want to change things. As long as I stay here, I have the Empress's ear. I can make things better. Maybe someday you will feel welcome in the city and will come home."

"You don't do this for me."

"I do it for you, and for the Cobriana, and Wyvern's Court, and all the thousands who died in Cjarsa's war. I cannot give you the white city, but I am doing all I can to protect the world you have. You know that Araceli would see Wyvern's Court destroyed if our Empress let her."

*"Our" Empress.* Only when it suited her purposes.

Still . . .

*The child Alasdair's scream.*

*Blood on the hawk child's hands.*

*Blood on my own.*

"And Oliza's abdication?" I asked. "Did you know of that?"

"The wyvern's magic disrupts my *sakkri*," Darien replied. "I have trouble seeing what she will do. Her abdication was as much a shock to me as it was to you. It certainly was not something I had planned."

"What about Araceli? Or Cjarsa?"

"Neither of them had a hand in it. I have enough power here to keep them from meddling . . . mostly." My mother hesitated. "Did they speak to you?" she asked, no doubt questioning my loyalty, as Oliza did.

"Of course," I replied. Let her take from that what she would; I owed this woman no answers. There was only one reason I wished to have her as an ally. "Regardless, my concern isn't for Oliza. I'm worried about Nicias, now that he isn't bound to her. You helped him leave the island once—"

I broke off, suddenly realizing that Darien was not on my side. She had helped Nicias leave the island, yes, but she had always wanted him beside her on Ahnmik.

"If you take Nicias from here . . ." There was no threat that would matter to my mother. I would never forgive her, but since when had she cared?

"Don't you see?" Darien argued. "Nicias has no place in Wyvern's Court—not now—and he could do so much good here. Araceli would listen to Nicias, because she wants her son's favor, and as prince, he would have power I can never dream of."

"My Empress," I said, petitioning for Cjarsa's attention. "Please, leave Nicias alone."

"It is not my will that would bring Nicias here," Cjarsa replied. "I have denied both Darien and Araceli permission to interfere with him. However, if he comes home of his own free will, I cannot refuse him his place."

"There is no free will. Not on Ahnmik."

"I will not take him from you," my Empress assured me. It was a cold comfort, and she knew it; she probably would not need to. "Be strong, *quemak'nesera*," she bid me, the words a dismissal.

My mother said nothing as I severed the magic between us so abruptly that I fell into the sound of Nicias's screams.


*Oliza's child, Keyi, was laughing, her red-blond hair rippling around her cherubic face. Her eyes were bright and as golden as a hawk's, but her eyelashes were pitch-black, an eerie contrast to her otherwise fair features. Her hands and arms were stained by twisting indigo magic that contorted and heaved across her flesh, but the child paid it no mind.*

*Keyi laughed. She was too young to understand ruin.*

*Sive Shardae wore not a mark upon her skin, but she was as still and silent as all Brysh's realm as Araceli lifted Aleya into her arms.*

*Sive's baby began to wail.*

*"You can't take Aleya!"*

*Keyi giggled as Nicias protested and struggled to reclaim the only surviving heir to the Tuuli Thea. The falcons had taken Salem's son Zenle; they couldn't take Aleya.*

*Araceli's Mercy held Nicias back, two of them gripping each of his arms.*

*Araceli held the baby as gently as porcelain, looking sadly into its frightened eyes. "I will return her to the avian throne when the time comes," she assured Nicias. "Be grateful . . . my grandson . . . that I do not have the heart to slay my own blood." She dropped her gaze to Keyi, who had begun to hum a little song. "Care for that one, if you wish. I will leave to you the decision of when she must be given back to Brysh."*

*"No," he pleaded.*

*Araceli turned with Aleya in her arms, and again Nicias shrieked, tearing into the guards holding him physically and magically. They knocked him to his knees as black-red slices of power rent his skin, leaving him shuddering on the ground. He could only watch as the falcons carried the little child away.*

*All of Nicias's monarchs were gone. Aleya and Zenle, taken. Oliza, Salem, Sive, Zane, Danica, Irene . . . The faces of the dead marched through his pained memory.*

*Keyi still laughed, though her hands—those tiny pink hands—were stained with the blood of thousands. She giggled, reaching for things only she could see: birds and butterflies, faeries and nymphs, raindrops, snowflakes, anything but the steel-hard sky, bleached as white as bone.*

I dragged myself from the vision, choking on screams as I struggled back to shore.

*Don't cry, my love; you do all you can.* I wept as I lay on the beach, too exhausted to move. *I'll do what I can, for you.*

Someone nudged my shoulder, roughly checking for life, and my body shuddered and began coughing up water, seeking air instead of raw power to sustain us.

Velyo Frektane looked at me with distaste. One of the two competing alpha wolves in the area, Velyo despised weakness. Nearly drowning in still water probably did not strike him as strong.

"I've heard that falcons can do that—just stop moving, eating, drinking," he remarked. "But I didn't know they could stop breathing."

"Breath belongs to *Mehay*," I replied, drawing in the air nonetheless. I could sustain myself for years on nothing but Ahnmik's power, as I had in the Halls of *shm'Ecl* before Nicias had taken me from there, but if I wanted to escape from that last vision, I needed to ground myself back to the world. "Ecl has no use for it."

The wolf let out a disdainful snort. "Well, sorry to interrupt your melodramatic expiration, but I thought Wyvern's Court might object to a dead cobra in our woods."

I would be shocked if they noticed.

But I accepted the wolf's help as I stood. When I touched his hand, I tried to ignore the images that it conjured. Oliza and her mate had each crossed paths with Velyo in the past.

"Do you need assistance back to Wyvern's Court?"

"I can make it."

He watched me skeptically as I wrung water from my hair; surely I looked less than capable to him, with my hair and clothes still dripping and my hands and arms streaked with dirt from my lying on the ground.

I was content not to earn the high regard of Velyo Frektane. He was a man who was used to power and getting his way even if it meant abusing those beneath him. I was too much a falcon to tolerate intimidation by or force from a wolf and—though I cringed to think it—too much a serpent to forgive the crimes he had committed in his past. After I'd chosen to ignore Araceli's hinted requests that I begin a war in Wyvern's Court shortly after I first woke here, it would have been a pity to start one accidentally by killing a wolf king.

So I walked away, not upset to hear the wolf scoff as I made a halfhearted attempt to brush mud from my skin and clothes.

Wondering if I would have to walk back to Wyvern's Court, I called silently for Najat and was pleased to find that the horse was not too far away in the woods. She came to me, and I climbed into the saddle and closed my eyes to rest as we returned slowly to Wyvern's Court. Najat knew the way home, far better than I.

# CHAPTER 8

The ride to Wyvern's Court seemed unnaturally long as I fought fatigue. I intended to tell Nicias that I had seen Oliza, and then I hoped to curl up somewhere to sleep.

I jumped as the peregrine dove through the treetops and returned to human form barely a breath from Najat's side. I expected Nicias to inquire immediately about Oliza, but his first words were "Are you all right?"

I nodded, pleasantly surprised by the query. "I spoke to Oliza. She and Betia are safe with friends who would never let welcome guests be hurt on their land. Oliza asked me to thank you for your concern and assure you that she would be fine."

Nicias reached out as I spoke, and brushed a streak of dirt from my cheek. The brief touch made my skin tingle.

"Thank you for going; it's good to know she is well. Are you *sure* you're all right?" I must have looked puzzled, because he added, "I don't know exactly what happened to you earlier, but I felt enough to worry."

"I didn't mean to trouble you. I know you have more to worry about than me," I said.

He winced. "I'm sorry."

"It wasn't a criticism."

"I know you didn't mean it to be, but I *do* feel responsible for you, and I feel like I've neglected—"

I held up a hand to stop him, before he could go further. "Nicias, I am an adult woman. Not a child. You pulled me from Ecl, and I—at least sometimes—thank you for that, but have you forgotten that I came back to save *your* life? You aren't my caretaker. And I don't want to be your ward."

I took a step back, horrified by what I had just said. Every heated word was true; of all the things I wished I could be to the peregrine, child was not one of them.

But to speak that way to Nicias . . .

When I forced myself to look up at him again, he was regarding me in a way I couldn't quite interpret. "You're right," he said after a few moments. "You're a long way from being helpless. I know that. But I can still care about you, even if you don't need me to."

"I . . ." I didn't know how to respond to that. I tried, haltingly, to explain. "The visions have been more difficult to control of late. There is too much going on. People are making decisions, *major* decisions, and every time they do . . ." I shuddered. "It's hard."

"Because of Oliza's abdication."

I nodded.

"What have you seen?" Nicias asked.

I shook my head. "Nothing specific enough that you could guard against it; I shouldn't even have mentioned it without knowing more."

Nicias looked at me as if he was trying to read my mind. If he did try, he might succeed, but the peregrine was a gentleman, and his own morals kept his magic from violating the privacy of my thoughts.

I reached forward and touched his arm.

"You should rest," I said, feeling the exhaustion in his limbs and realizing that he had been awake not just one night but many. "Your body hasn't learned yet how to go so long without sleep."

Nicias nodded, and I felt him sway slightly as if accepting for the first time how tired he was.

*You can invite me to join you,* I called mentally. *I wouldn't say no. I would carry you to sweet sleep . . . and perhaps I could find the same in your arms, unhaunted by Ecl.*

Nicias pulled away as he nodded again.

"You're right. I'm no good to anyone in this shape, least of all my . . . king."

I knew he had wanted to say *my queen.*

"Sweet dreams," I bid. Silently, I added, *Sweet dreams, my light, my heart.*

Once he had left, I did not know where to go. One of my father's traits had bred true; like a serpent, I did not do well with silent solitude. If I closed my eyes now, I knew I would see Keyi again. The child frightened me more than anything else in this world could.

I chose the candle shop on the northern hills.

Opal greeted me in the back room with a scowl, but the falcon didn't ask questions as I approached him; he never did. We didn't speak as he wrapped his arms around my waist, savoring the flavor of my magic and the scent of my skin.

It was a false comfort, an illusion, like so much of

Ahnmik's domain, but for now, being in someone's arms as I closed my eyes was enough. For a handful of hours, I slept deeply.

But then, again . . .

*Salem Cobriana, Diente, lay in my arms, dying. His body was cold; his red eyes had turned a tawny brown; his heartbeat raced, pushing the poison faster, deeper, while his lungs fought paralysis. I could barely feel him, his life, anymore. Slipping away.*

*I knew I could save him; I had that power, always had. I could use my magic to heal the tissues, destroy the poison . . . but terror gripped me. I could ask the magic for that much, and she would grant the favor, but she would ask even more in return. I could swim her dark, still waters, but I would drown. I shrieked for help, but none came.*

*None ever had; none ever would.*

*I covered Salem with my body, wishing I could give him my warmth, but did not reach out to him with the greedy magic that could save his life. I couldn't. Please . . .*

*Too late, Nicias reached his fallen monarch's side. He did what I would not, reaching out with his magic, but the attempt was clumsy. He had never had this type of training . . . and it was too late, anyway.*

*I felt Salem die, felt the last spark go out as Brysh claimed her own.*

I woke alone, despite having drifted into sleep in Opal's arms. He had not left long before—the bed was still warm where his body had lain—but it was long enough for that grisly vision of Salem to seep back into my mind.

It had changed. The cobra died of poison now, instead of at the hands of an angry mob.

The end result remained the same.

It was possible that Salem's death called to me so strongly simply because he was a cobra, as my father had been, but I feared there was more to it. To have such a vivid vision twice implied that it was more than a vague, far-off possibility. Fate, or more likely a conspirator, was actively working toward this future.

Fighting Fate was a pursuit for far stronger souls than mine.

The candle shop was quiet as I stepped into the front room. Opal, his hair still tousled from bed, glanced at me but did not even bother to say good morning. Gren and Spark were absent, probably tending their booth in the market, but Maya was there, keeping the fire hot and the tallow soft as she worked.

"I suppose you know that Salem Cobriana takes the throne tonight," Maya said, making it clear that she had not forgotten our argument.

Neither had I. "Gods and Fate willing, he will."

Maya scoffed. "Hai, you—"

"I could never become Diente with Salem Cobriana alive," I said bluntly. If Fate had destined that Salem Cobriana die, there was nothing I could do, but I would not let Wyvern's Court—Nicias's home, *my* home now—fall because this traitor had delusions of a bright new world. "If he falls and I suspect that you had a hand in it, my first order as queen will be to execute the four of you for treason."

In the frozen silence that followed my words, I picked up a small knife that Maya had been using to trim the wicks for her next batch of candles. As she watched with wide eyes, I drew the blade across the back of my hand, not wincing as I cut Ahnmik's symbol into my skin.

"This I swear by blood and blade and flame," I whispered. "To the god Ahnmik who holds all vows true. If Salem Cobriana falls, those responsible will know my wrath."

With a flick of my wrist, I let the droplets of blood that had gathered on my skin splash into the fire. Maya and Opal both recoiled as the flames turned indigo for an instant before collapsing again. As Maya had said, *they* were both *kajaes; they* had no power.

I was not as harmless.

"Do you hear me, Maya?"

She nodded mutely, her gaze locked on the wound on my hand, and the drops of blood there.

"And you will make my will clear to the others?"

"Yes," she whispered.

I wiped the knife on my arm, leaving a streak of blood there as I cleaned the blade. I had done what I could. Without another word, I stepped out of the house, with no plans ever to return.

# CHAPTER 9

I watched from the hillside as the people of Wyvern's Court prepared for Salem's coronation. From dawn to dusk, the air reeked of tension, fear, hope and despair, and the sweat of desperate excitement. I knew that the people felt abandoned by Oliza, and though they loved the cobra prince, they had been hurt badly enough that there was an edge of wariness in their jubilation as they gathered in the market square to witness the young dancer's rise to king.

By evening, all the members of both royal families were in attendance, with the exception of Oliza, and Salem's still missing mother. Danica Shardae and Zane Cobriana were standing just in front of the dais; Oliza's mother would still be queen of the avians after this night, but her father would have to relinquish his title. Nacola, once queen, and Sive Shardae, future heir to the avian throne, stood beside them. There was no need for the avian royal house to witness the serpiente succession, but their presence clearly showed

Shardae support for the Cobriana and hope for the continued alliance of Wyvern's Court.

I made my way down to the market square but refrained from approaching the royal family. They made no effort to seek me out. When Sive noticed me in the crowd, she smiled politely but edged closer to her alistair.

"Milady," Arqueete called out just then. The serpiente normally sold pastries in the early morning, but she was doing a brisk business in the ever growing crowd. "You haven't eaten today, have you?" she asked, looking me over.

When *had* I last eaten?

"It has been a while," I admitted.

"You need to take better care of yourself," she said. "I set aside some of those honey cakes I know you fancy, in case you came by. The dancer's nest is giving Salem and his mate an ornate formal ceremony, and it won't start until full dark. You have a few minutes yet to fortify yourself."

"The wolves are here," I observed, trying to distract the well-meaning but aggressive merchant. My appetite would return eventually, when the magic had calmed. Until then, trying to force food down my gullet would only bring it back up again.

"I know Kalisa Vahamil, but not the other one," Arqueete replied. "Are they mates?"

"Frektane and Vahamil are enemies," I said, already turning my attention to the white-haired man at the very edge of the market. The Obsidian guild had sent representatives here, too. Though they refused to be ruled by the Cobriana, the guild had not survived for as long as they had by being disinterested. They would know about everything that occurred that night.

As true dusk fell, dancers clad in elaborate silver and black *melos*, the traditional colors of the Cobriana royal house, went about lighting torches, until the market was as bright as at noontime. When finally the prince emerged with his queen-to-be, Rosalind, the image took my breath away. The next Diente and Naga made a beautiful pair. A ripple of appreciation ran through the crowd.

Then the peaceful moment was broken. Rosalind began to weep. And Salem—

*No.* That wasn't now. Salem was fine. Would be fine.

*Had* to be fine.

I was less interested in the elaborate ceremony than I was in the reactions of those watching it. Most serpents were enraptured by the royal pair, but more than a few exchanged concerned or outright skeptical glances. Were some of them beyond worried? Which ones might have treason on their minds?

Despite my cynical thoughts and the anxiety in the audience, when Salem kissed his mate, a tender sigh passed through the crowd. Couples among the serpiente moved closer together. Zane and Danica leaned against each other. I even saw Sive tentatively reach a hand toward her reserved alistair, though when her fingers brushed Prentice's, he looked startled and uncomfortable. She blushed and withdrew the attempted contact.

My eyes sought Nicias. He had positioned himself higher on the hills so he could see everything going on, and I was startled to find him looking toward me. He offered a tired half smile, and then his gaze moved on, scanning the crowd the same way mine had been.

I turned, and—

*   *   *

*The door opened and Nicias entered, his face nearly gray with exhaustion.*

*"Oh, fates . . . what has happened?" Oliza gasped, pulling away from Betia as she saw the pained expression of her former guard and always friend.*

I shuddered, pulling back from the vision at first—and then intentionally trying to move toward it. I needed to see what caused this future.

*Oliza stumbled back, caught by her mate. "No," she whispered.*

*"Sive and Danica are working to keep . . ." Nicias looked away. "Oliza . . . they need you."*

*Her eyes brimmed with tears as she realized the consequences of this horror. "I . . . I will speak to . . ." She turned to kiss Betia goodbye, her voice choked up as she whispered, "My love."*

*And then there was only fire.*

I was startled back from the vision when someone in the real world came to my side.

"It seems like you would have learned by now to be careful," I said as Vere Obsidian touched my arm. He was dressed as the dancers were, also wearing a black cloak embroidered with silver, which hid his white-viper features from the casual eye.

"I am always careful," he replied, "but being careful sometimes involves taking risks. I can see in your eyes when you start to drift away, and I can feel your magic waver when you are upset. What horrors do you see when you look at the new king?"

"Is Salem king already?"

The white viper nodded. "You must have lost quite a bit of time there. What was it you were seeing instead?"

"Why does it matter to you?"

He seemed to consider my words carefully. "Throughout history, the Cobriana have alternated between offering my people an olive branch and offering them a noose. I don't know this cobra. It worries me that when you look at him I can almost smell the blood."

"It isn't yours," I said.

"You've seen his reign?"

I shook my head. I had seen Oliza's reign, even though it had always ended in ice or fire. I had seen Sive's reign. The cobra had just been crowned king, and still, I could not see him rule.

"You mean for once the future is as much a mystery to you as to us mere mortals?" Vere joked.

"I—" Salem and his mate were moving toward us, through the crowd. "Do you care to introduce yourself to the current monarchy?"

The white viper hesitated for just a moment but then shook his head. "Not just yet. Take care of yourself, Hai." He squeezed my shoulder but was gone from my side before the Diente and his queen reached me.

"Hai, thank you for attending," Salem said, with what looked like a genuine smile.

The warm regard from the cobra unnerved me. I could only nod. "It seemed appropriate."

"Have you been introduced to Rosalind?"

"No, we haven't—" Halfway through offering my hand, I recoiled. For just a moment, I could almost taste the viper's tears. "I'm sorry. I . . ."

The dancer-queen, instead of looking insulted, looked relieved not to have to shake my hand.

Salem frowned. "Are you all right?"

Fortunately, before I had to answer, Sive found us in the crowd. "I'm sorry to interrupt," she said, touching Salem's wrist. "I was hoping I could get some advice." The hawk dropped her gaze, her expression more carefully controlled than she usually kept it around serpents.

"It's fine," I said, half curtsying, a habit from another world, as I excused myself.

Salem and Rosalind shrugged before turning their attention to Sive. I would always be a falcon to them. They didn't trouble themselves to worry about me.

# CHAPTER 10

I retreated to the hills where Nicias sat, his attention on the celebration.

"Are you all right?" Nicias asked as I sat beside him. "I saw you talking to Salem and Rosalind. You looked upset."

"Did I?" I asked. I couldn't remember the last time I had *looked* upset, even when I had felt it. I glanced back at the celebration now, where Rosalind was dancing with one of her nestmates, and Salem and Sive were having what appeared to be an intense conversation. Salem leaned close to whisper something to her, and she blushed so deeply I could see her cheeks redden from where we were.

At the same moment, Nicias exclaimed, "You're hurt!"

I tried to hide my hand from him, but he caught my wrist. "It's nothing; I cut myself." I could not lie to him, *would* not, and so I did not want him to ask about it.

"I can tell that." His voice sounded distant. "It looks like it stopped bleeding a while ago. The lines are almost gone. What happened, Hai?"

"I would rather not answer that," I said, more curtly than I meant to.

Nicias closed his eyes for a moment, taking a deep breath before he answered, "I won't force you to." Still, he did not release my hand. I could feel the soft hum of his magic like a summer breeze. It sent a shiver through me that had nothing to do with the weather.

"Salem," I began. "It was—stupid," I said, changing my mind about telling Nicias what had happened in Gren's house. None of those falcons would harm Salem, knowing what I would do. My gaze returned to the new serpiente king, who was dancing with his mate. Sive seemed to be trying to cajole Prentice into doing the same.

"I see the way you look at him," Nicias said. "I assumed he was related to your recent distress. I don't have nearly your control over *sakkri,* but I can almost see your visions when I reach for you," he said. "They troubled me enough that I spoke to Salem. I would like to assign extra guards to him, but he is very much a cobra. He is confident in his followers' loyalty and, like most of his line, believes a show of force will only breed trouble." He sighed heavily. "And, if I understand *sakkri,* it is entirely possible that he is correct and will be perfectly safe until we overreact and put him in danger. Unless you have seen any details . . ."

I shook my head, my eyes still on the crowd. "I have seen his death, but that is all I see, not what leads to it." Normally I would say that Nicias was right. Many futures that had been nearly impossible happened purely because of meddling that would not have occurred if there had been no prophecy. This, though, felt stronger. Softly, I added, "I've never considered myself loyal to the Cobriana, but I am not a traitor to them, either. If I knew how to protect him, I . . ." All my attention suddenly turned to Sive Shardae, who had just given up on trying to get Prentice to dance and wrapped her arms around his neck and kissed him.

"Hai?"

I turned back to Nicias, intending to reassure him that my moment of distraction had nothing to do with insincerity when a shout pierced the air.

*"Then leave me alone!"*

Nicias sprang to his feet, searching the crowd for the source, which I had already located. Sive had just shoved Prentice away and was glaring at him. Before I could try to convince Nicias that our presence wasn't needed at a lovers' quarrel, he started hurrying toward the argument. I followed, though it quickly became obvious even to Nicias that the cry had been born more of frustration than of fear.

Prentice moved after his pair bond, protesting. "Sive, please, I didn't mean—"

"Didn't mean *what*?" Sive demanded. "To insult me, slander me, and my family, and my loved ones, all at the same time?"

Prentice cringed. "I spoke poorly. You know that's not—"

"Maybe it isn't what you meant to *say*, but it is what you *meant*," she argued. "Or maybe you would like to give some more specific details about how I'm acting 'like a dancer'?"

"Can we please discuss this somewhere else?" he begged, stepping toward her and dropping his voice—as if it would matter when everyone around them had gone dead silent. It wasn't every day that one had a chance to see a hawk in hysterics.

"Somewhere else?" Sive cooed. "Somewhere *private*? Are

you sure it would be seemly for us to be alone together—especially given all the lewd *serpiente* *habits* I seem to have picked up? People might *talk*."

I had seen criminals in front of the Empress's mercy, yet in all my life, I had never seen a man's face turn so gray.

"That . . . isn't . . ."

Salem finally stepped forward. He touched his cousin's arm, making her jump. "I'm sorry; this is my fault. Sive asked me—"

"*Your* fault?" Prentice growled, his voice dropping. "I suggest you stay out of this, snake. You've had your hands all over her all night, and I've had to stand by and listen to people tell me that's 'just how serpents behave.' Maybe it's—"

"Sive isn't a child!" Salem shouted. "She is a woman, and she knows what she wants, so maybe—oh, never mind." He shook his head. "Sive, I'm sorry."

"Go away, Prentice," Sive whispered. "Please, just . . . just go away."

The raven hesitated, and anyone could see true anguish in his expression. Finally Prentice bowed his head. "As milady wishes."

He changed form and disappeared into the sky. Sive turned and leaned against Salem for a moment.

"Let's get you somewhere private," Salem said softly. Then he turned to the crowd with a fiery glare, daring the nearest fool to look him in the eye. "There's nothing to see. *Go.* There's nothing worth watching here. Leave her alone." Serpents turned away, not eager to incur the wrath of their new king by harassing the distraught hawk.

Nicias and I did as Salem wished, too, walking away from

the chaos. This was a private matter, not one for guards, and clearly not one for me.

"What was that about?" Nicias asked.

"I suspect it was about Sive trying very hard to catch some less-than-brotherly attention from her alistair," I said, recalling the moment earlier when Sive had reached for Prentice's hand. "Perhaps following advice she had received from Salem."

Nicias arched an eyebrow. "Considering the outrageous behavior serpiente consider casual, friendly contact, I'm certain I don't want to know what advice a serpiente dancer would give a woman regarding how to entice her mate."

"What advice would you have given her?" I wondered aloud.

Nicias, avian-raised gentleman that he was, blushed. "That's not the kind of conversation I am likely to have with the heir to the Tuuli Thea."

"Which is probably why Sive went to a serpent. What avian would have answered her question?"

Nicias jumped, and only then did I realize that I had been reaching for him. "I'm going to try to speak to Salem about security again, if I can get a private moment with him," he said, obviously trying to change the topic. "You should rest, if you can. I know how tired you are."

When Nicias said he knew, he meant it. He must have felt my weakness the moment he had touched my hand earlier.

Instead of pulling back, I moved closer, made brazen by his concern and the passion of serpents still celebrating in the marketplace. I brushed my lips over his soft skin. "Come with me?"

Nicias hesitated, then shook his head. "I have—"

"A duty, I know," I said. "I will still be here when you've done it."

He put his hands on my shoulders, using just enough force to put me back at arm's length. "If I really thought you wanted companionship, I would give it to you," he said softly. "If I thought that you felt any form of desire for me, even if that was all, I would consider staying. But I've seen the way you go to men like Opal to hide from your pain. I've seen the way you treat him, and the way you let him treat you. I won't be another man you use to help you find oblivion. I'm sorry."

I crumpled as he turned away, and dropped my head in my hands.

*It isn't like that with you*, I argued. *It was never like that with you . . . if only you would listen, if only you would see . . .* But Nicias had blocked me from his mind and did not hear my pleas.

I collapsed on the soft grass of the northern hills and watched him go to the new Diente's side. Nicias and Salem spoke at length, and then Salem's Naga pulled Nicias into the crowd, entreating him to dance.

I closed my eyes.

Nicias had a duty. It would be easier to turn the Mercy from the Empress than it would be to turn Nicias from his damned *duty*.

# CHAPTER 11

After Nicias left, I lay on the cool grass and closed my eyes, listening to the celebration from afar. Despite the serpents' swirled, half-formed magic, my mind remained oddly free of the violent visions that had plagued me for the past forty-eight hours.

Whatever was to be done, I knew, was done. One way or another, the decision that would either accept Salem as king or kill him had been made, and now I could hear the serpiente celebrating. Rosalind and her mate had withdrawn to a secluded den, but the king's people danced until dawn, when avian merchants began to emerge from their homes, determined not to be chased away by serpent festivities.

Perhaps, I thought, the world had shifted enough that this cobra was once again guarded by Ahnleh's grace. Maybe my conversation with Nicias, and his with Salem, had been enough to save him. That hope almost made me forget what a fool I'd been with Nicias and the way he had looked walking away from me.

Hope finally brought with it hunger. Ravenous, I descended into the market. There I found Arqueete, who was far too happy to give me breakfast when I admitted to my appetite.

"She looked so pale, though, when she left," I heard an avian man say as he passed me.

The person he had been speaking to answered, "It just doesn't seem . . ."

The conversation drifted out of my hearing range, but the merchant filled me in on their gossip. "Sive stayed for much of the celebration last night," Arqueete explained. "Apparently she looked upset when she went home."

I could imagine she had, after the fight with Prentice.

"She is all right, I assume?" I asked, vaguely aware that a couple of avian women were standing near us, listening.

Arqueete shrugged. "I haven't seen her since last night. She was pale, a little shaky, but she seemed to have calmed down from that argument."

Pale and shaky, a hawk? The serpent described her condition in an unconcerned tone, but anyone who had spent time with avians knew how much it took for them to become visibly upset. Then again, it took a lot to make one start screaming in the marketplace, too.

Another serpent, the flautist Salokin, approached the stall, drawn by our conversation. "I understand Sive's being upset. She just about threw herself at Prentice—an action I applaud, though her taste is questionable—and his response was less than enthusiastic. You should have heard what he said to her!" Salokin shook his head. "She'll be fine, though. A pretty girl like that isn't going to have any trouble finding someone else."

"True," the merchant answered. "Though, as for her *taste* . . ." She smirked. "Nah."

The avian women nearby were discussing the event, too, and I moved slightly toward them to hear better. "I just hope no serpent took liberties with her," one said. "I mean, she *is* still young, and very innocent, and even I know that serpiente have very different ideas of what's appropriate. I just hope no one took advantage of her."

"I think it would be good for her," Salokin commented, apparently also having eavesdropped on the women's conversation. "She's not ten; she's sixteen. A little fling never did a pretty girl harm."

Scandalized, the avian woman returned, "It does plenty of harm, especially when a lady has a very valiant alistair!"

"Valiant? Prentice?" another serpent scoffed. "On the most romantic night of the year, she has the audacity to try to *kiss* her *mate*—oh, the scandal!—and he puts her down like a child and tells her she's acting 'like a common serpiente whore.' "

"He did not!" one of the avians exclaimed.

"Oh, I'm sure those weren't his exact words," Arquecte interjected. "Even if the bird *knew* words like that, he would sooner die than speak them around a lady. Though that was pretty much the gist of it."

"You missed their earlier argument about Salem," Salokin said. "The Diente had just sworn to his mate, and Prentice was standing there telling Sive to stop flirting with her *cousin*."

"Only by marriage," Arqueete added under her breath.

"You have to admit, they do flirt," one of the avian ladies

said softly. "If she was my daughter, I would have called her to task over it."

"He's a serpent, and a dancer," one of the other avians said proudly, with her head held high. "Everyone knows that their form of friendly is simply forward. It doesn't mean anything."

As one of the two avian women cried, "Impossible!" I realized we had gathered quite a crowd.

"Stop this, stop it," another serpent said, breaking into the conversation. "Salem might not mind dancers gossiping about his affairs, but obviously Sive has been discreet on her side of the court."

Arqueete wasn't quite ready to change the subject. Speculating, she said, not nearly softly enough, "No wonder the hawk was feeling desperate—Salem's a mated man now."

"*Drop it,*" the third serpent snapped as one of the avian women gasped at the implication. "*He* has a mate and *she* has an alistair, and I'm sure neither Rosalind nor Prentice wants to know that Sive and Salem were together last night for some kind of . . ." He looked up and, realizing his words were reaching more people than he had intended them to, fell silent.

Worried, I looked at the surrounding faces, but even those who looked shocked also appeared slightly amused. There must have been enough serpiente influence on the avians of Wyvern's Court that they could feel scandalized without calling for blood. How progressive; Oliza would have been thrilled.

Then Salokin seemed to recall how the conversation had begun. "A woman isn't usually that upset after spending hours with her lover, and if she *was* involved with Salem, a little insult from a flustered raven like Prentice isn't likely to ruin her night."

Salokin's words caused an instant reaction, especially from the half dozen serpents who had come to Arqueete's stall now that the afternoon had begun.

"I hope you aren't implying—"

"I'm not implying anything," Salokin squeaked.

One of the avian women cleared her throat. "I think the discussion is over."

"I think someone should tell Prentice," the other avian woman remarked. "He'll forgive her, naturally."

"I'm sure he already knows," the first woman said.

My blood ran cold then, as suddenly I understood.

*Nicias!* I called out to him with all my magic and felt him respond.

I was immersed in another vision—only this time I knew I was witnessing the present, not some uncertain future.

*Prentice was furious. He had seen how pale his pair bond had looked when she'd finally returned home from Salem's coronation. She had refused to continue their earlier argument and had claimed that her pallor was from fatigue, that she had hardly slept since Oliza had made the announcement and the late-night festivities had been too much for her.*

*Then, the next morning, he had heard the rumors.*

*His heart was pounding with rage, but his face was composed as he stepped past the guards who were watching the serpent's door.*

*"I need to speak to Salem," he said.*

*Prentice sounded calm, and they knew he was Sive's alistair. They probably assumed he was carrying some message from her. One of them knocked on Salem's door.*

*The cobra was still sleeping, probably in the arms of his mate, but Prentice insisted that it was an emergency—that he needed to speak to Salem quickly, before it got later.*

"What is going on here?" Nicias demanded, in my real world.

I gasped, trying to move toward him. He had obviously landed just outside the crowd, which had become nastier in the moments I had been away from it.

"Nicias! You're one of Salem's guards now; you should deal with this," a serpiente merchant pleaded. "Sive was upset last night. Everyone knows that Salem has been flirting with her for months. They were alone together for part of last night—and this . . ." He spat a curse. "This pathetic excuse for a serpent dared suggest your king might have . . ." He struggled for words. "That she . . ."

"She was too upset to have spent those hours enjoying herself," someone said, an anonymous voice in a venomous crowd.

"Nicias," I shouted, trying to draw his attention to me.

*"I need to speak to you alone," Prentice insisted when Salem came to the door. "Without your Naga, please?"*

*Salem frowned, noticing the chill in Prentice's voice and assuming something was wrong. "Yes, of course. Rosalind, would you mind giving us a moment?"*

*The woman, who looked as if she had tugged on clothing as Prentice had waited at the door, gave Salem a playful smile. "I suppose." She kissed her mate on the cheek as she left. "I'll meet you in the nest, whenever you're free."*

Nicias's voice was cold as he demanded, "You're a serpent. Of all people, you know how serious a crime you are accusing Salem of. What proof do you have?"

"What proof do we need?" Salokin replied. "I saw the look on her face—"

"*I* saw no distress, only fatigue," Nicias said. "I heard her tell her alistair she was fine when she met back up with him. I saw nothing that would found this foul a rumor."

"Salem's a cobra," someone else said softly. "You're one of his guards. Of course you're going to be loyal to him."

"I'm loyal enough not to accuse the Diente, who last night was beyond any suspicion, of raping the heir to the Tuuli Thea."

"Nicias!" I shouted, and this time he turned to me. "They don't matter," I said quickly. "Prentice has already heard. He—"

Nicias had shifted shape and torn into the skies before I could explain that Salem was no longer in his room and Prentice was no longer in his; both were in a secluded spot.

Shoving people out of my way, I raced up the hills, my lungs burning and my heart longing for wings. I stumbled at the edge of the forest as Prentice drew his blade.

Salem dodged the first attack, shouting, "What is—" He rolled to avoid another attack. I could tell he didn't want to engage in the fight because he didn't want to harm his opponent.

I reached their side and struggled against visions as I dove at Prentice, bearing him to the ground. Again I shouted to Nicias, telling him where we were, and felt him back in the air, diving.

I threw Prentice away with strength I should not have had and ran to Salem's side. I had arrived in time to stop Prentice from landing a lethal blow, but there was a scratch across Salem's forearm that was already turning purple-black.

"No!"

Avian guards no longer used poison regularly, but Prentice had access to it. He had known he was up against a cobra.

Nicias landed and caught Prentice's wrists, but I was only barely aware. *A'she, she*—future, present—were blurring, blending, contorting and twisting—

Salem Cobriana lay in my arms, dying. His body was cold; his red eyes had turned a tawny brown; his heartbeat raced, pushing the poison faster, deeper, while his lungs fought paralysis. I could barely feel *him*, his life, anymore. Slipping away.

I knew I could save him; I had that power, always had. I could use my magic to heal the tissues and destroy the poison . . . but terror gripped me. I could ask the magic for that much, and she would grant the favor, but she would ask more than I wanted to give in return. I could swim her dark, still waters, but what if I drowned?

"Nicias!" I shrieked, even though I knew what the result would be. He had taken the time to immobilize Prentice, to guard our backs, and now it was too late for him to make any difference.

I covered Salem with my body, wishing I could give him my warmth, but did not reach out to him with the greedy magic that could save his life. I *couldn't*. Please . . .

I had fought so hard to stay in this world. Calling on my magic now could mean giving it all up and returning to the void darkness, where I would not even remember why I had fought at all.

Nicias reached his fallen monarch's side. He did what I would not, reaching out with his magic, but the attempt was clumsy. He had no training. . . .

*No.*

*Not this time.*

I knew where Salem's death led, and it was a darker path than Ecl.

I felt his life slip away, and I grabbed at it. He was trying to follow Brysh into the darkness of death. I bid goodbye to Wyvern's Court, and I dove after him.

# CHAPTER 12

*L*<sup></sup>*eben appeared to the Dasi, and they knelt in misguided worship.*

Maeve leaned against the creature, whispering in his ear with a smile, as Kiesha watched from the lonely darkness. The priestess of Anhamirak hid her tears.

Maeve wept as she was wrapped in the arms of the Nesera'rsh. She had done what she needed to protect her people, but she had lost . . . everything. Everything that mattered to her.
Without her, the balance ruptured, and the Dasi began to crumble.

Cjarsa, falcon priestess of Ahnmik, watched the first of her disciples fall to Ecl. Leben had given them wings, and he had given them madness. One was not worth the other.
This had to be stopped.

*   *   *

*Kiesha shrieked as magic that should have called rain for the crops brought lightning and deluge. She cradled a drowned infant in her arms. Her people were dying, and everything she did to try to help them only made it worse.*

*Araceli and Brassal, the priest of* Namid, *struggled; Araceli's daughter was caught in the middle, and at the end she was limp and cold. Brassal backed out of the room with his hands held in front of him; he stared at them as if they were alien growths instead of his own flesh.*

*The Dasi's altars were scorched, frozen, shattered–only ruin left behind–and their priests and priestesses struggled against the magic that cut their bodies and souls.*

*They cursed Maeve, who had enticed Leben into giving them these "gifts," the magic of their second forms. When people began to die, the new serpents blamed the falcons–those who worshipped death, sacrificed to it.*

*Magic and blades and fire and blood . . . so much blood, soaking the red sand.*

*"You say you wish to end this," Kiesha said, greeting the falcons.*

*"Before more lives are lost," Araceli said.*

*The hawk child Alasdair screamed as half of Kiesha's magic was shoved into her, and that scream echoed for generations: two thousand years of slaughter between the avians and the serpiente, which the falcons manufactured in an attempt to avoid the deaths of countless more.*

*Years later, the hawk child Danica screamed as Anjay tore his knife into her alistair's heart. A falcon mother screamed as that cobra was killed by another one of Alasdair's descendents.*

*I screamed as magic ripped into me and tore my wings away, and I fell from Ahnmik's skies.*

*Oliza screamed as the magic of her daughter, Keyi, destroyed her; and Nicias screamed as he fought the Mercy who had come to take Sive's daughter, Aleya, and Salem's son, Zenle, away—*

No!

That much I could stop.

The rest of these images were long gone, ash in the wind, but Keyi was still the future, and the future could be changed.

With one final shriek, I slammed into Salem's magic like a blade into water, gasping and choking as I forced myself deeper. The world swirled—violet, white, black, red. Distantly, I was aware that my body was somewhere.

I could hear my breath and my heartbeat slowing . . . slowing . . .

The shards of Anhamirak's magic in Salem were searing, and I felt them slice into my mind as I struggled to retain my focus. The poison—

There was a black cobra at the edge of my field of vision, but when I twisted to see, it was gone.

The poison. Falcons had created it; I needed to destroy it. I concentrated, and brought into view the places where Salem's undulating magic shuddered, the golden waves becoming black and charred.

The poison consisted of two parts. The primary ingredient was a toxin, which would cause little damage in the bodies of most shapeshifters; we healed too quickly for that.

However, there was a spell built into the poison, and I struggled to read it as it devoured even more of the magic that made Salem a serpent. The patterns kept shifting, melding themselves with the lines of that which they destroyed.

*So vulnerable*, I realized. The Cobriana had only half of the magic they had been created with; the other half had been used long before to form the avians. The falcons had cleverly fashioned the poison to meld with what remained of Anhamirak's power. Once it ate away at the magic that protected serpiente flesh, the base toxins could stop the heart and end the life.

I twisted about, wrapping that deadly magic around myself like spiderwebs. Strands ripped and shifted as I reached for them and altered the patterns to make the spell harmless.

I shoved the energy that made Salem's heart spasm into him. Again, again, again, until it beat on its own. I did the same for his lungs, making them rise and fall.

I surveyed the damage, and it was vast.

Left behind by the poison's onslaught was a battered, crippled remnant of the magic Salem should have had, *needed* to have. His body was performing the motions of life now, but his soul . . .

Was that lost?

I could force animation of Salem's body, but the poison had done so much damage that his mind and spirit had fled. I reached out as far as I could, trying to find him.

Again I saw a cobra at the edge of my vision, and I spun about, shouting, "Salem!"

Suddenly I slipped on a patch of black ice. On all fours, I scurried back as the ice began to crumble. Where—*Salem!* I screamed, but received no response.

Nothing.

Except a voice, an echo of the darkness I had once loved, whispering, *You have tried and failed, my love, my sweet. You have done all you can do, so rest now. Sweet failure grants no future decisions. It is over; let it be over.*

Ecl.

An icy breeze swirled through the illusion, and the skies darkened. Before me I could see a black castle, its dark and cold spires rising. Slipping, scrambling, I moved away from it, still reaching out with my magic. . . . I couldn't find anyone, anything, not even Nicias.

I had often wanted to return here since he had pulled me away, but I *couldn't*, not now.

*Why, my sweet? They do not need you. You have done all you can do and it was not enough. Rest.*

I crumbled, feeling the world go cold as the walls of my ancient black palace grew around me. I slammed my fists against them, and for a moment they rang like bells. Images of Wyvern's Court flashed in the darkness.

*People rioting and shouting. The serpiente screaming for blood, avians demanding justice, rumors rife, hatred stirred.* I recoiled without meaning to.

Then the sounds faded. Again I struck the black walls, but this time there was silence.

A falcon circled overhead, flickering into and out of the blackness of the sky.

I watched a woman cross the ice down below, her footsteps fatigued. She knelt by the gates. I tried to scream her name, but this land could hold no sound.

*Mother,* I shrieked, but Darien heard nothing.

She left behind pink roses, tucked into the chains that barred the door. Dimly I recalled that she had been here before; we both had been. This was an illusion formed of something less than memory—an echo of what once might have been.

Beasts prowled the land outside, ripping themselves out of the ice when threatened and then fading back into the void when my attention wandered. They were attracted by Anhamirak's warmth and held at bay only by my falcon magic. If I struggled, they returned, drawn like sharks to blood.

Soon even they faded away, and there was nothing. Then *I* ceased to be.

*Ka'hena'she.*

We are not.

*Ka'hena'o'she-ka'hena'a'she.*

We never were; we never will be. We return to the void we never left, for *Mehay* is the center of all, and all is the center of nothing.

Somewhere deep in that center, I glimpsed something quiet, a gentle vision of the world that still existed . . . somewhere.


*Sive was leaning against a post and trying very hard not to tremble. She was the heir to the avian throne now; she wasn't supposed to lose control this way.*

*Salem and Prentice, both gone. How could they both be gone?*

She had told the guards to take Prentice away. Now she had to strike from her mind the sound of his pleas, his begging her to understand that he had only been trying to protect her. Begging her to forgive him. Begging her not to let them execute him.

"Please, Shardae."

*Sky above, take the echo of those words from her brain. Take away the image of him kneeling before her, his hands bound and tears on his face, and let her rest.*

Someone walked up behind her and she tensed, wondering if the fiend who had plotted Salem's death by planting those vile rumors had made plans for hers as well. She was alone here; that was why she had come here instead of returning to the Rookery after she had addressed her people.

Silently, the stranger put his arms around her, holding her gently against him, as unimposing as he could be while still offering support. Suddenly Sive Shardae, heir to the Tuuli Thea, did something she had never done before.

She turned around, leaned against him, and began to cry.

Part of her was vaguely aware that he was a serpent, maybe a dancer, probably one of the many people who had loved and respected Salem Cobriana. But not, thank the gods, one of the many who blamed her for their king's death.

Tears fell silently from Sive's eyes as she let him hold her, as she listened to his heartbeat and matched her breathing to his and tried to think nothing.

# CHAPTER 13

To another, it might have been a tragic moment. To me, it held a quiet beauty. I struggled to see more, desperate to remember the gentle compassion and the way it had moved me, and again the ice trembled, this time allowing someone else's magic to slip through.

*Hai.*

A thought returned to my drifting mind, that single word: *Hai.* Vaguely, I remembered . . . that was me. . . .

*Hai!*

I thrashed as if in a drugged sleep, and again images pressed upon my mind. *Salem, poison, pain*—no, I didn't want that. *Sive, and a friendly stranger holding her.* Gentleness.

Someone was calling to me, and I could not help looking as outside my black palace the beasts groggily pulled themselves to the surface, hissing and snarling at an invader who sullied the darkness.

Echoes of what had been.

A panther leapt, drawing blood from the invader foolish enough to try to walk here. The crimson stain made the ice resonate, and I squeezed my eyes shut and crumpled into a ball, trying to block out the pain.

I had been here before.

"I won't leave you here!" the man shouted, but his voice was fading.

Serpents coiled around him, choking away the breath that with every exhalation made the ice near him steam.

I moved to the gates of my tower but was blocked by jagged ice before I could reach the interloper. He lifted his eyes to me, and they were as blue as opals. Nicias's tears fell and the tower fractured allowing me another step.

"Daughter of *shm'Ahnmik'la'Darien'jaes'oisna'ona'saniet' mana'heah'shm'Ecl* and Anjay Cobriana," he said. "Beautiful dancer Hai." I felt the words wrap around me as tightly as chains, and I moved forward once again.

The serpents shuddered and moved away from Nicias, their bodies contorting as if burned by his blood, red on their black scales. The panther continued to snarl, the sound a silent vibration through the ice. Finally I knelt beside Nicias, and he lifted a hand to touch my cheek.

"You cannot stay here," he told me. "I will not let you."

*Cold.*

I had never felt cold from him before, but the ice seemed to be seeping into Nicias as his blood flowed out. Too late, probably. At this point, it would be far easier to consign him to the void and follow him down.

*Rest with me,* someone whispered. My own voice, stolen by the darkness.

"Rest," Nicias echoed. He tried to shake his head and trembled.

Sive and her silent savior weren't the only ones comforting each other. I tried to draw on the compassion I could feel beneath the fury in Wyvern's Court, but blood was the only color in this land, the only heat, and it was feeding the creatures. They paced closer.

*What have I done?*

I had chosen this exile from reality; I had sought it, to escape the pain of my failures. I was meant to be here, but *he* was not. Nicias was light, and warmth, not this blackness. I held him against me as the monsters paced around us, and I felt the world quiver.

*It would be easier to let him fall.*

The knowledge tempted me too much.

"Nicias," I whispered. I kissed his forehead, trying to gather his warmth when everything around us was trying to take it away. "Nicias, my light. Please."

I shrieked into the darkness: *"You cannot have him!"* My voice faded into nothingness without so much as an echo.

The panther snarled, and I wanted desperately to scramble back into the palace to hide, but I couldn't give up on Nicias. If I fell now, Nicias would fall with me. I knew he would rather be dead than consigned to this void world.

"Please, Nicias," I prayed. "You're the only one who knows the way out of here. *Please . . .*"

I felt a sliver of awareness from him and tried to pull on it, dragging us both gruelingly across the sharp ice. Somehow, painfully, I found my way back to the *she.*

* * *

And then we were on a familiar bed—Nicias's, in his home in Wyvern's Court. My hands were gripping his so tightly I did not wonder why no one had separated us.

His skin writhed with my tarnished magic. Strips of power had lashed his arms, face, chest and back. His lungs barely moved and his heart barely beat, but I could fix that.

I gasped, my body going into spasms and my back arching in pain, as I lured the first loop of cutting magic away from him the only way I knew how. My magic preferred its owner. It cut into my body instead of his.

Another loop, and this time I cried out, feeling the skin on my back split. Blood seeped into my clothing. Another line, another slice, another shriek. How many times would I accidentally kill this peregrine?

Nicias stirred, drawing a breath as I removed the bands around his throat. His eyes opened. They held a dazed, lost look that nevertheless was one of the sweetest sights I had ever seen.

Exhausted, I wrapped my arms around Nicias's neck and laid my cheek against his shoulder, breathing deeply and trying to memorize his scent. My body was shaking from the pain it had absorbed and the effort of pulling us both back into this world, but the ache faded as Nicias took over the healing process.

"I couldn't leave you there," I whispered. "Why did you . . . why did you come for me?"

"I couldn't leave *you* there," he said.

Hungrily, I lifted my face to his, tasting his lips. Instead of the ashes of nothingness I had found with others, Nicias had a spark that drew me *here* and *now*. After a moment of surprise, he returned my kiss, his lips even softer than the feathers I felt at the nape of his neck.

I combed his hair back from his face with my fingers, savoring the silky texture.

He started to pull away, and I clung to him desperately.

"Please," I said. "Nicias, you drew me back from the Ecl and gave me the world. If you asked me to dance, I feel like I could fly. How could you ever doubt what you mean to me?" I whispered, addressing his fears before he could speak them. There were tears in my eyes, which had been dry for many years. "Please," I whispered. "Believe me. I love you."

He caressed my cheek; I closed my eyes, leaning toward his hand. "I believe you," he said.

"Then stay."

When I opened my eyes, he was shaking his head. "Hai, I left Salem unconscious, possibly dying, to go after you. I can't stay longer, not without knowing how he is."

Salem.

After risking so much, and experiencing a kind of hell that only a falcon could ever truly know, how could I possibly have forgotten who we had done it for?

I needed to know what would happen next.

I smiled wryly, realizing that Cjarsa had been wrong about one thing. Apparently a mongrel *could* understand things such as loyalty and duty . . . at least well enough to let go of this beautiful peregrine and say, "You're right."

Nicias kissed my forehead, lingering a moment longer before we both pulled back, and rose to face the world that Fate had left to us.

I would never be able to replace Nicias's love for his wyvern Oliza or supplant his responsibility to his Diente, Salem. But for now it was enough, for me, to see the reluctance in his movements as we stepped out his front door and into the bustle of the marketplace.

"I think I heard the doctor say she was taking Salem back to his room in the Rookery," Nicias said, leading the way to Wyvern's Court's royal keep.

When we reached the Rookery and ascended the stairs to the top floor, we found guards in front of Salem's door.

They nodded to Nicias in respectful greeting and said to us, "Sive Shardae is inside."

Nicias had just lifted his hand to knock when the door opened, revealing the young hawk, who did not manage to keep the sorrow and fatigue from her face.

"Nicias, Hai," she said. Her voice was still musical and calm, but exhaustion had given it a rough edge, and she didn't quite focus on us when she spoke. "We found you with Salem—" She drew a breath, trying to compose herself, and then said, "It is good to see you well."

"Thank you," Nicias answered her. "Has he woken yet?"

Sive shook her head. "Not yet, and the doctors do not know if he will. They say that by all rights he should be dead. The poison . . ." Her voice dropped, but resolutely she continued, "Prentice used the strongest poison he could get his hands on."

We knew it all too well. Neither of us had the courage to ask the next reasonable question, but Sive must have known what we were wondering.

"Prentice has officially been exiled from my people," she said, "and given over to the serpiente to face judgment. If

Salem survives, he will be the one to judge his attacker. If he dies, Prentice will be executed, in accordance with nest law."

She looked back at the door she had just come through, as if willing the cobra on the other side to wake.

"Oliza has returned," Sive added. "She is Salem's heir, and if he dies, she will need to take the serpiente throne."

Sive's gaze drifted out the window. On the ground below, I saw the image of a now familiar figure.

*Keyi darted among merchants, running into this one and that one as she evaded her mother, Oliza. The child was laughing as Oliza shook her head, smiling fondly.*

*Vere Obsidian sneaked through the crowd and took his daughter by surprise, lifting her around the waist.*

I reached for Nicias's hand, needing contact, comfort, *anything,* because in that moment I wasn't numb. I could feel despair, and hopelessness, and shame.

I had seen Keyi time and again. I had seen Salem's death. The visions had unsettled me, and I had stirred myself to speak to the Empress and the falcons, but what had I *done* to prevent this from happening?

Until the moment when the cobra had been dying in my arms, I had done little more than hope for the best . . . and now we would all suffer the consequences of my naïveté and weakness.

I, who could see quite clearly all our futures, had no excuse for this failure. I should have done something differently.

Was it too late, or could I still?

Sive leaned against the wall, whispering, "Salem should be king. Oliza should be allowed to be with the woman she loves. Prentice should—" She broke off. "Once Salem named his mate, he secured the title for his generation, and the succession never goes backward while there is a legitimate heir. Besides, an infertile couple can't rule the serpiente, and Irene hasn't had any children in the last twenty years."

Sive was rambling. Everyone in the room knew it, but she didn't seem able to help her own words.

Finally her eyes focused, on us. "Please. Is there anything you can do for him? *Please*."

"We'll try," Nicias promised her.

She reached out and caught my hand. "Hai, I know you and I have never been close. Your prophecies—the idea that our destiny might not be of our own design, might be completely out of our hands, terrifies me. But if you can tell me . . . please, will he wake? Do you know? Do you know who started those horrible rumors, or if . . . Is this my fault?"

Nicias gently took her hand off mine. "None of this was your fault," he said.

"I should go," she said to us. "I have obligations. I have to . . ."

"It's all right." I was not good at giving comfort, but I could try. "You do what you must. I swear to you, we will do everything we can for Salem."

"Th-thank you. I'm sorry, I—I should go," she whispered again, as if that one decision was still too difficult.

"Someone should go with her," Nicias said to one of the other guards as Sive started to walk away alone.

I shook my head. "She'll be fine."

"You can't be sure of that," the guard said. He looked from Nicias to me.

Nicias turned to me. "Hai, you're certain?"

"Yes, I am." Sive would be queen; she always reigned in the futures I envisioned, except when Oliza's child killed us all. "For now she needs time to be alone. She can't grieve if someone else is there."

But she wouldn't be alone. I could see her already snuggling close to the serpent who had first comforted her. He held her quietly, because someone needed to.

"Then we'll let her be alone."

"Yes, sir," the guard replied before we moved forward to check on Salem.

We entered the sickroom with Sive's despair heavy in our hearts, and it only settled deeper when I saw the cobra.

Salem was pale and still. His heartbeat was slow but even, and his breath rose and fell, yet I sensed no life from him. Normally my magic reacted to Anhamirak's fiery power in Kiesha's kin, but in this case I felt nothing.

Salem's body had survived, but that was all.

He would not wake.

He would live until his body starved, but he would never again open his garnet eyes. I knew that as surely as I knew Ecl's damning darkness. And I knew that nothing good would become of this world without him.

Behind me, I heard Keyi cry.

# CHAPTER 14

"No!" the child shouted.

Oliza frowned. "Keyi, you need to—"

"Don't wanna!" The child pouted and launched into a tantrum. "No, no, no!"

"Keyi, do I need to—"

Oliza cried out, recoiling from her daughter as golden red bands of magic whipped across her arms, drawing blood. Her eyes widened with sudden terror.

"Calm down, Keyi, please," she said.

Keyi continued to wail and stomp her feet, sending a stream of scalding magic at Oliza. Oliza screamed and fell, and only then did Keyi's tears stop.

"Mommy?"

Keyi hurried to Oliza's side, her eyes wide and afraid. "Mommy?" she wailed. "Mommy?" Her hands touched the blood as she shook Oliza, begging her to wake. "Mommy, come back! Mommy? Mommy, get up, please. I won't cry anymore. Mommy!"

"I need to talk to Oliza," Nicias was saying. "I—she—oh, gods."

"Nicias, you can't!" I cried, spinning toward him. "She can't rule. You know that."

He shook his head. "It isn't my decision."

*"It needs to be someone's,"* I snapped. "You of all people know the possible consequences if Oliza returns to the throne."

"And *you* of all people know that Araceli's predictions are not to be trusted," he replied. "Darien believes it is possible to protect any children Oliza might have, and Cjarsa trusts Darien's judgment. Since Oliza is returning only as Diente, she won't need to worry about choosing a mate the avians will accept—"

"Nicias, don't be a fool." Instinctively, I reached toward him magically, trying to show him. If he could only see what I had seen—

Nicias recoiled, slamming magical walls between him and me so fast that I felt as if I had been slapped.

"Nicias, please, listen to me." I begged without shame, but I could see in his eyes that it was no use. I had been careless in my haste and had warmed the seeds of mistrust that still lingered in Nicias from his time on Ahnmik. He had experienced firsthand how powerfully manipulative a falcon's persuasion magics could be, and he would not allow himself to be fooled a second time.

What he might never understand was that there was no magic more powerful than that his own mind could use to convince itself that it was right.

"Nicias, I have seen the future in which Oliza takes the throne. I have seen you screaming when—"

"You have said yourself, many times, that *sakkri* can be misleading. They can show us that which we most fear." Before I could argue, he added, "You are not the only falcon who can spin a *sakkri*, Hai. Your mother has hope."

"My mother can't see past Oliza's magic."

"And Cjarsa?"

Was wrong. I didn't know how, but Cjarsa was *wrong*. Yes, *sakkri* could be misleading, but this one was too real. I believed absolutely that if Oliza took the throne, this world would be destroyed. Cjarsa feared the return of a wyvern so much that I could not understand how she could possibly be fooled by the hope that Nicias would be able to keep us all safe by binding the magic. How could she not *see*? Long before, it had taken all of the four falcons' power to tear Anhamirak's magic in half to keep it subdued. How could anyone believe that one prince, who had begun to study his magic only a few months earlier, could do what the high priestesses of Ahnmik and Brysh and the priest of Ecl could not?

"I will try to warn her of the danger, but, Hai, Oliza is all we have left," Nicias said. "If you are afraid of what might happen, then *help* us. Your magic is as powerful as mine. I know it overwhelms you sometimes, but despite that handicap, you still wield it with more precision and power than I can. I do believe we can protect Oliza. I would like to have you on our side."

I closed my eyes, letting a million futures drift before them. I saw Keyi. I saw fire, and I saw ice. I saw Rosalind weeping, Sive cold and dead, Nicias shrieking—

"I love you," I said, opening my eyes. "I have come to care

for Wyvern's Court, and for Oliza. I do not know what Cjarsa does or does not know, or what my mother does or does not believe." All I knew was that my mother would risk much to prove Araceli wrong and to get Nicias back on the island. "But I . . . I swear, I will do all I can to keep Wyvern's Court safe."

*To Ahnmik, who holds all vows true, this I swear.*

"Speak to Oliza," I said. "I will be here when you return."

Oliza already didn't trust me; if Nicias wouldn't believe me, there was no use arguing with the wyvern. She would trust her loyal guard over any other falcon. However, I had spoken true when I had made my promise to Nicias.

Because he was wrong.

Oliza *wasn't* all we had left.

I walked through Wyvern's Court with a deep weight in my heart.

*Nicias, you gave me this pain,* I thought, weeping. *If it wasn't for you, I would never have loved this land. I would never have needed to fight for it.*

I found myself at the green marble plaza, at the very center of Wyvern's Court, regarding the tall marble statue there. The wyvern looked so proud and sure.

I knelt and pressed one hand to the statue's base. From this spot, I could feel the heartbeat of the land.

I could also hear the argument Nicias was having with Oliza. Though I was glad that some of my warnings had reached him, I knew they would not be enough.

"I'm not returning as wyvern; I'm returning as Diente," Oliza said when Nicias pointed out, as I had, that there had been many reasons for her to leave the first time. "I need to fill only the one role, so there will be no conflict as long as I choose a serpent for my mate."

"And your child?" Nicias asked.

This, too, Oliza had an answer to. "The Dasi's magic became unbalanced when Maeve left the coven, but there is a group where that balance has been preserved among her descendents."

"Obsidian."

"Yes. I wouldn't have been able to make the alliance as wyvern, but as Diente, I can. Their leader is . . ." Oliza's voice wavered a little. She had no words of love to speak. "He is not a bad man. He has been kind to me."

I could already hear the child I had seen in the woods, Obsidian's wyvern child, laughing.

I closed my eyes and sent my spirit outward as I whispered a prayer to Ahnmik.

"White falcon, give me strength. Help me do what must be done."

"Obsidian will make a good Nag. He leads well and is charismatic enough that I think he will be able to earn the favor of our people despite the prejudice against white vipers."

"Your people will be uneasy enough about your choosing a new mate," Nicias warned. "And even if you weren't pledged already, you know that the serpiente won't react well to anything they see as *a political marriage. It is going to be difficult to force a white viper on them at the same time."*

"I don't have a choice!" Oliza snapped, the words choked by sobs. "Gods . . . Salem." She bowed her head, no doubt struggling to compose herself, to stop thinking of her dying cousin and her abandoned love.

Prying myself away from Oliza and Nicias, I turned my prayers to another deity.

"Anhamirak," I said, "you have never answered me. The magic of my mother's ancestors ripped your serpiente worshippers in half, and all I have to call you by are the shreds left behind. I know that. But please, I'm struggling for your people now. Please, if ever you would help a mongrel, make it now."

*"It's the only option," Oliza was saying.*

*"It isn't a perfect solution, but . . . there might be some way you could adopt–"*

*Oliza shook her head. "If all I wanted was to be safe from my magic, that would be the answer–but if I must do this, make this choice, then I want more to show for it than survival. The Obsidian guild has been abused by the Cobriana for millennia. Anjay Cobriana promised them equality, but his death destroyed that chance. My father was pledged to a white viper, and then ended up executing her. I have a chance to make this right."*

*Oh, Oliza, there is no way to make this right.*

*"Ahnleh . . ."*

What could a mortal say to the merciless Fate?

I forced myself to my feet.

*A'le-Ahnleh* was the traditional end to a prayer. By the will of Fate.

"*A'le-la,*" I whispered defiantly.

By *my* will.

I had plans to make.

When Nicias returned to Wyvern's Court, his steps were heavy with sorrow and exhaustion, and his beautiful eyes were distant.

"My love," I said, greeting him.

He leaned against me. "I spoke to Oliza. She will be here in the morning and will speak to her parents, and then she will make the announcement of her return in the evening."

I wrapped my arms around him. "It's all right," I said. "We will make it all right. But you should rest for now."

He took a deep breath and whispered, "Stay with me tonight?"

"Yes," I said, the word a prayer. "Tonight."

And then, the next day, I would lose him.

He lowered his head, and we kissed. It was sweet, and gentle, and it made tears come to my eyes.

"Just hold me," I said. "I love you. Please believe that. Please trust me. I love you. I have always loved you."

He kissed me again and then picked me up in his arms and carried me inside to his bed.

We wove between us the magic known by every lover— that powerful spell of passion. We slept side by side beneath soft blankets. We dreamed, accompanied by the music of our breath and heartbeats.

Peregrine and gyrfalcon wings, hair like sunlight tangled with strands the deep tone of a cobra's scales, skin like alabaster next to skin the color of honey, coated with a sheen of sweat. This was bliss.

The morning came too soon.

I dressed and then pulled open a drawer in the bedside table. Silently, I removed a small bundle, which Nicias had brought back from Ahnmik at the behest of my mother, and which had remained here in his home. I had not wanted it.

I still did not want it. Nevertheless, I unwrapped the hand-carved box in which my mother had kept all her mementos of my father. With shaking hands, I retrieved my father's signet ring. I stared at it for a long time before slipping it on.

"Please trust me," I whispered again to Nicias when it came time for us to part. *Don't hate me,* I silently begged his still-sleeping form, *for what I am about to do.*

# CHAPTER 15

I looked back from the doorway, my heart pounding. Nicias looked so peaceful, lying there. Innocent. What I was about to do to him . . .

Suddenly he wasn't peaceful but once again screaming, fighting.

*"How can you do this to me?" he shrieked at the falcon who was holding Zenle Cobriana. "All your high ideals, all your dreams—you are no better than your Empress!"*

*Darien looked away sadly as she cradled the cobra child.*

*All she said was "This cannot be allowed to happen again."*

I shuddered. Nicias would probably never forgive me for what I was about to do, but *I* would never forgive myself if I didn't do it.

I saddled Najat and pounded into the woods with the word *traitor* echoing in my head.

At the edges of Obsidian land, I saw once again the child I had hoped I could banish.

*Keyi twirled among the trees, chasing fireflies in the night air, while her father watched her fondly with pale green eyes.*
*Vere Obsidian loved his daughter more than life itself, and that showed on every inch of his face.*

The white viper greeted me when I reached the camp, though he appeared distracted. "Hai, what brings you here so early in the day?"

Reasoning with Vere might get him to change his plans, but even if he backed out of his engagement to the wyvern princess, it did not mean she would change her mind.

"I came to offer my congratulations," I said instead. "I hear you are going to be king."

He looked away from me, toward the camp. "Apparently," he said.

"That's a bold move, for a man from a tribe that has sworn neither to lead nor to follow."

He nodded. "It is more than I would want, but Oliza's offer was . . ." He sighed. "This whole situation is appalling."

"Then why did you agree to it?"

"Oliza offered a pardon for all my people, without the

conditions her ancestors often tried to impose. They do not need to return to serpiente land or accept the Diente as king. She swore that the royal house would acknowledge the autonomy of the Nesera'rsh, as Maeve's coven once did, and that the Obsidian guild would be allowed to live as it wished, provided we break no serpiente laws."

"Do you love her?" I asked. As a rule, serpiente didn't believe in political marriage.

Vere shrugged. "I love my people."

"What of Betia?"

He winced. "I don't think I will ever be able to clear from my mind the expression on that woman's face when Nicias landed in front of Oliza. She knew what it meant before he said a word."

I'd learned enough. Now I had other visits to make.

"I will see you this evening, then."

"This evening."


My next visit was to the marketplace. It was still early, but I found Salokin speaking to Arqueete as she set out her wares for the day. They did not seem surprised to see me, and the way Arqueete dropped everything to give me her undivided attention the moment I approached told me where their loyalties lay.

The two serpents followed me, without question, to a less crowded area of the market.

"Salokin, you implied once that you might support me if I chose to assert my right as Anjay Cobriana's only child," I said, too softly for my voice to carry beyond these two. "If that is true, I need your vow on it."

His eyes widened as if I had asked him to sign his name

in blood. To a falcon, a spoken vow was much the same thing, though I did not think he knew that.

"I was loyal to your father," he answered firmly. "You are his child, his only heir. If you choose to step forward as Arami, then I swear I will be loyal to you."

Arqueete had put a hand on Salokin's arm to steady herself. She declared, "I served as a soldier beneath your father, before his death. I followed him to the Keep on the day he—" Her voice broke, but her fiery gaze remained on mine as she said, "I would have died in his place if I could have, and I would do the same for his heir. I swear it."

"I understand there are others?"

"Many others," Salokin answered immediately.

"When Oliza returns to Wyvern's Court to take the throne, I expect every serpent loyal to me to be in the crowd, at the front. Arqueete, if there are other trained soldiers in the group, I would appreciate their assistance. They are *not* to touch the princess. Make that very clear. They are simply to be there, in case I need them."

"Yes, milady."

I started to turn, then hesitated, looking back. "And, whoever is responsible for this . . . turn of events," I added, keeping all judgment clear from my voice, "I want them present. They should receive some recognition."

Salokin and Arqueete both nodded, deeply enough that they almost bowed. I did not know yet if they had started the rumors that had brought about Salem's demise, or just repeated them. Either way, I needed Salokin and Arqueete for a few hours more. It would be best to let them think I meant to reward them, until I was ready to act.

\*   \*   \*

I returned then to the candle shop on the northern hills, where I found Opal, Gren, Maya and Spark in heated conversation. The instant I stepped into the room, the four falcons began to proclaim their innocence.

"Hush," I snapped. "Not one of you is stupid enough to have planned this against my will. I am not the Mercy, who would arrest you all for wanting it to be done even when you had no hand in it."

They all calmed, but I could see the wariness on their faces.

"You have all spoken of me as queen of this land, many times. Do you still wish it?"

Maya was the first to react. She knelt beside me, and I felt a chill go down my spine. I had seen others grovel this way before the Empress, but I was no royal falcon—only a mongrel, desperate to pretend.

"Take the throne, and I will follow you," she swore.

One last visit.

Back in the cool shadows of the woods, I closed my eyes and reached for my mother.

*Darien?*

*Yes?*

There were many discussions we could have had in that moment. I sighed, *Take care of Nicias for me. I suspect he will come to you soon.*

*Hai, what are you doing?* Darien demanded.

*Fulfilling all your expectations,* I answered bitterly. I meant to leave it at that but couldn't stop myself from asking *How could you do this to me, to the world you claim to want to protect? How could you be so blind, to convince Nicias all is well and allow this horror?*

*I've told you. My* sakkri *are—*

*What of my Empress?* I asked. *Surely she can see far more than a mongrel can. She must know what will happen if Oliza takes the throne.*

I felt my mother shake her head on the distant Ahnmik as she stared out her window and over the white city. *Cjarsa has more power than you and I combined, but the void frightens her. She fears drowning in its illusions, so she holds back.*

The idea that Cjarsa might have such a powerful weakness was deeply unsettling. *If that's the case, then you're both blind here. Oliza listens to Nicias's counsel, and Nicias would listen to you. You could stop this with a few words to him, if you would just* trust *me.*

*I can't. Hai . . .* I felt her struggle to choose wording that would be kind. She settled on *You are a falcon despite your father's blood, and I have no way of knowing where your loyalties lie, but I know that they are not with me.*

Sometimes I myself wasn't sure.

Nicias's eyes opened as I returned to his room, my arms laden with a package of freshly baked pastries that Arqueete had given to me on my way back there.

"Good morning," Nicias said.

"Morning." I went to his side, my eyes feasting on the lines of his face—golden lashes, high cheekbones, soft lips, fair skin. "You looked so peaceful I didn't want to wake you."

He smiled, but I knew that he was wary. He had every right to be.

I kissed him, for perhaps the last time.

"I brought breakfast," I said. "We'll need it. I imagine it is going to be a very long day."

# CHAPTER 16

Oliza wore plum-violet—the serpiente color of mourning—to her coronation. Officially the color was in honor of her cousin, but Oliza had so much more than that to mourn, and everyone in the audience knew it.

Vere Obsidian was in such a deep shade of blue that it was almost black. I wondered how Oliza felt about her would-be mate's making an effort to avoid the Cobriana royal color, even though the difference in tone was discreet. His white-blond hair had been braided in back but was in no way hidden.

Both Vere and Oliza appeared grave as he helped her onto the dais.

Even once Oliza looked out over the crowd, the marketplace took a long time to hush, as serpiente continued to express their emotions, which ranged from relief at Oliza's return to fury. Even serpents who supported Oliza in general were disturbed by this turn of events.

Nicias, at the foot of the dais, swept the crowd with cool eyes. Only those who knew him well might have recognized how nervous he was.

He was not the only one. Oliza's parents appeared drawn and worn; for twenty years they had dreamed of the day their daughter would take the throne, but this was not the way any parent would have wished that dream to come true.

Sive stood at the far edge of the crowd, shunned by almost everyone but her avian guards; only a lone serpent had elected to stay by her side. Though she held herself straight, her eyes were swollen from crying.

Rosalind was not present. In fact, most of the dancers from the nest were missing. They had attended the coronation of one of their own, but they had chosen to stay by that fallen king's side rather than watch this farce. Their absence pleased me, as it meant my loyalists made up more of the crowd.

*How many?* I wondered.

There was only one way to find out.

I stepped forward.

Serpents stepped aside, some of them with confusion on their faces, but many with respectful nods, as I moved through the crowd. I kept my face neutral as I approached the bottom of the dais.

"Oliza Shardae Cobriana."

Oliza jumped as I called to her. Nicias, who was nearly next to me now, frowned and said my name. "Hai—"

I boosted myself smoothly onto the dais. "Oliza, a word with you."

"Hai, now is hardly the time," the wyvern replied.

"Now is the *only* time."

"Hai, what do you think you are doing?" Nicias asked.

I spoke clearly so my voice would be heard by the entire crowd.

"My father was the eldest of his generation, older brother to both Zane and Irene Cobriana. I recognized you as Arami, Oliza, because you held that place before my return, but then you gave up that title of your own free will. I recognized Salem because our people respected and followed him, and I wish he could still hold the throne—though from what I can tell of his injuries, he will not recover." The words hung in the air. I knew that every eye and every ear was focused on us at this moment. "I hope, milady wyvern, that you will gracefully step aside, and not attempt to force your way into a position you willingly abandoned."

"This is absurd," Zane said, objecting.

A pair of my followers, both of whom appeared to be soldiers, stepped between the cobra and the stage. "Let her speak," one of them said.

Oliza's voice was frosty when she said, "I stepped down because I knew I could not hold both thrones if I wanted to avoid another war. I never *abandoned* my people when they needed me, and I will not do so now."

"They do not need you now, either." More softly, praying Oliza would hear the truth in my words, I added, "And we both know what you really feared would happen if you took the throne."

Why was I the only one who could see Anhamirak's fire destroying us all? Why was I the only one who could hear the screams as the falcons slaughtered the survivors, leaving only children that the royal house could raise as it wished?

"Hai, this is madness," Oliza said.

Arqueete had come to the front and now pointed out, "It is not mad if it's true. She *is* rightfully Arami."

"*Oliza* is the rightful Arami," someone else shouted.

By now Nicias had climbed onto the stage. He stepped between Oliza and me, the pain of betrayal in his eyes. *"No."* The word was accompanied by angry magic that shuddered through me like the rumble of thunder. "Hai, I will not allow you to—"

I pulled back with a hiss. "Nicias Silvermead, if I am a cobra, then I am not a subject of the royal house of Ahnmik. You have told me this many times. That means *you* are not my prince." I wanted to recall the words the instant I shouted them, wanted to say *It's not true! Please, I meant nothing by it!* Instead, I continued. "Or is this the wish of that house? You say you turned down the falcon throne to stand behind Oliza, Nicias of Ahnmik. Are you here as a guard or a puppeteer?" Nicias was royal falcon born, but I had been Mercy raised. He did not have the experience to turn these allusions around as I spoke quickly, sowing distrust among all the serpiente around us.

"You know that isn't true. I am loyal—"

"Loyal to Oliza?" I asked, with obvious cynicism. "How can you claim to be loyal to the wyvern princess and then ask her to betray the sacred vows she swore to her true mate? How can you say you are loyal to Wyvern's Court and then participate in this sham ceremony in an attempt to—"

"An attempt to protect the throne from—"

"What? Its rightful heir?" I challenged him. "I am not a usurper, Nicias. I am Anjay Cobriana's daughter, and I will not abandon the responsibility of his legacy."

"Nicias, step aside."

Oliza's soft voice sent Nicias away, and I was left looking at the wyvern.

"Oliza, please, do not force this confrontation further," I implored. The crowd around us was beginning to get ugly. My followers were holding back Oliza's family and friends, including Zane Cobriana, but I knew that my loyalists would feel the need to protect me once her father reached the dais. "Neither of us wants blood to be spilled here today."

"I will not allow a *falcon* to usurp the serpiente throne."

I then let myself do something I had never done: I recoiled and shifted into my serpent half form. I had always thought of my cobra fangs and scales as dirty, but when I looked upon Oliza with garnet eyes and hissed, the action felt as natural as a falcon's cry once had.

"Falcon?" I asked. "I have as much cobra blood as you do, *wyvern*. My father would have been Diente had he not been slain by your mother's brother. Is your millennia-old prejudice against *my* mother's blood enough to deny me my rightful place?"

"*You have no rightful place here.*" Oliza was losing her temper and her poise as I twisted around her arguments.

I spun away from her as one of the serpents broke free from the crowd and leapt onto the dais. Sensing the blade and who it was intended for before anyone else noticed it, I pushed Oliza aside.

The blow, which had been meant for the wyvern, struck me in the side, piercing one of my lungs.

"*Stop!*"

My subjects pulled back as I shouted at them. I grabbed the wrist of the serpent who had just tried to end this debate with the death of my opponent, and dragged him forward.

"Oliza is my kin," I said, struggling for breath. "And she is my *heir*. I will not allow you, or any other, to harm her."

Two more serpents scrambled onto the dais. Before I could figure out if they were on my side or Oliza's, Nicias reacted for me. His magic lashed the would-be assassin, the other two serpents on the dais and several others who had been trying to reach us. They all fell back, hissing in pain and anger, and I suppressed a sad smile. In Nicias's attempt to defend his queen, he had cemented her connection to the royal falcon house in the minds of many serpents.

I collapsed to my knees and pulled the knife from my side. Coughing blood, I let my magic fill the wound. Falcons were harder to kill than serpents.

Kneeling, my hands bloody from a wound that had been intended for Oliza, I looked up at the wyvern. I knew the arguments she could make, but either she could not find the words, or she chose not to.

Instead, Oliza took one step back, then another.

"I will not let my pride drag us into a civil war here," she said, struggling to control her anger. "You are the only child of my father's eldest brother, and even though you have never claimed that parentage before, the Cobriana blood still shows true." She looked away as her voice wavered. "I gave my people up once to protect them. I will not let you create the strife I was trying to avoid. As long as my—*our*—people will support you, I will not challenge your claim to the serpiente throne."

She shifted before us all, something Oliza never willingly did. Her wyvern form soared into the skies, every movement betraying her fury and pain.

# CHAPTER 17

The crowd beyond the dais watched with a mixture of shock, understanding and—in the case of my followers—arrogance as Oliza left. Some retreated slowly, horrified, but most remained, turning their gazes to me with wide eyes.

Only one serpent still moved forward.

Zane Cobriana stepped, unchallenged, onto the dais. His garnet eyes burned, and I wondered whether he would attempt to speak to me or murder me outright without care for the consequences.

My defense came from an unexpected source. Vere Obsidian, who had stepped back from Oliza when I had ascended the dais, now moved protectively between me and the cobra.

"Get out of the way," Zane snarled.

"Do *not* give me orders, cobra," Vere replied coldly. "I am not your subject. *You* are not king to anyone right now. By your law, you lost that title when Salem took the throne. You have no more authority here than Hai does, and she at least has my respect."

"That is a *falcon*. She has no right to this throne!"

I struggled to my feet. "Yes, I am half falcon. But your daughter is half hawk. If wyvern blood makes an Arami unfit to rule, then you had best search harder for your sister, Irene. Or find yourself a new Naga, for law forbids your having a barren queen when you have no suitable heirs."

"Do not quote serpiente law at me—"

"I believe I need to, since *you* seem to have forgotten it," I said. "You have no right to keep your brother's heir from this throne."

The Cobriana were notorious for their temper, and as I saw the rage in Zane's eyes, I braced myself for a blow.

Vere caught the cobra's wrist.

"If you strike her, I swear to every god in this world, I will destroy you. I think a charge of treason would do quite nicely."

Zane's eyes widened. "She isn't Diente yet."

"Until she declares her mate. Yes, I'm aware of the laws, Zane. I learned them well as we waited for the day when you would name our Adelina *your* Naga. Instead, you broke my aunt's heart and then you executed her. Now you would drag your own Oliza from her beloved mate, and abuse your brother's daughter? And you wonder why the Obsidian guild refuses to kneel to you."

Zane glared. "Who are you to speak as if you understand what went on?"

"I am a subject of Anhamirak," Vere retorted, "and therefore free to speak my mind as I wish. I am a descendent of

Maeve, a child of the Obsidian guild, and therefore well versed in Cobriana politics. I am—"

*Are you still courting my father, Vere, or are you courting me now?* I remembered asking him. Now I relied on the answer he had given me.

"My mate," I declared. "Or did you think it was only for politics that I would interrupt this ceremony?" I spoke not for Zane but for those in our audience who still might object to this coup. Serpents liked romance; the idea of my challenging Oliza for love would appeal to them.

Vere looked surprised but did not protest. Instead, he wrapped an arm around my waist.

"Diente?"

I glimpsed a hawk out of the corner of my eye, but before I could react, a pale fist caught me under my jaw. Vere barely kept me on my feet as I stumbled backward, shocked, raising one hand to my bleeding lip.

My followers came to my defense, gripping the arms of the woman I now recognized as Danica Shardae, Oliza's mother, the avian queen. Zane had been enough of a threat that no one had even thought to watch for his mate.

"Release her!" I shouted to my guards, but they just looked at each other skeptically. "She is Oliza's mother. She has every right to be upset, and even if she did not, I have not done all this only to begin the war again by harming the Tuuli Thea!" At my glare, they reluctantly let go of the infuriated hawk, but this time they kept their attention on her.

Zane went to his mate's side as she spoke to me.

"Throughout my childhood, I was taught that a serpent couldn't be trusted," she said through clenched teeth. "Thousands of years of war were justified by that premise. Now my king, my pair bond, is a cobra. I love him. I trust him. I have learned that there is no evil inherent in serpiente blood.

"The head of my guard, Kel Silvermead," she continued, "is a falcon. She and her alistair, and their son, Nicias, are among the most loyal subjects Wyvern's Court could ever hope to have. So I know there is no innate flaw in falcons, either.

"But you, Diente, you are nothing but a soulless, bloodless *mongrel*. What you have done today . . ."

"It is better to be a soulless, bloodless mongrel," I replied cuttingly, "than an emotionless hawk who can't step down off her superior throne to look at the truth. Oliza is your daughter, and I know you want to protect her, but this is not her place."

"Oliza is more than my daughter," the Tuuli Thea said. "She is more than a princess; she is a symbol of a dream that took thousands of years to bring about, which you, raised on your island, can barely comprehend. When my daughter abdicated, she gave her crown to Sive and Salem, and her trust in them was enough to keep this land together. But now . . . now that's over. My people will leave Wyvern's Court. No matter what Sive or I may say, your betrayal will split this world in two."

"Better they leave in peace than stay and burn." At least this way they would have their precious freedom. It would take time for the serpiente to find their equilibrium again, and in the meantime there would be fights both within the serpiente and between them and the avians, but I had to believe that eventually the balance would return. Fate willing, they would never learn how close they had danced to a future in which the freedoms they worshipped were ripped away and replaced by lies, manipulations and rewritten history from the falcon empire.

Nicias stepped past me without a glance and touched Zane's shoulder respectfully. "Sir, milady Shardae, I am worried I will not be able to keep the crowd back if the three of you stay here. I do not believe that most in the crowd would harm you, but we have already had one would-be assassin."

Zane looked around with a heartbroken expression. Danica did not turn her golden-fire eyes from mine. They both knew what Nicias was really saying: This battle was over. The serpiente people had not rejected me, and that meant that no matter how much they hated this turn of events, they had no right to eject me from this dais.

"I am your kin, and I love this world," I said. I sincerely meant every word. "I will not betray it. I swear that to you both."

"Dien—sir?" Nicias said again, at the last moment changing his address from the title this cobra no longer held. "Lady Shardae?"

Slowly, the royal pair withdrew from the dais, leaving me alone with Vere Obsidian and a hundred pairs of serpiente eyes on us.

Too softly for those beyond the dais to hear, Vere whispered drily, "I never realized that you and I were so close."

"I have seen what will happen if Oliza rules," I explained. I planned my next words carefully before I spoke. "You asked me once what horrors I saw. Salem's death was only the beginning. I care for this world, and I am determined that it will not experience the bloodbath I can see so easily in its path. I have no desire to rule, but if I must—and I do believe that I must—then I want you beside me. It is the least I can do for you. And if you truly wish to honor my father, and help his daughter, then it is the most you can do for me."

Vere's expression was one of sweet concern, but his words were cool. "Aside from your lovely attempt at emotional blackmail, why would I wish to be your king, falcon?"

"Because you wanted to be king before," I answered. "You accepted Oliza's suit. I can match the terms she offered you."

I needed to block the path to every future in which the child Keyi could exist.

Among the serpiente, lovers came and went, but a couple sworn as mates never strayed. Those vows were even more sacred among the Nesera'rsh and so the Obsidian guild. If I could bind this man to me, I knew he would not visit Oliza's bed while I still lived.

"I feel like I am bartering for bread, not hearing a proposal."

"I can only offer what I have," I told him softly. "I cannot swear undying love. You would know it was a lie. I know that this land has never done you favors, and you certainly owe the Cobriana nothing, but I need you. Wyvern's Court needs you."

He nodded slowly. "Very well . . . cobra. Let's dance this step. Just lead the way."

I turned, at long last, to the enraptured crowd. I found myself shaking and had to lean against Vere for support.

My people were confused, frightened, utterly overwhelmed. Some of them had actively supported me, but most of them simply did not know what to do.

I did not know how to comfort them, so I chose honesty. "I love this world. I will not abandon her now that she needs me. If Salem wakes, I will willingly acknowledge him as my Diente. The rumors that led to his fall were false, as the avian queen-to-be herself has attested, and he is still the rightful king of this land. If Irene returns with another child, I will acknowledge that child as my heir. I will not allow the Cobriana line to diminish."

I said this to address the question of what would happen to their royal line when it was mixed with the blood of falcons and white vipers.

I said it also because Ahnmik's magic was too strong in me. I did not know if I would ever be able to have a child, and I certainly did not wish to rule until the end of time, as the falcon royals seemed content to do.

"I stand before you and swear a solemn vow to do what I must to protect this land, *my* land, until that day. I have also sworn to honor the promises made by Oliza regarding the Obsidian guild, which has been outcast from our society for too long. Wyvern's Court is meant to be a place without old hatred.

"And so I wish to present to you my mate, your Nag . . ." I hesitated, not sure how to introduce the white viper. Members of the Obsidian guild guarded their names, never sharing them with anyone but those to whom they were deeply connected.

"Vere Obsidian," he provided, loudly enough for the crowd to hear. More softly, he said to me, "Make it worth it, Diente."

*It's done.*

And yet there was so much more to come.

# CHAPTER 18

"I need to speak to my people and explain to them what happened here," Vere said to me as we stepped down off the dais. Two of my loyalists moved to flank us, guarding us from any of Oliza's or Zane's supporters who might have taken offense to any—or all—of what had just occurred.

"I'm still not entirely sure what *did* happen," Vere admitted. "I'm trusting you that there was a reason for this."

I nodded. "I assure you, there was. I will try to explain when we have a few moments alone."

For now, it would have to wait. Arqueete and Salokin found their way to the front of the crowd and knelt before me.

Arqueete grasped my hand. "Diente, I . . ." The rest of her words were lost to me as I instead heard what she had said to Salokin two days before.

\* \* \*

*"No one will believe it," Salokin said.*

*"No one needs to believe it except Prentice," Arqueete responded practically. "Do you really think that raven will stop to think about . . ."*

The vision faded, but I had heard enough. I withdrew my hand, taking a step back.

"Arqueete, Salokin . . ." Both serpents looked nervous when they heard my tone. "You're both under arrest, for conspiracy to commit regicide. In short, for treason."

"I . . ." Salokin's blue eyes widened. "Milady—"

"But we did it for you!" Arqueete protested. "And look where you are! It isn't treason to support the rightful heir to the throne."

"You *murdered* Salem Cobriana."

"We never touched him!" Salokin cried. "You were there. Prentice attacked him."

"I was also there in the market when you spread the rumors that sent Prentice after him. You might not have held the blade in your own hand, but you planned its use."

"No." Arqueete shook her head. "Milady, please, I beg your mercy. I did it only for you."

"My *Mercy*?" I echoed. "Be grateful I have none. Serpiente law says you will have a trial for this crime, and witnesses to speak on your behalf, if you can find any. It is more than I want to give you." I summoned one of my self-appointed guards, who was looking at Salokin and Arqueete in horror. "Arrest them. Bring them to the nest; Salem was not only a cobra but a dancer, and turning these two over to nest justice is the least I can do."

Salokin begged, "Please, Hai, don't do this."

I shook my head. "If you wish to redeem your honor, be honest with the dancers," I suggested. "If you wish to die a coward as well as a traitor, beg me further."

He went white and bowed his head before allowing my soldier to escort him to the nest.

"Milady, someone else to speak to you," another of my followers said to me.

I turned as if underwater. I did not need to be warned of Nicias's approach; I could sense it. Vere, who had stood silently beside me as I had dealt with the traitors, now stepped back to give us some space.

"Please, don't," I said softly.

"How convenient," Nicias observed, "to be able to execute the weapons you used to win this throne."

"You know I would never have harmed Salem," I said. "You may never forgive me for not allowing Oliza to return, but someday, you will at least believe that I did not wish for this."

He shook his head dismissively.

*Oh, gods. My sweet Ecl, Ahnmik, I wish I could reach for you now to take me back into my numbness.*

I lifted my gaze to his blue one and fought to keep the tears from spilling. *My Nicias, my light, you took me from the darkness.* I whispered silently to Nicias, and felt him listening briefly before he started to block me out again. *You took me from my black tower and taught me to feel again. Don't look at me with that fury, that awful look of betrayal.*

"I had no choice," I said aloud.

"No choice; of course."

"Nicias, *please,* you know as well as I do why Oliza cannot rule."

He shook his head again. "I don't know anything anymore. *Anything*. Hai, *I brought you here*. I defended you. I fell asleep with you in my arms and I thought—" He cleared his throat. "You slipped away while I slept to usurp my queen's throne, and now you dare tell me that you *had no choice*?"

The anguish in his voice was even worse than the anger. "I have to go," I whispered.

Fury smoldered in his gaze, and his body was rigid with the effort it took to keep his voice level as he continued. "Before you leave: I did not come here to criticize you. That isn't my *place*. I just came here to request that you release me from my obligations to Wyvern's Court."

"Nicias—"

He ignored my plea. "I do not feel it is appropriate for me to serve under the next Diente when I swore my loyalty to Oliza. I have been offered a position among the Royal Flight, effective once I leave."

*No,* I wanted to say, *I give no such permission.*

He would leave anyway, though. This was just a formality. Nothing I said would keep him here, after what I had done to him.

*Forgive me, my love,* I called silently. The words fell upon deaf ears.

Nicias did nothing more than frown, but the falcon shuddered at the prince of Ahnmik's obvious displeasure and turned to address Nicias's mate with a trembling voice.

"My Lady." His downcast eyes were unable to conceal his terror. "Please, forgive a foolish man his ill-conceived words."

"Do you apologize for my benefit," she asked, "or for my prince's?"

*Ahnmik's magic would not let this falcon lie, no matter how much she wished it would. The man looked at his* aona'ra *and cringed. Araceli's heir was not in a forgiving mood.*

Nicias would join the Royal Flight for a short time, but it would not be long before he would become restless. He would go to Ahnmik for valiant reasons, but the city would turn him into what he most hated—and it would be my fault.

How long would it take him, I wondered, to change into the cold, jaded prince I kept seeing lately? How long would it take him to forget Oliza—and me—and pick this other woman as his lover?

I could have saved him from that fate. I could have given him back Oliza. But the price, the destruction of Wyvern's Court, was one I knew he would never have chosen to pay.

So I damned him.

"Permission granted."

Nicias nodded. "Thank you." For a moment I thought he sounded regretful, but I did not know whether it was for leaving me or for saving me in the first place.

*It's done*, fateful words, echoed in the beat of his wings as he fled and in my pounding heartbeat.

"I'm sorry," Vere whispered. "But if what you have done is indeed for the best, he *will* someday realize that. First, though, he needs to calm down."

I shook my head. "I fear that by the time he calms down, he may be a very different man."

Vere started to reach for me, then hesitated, his mind surely on the peregrine who occupied my heart. I took the white viper's hand in mine, needing some kind of comfort but feeling just as awkward about it.

We had been . . . Had we been friends? I didn't even know if I could use that term. Now suddenly we had agreed to be mates. Even our reasons differed.

I turned to lean against Vere, closing my eyes for a moment. I did not love him, but as Oliza had said, he was a kind man. Of the two of us, I was far more likely to be cruel.

I opened my eyes again, prepared to suggest we move out of the marketplace, when suddenly I saw the child Keyi only a few feet away from us. Her pale blue eyes were gazing up at Vere with fascination. Her golden hair was rumpled, as if she had been playing.

I felt myself go cold.

"What is it?" Vere whispered as I pulled away from him.

Then he seemed to turn, and lift the girl in his arms, spinning her about.

*Why?*

I had done everything I could do, *everything*. What assassin's knife was going to find me, to allow this girl to live? I could think of no other way I would let her *a'she* come to pass.

She was laughing, this girl with so much blood on her hands.

I looked at the serpents who had surrounded me only moments before, and saw them all still and silent, their bodies glistening with the golden magic that would burn through this land like a storm.

I threw my mind into the power, screaming, *Why?*

*Ecl, my love.*

*Ahnmik, my master.*

*Anhamirak, my bane, please, I must know! There must be a way to stop this fire.*

Vere caught my hands, trying to call me back to the real

world. I felt his magic from Ahnmik soothe mine, even as Anhamirak's power shivered across my skin like . . .

Fire.

Like Oliza's wyvern.

Then the vision of the girl turned to me, and her eyes lit up as she said, "Mommy!"

Oliza was not the only one whose magic was unbalanced, made dangerous by Anhamirak's flames.

*No.*

Fate could not be so cruel.

When had it ever been gentle?

I shoved back from Vere, hard enough that only a serpent's reflexes kept him from falling. I felt the murmur in the crowd more than I heard it.

When I turned to run, people tried to stop me. Maya grabbed my arm, demanding an explanation, before Opal dragged her away.

I pushed past my followers and my enemies in a panicked daze, fleeing toward the only place I could think of: Wyvern's Nest.

# CHAPTER 19

Only a few feet from the nest, I slammed into Velyo as the wolf stepped in front of me.

"Diente," he said, greeting me with a nod.

"Frektane," I replied, gritting my teeth. I tried to step around him, and he blocked me. "What do you want?"

"I wanted to offer my congratulations," he said, "and I suppose an apology. I misjudged you."

"Fine. Forgiven," I said. "Now move aside."

"You look upset," he observed.

"And in a hurry," I returned.

"You did the right thing."

The right thing—this from Velyo Frektane, of all people. "I want no comfort from a man who murdered his own father to ascend to the throne."

"I did it for the good of my pack—just as you have done this for the good of Wyvern's Court. Oliza's weakness would have made her—"

"If Wyvern's Court had been ready for a wyvern queen, Oliza Shardae Cobriana—and her Naga, Betia Frektane—would have been the greatest monarchs this land had ever known," I snapped. "They are both strong, just and capable leaders . . . and they will prove it," I continued as the vision came to me, "when Betia succeeds *you* as alpha of the Frektane."

Velyo scoffed. "Your prophecies have become muddled again, Hai. There is no way I would allow that deviant back into our pack."

I had seen in *sakkri* this wolf with his angry hands on Oliza's mate. I had seen him try to repeat the crime with the wyvern. I had stolen Oliza's throne from her only minutes earlier, but there was one gift I could give to her and Betia now, so I gave it. "You want a prophecy, Velyo?" *Sometimes, speaking of a vision can set into motion the very events one is trying to prevent.* Or in this case, trying to cause. "Betia and Oliza *will* become the much-beloved queens of the Frektane tribe. Their son, an orphaned wolf cub they will adopt within the next few years, will inherit the title later. And you will have a say in none of it—because you will be dead within the next six months, at the jaws of one of the wolves you call your allies."

As I spoke the words, I felt Fate shiver, the future realigning itself until the possible events I had seen became a near certainty. Paranoia would eat at Velyo, and he would turn his fear on his allies until they would be forced to exterminate him.

"Enjoy your future," I said. "Now, I have my own to attend to." I pushed forward, shoving the horrified wolf out of the way, and stumbled through the doorway of the dancer's nest.

Inside, I was struck by the silence. Usually this place was

full of graceful bodies and joyous sounds, but now all I heard was a single voice.

Rosalind, Salem's mate, was singing a haunting, wordless melody. The others were silently dancing, their movements slow and careful.

They were praying, offering their worship to the gods in exchange for the health of one of their own.

The instant Rosalind noticed me, the mood shifted from sorrowful to angry.

"You aren't welcome here, falcon," she said. Her eyes were glazed with tears, and I could feel her pain like hail against my skin. "I don't care if you *are* Diente. You have no right to be here."

"I need to see Salem."

"So you can finish what your supporters started?" Rosalind said accusingly.

"So I can try to save him!" Serpents jumped, as startled as I was by how desperate I sounded. The dancers were the only rulers of their nest. My own magic would stop me if I tried to force my way past them.

Before Rosalind could respond, A'isha, the nest leader, placed a hand on her shoulder. "What can you do for him?"

"I don't know," I admitted. "But I have to—"

"We can't trust her!" Rosalind protested. "For all we know, it is her magic that is keeping him in this state."

A'isha shook her head. "I can't know your intentions for certain," she said to me, "but I will let you pass. If Salem's guard disagrees, you will leave."

"Thank you."

I pushed past, shaking off Rosalind when she tried to stop me. Behind me, I heard A'isha trying to calm the fearful woman.

I descended the stairs to the private rooms beneath the nest and found Salem's room easily. When I opened the door, Nicias looked up at me with disdain.

"Oh, gods," I whispered. "Nicias . . ."

"Get out of here," he ordered.

He knew that my vows to him were what kept me in this world, knew that my magic would tear at me to obey him. I fell to my knees to keep from turning around.

"You have to listen to me," I begged, fear, need and pain all too clear in my voice. "Oliza *cannot* take the throne. For her to do so would be disaster. You haven't seen— Dear Ahnmik, help me speak true and clearly," I prayed. "You haven't seen the visions I've been haunted by. You haven't seen Oliza murdered by her own child. You haven't seen Wyvern's Court burned to ash by Anhamirak's fire, or by the falcons when they come. . . ." My voice trembled. "I heard you scream, too, Nicias, my— Please, believe me, I would do everything in my power to keep you from that pain. I know you fear that *sakkri* can mislead, but not these," I whispered. "I have never seen visions this strong, this sure. I've tried and tried and I can't keep this land from burning."

He crossed the room as if he couldn't help himself, and lifted me to my feet. Even if he hated me, Nicias wasn't the type of man who could stand by and let a woman grovel.

His hands did not linger on mine. Coldly, he said, "So you set yourself up as queen of a land you never wanted. Then why are you here?"

"Because I can't rule, either," I whispered. I looked at Salem. "I swear to you, Nicias, I have never betrayed you. I swear it by blood, by fire, by flesh, by steel, by Ecl and by Ahnmik and by all that is and never will be. . . . I swear I have never lied to you and I have never betrayed you. I breathe this scorched air *for you*. Now, please, *believe me*. In every vision I see, this land falls. In every future I look to, I see you screaming. Salem Cobriana must take the throne, or our world *burns*."

"Ours?"

"You made your world mine," I said. "When you pulled me from Ecl, you gave me this land. At first I hated you for that. Now . . . I don't want this land to become the falcon crystal I see whenever I turn around. Let me try to help Salem."

"You couldn't help him before," he argued. "How can you help him now?"

"I'll dive deeper. . . . I don't know, maybe I can't do anything, but I need to try again. It's all I can do."

He stepped to the side, letting me past. When I moved toward the silent cobra, Nicias touched my arm.

"I'll try to hold you, to keep you from going too far."

I shook my head. "Don't pull me back. His life means more than mine."

Presuming there was any life left to save.

# CHAPTER 20

*Oh, gods, help me.* Diving into Salem's body again *hurt*. He wanted to die, but the magic I had wrapped into him previously kept him on this side of existence. His heart wanted to stop, but my power kept it beating.

His spirit was curled somewhere in the darkness, screaming in pain as it struggled to flee its corpse. Fear and agony ripped through me as his flesh prayed for release.

Had Salem been anyone else, I would have given him a gentle death, faced with such pleas. I was tempted to do so even now, but there was too much at stake.

*This world needs you,* I cried, begging him to return.

But how could he return when his body wouldn't take him? It wasn't . . . right. Stripped of its magic, it had no life, no place for a heart and a mind and a soul. It yearned for Brysh's embrace, after which there would be only silence and peace.

For him. For us, there would be only pain.

*Come to me,* I commanded, straining with every ounce of

my own magic. *Come to me.* I tried to wrap the words around him but felt him slipping away.

I cursed the *am'haj* poison. I slid my power over the ruined edges of his magic, trying to make him whole again, but Ahnmik can only destroy, and I had never had control over the hint of Anhamirak in my blood.

I tried to soothe Salem's pain and coax his terrified spirit back into this body, promising anything if he would return to this land. I felt him starting to fall into his final rest instead of rising.

I drew back and felt him shriek.

Salem could not survive without magic.

Wyvern's Court could not survive without Salem.

And Wyvern's Court needed to survive.

Therefore, Salem's body needed magic.

Suddenly I felt calm.

I had tried being gentle, coaxing and soothing and begging in much the same way that Ecl had whispered to me for years. *Come to me, and I will let you rest,* the void called. *Come to me, and I will take care of you. I will comfort you, and you will be at peace.*

But Anhamirak's power wasn't rooted in peace, gentleness and quiet entreaties. A cobra's magic, my father's magic, was what burned in me every moment of my life. It was fire and chaos; it was freedom, savage and natural, beyond civilization and law.

And it was desperation.

I slammed power into the cobra now, drowning his body in all the energy I had at my disposal. I held back nothing, baring every part of myself as I forced his flesh and soul to do as I willed.

Desperation was all I had left.

Finally I felt something in him react to the assault, drawn by the flicker of my father's magic. I had never been able to control Anhamirak's power, but now I used it as a lure, enticing Salem not with promises of rest—serpents didn't *rest*—but with heat.

*Now I have you.* I twined myself around and through every particle of his being, using Anhamirak to hold him close and Ahnmik to slice through the bonds between flesh and magic. I severed the rotten, tattered remnants of magic left by the *am'haj* poison, and felt Salem instinctively clutch at the familiar, healthy magic in my blood.

One more cut and—

I screamed as I felt the fabric of my reality rip. I struggled not to flee from the ice storm that struck me as my power slid away from me, seeking a more comfortable home.

Cold . . . so cold. Once, I had called Ecl cold, but that had been a blessed numbness compared to this. . . .

Back on the ice, I felt it cut into my hands and my knees as it began to shatter, as I fell into the darkness, choking on the frozen black water.

*Down,* someone said to me, a voice that sounded so familiar, so comforting. *Dive. Now.*

The beasts that used to dwell beneath the ice, forever drawn toward Anhamirak's warmth, ignored me. As I sank into the void, images of the past fluttered before me.

*I walked through the white city as a child and spoke to spirits others couldn't see. Oh, how the world shone so brilliantly. The voices of the Mercy who raised me faded as I listened to the songs the city wove. I could hear the colors of the sea and taste the moonlight and feel the shifting strands of Fate all around me.*

"When might I be able to see the Empress?"

This cobra had no fear at all. Though Anjay had been carried across the ocean by Pure Diamond falcons, who could as easily have dropped him into the sea, he had held his head high from the instant he had set foot on the white island—a place no Kiesha'ra had ever stood before.

"When she decides you are worth speaking to," Darien replied.

"How am I to convince her of my worth if you never let me so much as walk in the city?"

*My lady?*

*Let him see our land,* Cjarsa whispered through Darien's mind. *Give him beauty. There will be none in the world to which he must return.*


"I have always loved you, Darien." Years later, and still Cjarsa and my mother argued. "Always favored you. Always bent Ahnmik's rigid laws for you, though Ecl shrieks at me every time those laws are broken. I could not let a mongrel be trained in this land. Hai would never have survived if I had tried. But have you no faith at all that I might have worked toward this hena'she?"

My mother turned her back on her Empress, though she could not close her ears to Cjarsa's words or close her heart to her own hope.

"If I had let you care for your daughter, if I had not sent Kel to bring you to me and thus forced her into exile, if I had not twisted Fate as I willed with each step of the way, this Nicias would never have been born. Your daughter would never have risen from the darkness—"

"No." I interrupted them now.

Cjarsa was not surprised that I had been present and listening.

"It is little enough," she pointed out, "compared to your machinations to save Wyvern's Court. Why does it seem so impossible that I might work to save one child—the only child of my favored companion?"

"If you dared walk the line between Mehay and Ecl, where Fate is woven . . . but you do not. You fear it. You have feared it since the day you saw the first of your followers slide into Ecl. Araceli's terror led her to create the avian people. Yours led you to write the laws of this land, to bind you to it so Ecl could not take you."

"Enough!"

I had spoken without thinking, as if in a trance, but Cjarsa's command snapped me back from it.

"As you wish, my lady," I whispered.

Ecl'gah. Illusion, all of it.

"I am sorry to distress you," I said. I remembered the terror that had gripped me the day Nicias had first invaded my private illusion. His soul had stained that still and silent realm forever.

Cjarsa had no other world, no other place, and no one to call her from this white realm.


I did.


"Hai? Where are you, Hai?"

*   *   *

I could go back to Nicias. I paused, wondering. Memories of the past and the present poured through me, but I knew I could go back to him.

"Hai, listen to my voice."

So I did. It was simple. The water was cold, and deep, and dark, but I found its center, and there . . . I was.

# CHAPTER 21

I opened my eyes, though it did me little good. I thought I was still in the private room beneath the dancer's nest, but the lamps had burned out long before, leaving no light to see by. What I did know was that I was once again in Nicias's arms. I felt him stir, waking at the same time that I did.

"What happens if there comes a day when I'm not here to save you?" he asked me.

"Then . . . I'll find my way back on my own."

I struggled to gather my thoughts, remembering the last scene with Cjarsa. Had I really argued with the white Lady of Ahnmik? Or had that been another vision of another future? What possible future could I have in which I would so brazenly challenge my Empress?

My head began to pound as I remembered what we had been doing here.

"Salem . . ."

I pulled away from Nicias and closed my eyes for a

moment, trying to focus past the pain at my temples. The cobra wasn't here. I would have been able to sense him even with my unfocused magic.

"He's gone," Nicias said, coming to the same conclusion.

My limbs ached as I pushed myself to my feet, swaying before Nicias stood beside me and steadied me.

Together we groped our way through the darkness, toward the doorway and up the stairs, until we blinked at the sudden light and noise of the dancer's nest.

Before my eyes had a chance to adjust to the brightness from the central fire, Rosalind intercepted us, her posture guarded as she looked from me to Nicias.

"Salem's awake," I said. I could tell just by looking at the dancer before me. She was wearing a simple outfit made of two carefully wrapped and tied *melos,* one deep emerald in color, and one black with green stitching. At her temple was a symbol meaning *victory.* It was not an outfit for mourning.

"He is," she replied.

Other dancers had drifted toward us, though they left Rosalind plenty of space.

"Is he . . . well?" I remembered a jumble of sensations and panicked thoughts. I had no idea what I had done, in my desperation, to make the cobra wake, or what the consequences might be.

She hesitated, frowning.

Nicias understood before I did. "Hai isn't your enemy," he told Rosalind. "Salem was dying. If he is up now, it is entirely through Hai's efforts. She risked more than you can possibly imagine to go after him."

Rosalind cringed, looking away and then immediately back at me. "I'm sorry. With all that has happened . . . I don't understand any of it. From the moment that Oliza announced that she was going to abdicate—" She shook her head, making her long auburn hair ripple. "No. It started long before then."

It had started the day the young serpiente Arami, Zane Cobriana, and the avian heir to the Tuuli Thea, Danica Shardae, first sat together, in a room in the Mistari homelands, and decided that they would find a way to bring peace—no matter the cost.

Rosalind struggled to compose herself. "You were both unconscious for several days. We didn't know if you had fought, if you were responsible for Salem's recovery, or if you were our enemies. No one knew what to do. We spoke to your mother, Nicias, and she said there was probably nothing we *could* do, so we left you undisturbed. I am very glad that you are awake now."

"As am I," I said. "Where can we find Salem?"

"I'll bring you to him," Rosalind offered.


We found Salem in the market, making the rounds of the merchants there.

"We have been struggling to show solidarity with the avians," Rosalind explained as we approached the restored Diente. "Zane and Danica have been around to help, as well, but it has really been Sive who has done the most." I wondered if Rosalind had any doubts about Salem's relationship with the hawk, but I pushed the thoughts away as she embraced her mate. "Hai and Nicias are awake," she said unnecessarily.

Salem took a moment to assess the situation before saying, "I've heard many different theories on what happened. Do I have you to thank for my recovery, Hai?"

"Wyvern's Court needed its Diente."

His voice hardened somewhat. "I understand you briefly assumed that position in my absence."

"I had no intention of harming Oliza, nor did I desire to usurp any throne," I said frankly. "Wyvern's Court is my home. I did what I could to try to protect it."

Slowly, the cobra nodded. "Oliza tried to help calm people after you fell ill, but she was even less trusted than I was. She wasn't welcome in Wyvern's Court."

I winced. "I'm sorry I caused that hardship. I will make certain to clarify what happened, quickly."

Our conversation had drawn the attention of everyone in the market. Many of the people who watched us were my allies.

As odd as it felt to consider this cobra kin, it felt almost right when I let out a long breath and went down on one knee before Salem.

"Hai, this isn't necessary," he protested.

"Yes, it is," I said. "I was not behind the attempt to assassinate you, but I was the motive for it. If you were *shm' Ahnmik*, you would have me killed."

"I'm no falcon," he whispered.

"I have allies in your kingdom, Diente."

"So do I—but I wouldn't if I went about executing everyone who could possibly be a threat. You're innocent, Hai. You're *more* than innocent; you saved my life. Please, cousin, stand up."

It was the first time he had ever acknowledged any relationship between us. I didn't know how to reply.

He took my hands as I stood.

"Wyvern's Court has gone through a lot. Your help—and the help of your allies—would be greatly appreciated," Salem admitted. "When I stepped out of the dancer's nest without you beside me, even people who had protested your taking the crown were horrified. There was no way to convince them that we had not harmed you. Hopefully you will be able to calm them, now that you are awake."

"Have Salokin and Arqueete come to trial?" I asked.

"They both confessed," he said. "Out of loyalty to you, they said."

"And Prentice?"

"I asked that he be returned to the avians for trial. He was convicted of treason, grounded and exiled." Salem shook his head and moved on. "Those trials were the easiest part of the last few days. Most of our hours have been devoted to keeping people from rioting. If a few of your followers—the candlemaker, and a handful of others—had not stepped forward to speak to your loyalists, I do not think we would have been able to keep control at all."

"Gren?" Nicias asked. He had been so quiet behind me all this time that his voice startled me.

Salem nodded. "Maya was actually the one who spoke to me first. She had a few questions."

"You know who she is, then?" I asked.

"We spoke at length," he answered discreetly. "I don't know that I can do anything for her—I don't dare risk inciting Ahnmik's wrath—but at some point I would appreciate your council on the subject. Maya, Gren, Opal and Spark worked to keep Wyvern's Court from falling apart while you were gone. I don't want to ignore them now."

I admitted, "If I had not spoken to them, it is quite

possible that all four of them would have participated in the plot to have you killed. On Ahnmik, they would all be guilty of treason."

"And in Wyvern's Court, they are responsible only for the crimes they have committed, and for their actions, I owe them thanks." His tone clearly said he considered the discussion over and further debate irrelevant. "Though I am glad you convinced them to be on my side, and not the other."

I shrugged, still not used to his gratitude.

From above came a shriek—a sound that both chilled me and made my heart race. Salem, Nicias and I lifted our eyes to take in a quartet of falcons: three gyrfalcons and a peregrine.

The group banked, circling once before it dove, and then the Empress Cjarsa's Mercy landed before us.

# CHAPTER 22

Nicias started to draw his blade but hesitated as he beheld the gyrfalcon in the front. My mother. In Wyvern's Court. I started to step forward, but Nicias stopped me with a hand on my shoulder. His eyes focused upon the peregrine beside Darien, and I heard the ring of steel as he drew his weapon defensively upon seeing Lillian, the woman who only a few months before had been his lover.

The falcons fell back into formal postures, with their feet planted slightly apart and their right hands grasping their left wrists behind their backs, under the wings of their Demi forms. They did not acknowledge Nicias or me, focusing first on Salem.

"Salem Cobriana," Darien said, "I understand you are Diente now?"

Two of Salem's guards had materialized from the surrounding market, drawn by the falcons' cries, and stood beside him now as he said, "I am. And you are?"

The gyrfalcon answered, *"Shm'Ahnmik'la'Darien'jaes'-oisna'ona'saniet'mana'Leonecl'mana'heah.* And this is my working partner, *Lillian'jaes'mael'ona'saniet'mana'heah."* Darien and Lillian, working together?

Why were the Empress's elite messengers here? They had not come when Oliza had abdicated or when Salem had nearly been killed. Why *now*? I did not know whether to be overjoyed or frightened. The presence of the Empress's Mercy in this land could not be good.

Salem glanced at Nicias.

"What is the white Lady's Mercy doing in Wyvern's Court?" Nicias asked.

Only now did the two women turn to him. "You speak for the Diente?"

"I speak for my king," Nicias replied boldly.

Darien laughed a little, finally breaking from formality. "You, Nicias, are the only falcon on this earth who would dare call a cobra your king while standing before the finest of the Empress's Mercy."

"And you, Darien," Nicias said, "are the only falcon on this earth who would be forgiven for treason as many times as you have been."

She gave a little bow. "I am as loyal to my Empress as I should be. Now, to answer your question . . ." Her eyes, as they lifted to mine, were liquid silver. "The Empress felt a falcon wake."

Nicias argued, "Hai has been awake for months. Why come now?" This time, Lillian laughed, a sound that made Nicias tense. Her voice was soft and musical but cold as she spoke to the man who could have been her prince in another world. "You misunderstand," she said. "It did not matter to the Empress when a mongrel dancer opened her eyes. She was perhaps glad of it, because she favored the cobra child, but that was all, and it did not trouble her when again your Hai fell and reawakened several days ago, save that she felt the harm done to royal blood when you, Nicias, tried to save her.

"What interests *ona'la'Cjarsa*," Lillian continued, "is the shift in the magic she felt a day ago. A shift that felt like the birth of a pure-blood falcon."

"Then it isn't me you felt," I said bitterly, starting to turn away. My mother still had not even acknowledged her relationship to me, and I had no desire to speak with the woman who had once been Nicias's lover.

"Isn't it?" Darien whispered. "Hai . . . *shm'Ahnmik'-la'Hai-ra'o'la*." She called me a falcon and her daughter, and those words made me hesitate. "You spin *sakkri* stronger than most of the Mercy, mindwalk as simply as breathing, and have survived Ecl. Your features betray your cobra blood— the black hair and garnet eyes are not of Ahnmik—but it is Ahnmik's magic that holds you."

"It is Ahnmik's magic that has always cursed me," I returned.

My mother shook her head. She looked at Salem and asked him, "Do you know what my daughter has done for you, cobra?" When Salem did not respond, she asked Nicias, "Do you, Nicias?"

Nicias turned toward me, but I knew he could not tell what it was he saw.

Darien stepped forward and took my hand. "Your magic will never be as powerful as it was when it danced to Anhamirak's flame . . . when it was sparked by that which you gave to your king." She looked back at Salem and, almost angrily, informed him, "Would you tear open your soul and give it to another, cobra? That is what my daughter has done for you—given to you that which her father gave to her. Ahnmirak's magic—the magic our poison destroyed in your blood."

Salem's eyes widened. Instinctively, hearing my mother's words, I tried to call upon my own serpent form—

And found nothing.

I tried to draw across my skin the black scales—

And found nothing.

Desperately, I sought any magic I had left with which to change from this form—

And screamed as my body tried to return to the broken, battered falcon I had lost when I had fallen from the sky above the white city years before.

Nicias caught me, sheathing his blade to hold me in his arms, his magic reaching out to soothe me.

One last try. I reached this time for the magic that came from Ahnmik. I felt it ripple through me, rubbing against Nicias's power like a cat seeking attention. He jumped, startled, and I pulled back.

He glanced at Lillian, then back at me. "Darien is right. You feel like a pure-blood falcon now."

Lillian smiled a little. "At least I made a lasting impression."

"Like a knife blade," Nicias snapped. Then he dropped his gaze, shaking his head. "You were acting under orders."

"Mostly," Lillian replied. "If it makes you feel better, my interest in you wasn't all feigned."

"That doesn't really help, and it doesn't make me trust you now. Either of you," he added, turning to Darien, "no matter how you might have helped me in the past. You felt a pure-blood falcon wake. Cjarsa felt her wake. Now what do you want with her?"

With very few exceptions, a falcon was not allowed to live off the island. Nicias had been granted his pardon because he was Araceli's blood. His parents had sacrificed their magic and their falcon forms to stay here. What would Cjarsa ask of me?

*Will she let me stay?*

Did I *want* her to let me stay?

To see the white city again, to walk through it, not as *que-mak* but with magic as pure as all the rest . . .

But I still did not have my Demi or falcon form, and even if my magic was untainted now, the rest of my body was not. I was too dark; my father's cobra blood was still too evident.

Still . . .

"Naturally," Lillian replied, "the Empress wants her own returned."

"No," I whispered. I had never thought I would say that word in this context, but it slipped off my lips. "Wyvern's Court is my home now. I have—"

I broke off, about to say *I have responsibilities here.*

I had worked so hard for the court that leaving would feel like abandoning it. If I disappeared now, without a word to the serpiente, my followers would forever distrust Salem. I needed to stay, at least a little longer.

And then a little longer. I knew how this went. I knew the Cobriana; one did not easily name oneself one of them only to walk away. Even Oliza's abdication had been for her people. If I didn't walk away now, I would never be able to.

"You have . . . ?" my mother asked when I did not finish.

"Never mind."

"Our orders are to bring you to the city," one of the other falcons said. "Why are we even having this discussion?"

Lillian and my mother looked at each other, a meaningful glance that made Lillian sigh and say, "Please come with us willingly."

"May I have time to consider?" I asked, though I did not know why. I had no choices to consider except whether to fight or obey.

"Yes," my mother said, at the same moment that one of the others said, "No."

"Darien," Lillian warned.

"Yes, Lillian?" My mother's voice was falsely sweet.

"Hai," Lillian said, "please come home with us. Your place is on Ahnmik. You have power here, I know, enough that it probably makes the current monarchy nervous. How long do you think they will tolerate you—trust you—knowing that you once had enough favor to usurp the throne of their beloved—"

Suddenly I heard my mother's voice in my mind. I could tell by the way Nicias's gaze instantly turned to Darien that he heard her as well.

*Perhaps you* would *be happiest if you remained in Wyvern's Court,* she said. *If I knew that for certain, I would have insisted that Cjarsa leave you alone. I believe she would have let me have my way; she wants me by her more than she needs you on the island. But it must be your choice. I have been little enough a part of your life as it is. I should not be the one to decide what you do with it now.*

In that moment, it might have been nice if Darien had expressed a bias regarding my decision. It would have been comforting to know she cared, and it would have made choosing easier.

Instead, she turned her attention to Nicias to add, *Even you, Nicias, do not have that right. It is Hai's choice to make.*

*And if she says no?* Nicias asked.

*Let her look on the island with eyes not veiled by Ecl before she decides.*

*As I did?* he challenged again.

*My daughter does not have your naïveté,* Darien pointed out. *She knows how to use her power perfectly well. No one short of royal blood could use persuasion magics on her without her knowledge, and if they do, you are experienced enough to protect Hai, should you choose to accompany her.*

"Darien, if you are plotting with them, at least let us hear it," Lillian said. "I would like to know why we are being punished if the Lady takes us to task for something you've said."

"Have I spoken a word of treason to you?" Darien asked me and Nicias.

"No," I answered, considering her words.

"That's new," Lillian remarked. "Hai, are you coming with us willingly, or do we need to carry you?"

Nicias grasped my hand. "Araceli told me once that if I returned to the island, it would be as her heir. Is that still the case?"

"Of course," Lillian answered.

"If I understand correctly, that gives me authority over everyone but Cjarsa and Araceli themselves. Including you."

Lillian nodded warily. "We will follow our Empress's commands before yours, but yes, even Cjarsa's Mercy would be held to your will unless she said otherwise."

"Then these are my terms. If Hai goes to Ahnmik, I go with her," he said. "Anyone who tries to use magic to manipulate either of us, or who tries to separate us without

Hai's consent, I will consider to have acted against me—which, according to Ahnmik's laws, gives me every right to execute them. Or at least turn them over to you."

"*A'le*," Darien answered. "As you wish, *my lord*."

Her tone was so careful, so neutral, it betrayed her pleasure. My mother was concerned with assuring my freedom of choice, but she was not nearly as unbiased when it came to my prince.

# CHAPTER 23

I thought about all the times I had seen Nicias on Ahnmik . . . I had seen *myself* there, though I had never imagined that I could be the woman—the pure-blood falcon—I had often seen by his side. Now I understood.

"Milady." *The falcon did not kneel to me, but he bowed his head, his downcast eyes unable to conceal the terror within. "Please, forgive a foolish man his ill-conceived words."*

*Not incorrect, simply ill-conceived. If Nicias had not been nearby, his crass comments about* quemak *falcons would never have elicited any kind of stir.*

*"Do you apologize to me," I asked, "or to my prince?"*

*Ahnmik's magic would not let him lie, no matter how much the mongrel in question wished it would. The man looked at his prince and cringed. The* aona'ra *was not in a forgiving mood.*

\* \* \*

Perhaps too late, my mind made the crucial connections between the many *sakkri* I had spun in my life. I knew what would follow if Nicias and I went to Ahnmik now. How many times had I seen it, dreamed it, *wished* I could be that woman beside him?

The royal house would welcome us with open arms. Cjarsa would personally greet me. My mother would watch proudly as I took the trials—and passed, of course. I would be given a rank, and at last I would be able to begin formal study of the *jaes'Ahnmik* magic.

Someone would be able to heal my wings; now that the cobra's taint was gone from me, anyone powerful enough would be able to force-change me and give me back the sky and, with it, everything I had ever wanted. I would dance at the triple arches once again.

And Nicias . . . ah, my prince. He would be beside me. It would bother him at first when people were polite to me only because I had both his favor and Cjarsa's, but I had faced such disdain all my life, and I would convince him to ignore it and let things be.

My mother—my Empress and I would convince this lovely peregrine to accept many things.

I cringed, and though I wanted Nicias's company very much, I said, "You don't have to do this for me."

"I will return to Wyvern's Court after you make your decision, no matter what you do," Nicias replied. "Ahnmik isn't my world and I don't want it. I just don't trust them to let you decide without coercion. If you want to go alone, that is your choice, but I hope you will let me go with you—if only to allow me the comfort of knowing that you are not forced to stay."

*What if they try to force you to stay?* I asked, keeping the words from the ears and minds of the Empress's Mercy.

*Cjarsa's orders to Araceli to let me live my own life aren't likely to have changed,* he replied. *And if they have, I doubt your mother will fail to move Ecl and Mehay to get her way—as always.*

As always indeed. But my mother wanted Nicias on the island. *I* wanted Nicias on the island, too, but it was a selfish desire. I could not take him without eventually losing him.

In the end, Nicias was the only master of his fate; he would, or would not, go to the white city of his own volition. All I could hope to do was keep him from destroying himself for me.

If I went, I would miss him. I would miss Wyvern's Court, and even the Obsidian guild. I would regret not seeing Sive Shardae grow into the beautiful queen I knew she would become, and I would miss the cobra king to whom I had so recently offered my allegiance.

"Enough," one of the falcons snapped as I hesitated. "There is no room for negotiation. Hai is one of the Lady's subjects, and so is answerable to the Lady's commands."

"As are we all," Darien answered, and everyone knew exactly what she meant.

*Why?* Why did I delay?

This world of snakes and birds was filled with such impossible, contrary fools; they struggled daily against the tides of Fate, even when it would be so much wiser to give in.

They burned with an incredible, desperate passion, which perhaps only Anhamirak's followers could truly comprehend. Certainly there was no equivalent among the long-lived *shm'Ahnmik.*

In the white city, there was enough beauty to make the most hardened heart weep. There were music that resonated in the soul and colors that the eye could hardly comprehend.

Pure and crystalline and lovely, Ahnmik was clear of the grime and sweat of Wyvern's Court.

Without intending to, I let out a small sound. Nicias put a hand on my arm, but his eyes stayed on the Mercy, as if he was tying to discover what they had done to me.

"I want to go home," I said softly. "I want to speak to my—" I almost said *mother,* and that was what I meant, but I was not thinking of the mother who was standing before me. "My Empress."

"And if she chooses to see you, then you may," the impatient falcon replied. "Assuming we ever get back to the city."

Darien asked me, "You want to speak to her *now?*"

"The Empress does not grant audiences at the whims of a—"

Darien half lifted her hand and, without even turning, tossed enough magic at her fellow guard to make him stumble to his knees. Closing her eyes, my mother drew a half breath; I could feel her power reaching out with a petition.

To the magic of falcons, distance meant little. The many miles between Wyvern's Court and the island of Ahnmik were bridged by power, until suddenly my heart began to pound and I blinked back tears.

I was still in Wyvern's Court physically, but mentally I stood before my Empress.

"My Lady," I whispered.

"Darien has informed me that I must speak to you." There was some wry amusement in her tone; few people ever "informed" the white Lady of anything, much less told her she must do something.

"My Lady . . . you gave so much to me when I was a child, even though I was born *quemak.* I—"

"You are the only child of my favored companion, Darien," Cjarsa interrupted, her magic wrapping me almost like an embrace, gentle and comforting. "Your father's blood was not your fault. How could I do less than twist Fate herself to give you the chance to come home, whole and pure?"

The words differed a little from what she would have said to my mother, but I recognized the argument I had heard in my recent *sakkri*.

She must have sensed my slight withdrawal, for she continued to make her point.

"It is little enough," she pointed out, "compared to your machinations to save Wyvern's Court."

"My Lady . . ."

I thought about what my mother had told me when we had argued about Oliza. *Cjarsa has more power than you and I combined, but the void frightens her. She fears drowning in its illusions, so she holds back.* My mother's words had frightened me then, but I had not taken the time to understand the full implications of them.

Now Cjarsa had chosen her words carefully, avoiding stating any fact that Ahnmik's magic would reveal to be false.

"You never even looked to the future, did you?" I had nearly drowned trying to save Wyvern's Court. She had let me struggle on my own, and now she tried to take credit for all the incredible twists of Fate and Will that had led to this moment. "You would have seen the dangers of Oliza's reign if you had only *looked,* but you never even tried. You just let me . . ."

"I let you become queen," Cjarsa said.

"You let me tie myself to this realm," I said. "Do you wish me home, my Lady?"

"You are one of us, *shm'Ahnmik'la'Hai.* Your place is here."

Coldness seeped up my spine, as she neglected to answer the question.

"Lady, you know I would do anything you wished. From my earliest memory, you are there, teaching me to dance. You . . ." *You were the one who caught me when I fell and my wings were scoured from me.* "You were everything to me." *You were the one who healed what you could.* "Please, my Empress. *Do you want me to return to you?*"

She hesitated, and in that hesitation I heard the echo of all my last illusions shattering.

*You were the one,* I thought, *who held me . . . and you were the one who told me to rest. You were the one whose voice carried me into Ecl.*

"All you ever needed to say was that you wanted me," I said. "That day under the arches, if you had only given me a word of encouragement, I would have stayed in this world. I could have used my magic to heal my wings before they set so twisted I would never have them again. I could have . . ." My voice broke. "But instead, you told me to rest. I would be there still if Nicias had not come for me."

I waited, though I knew it was useless. Cjarsa did not continue to argue with me. I loved the white city, but there I was a mongrel, something to be tolerated. Even with "pure" magic, I would never be unblemished. I gathered myself together, drawing in a deep breath rich with the scents of wintertime in Wyvern's Court.

"I may finally be a falcon in your eyes, white Lady, but it is another land that holds my heart. I have no desire to return to Ahnmik. I . . . I have a place here," I said. I wasn't exactly certain what that place was, but over the past few days, I had started to discover a connection to this land that I had never had to Ahnmik.

Oliza did not trust me or like me. I made Sive nervous. The old Diente and Tuuli Thea, Zane and Danica, would probably never forgive me for what I had done to their daughter. And here, too, I would always be an outsider, a mixed-blood falcon.

But here, for a while, I had been needed.

Shaking with fear, I said, "Lady Cjarsa, I respectfully request your permission to stay here, as a citizen of Wyvern's Court and not as one of your subjects."

Such bold words. How could I have said them? How could I, who had been raised by the Lady's hand, even imply that I could be released from her authority?

*Brazen, as a cobra cannot help but be.* Somewhere in *sakkri*, I had heard Cjarsa say those words, about my father.

Cjarsa sighed, and I struggled not to tremble in the face of her disappointment. "Is this really what you want?" she asked.

"My Lady, if you tell me that you *want* me home, that you *want* me beside you, that I have ever been more to you than a nuisance, then I will fly to your side in an instant. But you won't, because Ahnmik will not let you lie that way.

"I saw the fear in your eyes when I was a child and I began to spin *sakkri* of the Dasi. You do not want me in your empire; you tolerated me for years to try to win back my mother's favor, but you never wanted me. Please, grant me permission to leave now."

Time stretched and seemed to slow as I waited for her reply.

"Permission granted."

*　　*　　*

I had tears in my eyes as I pulled myself out of the trance and away from the last time I would ever see the woman who had raised me.

I would probably love her all my life, as a child must love her mother. I certainly would not be able to hate her. I understood her fear too well to not forgive her.

"I don't understand," Darien said, standing beside where I knelt with one hand pressed to the soil of Wyvern's Court. "You told her no?"

"You said it would be her decision," Nicias pointed out. "Cjarsa has honored—"

"I never thought she would actually *choose* this!" Darien replied. "Hai, what do you have here? What place does any falcon have in a serpent and avian land?"

"Darien," Nicias said, intervening, "she made her decision."

I pushed myself to my feet, to face my mother. Looking into her Ahnmik silver eyes, I felt as if I was looking at a stranger.

"I have never been a falcon, not in your eyes, or the eyes of Ahnmik, or my Empress's or even my own. I was always . . . tainted. I'm cobra blood, Darien."

"You *used* to be," she asserted. "You know I loved your father, but I hated the curse he left you with. You've rid yourself of that now."

"The curse he left me with was passion," I replied. "And yes, it hurts, but it is *mine*. And the gift he left me with was Wyvern's Court."

"You would really stay here, when Cjarsa has offered you Ahnmik?" My mother looked at me with confusion. "Hai, all your life, I have struggled to give you this—"

"All my life, you have struggled to give *yourself* this," I said. "Struggled to win, against the Empress."

"Haven't you?"

"Darien . . . *Mother* . . . you are *shm'Ahnmik*. And the white god has no patience for right and wrong, or sacrifice, only power."

"You're one of us."

I shook my head. "In the first *sakkri* I ever saw, I watched through Kiesha's eyes as Cjarsa and Araceli ripped Anhamirak's magic in half. I screamed with the cobra, until my throat bled and I lost my voice for weeks. I should have known on that day that I would never be a falcon."

Those around me knew my heritage by my ebony hair. I knew that it was held somewhere even deeper than magic . . . and that it wasn't on the white island. It never had been.

"You will stay in this land, without a serpent form?" Darien asked, in a last desperate plea. "Hai, I do not understand you. You had Wyvern's Court in your hand, and you gave it up. You gave up your cobra form, and your position as Diente. Why else would you have done that, if not to come home?"

"I gave up my magic to save my cousin's *life*," I said. "I am more than my animal form. I am more than the magic the royal house of Ahnmik deemed right for the serpiente to retain. I am more than feathers or scales.

"*I am* Kiesha'ra."

# EPILOGUE

Months later, I still sometimes woke in the night, coated in sweat, with my heart pounding. Wrapped in Nicias's arms, I would open my eyes and take a deep breath to assure myself that the past half year had really happened.

As a child, I had centered my entire life on my Empress's desires; I had sought nothing more than to please her, even when she had sent me into Ecl. Now I had cut my ties to Ahnmik and was responsible for myself, for my own decisions, and for my own future. I had lost all guidance beyond myself and had chosen this heartache of decision that made serpents and avians so brilliantly alive: freedom.

Though flavored by tears, that freedom was the sweetest thing I had ever known.

After the weeks of chaos, from Oliza's abdication through Salem's resurrection, Wyvern's Court did not return instantly to rest. Both royal houses came together to try to heal their shaken world, like parents holding a child through her night terrors. There was much shuddering and wailing, but eventually the court returned to its precious balance of two worlds dancing together in defiance of Fate herself.

I was honored to say I was among the dancers.

On this night, I stood in the center of the Obsidians' camp, surrounded by all their guild, as well as some more unusual faces—the exiled falcons from the candle shop, and an uneasy-looking Sive Shardae, who was standing beside her serpiente companion. The only light came from a single lamp hanging on one of the nearest trees, and from the stars high above us.

Vere stood before me, dressed in black, with a silver *melos* about his waist.

"Your people have fared badly in all this," I said to him as we waited for the last guests to arrive. "First Oliza made you promises, and then I did, and now neither of us is in a position to keep them. I am sorry."

A rustling in the forest announced the arrival of three newcomers: Salem; his Naga, Rosalind; and Nicias, who had guided them here. Nicias came to my side and wrapped me in his arms.

Vere nodded a greeting and then continued our conversation. "You really think we have been mistreated by these events?" the white viper asked. "Look around. The cobra king and his mate are peaceful guests in our camp, traveling dancers and—albeit nervous—friends." He gestured at Sive, who was now deep in conversation with Maya. "You say we've come out badly, but look around. You'll see *Maeve'ra, Kiesha'ra, shm'Ahnmik* and the descendant of Alasdair standing together."

"It's an exception," I replied. "Tomorrow—"

"It is an exception that has never before occurred over the

course of thousands of years. And tomorrow, even if the fighting begins again, they will remember." He smiled in a way that said that he knew his words were dangerously optimistic, but that he couldn't help it. "I never wanted to be a king, Hai," he assured me. "I accepted your suit because I felt it was time to reach out and make alliances, but I am pleased with the way things have turned out."

His smile became a little more wistful as his gaze flickered from me to Nicias, but all he said was "Are you ready?"

I drew a long, deep breath, taking in all the scents of the wild forest, and raised my face to the night sky.

"I'm ready."

As I stepped onto the camp's center dais, I allowed myself once more to reach out to my lover and foe. Carefully, I asked Ecl's favor. There was only one thing I needed to know.

*It was a strange world, taken over by humanity and stretching farther than anyone had imagined. Vast oceans, unknown continents, machines that did the work of men . . . What an incredible world it had become in the centuries since my own life. And within that world:*

*Two women stood face to face, garnet eyes looking deeply into gold. The cobra began to laugh, then hugged the hawk joyously. The Tuuli Thea was crying, but they were sweet tears.*

*Both knelt beside a baby girl with white-blond hair and golden eyes. The next Tuuli Thea's father—a white viper, one of the few remaining children of Obsidian—leaned nearby, watching trustingly as the Diente picked up the hawk-viper child.*

*None of them knew what their ancestors had gone through—what risks had been taken, or what sacrifices had been made—to allow them to stand there unafraid.*

I pulled back from the vision as easily as I breathed, as I heard the drumbeat begin. Mentally, I sent a kiss to the familiar abyss, but the one it sent in return did not restrain me.

My eyes still closed, I lifted myself onto my toes, arching my back and crossing my wrists above my head. I listened to my heart as it began to beat in time with the drummer's rhythm. The flute, when it began to play, felt like an extension of my own breath.

My audience gasped as I unfurled wings the color of a cobra's scales, with a span of more than fifteen feet. Because my magic was finally under control, Nicias and—grudgingly—Oliza had been able to work together to heal them. Now, as I prepared to dance, I spread them wide.

Yes, I had finally embraced my Cobriana heritage, but who said snakes weren't meant to fly?

*My prayer is simple, my child, my child,*
*Please, do try to understand:*
*I've given you freedom, and left you with*
*choices.*
*Now you're at the beginning,*
*Again.*